# RUBÉN DARÍO:
## SELECTED WRITINGS

RUBÉN DARÍO (Félix García Sarmiento) was born in Metapa (re-named Ciudad Darío), a small town in Nicaragua, on January 18th, 1867. His parents soon separated. His mother took him to Honduras, but eventually returned to Nicaragua and Darío was raised in León. He was writing epitaphs in verse on commission by age eleven, and his first verses were published when he was thir-teen years old in the newspaper *El Termómetro*. In 1884, Darío worked as a presidential staff member under the regime of Adán Cárdenas, as well as in the National Library. He made his first trip to Chile in 1886, and debuted as a poet in book form with *Abro-jos* in 1887, but it was the combination of poetry and prose in *Azul . . .* (1888) that made him famous and transformed him into the lightning rod of the *Modernista* movement in the Spanish-speaking Americas. Soon after, Darío began contributing to the Argentine daily *La Nación,* a professional relationship that would last until his death. In Nicaragua, he married Rafaela Contreras Cañas, the first of three wives with whom he would have four children, two of whom died in infancy. A coup d'etat in Nicaragua in 1890 forced him to move to Guatemala and El Salvador. Darío was named secretary of the Nicaraguan delegation in charge of the four hundredth anniversary of Columbus's voyage across the Atlantic Ocean in 1892 and also made his first, revelatory trip to Spain. Rafaela Contreras Cañas died soon after. Months later, Darío married Rosario Murillo. In 1893 Darío met Paul Verlaine in Paris, and, in New York, José Martí, with whom he forged a friendship. In 1896 his books *Los Raros* [The Misfits] and *Prosas profanas y otros poemas* [Profane Prose and Other Poems] were published. He also started to serialize a novel called *El hombre de oro* [Man of Gold], which was influenced by Flaubert's *Salambó*. In 1898 the Spanish-American War took place and shook Darío to the core. He denounced the United States in a series of poems and articles written for various periodicals. A year later, he traveled to Barcelona, then to Madrid. His experiences in Spain would be de-scribed in the chronicles and literary portraits of *España contem-poránea* [Contemporary Spain] (1901). In 1899 he met Ramón

María Valle-Inclán, Juan Ramón Jiménez, as well as Francisca Sánchez, an illiterate peasant from Navalsáuz, whom Darío taught to read. The couple relocated in Paris, where he worked as a correspondent for *La Nación,* focusing on the *Exposition Universelle de Paris*. In 1903 he became consul of Nicaragua in Paris, where he had already met Antonio and Manuel Machado. From there he visited Barcelona and a year later traveled to Gibraltar, Morocco, and various locations in Spain. His book *Cantos de vida y esperanza: Los cisnes y otros poemas* [Songs of Life and Hope/Swans and Other Poems] appeared in 1905, followed a couple of years later by *El canto errante* [Wandering Song]. Darío was named to a diplomatic post in Spain by the Nicaraguan government in 1907 while he was in the country trying unsuccessfully to annul his marriage to Rosario Murillo. In 1909 he published *Alfonso XIII* and *El viaje a Nicaragua e Intermezzo tropical* [Voyage to Nicaragua and Tropical Intermezzo]. *Poema del otoño y otros poemas* [Autumn Poems and Other Poems] appeared in 1910, which is also when he visited Mexico to participate in the centenary commemoration of *El Grito de Dolores* [The Cry of Dolores] just as that country was about to be swept by a peasant revolution. While he was in Mexico City, Nicaraguan President José Madriz was deposed, and Darío abruptly left for Cuba. In 1911–12, he was contracted to edit and promote *Mundial Magazine*. His memoir *Historia de mis libros* [The Story of My Books] was serialized in *La Nación* in 1913. His health deteriorated and his cirrhosis of the liver became public knowledge. His last volume of poetry, *Canto a la Argentina y otros poemas* [Song to Argentina and Other Poems], was released in 1914, along with the first of three volumes of selected poems chosen by the poet and published in Madrid by Biblioteca Corona: *Muy siglo XVIII* [And Those that Come from the Eighteenth Century] (1914); *Muy antiguo y muy moderno* [Some Both Ancient and Modern] (1915); and *Y una sed de ilusiones infinita* [And a Thirst for Illusive Hope That's Endless] (1916). His autobiography, *La vida de Rubén Darío escrita por él mismo* [The Life of Rubén Darío, Written by Himself], appeared in 1915. He became gravely ill during a lecture tour of the United States, and returned to León, Nicaragua, early in 1916. Rubén Darío died on February 6, 1916. He was buried near the statue of Saint Paul, in the Cathedral of León.

A translator of some three dozen book-length works of literature, criticism, history, and memoir, ANDREW HURLEY is best known for his translation of Jorge Luis Borges's *Collected Fictions* (1998), as well as Reinaldo Arenas's "Pentagony" novels (1986–2000). He lives and works in San Juan, Puerto Rico.

GREG SIMON has published translations of poetry from the work of Spanish, Portuguese, German and Russian writers, and is the co-translator, with Steven F. White and Christopher Maurer, of Federico García Lorca's *Poet in New York* (1988).

STEVEN F. WHITE has edited and translated anthologies of contemporary poetry from Nicaragua, Chile, and Brazil. He is the author of *Modern Nicaraguan Poetry: Dialogues with France and the United States* (1993) and *El mundo más que humano en la poesía de Pablo Antonio Cuadra: Un estudio ecocrítico* (2002). He is a corresponding member of the Nicaraguan Academy of the Language and teaches Spanish at St. Lawrence University.

ILAN STAVANS is the Lewis-Sebring Professor in Latin American and Latino Culture and the Five-College 40th Anniversary Distinguished Professor at Amherst College. His books include *The Hispanic Condition* (1995), *The Riddle of Cantinflas* (1998), *On Borrowed Words* (2001), *Spanglish* (2003), and *Dictionary Days* (2005). He edited *The Oxford Book of Latin American Essays* (1997), *The Poetry of Pablo Neruda* (2003), and the four-volume *Encyclopedia Latina* (2005).

# Selected Writings

# RUBÉN DARÍO

# Selected Writings

Edited with an Introduction by
ILAN STAVANS

Translated by
ANDREW HURLEY, GREG SIMON,
*and* STEVEN F. WHITE

PENGUIN BOOKS

PENGUIN BOOKS

Published by the Penguin Group

Penguin Group (USA) Inc., 375 Hudson Street, New York, New York 10014, U.S.A.

Penguin Group (Canada), 90 Eglinton Avenue East, Suite 700, Toronto, Ontario, Canada M4P 2Y3
(a division of Pearson Penguin Canada Inc.)

Penguin Books Ltd, 80 Strand, London WC2R 0RL, England

Penguin Ireland, 25 St Stephen's Green, Dublin 2, Ireland (a division of Penguin Books Ltd)

Penguin Group (Australia), 250 Camberwell Road, Camberwell, Victoria 3124, Australia (a division of
Pearson Australia Group Pty Ltd)

Penguin Books India Pvt Ltd, 11 Community Centre, Panchsheel Park, New Delhi–110 017, India

Penguin Group (NZ), cnr Airborne and Rosedale Roads, Albany, Auckland 1310, New Zealand (a division
of Pearson New Zealand Ltd)

Penguin Books (South Africa) (Pty) Ltd, 24 Sturdee Avenue, Rosebank, Johannesburg 2196, South Africa

Penguin Books Ltd, Registered Offices:
80, Strand, London WC2R 0RL, England

1   3   5   7   9   10   8   6   4   2

LIBRARY OF CONGRESS CATALOGING IN PUBLICATION DATA

Darío, Rubén, 1867–1916.
[Selections. English & Spanish. 2005]
Selected writings / Ruben Dario ; edited with an introduction by Ilan Stavans ; translated by
Andrew Hurley, Greg Simon and Steven F. White.
p.   cm.—(Penguin Classics)
Includes index.
ISBN 0 14 30.39369
I. Stavans, Ilan.   II. Hurley, Andrew.   III. Simon, Greg.   IV. White, Steven F., 1955–
V. Title.   VI. Series.
PQ7519.D3A228 2005
861'.5—dc22       2005045224

Printed in the United States of America
Set in Adobe Sabon

# Contents

STORIES AND FABLES

# Introduction

"In truth, I live on poetry. I am naught but a man of art." Thus Rubén Darío, the Nicaraguan *homme de lettres* and indisputable leader of the *Modernista* movement that swept Latin America at the end of the nineteenth century and the early years of the twentieth, characterized himself. "I am good for nothing else," he went on. "I believe in God, and I am attracted to mystery. I am befuddled by daydreams and death; I have read many philosophers yet I know not a word of philosophy. I do espouse a certain Epicureanism, of my own sort: let the soul and body enjoy as much as possible on earth, and do everything possible to continue that enjoyment in the next life. Which is to say, *je vois la vie en rose.*"

At once visionary and agent provocateur, Darío witnessed the arrival of modernity in every aspect of life on this side of the Atlantic: from education to religion, from politics and the arts to science and technology. He wondered: What makes the Spanish language used in the Americas different from the language of the Iberian Peninsula? To what extent are these nascent nations—whose drive toward independence, in geographic terms, began in Mexico in 1810 and spread throughout the hemisphere—really autonomous, really independent of their "motherland"? From what cultural well ought artists and intellectuals in the Americas drink? What set of symbols and motifs might artists and poets call their own? Of course, the questioning was the result of Darío's discomfort with his surroundings, and it was not free of irony. "I detest the life and times it is my fate to live in," he declared. Darío was what we might today call "conflicted"; he was constantly pulled in contrary directions. While he felt himself a man of the Americas, at heart he was a cosmopolitan who looked to Europe as his prime source of inspiration, hoping to redeem himself and his people from the morose Spanish culture, which for Latin America had been the only connection to the outside world, but which had fallen into an embarrassing mediocrity. A man of deep Catholic faith, he understood poetry much in the way the Romantics did: as a bridge toward nature and the spiritual world. In searching for motifs to alleviate his sense of loss, he embraced the worldly and very "contemporary" French Symbolists—Baudelaire, Mallarmé, and Verlaine in particular— but he also felt the allure of the pre-Columbian past. "If there is any poetry in our America," Darío suggested, "it is in the old things; in Palenque and Utatlán, in the Indian of legend and the fine and sensual Inca, and in the great Moctezuma on his golden throne."

When approached *sub specie aeternitatis*, the poetry of Latin America appears to be defined by a cyclical battle of opposites: on one side are the Europeanized voices of the so-called aesthetes, whose poetry is disconnected from the social conditions from which it springs; on the other are the practitioners of an *engagé* art, who believe that the word has the power to change the world. Of course this tension, in some shape or form, lives at the heart of every poet. In Darío's case, it manifested itself more vividly than in anyone before him in the region, and the way he responded to it left a deep and lasting mark, to the point that one is able to declare, without fear of error, that the overall poetic tradition in the Spanish language on this side of the Atlantic is perfectly divisible into two halves: before and after Darío.

If the contribution of a single poet could be measured quantitatively, by the number of astonishing poems that have become an essential feature of a culture, then it is arguable that Darío stands as the most important poet ever to write in Latin America. From "Venus" to "Autumn Poem" and "Swans," from "Poets! Towers of God!" to "To Columbus" and "To Roosevelt," Darío achieves a pitch so faultless, a melodious style so controlled and authoritative, and a mannered tone, filled with Gallicisms, so influential not only to his successors but his contemporaries as well, as to make the reader believe that these pieces are integral to the universal order of Spanish-language letters. All artists dream of achieving perfection, but only a few might be said to succeed in their quest. Darío, in a handful of his compositions, makes the cut.

The first piece of criticism on Darío's work appeared in 1884, when he was twenty-one years old. Since then, he has been the subject of a veritable academic industry. Hundreds of book-length studies and thousands of monographs have been written by scholars on Darío. He has been a lightning rod for the *Modernista* movement that swept the intellectual world of Latin America as the nineteenth century came to a close. (It is no secret that most of these academic examinations tend to be innocuous, jingoistic, and altogether inundated by a hygienic theoretical jargon that specializes in killing the power of poetry. At times one feels that these exercises do little to explain his legacy.) Scholars have delved into the minutiae of his biography and his oeuvre, exploring every imaginable aspect of it from a myriad of perspectives, from the sociological to the political, from the philosophical to the semantic. Special emphasis has been placed on Darío's links to figures in world literature, with detailed concentration on his borrowings from the French intellectual orbit.

Beyond university circles, however, Darío's posterity is nothing if not contested, and often the assessment of Darío's legacy is so passionate as to be belligerent. Throughout his life not only was he often attacked for being either too daring or too imitative of foreign models, but his poetic revolution was also misunderstood. For some critics, such as philologist Raimundo Lida, Darío was not only the most admirable of all the *Modernista* poets but also one of the great modern Latin-American poets. And in an obituary published in 1916, Pedro Henríquez Ureña, the Dominican literary critic who delivered the Charles Eliot Norton Lectures at Harvard in 1940–41, was the first to equate Darío with Spain's two major Golden Age poets, Francisco de Quevedo and Luis de Góngora. Federico

García Lorca, in a conversation with Pablo Neruda at the PEN Club in Buenos Aires in 1933, argued, lyrically, that Darío "gave us the murmur of the forest in an adjective, and as masterful as Fray Luis de Granada, he made zodiacal signs out of the lemon tree, the hoof of a stag, and mollusks filled with terror and infinity. He launched us on the sea with frigates and shadows in our eyes, and built an enormous promenade of gin over the grayest afternoon the sky has ever known, and greeted the southwest wind as a friend, all heart like a Romantic poet, and put his hand on the Corinthian capital of all epochs with a sad, ironic doubt." Pablo Neruda responded: Darío's "red name deserves to be remembered, along with his essential tendencies, his terrible heartaches, his incandescent uncertainties, his descent into the hospitals of hell, his ascent to the castles of fame, his attributes as a great poet, now and forever undeniable." Neruda added: "Federico García Lorca, a Spaniard, and I, a Chilean, dedicate the honors bestowed on us today to that great shadow who sang more loftily than ourselves, and who saluted, in a new voice, the Argentine soil that we now tread."

But for others less diplomatic (and more racist, perhaps) in their judgment, such as Oxford don C. M. Bowra, Darío was a disappointing poet. Bowra compared the Nicaraguan unfavorably to W. B. Yeats, believing that Darío suffered from "his untutored simplicity and his complete lack of irony." Bowra added: "We must remember that he was a stranger from an underdeveloped land, that he had Indian blood in his veins and lacked the complexity and the sophistication which would belong to a European of his gifts and tastes." Luis Cernuda and Gastón Baquero, poets from Spain and Cuba respectively, saw Darío as either unoriginal or unworthy of his Latin-American origins, which, Baquero claimed, Darío seemed to reject in one poem after another. Baquero, we should note, changed his mind later in life; he dedicated one of his last books, *Memorial de un testigo* (A Witness's Memorial, 1966), to Darío. Is this proof of the kind of love/hate relationship that a solid number of Latin American poets have with the Nicaraguan? Indeed, since the twenties it has become a sport among young aesthetes to attack Darío in manifestos that proclaim a rupture, a rejection of his legacy, only to prove themselves *hijos de Rubén,* followers of the poet, in the years that follow.

The fact that youngsters throw stones at Darío proves that he has been, even for his opponents, a beloved enemy, an unmistakable and omnipresent landmark. We find this attitude in Pablo Antonio Cuadra and José Coronel Urtecho in Nicaragua itself, as well as in Spain and elsewhere in Latin America, as it was held by Vallejo, Neruda, Lorca, and a host of other, less gifted, poets. Manuel Gutiérrez Nájera, another *Modernista,* once said, apropos of one of the Nicaraguan's favorite animal motifs, the swan, that it was the duty of every follower of Darío to *"torcerle el cuello al cisne,"* to wring the bird's neck. Yet the work his accusers ended up producing has been remarkably *Dariano.* In any case, Cernuda and Baquero are part of the cadre of followers who have used the terms "decadent" and "melancholic" to attack the Nicaraguan poet. For them, the school of *Rubenistas* is about using symbols and meters that are foreign to the western shores of the Atlantic.

But what, in a culture such as ours, in which cross-fertilization is a sine qua non and the concept of purity in art is as elusive as it is artificial, can "foreignness" really mean? Latin-American literature in general, and poetry above all (not the poetry produced by pre-Columbian poets, of course, Nahuas such as Nezahualcoyotl and Axayacatl, but surely that which is the by-product of the colonial period and most crucially that which has been composed from Darío's generation onward), is really the result of a constant bombardment of outside influences. Foreign models first from Europe (Spain, France, Italy) and then from the United States, represented in figures such as Gustave Flaubert, Théophile Gautier, Edgar Allan Poe, and Walt Whitman, have exercised enormous power. Darío was neither bashful nor deceitful about these models. And his temperamental attraction to melancholy no doubt makes him a "typical" fin-de-siècle artist. As for his Decadence, it was an imitation of French Symbolism and Parnassianism, as well as of the remnants of the Romantic Movement that had swept Germany, Italy, and England, and that had not a few late repercussions in the United States. For a Nicaraguan to dream of a poetry firmly established in the motto *l'art pour l'art* might be seen, in and of itself, as an anachronism. But cannot poets of these lands also share in the feast of Western Civilization? Why should a Central American Decadent be less worthy than, say, his North American counterpart, or for that matter, Gautier himself?

Of Darío's *Rezeptionsgeshichte*, there are a number of essays worth reading for their clear and informed judgment. These include an illustrious exegetical essay by the Uruguayan critic José Enrique Rodó, author of the significant mediation *Ariel,* in which the Anglo and Hispanic sensibilities are for the first time contrasted in sharp philosophical terms. Rodó championed the *Modernista* aesthetic through lucid literary explorations. He focused on Darío as a stepping-stone for his generation, and in doing so left us an early thought-provoking analysis of Darío's poetry. Angel Rama, Pedro Salinas, and Max Henríquez Ureña (Pedro's brother) produced valuable commentaries. There is also a fine essay by Octavio Paz, the Nobel Prize winner who in more ways than one has been the inheritor of Darío's mantle: the poet as cultural commentator. In 1964, while in New Delhi on diplomatic service, Paz published a piece called "The Siren and the Seashell" (included in his book *Cuadrivio*), in which he convincingly dissects Darío's aesthetic and ideological revolution. It strikes me as one of the most convincing appraisals of Darío, his work, and his position in Latin American culture. It includes this argument, which helps us place the Nicaraguan in context:

> Darío was not only the richest and most ample of the Modernist poets: he was also one of our great modern poets. He was the beginning. At times he makes one think of Poe; at other times, of Whitman. Of the first, in that portion of his work in which he scorns the world of the Americas and is preoccupied solely by an otherwordly music; of the second, in that portion in which he expresses his vitalist affirmation, his pantheism, and his belief that he was, in his own right, the bard of Latin America as Whitman was of Anglo-America. In contrast to Poe, Darío did not enclose himself within his own spiritual adventure; neither did he have Whitman's ingenuous faith in progress and brotherhood. More than to

the two great North Americans, he could be compared to Hugo: eloquence, abundance, and that continuous surprise, that unending flow, of rhyme. Like the French poet's, his inspiration was that of the cyclopean sculpture; his stanzas are blocks of animated matter, veined with sudden delicacies: the striation of lighting on the stone. And the rhythm, the continuous swing that makes the language our enormous aquatic mass. Darío was less excessive and prophetic; he was also less valiant: he was not a rebel and he did not profess a horror of both miniaturism and titanism. More nervous, more anguished, he oscillated between contradictory impulses: one could say that he was a Hugo attacked by "decadent" ills. Despite the fact that he loved and imitated Verlaine above all (and above all others), his best poems have little resemblance to those of his model. He had superabundant health and energy; his sun was stronger, his wine more generous. Verlaine was a provincial Parisian; Darío a Central American globetrotter. His poetry is virile: skeleton, heart, sex.

Rubén Darío was born Félix Rubén García Sarmiento on January 18, 1867, in Metapa, a small town in what is now the municipality of Matagapa in Nicaragua. (It was eventually renamed Ciudad Darío.) His pen name, like that of Neruda (born Neftalí Ricardo Reyes Basoalto), was adopted later: it combines his second forename and the second last name of his father, Manuel García Darío. (His mother was Rosa Sarmiento Alemán.) He was baptized a Christian. His parents separated soon after his birth. His mother took him to Honduras, but eventually returned to Nicaragua, where Darío was raised in León.

In his autobiography, published in 1915 and known in Spanish as *La vida de Rubén Darío escrita por él mismo* (The Life of Rubén Darío, Written by Himself ), a volume which, as critics have pointed out, is filled with deliberate omissions as well as unintended errors, Darío reflected on the colonial landscape that surrounded him as a child. León, he said, was filled with cupolas, stone-paved streets, and fortresses. There were legends of decapitated priests on horses running wild; relatives would tell him ghost stories. Clearly, these stories and this setting instilled in him a sense of mystery and even religious devotion.

Anecdotes about Darío's precociousness abound. He himself stated that he learned to read at the age of three. And in his autobiography he tells us that at ten he discovered in a closet the first books he would read; among them were the Bible, *Don Quixote, The Arabian Nights,* works by Cicero and Madame de Staël, and a volume of Golden Age Spanish comedies. He attended public school but also studied at the Iglesia de la Recolección in León under the tutelage of the Jesuits—who had been expelled from Guatemala. It was also in those early years that he began to write poetry; as he put it, "I would never commit a single error in rhythm." Shortly after, Darío, at eleven, was writing epitaphs in verse on commission. His first poems were actually published in periodicals when he was thirteen years old; the newly formed newspaper *El Termómetro* featured a number of them. By the way, it is also said, implausibly, that before he reached twenty years of age Darío knew the entire *Diccionario de la Real Academia Española* by heart.

In 1884, at seventeen, several important events took place in Darío's life. At this time he was working as a presidential staff member under the regime of Adán Cárdenas, as well as in the National Library. The first life-changing event was Darío's appointment to what would be the first of several diplomatic posts. The other was the start of his contributions to the Argentine daily *La Nación,* a professional relationship that would last until Darío's death. And of course Darío's connection to the library would also prove to be invaluable. Throughout his life, he surrounded himself with books. The act of reading is ubiquitous in him: it appears in his poems, as book-reviewing in his journalism, and as a leitmotif in his prose; he even has a volume called *The Story of My Books.*

It was also at this period that Darío married for the first time, in a ceremony that took place in Nicaragua. His wife was Rafaela Contreras Cañas. She would be the first of three wives, with whom he would have four children, two of them dying in infancy. His first trip out of Nicaragua took him to Chile in 1886. In Chile, Darío found an atmosphere conducive to his revolutionary aesthetics, and in fact it was here that he made his debut as a poet in book form, with *Abrojos* in 1887. But it was *Azul . . . (Azure)*, a tiny volume published by Imprenta y Litografía Excelsior in Valparaíso—a thriving Chilean city of a hundred thousand citizens at the time—that not only remained one of Darío's all-time personal favorites but almost overnight made him famous in the Spanish-speaking world and turned him into the consummate leader of the *Modernistas*. The volume, combining poetry and prose, vies with Borges's *Ficciones* as the single most influential book-length publication ever to appear in Latin America. (*One Hundred Years of Solitude*, by Gabriel García Márquez, is next in importance.) Reaction to the book was mixed, but on balance gratifying. "I was greeted with incomprehension, astonishment, and censure from the professors, but cordial applause from my companions," Darío wrote. What made the volume so terribly important? "My success—it would be absurd not to confess it—has been due to novelty." He went on to explain:

> The origin of the novelty was my recent encounter with the French authors of the Parnassus, for at the time the Symbolist struggle was just beginning in France and so was not known abroad, much less in our Americas. . . . Accustomed as I was to the eternal cliché of the Spanish *Siglo de Oro* and Spain's indecisive modern poetry, I found in those French writers a mine of literary gold that was there to be explored, and exploited: I applied their way of employing adjectives, certain syntactical habits, a verbal aristocracy, to my Spanish. The rest was given by the character of Spanish itself, and the talent of yours truly. And I, who know Baralt's *Dictionary of Gallicisms* by heart, realized that not just a well-chosen Gallicism but also certain particularities from other languages might be extremely useful, might even be of incomparable efficacy in a certain type of "transplant."

It is the elements of French culture that make Darío tick. In 1899 he wrote in a letter to the Iberian philosopher Miguel de Unamuno: "I am embarrassed to admit it, but I do not think in Castillian Spanish. Rather, I think in French! Or, better still, I think *ideographically*, which is why my work is not 'pure.' I am referring to my most recent books. My first works, up to

*Azul . . .*, come from an undeniably Spanish stock, at least in their form." While Paris was Darío's center of cultural gravity, one ought to keep in mind that he was imagining the metropolis from his sojourns in Nicaragua and Chile. He would never be more Parisian than when he was still unacquainted with Paris, imagining its landscape through readings of his favorite authors. Notice also the use of the ellipsis after *Azul . . .* : Darío seems to invite the reader to enter with him that realm of dreams he is so eagerly striving for. His Catholic worldview had, as its counterpoint in the poetry, heterodox, pagan concepts. He styled himself a dilettante, and all in all succeeded in mastering that "profession." The poetic and prose experiments followed a similar approach: "the application to Spanish of certain verbal superiorities from other languages, in this case mainly French," Darío explained. For yes, the material is aristocratic in nature; it is also unapologetically erudite. The author exploits the etymology of words. He lets his style be driven by a melodious inner voice, focusing on rhythm not only in his stanzas, which are governed by syllabic meter, but also in his prose.

*Azul . . .* contains classic pieces like "About Winter" and "To a Poet." And in a literary mode that Darío would repeatedly return to, he included in this volume what he called *medallones,* a text written in homage—in the form of an ornament, a medallion—to an influential figure, Whitman for instance. Darío saw the good gray poet simultaneously as an emperor and a priestly presence who strove toward true democracy by encouraging the sailor to row, the eagle to fly, and the laborer to work. Darío praised Whitman in this way:

> His boundless soul resembles a mirror.
> His weary shoulders deserve the best cloak.
> He sings his song like a modern seer,
> strumming on a lyre cut from ancient oak.

Yes, much like Borges and Neruda after him, Darío thoroughly admired Whitman. The very name of the American master required him to take a breath. "Whitman, maestro

Whitman," sighed the Nicaraguan poet, "broke all the rules and, guided by instinct, went back to the Hebrew line. And I must concur with the diagnosis of the Jew Nordau with respect to the immense poet of *Leaves of Grass,* that rare, strange— passing strange, *degenerate*—Whitman, yet honored, too, Maeterlinck's master, that strong, cosmic Yankee. We, dear maestro, the young poets of the Spanish Americas, are preparing the way, because our own Whitman must be soon to come, our indigenous Walt Whitman, filled with the world, saturated with the universe, like that other Whitman of the north, chanted so beautifully by 'our' Martí. And no one would be surprised if in this vast cosmopolis, this alembic of souls and races, where Andrade of the symbolic *Atlántida* lived his life and this young savage Lugones has just appeared, there might appear some precursor of that poet heralded by the enigmatic and terrible Montevideo madman, in his prophetic and terrifying book."

In this Penguin Classics anthology, *azul,* "blue" in Spanish, is not translated as blue. As Andrew Hurley suggests in his translator's note to the section of stories and fables, the alternative choice, *azure,* is closer in spirit to Darío's intention: while avoiding associations with "the blues" and "being blue," it foregrounds an association Darío made with fairy tales (*"cuentos azules"* in Spanish) filled with princesses, castles, and knights in shining armor (or "Prince Charmings," *"príncipes azules,"* literally "blue knights," in Spanish). The title of that first influential collection, in Darío's view, pointed to the color of daydreams, an azure found in the work of Victor Hugo, "the color of art, a Hellenic, Homeric color, a color oceanic and firmamental, the *coeruleum* which in Pliny is the simple color that resembles the sky, and sapphires."

In any case, *Azul . . .* ought to be read as an itinerary of sorts, announcing the direction Darío would take in his life-long oeuvre. Most of the attention it commands comes from its crystalline stanzas. But it also contains stories such as "The Bourgeois King," subtitled "A Cheering Tale," about a pompous monarch who hires a poet to play the organ in his garden parties, "near the swans." The fairy tales function as an excuse for Darío to analyze two social types: an emerging bourgeoisie in Latin America, uninterested in art, and the artist with lofty ideals. The poet is clearly Darío's alter ego. He states: "My lord, for long years I have sung the word of the future. I was born in the time of the dawn and I have spread my wings in the hurricane. I seek the chosen race that awaits, with hymns upon their lips and lyres in their hands, the rising of the great sun. . . ." And: "I have caressed great Nature, and I have sought, in the warmth of the ideal, the verse that lies in the star at the end of the heavens, the pearl in the depths of ancient Ocean. I have sought to boom, to crash! For the age of the great revolutions is coming, with a Messiah that is all Light, and Agitation, and Power, and we must receive his spirit with a poem that is a triumphal arch, with lines of iron, and lines of gold, and lines of love." The survival of this hungry artist depends on the bourgeois king. At the end of the story, Darío has him perish "thinking that the sun would rise the next day, and with it, the ideal . . . and that art would wear not wool pants, but a mantle of gold, and flames. . . . And the next day the king and his courtiers found him there, the poor devil of a poet, like a swallow frozen in the ice, with a bitter smile on his lips."

In comparison with Darío's poetry, his stories have commanded limited attention. They are skillfully written, but they suffer for their ambitions, in that they rarely generate the genuine psychological terror achieved by Poe and Stevenson, and also from the fact that their author died too soon to benefit, as Borges did so exotically, from the discoveries of Sigmund Freud. Still, they are marvelous in the traditional sense of the term: filled with precious marvels. And they ought to be read in their own historical context. As a fin-de-siècle literari, Darío employed images and symbols, much in the way the nineteenth-century Romantics did. He wasn't interested in plot. Instead, his objective was to communicate "truths." What makes him so compelling, I would argue, is his perversity—perversity of spirit, sexual perversity. In "The Ruby," for instance, the precious stone is created by means of the blood of a woman that has been kidnapped and maybe raped. Thus, the gems that result from it are dependent on violence, wounding, abuse, violation of all sorts. There is also the dance-read-as-sexual-dalliance of "The Palace of the Sun," the "murder" of art by a jealous wife in "The Death of the Empress of China," and "El Fardo" and countless other similar stories in which the artist-figure is insensitive to the pain of others. It is in his stories that Darío is at his most Decadent and the humanistic paradigm is inverted. For what is Decadence if not a form of writing obsessed with style, in which the subject tends toward the perverse, dark, and sinful, and in which sensation is more important than morality? In his fiction Darío does tend to be overly allegorical for the pre-Chekhov and pre-Joyce reader, delegating plot to a secondary role and coming up with characters that might serve as mouthpieces for/of his aesthetic and other ideas. This, after all, is what the French short story was at the time, and the short story often written in English when Nathaniel Hawthorne and Herman Melville were active. Such is the case of "The Deaf Satyr," also in *Azul . . .* , a Greek story set on Mount Olympus, in which the poet Orpheus sings his songs in the woods. Orpheus, the poet, "sickened by mankind's misery," decides to seek refuge in the woods, "where the trees and rocks might understand him and listen to him in ecstasy, and where, when he played his lyre, he might make all things tremble with harmony and the fire of love." He sings his song to a deaf satyr, who, following his ass's advice, exiles Orpheus from the woods. Again, the portrait of the artist is disheartening: the poet, seeking communion with nature and community, finds only rejection.

In the preceding pages I have spoken, time and again, about the *Modernista* revolution. Let it not be confused with the term *Rubenista,* which means a follower of Darío. *Modernismo* was an ambitious way of reappraising the world. But what was it really about? And why should the term be written in Spanish and italicized? What constitutes an artistic movement? Should *Modernismo* be considered such a movement? These questions, particularly the latter ones, have, again, an embattled quality to them, in tune with the critique Darío faced in life as a *Modernista.* For intellectuals of his time—and scores of others since then—have often suggested that Darío's poetics encapsulated impossibly disparate ambitions. A new bourgeois sensibility like the one Darío was announcing, an interest in occult religion, a Pythagorean understanding of music and the spiritual realm, and a desire to write Spanish following French syntax are efforts so disparate in their very nature that it seems impossible to bring them together under a single rubric. No wonder Miguel de Unamuno complained in 1918: "I don't exactly know what this business of *Modernistas* and *Modernismo* is. Such diverse and opposing things are given these names that there is no way to reduce them to a common category." Others have agreed with Unamuno, arguing that almost a century after Darío's death—and thus, after the demise of the overall intellectual and social upheaval he expounded—today we still have no clear vision of what it was all about.

But these complaints are unjustified. In recent years there has been an effort to conceptualize *Modernismo* in ways unattainable to Unamuno. Clearly, *Modernismo* was, more than anything else, a metaphysical pursuit by a cadre of intellectuals disenchanted with institutionalized religion and with the ideological currents available. In Darío's case, he was influenced by Pythagoreanism, a view (adapted by Spinoza in the Renaissance) suggesting that the entire universe is permeated by, and manifests, the divine. An essential ingredient of this worldview is the concept of harmony. God is a harmonious entity and so is nature, made of eternal male and female elements. The Pythagoreans sought a unity of life based on their faith in a universe that was orderly, intelligible, and logical, and on the need to find balance between the masculine and feminine sides of the self. The search for unity leads to the concept of a mirror between the microcosm of humanity and the macrocosm that is the universe. The *Modernistas* sought to understand their surroundings through theories such as this one. They perceived the poet to be a biblical character of sorts, whose talent, much like that of the prophet, lay in his ability to perceive the layers and connections that make reality what it is. The poet was able to communicate with the higher spheres through his intellect and

song, and he (for these were male-dominated times) needed to
offer those gifts to the people even if the message might be
misunderstood and rejected. This haughty attitude toward art
was typical in the twilight of the nineteenth century. Among the
*Modernistas* in Latin America, it sometimes found itself mixed
with politics. That is the case of the Cuban José Martí, of
course, and, as I will discuss later, also with Darío, although to
a far lesser extent.

The term Modernism—in spite of the way Paz, or better, his
translators, and others use it—should not be confused with its
Spanish version, *Modernismo*. As it turns out, the meaning of
the words in the two languages is diametrically different, iden-
tifying trends that belong to radically divergent cultural land-
scapes. (Hence my use, throughout, of the italicized Spanish.)
"Modernism" is the rubric used in Europe and the United
States to designate the artistic generation between the world
wars (the dates range from approximately 1914 to the mid-
fifties), personified by, among others, T. S. Eliot, Ezra Pound,
James Joyce, Virginia Woolf, and Gertrude Stein. Their pursuit
was aesthetic in nature as well as political and linguistic. They
believed that the patterns of life at the end of the Industrial Rev-
olution, as they applied to art and philosophy, were outmoded
and needed to be revitalized, sometimes by "renewing" old
forms, genres, authors. Thus, in the area of literature, the prac-
titioners of Modernism sought to invigorate the page by making
language less rigid, more flexible. They embraced concepts such
as "stream of consciousness" in order to portray characters in
nontraditional ways—from inside out, so to speak. All of this
makes the Modernists in Europe closer to what are called the
*Vanguardistas* of Latin America (e.g., César Vallejo, et al.).

In contrast, the *Modernistas* in Latin America appeared
earlier on the cultural map. Their revolution occurred roughly
between 1885 and 1915 (or, with Darío's death, a year later)
and although it spilled into other artistic areas, its central
tenets apply to literature almost exclusively, and to poetry
most vividly. The writers of the *Modernista* movement are
much closer in spirit to the Romantics in Europe, whose

poetic search is also for unity and harmony in the universe at large. Latin America never had a Romantic movement per se; indeed, it skipped it, because by the time that particular aesthetics arrived on this side of the Atlantic the region was consumed with ideas of independence and revolution. Politics mingled inextricably with daily affairs and there was no time to be concerned with that sublime and tragic sense of life. But by the end of the nineteenth century, nations such as Mexico, Argentina, and Colombia had become autonomous, and they were focused on finding their own collective identity. Others, such as Cuba and Puerto Rico, would be at the junction of the Spanish-America War of 1898, through which Spain lost its colonies in the Caribbean Basin and the region entered the orbit of a new imperial power, the United States. Thus, *Modernismo* is, in essence, a loose Latin American version of Romanticism, infused with an understanding of language and politics that is influenced by global events at the time and by post-Romantic artistic movements in Europe such as Symbolism and Parnassianism, which embraced an esoteric, somewhat hermetic conception of art. The poet, in the view of these movements, connected with archetypes embedded in the cultural consciousness. Aside from Darío, the movement included Martí, Colombian José Asunción Silva, Mexican Manuel Gutiérrez Nájera, and Argentine Leopoldo Lugones. Through his combination of literature and essays, Martí, like Darío, was an assiduous correspondent to newspapers such as *La Nación* in Buenos Aires, and his readers soon made him an idol—and, with his death on the battlefield in 1895 in the struggle for Cuban independence, a martyr as well. But while these two authors have much in common, they are also quite different. Darío, for one thing, is an aesthete, even though he wrote copiously on the imperial hopes of the United States in the Spanish-speaking hemisphere. While Martí remained focused on Cuba no matter where he was throughout the Americas and in exile in Key West and New York, Darío wandered the globe. Darío's itinerant agenda as a diplomat, journalist, and traveler brought him to distant regions—distant at least for a citizen of a small, impoverished nation such as Nicaragua.

Darío was comfortable with the effort behind *Modernismo,* although he grew suspicious of the rubric itself. In his eyes the movement should have represented progress in a myriad of areas, from science to technology, from economics to education. He envisioned—and with enormous enthusiasm—a transition for the Americas from an awkward, dependent region still lingering in its mediocrity, stuck in a dogmatic tradition, and blindly loyal to a feudal Spain, to a fully cosmopolitan society attuned to the principles and fashions of the West. This, for him, was the announcement of a new type of life. This *Modernismo,* he stated, "is beginning to give us a place apart, a place that is independent." It must be kept in mind that with the exception of the luminous seventeenth-century Mexican nun Sor Juana Inés de La Cruz and an improbably small cadre of *americanistas,* the number of authors from the New World that were recognized at all in Spain was insignificant. So for Darío and his peers, recognition in Madrid was important, since it meant legitimacy: if the former colonial power could validate their work, the status of that work was automatically more solid, less ethereal.

There was much debate in Spain at the time about the accuracy of describing the overall effort as *Modernismo* and about the ultimate endurance of the work. Juan Valera, in a column called "American Letters" for the literary supplement of the newspaper *El Imparcial,* expressed his enthusiasm. He remarked on Darío's French tone and the highly polished Spanish of the pieces. Valera eventually wrote to Darío: "None of the men of letters of the Peninsula that I have known with more cosmopolitan spirit, and that have resided for a longer time in France, and that have spoken French and other foreign languages better, have ever seemed to me so deeply filled with the spirit of France as you, sir: not Galiano, not Eugenio de Ochoa, not Miguel de los Santos Alvarez." Valera added a little later: "It seems that here, a Nicaraguan author who never set foot out of Nicaragua except to go to Chile, and who is an author so *à la mode de Paris* and with such 'chic' and distinction, has been able to anticipate fashion and even modify and impose it."

In 1890, a couple of years after *Azul . . .* was published, a coup d'etat in Nicaragua forced Darío to move to Guatemala, then to El Salvador. In 1891, his son Rubén Darío Contreras was born in Costa Rica. In 1892 he also made his first, revelatory trip to Spain, a country with which he had an emotional relationship described in the chronicles and literary portraits of *España contemporánea* (Contemporary Spain, 1901). This was the four hundredth anniversary of Columbus's so-called discovery of the Americas, and Darío was on the verge of replicating, at the aesthetic level, Simón Bolívar's effort to achieve continental independence from Spain. Over time he met several Spanish writers with whom he established a lasting friendship; some of them, including Ramón María Valle-Inclán, Antonio and Manuel Machado, and Juan Ramón Jiménez, later to win the Nobel Prize for literature, became supporters or wrote prologues for his books. It was also at this time that Rafaela Contreras Cañas died. Shortly after, Darío married his second wife, Rosario Murillo.

Darío finally traveled to Paris in the early 1890s. There he at last met one of his idols, Paul Verlaine, and, on a trip to New York, he forged a friendship with Martí. Three years later, in 1896, now known as the *annus mirabilis* in Darío's career, two of his most important books, *Los raros* (The Misfits) and *Prosas profanas y otros poemas* (Profane Prose and Other Poems), were published by Imprenta Pablo E. Coni, their publication costs paid by Carlos Vega Belgrano, editor of Argentina's *El Tiempo,* a newspaper for which Darío regularly wrote. These two efforts are fascinating in that they push Darío's aesthetic views to new dimensions. *Los raros,* published in Argentina, includes profiles of characters Darío is attracted to (Poe, Verlaine, Rachilde, Villiers de Lisle d'Adam, et al.). Their appeal is to be found in the desire they nurture to not adapt their needs to society, to break rules, to rebel. In *Prosas profanas,* on the other hand, the term "profane" is crucial: Darío strove for a poetics akin to his age, connected to Catholicism but seeking alternative modes of faith. He looked toward mythology, and he also looked toward pre-Columbian history. His memoir *Historia de mis libros* (The Story of My Books), serialized in Buenos Aires's *La Nación* in 1913, along with his autobiography, allow us to understand Darío's own perception of his poetic mission. In that first book, he writes: "[In] all the Spanish Americas, no one held any end or object for poetry save the celebration of *native* glories, the events of Independence, the *American* nature: an eternal hymn to Junín, an endless ode to the agriculture of the torrid zone, and stirring patriotic songs. I did not deny that there was a great treasure trove of poetry in our prehistoric times, in the Conquest, and even in the colony, but with our subsequent social and political state had come intellectual dwarfism and historical periods more suitable for the blood-dripping penny dreadful than the noble canto. Yet I added: 'Buenos Aires—cosmopolis! And tomorrow!' The proof of this prophecy can be found in my recent 'Canto to Argentina.'"

This volume again contains classical examples of Darío's aesthetics, including a sonatina about a princess, an early poem about a swan, and a couple of poems that might well be considered his *ars poetica*: "Love Your Rhythm" and "I'm Hunting a Form." In the former, Darío, in a self-referential voice, maps out his poetic pursuit, offering a vision of the poet as a medium between the earthly and celestial spheres. The poem includes this stanza:

> The celestial oneness you surely are
> will make worlds sprout in you that are diverse,
> and if your meters start to sound dispersed,
> use Pythagoras to unite your stars.

The sonnet "I'm Hunting a Form," on the other hand, is the most representative of Darío's confessional pieces. It mixes classical and mythical ingredients, from the Venus de Milo to Sleeping Beauty, concluding with the swan, specifically its question mark–shaped neck, as a symbol of doubt. This is a memorable disquisition on the evasiveness and vulnerability of poetry. The last two stanzas read:

> I can only find words that never seem to stay,
> pieces of a song from a flute, which slip away,
> the ship of those dreams, which drift aimlessly in space.
>
> And under my Sleeping Beauty's open window,
> the soft and steady crying of the fountain's flow,
> and the swan's great white neck, with its questions, its grace.

On the other hand, *Los raros* is, in my estimation, one of Darío's most bizarre, most daring works. Mexican critic Jaime Torres Bodet once said that the book contains portraits of artists better known for their proclivity toward the uncanny than for their authentic genius, and more apt to produce episodic—that is, forgettable—art than art that is likely to endure throughout the ages. But a mere list of those discussed by Darío instantaneously proves the thesis wrong: Martí, Poe (who, according to Dario, "passed his life, one might say, under the floating influence of a strange mystery"), Ibsen, Verlaine, Léon Bloy, and Isadora Duncan, to name only a handful. Darío does not attempt to deliver a balanced view. Instead, he is interested in an open, confessed display of subjectivity. His portraits are about exceptional natures, about freedom in art, about talents whose life, like Darío's, is spent "hunting a form that my style can barely trace." Needless to say, Darío's choice of a subject for a book was, in a way, a self-justification. After all, he, too, was *un raro,* an eccentric who had a huge influence on literature and was recognized as something of a genius. This, by the way, wasn't the first time he had embraced a tangential approach to writing: Darío was often known to choose a theme in order to talk about himself and his place in society, the place of his poetry in society, and the place of the artist in society. The argument in *Los raros* is that those who rebel, those who assert their difference, are those whom, in the long run, we most prize.

It should be added that at this time Darío also started to serialize a novel called *El hombre de oro* (Man of Gold), which was influenced by Flaubert's *Salambó*. As for Whitman, who also tried his luck at writing a novel, for Darío the excursion was not a high point in his career: the volume is more derivative than anything else he ever did, abstruse, distracted. He clearly did not have a talent for long fictional narratives. Nor would he stop traveling and getting himself romantically involved. Then there were the newspaper deadlines to meet, for journalistic squibs were, in the end, his only regular means of support. Actually, these two elements, women and journalism, played a crucial role as Darío's career entered its last creative stage. Women sometimes seemed almost the entire focus of his attention. He was known as a regular visitor of prostitutes. He also wrote profusely on women. In the short story "The Ruby," one of the characters says: ". . . I have been but a slave to one, an almost mystical adorer of the other." Sometimes Darío discussed their role as labor at the dawn of the twentieth century in societies such as Germany, England, and the United States, in order to persuade people that in Latin America "the working mother will make hardworking children, and good citizens"; he also talks of the Nicaraguan woman as possessing "a kind of Arabian languor, a native-born insouciance, joined to a natural elegance and looseness in her movements and her walk." But when Darío talks about Spanish women, his lyricism is unequaled. He chants:

> Nature proceeds and teaches logically; Nature has ordered the creatures and things of the earth according to their place on it, and Nature knows why the Scandinavians are blond and Abyssinians black, why the English have swan's necks and Flemish women opulent handholds. Spanish females were given several models, depending upon their region in the Peninsula, but the true type, the type best known through poetry and art, is the olive-skinned beauty, somewhat *potelée,* neither tall nor short, with wondrous large dark eyes and wavy black hair that falls in cascades, all this animated by a marine, Venusian quality that has no name in any other language: *sal*.

As his first and second marriages attest, Darío also sought to commit himself to women, even though his itinerant life often unraveled those commitments. But the picture that emerges in short stories like "The Palace of the Sun" is never that simple. In it the Nicaraguan talks of anemic maidens overwhelmed by melancholy, a favorite *fin-de-siècle* malady. Darío talks of "something better than arsenic and iron for rekindling the crimson of lovely virginal cheeks." What does he recommend? The message is allegorical. He tells the mothers of those maidens, "your enchanting little birds' cages must be opened, especially when the spring-time comes and there is ardor in the veins and sap, and a thousand atoms of sunlight are buzzing in the garden like a swarm of gold among the half-open roses." When describing the female body, the Nicaraguan's language is invariably lush. He talks of the "pink flesh" of precious princesses, describing them as "gay, delicious songbird[s] of black eyes and red mouth." They are voluptuous in their innocence, nymphs that become not only love objects but idols to be adored. In "The Ruby," Darío states: "My human woman loved a man, and from her prison she was sending him her sighs. The sighs passed through the pores of the earth's skin and found him, and he, still loving her, would kiss the roses in a certain garden, and she, his beloved, would have sudden convulsions . . . in which she would pucker her pink, cool lips like the petals of a damask rose." In the spirit of the Romantics, Darío seems infatuated by a woman's nakedness, which he describes by invoking flowers—roses, lilies, ivory hillocks crowned with cherries. His infatuation reaches such a degree that it often makes him lose all inhibitions. Voyeurism leads to lust, and lust might result in violent possession. This approach might appear scandalous to our eyes, but think of popular examples in Darío's age, like Bram Stoker's *Dracula,* first published in 1897, as well as Alexandre Dumas's play *La dame aux camélias,* on which Giuseppe Verdi's *La Traviata* is based. Women in them are discontented beings or sheer objects of uncontrollable male desire, or both. Surely Darío was not unique in his fixations.

In 1899, Darío, again traveling to Spain—first to Barcelona, then to Madrid—met Francisca Sánchez, an illiterate peasant from Navalsáuz, whom Darío taught to read. The couple relocated in Paris, where he worked as a correspondent for *La*

*Nación,* focusing on the *Exposition Universelle de Paris.* His pieces for *La Nación* were at times reportage and others columns and op-eds. And this was only the principal newspaper he worked for. His articles were reprinted in others elsewhere in the Spanish-speaking world, as well as in weekly and monthly magazines. Plus, on occasion Darío worked as an editor himself for a periodical. This effort needs to be seen in context. Latin America was swept by a spirit of independence that had begun in 1810. Throughout the century, the nations of the continent strove to break away from Spain as an imperial power and to establish autonomous, self-sufficient nation-states all across the hemisphere. By the conclusion of the nineteenth century, a new bourgeoisie was on the rise in major urban centers on this side of the Atlantic, from Mexico to Peru to Argentina. This was also the period in which positivistic thinking penetrated the region, encouraging the educated classes to endorse science and technology as approaches that needed to replace the awkwardness of religion, which had prevailed as a system of thought throughout the colonial age. Modernity, then, arrived just as open markets and free thinking made inroads among the educated.

In substantial ways, the *Modernista* revolution was an intellectual modality that needs to be seen as intimately related to the consolidation of capitalism in Latin America. I hinted at this in the brief discussion of Darío's short story "The Bourgeois King," but in fact this socioeconomic aspect might be found in numerous places in his work, from *Azul . . .* through *Los raros* to *El canto errante* (The Wandering Song). Angel Rama, in his book *Rubén Darío y el modernismo,* disagrees with scholars who suggest that *Modernismo* was a reaction to capitalism. Instead, he suggests that it is a by-product of it. Rama analyzes Darío's self-awareness as a dilettante, his view of the poet as a conduit expressing dissatisfaction with contemporary life, his faith in Catholicism as a way to satisfy humans' ancient desire to communicate with the supernatural, and so on. One should also add to this Darío's role as a journalist, the only way a Nicaraguan of humble means or background could support both his career as a poet and also his role as a diplomat, which enabled him to travel far and wide and gain exposure to aspects of Western civilization he would otherwise not have had access to. Indeed, at the time the average middle-class citizen of a Central American country never even dreamed of traveling within the region, let alone abroad. In that sense, Darío, thus, is a *rara avis*: year by year, most of his life was spent overseas. Guatemala, Chile, Spain, and France were important destinations, and for a while became homes, too; and Darío also traveled to Gibraltar and Morocco, Italy, Cuba, and Mexico, where, by the way, he participated, in 1910, in the hundredth anniversary commemoration of *El Grito de Dolores,* the battle-cry for independence.

Did Darío ever consider his roles as journalist and diplomat as important as that of poet? No, he never did. He was a poet first and foremost. None of his diplomatic work left any imprint. Actually, he often convinced friends and acquaintances to name him to a post for no other reason than to be far away from Nicaragua. As a journalist, on the other hand, he was unquestionably prolific as well as influential. Darío was active at a time when the perceptions of journalism were already being differentiated between the European model and its counterpart in the United States. In the Old Continent the view was that newspapers offered the facts with little embellishment: the duty of reporters was to be succinct in conveying the news. But on this side of the Atlantic, and especially in Latin America, the approach was to mix journalism and literature, to entertain as well as to inform. It is easy to see where Darío's sympathies fell. He wrote: "Today, and always, 'journalists' and 'writers' must of necessity be confused with one another. Most essayists are journalists. Montaigne and de Maistre are journalists in the broad sense of the word. All observers of, and commentators on, life have been journalists. Now, if you are referring simply to the mechanical aspect of the modern profession, then we can agree that the only persons who merit the name *journalist* are commercial 'reporters,' those who report on daily events—and even these may be very good writers who with a grace of style and a pinch of philosophy are able to turn an arid affair into an interesting page. There are political editorials written by thoughtful, high-minded men that are true chapters of fundamental books.

There are chronicles, descriptions of celebrations or ceremonies, written by reporters who are artists, and these chronicles might not be out of place in literary anthologies. The journalist who writes what he writes with love and care is as much a 'writer,' an 'author' as any other. . . . The only person who merits our indifference and time's oblivion is he who premeditatedly sits down to write, for the fleeting moment, words without the glow of burnishing, ideas without the salt taste and smell of blood. . . . Very beautiful, very useful, and very valuable volumes could be made up if one were to carefully pick through newspapers' collections of 'reports' written by many persons considered to be simple 'journalists.' "

In 1905, just as the expectations for the century were settling in, Darío offered his greetings to *"la nueva era"* by publishing his book *Cantos de vida y esperanza: Los cisnes y otros poemas* (Songs of Life and Hope: Swans and Other Poems). The volume appeared under the aegis of the Taller de la Revista de Archivos. It might be significant to remember that much like the rest of Darío's books, this perennial classic had a first printing of only five hundred copies, which took a while to be sold. Then as now, poetry, needless to say, was not an item destined for mass consumption. Of Whitman, too, it is known that several decades after publishing *Leaves of Grass*, only three hundred had been sold. In spite of this "eternal truth," Darío was dismayed. Not that he was a popularist, but he surely disliked one aspect of the elitism of poetry: "Ask booksellers how many editions they have published and how many copies they have sold of great poetry, of books of travel, of novels—ask them, and the reply will be terribly mortifying to your spirit! . . ."

*Azul* . . . , *Prosas profanas*, and *Cantos de vida y esperanza* form a triptych wherein Darío's stylistic mission is best understood. However, compared with the other two, in *Cantos* Darío strikes a decidedly amending tone, reformulating his own aesthetics, arguing with his antagonists, and generally looking at his own place as a poet not only at the past and present time but also into posterity. I for one see this volume as Darío's most compact and complete single volume, but one dealing less with innovation than with recapitulation. At a time when poets died young—among the *Modernistas* Martí died at the age of 42, Rodó at 46, José Asunción Silva at 31, and Gutiérrez Nájera at 36, only Lugones lived to the "advanced" age of 64—Darío was almost 40 years old, a mature man by the standards of his period. His mood makes him look back and reconsider his previous work. He also feels the need to expand, to look beyond his horizon. Octavio Paz wrote that Darío "expresses himself [here] more soberly, more profoundly, but his love for the brilliant word does not diminish. Nor does his taste for rhythmic innovation disappear; on the contrary, these innovations are surer and more daring." *Cantos de vida y esperanza* includes poems to Cervantes and Goya, songs to melancholy, and more than sixty other poems, his most prolific production ever. The book also reflects Darío's political transformation at the time of the Spanish-American War in 1898. The struggle shook him to the core. He denounced the United States in a series of poems and articles written for various periodicals. Still, he perceived the United States—or better, he misunderstood it—as a godless empire whose hemispheric fortune was on the rise. He simultaneously admired and detested it, thinking that the best solution for a hemispheric harmony was a neighborly pact between north and south. His poem to Theodore Roosevelt includes one of the most famous words Darío ever wrote: the monosyllabic *no*. This might sound preposterous; after all, how often does the word appear in his oeuvre? Thousands of times, no doubt. But its position in the poem "To Roosevelt" is exemplary and has been read as a political statement. Herein a fragment:

> You're arrogant and you're strong, exemplary of your race;
> you're cultivated, you're skilled, you stand opposed to Tolstoy.
> You're a tamer of horses, you're a killer of tigers,
> you're like some Alexander mixed with Nebuchadnezzar.
> (You must be the Energy Professor
> as the crazies today might put it)
>
> You think that life is one big fire,
> that progress is just eruption,

that wherever you put bullets,
you put the future, too.


                              No.


The U.S. is a country that is powerful and strong.
When the giant yawns and stretches, the earth feels a tremor
rippling through the enormous vertebrae of the Andes.
If you shout, the sound you make is a lion's roar.
Hugo once said this to Grant: "You possess the stars."
(The Argentine sun at dawn gives off hardly any light;
and the Chilean star is rising higher . . . ) You're so rich,
you join the cult to Hercules with the cult to Mammon.
And lighting the broad straight path that leads to easy conquests,
Lady Liberty raises her torch in New York City.

But our own America, which had plenty of poets
even from the ancient times of Netzahualcoyotl,
and which retained the footprints from the feet of Great Bacchus,
and, over the course of time, learned the Panic alphabet:
it sought advice from the stars, and knew of Atlantis,
whose name was a legacy, resonating in Plato.
Even from the most remote moments in its boundless life,
it has lived by light and fire, by fragrances and by love:
America of the great Moctezuma and Inca,
America redolent of Christopher Columbus,
Catholic America and Spanish America,
the place where once long ago the noble Cuátemoc said,
"I'm not on a bed of roses!" Yes, that America,
trembling from its hurricanes and surviving on its Love . . .
It lives with you, with your Saxon eyes and barbaric souls.
And dreams. And loves, and vibrates; it's the daughter of the Sun.
Be careful. Spanish America is alive and well!
There are myriad loose cubs now from the Spanish Lion.
Roosevelt, you'd need to be transfigured by God himself
into the dire Rifleman and the powerful Hunter
to finally capture us in your talons of iron.


This, clearly, is a defiant ideological poem. But it also strikes a
religious chord, for Darío ends it by telling Roosevelt: "And
you think you have it all, but one thing is missing: God!" In this

sense it showcases a view of the United States that is nearsighted: the Nicaraguan sees Latin America as a site where faith is essential, unlike its Anglo-Saxon counterpart, which he portrays, mistakenly, as less devout. Did Darío not understand the principal puritan beliefs? Significantly, his North American idols, as stated before, are Whitman and Poe. But what about Emerson and even Hawthorne? Was it his troubled Catholicism that made it impossible for him to connect with a core Protestant constituency north of the Rio Grande?

In 1848, almost half a century before the Spanish-American War, the United States, by signing the Treaty of Guadalupe Hidalgo, acquired a large portion of Mexico's territory—largely what today is known as the Southwestern states. What were Darío's views on the Mexican population in places like Arizona, Colorado, and New Mexico? He ignored it. And yet, in "To Roosevelt," he announced that Spanish America, in spite of American imperialism, is alive and well. And in the poem "The Swans," he reiterates this view but also foresees, tangentially, the growth of a Latino community within the United States. His view is not comforting, though. Should this demographic transformation be applauded or condemned, he wonders? Herein two crucial stanzas:

> Hispanic America and Spain as a whole country
> are fixed on the origin of their fatal destiny.
> I am questioning the Sphinx about what it can foresee
> with the question mark of your neck, asking the air for me.
>
> Are we to be overrun by the cruel barbarian?
> Is it our fate that millions of us will speak in English?
> Are there no fierce shining knights, no valiant noblemen?
> Shall we keep our silence now, to weep later in anguish?

Seen from another perspective, this poem, also part of *Cantos de vida y esperanza,* brings Darío back to his enduring symbol, the swan, made famous in *Azul* . . . What tigers and mirrors are to Borges, what houses and the ocean are to Neruda, the swan is to Darío. But in 1905 the poet's act of return makes the bird less a chimera and an artifact of fairy tales than an outright symbol, though, at this stage in his life, the swan is a symbol infused with a political pathos. Darío announces: "What sign do you form, oh, Swan, with the curve of your neck's shape / when the wandering dreamers who are filled with grief pass by? / Why is it you are silent, white, lovely in this landscape, / a tyrant to these waters, heartless to these flowers? Why?"

However, *Cantos de vida y esperanza* also includes the poem "Poets! Towers of God!", in which Darío establishes, once and for all, his Pythagorean approach to poetry and poets:

> Poets! Towers of God!
> You bear storms that are infernal
> like a jagged mountain range,
> like a heavenly lighting rod,
> breakwaters of the eternal,
> high summits that will never change!

The rest of the stanzas emphasize Darío's opinion that "while on one side a poet leans toward nature, and in that he approaches the estate of the plastic artist, on the other side, he is of the race of priests, and in that he rises toward the divine." For this reason, the poem is a manifesto: an elegy to poetry as the seeker of harmony. It is also a hymn to elitism.

Darío was quite productive in his last decade of life. At just the moment he was unsuccessfully trying, from his post as a diplomat in Spain, to annul his marriage to Rosario Murillo and, as Francisca was giving birth to Rubén Darío Sánchez, nicknamed Guicho, Darío himself was publishing, in 1907, *El canto errante*. This is a volume in which Darío comes to terms with his own mortality, a subject that is part of the poem "Lo fatal" (Destined to Die) but that increasingly permeates all his work as he approaches his end. By our standards, he was still young. But unhealthy habits (alcohol, visits to prostitutes) got the best of him. Not surprisingly, though, his physical decline encouraged his poetic ambition. His next collection, *Poema de otoño y otros poemas* (Autumn Poem and Other Poems), released in 1910, includes pieces about death and eternal peace. For instance, the poem "Vesperal" includes these lines:

Now that the siesta's done,
now that the twilight hour is drawing near
and the tropical sun

that charred this coast has almost disappeared,
there's a gentle, cool zephyr breathing here
through the western sky's trees of illusion
lit by purple flames in the atmosphere.

Darío seems to ask: Might I claim for myself a place in Western
civilization as a whole? The answer in his view was inconclusive,
yet he did not give up his quest. He recognized at that point his
enormous influence over Spanish-language poetry, the way he
had brought fresh life into a culture known, until him, for its al-
lergy to innovation. Symbolically, the image of Jesus Christ is
solidly present in his poetry of the period. His poem "To Colum-
bus," included in *El canto errante,* was written some years ear-
lier to commemorate the four hundredth anniversary of the
Genoese admiral's voyage across the Atlantic. He portrays the
navigator as a bringer of misery to the Americas, and he indicts
him for the abuses. But he also sees Columbus's messianic ghost
wandering the continent, a witness of his own atrocities:

The cross you brought us never seems to diminish.
When will corruption in revolutions be shown?
Not in the works of women who will demolish
the keen language of Cervantes and Calderón.

Christ is wandering through the streets, diseased and lean.
Barrabas has slaves, military distinction.
The lands of Chibcha, Cuzco, Palenque have seen
their panthers tamed, beribboned, brought to extinction.

The horror, the wars, the constant malarias
are doomed paths from which our luck has not recovered:
Poor Admiral, yes, you, Christopher Columbus,
pray to God for the world you discovered!

A couple of years later Darío brought out *Alfonso XIII* and *El
viaje a Nicaragua e Intermezzo tropical* (Voyage to Nicaragua

and Tropical Intermezzo), after which he released his collection *Poema del otoño y otros poemas* (Autumn Poems and Other Poems). His health deteriorated rapidly in the years following World War I. It is no secret that he was drinking heavily. His alcoholism often spiraled out of control and got the better of him. Finally his cirrhosis became public knowledge. His last volume of poetry, *Canto a la Argentina y otros poemas* (Song to Argentina and Other Poems), was released in 1914. The title poem—the longest in a long career—was written in 1910 and includes material that deals with the social and commercial changes occurring in Latin America in the early part of the twentieth century, especially the dramatic changes Argentina had undergone in order to become modern. For instance, Darío refers to the Jewish immigrants from Eastern Europe who had arrived in Argentina and settled in communes in the province of Entre Ríos and elsewhere. Overall, this is a panoramic piece about freedom and independence. It includes these stanzas:

> Commerce, the great cities' forces,
> rumbling of iron and towers,
> swift hippogriff shielded in steel,
> electric roses and flowers
> plucked from the Arabian Nights,
> Babylonian pomp, bells, lights,
> trumpets, rumbling wheels, yoked oxen,
>
> voices of pianos from parlors,
> profound and piercing human moans,
> children singing as one in class,
> people hawking things in the street,
> one tense fiber keeping the beat,
> living in life's most vital core
> the way a heart goes on beating,
> the way this crowd goes on breathing
> in the chest of the city they adore.

This poem allows modern readers to see Darío's views of minorities. It is indisputable that by our standards, his views are, to use the jargon of our own day, politically incorrect. His opinion of Jews, for instance, is troubling. While in a portion of

"Canto a la Argentina" that is not included in this volume, he commands:

> Sing Jews of the Pampa!
> Young men of rude appearance,
> sweet Rebeccas with honest eyes,
> Reubens of long locks,
> patriarchs of white
> dense, horselike hair.
> Sing, sing old Sarahs
> and adolescent Benjamins
> with the voice of our heart:
> "We have found Zion!",

in a poem called "Israel" his portrait of Jews rotates around their need to believe in Christ. Likewise, he approached blacks as inferior people. And while he idealized the pre-Columbian past, he never directly addressed the plight of the indigenous people contemporary to him. Still, within Nicaragua his relatively enlightened attitude was appreciated. Pablo Antonio Cuadra, arguably one of the most significant post-*Rubenista* poets in Nicaragua, who died in 2002, argued: "Darío was the first in the tradition of our *literatura culta,* the nation's high-brow letters, not only to point to *lo indio* as a fountain of literary originality and authenticity but also to proclaim, against the complexes and prejudices of his age, *mestizo* pride."

As a whole the issue of minorities in Darío is a controversial one and is in need of revaluation. Clearly, it is intimately linked in Latin America to questions of class. How did he view the difference between whiteness and brownness, between the Europeanized elite in Central America whose roots were in the Iberian Peninsula, and the rest of the population? What about immigration and the effort at the end of the nineteenth century by various governments on this side of the Atlantic to "recolonize" the provinces by opening the doors to Italian, German, and Jewish newcomers? Similarly, it is important to reassess Darío's understanding of the duality between center and periphery, which I glanced at earlier on in this introduction. To what extent did his "colonial" mentality become the engine that made him conquer Spain by storm? And what is one to say about his approach to sex, death, and the human body in general? The reader of Darío's prose in particular is likely to find an unsettling answer to this question.

In the end, though, what was the secret of Darío's success? He himself answered the question thus: "My success—it would be absurd not to confess it—has been due to novelty. . . . And this novelty, what has it consisted of? A mental gallicism. When I read Groussac I did not know he was a Frenchman writing in Spanish. But he taught me to *think in French*; after that, my young, happy heart claimed Gallic citizenship." As World War I was raging, Darío published the first of three volumes of his selected poems, which he himself chose and organized. It appeared in Madrid under the auspices of Biblioteca Corona: *Muy siglo XVIII* (And Those that Come from the Eighteenth Century, 1914). Two other volumes followed, completing a trilogy in which Darío sought to reconfigure his work thematically. These were *Muy antiguo y muy moderno* (Some Both Ancient and Modern, 1915) and *Y una sed de ilusiones infinita* (And a Thirst for Illusive Hope That's Endless, 1916). It was around the time of the third volume's publication that Darío fell gravely ill during a lecture tour of the United States. He returned to León, Nicaragua, early in 1916, where he underwent various surgical operations. He died on February 6, 1916, and was buried near the statue of Saint Paul, in the Cathedral of León.

His "contradictory identities," as they've been described, had by then placed Nicaragua, a minuscule Central American nation of approximately 120,254 square kilometers—roughly the size of Vermont—and a population today of a little over five million people, on the cultural map, even though, as David Whisnant put it in *Rascally Signs in Sacred Places: The Politics of Culture in Nicaragua,* Darío's supporters and opponents in the country have seldom been able "either to tolerate or to process the complex nuances and contradictions of his thought and work." Still, to this day his contribution is seen, internally, not only as a literary hiatus but as a veritable geopolitical transformation. Pablo Antonio Cuadra emphasized this when he wrote: "A country must compare the benefit of its great poets to that of its great ports." Cuadra compared Darío to New York. "The number of connections, the amount of knowledge, and the ethical and aesthetic values that came to Nicaragua through Rubén are incommensurable."

Efforts at translating Darío into other languages date back to the last third of his career. French culture, obviously, was fitted for his vision. His poems and nonfiction were appearing in magazines in Paris by the first years of the twentieth century. He was also translated into Portuguese, German, and Italian, among other European languages. In English, his career has not always been a happy one. His rhythmic stanzas establish a sort of symmetry between form and content that is quite difficult to recapture in Shakespeare's tongue. Still, there have been efforts made, especially since the sixties, to render the Nicaraguan in a convincing way.

This anthology represents the most ambitious attempt ever to make the Nicaraguan poet comfortable in English. A selection of the most representative prose, stories and fables, and journalism, and a dozen letters to relatives and friends, are featured together with the poetry for the first time. Intriguingly, this volume also brings together different translation strategies. The compilation is divided into two parts, each briefly prefaced by its respective translators. The first section is devoted to poetry and it appears in bilingual format. The English renditions are by Greg Simon and Steven F. White. The organization is thematic rather than chronological. Instead of representing the arc of Darío's poetry from his debut to his posthumous stanzas, the material is showcased in the way Darío himself arranged it when he released the three volumes published in Madrid by Biblioteca Corona between 1914 and 1916. Three sections are titled after lines he had used early in *Cantos de vida y esperanza* and they represent modalities of his temperament, so to speak: a connection with the past, his urbane worldview, his transition as a modern voice, and his philosophical and religious pursuits. A fourth section is an intelligent approximation to yet another section Darío might have intended to publish but was unable to do so before he died. Darío's development as a poet is of primary importance in the Spanish-speaking world. When did he first come across motifs like the swan and the princess? In what kinds of rhythmic experimentation did he engage at various stages of his career? In order to give even a vague semblance of his aesthetic transformation, there are dates of composition in brackets after each of the Spanish originals. When the date is preceded by a "p," it means the information is lacking and the date included is that of publication in book form. Some of the dates are a range of years; this is a reference to Darío's uncollected poetry, known to scholars as *poesía dispersa.*"

The second part of this volume, devoted to Darío's fiction, essays, reportage, and travel writing, has been translated by Andrew Hurley. This section is cataloged not by theme, but rather by genre. It first concentrates on his stories and fables, which include myths and legends, tales of horror and the grotesque, and a handful of prose poems, and then moves to the part of Darío's work that remains least known in English: his nonfiction, including the pieces on Poe, Verlaine, Martí, Ibsen, and Isidore Ducasse (aka Count of Lautréamont) from *Los raros.* This section also includes op-eds and political pieces on crime, the iron industry, and cosmopolitan life. Translations of Darío's important forewords to *Azul . . .*, and *Los raros* are also included, as well as Darío's commentary on Marinetti and futurism and on a new French rendition of *The Book of a Thousand Nights and A Night.* His itinerant pieces on countries he visited, such as Spain, France, Italy, Germany, and Hungary are provocative. (It is regrettable that the Nicaraguan never looked at the landscape of the Americas with the same consideration he devoted to Europe.) For him the Old Continent was a destination that piqued his curiosity, whereas this side of the Atlantic Ocean was a mere place of departure. Darío, of course, was a decadent. For him, as for most of his peers in Latin America, a journey to the center of Western Civilization was a rite of passage. (Has this asymmetrical approach finally changed? Perhaps only by expanding the destination to the United States as well. At the end of the twentieth century, a visit to New York, not Paris, was de rigueur for any serious young Mexican, Argentine, Venezuelan, Columbian . . . writer whose goal was to shape a promising career.) Darío's prose did not go through stylistic changes the way his poetry did, nor did it have the same impact on his readership. In it the Nicaraguan reacts to his immediate circumstance: people, places, books. Chronology is considerably less significant in this, so the material doesn't include bracketed dates.

I've been a devoted reader of his oeuvre since my teens, when I first read *Los raros* during my college years in Mexico and was overwhelmed by his sonnets, memorizing dozens of poems, starting with "*De invierno*" (About Winter) and "*Lo fatal*" (Destined to Die). After I immigrated to the United States in 1985, it became my dream to see Rubén Darío find a space of his own in the English language in a way that wouldn't make him sound awkward. The power of his verbal art and his astounding influence more than justify the endeavor. It took a long time to complete the task but the energy and encouragement I received from numerous people allowed me—and the team we finally put together—to remain focused. In this volume I did not just seek to introduce Darío in a comprehensive, responsible fashion, offering a context against which to understand his contribution. I also wanted readers to appreciate his polyphonic talents. That polyphony, in my eyes, at least, suggests that there are at least two Daríos, if not more: one a glorious poet, the other an emblematic narrator. Since I wanted him to have as close to a perfect pitch in Shakespeare's tongue as he has in Cervantes's, I sought different translators who would be able to give the Nicaraguan the exact touch he requires in the different genres he mastered. Intriguingly, the approaches taken by Simon and White in the poetry part, and by Hurley in its prose counterpart, offer alternative lessons in the art of translation. The reader will quickly notice that the language used in each of these parts is different: for the poetry, the translators have intentionally brought Darío to the present tense, making him current today. Their renditions answer the question: How does this late-nineteenth-century *Modernista* sound to today's ears? Hurley's approach moves in the opposite direction, bringing the contemporary reader to the past. He does not reimagine Darío's fiction and nonfiction using present-day colloquialisms. Instead, he makes use of the English of the time to place the Nicaraguan in a period to which he belongs in chronological terms. Hurley states that "Just as in Spanish Darío reminds one of the English and French writers that were pursuing similar themes and aesthetic concerns at the same time as he (because he was, in fact, 'translating' them), so I have wanted Darío, in English, to sit firmly in that tradition. Thus, a 'timeless' yet identifiably fin-de-siècle language and style seemed called for, and I simply 'back-translated' Darío into a tradition the English reader is already perfectly familiar with."

This double strategy might be disruptive to some, resulting in a composite picture of Darío that is schizophrenic. But the opposite is true. The Rubén Darío showcased in this anthology is a man for all seasons. It is our duty to appreciate him in full in each and every one of them. After all, he was a polymath, a sum of parts. Why simplify him? Shouldn't each of those parts command our attention? Neither of the translating methods used in these pages is better than the other. They are mere stratagems, for the translator is also an artist, and an approach to the work depends on an understanding of the world. The same question of approach, I might add, might be faced by a novelist today whose task it is to locate his plot in Dickens's London: should he recreate the past in content only, making use of the jargon we employ nowadays? Or might it be better to deliver the storyline as if the author of *David Copperfield* had written it himself? As long as each of the approaches is embraced not only thoroughly but convincingly, their worth is indisputable and that, I'm happy to report, is the case in this Penguin Classic volume. I would go as far as to argue that the approach taken for the two parts is precisely the one required. Darío's poetry tends toward the hermetic. Why eclipse his esoteric views even more by presenting them in a language that is alien to readers today? Why make his poetic remoteness even more isolated? Conversely, his stories, legends and journalism were often written on deadline, are originally meant for a wider readership. This, it strikes me, is reason enough to use them as a springboard to

understand Darío's frame of mind as well as the type of lan-
guage he used and the age in which he lived.

Translation was a topic that concerned Darío dearly, just as it
concerned other giants of Latin American poetry: Borges,
Neruda, Vallejo, Paz . . . The Nicaraguan believed that in order
to translate a work of poetry, one must be a poet. But Darío did
not so much engage in the act and art of translation as read
translations devotedly and enthusiastically. Upon reading the
J. D. Mardrus rendition of the *1001 Nights,* he commented:
"Of myself, I will say that no book has so liberated my spirit
from the wearinesses of our common existence, our daily aches
and pains, as this book of pearls and gems, magic spells and en-
chantments, realities so ungraspable and fantasies so real. Its
fragrance is sedative, its effluvia calming, its delights refreshing
and comforting. Like any modifier of thought, but without the
inconveniences of venoms, alcohols, or alkaloids, it offers the
gift of an artificial paradise. To read certain tales is to enter a
pool of warm rosewater. And in all, there is delight for the five
senses—and for others that we hardly suspect." Obviously the
Rubén Darío encountered in the following pages is, inevitably, a
reinvented one, a poet remapped in a language not his own. But
in my view the collaborative effort is brilliant. It should allow
the uninitiated to appreciate the pearls and gems, magic spells
and enchantments, as well as the emblematic aesthetic view-
point this superb *homme de lettres* left for us. His "artificial
paradise" is more than worth exploring, for through his oeuvre
he surely liberated an entire continent from its own soporific
existence.

                                                    —Ilan Stavans

# Suggestions for Further Reading

Acevedo Marrero, Ramón Luis. *El discurso de la ambigüedad: La narrativa modernista hispanoamericana.* San Juan, P.R.: Isla Negra, 2002.

Anderson Imbert, Enrique. *La originalidad de Rubén Darío.* Buenos Aires: Centro Editor de América Latina, 1967.

Arellano, Jorge Eduardo. *Azul . . . de Rubén Darío: Nuevas perspectivas.* Washington, D.C.: Organización de los Estados Americanos, 1993.

Arellano, Jorge Eduardo and José Jirón Terán, eds. *Investigaciones en torno de Rubén Darío.* Managua: Dirección General de Bibliotecas y Archivos, 1981.

Baquero, Gastón. *Darío, Cernuda y otros temas poéticos.* Madrid: Editora Nacional, 1969.

Bourne, Louis. *Fuerza invisible: Lo divino en la poesía de Rubén Darío.* Málaga: Campus de Teatinos, Universidad de Málaga, 1999.

Concha, Jaime. *Rubén Darío.* Madrid: Ediciones Júcar, 1975.

Cuadra, Pablo Antonio. *Aventura literaria del mestizaje y otros ensayos.* San José, Costa Rica: Libro Libre, 1988.

Darío, Rubén. *Muy siglo xviii.* Madrid: Biblioteca Corona, 1914.

———. *Muy antiguo y muy moderno.* Madrid: Biblioteca Corona, 1915.

———. *Y una sed de ilusiones infinita.* Madrid: Biblioteca Corona, 1916.

———. *Eleven Poems of Rubén Darío.* Trans. by Thomas Walsh and Salomón de la Selva. New York: G. P. Putnam's Sons, 1916.

———. *Autobiografía*. Madrid: Editorial Mundo Latino, 1918.

———. *Epistolario*. Prólogo de Alberto Ghiraldo. Madrid: Biblioteca Rubén Darío, 1932.

———. *Antología poética*. Selección, Estudio Preliminar, Cronología, Notas y Glosario de Arturo Torres Rioseco. University of California Press: Berkeley and Los Angeles, 1949.

———. *Cuentos Completos*. Ed. Ernesto Mejía Sánchez. México: Fondo de Cultura Económica, 1950.

———. *Obras completas*. 4 vols. Ed. by M. Sanmiguel Raimúndez. Madrid: Afrodisio Aguado, 1950.

———. *Poesías completas*. Ed. by Alfonso Méndez Plancarte. Madrid: Aguilar, 1961.

———. *Cartas de Rubén Darío. Epistolario inédito del poeta con sus amigos españoles*. Ed. by Dictino Álvarez Hernández. Madrid: Taurus, 1963.

———. *Selected Poems of Rubén Darío*. Trans. by Lysander Kemp. Austin: University of Texas Press, 1965.

———. *Antología poética*. Managua: Editorial Hospicio, 1966.

———. *Poesía*. Ed. by Ernesto Mejía Sánchez. Caracas: Ayacucho, 1977.

———. *Opiniones*. Managua: Nueva Nicaragua, 1990.

———. "Número monográfico dedicado a Rubén Darío." *Poesía* (Madrid) 34 & 35 (1991).

———. *La vida de Rubén Darío escrita por él mismo*. Caracas: Biblioteca Ayacucho, 1991.

———. *Azul . . . Cantos de vida y esperanza*. Ed. and intro. by José María Martínez. Madrid: Cátedra, 1995.

———. *Cuentos*. Ed. by José María Martínez Domingo. Madrid: Cátedra, 1997.

———. *Poesía erótica*. Ed. by Alberto Acereda. Madrid: Hiperión, 1997.

———. *Epistolario selecto*. Ed. by Pablo Zegers and Thomas Harris, prólogo by Jorge Eduardo Arellano. Santiago, Chile: LOM Ediciones, 1999.

———. "Rubén Darío y Nicaragua (Antología)." *El Pez y la Serpiente* 33 (enero–febrero 2000).

———. *Y una sed de ilusiones infinita*. Ed. by Alberto Acereda. Barcelona: Lumen, 2000.

———. *Cartas desconocidas de Rubén Darío, 1882–1916*. Ed. by José Jirón Terán, Julio Valle-Castillo, and Jorge Eduardo Arellano. Managua: Academia Nicaragüense de la Lengua, 2000.

———. *Selected Poems of Rubén Darío: A Bilingual Anthology*. Ed., trans. and with an intro. by Alberto Acereda and Will Derusha. Lewisburg: Bucknell University Press, 2001.

———. *Songs of Life and Hope / Cantos de vida y esperanza*. Ed. and trans. Will Derusha and Alberto Acereda. Durham: Duke University Press, 2004.

Darío, Rubén and César Vallejo. *Heraldos del nuevo mundo*. Ed. by Álvaro Urtecho and Ricardo González Vigil. Managua: Banco Central de Nicaragua and Embajada del Perú en Nicaragua, 1999.

Ellis, Keith. *Critical Approaches to Rubén Darío*. Toronto; Buffalo: University of Toronto Press, 1974.

Fernández, Jesse. *El poema en prosa en Hispanoamérica: Del modernismo a la vanguardia: estudio crítico y antología*. Madrid: Hiperión, 1994.

Fernández, Teodosio. *Rubén Darío*. Madrid: Historia 16; Quorum, 1987.

Gibson, Ian. *Yo, Rubén Darío: Memorias póstumas de un rey de la poesía*. Madrid: Aguilar, 2002.

Henríquez Ureña, Max. *Breve historia del modernismo*. México: Fondo de Cultura Económica, 1962.

LoDato, Rosemary C. *Beyond the Glitter: The Language of Gems in Modernista Writers Rubén Darío, Ramón del Valle-Inclán, and José Asunción Silva*. Lewisburg: Bucknell University Press, 1999.

Jrade, Cathy Login. *Rubén Darío and the Romantic Search for Unity: The Modernist Recourse to Esoteric Tradition*. Austin: University of Texas Press, 1983.

Mejía Sánchez, Ernesto, ed. *Estudios sobre Rubén Darío*. México: Fondo de Cultural Económica, 1968.

Moser, Gerald M. and Hensley C. Woodbridge. "Colaboraciones rubendarianas en *El Cojo Ilustrado* de Caracas: 'La

Klepsidra' y 'La Guerra.' " *Boletín Nicaragüense de Bibliografía y Documentación* 104 (julio–septiembre 1999):13–14.

Paz, Octavio. "El caracol y la sirena: Rubén Darío." In *Cuadrivio: Darío, López Velarde, Pessoa, Cernuda.* México: J. Mortiz, 1965.

———. *The Siren & the Seashell, and Other Essays on Poets and Poetry.* Trans. by Margaret Sayers Peden. Austin: University of Texas Press, 1976.

Rama, Ángel. *Rubén Darío y el modernismo.* Caracas: Alfadil Ediciones, 1985.

Rodó, José Enrique. *Obras completas.* Ed. by Emir Rodríguez Monegal. Madrid: Aguilar, 1967.

Salinas, Pedro. *La poesía de Rubén Darío: Ensayo sobre el tema y los temas del poeta.* Buenos Aires: Losada, 1948.

Schulman, Iván A. *Nuevos asedios al modernismo.* Madrid: Taurus, 1987.

Schulman, Iván A. and Manuel Pedro González. *Martí, Darío y el modernismo.* Madrid: Gredos, 1969.

Skyrme, Raymond. *Rubén Darío and the Pythagorean Tradition.* Gainesville: University Presses of Florida, 1975.

Torres, Edelberto. *La dramática vida de Rubén Darío.* Barcelona: Grijalbo, 1966.

Valle-Castillo, Julio. "Un manuscrito y dos poemas inéditos de Rubén Darío." *Nuevo Amanecer Cultural* (15 de enero de 2000):1–3.

Whisnant, David. *Rascally Signs in Sacred Places: The Politics of Culture in Nicaragua.* Chapel Hill: University of North Carolina Press, 1995.

Woodbridge, Hensley C. *Bibliografía selectiva clasificada y anotada.* León: UNAN, 1975.

———. *Rubén Darío: A Selective Classified and Annotated Bibliography.* Metuchen, N.J.: Scarecrow Press, 1975.

———. *Bibliografía selectiva clasificada y anotada (suplemento para los años 1974–76).* León: UNAN, 1977.

———. *Bibliografía activa de Rubén Darío (1883–1980): una bibliografía selectiva clasificada y anotada (suplemento II para los años 1975–78).* Managua: Biblioteca Nacional Rubén Darío, Ministerio de Cultura, 1981.

Ycaza Tigerino, Julio and Eduardo Zepeda-Henríquez. *Estudio de la poética de Rubén Darío.* Managua: Comisión Nacional del Centenario Rubén Darío, 1867–1967, 1967.

Zavala, Iris. M. *Rubén Darío bajo el signo del cisne.* Río Piedras, P.R.: Editorial de la Universidad de Puerto Rico, 1989.

# A Note on the Text

No critical edition of Rubén Darío's complete works is available. The most authoritative sources in Spanish are the four-volume *Obras completas* (Afrodisio Aguado, 1950), edited by M. Sanmiguel Raimúndez; *Poesías completas* (Aguilar, 1961), edited by Alfonso Méndez Plancarte, famous also for his work on Sor Juana Inés de la Cruz and San Juan de la Cruz; *Poesía* (Ayacucho, 1977), edited by Ernesto Mejía Sánchez; and *Azul... Cantos de vida y esperanza* (Cátedra, 1995), edited by José María Martínez. The guiding rod in this Penguin Classics volume was the M. Sanmiguel Raimúndez edition. In translating the poetry, Greg Simon and Steven F. White used the three-volume anthology released by Biblioteca Corona, compiled by Darío himself, which suggests a thematic, rather than chronological, approach to his oeuvre: *Muy siglo xviii* (1914), *Muy antiguo y muy moderno* (1915), and *Y una sed de ilusiones infinita* (1916). Section 3 is based on the speculation of Pablo Antonio Cuadra and Eduardo Zepeda-Henríquez, who, in their anthology *Antología poética* (Hospicio, 1966), extend Darío's own strategy in the Biblioteca Corona volumes by proposing an additional grouping of poems that might be entitled *Audaz, cosmopolita*. In translating the prose, Andrew Hurley used the M. Sanmiguel Raimúndez edition; *Cuentos completos* (Fondo de Cultura Económica, 1950), edited by Ernesto Mejía Sánchez; as well as *Cuentos* (Cátedra, 1997), edited by José María Martínez. Finally, the sources for Darío's correspondence as translated by Steven F. White are *Epistolario* (Biblioteca Rubén Darío, 1932), edited by Alberto Ghiraldo; *Cartas de Rubén Darío: Epistolario inédito del poeta con sus amigos españoles* (Taurus, 1963), edited by Dictino Álvarez Hernández; *Epistolario selecto* (LOM Ediciones, 1999), edited by Pablo Zegers and Thomas Harris; and *Cartas desconocidas de Rubén Darío, 1882–1916* (Academia Nicaragüense de la Lengua, 2000), edited by José Jirón Terán, Julio Valle-Castillo, and Jorge Eduardo Arellano.

# Selected Writings

# POEMS

# TRANSLATORS' NOTE

*Horseman on a rare Pegasus,*
*who reached an impossible realm . . .*
*— R. D.*

Many commentators on the poetry of Rubén Darío correctly praise the Nicaraguan for introducing elements of syntactical freedom into Spanish prosody. Almost all of them go on to mention the other prosodic development that would become predominant with Darío's peers, and the poets who followed them: free verse. But a translator of Darío soon discovers that most of his lines were composed to meet strict metrical standards, fortified by rhyme. That his alexandrines also contained the power to liberate late-nineteenth-century poetic thinking in Spanish was a testament to Darío's aggressiveness as a poet. His work was modern in the sense that it was disruptive and disturbing. It juxtaposed the seeds of Darío's native Catholicism and the Symbolist poetry he found himself surrounded by for most of his life, in his own words, "against a tempestuous pagan instinct . . . complicated by the psychophysical need for thought-modifying stimulants, dangerous combustibles, suppressors of disturbing perspectives . . . which put at risk the cerebral machine and the vibrating tunic of nerves." The tyranny of tin-pot dictators and a lack of money curtailed the life Darío wanted to live as a man. But almost miraculously, the tyranny of metrical composition liberated Darío as a poet. In verse, Darío was finally free to be himself.

He was obsessed by white things: swans, stars, shells, the caps of ocean waves, bulls, women, buildings, sand, wine, and fear. Yes, fear is white, white-hot, and Darío feared, most of all, that he would be forgotten. His answer: make it impossible to ignore or not memorize his work by carving it into metric stone. "Governments change," Mallarmé wrote, "prosody remains ever intact." Because his family was penurious, Darío was forced to make his living as an itinerant journalist and diplomat. But he filled his secret life, his life away from the official functions, women, and alcoholic binges, with horizontal columns of the next best thing to stone: words. "In truth," he wrote, "I live on poetry. My dreams have a Solomonic magnificence. I love beauty, power, grace, money, luxury, kisses, and music . . ."

Most of this age-old wish list went unrequited during Darío's lifetime, but it is undeniable that his writing shimmers with beauty and strains with verbal harmony and grace. "[E]ach word has a soul," he tells us, and to understand this "lexical aristocracy," to delve into the interior, ideal melody that words create when they are placed in conjunction with each other, Darío believed a poet must apply "a grounding in knowledge of the art to which one consecrated oneself, an indispensable erudition, and the necessary gift of good taste." Yes, the soul of a word has its mysteries, those elements of usage, spelling, and language of origin, but it is also full of history. For the key to unlocking the power of the word-soul, Darío wrote that he "looked toward the past, toward ancient mythologies and splendid histories. . . ."

Darío became a hunter, imagining himself the twin of Nimrod, an ancient Persian king who founded Nineveh and Babylon, and who, after his descendants conquered Jerusalem, was identified by the Jews as an Antichrist. Darío, who was once jailed for antireligious sedition himself, sought to be one of the enchanted hunters who seek the forms in which words will find their resting places, where they will reveal the images in their souls. This movement of knowledge is literature, as Roberto Calasso defines it, "divine material that molds itself into epiphanies and enthrones itself in the mind. . . ." Literature is found at the primordial hunting grounds where humans can encounter the gods, gaze at them, even emulate and name them, at the risk of glory or death.

The glossary at the end of this volume supports and amplifies the translations from the immense poetic output of Rubén Darío. It contains a fraction of the names, places, and occasionally untranslatable words that fill the one thousand three hundred pages of his *Poesías completas*. While Darío's vocabulary perfectly reflects the diversity of cultures and mythologies he touched upon in his extensive readings and travels, a reader will quickly notice that this vocabulary is dominated by the masculine gender, as is the list of names of the world's leading Symbolist poets. (In fact, there are *no* women on that list.) Poets are warrior-poets, and the women they master or win for themselves during their trials of strength are most often represented as victims, seductresses, or breeding stock.

In the annals of poetry, such gender loyalty is hardly unique. Poets tend to make life choices based on what works best for their art. The Muse is unpredictable, and in our next translation project we might very well find a poet completely dedicated to another gender. Salomé's, for example, who despite the seeming callousness of her attitude toward the health of the men around her, has inspired many famous admirers throughout history, both male and female, including an active cult still devoted to decapitation.

Those of us who live in a time in history when equality for women is rightfully ascendant (though by no means perfected) might wish for more enlightenment in the poetry we are reading and translating. But such hindsight, while politically correct, is insufferable. A selection of *Darío profundo* is simply a selection of modern poetry of the highest order, driven by loyalty to the same manic flood of words that impelled Darío from the age of three.

As Ilan Stavans stated it in the introduction to this anthology, the ordering principle of the section on poetry in this anthology is an approximation of Darío's own strategy for representing his verse, in keeping with three ornate little volumes (from Madrid's Biblioteca Corona) that appeared at the end of the poet's life in 1914, 1915, and 1916. Darío chose a stanza from the *"Preludio"* to his landmark work, *Cantos de vida y espe-ranza*, to provide the titles for the only anthologies the poet or-ganized himself: *Y muy siglo diez y ocho, Y muy antiguo y muy moderno*, and *Y una sed de ilusiones infinita*. No doubt it was a truncated project. Indeed, Nicaraguan Darío specialists Eduar-do Zepeda-Henríquez and Pablo Antonio Cuadra believe that Darío may very well have intended to publish a fourth volume that might justifiably have been entitled *Audaz, cosmopolita,* a convincing speculation that has been incorporated into our se-lection. Darío's audacious and cosmopolitan sensibility certainly warrants the inclusion here of poems such as "Tutecotzimí" (a celebration of the poet's indigenous heritage that perturbed his racist contemporaries in Spain), "Black Dominga" (a doorway to the future *movimiento de la negritud*), "To Roosevelt" (the quintessential Latin American poem of finely honed political denunciation), and "The Great Cosmopolis" (a vision of New York City that resonates with Lorca's subsequent treatment of this urban center in 1929–30).

Can Darío be found in the harmony of a hemistich, or is he in the caesura, which functions in his work as a kind of fulcrum of silence between one hemistich and another? Perhaps it ulti-mately became possible for us as translators to hear Darío mov-ing with such certainty and grace across his deeply folded soundscape as we attempted to find compressed English equiva-lents to alexandrines and hendecasyllables. We relished the idea of these formal challenges, these Pythagorean proposals, as new doorways to the slightly dissonant harmonics of rhyme and slant rhyme in English. Often we found ourselves abandoning a fully rational approach to our work in favor of one that is more subjective since, in Douglas Robinson's words, "humans translate truly, restoratively, only when they hear and become a responsive part of the translating of spirit." In any event, translations are a kind of afterlife, a thick vine of the souls, per-haps, from which, as Walter Benjamin says, "the life of the originals attains in them . . . its ever renewed latest and most abundant flowering."

Steven F. White gratefully acknowledges the ongoing guidance of Jorge Eduardo Arellano, Julio Valle-Castillo, and Don José Jirón Terán (1916–2004). He also thanks *Banisteriopsis caapi* and *Psychotria viridis* for their collective insights into Rubén's eternal harmonies.

—Greg Simon and Steven F. White

## PRELUDIO (FRAGMENTO)

*A J[osé] Enrique Rodó.*

Yo soy aquel que ayer no más decía
el verso azul y la canción profana,
en cuya noche un ruiseñor había
que era alondra de luz por la mañana.

El dueño fui de mi jardín de sueño,
lleno de rosas y de cisnes vagos;
el dueño de las tórtolas, el dueño
de góndolas y liras en los lagos;

y muy siglo diez y ocho y muy antiguo
y muy moderno; audaz, cosmopolita;
con Hugo fuerte y con Verlaine ambiguo,
y una sed de ilusiones infinita.

\*    \*    \*    \*    \*

La virtud está en ser tranquilo y fuerte;
con el fuego interior todo se abrasa;
se triunfa del rencor y de la muerte. . . .

[1904]

# PRELUDE *(FRAGMENT)*

*to J[osé] E[nrique] Rodó*

Why, only yesterday I was reciting
poems with azure lines and songs that were profane.
And there was a nightingale in my writing
that became a radiant lark when morning came.

I was the master of my garden of dream
filled with roses and the rippling a swan makes,
master of turtledoves and all that's serene—
music of harps and gondolas on lakes.

And those that come from the eighteenth century;
some both ancient and modern; some audacious,
cosmopolitan; Hugo, yes!, Verlaine, maybe;
and a thirst for illusive hope that's endless.

\* \* \* \* \*

Virtue consists of being strong and tranquil;
your inner fire will turn anything to ash
and lift you above anger and death as well.

# I.
# And Those That Come from the Eighteenth Century

# CARACOL

*A Antonio Machado*

En la playa he encontrado un caracol de oro
macizo y recamado de las perlas más finas;
Europa le ha tocado con sus manos divinas
cuando cruzó las ondas sobre el celeste toro.

He llevado a mis labios el caracol sonoro
y he suscitado el eco de las dianas marinas,
le acerqué a mis oídos y las azules minas
me han contado en voz baja su secreto tesoro.

Así la sal me llega de los vientos amargos
que en sus hinchadas velas sintió la nave Argos
cuando amaron los astros el sueño de Jasón;

y oigo un rumor de olas y un incógnito acento
y un profundo oleaje y un misterioso viento . . .
(El caracol la forma tiene de un corazón)

                                              [p 1905]

# SEASHELL

*To Antonio Machado*

On the beach I found a golden seashell.
It was massive and studded with fine pearls.
Europa stroked it with divine fingers
as she rode waves on a celestial bull.

With my lips, I played the shell's melody.
Deep in the azure mines of its whispers,
it told me about its secret treasures
under the echoing sea's reveille.

The salt pervades me in a bitter breeze,
and while the stars blessed Jason's reveries,
it swelled the Argonaut's white sails. I start

to hear the murmuring waves speak inside
the cryptic winds and the most profound tide . . .
(The shell was formed in the shape of a heart.)

# MARINA

Como al fletar mi barca con destino a Citeres
saludara a las olas, contestaron las olas
con un saludo alegre de voces de mujeres.
Y los faros celestes prendían sus farolas,
mientras temblaba el suave crepúsculo violeta.
"Adiós—dije—países que me fuisteis esquivos;
adiós peñascos enemigos del poeta;
adiós costas en donde se secaron las viñas
y cayeron los términos en los bosques de olivos.
Parto para una tierra de rosas y de niñas,
para una isla melodiosa
donde más de una musa me ofrecerá una rosa."
Mi barca era la misma que condujo a Gautier
y que Verlaine un día para Chipre fletó,
y provenía de
el divino Astillero del divino Watteau.
Y era un celeste mar de ensueño,
y la luna empezaba en su rueca de oro
a hilar los mil hilos de su manto sedeño.
Saludaba mi paso de las brisas el coro
y a dos carrillos daba redondez a las velas.
En mi alma cantaban celestes filomelas,
cuando oí que en la playa sonaba como un grito.
Volví la vista y vi que era una ilusión
que dejara olvidada mi antiguo corazón.
Entonces, fijo del azur en lo infinito,
para olvidar del todo las amarguras viejas,
como Aquiles un día, me tapé las orejas.
Y les dije a las brisas: "Soplad, soplad más fuerte;
soplad hacia las costas de la isla de la Vida."
Y en la playa quedaba desolada y perdida
una ilusión que aullaba como un perro a la Muerte.

[1898]

# SEASCAPE

I embarked on a chartered ship to Cythera,
and I greeted the waves, which answered as they churned
with the welcoming voices of a plethora
of women. And lighthouses lit astral lanterns
while the gentle, gathering dusk turned violet.
I said, "Farewell, countries that once eluded me.
Farewell, cliffs! You are enemies of the poet!
Farewell to the dry coast where the vineyard withers
and the shoreline ends in tree after olive tree.
I'm bound for a land of little girls and flowers,
for an island of melodious tunes
where I'll be presented with roses by a Muse."
My ship is the same one that transported Gautier
and also Verlaine to Cyprus once as cargo.
It sailed away
from the sacred Shipyard of the divine Watteau.
And the moon began to ply its distaff of gold
over this great celestial sea of reveries,
spinning thousands of threads to make its silken cloak.
A choir greeted my passage in the marine breeze,
and with two sets of tackle, it made the sails round.
In my soul, celestial nightingales made a sound
that I could hear echoing on shore like a cry.
I turned to look and saw it was an illusion
that my ancient heart had let go and forgotten.
Then, fixed on the infinite azure of the sky,
to erase all the old bitterness in the breeze,
one day I covered my ears like Achilles.
And I said to the wind, "Blow, blow with all your strength.
Send me toward the shoreline of the island of Life."
And on the sand stood a desolate thing, ghostlike,
abandoned, and howling like a wild dog at Death.

## LOS CISNES

*A Juan R[amón] Jiménez.*


¿Qué signo haces, oh Cisne, con tu encorvado cuello
al paso de los tristes y errantes soñadores?
¿Por qué tan silencioso de ser blanco y ser bello,
tiránico a las aguas e impasible a las flores?

Yo te saludo ahora como en versos latinos
te saludara antaño Publio Ovidio Nasón.
Los mismos ruiseñores cantan los mismos trinos,
y en diferentes lenguas es la misma canción.

A vosotros mi lengua no debe ser extraña.
A Garcilaso visteis, acaso, alguna vez . . .
Soy un hijo de América, soy un nieto de España . . .
Quevedo pudo hablaros en verso en Aranjuez . . .

Cisnes, los abanicos de vuestras alas frescas
den a las frentes pálidas sus caricias más puras
y alejen vuestras blancas figuras pintorescas
de nuestras mentes tristes las ideas obscuras.

Brumas septentrionales nos llenan de tristezas,
se mueren nuestras rosas, se agostan nuestras palmas,
casi no hay ilusiones para nuestras cabezas,
y somos los mendigos de nuestras pobres almas.

# THE SWANS

*To Juan R[amón] Jiménez*

What sign do you form, oh, Swan, with the curve of your
    neck's shape
when the wandering dreamers who are filled with grief pass
    by?
Why is it you are silent, white, lovely in this landscape,
a tyrant to these waters, heartless to these flowers? Why?

I give you my greetings now as if these lines were Latin
and I were Ovid, greeting you in verse from years long past.
Because the same nightingales have one song they imagine
and in whatever language their songs are always steadfast.

For you, the language I speak is not, I think, so foreign,
since you met Garcilaso, perhaps, in another time.
America is my father, but I'm a grandson of Spain.
In Aranjuez, Quevedo addressed words to you that rhyme.

Swans, let your spreading wings be like fans to stir a
    breeze
to caress pale foreheads with fingers that are cool and kind.
And help us, with the whiteness of your picturesque bodies,
to distance the dark ideas from every sorrowful mind.

The mist from the northern realms fills us with such great
    sadness.
Our roses wither and rot, the palms we cared for are dry.
Hardly any illusions are left to nourish and bless
our heads, since we're but paupers with poor souls until we
    die.

Nos predican la guerra con águilas feroces,
gerifaltes de antaño revienen a los puños,
mas no brillan las glorias de las antiguas hoces,
ni hay Rodrigos ni Jaimes, ni hay Alfonsos ni Nuños.

Faltos del alimento que dan las grandes cosas,
¿qué haremos los poetas sino buscar tus lagos?
A falta de laureles son muy dulces las rosas,
y a falta de victorias busquemos los halagos.

La América Española como la España entera
fija está en el Oriente de su fatal destino;
yo interrogo a la Esfinge que el porvenir espera
con la interrogación de tu cuello divino.

¿Seremos entregados a los bárbaros fieros?
¿Tantos millones de hombres hablaremos inglés?
¿Ya no hay nobles hidalgos ni bravos caballeros?
¿Callaremos ahora para llorar después?

He lanzado mi grito, Cisnes, entre vosotros,
que habéis sido los fieles en la desilusión,
mientras siento una fuga de americanos potros
y el estertor postrero de un caduco león . . .

. . . Y un Cisne negro dijo: "La noche anuncia el día".
Y uno blanco: "¡La aurora es inmortal, la aurora
es inmortal!" ¡Oh tierras de sol y de armonía,
aun guarda la Esperanza la caja de Pandora!

                                                    [p 1905]

People say we'll be at war with the eagles that are fierce,
hawks from another era will come to dispute our space,
but no former glory shines on our sickles from past years,
no men like Rodrigo, James, Alphonse, or Nuño these days.

Since there is no sustenance for poets in some great thing,
what are we supposed to do, except try to find your lakes?
There are no laurels for us, though roses are consoling.
Rather than seek victories, let's content ourselves with praise.

Hispanic America and Spain as a whole country
are fixed on the origin of their fatal destiny.
I am questioning the Sphinx about what it can foresee
with the question mark of your neck, asking the air for me.

Are we to be overrun by the cruel barbarian?
Is it our fate that millions of us will speak in English?
Are there no fierce shining knights, no valiant noblemen?
Shall we keep our silence now, to weep later in anguish?

Swans, now you have heard my cry echo in your company
because you have been faithful in my disillusionment,
while I watch the skittish colts of Latin America flee,
and the death throes of a Spanish lion whose life is spent.

And a black Swan said: "The night heralds the dawn that will
    come."
And a white one added: "The sunrise will always abide,
always!" Oh, people from the lands of harmony and sun,
rest assured, Pandora's box safely carries Hope inside.

# LEDA

El cisne en la sombra parece de nieve;
su pico es de ámbar, del alba al trasluz;
el suave crepúsculo que pasa tan breve
las cándidas alas sonrosa de luz.

Y luego, en las ondas del lago azulado,
después que la aurora perdió su arrebol,
las alas tendidas y el cuello enarcado,
el cisne es de plata, bañado de sol.

Tal es, cuando esponja las plumas de seda,
olímpico pájaro herido de amor,
y viola en las linfas sonoras a Leda,
buscando su pico los labios en flor.

Suspira la bella desnuda y vencida,
y en tanto que al aire sus quejas se van,
del fondo verdoso de fronda tupida
chispean turbados los ojos de Pan.

[1892]

# LEDA

The swan composed of snow floats in shadow,
amber beak translucent in the last light.
The white and innocent wings in the glow
of the short-lived dusk are rose tipped and bright.

And then, on ripples of the clear blue lake,
when the crimson dawn is over and done,
the swan spreads his wings and lets his neck make
an arch, silver and burnished by the sun.

Grand, as he ruffles his silken feathers,
this bird from Olympus bearing love's wound,
ravishing Leda in roiling waters,
thrusting at petals of her sex in bloom . . .

When at last her sobbing is heard no more,
the stripped, mastered beauty lets out a sigh.
From the tangled green rushes by the shore,
sparkle-eyed Pan watches, and wonders why.

## A GOYA

Poderoso visionario,
raro ingenio temerario,
por ti enciendo mi incensario.

Por ti, cuya gran paleta,
caprichosa, brusca, inquieta,
debe amar todo poeta;

por tus lóbregas visiones,
tus blancas irradiaciones,
tus negros y bermellones;

por tus colores dantescos,
por tus majos pintorescos,
y las glorias de tus frescos.

Porque entra en tu gran tesoro
el diestro que mata al toro,
la niña de rizos de oro,

y con el bravo torero,
el infante, el caballero,
la mantilla y el pandero.

Tu loca mano dibuja
la silueta de la bruja
que en la sombra se arrebuja,

y aprende una abracadabra
del diablo patas de cabra
que hace una mueca macabra.

# TO GOYA

Rare and daring man of genius
with your visions of the endless,
for you I light fragrant incense.

To the greatness of your palette
that's capricious, brash, incited,
and beloved by every poet;

to the darkness in your visions,
to your whitened emanations,
to your black and your vermilions.

From you all Dante's colors flow.
From you, lovely human forms glow.
From you, glorious frescoes.

Because, within your plentiful
brush lie the killer of the bulls
and the girl with her golden curls,

and with those valiant bullfighters
are knights-errant, and the King's heirs,
black shawls, and tambourine players.

And with one crazy hand you sketch
the grim silhouette of a witch
concealing herself in a ditch,

and you show the way to cast a spell
of split goat hoofs and the devil
whose smile rises straight out of hell.

Musa soberbia y confusa,
ángel, espectro, medusa:
tal aparece tu musa.

Tu pincel asombra, hechiza,
ya en sus claros electriza,
ya en sus sombras sinfoniza;

con las manolas amables,
los reyes, los miserables,
o los Cristos lamentables.

En tu claroscuro brilla
la luz muerta y amarilla
de la horrenda pesadilla,

o hace encender tu pincel
los rojos labios de miel
o la sangre del clavel.

Tienen ojos asesinos
en sus semblantes divinos
tus ángeles femeninos.

Tu caprichosa alegría
mezclaba la luz del día
con la noche oscura y fría:

Así es de ver y admirar
tu misteriosa y sin par
pintura crepuscular.

De lo que da testimonio:
por tus frescos, San Antonio;
por tus brujas, el demonio.

[p 1892]

Muse of arrogance, so confused,
angel, phantom, or medusa—
these are the forms that make your muse.

Your brush: bewitching artistry,
electrifying clarity,
shading like a full symphony;

the working poor and royalty,
and those locked in life's misery,
and the Christs beyond all pity.

In your splendid chiaroscuro,
the light is macabre and yellow
in the nightmarish horror show.

Or do you set your brush aflame
to give red honeyed lips a name
and make carnations bleed again?

Your angels, who are feminine,
carry in sacred expressions
the deadly eyes of assassins.

Your enraptured flights of fancy
mix the light of the days to be
with nights that are dark and wintry.

To admire is simply to see
your paintings' matchless mystery,
their crepuscular quality.

You left us your testimony:
in your frescoes—St. Anthony;
in your witches—our deviltry.

## EL POETA Y EL REY

Llevaron un día ante el Rey
a un hombre solitario . . .
El trono le deslumbraba
y mirándole de soslayo
el monarca quiso saber
qué elementos componían
las trazas del raro ser . . .

Indulgente y patriarcal
con suavidad preguntó:
¿Tienes nombre?
—No, Señor.
Patria por casualidad?
—El mundo es mi vecindad.
Por qué tanta la amargura
que de tu garganta brota?
¿Eres libre, eres ilota?
—Libre soy, mas triste cosa:
Yo, Señor . . . yo soy
                    Poeta!

                         [1887]

## THE POET AND THE KING

One day, a solitary man
was brought before the King.
From the dazzling throne
the Monarch looked down upon him
and wanted to know
what elements made up the life
of this strange being.

Indulgent and patriarchal,
the King began with a gentle question:
*"Do you have a name?"*
"No, Sire."
*A homeland, by any chance?*
"The whole world is where I live."
*Why does such bitterness
blossom in your voice?
Are you a free man or a slave?*
"I am free, yes, but, sad to say,
Sire, I am a poet!"

# INTERROGACIONES

—¿Abeja, qué sabes tú,
toda de miel y oro antiguo?
¿Qué sabes, abeja helénica?
—Sé de Píndaro.

—León de hedionda melena,
meditabundo león,
¿sabes de Hércules acaso . . . ?
—Sí. Y de Job.

—Víbora, mágica víbora,
entre el sándalo y el loto,
¿has adorado a Cleopatra?
—Y a Petronio . . .

—Rosa, que en la cortesana
fuiste sobre seda azul,
¿amabas a Magdalena? . . .
—Y a Jesús . . .

—Tijera que destrozaste
de Sansón la cabellera,
¿te atraía a ti Sansón?
—No. Su hembra . . .

—A quién amáis, alba blanca,
lino, espuma, flor de lis,
estrellas puras, ¿a Abel?
—A Caín.

—Águila que eres la Historia,
¿dónde vas a hacer tu nido?
¿A los picos de la gloria? . . .
—Sí. ¡En los montes del olvido!

[p 1907]

# QUESTIONS

—What is it that you've come to know,
bee of honey and ancient gold?
What do you know, Hellenic bee?
—All about Pindar.

—Lion with your fetid mane,
contemplative lion,
would you know about Hercules?
—Of course. And Job.

—Serpent, magic serpent,
amid sandalwood and lotus,
did you adore Cleopatra?
—And Petronius.

—Rose, when you caressed
the courtesan's blue silk,
were you in love with Magdalene?
—And Jesus, too.

—Scissors, when you destroyed
Samson's hair,
were you attracted to Samson?
—No. To his woman.

—And as for you, white dawn,
flax, sea-foam, fleur-de-lis, pure stars,
is it Abel you love?
—It's Cain.

—Eagle, symbol of History,
where will you build your nest?
On the peaks of glory?
—Yes. In the mountains of oblivion!

# COLOQUIO DE LOS CENTAUROS
## *(FRAGMENTO)*

*A Paul Groussac*

### Quirón

¡Himnos! Las cosas tienen un ser vital; las cosas
tienen raros aspectos, miradas misteriosas;
toda forma es un gesto, una cifra, un enigma;
en cada átomo existe un incógnito estigma;
cada hoja de cada árbol canta un propio cantar
y hay un alma en cada una de las gotas del mar;
el vate, el sacerdote, suele oír el acento
desconocido; a veces enuncia el vago viento
un misterio; y revela una inicial la espuma
o la flor; y se escuchan palabras de la bruma;
y el hombre favorito del Numen, en la linfa
o la ráfaga encuentra mentor—demonio o ninfa.

[p 1896]

# COLLOQUY OF THE CENTAURS
## *(FRAGMENT)*

*To Paul Groussac*

### Chiron

Hymns! All things possess a vital being,
strange appearances, weird ways of seeing.
All shapes are gestures, codes, and enigmas.
In every atom are hidden stigmas.
Each leaf on the trees sings with its own goal.
Each drop of ocean contains its own soul.
The prophet, the priest can hear the unknown
accents that sometimes vague winds will intone.
Perhaps the sea foam and flower exist
to bare initials or words in the mist.
As he guards our pools and winds, the Numen
sees us select a guide—nymph or demon.

# NUMEN

¡Pasa "el Dios," se estremece el inspirado
y brota el verso como flor de luz;
y quedan en el fondo del cerebro
un rostro de mujer, un sueño azul! . . .

[1887]

# NUMEN

The "God" goes by, someone trembles, inspired.
A line of poetry flowers like light;
and what will remain deep within the brain
is a woman's face, a dream of azure!

# PEGASO

Cuando iba yo a montar ese caballo rudo
y tembloroso, dije: "La vida es pura y bella",
entre sus cejas vivas vi brillar una estrella.
El cielo estaba azul y yo estaba desnudo.

Sobre mi frente Apolo hizo brillar su escudo
y de Belerofonte logré seguir la huella.
Toda cima es ilustre si Pegaso la sella,
y yo, fuerte, he subido donde Pegaso pudo.

¡Yo soy el caballero de la humana energía,
yo soy el que presenta su cabeza triunfante
coronada con el laurel del Rey del día;

domador del corcel de cascos de diamante,
voy en un gran volar, con la aurora por guía,
adelante en el vasto azur, siempre adelante!

                                        [p 1905]

# PEGASUS

When it was time for me to mount that coarse,
trembling horse, I said, "Life's beautiful, pure."
The eyes I saw had a star's vital force.
I was naked, the sky a deep azure.

To my head, Apollo's bright shield was bound.
Bellerophon taught me to track those flights.
Each peak Pegasus touches is renowned.
I'm strong. With Pegasus, I've climbed all heights.

The knight-errant of human energy,
I raise my triumphant head and proceed,
crowned with laurels by the day's Royalty.

As tamer of the great diamond-hoofed steed,
I soar with the aurora as my guide
on the vast azure journey of my ride.

# II.
# Some Both Ancient and Modern

# EHEU!

Aquí, junto al mar latino,
digo la verdad:
Siento en roca, aceite y vino
yo mi antigüedad.

¡Oh, qué anciano soy, Dios santo,
oh, qué anciano soy! . . .
¿De dónde viene mi canto?
Y yo, ¿adónde voy?

El conocerme a mí mismo
ya me va costando
muchos momentos de abismo
y el cómo y el cuándo . . .

Y esta claridad latina,
¿de qué me sirvió
a la entrada de la mina
del yo y el no yo? . . .

Nefelibata contento,
creo interpretar
las confidencias del viento,
la tierra y el mar . . .

Unas vagas confidencias
del ser y el no ser,
y fragmentos de conciencias
de ahora y ayer.

Como en medio de un desierto
me puse a clamar;
y miré el sol como muerto
y me eché a llorar.

[1907]

# EHEU!

Standing beside the Latin sea,
I want to speak my mind.
In these rocks, olive oil, and wine
is my antiquity.

How did I get old? How?
My time has almost come.
And where is my song really from?
Where am I heading now?

Because coming to self-knowledge,
with its Whens and What-ifs,
has taken me to the abyss—
right to the very edge.

And all this Latin clarity?
What is the point of that
when I'm looking down the mineshaft:
To be or not to be.

I'm Nephelibata, happy
that I can understand
the deepest secrets of the land,
and the wind and the sea.

I and not-I is a hard way,
vague secrets I can guess,
the shards of human consciousness
from now and yesterday.

I saw the sun, ready to die,
lost in my desert dream,
and the best I could do was scream.
Then I began to cry.

# REENCARNACIONES

Yo fui coral primero,
después hermosa piedra,
después fui de los bosques verde y colgante hiedra;
después yo fui manzana,
lirio de la campiña,
labio de niña,
una alondra cantando en la mañana;
y ahora soy un alma
que canta como canta una palma
de luz de Dios al viento.

[1890]

# REINCARNATIONS

First I was a bed of coral,
then a beautiful gem,
then green and hanging ivy on a stem;
then I was an apple,
a lily growing in the fields,
a young girl's lips as she yields,
a skylark singing in the morning;
and now I am like a palm
in Jehovah's light, a soul or a psalm
that is sung to the wind.

# METEMPSICOSIS

Yo fui un soldado que durmió en el lecho
de Cleopatra la reina. Su blancura
y su mirada astral y omnipotente.
         Eso fue todo.

¡Oh mirada! ¡oh blancura y oh aquel lecho
en que estaba radiante la blancura!
¡Oh la rosa marmórea omnipotente!
         Eso fue todo.

Y crujió su espinazo por mi brazo;
y yo, liberto, hice olvidar a Antonio.
(¡Oh el lecho y la mirada y la blancura!)
         Eso fue todo.

Yo, Rufo Galo, fui soldado, y sangre
tuve de Galia, y la imperial becerra
me dio un minuto audaz de su capricho.
         Eso fue todo.

¿Por qué en aquel espasmo las tenazas
de mis dedos de bronce no apretaron
el cuello de la blanca reina en broma?
         Eso fue todo.

Yo fui llevado a Egipto. La cadena
tuve al pescuezo. Fui comido un día
por los perros. Mi nombre, Rufo Galo.
         Eso fue todo.

            [1893]

# METEMPSYCHOSIS

I was a soldier, and Cleopatra the Queen
took me to her bed for sex. Her whiteness,
the unearthly omnipotence of her gaze.
        Then it was over.

Oh, that gaze, that white skin, and that bed
where a dazzling whiteness reigned supreme.
Oh, that omnipotent, marble-colored rose!
        Then it was over.

I could have snapped her spine with my hands.
I was the slave set free who made her forget Antony.
(Oh, her bed, her gaze, and her whiteness!)
        Then it was over.

My name is Rufus Gallus. I was a soldier
with Gallic blood, and that imperious cow
blessed me with a bold minute of her whim.
        Then it was over.

When her body arched in orgasm, why didn't
my bronze fingers encircle the white queen's neck,
and close even tighter, in playful jest?
        Then it was over.

I was taken to Egypt with a chain
around my neck. Then one day I was devoured
by dogs. My name? Rufus Gallus.
        Then it was over.

# RAZA

Hisopos y espadas
han sido precisos,
unos regando el agua
y otras vertiendo el vino
de la sangre. Nutrieron
de tal modo a la raza los siglos.

Juntos alientan vástagos
de beatos e hijos
de encomenderos, con
los que tienen el signo
de descender de esclavos africanos,
o de soberbios indios,
como el gran Nicarao, que un puente de canoas
brindó al cacique amigo
para pasar el lago
de Managua. Eso es épico y es lírico.

[1907]

# RACE

Holy water and swords
have both been essential—
the former to spread blessings,
the latter to spill the wine
of blood. Together, like this,
they nourished our race for centuries.

And jointly they feed the scions
of the blessed as well as the sons
of the owners of land, with
those who have the sign
of descent from African slaves
or the proudest Indian,
like the great Nicarao, who was given
a bridge of canoes by a friendly cacique
to cross Lake
Managua. And that's epic and it's lyric.

# REVELACIÓN

En el acantilado de una roca
que se alza sobre el mar, yo lancé un grito
que de viento y de sal llenó mi boca:

A la visión azul de lo infinito,
al poniente magnífico y sangriento,
al rojo sol todo milagro y mito.

Y sentí que sorbía en sal y viento
como una comunión de comuniones
que en mí hería sentido y pensamiento.

Vidas de palpitantes corazones,
luz que ciencia concreta en sus entrañas
y prodigio de las constelaciones.

Y oí la voz del dios de las montañas
que anunciaba su vuelta en el concierto
maravilloso de sus siete cañas.

Y clamé y dijo mi palabra: "¡Es cierto,
el gran dios de la fuerza y de la vida,
Pan, el gran Pan de lo inmortal, no ha muerto!"

Volví la vista a la montaña erguida
como buscando la bicorne frente
que pone el sol en la alma del panida.

Y vi la singular doble serpiente
que enroscada al celeste caduceo
pasó sobre las olas de repente

# REVELATION

From cliffs that were high and rocky,
my mouth engorged with wind and salt,
I launched my cry above the sea

into the infinite cobalt
vision and the blood-red sunset
that myths and miracles exalt.

I drank salt wind and won't forget
the communion of communions
that left my mind's meaning wounded.

Each beating heart and the living cells,
science-fired gut shining within,
constellations and their marvels.

I heard the mountain god begin
to speak with the music he knew—
a concert he played on seven

pipes. And then I shouted, "It's true!
Pan, great god of vitality,
is alive and immortal, too!"

I stared at the peak and could see,
almost, double horns on a head,
a sunlit soul, Pan's devotee.

The single double serpent sped
over waves. It was coiled around
a caduceus transported

llevada por Mercurio. Y mi deseo
tornó a Thalasa maternal la vista,
pues todo hallo en la mar cuando la veo.

Y vi azul y topacio y amatista,
oro, perla y argento y violeta,
y de la hija de Electra la conquista.

Y escuché el ronco ruido de trompeta
que del tritón el caracol derrama,
y a la sirena, amada del poeta.

Y con la voz de quien aspira y ama,
clamé: "¿Dónde está el dios que hace del lodo
con el hendido pie brotar el trigo

que a la tribu ideal salva en su exodo?"
Y oí dentro de mí: "Yo estoy contigo,
y estoy en ti y por ti: yo soy el Todo".

[p 1907]

by Mercury. I was spellbound
by the thalassic mother, blessed
by this sea of all that I've found.

I saw blue, topaz, amethyst,
gold, pearls, silver, and violet,
and Electra's daughter's conquest.

And I heard the piercing trumpet
as it poured from the triton's shell
and mermaids loved by the poet.

And as one who longs to love well,
I cried out, "Where's the god who brings
forth wheat from mud, and plants that grew

to free this tribe from its wanderings?"
An inner voice said: "I'm with you,
in you, for you: I am All Things."

# LA CANCIÓN DE LOS PINOS

¡Oh pinos, oh hermanos en tierra y ambiente,
yo os amo! Sois dulces, sois buenos, sois graves.
Diríase un árbol que piensa y que siente,
mimado de auroras, poetas y aves.

Tocó vuestra frente la alada sandalia;
habéis sido mástil, proscenio, curul,
¡oh pinos solares, oh pinos de Italia,
bañados de gracia, de gloria, de azul!

Sombríos, sin oro del sol, taciturnos,
en medio de brumas glaciales y en
montañas de ensueños, oh pinos nocturnos,
¡oh pinos del norte, sois bellos también!

Con gestos de estatuas, de mimos, de actores,
tendiendo a la dulce caricia del mar,
¡oh pinos de Nápoles, rodeados de flores,
oh pinos divinos, no os puedo olvidar!

Cuando en mis errantes pasos peregrinos
la Isla Dorada me ha dado un rincón
do soñar mis sueños, encontré los pinos,
los pinos amados de mi corazón.

Amados por tristes, por blandos, por bellos.
Por su aroma, aroma de una inmensa flor,
por su aire de monjes, sus largos cabellos,
sus savias, ruidos y nidos de amor.

¡Oh pinos antiguos que agitara el viento
de las epopeyas, amados del sol!

# THE SONG OF THE PINES

Pine trees! Brothers on land and in the air,
I love you all! You're sweet, good, and somber.
One might say that you're trees who think and care,
pampered by sunrises, poets, and birds.

The winged sandal must have grazed your brow.
You're masts, proscenia, and a curule chair.
Solar pines! Pines from Italy! How
bathed you are in grace and blue glory there.

Without the sun's gold, you can be gloomy,
covered in glacial mists and dew.
Pines at night in mountains of reverie,
pines from northern climes, you're beautiful, too.

You move like mimes, actors, or a statue,
stretching toward the sweet caress of the sea.
Sacred pines, I will never forget you!
Pines from Naples, loved by flowers and me!

While wandering on my pilgrim's journey,
where I can dream my dreams, I found lovely
pines on Golden Island that granted me
a heartfelt place for you, a place to be.

Loved because they're so sad, so soft and fair,
or for their fragrance like some immense bloom,
for a certain monkish air and long hair:
their sounds, their nests of love, their sap's perfume.

Ancient pines shaken by the wind's presence
in epic poems and loved by the sun!

¡Oh líricos pinos del Renacimiento,
y de los jardines del suelo español!

Los brazos eolios se mueven al paso
del aire violento que forma al pasar
ruidos de pluma, ruidos de raso,
ruidos de agua y espumas de mar.

¡Oh noche en que trajo tu mano, Destino,
aquella amargura que aun hoy es dolor!
La luna argentaba lo negro de un pino,
y fui consolado por un ruiseñor.

Románticos somos . . . ¿Quién que Es, no es romántico?
Aquel que no sienta ni amor ni dolor,
aquel que no sepa de beso y de cántico,
que se ahorque de un pino: será lo mejor . . .

Yo no. Yo persisto. Pretéritas normas
confirman mi anhelo, mi ser, mi existir.
¡Yo soy el amante de ensueños y formas
que viene de lejos y va al porvenir!

[1907]

Lyric pines growing in the Renaissance
and in the soil of some Spanish garden!

Aeolian arms sway together
when a violent gust with its fury
makes silken sounds, sounds of feathers
as it passes, sounds of surf and sea.

There was that night when the hand of Fate
brought the bitter sorrows that enfold me.
The moon used silver on the pine to plate
its blackness. A nightingale consoled me.

We're Romantics. . . . Is there anyone who Is,
who isn't? If you've never met the test
of love and pain, or never sung a kiss,
hang yourself from a pine: it's for the best . . .

Not me. The ways of yesterday assure
my longing and my being. I endure
with reveries and shapes as their lover
from far away, heading toward the future.

# CANTO DE LA SANGRE

*A Miguel Escalada.*

Sangre de Abel. Clarín de las batallas.
Luchas fraternales; estruendos, horrores;
flotan las banderas, hieren las metrallas,
y visten la púrpura los emperadores.

Sangre del Cristo. El órgano sonoro.
La viña celeste da el celeste vino;
y en el labio sacro del cáliz de oro
las almas se abrevan del vino divino.

Sangre de los martirios. El salterio.
Hogueras, leones, palmas vencedoras;
los heraldos rojos con que del misterio
vienen precedidas las grandes auroras.

Sangre que vierte el cazador. El cuerno.
Furias escarlatas y rojos destinos
forjan en las fraguas del oscuro Infierno
las fatales armas de los asesinos.

¡Oh sangre de las vírgenes! La lira.
Encanto de abejas y de mariposas.
La estrella de Venus desde el cielo mira
el purpúreo triunfo de las reinas rosas.

Sangre que la Ley vierte.
Tambor a la sordina.
Brotan las adelfas que riega la Muerte
y el rojo cometa que anuncia la ruina.

# SONG OF BLOOD

*To Miguel Escalada*

Blood flowing from Abel. Trumpet calls in battle.
Struggles between brothers. Commotion and horror.
Flags floating in the air. Machine guns wound, rattle.
And, dressed in purple robes, every great emperor.

Blood that's flowing from Christ. The organ's rich fullness.
The celestial vineyard yields the celestial mead.
And at the hallowed brim of the golden chalice,
the souls are all sipping the wine that's now sacred.

Blood flowing from martyrs. Strings of the psaltery.
Great bonfires and lions, the palms of victory.
The bright crimson heralds that come from mystery
usher in the great dawns with endless pageantry.

Blood that the hunter spills. The horn he knows so well.
Scarlet-colored furies on the red roads of fate
forge on ringing anvils in the darkness of Hell,
the deadliest weapons that murderers create.

Oh, blood of the virgins! There's the sound of the lyre.
The spell of butterflies, enchantment of the bee.
The star of Venus shines, and watches with its fire
purple hues of triumph, the stains of royalty.

The blood that's spilled by the Law.
Muffled rolling of the drum.
Death waters the blooming oleanders it saw.
The red comet announces ruin that will come.

Sangre de los suicidas. Organillo.
Fanfarrias macabras, responsos corales,
con que de Saturno celébrase el brillo
en los manicomios y en los hospitales.

[1894]

Blood of the suicides. Choral prayers for the dead.
Macabre sorts of fanfare, hand organ in the street.
In places where the sick and the insane are led,
we celebrate the shining pool at Saturn's feet.

# FLORES LÍVIDAS

Las sonrisas sin encías
y las miradas sin ojos,
las visiones de los sueños,
de los pálidos neuróticos,
invisibles enemigos,
implacables odios póstumos,
hacen que dé su flor lívida
el rosal del manicomio,
que crece y que tiene savia
con la sangre de los locos.

[1889–93]

## LIVID FLOWERS

There are smiles that possess no gums,
staring that consists of no eyes,
visions that emerge in the dreams
of neurotics with their pale skin,
those invisible enemies,
implacable posthumous hatreds,
and it all makes the asylum's
rosebushes bloom with livid flowers,
growing and coursing with the sap
from the blood of these lunatics.

# DE OTOÑO

Yo sé que hay quienes dicen, ¿Por qué no canta ahora
con aquella locura armoniosa de antaño?
Esos no ven la obra profunda de la hora,
la labor del minuto y el prodigio del año.

Yo, pobre árbol, produje, al amor de la brisa,
cuando empecé a crecer, un vago y dulce son.
Pasó ya el tiempo de la juvenil sonrisa:
¡Dejad al huracán mover mi corazón!

[p 1905]

# ABOUT AUTUMN

I know there are those who say: "Why doesn't he sing
now with that same musical madness of years past?"
But these people can't see the deep work of timing,
each minute's labor, the year's marvel made to last.

The poor tree that I am produced a soft, sweet song
of my love for the breeze when I grew strong and tall.
The time of youthful happiness is now long gone:
let the hurricane try to move my heart at all!

## EN UNA PRIMERA PÁGINA

Cálamo, deja aquí correr tu negra fuente.
Es el pórtico en donde la Idea alza la frente
luminosa y al templo de sus ritos penetra.
Cálamo, pon el símbolo divino de la letra
en gloria del vidente cuya alma está en su lira.
Bendición al que entiende, bendición al que admira.
De ensueño, plata o nieve, ésta es la blanca puerta.
Entrad los que pensáis o soñáis. Ya está abierta.

[1906]

# ON A FIRST PAGE

Calamus, here, from your sharp tip, let your dark fountain
    flow.
The Idea lifts its lucent head in this portico,
then enters the temple where it observes its rituals.
Calamus, set down the letters, those sanctified symbols,
in glory of the prophet whose soul exists in his lyre.
Bless all those who understand and bless all those who
    admire.
This is the blank doorway of silver, snow, or reverie.
If you can think or dream, come in. It's open already.

## LA PÁGINA BLANCA

*A A{ntonino} Lamberti*

Mis ojos miraban en hora de ensueños
la página blanca.

Y vino el desfile de ensueños y sombras.
Y fueron mujeres de rostros de estatua,
mujeres de rostros de estatuas de mármol,
¡tan tristes, tan dulces, tan suaves, tan pálidas!

Y fueron visiones de extraños poemas,
de extraños poemas de besos y lágrimas,
¡de historias que dejan en crueles instantes
las testas viriles cubiertas de canas!

¡Qué cascos de nieve que pone la suerte!
¡Qué arrugas precoces cincela en la cara!
¡Y cómo se quiere que vayan ligeros
los tardos camellos de la caravana!

Los tardos camellos
—como las figuras en un panorama—,
cual si fuese un desierto de hielo,
atraviesan la página blanca.

Éste lleva
una carga
de dolores y angustias antiguas,
angustias de pueblos, dolores de razas;
¡dolores y angustias que sufren los Cristos
que vienen al mundo de víctimas trágicas!

# THE BLANK PAGE

*To Antonino Lamberti*

I was contemplating the blankness of the page
         during my reverie.

And then came the parade, lucid dreams, and shadows.
And I saw the women with their sculpted faces,
women like statues with faces of marble.
They were so sad, so sweet, so gentle and pallid!

And then there were visions of the strangest poems,
of the strangest poems filled with kisses and tears,
and stories that would leave the head of any man
covered with graying hair in one cruel instant.

What snow-colored helmets that destiny issues!
What premature wrinkles are chiseled in faces!
And how each of us hopes that all the slow camels
are carrying light loads when caravans journey.

And all the slow camels,
like some tiny figures in a panorama,
as if it were a desert made of ice,
make their way through the blankness of the page.

        This one carries
        a heavy load
of sorrow and anguish as old as time,
the anguish of nations, the sorrow of races;
the sorrow and anguish that any Christ suffers
who comes into the world as some tragic victim!

Otro lleva
en la espalda
el cofre de ensueños, de perlas y oro,
que conduce la reina de Saba.

Otro lleva
una caja
en que va, dolorosa difunta,
como un muerto lirio la pobre Esperanza.

Y camina sobre un dromedario
la Pálida,
la vestida de ropas obscuras,
la Reina invencible, la bella inviolada:
la Muerte.

Y el hombre,
a quien duras visiones asaltan,
el que encuentra en los astros del cielo
prodigios que abruman y signos que espantan,
mira al dromedario
de la caravana
como el mensajero que la luz conduce,
¡en el vago desierto que forma la página blanca!

[1896]

This one carries
upon its back
coffers of reveries filled with pearls and fine gold,
proceeded by the Queen of Sheba.

The next one carries
a coffin
that transports the disconsolate remains
of poor Hope, like a lily that has died.

And riding another dromedary,
the Pale Lady,
the one who is dressed in the darkest robes,
the invincible Queen, inviolate beauty,
regal Death.

And the man
who's been assaulted by these harsh visions,
the one who finds in the stars of the sky
marvels that astonish and signs that produce fear,
he considers the camel
in the slow caravan
as a true messenger preceded by the light,
in the shifting desert sands that shape the blank page.

## DE INVIERNO

En invernales horas, mirad a Carolina.
Medio apelotonada, descansa en el sillón,
envuelta con su abrigo de marta cibelina
y no lejos del fuego que brilla en el salón.

  El fino angora blanco junto a ella se reclina,
rozando con su hocico la falda de Alençón,
no lejos de las jarras de porcelana china
que medio oculta un biombo de seda del Japón.

  Con sus sutiles filtros la invade un dulce sueño:
entro, sin hacer ruido; dejo mi abrigo gris;
voy a besar su rostro, rosado y halagüeño

  como una rosa roja que fuera flor de lis.
Abre los ojos, mírame con su mirar risueño,
y en tanto cae la nieve del cielo de París.

[1889]

# ABOUT WINTER

Here's Carolina on a winter's day,
languorous, slumped in a comfortable chair,
wrapped in a coat of fur like Cybele
next to the fireplace that shines over there.

The white Angora cat found the right place—
the snug Alençon skirt she wears inside—
not far from the Chinese porcelain vase
that her folding Japanese silk screens hide.

A sweet dream occupies her with its spell:
I come in, take off my gray coat, softly
kiss the alluring face I know so well

like a rose that might be a fleur-de-lis.
She stirs, looks at me with her sunny eyes,
and, meanwhile, snow falls from Parisian skies.

# VESPERAL

Ha pasado la siesta
y la hora del Poniente se avecina,
y hay ya frescor en esta
costa, que el sol del Trópico calcina.
Hay un suave alentar de aura marina,
y el Occidente finge una floresta
que una llama de púrpura ilumina.

Sobre la arena dejan los cangrejos
la ilegible escritura de sus huellas.
Conchas color de rosa y de reflejos
áureos, caracolillos y fragmentos de estrellas
de mar forman alfombra
sonante al paso en la armoniosa orilla.

Y cuando Venus brilla,
dulce, imperial amor de la divina tarde,
creo que en la onda suena
o son de lira, o canto de sirena.
Y en mi alma otro lucero como el de Venus arde.

[1907]

# VESPERAL

Now that the siesta's done,
now that the twilight hour is drawing near
and the tropical sun
that charred this coast has almost disappeared,
there's a gentle, cool zephyr breathing here
through the western sky's trees of illusion
lit by purple flames in the atmosphere.

Scrawled across beaches, the crabs have written
the illegible message of their trails.
There are pink-colored shells and some golden
reflections. Pieces of starfish and snails
form a clicking carpet
as I walk the harmonious shoreline.

When Venus starts to shine
in the holy last light, a regal love returns,
and I hear the waves' choir—
a mermaid's song or the sound of a lyre.
And in my soul, another star like Venus burns.

# VÉSPER

Quietud, quietud. . . Ya la ciudad de oro
ha entrado en el misterio de la tarde.
La catedral es un gran relicario.
La bahía unifica sus cristales
en un azul de arcaicas mayúsculas
de los antifonarios y misales.
Las barcas pescadoras estilizan
el blancor de sus velas triangulares
y como un eco que dijera: "Ulises,"
junta alientos de flores y de sales.

[p 1907]

# VESPER

Peace and more peace . . . now the city of gold
has entered the mystery of twilight.
The cathedral is one great reliquary.
The bay brings together its glass crystals
in a blue both archaic and major,
drawn from antiphonaries and missals.
The fishing boats have a stylized version
of whiteness with their triangular sails,
an echo, perhaps, that cries, "Ulysses!"
and mixes the salty air with flowers.

# SINFONÍA EN GRIS MAYOR

El mar como un vasto cristal azogado
refleja la lámina de un cielo de zinc;
lejanas bandadas de pájaros manchan
el fondo bruñido de pálido gris.

El sol como un vidrio redondo y opaco
con paso de enfermo camina al cenit;
el viento marino descansa en la sombra
teniendo de almohada su negro clarín.

Las ondas que mueven su vientre de plomo
debajo del muelle parecen gemir.
Sentado en un cable, fumando su pipa,
está un marinero pensando en las playas
de un vago, lejano, brumoso país.

Es viejo ese lobo. Tostaron su cara
los rayos de fuego del sol del Brasil;
los recios tifones del mar de la China
le han visto bebiendo su frasco de *gin*.

La espuma impregnada de yodo y salitre
ha tiempo conoce su roja nariz,
sus crespos cabellos, sus bíceps de atleta,
su gorra de lona, su blusa de dril.

En medio del humo que forma el tabaco
ve el viejo el lejano, brumoso país,
adonde una tarde caliente y dorada
tendidas las velas partió el bergantín . . .

# SYMPHONY IN GRAY MAJOR

The sea like some giant crystal of quicksilver
reflects the metal plate of a sky of rolled zinc.
Far away there are flocks of birds forming a stain
on a polished background of a pale shade of gray.

The sun, a piece of glass, both rounded and opaque,
walks toward its zenith with a sick person's steps.
The breezes from the sea take a rest in the shade,
using as a pillow what their black trumpets play.

The waves, moving their bellies made of lead,
seem to be moaning under the great wharf.
Sitting on a cable and puffing on his pipe,
there is a mariner, thinking about beaches
in some distant country, lost on a foggy day.

That sea-wolf is ancient. The burning rays of light
from the Brazilian sun toasted him to a crisp.
The harshest typhoons on the South China Sea
found him drinking his gin in a protected bay.

Iodine and nitrate fecundate the sea-spray
that has known his red nose for a very long time,
and his curly hair, too, and his athlete's biceps,
his hat made of canvas, his shirt ripped in a fray.

In the midst of the smoke from clouds of tobacco
the old man can discern the country lost in fog,
where on one afternoon that was golden and warm,
the brigantine weighed anchor and then sailed away.

La siesta del trópico. El lobo se aduerme.
Ya todo lo envuelve la gama del gris.
Parece que un suave y enorme esfumino
del curvo horizonte borrara el confín.

La siesta del trópico. La vieja cigarra
ensaya su ronca guitarra senil,
y el grillo preludia un solo monótono
en la única cuerda que está en su violín.

[1891]

Tropical siesta. The sea-wolf is sleeping.
The gamut of the gray enshrouds everything now.
It seems like some gentle and huge stump of paper
for shading the lines that frame the curved sky today.

Tropical siesta, and the old cicada
practices its guitar so hoarse and so senile.
The cricket tries out a monotonous solo
on the one-stringed violin it knows how to play.

## EN EL PAÍS DE LAS ALEGORÍAS

En el país de las Alegorías
Salomé siempre danza,
ante el tiarado Herodes,
eternamente.
Y la cabeza de Juan el Bautista,
ante quien tiemblan los leones,
cae al hachazo. Sangre llueve.
Pues la rosa sexual
al entreabrirse
conmueve todo lo que existe,
con su efluvio carnal
y con su enigma espiritual.

[p 1905]

# IN THE LAND OF ALLEGORIES

In the land of Allegories,
Salomé always dances
before Herod and his miter,
eternally.
And the head of John the Baptist,
who has made the lions tremble,
falls at the stroke of an axe. Blood flows.
For when the sexual rose
begins to open,
it moves all that exists
with the carnality it secretes
and the spilling of the sacred secrets.

# SANTA ELENA DE MONTENEGRO
## *(FRAGMENTO)*

\* \* \* \* \*

El hambre medioeval va por
sendas de sulfúreo vapor
y olor de muerte. ¡Horror, horror!

Ladran con un furioso celo
los canes del diablo hacia el cielo
por la boca del Mongibelo.

Tiemblan pueblos en desvarío
de hambre, de terror y de frío . . .
¡Dios mío! ¡Dios mío! ¡Dios mío! . . .

Como en la dantesca Comedia,
nos eriza el pelo y asedia
el espanto de la Edad Media.

Pasan furias haciendo gestos,
pasan mil rostros descompuestos;
allá arriba hay signos funestos.

Hay pueblos de espectros humanos
que van mordiéndose las manos.
Comienzan su obra los gusanos.

Falta la terrible trompeta.
Mas oye el alma del poeta
crujir los huesos del planeta.

[1908]

# ST. HELEN OF MONTENEGRO
## *(FRAGMENT)*

\* \* \* \* \*

Through the smoky plumes of sulfur,
that stalking medieval hunger
with the smell of death, the horror!

Barking with furious envy,
the Devil's dogs assail the sky
as the Mongibelo flows by.

People tremble, delirious
from hunger, cold, the fear of this.
Dear God! Sweet Father of Jesus!

Throughout his *Commedia*'s pages,
Dante's hair bristled at sieges,
terrors of the Middle Ages.

The furies pass, tempers explode,
a thousand faces decompose,
dire signs that the sky will impose.

Throngs of ghastly human specters
are gnawing at their own fingers.
Worms are adding to their oeuvres.

The shrill trumpet is still silent,
but there's a sound for the poet—
creaking boneyards of this planet.

# CANCIÓN DE OTOÑO EN PRIMAVERA

*A [Gregorio] Martínez Sierra*

Juventud, divino tesoro,
¡ya te vas para no volver!
Cuando quiero llorar, no lloro . . .
y a veces lloro sin querer . . .

Plural ha sido la celeste
historia de mi corazón.
Era una dulce niña, en este
mundo de duelo y aflicción.

Miraba como el alba pura;
sonreía como una flor.
Era su cabellera obscura
hecha de noche y de dolor.

Yo era tímido como un niño.
Ella, naturalmente, fue,
para mi amor hecho de armiño,
Herodías y Salomé . . .

Juventud, divino tesoro,
¡ya te vas para no volver!
Cuando quiero llorar, no lloro . . .
y a veces lloro sin querer . . .

Y más consoladora y más
halagadora y expresiva,
la otra fue más sensitiva
cual no pensé encontrar jamás.

## AUTUMN SONG IN SPRING

*To [Gregorio] Martínez Sierra*

Treasured days of my youth and boyhood,
you're gone and won't be back again!
You know I'd cry if only I could,
then tears come and I wish they'd end.

The celestial history of my heart
is best told in plural. She
was a sweet girl playing the first part
set in this world's great misery.

The purest sunrise describes her gaze
and she'd smile with a flower's light.
Her hair was the dark series of waves
fashioned by sorrow and by night.

I was as timid as any boy.
But she, one could easily say,
disposed of my ermine love and joy
like Herodias and Salomé.

Treasured days of my youth and boyhood,
you're gone and won't be back again!
You know I'd cry if only I could,
then tears come and I wish they'd end.

The next gave more solace, and was more
alive and full of flattery,
a woman sensitive to her core,
unique in my life and lovely.

Pues a su continua ternura
una pasión violenta unía.
En un peplo de gasa pura
una bacante se envolvía . . .

En sus brazos tomó mi ensueño
y lo arrulló como a un bebé . . .
y le mató, triste y pequeño,
falto de luz, falto de fe . . .

Juventud, divino tesoro,
¡te fuiste para no volver!
Cuando quiero llorar, no lloro . . .
y a veces lloro sin querer . . .

Otra juzgó que era mi boca
el estuche de su pasión;
y que me roería, loca,
con sus dientes el corazón.

Poniendo en un amor de exceso
la mira de su voluntad,
mientras eran abrazo y beso
síntesis de la eternidad;

y de nuestra carne ligera
imaginar siempre un Edén,
sin pensar que la Primavera
y la carne acaban también . . .

Juventud, divino tesoro,
¡ya te vas para no volver!
Cuando quiero llorar, no lloro . . .
y a veces lloro sin querer.

¡Y las demás! En tantos climas,
en tantas tierras siempre son,

Her passion, fierce and energetic,
merged with an endless tenderness.
Her peplos of some pure sheer fabric
covered an adept of Bacchus.

In her arms, she rocked my reverie
and sang it a sweet lullaby.
Then she killed this creature, too tiny,
too bereft of faith and light to die.

Treasured days of my youth and boyhood,
you're gone and won't be back again!
You know I'd cry if only I could,
then tears come and I wish they'd end.

My mouth was the place where another
kept the jewels of her passion safe.
And this madwoman, my lover,
used her teeth to gnaw my heart away.

What she wanted was like a gun sight
that she trained on love of excess,
since myriad kisses and delight
were eternity's synthesis.

And from our nearly weightless skin
she would fabricate some Eden
without realizing that the Spring
or our flesh is a transient thing.

Treasured days of my youth and boyhood,
you're gone and won't be back again!
You know I'd cry if only I could,
then tears come and I wish they'd end.

All the women I've known in my time
are from many lands and climates.

si no pretextos de mis rimas
fantasmas de mi corazón.

En vano busqué a la princesa
que estaba triste de esperar.
La vida es dura. Amarga y pesa.
¡Ya no hay princesa que cantar!

Mas a pesar del tiempo terco,
mi sed de amor no tiene fin;
con el cabello gris, me acerco
a los rosales del jardín . . .

Juventud, divino tesoro,
¡ya te vas para no volver!
Cuando quiero llorar, no lloro . . .
y a veces lloro sin querer . . .
¡Mas es mía el Alba de oro!

                                        [p 1905]

If they're not my pretexts for a rhyme,
they float through my heart as spirits.

In vain did I look for the princess
who was sad from so much waiting.
Life is hard, bitter, of great duress,
and there's no princess left to sing!

In spite of time that's so unyielding,
thirst for love is my parched burden.
With gray hair, I'm always moving
toward the roses in the garden . . .

Treasured days of my youth and boyhood,
you're gone and won't be back again!
You know I'd cry if only I could,
then tears come and I wish they'd end.
But the Dawn is mine! And it's golden!

# MARCHA TRIUNFAL

¡Ya viene el cortejo!
¡Ya viene el cortejo! Ya se oyen los claros clarines.
La espada se anuncia con vivo reflejo;
ya viene, oro y hierro, el cortejo de los paladines.

Ya pasa debajo los arcos ornados de blancas Minervas y
    Martes,
los arcos triunfales en donde las Famas erigen sus largas
    trompetas,
la gloria solemne de los estandartes
llevados por manos robustas de heroicos atletas.
Se escucha el ruido que forman las armas de los
    caballeros,
los frenos que mascan los fuertes caballos de guerra,
los cascos que hieren la tierra
y los timbaleros,
que el paso acompasan con ritmos marciales.
¡Tal pasan los fieros guerreros
debajo los arcos triunfales!

Los claros clarines de pronto levantan sus sones,
su canto sonoro,
su cálido coro,
que envuelve en un trueno de oro
la augusta soberbia de los pabellones.
Él dice la lucha, la herida venganza,
las ásperas crines,
los rudos penachos, la pica, la lanza,

# TRIUMPHAL MARCH

Here come the attendants!
Here come the attendants! You hear them? They're loud
   now!
   The trumpets!
There's one sword and more swords with long blades of
   brilliance!
There's gold and iron on paladins and their bright helmets.

They pass beneath arches with statues of Mars and Minerva
   whose whiteness is awesome,
the arches of triumph where often the gods show their favor
   with horns and great fanfare,
the glory of banners so lofty and solemn,
transported by athletes who swept into view when they ran
   there.
The weapons of horsemen are making their music by
   jingling and clashing,
and so do the bridles of powerful horses for riding
with hooves that wound landscapes by fighting—
now cymbals are crashing
with bellicose rhythms when everything matches
and this is how soldiers are passing
beneath the triumphant white arches.

The echoing trumpets will suddenly build up their accents,
their song that's sonorous,
their warm-hearted chorus,
their cover of thunder that's aurous
above the bright banners' magnificent presence.
He mentions the combat, the wounds, and the vengeance,
the harsh manes of war-steeds,
the coarse crests on helmets, the pike, and the long lance,

la sangre que riega de heroicos carmines
la tierra;
los negros mastines
que azuza la muerte, que rige la guerra.

Los áureos sonidos
anuncian el advenimiento
triunfal de la Gloria;
dejando el picacho que guarda sus nidos,
tendiendo sus alas enormes al viento,
los cóndores llegan. ¡Llegó la victoria!

Ya pasa el cortejo.
Señala el abuelo los héroes al niño:
ved cómo la barba del viejo
los bucles de oro circunda de armiño.
Las bellas mujeres aprestan coronas de flores,
y bajo los pórticos vense sus rostros de rosa;
y la más hermosa
sonríe al más fiero de los vencedores.
¡Honor al que trae cautiva la extraña bandera;
honor al herido y honor a los fieles
soldados que muerte encontraron por mano extranjera!
¡Clarines! ¡Laureles!

Las nobles espadas de tiempos gloriosos,
desde sus panoplias saludan las nuevas coronas y lauros:
las viejas espadas de los granaderos, más fuertes que
     osos,
hermanos de aquellos lanceros que fueron centauros.
Las trompas guerreras resuenan;
de voces los aires se llenan . . .
—A aquellas antiguas espadas,
a aquellos ilustres aceros,
que encarnan las glorias pasadas . . .

the blood that's like water, for heroes and red deeds,
this humus,
the barking of black breeds
that death has incited and war will make monstrous.

Golden music like fountains
announces the coming of more things
from faraway places.
The condors abandon the peaks of the mountains
where they nest in safety and stretch out their great wings
to witness this triumph and offer their graces.

The retinue lengthens
and grandfathers point out the heroes to children:
they see how the beard of that victor
has golden soft ringlets surrounded by rich fur.
The beautiful women have fashioned some crowns of sweet
    blossoms,
and their faces are like roses under the porticos.
The fairest one poses
and smiles at a hero, who longs for her welcome.
Let us honor those who have captured the strange-looking
    banner!
The wounded are honored and so are the faithful
combatants who died at the hands of some faraway
    soldier!

The noblest soldiers from long-ago glories
salute the new garlands and laurels of splendor while wearing
    their panoplies:
the swordsman of yore here, sons of the grenadiers, no bear
    could be stronger,
and brothers of lancers who are the old centaurs no longer.
A warrior's trumpet rejoices.
The heavens are filling with voices.
To honor the oldest soldiers,
those illustrious bearers of steel,
no human has ever been bolder.

Y al sol que hoy alumbra las nuevas victorias ganadas,
y al héroe que guía su grupo de jóvenes fieros,
al que ama la insignia del suelo materno,
al que ha desafiado, ceñido el acero y el arma en la mano,
los soles del rojo verano,
las nieves y vientos del gélido invierno,
la noche, la escarcha
y el odio y la muerte, por ser por la patria inmortal,
¡saludan con voces de bronce las tropas de guerra que tocan
   la marcha
triunfal! . . .

[1895]

Let's revel in triumphs and let the sun shine on their shoulders.
And here's to the hero who shepherds his men through the
    ordeal,
to the men who adore the flag of their country,
to those who have challenged, with girded steel bodies, and
    wielding their weapons,
the summers and their fiercest suns,
as well as the winter that's frigid and snowy,
and frost in the darkening arch,
and hatred and dying because their own homeland's immortal.
The soldiers of wartime compel them with voices of metal:
                    Play the triumphal march!

# EPÍSTOLA
## (FRAGMENTO)

*A la señora de Leopoldo Lugones*


¿Por qué mi vida errante no me trajo a estas sanas
costas antes de que las prematuras canas
de alma y cabeza hicieran de mí la mezcolanza
formada de tristeza, de vida y esperanza?
¡Oh qué buen mallorquín me sentiría ahora!
¡Oh cómo gustaría sal de mar, miel de aurora,
al sentir como en un caracol en mi cráneo
el divino y eterno rumor mediterráneo!
Hay en mí un griego antiguo que aquí descansó un día
después que le dejaron loco de melodía
las sirenas rosadas que atrajeron su barca.
Cuanto mi ser respira, cuanto mi vista abarca,
es recordado por mis íntimos sentidos,
los aromas, las luces, los ecos, los ruidos,
como en ondas atávicas me traen añoranzas
que forman mis ensueños, mis vidas y esperanzas.

Mas ¿dónde está aquel templo de mármol, y la gruta
donde mordí aquel seno dulce como una fruta?
¿Dónde los hombres ágiles que las piedras redondas
recogían para los cueros de sus hondas? . . .

[1906]

# A LETTER
## *(FRAGMENT)*

*To the wife of Leopoldo Lugones*

Why has my vagrant life not brought me, until today,
to this healthy coast before my prematurely gray
soul and hair transformed me into some strange mix
of sadness, life, and hope nothing can fix?
By now, I'd be fitting into Mallorca's scene,
and I'd know what ocean salt and honeyed dawns mean!
I'd feel as if I heard a seashell in my brain—
the divine, eternal Mediterranean.
There must be some old Greek in me, who rested here
when a few rosy mermaids began to appear,
attracted to his boat, hoping to drive him mad
with song. Everything I see and breathe I had
already in memories of cherished feelings—
those aromas, lights, noises, and the echoings.
They bring me an atavic wave of memories
that gives shape to my lives, my hopes, and reveries.

But where are the grotto and the marble temple
where I savored that sweet breast like a fresh apple?
Where are all those agile men who were gathering
a legion of stones for the leather straps of their slings?

# RETORNO
## *(FRAGMENTO)*

A través de las páginas fatales de la historia,
nuestra tierra está hecha de vigor y de gloria,
nuestra tierra está hecha para la Humanidad.

Pueblo vibrante, fuerte, apasionado, altivo;
pueblo que tiene la conciencia de ser vivo,
y que, reuniendo sus energías en haz
portentoso, a la Patria vigoroso demuestra
que puede bravamente presentar en su diestra
el acero de guerra o el olivo de paz.
        * * * * *
Si pequeña es la Patria, uno grande la sueña.
Mis ilusiones, y mis deseos, y mis
esperanzas, me dicen que no hay patria pequeña.
Y León es hoy a mí como Roma o París.

[1907]

# RETURN
## *(FRAGMENT)*

. . . on every fatal page of its history,
our land has been forged from passion and glory,
our land has been created for Humanity.

Its people are vibrant, passionate, proud, honest—
a people aware of what it means to exist,
who cut down and gather their energies in sheaves
of promise, and demonstrate well for their country
how they're able to raise their right hands and bravely
hold the steel of war or the olive branch of peace.

\*     \*     \*     \*     \*

If one's country is small, it grows bigger in dreams.
My illusions, desires, my hopes of home
convince me no country is as small as it seems.
Today, for me, León is my Paris, my Rome.

# TERREMOTO

Madrugada. En silencio reposa la gran villa
donde de niño supe de cuentos y consejas,
o asistí a serenatas de amor junto a las rejas
de alguna novia bella, timorata y sencilla.

El cielo lleno de constelaciones brilla,
y su oriente disputan suaves luces bermejas.
De pronto, un terremoto mueve las casas viejas
y la gente en los patios y calles se arrodilla

medio desnuda, y clama: "¡Santo Dios! ¡Santo fuerte!
¡Santo inmortal!" La tierra tiembla a cada momento.
¡Algo de apocalíptico mano invisible vierte! . . .

La atmósfera es pesada como plomo. No hay viento.
Y se diría que ha pasado la Muerte
ante la impasibilidad del firmamento.

[1912]

# EARTHQUAKE

Dawn. It was here in the great still villa that I
heard as a child so many fables and stories,
or serenades by the window bars in the breeze,
courting some girl who was dazzling, simple, and shy.

The constellations revolve in the brilliant sky,
and a few soft crimson lights argue in the East.
All at once, an earthquake brings people to their knees.
They pray half-naked in courtyards and streets, and cry:

"Dear God! Immortal Saints! Save us from being damned!"
Houses crumble. The earthquake shakes again and again.
The apocalypse pours from an invisible hand.

There's not the slightest breath of wind in this leaden
air, and one could say death passed over this land
under the indifferent gaze of our heaven.

# ALLÁ LEJOS

Buey que vi en mi niñez echando vaho un día
bajo el nicaragüense sol de encendidos oros,
en la hacienda fecunda, plena de la armonía
del trópico; paloma de los bosques sonoros
del viento, de las hachas, de pájaros y toros
salvajes, yo os saludo, pues sois la vida mía.

Pesado buey, tú evocas la dulce madrugada
que llamaba a la ordeña de la vaca lechera,
cuando era mi existencia toda blanca y rosada;
y tú, paloma arrulladora y montañera,
significas en mi primavera pasada
todo lo que hay en la divina Primavera.

[p 1905]

## FAR AWAY

Ox whose steaming clouds of breath I saw as a boy
beneath the Nicaraguan sun, golden, aflame,
on a fertile hacienda of harmonious joy
in the tropics. Dove in the dense forests that name
the wind's music, axes, birds, wild bulls—you became
what I am now, what no forgetting can destroy.

Heavy ox, you evoke the sweetness of the dawn
that called to wake me in time to do the milking.
This was when my life was a white and rosy song,
native to these mountains, a mother dove cooing
all that had meaning in my spring forever gone,
and the whole kingdom of a future holy Spring.

# III.
## Some Audacious, Cosmopolitan

## TUTECOTZIMÍ *(FRAGMENTO)*

Al cavar en el suelo de la ciudad antigua,
la metálica punta de la piqueta choca
con una joya de oro, una labrada roca,
una flecha, un fetiche, un dios de forma ambigua,
o los muros enormes de un templo. Mi piqueta
trabaja en el terreno de la América ignota.

¡Suene armoniosa mi piqueta de poeta!
¡Y descubra oro y ópalos y rica piedra fina,
templo, o estatua rota!
Y el misterio jeroglífico adivina
la Musa.

De la temporal bruma surge la vida extraña
de pueblos abolidos; la leyenda confusa
se ilumina; revela secretos la montaña
en que se alza la ruina.
                    * * * * *
                Cuando el grito feroz
de los castigadores calló y el jefe odiado
en sanguinoso fango quedó despedazado,
viose pasar un hombre cantando en alta voz
un canto mexicano. Cantaba cielo y tierra,
alababa a los dioses, maldecía la guerra.
Llamáronle:—"¿Tú cantas paz y trabajo?"—"Sí"
—"Toma el palacio, el campo, carcajes y huepiles;
celebra a nuestros dioses, dirige a los pipiles".

Y así empezó el reinado de Tutecotzimí.

                                      [1890]

# TUTECOTZIMÍ *(FRAGMENT)*

Digging in the topsoil of the ancient city
the pick's metallic point strikes something very hard:
some golden gem, perhaps, a stone that's been carved,
an arrow, fetish, some god's ambiguity,
or the enormous walls of some temple. My tools
open America's still undiscovered lands.

Let poetry's tools sing like harmonious jewels!
Let them discover fine, rich stones, gold, or opal,
temples, or statue's hands.
And mysterious hieroglyphics that foretell
my own Muse.

From the thick mist of time emerges the strangeness
of annulled peoples' lives, and legends, once confused,
now shine. The mountain reveals its secret access
to ruins underneath the plants of the jungle . . .
                    *   *   *   *   *
                    Then the ferocious cry
of the oppressors stopped. Their reviled leader's heart
would beat no more, his bloody body torn apart.
And then, singing loudly, a person journeyed by.
He sang to earth and sky and used an Aztec song
to praise the gods and curse all wars as being wrong.
The people cheered: "Can you bring peace and work?"
    "I can."
"Take this palace, these fields, arms, and *huepiles*, please;
lead the Pipil nation and praise our deities."

That's how the reign of Tutecotzimí began.

## LA NEGRA DOMINGA *(FRAGMENTO)*

¿Conocéis a la negra Dominga?
Es retoño de cafre y mandinga,
es flor de ébano henchida de sol.
Ama el ocre y el rojo y el verde
y en su boca, que besa y que muerde,
tiene el ansia del beso español.

Serpentina, fogosa y violenta,
con caricias de miel y pimienta
vibra y muestra su loca pasión:
fuegos tiene que Venus alaba
y envidiara la reina de Saba
para el lecho del rey Salomón.

Vencedora, magnífica y fiera,
con halagos de gata y pantera . . .

muestra dientes de carne de coco
con reflejos de lácteo marfil.

[1892]

# BLACK DOMINGA
## *(FRAGMENT)*

Have any of you met black Dominga,
that cross between *cafre* and *mandinga*?
She's an ebony bloom looking for bliss.
She adores ochre colors, red and green.
She is the best nibbler you've ever seen,
and all she yearns for is a Spaniard's kiss.

Like a passionate serpent that's on fire,
she's the honey and pepper of desire.
She's crazy with passion. Don't be misled:
she's the fiery lover Venus praised,
and the Queen of Sheba wished she'd saved
for King Solomon and their nights in bed.

Triumphant, fierce, and proud in her grandeur
with a stalking panther's feline allure . . .

she flashes her teeth like coconut meat,
reflecting an ivory, milky light.

# A COLÓN

¡Desgraciado Almirante! Tu pobre América,
tu india virgen y hermosa de sangre cálida,
la perla de tus sueños, es una histérica
de convulsivos nervios y frente pálida.

Un desastroso espíritu posee tu tierra:
donde la tribu unida blandió sus mazas,
hoy se enciende entre hermanos perpetua guerra,
se hieren y destrozan las mismas razas.

Al ídolo de piedra reemplaza ahora
el ídolo de carne que se entroniza,
y cada día alumbra la blanca aurora
en los campos fraternos sangre y ceniza.

Desdeñando a los reyes nos dimos leyes
al son de los cañones y los clarines,
y hoy al favor siniestro de negros Reyes
fraternizan los Judas con los Caínes.

Bebiendo la esparcida savia francesa
con nuestra boca indígena semiespañola,
día a día cantamos la *Marsellesa*
para acabar cantando la *Carmañola*.

Las ambiciones pérfidas no tienen diques,
soñadas libertades yacen deshechas.
¡Eso no hicieron nunca nuestros Caciques,
a quienes las montañas daban las flechas!

Ellos eran soberbios, leales y francos,
ceñidas las cabezas de raras plumas;

# TO COLUMBUS

Ill-fated admiral! Your poor America,
your beautiful, hot-blooded Indian virgin,
the pearl of your dreams, is now some hysterical
woman who has convulsions, tics, and pallid skin.

A disastrous spirit has occupied your land.
Where once united tribes lifted their maces high,
an endless civil war has gotten out of hand:
those of the same race fight and watch each other die.

Now the pagan idols of stone have been replaced
by idols of flesh that have taken their throne,
and every day dawn after white dawn has embraced
fraternal fields with blood and ashes of our own.

Disdaining the monarchy, we made our own laws
to the sound of trumpets and all our great weapons.
Now there's support for sinister black Kings because
men like Judas and Cain can be the best of friends.

It's droplets of refined French sap we're drinking,
that our half-Spanish, half-indigenous mouth sips.
Day after day it's the "Marseillaise" we sing,
though we end with the *"Carmañola"* on our lips.

There is no limit to treacherous ambition.
Dreams of freedom are scattered among the nations.
Our caciques never made this supposition.
Their arrows came to them as gifts from the mountains.

They were proud, trustworthy, and forthright in those days.
They had feathered diadems, wore exotic things.

¡ojalá hubieran sido los hombres blancos
como los Atahualpas y Moctezumas!

Cuando en vientres de América cayó semilla
de la raza de hierro que fue de España,
mezcló su fuerza heroica la gran Castilla
con la fuerza del indio de la montaña.

¡Pluguiera a Dios las aguas antes intactas
no reflejaran nunca las blancas velas;
ni vieran las estrellas estupefactas
arribar a la orilla tus carabelas!

Libres como las águilas, vieran los montes
pasar los aborígenes por los boscajes,
persiguiendo los pumas y los bisontes
con el dardo certero de sus carcajes.

Que más valiera el jefe rudo y bizarro
que el soldado que en fango sus glorias finca,
que ha hecho gemir al zipa bajo su carro
o temblar las heladas momias del Inca.

La cruz que nos llevaste padece mengua;
y tras encanalladas revoluciones,
la canalla escritora mancha la lengua
que escribieron Cervantes y Calderones.

Cristo va por las calles flaco y enclenque,
Barrabás tiene esclavos y charreteras,
y las tierras de Chibcha, Cuzco y Palenque
han visto engalonadas a las panteras.

Duelos, espantos, guerras, fiebre constante
en nuestra senda ha puesto la suerte triste:
¡Cristóforo Colombo, pobre Almirante,
ruega a Dios por el mundo que descubriste!

[1892]

If only white people could have had the same ways
as Atahualpa, Moctezuma, and other great kings.

When the iron race of the Spaniard's seeds
were sown in America's wombs and grew,
there was a mix of great Castille's heroic deeds
with an indigenous mountain fortitude, too.

Would that God had never let waters that had been
unbroken reflect the whiteness of your sails, or
allowed the astonished stars to look down on
your caravels as they dropped anchor on this shore.

If only the mountains could bear witness again
to the great forests where each aborigine
with arrows went hunting the puma and bison,
free as eagles, free as a people can be.

Let the gallant and primitive chief be esteemed
more than the muddy soldier who built your glories,
torturing under wheels the Chibcha king (who screamed)
and, trembling, dug up your icy Incan mummies.

The cross you brought us never seems to diminish.
When will corruption in revolutions be shown?
Not in the works of women who will demolish
the keen language of Cervantes and Calderón.

Christ is wandering through the streets, diseased and lean.
Barrabas has slaves, military distinction.
The lands of Chibcha, Cuzco, Palenque have seen
their panthers tamed, beribboned, brought to extinction.

The horror, the wars, the constant malarias
are doomed paths from which our luck has not recovered:
Poor Admiral, yes, you, Christopher Columbus,
pray to God for the world you discovered!

# CANTO A LA ARGENTINA
## (FRAGMENTO)

Tráfagos, fuerzas urbanas,
trajín de hierro y fragores,
veloz, acerado hipogrifo,
rosales eléctricos, flores.
miliunanochescas, pompas
babilónicas, timbres, trompas,
paso de ruedas y yuntas,
voz de domésticos pianos,
hondos rumores humanos,
clamor de voces conjuntas,
pregón, llamada, todo vibra,
[pulsación de una tensa fibra,]
sensación de un foco vital,
como el latir del corazón
o como la respiración
del pecho de la capital.

¡Que vuestro himno soberbio vibre,
hombres libres en tierra libre!
Nietos de los conquistadores,
renovada sangre de España,
transfundida sangre de Italia,
o de Germania, o de Vasconia,
o venidos de la entraña
de Francia, o de la Gran Bretaña,
vida de la Policolonia,
savia de la patria presente,
de la nueva Europa que augura
más grande Argentina futura.

# SONG TO ARGENTINA
## *(FRAGMENT)*

Commerce, the great cities' forces,
rumbling of iron and towers,
swift hippogriff shielded in steel,
electric roses and flowers
plucked from the Arabian Nights,
Babylonian pomp, bells, lights,
trumpets, rumbling wheels, yoked oxen,
voices of pianos from parlors,
profound and piercing human moans,
children singing as one in class,
people hawking things in the street,
one tense fiber keeping the beat,
living in life's most vital core
the way a heart goes on beating,
the way this crowd goes on breathing
in the chest of the city they adore.

Let your proud banner fly for all to see,
free men in a land that is free!
Grandchildren of the conquistador,
renewed blood from the motherland Spain,
and transfusions from Italy,
and the land of the Basques, and Germany,
and all European terrain,
somewhere in France or Great Britain,
life in this poly-colony,
sap for this country before us,
from the new Europe that can foresee
Argentina's future prosperity.

¡Salud, patria, que eres también mía,
puesto que eres de la humanidad:
salud, en nombre de la Poesía,
salud en nombre de la Libertad!

[1910]

Here's to you, since you're also my country,
and to your diverse humanity.
Prosper, in the name of Poetry.
Prosper, in the name of Liberty!

# A MOISÉS ASCARRUNZ

*Y para sus hermanos muertos
en los campos de batalla.*

Maldigo la quijada del asno, el enemigo,
Odio la flecha, el sable, la honda, la catapulta;
maldigo el duro instinto de la guerra, maldigo
la bárbara azagaya y la pólvora culta;

y a quien ahoga en sangre la cosecha de trigo
y a quien ciego de rabia la Cruz de Paz insulta;
a Bonaparte o César, a Marat o a Rodrigo,
príncipe de soldados o rey de turbamulta.

Los maldigo por tantas tristes almas de duelo
que van todos los días por la senda del cielo
precedidas por Cristo, a pedir paz y luz;

por Cristo que solloza, que palidece y sufre
mientras un negro incendio de salitre y azufre
obscurece a los hombres la visión de la Cruz.

[1899]

# TO MOISÉS ASCARRUNZ

*And to his brothers who died on the battlefields.*

I curse the jawbone of the ass, the enemy.
I detest all swords, catapults, slings, and arrows.
And I curse every war's unyielding tendency,
its genteel gunpowder, its brute darts for crossbows.

I curse all those who cause spilled blood to drown the wheat
and those who desecrate the Cross of Peace in rage:
Bonaparte and Caesar, Rodrigo and Marat,
soldiers, princes, kings, and mobs no one can assuage.

I curse them in the name of all the souls who die
and make their daily mournful journey through the sky,
led by Christ as they seek peace and light for their loss.

And in the name of Christ who cries and will suffer
while a great fire rages of nitrate and sulfur,
eclipsing humanity's vision of the Cross.

## A ROOSEVELT

¡Es con voz de la Biblia, o verso de Walt Whitman,
que habría que llegar hasta ti, Cazador!
¡Primitivo y moderno, sencillo y complicado,
con un algo de Wáshington y cuatro de Nemrod!

Eres los Estados Unidos,
eres el futuro invasor
de la América ingenua que tiene sangre indígena,
que aun reza a Jesucristo y aun habla en español.

Eres soberbio y fuerte ejemplar de tu raza;
eres culto, eres hábil; te opones a Tolstoy.
Y domando caballos, o asesinando tigres,
eres un Alejandro-Nabucodonosor.
(Eres un profesor de energía,
como dicen los locos de hoy)

Crees que la vida es incendio,
que el progreso es erupción;
en donde pones la bala
el porvenir pones.
                                        No.

Los Estados Unidos son potentes y grandes.
Cuando ellos se estremecen hay un hondo temblor
que pasa por las vértebras enormes de los Andes.
Si clamáis, se oye como el rugir del león.
Ya Hugo a Grant lo dijo: "Las estrellas son vuestras".
(Apenas brilla, alzándose, el argentino sol
y la estrella chilena se levanta . . . ) Sois ricos.

# TO ROOSEVELT

The voice of the Bible, or a stanza by Walt Whitman—
isn't that what it would take to reach your ears, Great Hunter?
You're primitive and modern, simple and complicated,
made of one part Washington and perhaps four parts Nimrod!

You yourself are the United States.
You will be a future invader
of naïve America, the one with Indian blood,
that still prays to Jesus Christ and still speaks the Spanish
    tongue.

You're arrogant and you're strong, exemplary of your race;
you're cultivated, you're skilled, you stand opposed to Tolstoy.
You're a tamer of horses, you're a killer of tigers,
you're like some Alexander mixed with Nebuchadnezzar.
(You must be the Energy Professor
as the crazies today might put it)

You think that life is one big fire,
that progress is just eruption,
that wherever you put bullets,
you put the future, too.
                         No.

The U.S. is a country that is powerful and strong.
When the giant yawns and stretches, the earth feels a tremor
rippling through the enormous vertebrae of the Andes.
If you shout, the sound you make is a lion's roar.
Hugo once said this to Grant: "You possess the stars."
(The Argentine sun at dawn gives off hardly any light;
and the Chilean star is rising higher . . . ) You're so rich,

Juntáis al culto de Hércules el culto de Mammón;
y alumbrando el camino de la fácil conquista,
la Libertad levanta su antorcha en Nueva-York.

Mas la América nuestra, que tenía poetas
desde los viejos tiempos de Netzahualcoyotl,
que ha guardado las huellas de los pies del gran Baco,
que el alfabeto pánico en un tiempo aprendió;
que consultó los astros, que conoció la Atlántida,
cuyo nombre nos llega resonando en Platón,
que desde los remotos momentos de su vida
vive de luz, de fuego, de perfume, de amor,
la América del grande Moctezuma, del Inca,
la América fragante de Cristóbal Colón,
la América católica, la América española,
la América en que dijo el noble Guatemoc:
"Yo no estoy en un lecho de rosas"; esa América
que tiembla de huracanes y que vive de Amor;
hombres de ojos sajones y alma bárbara, vive.
Y sueña. Y ama, y vibra; y es la hija del Sol.
Tened cuidado. ¡Vive la América española!,
hay mil cachorros sueltos del León Español.
Se necesitaría, Roosevelt, ser por Dios mismo,
el Riflero terrible y el fuerte Cazador,
para poder tenernos en vuestras férreas garras.

Y, pues contáis con todo, falta una cosa: ¡Dios!

[1904]

you join the cult to Hercules with the cult to Mammon.
And lighting the broad straight path that leads to easy
    conquests,
Lady Liberty raises her torch in New York City.


But our own America, which had plenty of poets
even from the ancient times of Netzahualcoyotl,
and which retained the footprints from the feet of great
    Bacchus,
and, over the course of time, learned the Panic alphabet:
it sought advice from the stars, and knew of Atlantis,
whose name was a legacy, resonating in Plato.
Even from the most remote moments in its boundless life,
it has lived by light and fire, by fragrances and by love:
America of the great Moctezuma and Inca,
America redolent of Christopher Columbus,
Catholic America and Spanish America,
the place where once long ago the noble Cuátemoc said,
"I'm not on a bed of roses!" Yes, that America,
trembling from its hurricanes and surviving on its Love . . .
It lives with you, with your Saxon eyes and barbaric souls.
And dreams. And loves, and vibrates; it's the daughter of the
    Sun.
Be careful. Spanish America is alive and well!
There are myriad loose cubs now from the Spanish Lion.
Roosevelt, you'd need to be transfigured by God himself
into the dire Rifleman and the powerful Hunter
to finally capture us in your talons of iron.


And you think you have it all, but one thing is missing: God!

# SALUTACIÓN AL ÁGUILA

*. . . May this grand Union have no end!*
— FONTOURA XAVIER

BIEN vengas, mágica Águila de alas enormes y fuertes
a extender sobre el Sur tu gran sombra continental,
a traer en tus garras, anilladas de rojos brillantes,
una palma de gloria, del color de la inmensa esperanza,
y en tu pico la oliva de una vasta y fecunda paz.

Bien vengas, oh mágica Águila, que amara tanto Walt
    Whitman,
quien te hubiera cantado en esta olímpica jira,
Águila que has llevado tu noble y magnífico símbolo
desde el trono de Júpiter, hasta el gran continente del Norte.

Ciertamente, has estado en las rudas conquistas del orbe.
Ciertamente, has tenido que llevar los antiguos rayos.
Si tus alas abiertas la visión de la paz perpetúan,
en tu pico y en tus uñas está la necesaria guerra.

¡Precisión de la fuerza! ¡Majestad adquirida del trueno!
Necesidad de abrirle el gran vientre fecundo a la tierra
para que en ella brote la concreción del oro de la espiga,
y tenga el hombre el pan con que mueve su sangre.

No es humana la paz con que sueñan ilusos profetas,
la actividad eterna hace precisa la lucha:
y desde tu etérea altura tú contemplas, divina Águila,
la agitación combativa de nuestro globo vibrante.

Es incidencia la historia. Nuestro destino supremo
está más allá del rumbo que marcan fugaces las épocas.

# SALUTING THE EAGLE

*... May this grand Union have no end!*
*—FONTOURA XAVIER*

Welcome, magical Eagle! With strong and enormous wings
you cast your great continental shadow throughout the South.
In your talons, ringed in the most brilliant of reds,
you bring a palm of glory, the color of limitless hope.
In your beak is the olive branch of a vast and fertile peace.

Welcome, oh magical Eagle that Walt Whitman loved so well.
He would have sung your praises in this Olympic repast.
You have carried the noble and magnificent symbol you are
from the throne of Jupiter to the great continent of the North.

Of course you have battled in the harsh conquests of the globe.
Of course you have been keen to carry ancient bolts of
    lightning.
Yet your open wings have symbolized enduring peace
and in your beak and your claws is the necessary war.

The precision of force! Majesty acquired from thunder!
The need to open the great fertile womb of the earth
so that the concretion of gold and wheat can sprout,
so that humans might have the bread that moves their blood.

Deluded prophets have dreamed a peace that is not human.
Eternal activity entails eternal struggle:
and from your ethereal heights, divine Eagle, you contemplate
the combative confusion of our vibrant world.

History is incidental. Our supreme destiny
is beyond the course set out by fleeting epochs.

Y Palenke y la Atlántida no son más que momentos soberbios
con que puntúa Dios los versos de su augusto Poema.

Muy bien llegada seas a la tierra pujante y ubérrima,
sobre la cual la Cruz del Sur está, que miró Dante
cuando siendo Mesías, impulsó en su intuición sus bajeles,
que antes que los del sumo Cristóbal supieron nuestro cielo.

*E pluribus unum!* ¡Gloria, victoria, trabajo!
Tráenos los secretos de las labores del Norte,
y que los hijos nuestros dejen de ser los retores latinos,
y aprendan de los yanquis la constancia, el vigor, el carácter.

¡Dinos, Águila ilustre, la manera de hacer multitudes
que hagan Romas y Grecias con el jugo del mundo presente,
y que, potentes y sobrias, extiendan su luz y su imperio
y que, teniendo el Águila y el Bisonte del Hierro y el Oro,
tengan un áureo día para darles las gracias a Dios!

Águila, existe el Cóndor. Es tu hermano en las grandes alturas.
Los Andes le conocen y saben que, como tú, mira al Sol.
*May this grand Union have no end,* dice el poeta.
Puedan ambos juntarse, en plenitud de concordia y esfuerzo.

Águila, que conoces desde Jove hasta Zarathustra
y que tienes en los Estados Unidos monumento,
que sea tu venida fecunda para estas naciones
que el pabellón admiran constelado de bandas y estrellas.

¡Águila que estuviste en las horas sublimes de Pathmos,
Águila prodigiosa, que te nutres de luz y de azul,

And Palenque and Atlantis are nothing more than proud
    moments
God uses to punctuate lines in his august Poem.


Welcome again to this forceful and plenteous land,
guarded by the Southern Cross above, that Dante saw
when he was the Messiah and used intuition to propel his
    vessels
beneath our skies even before the great Columbus.


*E pluribus Unum!* Glory, victory, work!
Give us the secret of the way you labor in the North,
the way our children might cease to be cut from Latin cloth
and learn perseverance, vigor, character from the Yankees.


Give us, illustrious Eagle, the way to make multitudes
who will build another Rome and Greece with the juice of the
    world they know,
and let them extend their light and their empire with sober
    strength,
using the Eagle, the Iron Bison, and Gold as their models,
and let them have a golden day for which they can give thanks
    to God!


But, Eagle, don't forget the Condor. He's your brother on the
    great heights.
The Andes know him, and know, like you, that he looks at the
    Sun.
*May this grand Union never end,* says the poet.
Let the two of you join in a plenitude of harmony and strength.


Oh, Eagle, whose knowledge spans Jupiter to Zarathustra,
the United States is a monument raised to you.
Let your presence be fertile for these many nations
that admire its banner of constellations and stripes.


Oh, Eagle, you were there for the sublime hours in Patmos.
Prodigious Eagle, you feed on celestial light.

como una Cruz viviente, vuela sobre estas naciones,
y comunica al globo la victoria feliz del futuro!

Por algo eres la antigua mensajera jupiterina,
por algo has presenciado cataclismos y luchas de razas,
por algo estás presente en los sueños del Apocalipsis,
por algo eres el ave que han buscado los fuertes imperios.

¡Salud, Águila! Extensa virtud a tus inmensos revuelos,
reina de los azures, ¡salud! ¡gloria! ¡victoria y encanto!
¡Que la Latina América reciba tu mágica influencia
y que renazca un nuevo Olimpo, lleno de dioses y héroes!

¡Adelante, siempre adelante! *¡Excélsior!* ¡Vida! ¡Lumbre!
¡Que se cumpla lo prometido en los destinos terrenos,
y que vuestra obra inmensa las aprobaciones recoja
del mirar de los astros, y de lo que Hay más Allá!

[1906]

Like a living Cross, fly over these nations
and communicate to the world the future's joyous triumph!

There's a reason you're Jupiter's ancient messenger
and you've witnessed cataclysms and struggles between races
and you're present in the dreams of the Apocalypse
and you're the bird that strong empires have sought.

Here's to you, Eagle, and your sweeping virtue on the long
    flights
throughout your blue domain! Health! Glory! Triumph and
    allure!
Let Latin America receive your magical influence
and let a new Olympus be born, full of gods and heroes!

Onward, always onward! Excelsior! Life! Light!
Let the promise of earthly destinies be fulfilled
and let your immense work receive the praise it deserves
under the watchful eyes of the stars and Heaven above!

# LA GRAN COSMÓPOLIS

*(Meditaciones de la madrugada)*

Casas de cincuenta pisos,
servidumbre de color,
millones de circuncisos,
máquinas, diarios, avisos
y ¡dolor, dolor, dolor . . . !

¡Éstos son los hombres fuertes
que vierten áureas corrientes
y multiplican simientes
por su ciclópeo fragor,
y tras la Quinta Avenida
la Miseria está vestida
con ¡dolor, dolor, dolor . . . !

¡Sé que hay placer y que hay gloria
allí, en el Waldorff Astoria,
en donde dan su victoria
la riqueza y el amor;
pero en la orilla del río,
sé quiénes mueren de frío,
y lo que es triste, Dios mío,
de dolor, dolor, dolor . . . !

Pues aunque dan millonarios
sus talentos y denarios,
son muchos más los calvarios
donde hay que llevar la flor
de la Caridad divina
que hacia el pobre a Dios inclina
y da amor, amor y amor.

# THE GREAT COSMOPOLIS

### (Meditations at Dawn)

Homes in a fifty story high-rise,
a serving class of color,
millions of people circumcised,
machines, billboards, newspapers,
and grief, layer upon layer!

So these must be the strong men
who spread their golden needs
and multiply their seeds
with a Cyclopian fervor,
while all along Fifth Avenue
Misery is in full view
and grief, layer upon layer!

I know there's glory and pleasure
at the Waldorf-Astoria in good measure
where there's lots of treasure,
love, triumph, the rich getting richer.
But on the banks by the river,
the dying are cold and shiver,
and worse still, God lives here,
in grief, layer upon layer.

Even though each millionaire
passes out pennies to assuage despair,
there's many a Calvary where
one must carry the flower
of divine Charity
so God can care for the needy
with love, layer upon layer.

Irá la suprema villa
como ingente maravilla
donde todo suena y brilla
en un ambiente opresor,
con sus conquistas de acero,
con sus luchas de dinero,
sin saber que allí está entero
todo el germen del dolor.

Todos esos millonarios
viven en mármoles parios
con residuos de Calvarios,
y es roja, roja su flor.
No es la rosa que el Sol lleva
ni la azucena que nieva,
sino el clavel que se abreva
en la sangre del dolor.

Allí pasa el chino, el ruso,
el kalmuko y el boruso;
y toda obra y todo uso
a la tierra nueva es fiel,
pues se ajusta y se acomoda
toda fe y manera toda,
a lo que ase, lima y poda
el sin par Tío Samuel.

Alto es él, mirada fiera,
su chaleco es su bandera,
como lo es sombrero y frac;
si no es hombre de conquistas,
todo el mundo tiene vistas
las estrellas y las listas
que bien sábese están listas
en reposo o en vivac.

Aquí el amontonamiento
mató amor y sentimiento;

The mansion that is so fine
with its grand design
goes where everything will shine
in an ambience each person suffers,
with its conquests of steel,
its money struggles, the major deal,
without knowing what's real—
the grief that grows in layers.

Each and every millionaire
sits in a Grecian marble chair
in the remains of Calvary's despair,
and red is their flower's color.
It's not the rose that the Sun brings
or the snow-white lily of spring,
but the carnation that shrinks,
in bloody grief, layer upon layer.

Chinese and Russians live here,
and many a Kalmuck and Prussian appear,
and any work they decide to try
in this new land, is a way to say, "I am!"
since one has to adjust
to new faiths and customs as you must
since polishing and making cuts
is the job of peerless Uncle Sam.

He's tall with fierce eyes that glow.
His coat is his flag, you know,
so is his hat and tuxedo.
He might not be a ladies' man
but everyone can see his plan
with his stars and stripes in hand
ready to fight in any land
on guard and fast or at ease and slow.

Here, all the things heaped to the ceiling
killed off love and feeling;

mas en todo existe Dios,
y yo he visto mil cariños
acercarse hacia los niños
del trineo y los armiños
del anciano Santa Claus.

Porque el yanqui ama sus hierros,
sus caballos y sus perros,
y su *yacht*, y su *foot-ball;*
pero adora la alegría,
con la fuerza, la armonía:
un muchacho que se ría
y una niña como un sol.

[1914]

but this God, this God's Laws
are in all the wide-eyed children who stare
and receive such tender loving care
from an old man dressed in fur in a sleigh: "There!
Look! Here comes Santa Claus!"

The Yankee loves his chains, of course,
every dog and any horse,
his yacht and the football game he won.
But he truly adores happy days,
harmony and forceful ways:
a boy who laughs and plays
and a girl who looks like the sun.

# WALT WHITMAN

En su país de hierro vive el gran viejo,
bello como un patriarca, sereno y santo.
Tiene en la arruga olímpica de su entrecejo
algo que impera y vence con noble encanto.

Su alma del infinito parece espejo;
son sus cansados hombros dignos del manto;
y con arpa labrada de un roble añejo
como un profeta nuevo canta su canto.

Sacerdote, que alienta soplo divino,
anuncia en el futuro, tiempo mejor.
Dice al águila: "¡Vuela!"; "¡Boga!", al marino,

y "¡Trabaja!", al robusto trabajador.
¡Así va ese poeta por su camino
con su soberbio rostro de emperador!

[1890]

# WALT WHITMAN

The good gray man lives in his iron land
like a patriarch, serene and saintly.
The Olympian furrow of his grand
brow rules and conquers with nobility.

His boundless soul resembles a mirror.
His weary shoulders deserve the best cloak.
He sings his song like a modern seer,
strumming on a lyre cut from ancient oak.

He is a priest of that first breath's holy
omen of better times for the future.
He tells the sailor, "Row!" and says, "Fly free!"

to eagles; "Work!" to the strong who labor.
Our poet continues on his journey
with the proud visage of an emperor.

# AGENCIA . . .

¿Qué hay de nuevo? . . . Tiembla la tierra.
En La Haya incuba la guerra.
Los reyes han terror profundo.
Huele a podrido en todo el mundo.
No hay aromas en Galaad.
Desembarcó el marqués de Sade
procedente de Seboím.
Cambia de curso el *gulf-stream*.
París se flagela de placer.
Un cometa va a aparecer.

Se cumplen ya las profecías
del viejo monje Malaquías.
En la iglesia el diablo se esconde.
Ha parido una monja . . . (¿En dónde? . . . )
Barcelona ya no está bona
sino cuando la bomba sona . . .
China se corta la coleta.
Henry de Rothschild es poeta.
Madrid abomina la capa.
Ya no tiene eunucos el papa.
Se organizará por un bill
la prostitución infantil.
La fe blanca se desvirtúa
y todo negro *continúa*.
En alguna parte está listo
el palacio del Anticristo.
Se cambian comunicaciones
entre lesbianas y gitones.
Se anuncia que viene el Judío
errante . . . ¿Hay algo más, Dios mío? . . .

[p 1907]

# WIRE SERVICE

This just in—The Earth Quakes!
4-Stars brew war at The Hague.
The Royals are running scared.
Something stinks around the world.
There is no more balm in Gilead.
Wicked times for Marquis de Sade—
the last man out of Zeboim.
Terror tides in the Gulf Stream.
Paris whipped for pleasure.
Comet coming closer.
All that I have prophesied
will come true, says Malachi.
Devil finds faith in churchyard.
Nun gives birth to child. (Had you heard?)
Barcelona is a tomb—
ready to blow like a bomb.
In China pigtails are cut.
Henry de Rothschild: Poet.
In Madrid the cape is passé.
Pope says eunuchs gone today.
Parliament's latest bill—
child prostitution is legal.
What was white is now dead.
What is black is still ahead.
Where do we go to find grace?
Try the antichrist's grand estate.
The first words spoken between
faggots and lesbians.
Nearly home, our Wandering Jew?
My God, what else is new?

# IV.
# And a Thirst for Illusive Hope
# That's Endless

## YO PERSIGO UNA FORMA . . .

Yo persigo una forma que no encuentra mi estilo,
botón de pensamiento que busca ser la rosa;
se anuncia con un beso que en mis labios se posa
al abrazo imposible de la Venus de Milo.

Adornan verdes palmas el blanco peristilo;
los astros me han predicho la visión de la Diosa;
y en mi alma reposa la luz como reposa
el ave de la luna sobre un lago tranquilo.

Y no hallo sino la palabra que huye,
la iniciación melódica que de la flauta fluye
y la barca del sueño que en el espacio boga;

y bajo la ventana de mi Bella-Durmiente,
el sollozo continuo del chorro de la fuente
y el cuello del gran cisne blanco que me interroga.

[1900]

# I'M HUNTING A FORM

I'm hunting a form that my style can barely trace,
the budding of thought that wants to become a rose;
first it lands on my lips like a kiss, then it goes
to Venus de Milo's impossible embrace.

There are green palms along the columned gallery;
the stars have shown me a vision of the goddess.
And in my soul, light extends itself in fullness
like the moon's bird skimming the lake's tranquility.

I can only find words that never seem to stay,
pieces of a song from a flute, which slip away,
the ship of those dreams, which drift aimlessly in space.

And under my Sleeping Beauty's open window,
the soft and steady crying of the fountain's flow,
and the swan's great white neck, with its questions, its grace.

## LA ESPIGA

Mira el signo sutil que los dedos del viento
hacen al agitar el tallo que se inclina
y se alza en una rítmica virtud de movimiento.
Con el áureo pincel de la flor de la harina

trazan sobre la tela azul del firmamento
el misterio inmortal de la tierra divina
y el alma de las cosas que da su sacramento
en una interminable frescura matutina.

Pues en la paz del campo la faz de Dios asoma.
De las floridas urnas místico incienso aroma
el vasto altar en donde triunfa la azul sonrisa.

Aun verde está y cubierto de flores el madero,
bajo sus ramas llenas de amor pace el cordero
y en la espiga de oro y luz duerme la misa.

                                                        [1899]

# THE EAR OF WHEAT

Consider the subtle sign that the wind's fingers
create when they shake the stalks of the plants that bend
then rise into rhythms of the air that lingers.
The flour's flowers, those brushes loaded with golden

strokes compose on the sky's canvas of blue colors,
painting mysteries that the sacred lands extend
and the sacraments that the soul of things confers
in the freshness of these mornings that never end.

Then, from the peace of the fields, God's face emerges.
From flower-charged urns mystic incense surges,
fills the vast altar that the blue smile's triumph keeps.

The wood is still green and has blossoms that amaze.
Beneath its branches full of love, the lamb will graze,
and in each gold ear of wheat, the Eucharist sleeps.

# ANTONIO MACHADO

Misterioso y silencioso
iba una y otra vez.
Su mirada era tan profunda
que apenas se podía ver.

Cuando hablaba tenía un dejo
de timidez y de altivez.
Y la luz de sus pensamientos
casi siempre se veía arder.

Era luminoso y profundo
como era hombre de buena fe.
Fuera pastor de mil leones
y de corderos a la vez.
Conduciría tempestades
o traería un panal de miel.

Las maravillas de la vida
y del amor y del placer.
Cantaba en versos profundos
cuyo secreto era de él.

Montado en un raro Pegaso,
un día al imposible fue.
Ruego por Antonio a mis dioses;
ellos le salven siempre. Amén.

[1905–1907]

# ANTONIO MACHADO

Mysteriously, silently,
he went there time and time again.
His gaze had such profundity
that he himself went unseen.

His words had a slight taste
of apprehension and disdain.
And the brilliance of his thinking
almost always cast its flames.

He was luminous and profound,
and also a man of good will.
He could shepherd prides of lions
and flocks of lambs at the same time.
He would harness any tempest
or bring home bees and honeycombs.

All the marvels that flow from life
and the love that brings us pleasure . . .
He could sing the most profound lines
whose secret belonged just to him.

Horseman on a rare Pegasus,
who reached an impossible realm . . .
I shall always pray to my gods:
Watch over Antonio! Amen.

# A JUAN RAMÓN JIMÉNEZ

## *Atrio*

¿Tienes, joven amigo, ceñida la coraza
para empezar, valiente, la divina pelea?
¿Has visto si resiste el metal de tu idea
la furia del mandoble y el peso de la maza?

¿Te sientes con la sangre de la celeste raza
que vida con los números pitagóricos crea?
¿Y, como el fuerte Herakles al león de Nemea,
a los sangrientos tigres del mal darías caza?

¿Te enternece el azul de una noche tranquila?
¿Escuchas pensativo el sonar de la esquila
cuando el Ángelus dice el alma de la tarde? . . .

¿Tu corazón las voces ocultas interpreta?
Sigue, entonces, tu rumbo de amor. Eres poeta.
La belleza te cubra de luz y Dios te guarde.

[1900]

# TO JUAN RAMÓN JIMÉNEZ

*Atrium*

Have you put on your armor, my young friend?
Are you ready to wage the holy war?
Can the metal of your ideas fend
off two-handed sword-blows, the hard hammer?

Do you have the cosmic race's iron
blood to wield Pythagorean numbers?
Hercules killed the Nemean lion:
will you hunt down the fierce, evil tigers?

Do still nights help you make heartfelt choices?
Are you hearing the Angelus bell toll
and speak all about the afternoon's soul?

Can your heart translate the hidden voices?
Follow your path toward love. You're a poet.
May God and beauty cover you with light.

# CANTO DE ESPERANZA

Un gran vuelo de cuervos mancha el azul celeste.
Un soplo milenario trae amagos de peste.
Se asesinan los hombres en el extremo Este.

¿Ha nacido el apocalíptico Anticristo?
Se han sabido presagios y prodigios se han visto
y parece inminente el retorno del Cristo.

La tierra está preñada de dolor tan profundo
que el soñador, imperial meditabundo,
sufre con las angustias del corazón del mundo.

Verdugos de ideales afligieron la tierra,
en un pozo de sombra la humanidad se encierra
con los rudos molosos del odio y de la guerra.

¡Oh, Señor Jesucristo!, por qué tardas, qué esperas
para tender tu mano de luz sobre las fieras
y hacer brillar al sol tus divinas banderas!

Surge de pronto y vierte la esencia de la vida
sobre tanta alma loca, triste o empedernida
que amante de tinieblas tu dulce aurora olvida.

Ven, Señor, para hacer la gloria de ti mismo,
ven con temblor de estrellas y horror de cataclismo,
ven a traer amor y paz sobre el abismo.

Y tu caballo blanco, que miró el visionario,
pase. Y suene el divino clarín extraordinario.
Mi corazón será brasa de tu incensario.

[1904]

# SONG OF HOPE

A great flock of crows is staining the sky.
The winds of millennial plagues blow by.
In the far eastern war, many men die.

Is this a sign of the Antichrist's birth?
Apocalyptic omens of the earth
that foreshadow Christ's imminent return?

The globe is pregnant with a pain so deep
the imperial dreamer gets no sleep
and in his own chest feels the world's heartbeat.

Torturers plagued the earth with their ideals.
Humans drown in what a dark pool conceals:
three Greek syllables that hatred reveals.

Oh, Lord Jesus, what are you waiting for?
Extend your hand of light over the hordes
and make your holy banners shine once more.

Show yourself right now and pour life's essence
over souls gone mad without your presence,
who forgot your dawn in their dark offense.

Come, Lord, and make manifest your glories.
Make stars tremble, cast out calamities,
bridge the abyss with your love and your peace.

Let your visionary white horse renew
us and let the divine trumpets sound, too.
My heart will burn like incense within you.

# AMA TU RITMO . . .

Ama tu ritmo y ritma tus acciones
bajo su ley, así como tus versos;
eres un universo de universos
y tu alma una fuente de canciones.

La celeste unidad que presupones
hará brotar en ti mundos diversos,
y al resonar tus números dispersos
pitagoriza en tus constelaciones.

Escucha la retórica divina
del pájaro del aire y la nocturna
irradiación geométrica adivina;

mata la indiferencia taciturna
y engarza perla y perla cristalina
en donde la verdad vuelca su urna.

                                        [1899]

# LOVE YOUR RHYTHM . . .

Love your rhythm and rhythmize your deeds.
Obey its laws, as in your poetry.
You're a cosmos in a cosmos set free.
Be the fountain of songs that your soul needs.

The celestial oneness you surely are
will make worlds sprout in you that are diverse,
and if your meters start to sound dispersed,
use Pythagoras to unite your stars.

Hear divine rhetoric in each feather
of every bird that takes to air, and learn
nighttime geometric heat and weather.

Kill all indifference that is taciturn
and string pearl on crystal pearl together
in the place where truth tips over its urn.

# NOCTURNO

Quiero expresar mi angustia en versos que abolida
dirán mi juventud de rosas y de ensueños,
y la desfloración amarga de mi vida
por un vasto dolor y cuidados pequeños.

Y el viaje a un vago Oriente por entrevistos barcos,
y el grano de oraciones que floreció en blasfemia,
y los azoramientos del cisne entre los charcos
y el falso azul nocturno de inquerida bohemia.

Lejano clavicordio que en silencio y olvido
no diste nunca al sueño la sublime sonata,
huérfano esquife, árbol insigne, obscuro nido
que suavizó la noche de dulzura de plata . . .

Esperanza olorosa a hierbas frescas, trino
del ruiseñor primaveral y matinal,
azucena tronchada por un fatal destino,
rebusca de la dicha, persecución del mal . . .

El ánfora funesta del divino veneno
que ha de hacer por la vida la tortura interior,
la conciencia espantable de nuestro humano cieno
y el horror de sentirse pasajero, el horror

de ir a tientas, en intermitentes espantos,
hacia lo inevitable, desconocido, y la
pesadilla brutal de este dormir de llantos
¡de la cual no hay más que Ella que nos despertará!

                                                  [p 1905]

# NOCTURNE

I want to erase my anguish in verse
that will describe my youth of reveries,
roses stripped to make my bitter life worse
after all the vast pain and small worries.

And the journey East on that ship of fools,
prayer-seeds that blossomed into blasphemy,
the irritating swan among the pools,
fake blue nights, bohemian revelry.

Clavichord that played the void in silence,
you stole from me the sonata's delight,
orphaned boat, well-known tree, and hidden nest
that pacified the sweet and silver night.

The hope that is scented with these fresh herbs,
the nightingale's song at dawn in the spring,
the fate of the lily to be severed,
cursed by vice, gleaning for what joy will bring . . .

Death's amphora of sanctified poison
will transform life into inner torture.
We fear the clay that makes us so human,
our fleeting being. And there's the horror

of groping in dark fear that comes and goes,
cruel nightmares of this sleeping pierced by screams,
lost in the foreordained that no one knows,
for only She will wake us from these dreams.

# ADIÓS

Adiós primavera en flor!
Adiós fuentes de aguas puras!
Adiós bosques de verduras
y aromas de floración!

Adiós mi fiel corazón . . .
con todas sus alegrías
de las dichas, de los días
de esa tan bella estación!

Adiós a la edad inquieta
ya mi vida se penetra . . .
en otra sombría senda.

Solo desnudo, y temblando
ante lo no conocido
            espero
No sea el destino severo,
y que lo que vea,
            entienda!

                              [p 1910]

# GOOD-BYE

Good-bye to the flowers of spring!
Good-bye fountains of pure water!
Good-bye deep forest greenery
and the fresh scents of flowering!

Good-bye to you, my faithful heart . . .
with the joyousness that rises
from the very best, from the days
of the most beautiful season!

Good-bye to the restless era
that has penetrated my life
on another darkening path.

By myself, naked and trembling
before the unknown, I still pray
fate will not treat me severely,
and I'll understand what I see!

## FLOR DE LUZ

Apareció mi alma como de la corola
de un lirio. Ella sabía estar desnuda y sola.
Sola, como en el agua, o en el viento. Ligera,
transparente, sutil, maravillosa. Era
como una divina flor de luz, o un divino
pájaro que en el aire acaba de nacer.
No sabía ni oír, ni ver, ni comprender;
y aún no sabía adónde iba,
ni lo que era materia aquí abajo, ni arriba . . .

[1911–1914]

# FLOWER OF LIGHT

My soul emerged into life as if she had come
from a lily's corona. And she was at one
with being naked, alone, as if she were lost
in water or wind, weighing nothing, gently tossed
into transparency, divine flower of light.
She resembled a bird that was born in midair
with no inkling of how to see or know or hear.
And still she had no idea where she would go,
or what matter is in the sky or here below.

# ALMA MÍA

Alma mía, perdura en tu idea divina;
todo está bajo el signo de un destino supremo;
sigue en tu rumbo, sigue hasta el ocaso extremo
por el camino que hacia la Esfinge te encamina.

Corta la flor al paso, deja la dura espina;
en el río de oro lleva a compás el remo;
saluda el rudo arado del rudo Triptolemo;
y sigue como un dios que sus sueños destina . . .

Y sigue como un dios que la dicha estimula,
y mientras la retórica del pájaro te adula
y los astros del cielo te acompañan, y los

ramos de la Esperanza surgen primaverales,
atraviesa impertérrita por el bosque de males
sin temer las serpientes, y sigue, como un dios . . .

                                                    [1900]

# OH, MY SOUL!

Oh, my soul! You must persist in your sacred ways!
All things exist under a sign of destiny.
Follow the long road to the Sphinx's mystery.
Follow the path to the setting sun of your days.

Pick flowers as you go, but let the thorns remain.
Use oar and gold river to keep the beat steady.
Greet Triptolemus and his crude plow, bow slowly,
then move on, like a god whose dreams are his domain.

And move on like a god inspired by ecstasy,
and as the rhetoric of birds makes you worthy
and your constellations are a holy presence,

and all the branches of Hope blossom in the spring—
make your bold way through the forest of wrongdoing.
Move on, like a god, without fearing the serpents.

## POEMA DEL OTOÑO *(FRAGMENTO)*

*A Mariano Miguel de Val*

El corazón del cielo late
por la victoria
de este vivir, que es un combate
y es una gloria.

Pues aunque hay pena y nos agravia
el sino adverso,
en nosotros corre la savia
del universo.

Nuestro cráneo guarda el vibrar
de tierra y sol,
como el ruido de la mar
el caracol.

La sal del mar en nuestras venas
va a borbotones;
tenemos sangre de sirenas
y de tritones.

A nosotros encinas, lauros,
frondas espesas;
tenemos carne de centauros
y satiresas.

En nosotros la Vida vierte
fuerza y calor.
¡Vamos al reino de la Muerte
por el camino del Amor!

[p 1909]

# AUTUMN POEM *(FRAGMENT)*

*To Mariano Miguel de Val*

The heartbeat of the sky within
wants a victory
for the lifelong battle to win
at least some glory.

Though we feel pain and are victims
of our destiny,
a cosmic sap flows in our limbs
and through our body.

Our skulls retain the harmony
of the sun and land,
just like the music of the sea
from shells in our hand.

The salt-sea courses in your veins,
bubbling within you.
And inside, a mermaid's blood reigns
with the tritons', too.

Our flesh is made of oak, thick ferns,
and a laurel tree,
home for when the centaur returns
and the satyrs breed.

Life gives our each and every breath
the strength to explode.
We'll head to the kingdom of Death
down Love's holy road!

# NOCTURNO

Silencio de la noche, doloroso silencio
nocturno . . . ¿Por qué el alma tiembla de tal manera?
Oigo el zumbido de mi sangre,
dentro mi cráneo pasa una suave tormenta.
¡Insomnio! No poder dormir, y, sin embargo,
soñar. Ser la auto-pieza
de disección espiritual, ¡el auto-Hamlet!
Diluir mi tristeza
en un vino de noche
en el maravilloso cristal de las tinieblas . . .
Y me digo: ¿a qué hora vendrá el alba?
Se ha cerrado una puerta . . .
Ha pasado un transeúnte . . .
Ha dado el reloj trece horas . . . ¡Si será Ella! . . .

                                                    [p 1907]

# NOCTURNE

Silence of the night, painful silence,
Nocturne . . . Why does my soul tremble like this?
I hear the low hum of my blood.
I watch a calm storm pass inside my skull.
Insomnia! Not to sleep, and perchance
to dream. To be the whole soliloquy
of spiritual dissection, my Hamlet-I!
To dissolve my sadness
in one night's wine,
in the marvelous crystal darkness . . .
And then I wonder: When will it be dawn?
A door just closed . . .
Someone is passing on the street . . .
The clock strikes three . . . It must be Her!

# "¡TORRES DE DIOS! ¡POETAS!"

¡Torres de Dios! ¡Poetas!
¡Pararrayos celestes,
que resistís las duras tempestades,
como crestas escuetas,
como picos agrestes,
rompeolas de las eternidades!

La mágica esperanza anuncia un día
en que sobre la roca de armonía
expirará la pérfida sirena.
¡Esperad, esperemos todavía!

Esperad todavía
El bestial elemento se solaza
en el odio a la sacra poesía
y se arroja baldón de raza a raza.

La insurrección de abajo
tiende a los Excelentes.
El caníbal codicia su tasajo
con roja encía y afilados dientes.

Torres, poned al pabellón sonrisa.
Poned ante ese mal y ese recelo
una soberbia insinuación de brisa
y una tranquilidad de mar y cielo . . .

[1903]

## "POETS! TOWERS OF GOD!"

Poets! Towers of God!
You bear storms that are infernal
like a jagged mountain range,
like a heavenly lightning rod,
breakwaters of the eternal,
high summits that will never change!

Hope with its magic announces the day
when, thrown against the shoals of harmony,
the treacherous mermaid will pass away.
But wait, and don't lose your patience with me!

Be patient with me.
The bestial crowd takes great solace
in its hatred of sacred poetry,
hurling insults regardless of their race.

The insurrection from beneath
always targets the elite.
The cannibals with their red gums and teeth
love and covet their bloody chunk of meat.

Over that evil and that suspicion,
towers, let your smile be flag and country.
Be proud and let the slightest hint of wind
bring you the composure of sky and sea.

## A UN POETA *(FRAGMENTO)*

Sabe que, cuando muera, yo te escucho y te sigo:
que si haces bien, te aplaudo; que si haces mal, te riño;
si soy lira, te canto; si cíngulo, te ciño;
si en tu cerebro, seso; y si en tu vientre, ombligo.

[1911–1914]

# TO A POET
## *(FRAGMENT)*

Even after I die, I will hear your words and remain.
If you do well, I'll applaud. If you don't, you'll be disgraced.
I'll be a harp to sing you, the alb's cord around your waist.
Think of me as your navel or living inside your brain.

## A PHOCÁS EL CAMPESINO

Phocás el campesino, hijo mío, que tienes,
en apenas escasos meses de vida, tantos
dolores en tus ojos que esperan tantos llantos
por el fatal pensar que revelan tus sienes . . .

Tarda en venir a este dolor adonde vienes,
a este mundo terrible en duelos y en espantos;
duerme bajo los Ángeles, sueña bajo los santos,
que ya tendrás la Vida para que te envenenes . . .

Sueña, hijo mío, todavía, y cuando crezcas,
perdóname el fatal dón de darte la vida
que yo hubiera querido de azul y rosas frescas;

pues tú eres la crisálida de mi alma entristecida,
y te he de ver en medio del triunfo que merezcas
renovando el fulgor de mi psique abolida.

                                          [1905]

## TO PHOCÁS, TILLER OF FIELDS

Phocás, tiller of fields, my son, you've known
in just a few months of life so many
sorrows in your eyes that await any
hardship your fatal furrowed brow has shown.

Take your time coming to this pain that's grown
in this terrible world of agony.
Sleep, dream beneath angels and the saintly.
Soon enough, Life will poison what you've sown.

Dream, my son, please, and when you've come of age,
forgive me for giving you the deadly
gift of life, not fresh roses or blue sage.

You're the chrysalis of my unhappy
soul and the fitting triumph over rage,
restoring light to my annulled psyche.

## "DIVINA PSIQUIS, DULCE
## MARIPOSA INVISIBLE"

1

¡Divina Psiquis, dulce mariposa invisible
que desde los abismos has venido a ser todo
lo que en mi ser nervioso y en mi cuerpo sensible
forma la chispa sacra de la estatua de lodo!

Te asomas por mis ojos a la luz de la tierra
y prisionera vives en mí de extraño dueño;
te reducen a esclava mis sentidos en guerra
y apenas vagas libre por el jardín del sueño.

Sabia de la Lujuria que sabe antiguas ciencias,
te sacudes a veces entre imposibles muros,
y más allá de todas las vulgares conciencias
exploras los recodos más terribles y obscuros.

Y encuentras sombra y duelo. Que sombra y duelo
   encuentres
bajo la viña en donde nace el vino del Diablo.
Te posas en los senos, te posas en los vientres
que hicieron a Juan loco e hicieron cuerdo a Pablo.

A Juan virgen y a Pablo militar y violento,
a Juan que nunca supo del supremo contacto;
a Pablo el tempestuoso que halló a Cristo en el viento.
y a Juan ante quien Hugo se queda estupefacto.

2

Entre la catedral y las ruinas paganas
vuelas, ¡oh Psiquis, oh alma mía!
—como decía

# DIVINE PSYCHE, SWEET INVISIBLE BUTTERFLY!

### 1

Divine Psyche, sweet invisible butterfly!
You've risen from the deep abysses and the dark
into my nervous system, my body, and my
sentient sculpture of mud to shape a sacred spark.

You gaze through my eyes at the lands and light you crave,
yet you are but a prisoner in me, it seems.
My senses at war have reduced you to a slave
with almost no freedom in the garden of dreams.

Learned in ancient sciences of prurience,
you hurl yourself at times against hard surfaces,
and, beyond the limits of each vulgar conscience,
you explore the most obscure terrible places.

You find shadows and grief, and I know what you know:
you live in vines that gave birth to the Devil's wine;
you land on breasts and then on parts farther below,
where Paul became sane and John truly lost his mind.

John was chaste, Paul a soldier against those who sinned.
John would not know the rapture of being ravished.
Paul was enraged until he found Christ in the wind
and John was the one who left Hugo astonished.

### 2

Between pagan ruins and cathedral
you fly, Oh, my soul, my Psyche!
said Edgar to me

aquel celeste Edgardo,
que entró en el paraíso entre un son de campanas
y un perfume de nardo—,
entre la catedral
y las paganas ruinas
repartes tus dos alas de cristal,
tus dos alas divinas.
Y de la flor
que el ruiseñor
canta en su griego antiguo, de la rosa,
vuelas, ¡oh, Mariposa!,
a posarte en un clavo de nuestro Señor.

                                              [p 1905]

as his earthly body
entered paradise on the tolling bell
with the smell of spikenards so lovely—
between pagan ruins
and cathedral,
you spread your two crystalline wings,
wings of the eternal.
When the flowers exhale
and then the nightingale
sings from the rose in ancient Greek,
you float, oh, Butterfly, and seek
a place on our Lord, on the Cross—a nail.

# FILOSOFÍA

Saluda al sol, araña, no seas rencorosa.
Da tus gracias a Dios, oh sapo, pues que eres.
El peludo cangrejo tiene espinas de rosa
y los moluscos reminiscencias de mujeres.
Sabed ser lo que sois, enigmas siendo formas;
dejad la responsabilidad a las Normas,
que a su vez la enviarán al Todopoderoso . . .
(Toca, grillo, a la luz de la luna; y dance el oso.)

[p 1905]

# PHILOSOPHY

Say hello to the sun, spider. Don't feel forlorn.
Offer thanks to God, oh, Toad, that you are alive.
The crab's shell defends itself with a rose's thorn—
a point of resemblance between mollusks and wives.

Enigmas given form—accept what you are;
you can leave responsibility to the Law,
which in turn will leave it to the Omnipotent . . .
(Crickets! Sing the moon! Bears! Dance to your heart's
    content!)

# AUGURIOS

*A E[ugenio] Díaz Romero*

Hoy pasó un águila
sobre mi cabeza,
lleva en sus alas
la tormenta,
lleva en sus garras
el rayo que deslumbra y aterra.
¡Oh águila!
Dame la fortaleza
de sentirme en el lodo humano
con alas y fuerzas
para resistir los embates
de las tempestades perversas,
y de arriba las cóleras
y de abajo las roedoras miserias.

Pasó un buho
sobre mi frente.
Yo pensé en Minerva
y en la noche solemne.
¡Oh buho!
Dame tu silencio perenne,
y tus ojos profundos en la noche
y tu tranquilidad ante la muerte.
Dame tu nocturno imperio
y tu sabiduría celeste,
y tu cabeza cual la de Jano,
que, siendo una, mira a Oriente y Occidente.

# AUGURIES

*To Eugenio Díaz Romero*

Today, an eagle passed
over my head,
carrying a storm
on its wings,
carrying the flashing
and awesome lightning in its claws.
Oh, eagle!
Give me the strength
to be in the human mud yet feel
the wings; and the force
to resist the wild seas
of perverse tempests,
the anger from above
and from below, gnawing miseries.

An owl passed
over my forehead.
Minerva crossed my mind
as well as the solemn night.
Oh, owl!
Give me your steadfast silence,
your eyes deep in the night,
your calm in facing death.
Give me your nocturnal empire,
your celestial wisdom,
your head like that of Janus,
who looks both East and West at once.

Pasó una paloma
que casi rozó con sus alas mis labios.
¡Oh paloma!
Dame tu profundo encanto
de saber arrullar, y tu lascivia
en campo tornasol; y en campo
de luz tu prodigioso
ardor en el divino acto.
(Y dame la justicia en la naturaleza,
pues, en este caso,
tú serás la perversa
y el chivo será el casto.)

Pasó un gerifalte. ¡Oh gerifalte!
Dame tus uñas largas
y tus ágiles alas cortadoras de viento,
y tus ágiles patas,
y tus uñas que bien se hunden
en las carnes de la caza.
Por mi cetrería
irás en jira fantástica,
y me traerás piezas famosas
y raras,
palpitantes ideas,
sangrientas almas.

Pasa el ruiseñor.
¡Ah divino doctor!
No me des nada. Tengo tu veneno,
tu puesta de sol
y tu noche de luna y tu lira,
y tu lírico amor.
(Sin embargo, en secreto,
tu amigo soy,
pues más de una vez me has brindado,
en la copa de mi dolor,
con el elíxir de la luna
celestes gotas de Dios . . . )

A dove passed
and nearly brushed my lips with its wings.
Oh, dove!
Give me your song's profound gift
to soothe, and the lust you show
in radiant fields, and in fields
of light your prodigious
passion in the divine act.
(And give me the justice one finds in nature,
since, in this case,
you are perverse
and the goat is chaste.)

A falcon passed. Oh, falcon!
Give me your long claws,
your agile wings that cut through wind,
your agile talons
that sink so well
into the prey of your hunt.
With me as your falconer
you'll be on a fantastic tour
and you'll return to bring me
pieces that are famous
and rare, pulsing ideas,
bloody souls.

The nightingale passes.
Ah, divine healer!
Give me nothing. I have your poison,
your sunset,
your moonlit night and your lily,
your lyrical love.
(And yet, in secret,
I'm your one true friend,
since more than once you've poured
the elixir of the moon
into the cup of my sorrow,
those celestial droplets of God . . . )

Pasa un murciélago.
Pasa una mosca. Un moscardón.
Una abeja en el crepúsculo.
No pasa nada.
La muerte llegó.

[p 1905]

A bat goes by.
So does a fly. Then a hornet.
A bee at dusk.
Then nothing.
Death has come.

## PÁJAROS DE LAS ISLAS . . .

Pájaros de las islas, en vuestra concurrencia
hay una voluntad,
hay un arte secreto y una divina ciencia,
gracia de eternidad.

Vuestras evoluciones, academia expresiva,
signos sobre el azur,
riegan a Oriente ensueño, a Occidente ansia viva,
paz a Norte y a Sur.

La gloria de las rosas y el candor de los lises
a vuestros ojos son,
y a vuestras alas líricas son las brisas de Ulises,
los vientos de Jasón.

Almas dulces y herméticas que al eterno problema
sois en cifra veloz
lo mismo que la roca, el huracán, la gema,
el iris y la voz.

Pájaros de las islas, ¡oh pájaros marinos!
Vuestros revuelos, con
ser dicha de mis ojos, son problemas divinos
de mi meditación.

Y con las alas puras de mi deseo abiertas
hacia la inmensidad,
imito vuestros giros en busca de las puertas
de la única Verdad.

                                        [1906–1907]

# ISLAND BIRDS

Island birds, in your gathering presence
there is a will to be,
a secret art and a divine science,
grace of eternity.

Your maneuvers reveal expressive schools,
and azure auguries,
an East of dreams, a West where longing rules,
a North and South of peace.

Dazzling roses and simple fleurs-de-lis
are the gifts of your eyes.
Your lyric wings create Ulysses' breeze
and Jason's windy skies.

Sweet, hermetic souls, the lasting problem
is coded fast in you
and in the rock, the hurricane, the gem,
the iris, our speech, too.

Island birds, birds that live to ply the seas,
your circles overhead
cheer my eyes, but perplex my reveries—
you, signs of the sacred.

I sail on open wings of my desire
into immensity,
seeking the way in your widening gyre.
Truth: the one, the only . . .

# NOCTURNO

*A Mariano de Cavia.*

Los que auscultasteis el corazón de la noche,
los que por el insomnio tenaz habéis oído
el cerrar de una puerta, el resonar de un coche
lejano, un eco vago, un ligero ruido . . .

En los instantes del silencio misterioso,
cuando surgen de su prisión los olvidados,
en la hora de los muertos, en la hora del reposo,
¡sabréis leer estos versos de amargor impregnados! . . .

Como en un vaso vierto en ellos mis dolores
de lejanos recuerdos y desgracias funestas,
y las tristes nostalgias de mi alma, ebria de flores,
y el duelo de mi corazón, triste de fiestas.

Y el pesar de no ser lo que yo hubiera sido,
la pérdida del reino que estaba para mí,
el pensar que un instante pude no haber nacido,
¡y el sueño que es mi vida desde que yo nací!

Todo esto viene en medio del silencio profundo
en que la noche envuelve la terrena ilusión,
y siento como un eco del corazón del mundo
que penetra y conmueve mi propio corazón.

                                                      [p 1905]

# NOCTURNE

*To Mariano de Cavia*

For those who've heard the night's heart by auscultation
in your endless insomnia, there's a closing door,
a passing carriage, whose loud reverberation
echoes until you cannot hear it anymore.

In those moments with their mysterious silence,
when those you've forgotten break free from their prison,
when you should sleep, but the dead assert their presence,
you'll understand these lines and their bitter vision.

Like an empty glass in which I pour my sorrows,
my distant memories, misfortunes, and disgrace,
the nostalgia that my soul, drunk on flowers, knows,
and my heart forever mourning, undone by fêtes . . .

The burden of not being what I could have been,
and losing the kingdom that was ready for me,
or never being born with a chance to begin
living after my birth, my life, this reverie!

Through the deepest silences, here is all I'll know:
night enfolds the earthly realm where illusions start,
and I feel like the world's heart, feel like its echo
as it penetrates, moves, and touches my own heart.

# LA VICTORIA DE SAMOTRACIA

*A mi viejo amigo {Alberto} Gache*

La cabeza abolida aún dice el día sacro
en que, al viento del triunfo, las multitudes plenas
desfilaron ardientes delante el simulacro,
que hizo hervir a los griegos en las calles de Atenas.

Esta egregia figura no tiene ojos y mira,
no tiene boca y lanza el más supremo grito;
no tiene brazos y hace vibrar toda la lira,
y las alas pentélicas abarcan lo infinito.

[1914]

# VICTORY OF SAMOTHRACE

*To my old friend Alberto Gache*

The abolished head still speaks of the parade
that sacred day, when masses marched in triumphant winds
and, ardent, bowed before this simulacrum made
to make Greeks teem in the streets of Athens.

This illustrious figure sees though it has no eyes.
It has no arms, and yet its entire lyre sings.
It has no mouth, yet unleashes its supreme cries,
embracing infinity with Pentelic wings.

## TRISTE, MUY TRISTEMENTE . . .

Un día estaba yo triste, muy tristemente
viendo cómo caía el agua de una fuente;

era la noche dulce y argentina. Lloraba
la noche. Suspiraba la noche. Sollozaba

la noche. Y el crepúsculo en su suave amatista,
diluía la lágrima de un misterioso artista.

Y ese artista era yo, misterioso y gimiente,
que mezclaba mi alma al chorro de la fuente.

[1916]

# SAD, SADLY CALLING

One day when I was sad, sadly calling
to a fountain, its water was falling,

and the night, sweet and silver, was crying.
The night was sobbing. The night was sighing.

And the dusk, in its gentle amethyst,
diffused the tear of a cryptic artist.

I was the cryptic artist's moaning dream,
and I mixed my soul with the fountain's stream.

# AUTORRETRATO A SU HERMANA LOLA

Este viajero que ves,
es tu hermano errante. Pues
aún suspira y aún existe,
no como le conociste,
sino como ahora es:
viejo, feo, gordo y triste.

[1904]

# SELF-PORTRAIT FOR HIS SISTER LOLA

The traveler before your eyes
is your wandering brother, who
still lives and breathes to your surprise,
not how he was when he left you,
but how he became after that:
old and ugly and sad and fat.

# EXTRAVAGANCIAS
## *(FRAGMENTO)*

Hermano: estoy enfermo de un mal solemne y grave
que me es desconocido. Alguien dice que sabe
a ciertas convulsiones de la vida moderna.
Es como sed de luz, y quiero una linterna
que me guíe al ignoto remedio de mis males,
y así sanaré solo, ya que no hay hospitales
ni médicos que sepan algo de mi pereza,
de mi *spleen,* de mis ansias.
                            En fin, no sé qué es esa
locura que me envuelve;
mi mente piensa mucho, pero nada resuelve
acerca del remedio que necesito, hermano,
para tomar el tren hacia lo arcano,
sano . . .

                                              [1911–1914]

# EXTRAVAGANCES
## *(FRAGMENT)*

I'm sick, my friend, with an illness serious and grave
that I cannot explain. It seems no one can save
me from certain convulsions of the modern age.
It's like some thirst for light, a lantern to assuage
and guide me toward some unknown cure for my ills
so I might soon improve, because no hospitals,
no doctors have a clue about my lethargy,
my spleen, my anxiety.
                What could it be,
this madness that envelops me?
My mind solves nothing, yet it's thinking constantly
about the medicine I really need, my friend,
so that I can catch a train to an arcane end,
healthy . . .

## LOS HUÉSPEDES
### *(FRAGMENTO)*

*De Jacques de Nittis*

Y en lo inconsciente de nuestras almas, a veces,
rumores lejanos que surgen de antes,
tumulto desencadenado por súbitas ráfagas,
el pueblo prisionero de las almas ancestrales
se subleva; y he aquí surgir, brutales y desnudos.
—huéspedes desmesurados que dormían desconocidos—
los deseos, turba que no fue saciada,
en nuestra alma, tan vieja y larga como la Vida.

[1897]

# THE GUESTS
## *(FRAGMENT)*

### *From Jacques de Nittis*

Sometimes, in our collective unconscious,
murmurs from long ago emerge,
tumultuous gusts of wind unleashed,
and the people, imprisoned by ancestral souls,
revolt. Brutal and naked desires awakened
like unruly guests no one knew were there,
a mob that was never satisfied
in our souls as old and long as Life.

## VENECIA

Tristeza, tristeza. No es el alma
La triste, la flaca. Es este cuerpo
Que agitan las ráfagas misteriosas
Martirizadoras de los nervios.
Hay un raro huésped en mi carne,
Que mueve mis músculos, mis huesos.

[¿1901?]

# VENICE

Sadness, only sadness. It's not the soul
that's sad and wastes away, but this body
wracked by mysterious gusts
blowing from the martyrdom of my nerves.
There is a strange guest in my flesh,
moving my muscles and my bones.

# MELANCOLÍA

*A Domingo Bolívar.*

Hermano, tú que tienes la luz, dime la mía.
Soy como un ciego. Voy sin rumbo y ando a tientas.
Voy bajo tempestades y tormentas,
ciego de ensueño y loco de armonía.

Ese es mi mal. Soñar. La poesía
es la camisa férrea de mil puntas cruentas
que llevo sobre el alma. Las espinas sangrientas
dejan caer las gotas de mi melancolía.

Y así voy, ciego y loco, por este mundo amargo;
a veces me parece que el camino es muy largo,
y a veces que es muy corto . . .

Y en este titubeo de aliento y agonía,
cargo lleno de penas lo que apenas soporto.
¿No oyes caer las gotas de mi melancolía?

[p 1905]

# MELANCHOLY

*To Domingo Bolívar*

You, my brother, holding the light—Lend me
some. I'm blind. Can't find my way in the dark.
Can't escape the tempests or storms. Music
and blinding dreams have driven me crazy.

That is my curse. To dream. Poetry
is an iron vest with a thousand darts.
It's wrapped around my soul, its bloody barbs
wet with endless drops of melancholy.

I roam the bitter world, insane and blind,
and I think, at times, that the way I find
is long—or very short . . .

So, torn between courage and agony,
it's hard to bear the burdens of my heart.
Can't you hear those drops, that melancholy?

# AY, TRISTE DEL QUE UN DÍA . . .

Ay, triste del que un día en su esfinge interior
pone los ojos e interroga. Está perdido.
Ay del que pide eurekas al placer o al dolor.
Dos dioses hay, y son: Ignorancia y Olvido.

Lo que el árbol desea decir y dice al viento,
y lo que el animal manifiesta en su instinto,
cristalizamos en palabra y pensamiento.
Nada más que maneras expresan lo distinto.

[p 1905]

# ONE DAY, UNDONE, HE SIGHED

One day, undone, he sighed then fixed his eyes on this:
his inner sphinx. He asked, but he's just an Absence.
He begs for eurekas from sorrow or from bliss.
There are two gods: Oblivion and Ignorance.

What the tree wants to say when it speaks to the wind
and what all the animals instinctively show
is the language growing like crystals in our mind,
simply behaviors for expressing what we know.

# PASA Y OLVIDA

*Ese es mi mal: Soñar.*

Peregrino que vas buscando en vano
un camino mejor que tu camino,
¿cómo quieres que yo te dé la mano,
si mi signo es tu signo, Peregrino?

No llegarás jamás a tu destino;
llevas la muerte en ti como el gusano
que te roe lo que tienes de humano . . . ,
¡lo que tienes de humano y de divino!

¡Sigue tranquilamente! ¡Oh caminante!,
todavía te queda muy distante
ese país incógnito que sueñas . . .

 . . . Y soñar es un mal. Pasa y olvida,
pues si te empeñas en soñar, te empeñas
en aventar la llama de tu vida.

[1911–1914]

# KEEP WALKING, TRY TO FORGET

*That is my curse. To dream.*

Wayfarer, you may be seeking in vain
a road that would be better than your road.
If I gave you a hand, what would you gain?
My sign is your sign, the very same road.

Because you carry death, you'll never find
your destination. There's a worm within,
eating everything you have that's human—
your human parts and also the divine.

My advice to you is to walk in peace,
to go the whole distance and never cease
moving toward the unknown land of dreaming . . .

that curse. Keep walking, and try to forget!
For if you dream, if you search for meaning,
you'll fan life's flame and burn yourself to death.

# THÁNATOS

*En medio del camino de la Vida* ...
dijo Dante. Su verso se convierte:
En medio del camino de la Muerte.

Y no hay que aborrecer a la ignorada
emperatriz y reina de la Nada.
Por ella nuestra tela está tejida,
y ella en la copa de los sueños vierte
un contrario nepente: ¡ella no olvida!

[p 1905]

# THANATOS

*In the middle of the road of life . . .* said
Dante, which is a line that can be read
as *In the middle of the road of Death.*

There's no reason to abhor or ignore
the empress and the queen of Nothingness—
she wove the cloth of life in which we dress,
and in her own cup of dreams, she will pour
an anti-nepenthe—she won't forget!

## SPES

Jesús, incomparable perdonador de injurias,
óyeme; Sembrador de trigo, dame el tierno
pan de tus hostias; dame, contra el sañudo infierno,
una gracia lustral de iras y lujurias.

Dime que este espantoso horror de la agonía
que me obsede, es no más de mi culpa nefanda,
que al morir hallaré la luz de un nuevo día
y que entonces oiré mi "¡Levántate y anda!"

[p 1905]

# SPES

Jesus, forgiver of trespass beyond compare,
hear me; sower of wheat, please give me the gentle
bread of your hosts; give me, against the wrath of hell,
a blessing that will cleanse rage, lust, despair.

Tell me that these grim thoughts of pain and agony
that plague my mind are just my own guilt-laden fears,
and when I die I'll find the light of a new day,
and that the words, "Stand up and walk!" will reach my ears.

## LA DULZURA DEL ÁNGELUS . . .

La dulzura del ángelus matinal y divino
que diluyen ingenuas campanas provinciales,
en un aire inocente a fuerza de rosales,
de plegaria, de ensueño de virgen y de trino

de ruiseñor, opuesto todo al rudo destino
que no cree en Dios . . . El áureo ovillo vespertino
que la tarde devana tras opacos cristales
por tejer la inconsútil tela de nuestros males

todos hechos de carne y aromados de vino . . .
Y esta atroz amargura de no gustar de nada,
de no saber adónde dirigir nuestra prora

mientras el pobre esquife en la noche cerrada
va en las hostiles olas huérfano de la aurora . . .
(¡Oh, suaves campanas entre la madrugada!)

                                                            [1905]

# THE SWEET MORNING ANGELUS

The sweet morning Angelus, its divinity
diffused by the chiming of bells from the province,
the roses that exhale an air of innocence,
the dreams of the virgin, and the sweet litany

of nightingales: all oppose the rough destiny
of not believing in God . . . Twilight is ready
to spin a ball of gold thread behind dark windows,
to start weaving our iniquities' seamless clothes,

vices redolent of wine and carnality.
The loathsome bitterness of not liking a thing,
of having no idea where to steer our prow

as the poor skiff moves through the stormy night, losing
its way among hostile waves like an orphan now . . .
Oh, gentle bells, which break the day with their tolling.

# LO FATAL

*A René Pérez.*

Dichoso el árbol que es apenas sensitivo,
y más la piedra dura porque esa ya no siente,
pues no hay dolor más grande que el dolor de ser vivo,
ni mayor pesadumbre que la vida consciente.

Ser, y no saber nada, y ser sin rumbo cierto,
y el temor de haber sido y un futuro terror . . .
Y el espanto seguro de estar mañana muerto,
y sufrir por la vida y por la sombra y por

lo que no conocemos y apenas sospechamos,
y la carne que tienta con sus frescos racimos,
y la tumba que aguarda con sus fúnebres ramos,
¡y no saber adónde vamos,
ni de dónde venimos! . . .

                                                  [p 1905]

# DESTINED TO DIE

*To René Pérez*


Trees are lucky because they barely sense a thing.
Stones, as well, because they're hard, beyond all feeling.
No pain's greater than the pain of being aware.
Human consciousness produces the worst despair.

To be, yet know nothing with no clear way to go,
the fear of having been, a future terror, too,
the unerring dread of being dead tomorrow,
and suffering through life and through shadows and through

the unknown and what one cannot anticipate,
the temptation of flesh, the fresh fruit still to come,
our tombs and the memorial laurels that await,
not knowing where we're going
or even where we're from!

# STORIES AND FABLES

# TRANSLATOR'S NOTE

*. . . Rubén Darío, whom we spend half our lives denying,
only to realize later that without him we would not speak
our own language—that is, without him we would speak a
stiff, stilted, insipid tongue.*

—PABLO NERUDA, "JOURNEY TO THE
HEART OF QUEVEDO"

Darío tells his readers in "The Story of His Books: *Azure . . .*"
that his masters in the art of writing were French; he read
Théophile Gautier, the Flaubert of *The Temptation of St. Anthony,* Catulle Mendès (both in the original and translated into
Spanish), Paul de Saint-Victor, and from them he got an instantly dazzling conception of style. His incorporation of the
Gallic adjective, Gallic syntactical habits, and, undeniably, a
certain Gallic attitude—arch and knowing and slightly world-weary and most decidedly "decadent"—was indeed theretofore
unknown in Spanish, and so one can make the argument that
Rubén Darío was as important a "translator" for Spanish culture as the great German translators and translation theorists
were to German culture in the nineteenth century, opening the
closed land and literature to new currents of thought and imagination and poetics and aesthetics, and to new possibilities in
the language. And from that, as though as an expression of the
gratitude of Spanish youth, fame came almost overnight to the
young poet. Schools of poets grew up around his poetry and
stories, and his repertory of words and images and meters and
"influences" was appropriated ad nauseam by writers both
younger *and* older. And Spanish culture was forever changed,
just as translations, cultural cross-pollinations, have made happen for thousands of years, as one culture has embraced another culture's graces.

So how does one translate into English a writer who has

himself "translated" French literature of the late nineteenth
century into Spanish, with all those entanglements of European-
American-Latin American culture and literature, all those bor-
rowings and emulations and apprenticeships? First of all, one
starts by presuming that the themes and images and structures
pretty much take care of themselves, and that what one has to
labor to achieve is a particular *style*. Then one begins by believ-
ing Neruda, who says that Rubén Darío created the (Spanish)
language that people spoke in the early part of the twentieth
century. That would argue for a relatively "modern" syntax.
On the other hand, Darío's images and themes and treatments
and attitudes are clearly those of his time, not ours, and not
much in fashion today—and we recognize them (speaking now
of the prose, which is my purview here) in Poe and Wilde and
Huysmans and others: authors of an earlier day, with a very
particular manner of expression.

These are the considerations that led to my choice of a trans-
lation strategy, or mode: Just as in Spanish Darío reminds one
of the French writers that were pursuing similar themes and
aesthetic concerns at the same time as he (because he was, in
fact, "translating" them), so I have wanted Darío, in English, to
sit firmly in that tradition. Thus, a "timeless" yet identifiably
fin-de-siècle language and style seemed called for, and I simply
"back-translated" Darío into a tradition the English reader is
already familiar with through Poe, Wilde, and Huysmans.

Let me mention two particular decisions that came to seem in-
evitable over the course of my translation: First, that wherever
Darío used the word *azul,* I would say not "blue," which is the
standard and baseline translation for the word, but rather
"azure." *Azul* meant so much to Darío—his first volume of po-
ems, the poems that made him famous, bore that name, and it sig-
nified blue skies and the ocean and hope and spring, but also, in
Spanish, is associated with "fairy tales" *(cuentos azules)* and
"knights in shining armor" *(príncipes azules;* also translated as
"Prince Charming")—the world of daydreams, and of dreams-
that-we-wish-would-come-true, as the song in Disney's *Cinderella*
has it. Darío dreamed his entire life—dreamed against a reality he
felt had not dealt him the lot he merited; dreaming represented

escape from the quotidian world and into the empyrean. The word *azul,* then, needed to be something more than just "blue," with its associations of feeling blue, singing the blues, and so on. "Azure" seemed just right.

The second decision was to use French borrowings throughout. There is simply no question that Darío incorporated an unprecedented number of gallicisms into the rather dour and colorless ("insipid," Neruda says) Spanish of his day; he thought, often, in a kind of French-Spanish patois. I decided that the English used to represent him should indicate that hybridity, and so my translations are full—I hope not obtrusively full—of French phrases and other foreign words and expressions, un-English'd. It was a way, too, of indicating Darío's remarkable cosmopolitanism—underscoring the almost incredible range of cultural references in his stories and essays.

*Lost in translation:* This phrase grates on the ear, patience, and professional and creative pride of literary translators everywhere. The general public and many reviewers of translations appear not to recognize that the phrase is a truncation: Robert Frost is famously but probably apocryphally quoted as saying (with a gleam in his eye), "Poetry is what's lost in translation." When one hears it put that way, as a quip-cum-definition of poetry (and an exceptionally clever way of dodging the question "How would you define poetry, Mr. Frost?"), some of the sting of the aphorism is assuaged. But when a translator is asked by an interviewer straight out, on radio, and without warning, what his translation has lost (as though he wouldn't put back whatever it was if he knew, and could!), he has to come up with a response that is not too curt, not too thin-skinned. And so what I once not at all famously replied (frostily dodging the question) was not that my translation had lost anything, but that with time, the shock of the new caused by a great writer's innovations to the language had been lost to readers of today.

Rubén Darío will probably not seem new or shocking, and certainly not contemporary to us, in my translations here, just as Rubén Darío no longer seems new or shocking, or contemporary, either, in Spanish. He lies firmly in the past. And yet he exerts a timeless fascination, as Poe does, and Wilde, and

Huysmans, who have unquestionably influenced generation upon generation of writers and who are still read today. They are "classics." And so, even when the shock of the new has become dulled, what we know when we read these innovator-classics is that they created new ways of writing, opened new windows of the imagination to and for their contemporaries and those who followed. Rubén Darío's charms are manifold and manifest, and we hope that this volume may allow them to be appreciated as they should be, for the first time in English in such abundance and breadth.

—ANDREW HURLEY

# On Poetry and the Poet

# THE BOURGEOIS KING

*A cheering tale*

Friend! The sky is dark, the wind is cold, the day is sad. What say you to a cheering tale, to dispel the gray mists of melancholy? . . . A tale such as this one, say:

Once, in a grand and brilliant city there was a powerful king who had rich, capricious apparel, naked slave-girls both black-skinned and white, long-maned steeds, bright new weapons, lean swift greyhounds, and huntsmen with brass horns, who filled the air with fanfares. Was this king a poet? No, my friend, he was the Bourgeois King.

This sovereign was very fond of the arts, and with great largesse he would favor his musicians, his makers of dithyrambs, his painters, sculptors, and apothecaries, his barbers and fencing masters.

When he went out into the leafy forest, to hunt the roe or bring to earth the bloody, wounded boar, he would bid his professors of rhetoric to improvise allusive songs. His servants would fill glasses with that golden wine that bubbles in the cup, and women would clap their hands and perform elegant, rhythmic dances. He was a Sun King, in his Babylon filled with music, laughter, and the sounds of revelry. When he wearied of the tumult of the city, he would go out hunting, and the woods would ring with the noise of his retinue. The sound would frighten the birds from their nests, and the shouts and calls would echo in the hidden depths of caves. Dogs of elastic gait would race through the undergrowth, parting it as they went, and hunters would strain forward, leaning over the long necks of their horses, their faces flushed, their hair tousled, their purple mantles rippling out behind them as they pursued their prey.

The king had a magnificent palace, in which he had amassed rich treasures and marvelous *objets d'art*. A path that wound through fields of fragrant lilacs and past broad pools of water led to this palace, and long-necked swans bade visitors welcome even before the tall-standing footmen and palace pages. At the entrance was a stairway lined with alabaster and smaragdite columns and flanked with marble lions, like those of the throne of Solomon. The palace breathed Refinement. In addition to the swans, the king, a lover of harmony, of cooing, of twittering and chirping, had a vast aviary, and to soothe his spirit he would go out to sit on a nearby bench, where he would read novels by M. Ohnet, or lovely books of grammar or pretty criticism. For the king was, indeed, a puissant defender of scholarly correctness in writing, and of absolute neatness in the arts. His sublime soul loved polish, and good spelling.

*Japonaiserie! Chinoiserie!* For the luxury of it, period. Well might his riches afford a salon worthy of the good taste of a Goncourt, the millions of a Croesus: bronze chimeras with open jaws and coiled tails, in fantastic, wondrous groupings; lacquers from Kyoto with inlaid leaves and branches of a monstrous flora, animals of an unknown fauna; butterflies with rare wings upon the walls; many-colored fish and gamecocks; masks with hellish grimaces and eyes that seemed alive; pikes and halberds with ancient blades, their handles emblazoned with dragons devouring lotus flowers; in vessels of porcelain as thin as eggshell, tunics of yellow silk, as though spun from spider webs, with embroidery of red cranes and green rice plants; and vases of great antiquity, with designs of Tartar warriors in kidney-length coats of shaggy fur, bearing tensed bows and quivers of sharp arrows.

The Greek Hall was filled with marbles depicting goddesses, muses, nymphs, and satyrs. The Hall of the Age of Gallantry contained paintings by the great Watteau and Chardin—two, three, four, so many salons and halls!

And this Maecenas would stroll through them all, his face filled with majesty, his belly happy, and his crown perched upon his head like the King of Hearts in a deck of playing cards.

One day a strange species of man was brought before the throne where the king sat surrounded by courtiers, rhetoricians, and riding and dancing masters.

"What sort of man is this?" the king asked.

"My lord, he is a poet."

The king had swans in the pool, canaries, swallows, and mockingbirds in the aviary, but a poet was something new and strange.

"Bring him here."

And the poet said:

"My lord, I have not eaten."

And the king said:

"Speak and you shall eat."

And so he began:

"My lord, for long years I have sung the word of the future. I was born in the time of the dawn and I have spread my wings in the hurricane. I seek the chosen race that awaits, with hymns upon its lips and lyres in its hands, the rising of the great sun. I have fled the inspiration of the unhealthful city and the boudoir reeking of perfume, I have fled the muse of flesh that fills the soul with trifles and covers the face with rice-powder. I have smashed the fawning, loose-stringed harp against the goblets of Bohemian crystal and the pitchers filled with sparkling wine that inebriates without giving strength; I have put off the mantle that made me appear to be an actor, or a woman, and I have dressed in a more savage, splendid way: my rags are crimson. I have gone to the jungle, where I have become vigorous, sating myself upon fecund milk and the liquor of new life, and to the banks of the harsh sea, where, shaking my head in the black, strong tempest like a proud angel, or an Olympian demigod, I have rehearsed iambs, the ringing madrigal forgotten.

"I have caressed great Nature, and I have sought, in the warmth of the ideal, the verse that lies in the star at the end of the heavens, the pearl in the depths of ancient Ocean. I have sought to boom, to crash! For the age of the great revolutions is coming, with a Messiah that is all Light, and Agitation, and Power, and we must receive his spirit with a poem that is a triumphal arch, with lines of iron, and lines of gold, and lines of love.

"My lord, art lies not in the cold trappings of marble, nor in highly polished paintings, nor in the excellent M. Ohnet. Art does not wear rich wool pants, or speak Bourgeois, or dot all its *i*'s. Art is august, and it wears mantles of gold, or flames, or nothing at all, and walks about quite naked, or it kneads fever into its clay, and paints with light, and is opulent, and beats its wings like the eagles, swipes its claws like the lions. My lord, between an Apollo and a goose, give preference to Apollo, though Apollo be of fired earth and the goose of finest marble.

"Oh, poesy!

"And yet, my lord—Poetry may prostitute itself. It may sing songs to the beauty mark upon a woman's cheek, or concoct syrupy rhymes. Not to mention, my lord, that the cobbler criticizes my hendecasyllables, and the professor of pharmacology adds semicolons to my inspiration. And what is worst of all, my lord, is that you give your blessing to all this! . . . The ideal, the ideal . . ."

The king interrupted:

"My courtiers, you have heard him. What shall be done?"

And a philosopher, according to custom, replied:

"If you please, my lord, he might earn his board with a hand-organ. We could put him in the garden, near the swans, for those times when you go out for a walk."

"Indeed," said the king. Then turning to the poet, he said:

"You will turn the hand-crank. You will close your mouth. You will provide us with music from a music-box that plays waltzes, quadrilles, and gallopes, unless you prefer to starve. Piece of music for crust of bread. But no more prattling, and no more talk of ideals. Go."

And from that day forth, the starving poet might be seen on the bank of the swans' pool, turning the crank on the hand-organ—*tra-la-la, tra-la-lee* . . . embarrassed by the glances of the great sun! And when the king strolled anywhere nearby? *Tra-la-la, tra-la-lee!* Was the stomach in need of filling?

*Tra-la-la, tra-la-lee!* All to the mockery of the birds flying free, who came to drink dewdrops from the blooming lilacs, the buzzing of the bees that stung his face and filled his eyes with tears . . . bitter tears that rolled down his cheeks and fell to the black earth!

And winter came, and the poor man was chilled in body and soul. And his brain seemed almost petrified, and the grand anthems were forgotten, and the poet from the mountain crowned with eagles was naught but a poor devil cranking a hand-organ: *Tra-la-la, tra-la-lee!*

And when the snow fell, the king and his vassals forgot about the poet. They gave the birds warm shelter, but the poet they left out in the glacial wind that nipped at his flesh and burned his face.

And one night when the white rain of tiny crystal feathers was falling fast, there was a feast within the palace, and the light of the chandeliers laughed gaily down upon the marbles, upon the gold, upon the tunics of the ancient porcelain mandarins. And the people inside madly applauded the toasts raised by the professor of rhetoric, which were studded with dactyls, anapests, and phyrrics, while in crystal goblets the champagne's fleeting bubbles burst and sparkled. Night of winter, night of revelry! And the poor wretch out by the swans' pool, shivering with cold, insulted by the north wind, covered with snow, standing stiff in the implacable whiteness of the garden, in the gloomy night, turned the hand-crank to keep himself warm, and the wild music of gallopes and quadrilles echoed among the leafless trees. And then he died, thinking that the sun would rise the next day, and with it, the ideal . . . and that art would wear not wool pants, but a mantle of gold, and flames. . . . And the next day the king and his courtiers found him there, the poor devil of a poet, like a swallow frozen in the ice, with a bitter smile on his lips, and his hand still on the hand-crank.

Oh, my friend! The sky is dark, the wind is cold, the day is sad. The gray mists of melancholy fill the air. . . .

But how a kind word, a squeezing of the hand can warm us! And with that moral to my tale, adieu.

# THE DEAF SATYR

*A Greek story*

Near Olympus there lived a satyr, and he was the old king of the forest. Long years ago the gods had told him: "Here, disport yourself, the woods are yours. Be a happy rascal—chase nymphs and play your flute." Life was great fun for the satyr.

One day, as father Apollo was strumming his sacred lyre, the satyr emerged from the woods within which lay his domain, and he had the audacity to scale the sacred mount, where he surprised the long-haired god at his music. To punish the satyr, the god struck him deaf—as deaf as a post. In vain did the birds of the dense woods scatter birdsong on the air and fill the breeze with cooing. The satyr could hear nothing. Philomela would come and perch above his grape-wreathed brow, to sing him songs that made rivulets stop flowing and turned pale roses red. The satyr would sit impassive, or laugh his rude laughter, or leap up, lecherous and gay, when through the leafy branches he caught a glimpse of some round, white thigh caressed by the sun's soft golden light.

All the animals came to sit around him, for he was their master, who was to be obeyed. And before him, to cheer his spirit, danced choruses of bacchantes in their wild feverish dance, and the harmony was accompanied by adolescent fauns, like lovely ephebes, who caressed him reverently with their smiles. And although he could hear no voice, not even the sound of the rattlesnake, still there were other ways by which he took his enjoyment.

And so passed the life of this bearded, goat-footed king.

He was a capricious satyr.

He had two court counselors: a lark and an ass. The lark fell in the hierarchy of the rustic court, for she lost the king's ear when the satyr became deaf. Before, if he tired of his lecherous pursuits he would sweetly play his flute, and the lark would accompany him. Afterward, in the wide forest, where not even Olympian thunder was heard by the monarch of the woods, the patient long-eared ass allowed him to ride, while the lark, at the apogee of dawn, would fly skyward from his hands, singing.

The woods were immense. The lark had been given the treetops; the ass, the greensward under the trees. The lark was kissed by the first rays of the dawn; she drank dewdrops from the new sprouts and woke the oak tree saying, "Old oak, awake!" She took delight in the kiss of the sun, and she was loved by the morning star. And the deep azure of the sky, so immense, knew that she, so tiny, existed within its immensity. The ass (though he had not yet conversed with Kant) was an expert in philosophy, as Victor Hugo has told us. The satyr, who watched him graze in the meadows, moving his ears gravely, had a high idea indeed of this thinker. (In those days, unlike our own, the ass had not yet developed a reputation.) As the satyr watched him chew, he would never have imagined that Daniel Heinsius was to praise him in Latin; Passerat, Buffon, and the great Hugo in French; and Posada and Valderrama in Spanish.

The ass was a patient creature, and if the flies stung him he would flick them away with his tail; he would kick his heels in the air from time to time, and in the great nave of the forest lift up his throat's strange song. And he was greatly pampered there. When he lay down on the soft black earth for his afternoon siesta, the grasses and flowers offered him their fragrance and the great trees spread their leaves over him, for shade.

It was during this time that Orpheus, the poet, sickened by mankind's misery, decided to flee to the woods, where the trees and rocks might understand him and listen to him in ecstasy, and where, when he played his lyre, he might make all things tremble with harmony and the fire of love. For when Orpheus strummed his lyre, a smile would come to Apollo's face, and Demeter would shiver with pleasure; the palm trees would release their pollen, seeds would burst, lions would softly shake their golden manes. Once, a carnation, transformed into a red butterfly, fluttered up off its stalk, and a star, fascinated, descended and became a fleur-de-lis.

What better forest could there be than this one belonging to the satyr? He lived a life of pure delight here, and was treated like a demigod. The woods were all happiness and dancing, beauty and lustful voluptuousness. Nymphs and bacchantes were always caressed yet always virgins; there were grapes and roses and the sound of zithers; and the caper-footed king, as intoxicated and expressive as Silenus, would dance before his fauns.

Orpheus, proud, radiant, went to that forest with his crown of laurel, his lyre, his high poetic brow.

He came to the hairy, half-savage satyr, and to beg his hospitality, he sang. He sang of great Jove, of Eros and Aphrodite, of regal centaurs and ardent bacchantes. He sang of Dionysius' cup, and of the vine-wreathed staff that wounds the happy air, and of Pan, the emperor of the mountains and sovereign of the woods, the satyr-god who, like Orpheus himself, would sing. He sang of the intimacies of the air of great mother earth. And thus from him issued the harmonies of an Aeolian harp, the whisper of a grove, the hoarse murmur of a seashell, and the chorded notes that emerge from a pipe of Pan. He sang of poetry, which descends from heaven and gives pleasure to the gods, the song that accompanies the barbitos in the ode and the tympanum in the paean. He sang of warm snowy breasts and goblets of hammered gold, and the beak of the bird and the glory of the sun.

And even as he began his song, the light shone brighter. The enormous trees were moved, and there were roses that dropped their petals, lilies that drooped in languor, as though in a sweet swoon. For the music of Orpheus' lyre made lions moan, made pebbles cry. The most furious bacchantes fell silent, and they listened to him as though entranced. A virgin naiad, whose beauty had never been profaned by even a single glance from the satyr, shyly stole near the singer and said to him, "I love you." Philomela fluttered down to perch upon the lyre, like the Anacreontic dove. The only echo within the grove was that of the voice of Orpheus; all Nature listened to his song. Venus, who happened to be passing nearby, asked from afar in her divine voice: "Is that by chance Apollo that I hear?"

And in all that immensity of wondrous harmony, the one creature who heard nothing was the deaf satyr.

When the poet ended, he said to the satyr:

"Has my song pleased you? If it has, I shall bide with you in the forest."

The satyr looked toward his two councillors. They would have to resolve what he himself could not understand. His look was querying.

"Sire," said the lark, straining to raise his voice above a chirp, "he who has sung so beautifully must be allowed to stay with us. His lyre is beautiful, and has great power. He has offered you the grandeur, the rare light that you have seen today in your woodland. He has made you a gift of his harmony. Sire, I know about these things. When the naked dawn comes, and the world awakes, I fly up into the profound heavens and from on high pour down the invisible pearls of my trilling song, and in the morning's light my melody floods the breeze, and is the delight of the air. And I tell you that Orpheus has sung well, for he is chosen of the gods. The entire forest has been intoxicated by his music. The eagles have come close, to soar over our heads, the flowering bushes have softly waved their mysterious censers, the bees have left their hives to come hereby to listen. And as for me, oh, my lord! if I were in your place I would crown him with my wreath of grapes and vines, and pass him my vine-twined staff. There are two great potencies: the real and the ideal. What Hercules would do with his mighty arms, Orpheus does with his inspiration. With one blow, the muscled god would crush Athos himself. But with the power of his triumphant voice, Orpheus would tame his lion Nemea and his wild boar Erimanthus. Some men are born to forge metal, others to wrest from the fertile soil the tender stalks of wheat, others to fight in bloody war, and others yet to teach, to glorify, and to sing. If I am your cup-bearer and I give you wine, your palate is pleased; if I offer you a hymn, it delights your soul.

While the lark was singing these words, Orpheus accompanied her upon his lyre, and a vast, thrilling breath of music rose from the green and fragrant woods. The deaf satyr began to grow impatient. Who was this strange visitor? Why had the wild, voluptuous dancing stopped? What were his two councillors saying?

Ah, the lark had sung, but the satyr had not heard! At last he turned his glance upon the ass.

The ass's opinion was required? Well then, standing before the immense, echoing forest, under the sacred azure sky, the ass shook his head, from one side to the other—stubborn, silent, like a wise man meditating.

At that, the satyr wounded the ground with his cleft foot, thrust his face forward angrily, and without hearing a thing, raised his finger and pointed Orpheus the way out of the forest, exclaiming:

"No! . . ."

The echo of his cry reached nearby Olympus, and there, where the gods were sporting, it inspired a chorus of laughter that was later called Homeric.

Orpheus, his heart downcast, made his way out of the deaf satyr's woods, almost ready to hang himself from the first laurel tree he came upon.

He did not hang himself, but he did marry Eurydice.

# MY AUNT ROSA

The young woman sobbing at one end of the large, comfortable sitting room had been "spoken to," as people used to say, but in that common proceeding within families it had been learned, or determined, that she was not so much to blame. No, the person upon whose head fell most of the reprobation was "this boy who one would think was always off in the clouds somewhere, and who'll drive me to an early grave!"

My own head was lowered, but (happy, deliciously guilty) it still held the dazzling image of paradise found: a blond, fifteen-year-old paradise, all roses and lilies and fruit of good and evil, fruit of the first harvest, when the grape's sweetness still has a hint of tartness. . . .

My father, a tyrant, was thundering on . . .

"Because you think yourself a man, but you're no more than a dawdling boy . . . an idle boy chasing butterflies in the garden. . . . Roberto, look at me when I talk to you! I've forgiven you many things. You are hardly a model student. Your mathematics teacher says you're an utter failure, in fact, and I'm beginning to believe he is right. You hardly speak, and when you do, it's to yourself. The day they booted you out of school, your mother found love notes in among your schoolbooks. Is this the work of a serious student? Well, this thing now is serious. What you've done this time deserves the strictest punishment, and punished you shall be. This is what all that idling about and dreaming has brought you to! Dreaming indeed!

"Tell me, d'you really think you're of an age to take responsibility for this, like a man? I vow to teach you your responsibilities, with a severity I've never shown before. You want to be

a man? I'll teach you to be a man! You'll do the work of a man.
Oh, lolling about, playing at being in love, doing things worse
than poetry is hardly worthy of a young person who wants to
be a gentleman. Poetry indeed! And after the poetry, or poetast-
ing, we've come to *this!* . . . You rascal!"

He had never preached at me this way.

"But I want to get married!" I managed at last to exclaim,
like some offended Poil-de-Carotte.

At that, after a burst of laughter *à deux* over what I'd said
(which must indeed have been quite ridiculous), it was my
mother who came at me next.

"Get married! What will you marry on? How will you sup-
port your wife? Do you honestly think you can patch up this
atrocity you've committed? *I want to get married!* . . . Have
you ever in your life seen schoolboys marry? For you're no
more than a schoolboy, Roberto. And your father is right: those
absurd stories, those verses of yours, those useless scraps of pa-
per are the cause of it all. They are the reason you spend your
days daydreaming and never study. Idleness is the devil's work-
shop, boy. What you've done comes from idleness, because if
you would just do something useful, you wouldn't have those
evil thoughts . . .

"And our hesitation to call you to task over your behavior
has not improved things—in fact, you've gone from bad to
worse. We should have sent you to the country long ago,
to work in the fields! You won't have a career? Then to the fields
with you! Your father gave a great deal of thought to a career in
business for you, but you wouldn't have it, and only after I
pleaded with you on bended knee did you agree to go to school,
and even promised me you'd become a lawyer . . . But what
have you done since? You haven't even entered the university
yet. *I want to get married!*

"What do you suppose there'll be to eat in your house? Be-
cause you'll need a house. Married at sixteen! What are you
and your wife going to eat? Poetry, flowers, stars? . . . You'll
throw all that paper in the fire this minute, young man. . . . And
give me those letters that silly girl has written you . . . Go on

now, start packing, because you're off to the country—no
backtalk, now, I mean it—to work on a farm. That'll make you
a man! . . . You want to be a grown-up? Then you'll work like
one! You rascal!"

And the paternal thunder once again:

"Well said, my dear!"

You, divine Spring, and you, imperial Dawn, know whether I
was in truth that dreadful character painted by my parents. For
it was my own springtime, and the dawn of my young man-
hood, and in my body and in my soul there blossomed, in all its
magnificence, the grace of life and love. My poetic dreams had
already unfurled their azure canopies, their tents of wondrous
gold. My visions were triumphant mornings, and nights of silk
and perfume in the light of a full moon. My star was Venus; my
birds, fabulous peacocks and lyrical nightingales; my fruits, the
symbolic apple and the pagan grape; my flower, the rosebud,
for I dreamt that it adorned women's snowy breasts; my music
was Pythagorean, which, like Pan, was everywhere; my yearn-
ing was to kiss, love, live; my ideal incarnate, the blond creature
whom I had come upon one day at her bath. I was adolescent
Actaeon before my white goddess—silent, but bitten by the
ravenous dogs of desire. Yes, I was the burglar of life, the ban-
dit of dawn; yes, father and mother mine, you were right to
thunder at my sixteen years, for I was about to put on my coat
and tie and enter April, step into the butcher shop of May, and
celebrate the triumph of youth and love, the omnipotent glory
of sex, in all the stirring reveille of my blood. And while I was
listening to your reproaches, standing in the tempest of your
wrath with me, I was staring at the most luxuriant, perfumed
head of blond hair as it blazed like a royal standard, and I was
thinking of the red corolla of the two prettiest lips, behind
which lay the otherworldly honey of the sweetest fruit, and I
was listening to the amorous voice that had first awakened me
to the passion of passion, and under my nervous, hungry fin-
gers, all the dovelike treasure, all the gold and marble and
ruby—the swan's white wing, the wave, the lyre! No, I was not,
quite, the guilty one. I was no more than a new instrument in

the infinite orchestra, and however furiously, however madly, however loudly I played, I amounted to no more than the tiniest sparrow in the trees, the smallest fish in the ocean.

I was to go and pack. Pack, and be cast from the paradise I had conquered, my throne of love, my city of marble, my garden of enchanted flowers, my bower of inebriating perfume . . . And so, head down, sad, I believed this was the eve of my execution, and that my departure would be a voyage to the land of Death.

Because what was the world but death, if I was far from all that was life to me?

So I sat alone in the garden, while my parents sent their niece, "for reasons that they would explain later," home to her own parents.

I was stunned—wrenched from my destiny, from my lovely angel of flesh, from my dreams, from everything and everyone. . . . Oh, black existence! And since I was quite long-haired and romantic then, I could not stop thinking about an old pistol. . . . I knew what armoire it was kept in . . . I would write two letters: one for my parents and one for. . . . And then . . .

"Psst! Psst!"

And then I'll shoot myself as I speak the name of the most beloved of . . .

"Psst! Psst!"

Heavens! My aunt Rosa was motioning to me from a window that opened onto the garden, motioning to me with a look that promised some consolation, in the midst of so much misfortune.

"Yes, Aunt Rosa!"

And in four bounds I reached her window, which was just above a little garden-bed perfumed with flowering orange trees, visited often by doves and hummingbirds.

Allow me to introduce my aunt, Rosa Amelia. At the time we are speaking of she had reached the virgin age of fifty. In her youth she had been quite a beauty, as witnessed by a miniature she wore about her neck. Now her hair had grown white—*mais où sont les neiges d'antan?*—and her body had lost the lithe elegance of former times, but her face still had the soft freshness of

an apple, though a bit pale: the face of an aristocratic abbess, il-
luminated duskily by a fleeting, melancholy smile. In that youth,
Rosa, when she was still a rose and, among all the lovely young
women, a princess, had had a suitor, whom she had loved
greatly. But he did not please the family, and then the wedding
was embittered forever, because the young man died. My aunt,
so beautiful, began to fade and wither, and she withered, and
withered . . . until, her flowering bough dry upon the tree, the
poor woman remained a spinster for the rest of her days.

She had the consolation, however, of adoring her nieces and
nephews as though they were her own children, and of making
lovely bouquets and matches of the matrimonial kind, sending
off anyone that approached her to the epistle of St. Paul.

"I heard everything!" she told me. "And I know what's hap-
pened. Don't be so downcast."

"But I'm being sent to the country, and I won't be able to
see her."

"That doesn't matter, child. Does she love you? Good! And
do you love her? Good again! And so you two shall marry, your
Aunt Rosa promises."

And then, after a pause, and giving a great sigh, she went on
in this way:

"My dear, you must not waste the most beautiful time of
your life. One is young but once, and the poor soul that lets the
time of flowers pass without cutting a few will never find them
again, as long as he lives. Look at this white hair—once it was
lovely black. I loved, but I could not obey the law of love, and
so I go to my grave with the most grievous sadness. You love
your cousin, and she loves you. You do mad things, you have let
yourselves be swept up by the whirlwind. That is not prudent,
but it is certainly natural enough, and God surely cannot be too
angry with you. So, Roberto, my dear, trust me—your Aunt
Rosa will see you married. You are still very young, though. In
three or four years, you can have one another. Meanwhile, pay
no attention to your father—love her!

"You're going off to the country. I'll keep the fire lit here—
you write me (oh, sublime aunt!), and I will pass on your

letters. . . . They laugh at you because you want to get married!
Well, get married you shall. But go first to the country for a
while; after what's happened, she shall be your wife. And she's
surely mad for you!"

Having said this, she pulled back from the window, as
though slipping back into her rooms. And this is the hallucina-
tion I had then: My aunt still remained close to me, but was
changed by a marvelous power. Her white, combed hair—the
hair of an aging spinster—was changed into a thick mane of
gold. Her pearl-gray dress vanished, and the most divine of
nudes appeared, perfumed by the rarest and most subtle fra-
grance, as though sacred snowy flesh exuded a diaphanous haze
of light. Through her azure eyes shone the delightfulness of the
universe, and her mysterious red mouth spoke to me in the lan-
guage of the lyre:

"I am the immortal Anadyomene, the glorious patron saint of
swans! I am the wonder of all things, whose presence stirs the
arcane nerves of the world. I am the divine Venus, empress of
kings, mother of poets; my eyes are more powerful than
Jupiter's brow, and I have enchained Pan with my girdle. Spring
is my herald, with its trumpet, and Dawn my tambor-player. All
the gods of Olympus have died, save this goddess who is im-
mortal, and all the other deities will disappear, while my face
shall cheer the world's sphere for all time. Oh, holy Puberty, tri-
umph and sing in your season! Bloom, May; bear fruit, Au-
tumn. The sin of May is the world's greatest virtue. The doves
that draw my chariot through the air have multiplied to the four
corners of the earth, and they take messages of love from north
to south, from east to west. My roses bleed in all climes, and of-
fer up their balm to all races. The time will come when the au-
gust liberty of kisses will fill the world with music. Unhappy the
soul who does not enjoy the sweetness of his dawn, and who al-
lows the flower or grape to wither, or to rot, on the stalk or
vine. Happy, though, the youth who is called Bathyllus, and the
old man named Anacreon!"

On a mule with rich saddle and bridle, and in the company
of a good black valet, I departed for the farm. There I wrote
more poetry than ever, and some time later I journeyed far

away. I never saw my cousin again until she was a widow, and a mother of many children. And my Aunt Rosa I never saw again ever, because she went to the other world with her dry orange-blossoms.

Allow me, across time and despite the tomb, to send her a kiss.

# TALE OF THE SEA

Yes, my friend, a story of the sea—a legend, rather, or perhaps more accurately, a tale. It was told me by a fisherman whose brow looks as though it were made of rock, one evening when I had traveled out to the lighthouse at Punta Mogotes. Do you recall those plans of yours for a novel about the lighthouse? Well, you had good reason to believe that the elements of novels and poetry soar like seabirds around these light-machines. It was near the lighthouse that the fisherman told me the story, because it was there that he'd seen old María pass by—like a specter, or a shadow. Who is old María? This is her story. You can tell it to your prettiest lady friend, someday when she's laughing hardest.

There, near the lighthouse, is the old lady's rundown dwelling. In years gone by, it had been very gay. The fishermen had had their celebrations there; the old man, who had been one of the first fishermen in Mar del Plata, was still alive. There was always, on those nights of revelry, the music of a guitar. But that was many years ago. Since then, the old lady has cried many a tear, and people no longer go to the house to laugh and dance as they once did.

Back then the best thing about the house, the prettiest thing on all that coast—saving, of course, the dawn that one savored there every day—was that fisherman's daughter, the daughter, too, of old María, who today is a wrinkled, withered Magdalene, a grieving soul more bitter from the tears she's shed than from the rigors of the sea. The girl was as healthy as a bright new apple, and there was no greater natural beauty in all the countryside around than hers.

When her father returned from his fishing, she would help him pull the nets up out of the waves; she would prepare the meals in the poor hut, and she was more the mother of the house than the mother herself. She was a strong, robust girl, and she had a lovely masculine strength about her; healthy, there was no wind off the ocean that didn't bring her a gift from distant islands; rosy pink, her coral was the field on which the prettiest flowers of her blood blossomed; innocent and natural, a seagull. She was of an age— thirteen? fourteen? twenty? She might have been any of those, for pristine opulence manifested itself in that winning, lovely work of nature's art.

A wondrous mass of hair, two frank eyes filled with innocent yet savage light, a bosom like a back-held wave, and a voice, a laughter that was free and thrilling, like the ocean-spray and the wind.

One spring came, at last, more tempestuous than any winter. The lovely seagull looked to the four points of the compass, as though trying to see from which direction something unknown was about to come.

"Daughter," said old María, "something is not right with you—what might it be?" The seagull gave no reply. She was un-quiet, pacing back and forth as though driven by some strange gust toward a place she knew not, did not want, yet inexorably went toward.

What had happened was as simple as a whitecap or a breath of air.

Who was the young man who had, in an instant, snared the free-spirited sea bird? Or was it she herself who sought the hand that was to snatch her up? Then it was summer. And no one ever found out whether it was a sailor or a gentleman from the city. All anyone knew was that the young woman—did I mention her name? her name was Sara—was about to have a child.

People say that she had a friend, a girl in the village, to whom she confided her dreams. And they say that Sara told this friend that she was going to go away—happily, she said—to Buenos Aires; that there was a man that loved her greatly, an elegant, gentle, well-positioned young man, of good family and some wealth. People say that, but no one will vow that this was true. What is true, though, indisputably, is that the little fisherwoman's belly grew bigger day by day. The colors of the apple faded, the eyes filled with savage light grew sad from seeing so many things come and go that were not those things yearned after by the simple, rustic daughter of nature, beloved by the sea.

And just during those months, the father died—not drowned by the waves, on a fishing day, but rather spent by struggling against the salt wind and salt sea.

María, the mother, fell ill, became almost an invalid, and poor Sara became the only doer in that seaside hut.

Old María, people say, turned strange when she became bedridden. Her gray eyes, her gray hair, the movements and gestures of her thin arms showed that her miserable soul was in the throes of delirium.

Sara cooked the meals, Sara washed, Sara went to town to fetch what was needed. . . . And she always looked toward one spot on the road: she was always expecting someone to appear.

Until the day came when she, too, had to take to her bed, her sad, miserable bed, where a child was stillborn. . . . Born dead, or did the mother kill it?—for people say that on that day, the mother was heard howling at the wind like a she-wolf.

I urged the man of the sea who was telling me the story—which is perhaps a legend, and perhaps a simple tale—to go on, and this is more or less what he said:

"Yes, sir, it was a stormy night. I'm a neighbor of old María's. When the husband was alive, I'd go to the parties, there in the house. We'd all sing, and dance . . . but since the old man died, there've been no more festivities. María got sick; Sara was like Providence itself. She'd been disgraced by then. While the child was coming, I've never seen a more bitter-looking face. María looked like she was going to die. She would walk up and down the shoreline, making us all sad. Oh, what grief in that house. Oh, what grief in those eyes!

"And it was one night when she went down to the sea, a stormy night. The lightning and thunder hadn't started yet, but the seas were rough. Out in the distance, you could see something like cannon-bursts, but without any noise. The sky had not a star, no light up there at all, and the waves were treacherous, and angry. That's the way the storms are in these seas of ours. That's the way they begin. The lighthouse-keeper knows from the evening clouds what's coming, as does the fisherman, and the sailor. And down here on earth, the ocean begins to look just like the clouds.

"The wind comes from one direction and then another. Then comes the lightning, and the thunder, and the lightning-bolts are striking all around, out on the dark water—which will have your boat in a minute if you let it. A night like that it was, sir.

"The old lady was bad sick. The baby was born and Sara turned crazy. What time it was born, nobody knows, but I think it must have been just about sunrise, because it was a little after that that I heard old María, out there yelling and screaming. I hadn't been able to sleep, thinking about the storm, when I heard something like a scream in that house next door, in María's little house there. I wonder what's happening, I said, and seeing that those two women were over there alone, I got dressed, picked up my gun, and went over there, to the house. That was when I saw a figure like a dead person going off toward the ocean—it was a figure wrapped in a white sheet. The lightning flashes from the storm that was coming on lit up that whole ocean out there. The white thing walked out into the water, farther and farther out. . . . And then I got to the house, old María's house, and I saw her, stumbling about from how weak she was, with her arms stretched out toward the white sheet, crying, moaning, crying, moaning. . . .

" 'Sara! . . .'

"The sick old lady had gotten up, and she was stretching out her thin, withered arms, and calling, although now weaker and weaker:

" 'Sara! Sara! . . .'

"The white figure kept walking out into the water, farther and farther out . . .

"I didn't realize this until later; I didn't realize because at first I was scared—truly scared, sir, I'll tell you.

" 'Sara! . . .' until the white figure disappeared into the water, in that storm that was coming on. I held onto the sick old lady, to keep her from going after her—she was delirious, and almost naked, out there in the cold of the night. We never found the body of that poor girl."

# THE BALE

Far out on the line, as though drawn by a blue pencil, that divided the ocean from the sky, the sun was going down, with its gold dust and its wisps of purplish cloud, like an immense disk of red-hot iron. The customs dock was beginning to grow quiet; the guards were making their rounds, their berets pulled down to their eyebrows. The huge arm of the crane stood immobile, the stevedores were heading back to their homes. The water was murmuring under the pier, and the wet salt breeze, which blows seaward as the night begins to fall, kept the nearby skiffs rocking and swaying on the water.

All the boatmen had already gone; the only one left was old Tío Lucas, who had sprained an ankle this morning when he was lifting a barrel onto a cart, but who, though limping, had worked all day long. He was sitting on a rock with his pipe in his mouth, and he was looking out sadly at the ocean.

"Eh, Tío Lucas! Taking a rest?"

"That I am, sir."

And there began the chat—that pleasant, easygoing chat that I enjoy having with the strong, brave, rough men who live a life of fortifying labor, the life that gives good health, and strength to the muscles, and is nourished on beans and the frothy blood of life.

I had a particular fondness for this uncouth old man, and I listened to his stories with interest—they were all brief and to the point, like the unlettered man himself, but they came from the heart. Oh, so he'd been a soldier! So as a young man he'd been a soldier under Bulnes! So there was still resistance when the cavalry went into Miraflores! And he's married, and he had a son, and . . .

And Tío Lucas interrupts me:

"Yes, sir—he died two years ago."

Those eyes, small, bright under the hirsute gray eyebrows, threatened to overflow.

"How did he die, you say? At his work, trying to put food on the table for all of us—my wife, the little ones, and me, sir, for at the time I was not well."

And then, as night fell, and the waves were mantled with sea mist, and the city turned on its lights, he put out his black pipe and tucked it behind his ear and sat on that rock that served us as a chair, and he stretched, and then he crossed his skinny yet muscular legs, his pants legs rolled up above his ankles, and he told me the story:

He was a good, honest young fellow, and very hard-working. They had wanted to send him to school from the time he was big enough, but the poor cannot be given leave to learn to read when there are hungry ones crying for food around the table.

Tío Lucas was married, and there were many children.

His wife was cursed with the poor people's belly: fertility. There were, then, many mouths open for bread, many dirty little ragamuffins picking through the garbage, many thin bodies trembling with cold. Someone had to go out to get something to eat, and clothes for their backs, and to do that, work like a mule.

When the boy grew up, he helped his father. A neighbor, the blacksmith, took him in to teach him the trade, but since the boy was so weak, no more than skin and bones, and at the forge a fellow had to have his shoulder to the wheel, so to speak, the live-long day, the boy soon fell ill, and he returned to the family's rundown little dwelling.

He was very ill indeed! But he didn't die. He lived, despite the fact that they lived in conditions of utter human poverty—four old, ugly, ramshackle walls in a squalid street of lost women. The street stank at all hours of the day and night. It was lit at night by feeble streetlights, and behind many of its doors one could hear zithers and acordions, and the constant calls of procurers and madams, and the hullabaloo of sailors coming to the brothels, desperate from the chastity of long sea journeys, drinking themselves tipsy and yelling and kicking like the very damned. Yes, among the poorest of the poor, and in that infernal racket from the revelry of the fleshpots, the young fellow lived, and he was soon hale and hearty once more, and up and about.

And then he turned fifteen.

Tío Lucas, saving, scrimping, and sacrificing sometimes even the necessities of life, had managed to buy a little boat. He became a fisherman.

When dawn came, he would go down to the water with his strapping son, carrying the day's fishing gear. One would row while the other baited the hooks. Then, singing the sad songs of the fishermen of those waters, and with the oar, dripping saltwater, triumphantly high, they would return to the shore in hopes of selling what they'd caught out there in the cool wind and the opacities of the fog.

If sales were good, they'd go out again in the evening.

One winter evening there was a storm. Out on the water, father and son, in the little boat, were pummeled by the madness of wave and wind. Catch and all were lost, but they had to look to saving their own skins. They struggled mightily to reach the beach. They were close—but a gust of wind pushed them against a rock, and the boat was smashed to pieces. They got out with no more than a few bruises, thank God! as Tío Lucas put it. After that, they both hired out as stevedores.

Yes, stevedores! On the big black, flat ships, they would hang from the shrieking chain that dangled like an iron serpent from the massive crane, which resembled nothing more than the hangman's gibbet. They would stand and row in unison with the others. They would go out to the steamships with the customs lighter and come back in again. And they would call out *hiooeeep!* when they pushed the heavy crates and bundles over to the powerful hook that would lift them high off the deck, swinging like a pendulum. Yes, stevedores! the old man and the boy, the father and the son, both straddling a crate, both pushing and sweating, both earning their day's wages, for them and for their beloved leeches back in the ramshackle rooms they all shared.

They would go off to work every day, wearing old clothes, their waists tied round with colorful bandannas, their feet clattering along in the rough-sewn, heavy shoes that they would remove when the work day began, throwing them off into some corner of the ship's deck.

The day's work would begin, the loading and unloading. The father was watchful:

"Careful, boy, you'll crack your head there! That rope'll take your hand off! Don't bang your shins!" And in his own way, with the brusque words of an old laborer and a loving father he would teach, train, guide his son.

Until one day Tío Lucas couldn't get out of bed, because his joints were swollen with rheumatism and his bones ached.

Oh, but medicine and food had to be bought, there was no getting around that!

"Son, off to work. Today's Saturday, and it's payday."

And so the son went off, almost running, without breakfast, to his daily routine.

It was a beautiful clear day, and the sun was golden. On the docks, the railcars rolled along on their rails, the pulleys creaked, the chains clanked. The bustle and confusion on the piers was dizzying—the noise of iron, the rumblings everywhere, and the wind passing through the forest of masts and rigging of the ships at anchor there.

Under one of the davits on the pier, Tío Lucas's son worked with other stevedores, unloading as fast as they could. They had to empty the ship filled with bales. From time to time, the long chain, clanking like an iron rattle as it rolled over the pulley-wheel, would snake downward with its enormous hook, and the boys would tie a double strand of thick rope about the bale and hook it onto the chain, which would lift the bale like a fish on a fishhook, or the weight on a sounding-line—sometimes the bales would rise straight up, and sometimes they would swing from side to side, like the clapper of a bell.

The cargo was stacked. From time to time the waves would slowly rock the ship filled with bales. The bales formed a sort of pyramid in the center. There was one that was very heavy, very heavy. It was the largest of them all—wide, fat, and smelling of tar. It was in the very bottom of the hold. A man standing atop it looked a very small figure against the massive pedestal he stood upon.

This bale looked like all the other prosaic goods of import wrapped in canvas and bound with bands of iron. On its sides, in the midst of black lines and triangles, there were letters that looked out like eyes—letters in "diamonds," Tío Lucas called them. Its iron straps were held with rough thickheaded rivets, and in its belly the monster must have had, at least, lemons and percales.

It was the last one left.

"Here comes the bruiser!" said one of the stevedores.

"The big-bellied one!" said another.

And Tío Lucas's son, who was eager to finish the day's work, was getting ready to collect his pay and go off to breakfast; he tied a checkered bandanna around his neck.

The chain snaked downward, dancing in the air. A large noose was tied to the bale and tested to make certain it would hold, and then someone called out, "Hoist away!" while the chain, creaking, pulled on the mass, slowly raising it into the air.

Some of the stevedores stood below to watch the enormous weight rise, and some were preparing to go ashore, when they saw a terrible thing. The bale, the enormous, heavy bale, slipped from its ropes, like a dog that slips its collar, and it fell on Tío Lucas's son, who lay now crushed between the bale and the guardrail of the boat, his kidneys ruined, his backbone fractured, black blood flowing from his mouth.

That day there was no bread or medicine in Tío Lucas's house—the crushed and mutilated body lay there, until, embraced tearfully by the rheumatic father, wept and wailed over by the mother and the other children, it was carried to the cemetery.

———

I bade good evening to the old stevedore, and with elastic step I left the pier, taking the road home and spinning philosophy with all the deliberateness of a poet, while a glacial breeze, which blew in from far out at sea, tenaciously nipped my nose and ears.

# Fantasy, Horror,
and the Grotesque

# THE LARVA

They were talking about Benvenuto Cellini and one of them had smiled at the great artisan's declaration in his *Life*, that he had once seen a salamander. At that provocation, Isaac Cocomano said:

"You scoff? O ye of little faith, I swear to you that I have seen, as clearly as I am seeing all of you now, if not a salamander, then a larva or an Empusa. I will tell you the story, and I will be brief. . . ."

I was born in a country where, as in almost all of the Americas, the people practiced witchcraft and their warlocks and witches communicated with the invisible world. The mysteries of the native peoples and their religions did not disappear with the arrival of the conquistadors. No, and in fact under Catholicism, there were perhaps even more numerous cases of the evil eye, demonism, the evocation of strange forces than before the Spaniards came. In the city where I spent my early years people talked—and I remember this well, as though it were an everyday occurrence—about apparitions, the sudden presence of demons, ghosts, and sprites. In one poor family that lived near my house, for example, the ghost of a Spanish colonel appeared to a young man and revealed to him that a treasure was buried in the garden. The young man died from this extraordinary visit, but the family profited well enough—they became rich, as their descendants are still today. There was a bishop that appeared to another bishop, to tell him where he might find a document lost in the archives of the cathedral. The devil carried off a woman through a window in a certain house that I recall

quite clearly. My grandmother assured me of the frightful
nighttime roaming of a headless friar and of a huge hairy hand
that appeared of its own locomotion, like some hellish spider. I
heard about all these things as a boy. But what I *saw,* what I
touched—what I saw and touched from the world of shadows
and tenebrous arcana—*that* came when I was fifteen.

In that city, much like other Spanish provincial cities, all the
residents shut up the doors of their houses at eight o'clock in
the evening, or nine at the latest. The streets were left solitary
and silent. The only sound to be heard was the soft call of the
owls nesting in the eaves, or the distant barking of the dogs on
the outskirts of the city.

Anyone who went out to fetch a doctor or a priest, or on
some other urgent nighttime errand, had to make his way down
ill-cobblestoned streets full of pitfalls for the unwary and lighted
by no more than oil lanterns on posts, which cast but the faintest
beams.

From time to time one would hear the echoes of tunes played
on guitars and zithers, or of singing. These were the serenades *à
l'espagnole,* the airs and romances that spoke tender words of
love from lover to lover. Sometimes these would be but a single
guitar and the serenading suitor, a young man of scanty means,
but sometimes there would be a quartet, or septet, or entire or-
chestra, with a piano, which some wealthy gentleman would
hire to declare his love or plead his case to the lady of his
dreams, under her windows.

I was fifteen, with grand yearnings for life and the wide
world. And one of the things I yearned for most fervently was
to be able to go out into the streets and accompany the others
on one of those serenades. But how was I to do this?

Every night, after the rosary beads had been spelled, the
great-aunt that watched over my childhood was careful to walk
through the house, closing and locking all the doors, and then
she would carry the keys with her to her room, leaving me well
tucked in under the canopy of my four-poster bed. But one day
I learned that that same evening there was to be a serenade. And
more: one of my friends, as young as I, was to attend the event,

whose enchantments he painted to me in the most tantalizing colors. I spent every hour of the day before that evening restlessly, thinking and rethinking my plan of escape. And so, when my great-aunt's visitors had gone—among them a priest and two attorneys who had come to discuss politics or play a game of cards—and the prayers had been prayed and everyone was tucked in bed, I could think of nothing but putting into practice my plan to steal a key from the venerable lady.

After three hours had passed, it was not hard to carry out my plan, for I knew where she left the keys—and besides, she slept the sleep of the righteous. Master of that which I'd sought, and knowing which door it opened, I reached the street just at the moment when, in the distance, the sound of violins, flutes, and cellos began to be heard. I considered myself a man. Drawn by the melody, I soon reached the place where the serenade was being sung. While the musicians played, the members of the serenade drank beer and liquors. Then a tailor, in the role of don Juan, sang first "In the Light of the Pale Moon" and then "Remember when the Dawn . . ."

I enter into such detail so that you will see how everything that happened on that night so extraordinary for me has remained in my memory. From the windows of that Dulcinea they resolved to go to another's. We passed through the Plaza de la Catedral. And then . . .

I have said that I was fifteen, that we were in the tropics, and that all the yearnings—the urges, shall I say—of youth were awakening in me. . . . And there I was, in the prison of my house, which I never left save to go to school, and under my great-aunt's stern vigilance, and with those primitive customs of our culture. . . . I was ignorant, as I must be, of all the mysteries. Thus, imagine my delight when, as I passed through the Plaza de la Catedral, after the serenade, I saw, sitting on a curbside, wrapped in her rebozo, as though asleep, a woman. I stopped.

Young? Old? A beggar? A madwoman? What did I care! I was in search of some dreamed-for revelation, some yearned-after adventure.

The serenaders walked on, leaving me behind.

———

The light from the plaza's lamps was pale. I approached. I spoke: I will not tell you that I spoke sweet words, for they were ardent, urgent. And as I received no reply, I leaned down and touched the back of that woman who would not answer me and in fact was doing all she could to prevent me from seeing her face. I was haughty; I cajoled and chaffed; I spoke to her suggestively. And when I believed that victory at last was mine, the figure turned toward me, uncovered her face, and oh! what horror of horrors! Her face was slimy and misshapen, as though the flesh had all decayed: one eye hung over the bony, suppurating cheek and there came to my senses a reek of putrefaction. From the creature's horrible mouth there came what seemed to be hoarse laughter, and then that *thing*, making the most macabre of grimaces, produced a sound that I might try to imitate in this way:

"*Kggggg!*"

My hair standing on end, I jumped back and gave a shriek. I called out to my companions.

By the time some of the young men from the serenade arrived, the *thing* had disappeared.

"I give you my word of honor," Isaac Cocomano concluded, "that what I have told you is completely true."

# THANATOPHOBIA[1]

My father was the celebrated Dr. John Leen, member of the Royal Society for Psychic Research in London and very well known in the scientific world for his studies of hypnotism and his famous *Report on the Creature Known as Old*. He died not long ago, and may he rest in peace.

James Leen emptied most of his beer into his belly and then went on:

You have all laughed at me and what you call my worrying and foolishness. I forgive you, because, frankly, there are more things in heaven and earth than are dreamed of in your philosophy, as the great Will once said.

You do not know that I have suffered greatly, that I still suffer greatly—the bitterest of tortures—on account of your laughter. . . . Yes, I admit it: I cannot sleep without a light, I cannot bear being alone in an empty house; I tremble at the mysterious sound that in the twilight hours just after dusk and just before dawn emerges from the underbrush along the path; I do

1. The *Cuentos* edited by José María Martínez (Madrid: Cátedra, 1997) gives this, "Thanatophobia," as the title of a story known in other collections as "Thanatopia." Martínez provides the following information, which has led me to adopt the title as it appears here: [This story] "appeared for the first time in *La Tribuna,* in Buenos Aires, in November of 1897, specifically on November 2, the day the Church calls All Souls Day, which in part explains the tone and content of this tale. We have preferred the title of that first publication to that proposed by Mejía Sánchez ("Thanatopia"). . . ." I, too, believe the title as given here more befits the story.

not like to see an owl or bat fly up; I never, in any city where I may go, visit its cemeteries; I am burned by the fires of martyrdom when I am exposed to conversations dealing with macabre events, and when I must be exposed, my eyes wait only to close, in love of sleep, until the light reappears.

I have a horror of what—oh, God!—I am about to speak of: death. You will never make me remain in a house where there is a dead body, even that of my dearest friend. Oh, those are the most appalling words in the language: *dead body*. . . . You have laughed at me, and still do—so be it. But allow me to tell you the truth of my secret. I have come to the Republic of Argentina *a fugitive, having lived five years as a prisoner, held as a miserable captive by my father, Dr. Leen,* who, although a great and wise man, I suspect was an equally great scoundrel. On his orders I was taken to an asylum for the insane—on his orders, for he feared that I might perhaps one day reveal that which he intended forever to hide . . . that which you are about to learn, for it is impossible for me to keep silent any longer.

I tell you that I am not drunk. I am not and have never been insane. He ordered my reclusion because. . . . You shall hear.

Thin, blond-haired, nervous, seized by a frequent tremor, or shiver, James Leen raised his head at that table in the beer garden where, surrounded by friends, he spoke these words to us. Is there anyone in Buenos Aires who does not know him? He is not an eccentric in his daily life. From time to time he suffers these strange fits. As a professor, he is one of the most estimable in one of our private schools, and as a man of the world he is, though a bit quiet, one of the finest young elements of the Cinderella dances that are held among the city's higher reaches of society. And so that night he went on with his strange tale, which we dare not call mere *fumisterie,* given the character of our friend. But we shall let our readers judge the thing for themselves:

I lost my mother when I was very young, and I was sent on my father's orders to a public school, as we call them in England, in Oxford. My father, who never showed his affection for me, would come from London once a year to visit me at that school ere I grew up, solitary in my spirit, without affection, without praise.

There, I learned to be sad. Physically, I was the image of my mother, I've been told, and *I suppose that was why the doctor tried to see me as little as possible.* I shall say no more about this. I hope you will excuse the way in which I choose to narrate my story.

Whenever I have touched upon this subject, I have felt myself stirred by a familiar force. *Try to understand me.* I was saying, then, that I lived as a boy solitary in my spirit, learning sadness in that school with its black walls, which I can still see in my imagination on moonlit nights. . . . Oh! how I learned to be sad. I still see, through a window in my room, the poplars, the cypresses, bathed in a pale and spectral moonlight. . . . *Why were there cypresses at that school?* . . . and throughout the park, decaying old Termini, leprous with time—the perches for those owls raised by the hateful septuagenarian headmaster. . . . *Why did the headmaster raise owls?* . . . And I would hear, in the silent depths of the night, the flight of those nocturnal animals and the creaking of the tables and one midnight, I swear to you, I heard a voice: "James!" Oh, such a voice!

When I turned twenty, a visit from my father was announced to me one day. *I was thrilled, despite the fact that I felt an instinctive repulsion for him;* I was thrilled, because just then I needed to unburden myself to someone, *even him.*

He arrived in a much more amiable temper than many times before, and although he did not look directly into my eyes, his deep voice sounded somehow well-disposed to me. I told him that I wished, finally, to return to London, that I had completed my studies, and that if I remained in that house any longer I would die of sadness. . . . His deep voice again sounded somehow well-disposed toward me:

"I have fully planned, James, to take you with me this very day. The headmaster has told me your health is not good, that you are often sleepless, that you hardly eat. Too much studying is bad for a lad, as are all things in excess. But," he said, "I have another reason for taking you to London. At my age, I have needed a helpmate, and I have found her. You have a stepmother, who ardently desires to know you, and I wish to present you. You shall come away with me today, then."

A stepmother! And suddenly there came into my memory the image of my sweet, pale-skinned, blond-haired mother, who loved me so much when I was a boy, and petted and spoiled me. She had been abandoned almost always by my father, who spent nights on end, and days alike, in his horrid laboratory, while that poor delicate flower wasted away. . . . A stepmother! I would go, then, to bear the tyranny of Dr. Leen's new wife, no doubt a dreadful bluestocking, or cruel know-it-all, or shrewish witch. . . . Forgive those words. Sometimes I don't know exactly what I'm saying—or perhaps I know all too well . . .

I had not a word of reply for my father, but that afternoon, as he wished, we boarded the train that would take us to our townhouse in London.

From the moment we arrived, from the moment I stepped through the grand antique door, which was followed by a dark stair that led upstairs, to the sitting room, I was disagreeably surprised: In the house there was not one of our old servants.

Four or five decrepit old things, wearing loose—or overlarge— black livery, paid their respects as we passed, with slow, mute bows or curtsies. We entered the large sitting room. Everything was changed: the furniture that had once been there had been replaced by other pieces, of a cold, unwelcoming taste. The only thing that remained of all the furnishings was a large portrait of my mother at the far end of the room—the work of Dante Gabriel Rossetti—and it was covered with a long crêpe veil.

My father led me to my rooms, which were not far from his laboratory. He bade me good night. Out of some inexplicable courtesy, I asked after my stepmother. He answered me slowly, taking care to pronounce each syllable in a voice combining tenderness and fearfulness *that I did not then understand*:

"You will see her later. . . . You will most surely see her . . . James, my son James, good-night. I assure you, you will see her later . . ."

Angels and ministers of grace, why did you not take me with you? And you, mother, my sweet little mother, my sweet Lily, why did you not come down to take me away at that instant? Oh, had I been swallowed up by an abyss or pulverized by a falling rock, or reduced to ashes by a bolt of lightning! . . .

It was that same night. With a strange weariness of body and spirit, I had lain down on the bed, dressed just as I had come in from the journey. As though in a half sleep, or dream, I remember hearing one of the old creatures in the house's service creep up to my bed, muttering lord knows what words and looking at me vaguely with a pair of tiny wall-eyes that gave the impression of a bad dream. Then I saw him light a candelabra with three wax candles. When I woke up around nine, the candles were burning in my room.

I washed. I changed clothes. Then I heard footsteps, and my father appeared. For the first time—*for the first time!*—I saw his eyes fixed on mine. Indescribable eyes, I assure you: eyes such as you have never seen before, or ever will; eyes whose retina was almost red, like a rabbit's; eyes that would make you tremble, for the strange way they looked at you.

"Let us go down, son; your stepmother is waiting for you. She is there, in the sitting room. Come."

There, in a high-backed armchair, like those in choir stalls, a woman was seated.

She . . .

And my father spoke:

"Come closer, my little James, come closer!"

I approached mechanically. The woman put out her hand to me. . . . I then heard, as though it came from the great portrait, the great portrait draped in mourning, that same voice I had heard in Oxford, but very sad, so much sadder: "James!"

I put out my hand. The contact with the woman's hand turned my blood to ice, and horrified me. The hand was stiff, and cold, cold. . . . And the woman was not looking at me. I stammered out a greeting, some polite words.

And my father spoke again:

"My wife, this is your stepson, our beloved James. Look at him, here he is. Now he is your son, too."

And my stepmother looked at me. My jaws locked, one against the other. I was seized with horror: *Those eyes had no*

*light in them at all; there was no gleam of life.* An idea began to
take shape within my brain—maddening, horrible, horrible.
Then suddenly, there was an odor, an odor . . . *that odor,* my
God! That odor . . . I don't want to tell you. . . . Because you
already know, yet I assure you: I smell that odor yet, and it
makes my flesh crawl.

And then there emerged from those white lips, from that
pale, pale, pale female figure, *a voice like that from a cavern, or
a tomb*:

"James, our beloved James, my son, come closer. I want to
give you a kiss on the forehead, and one on the eyes, and one on
the lips. . . ."

I could bear no more. I cried out.

"Mother, help me! Angels of God, help me! Heavenly pow-
ers, ministers of grace, help me! I want to leave this place soon,
soon—take me away from here!"

I heard the voice of my father:

"Calm yourself, James, calm yourself, my son. Hush, my son."

"No!" I shouted louder, now struggling with the old servants
of the house. "I'll leave this place and tell the world that Dr.
Leen is a cruel murderer, that his wife is a vampire, and that my
father has married a dead woman!"

# HUITZILOPOXTLI

*A Mexican legend*

Some time ago, I was sent by a newspaper on a commission to Mexico. I was to depart from a certain city on the United States border and travel southward to a certain place where a detachment of Carranza's army was to be found. There, I was to be given a letter of introduction and a safe-conduct so that I might penetrate into a part of the territory that was controlled by Pancho Villa, the formidable fighter and military leader. . . . I was to see a friend, a lieutenant in the Revolution's militia, who had promised to give me information for a news story. He had assured me that I had nothing to fear during my stay in his field of operations.

I made the trip by automobile, to a point a little beyond the border, in the company of two gentlemen: Mr. John Perhaps, a physician and also something of a journalist himself, in the service of U.S. newspapers, and Colonel Reguera, or, to be more exact, Father Reguera, one of the strangest and most fearsome men I have ever known in my life.

Father Reguera is an old friar who, young in the times of Maximilian (and an imperialist, of course) changed emperors in the days of Porfirio Díaz, though nothing else about him changed. He is an old Basque friar who believes that all things are disposed by divine will. Especially the divine right of command, which for him is unquestionable.

"Porfirio won," he would say, "because God willed it so, because it was meant to be."

"Don't talk rubbish!" replied Mr. Perhaps, who had been in Argentina.

"But Porfirio had no communication with the deity. . . . Anyone who doesn't respect the mystery, the devil take him! And Porfirio made us all take off our cassocks when we were out in the street. Madero, on the other hand . . ."

In Mexico, the earth is filled with mystery. Every Indian that lives, breathes the mystery with every breath. And the fate of the Mexican nation is still in the power of the Aztecs' primitive deities. In other places, people say "Speak of the . . . and he will appear." Here, one does not have to speak. The Aztec, or Maya, mystery lives in every Mexican, however much racial mixing there is in his blood.

"Colonel, have a whisky!" said Mr. Perhaps, offering him his bottle of *ruolz*.

"I prefer this," replied Father Reguera, and with one hand he held out to me a little piece of folded-up paper containing salt that he'd pulled out of his pocket, while with the other he extended his canteen full of tequila.

We drove and drove, and finally came to the edge of a forest, where we heard a shout: "Halt!" We halted. We could not go any farther. A small band of Indian soldiers, barefoot, with their enormous sombreros and their rifles at the ready, prevented us.

Reguera parlayed with the main person, who also knew the Yankee. Everything turned out all right. We had two mules and a fly-bitten nag to take us to our destination. The moon was out when we began our march. We plodded along. Suddenly, turning to the old friar, I said:

"Reguera, how do you want me to address you—colonel or father?"

"However you bloody well feel like!" guffawed the parchment-skinned personage.

"I ask," I said, "because I must ask you about some things that have me a bit concerned . . ."

The two mules were trotting along nicely, and only Mr. Perhaps would have to stop from time to time—to tighten the cinch on his poor spavined steed, he said, although the principal reason was his need for whisky.

I let the Yankee go on ahead, and then, pulling my mule close to Padre Reguera's, I said to him:

"You are a brave and practical man, and getting on in years. You are respected and loved by all the Indian peoples hereabouts. Tell me, in confidence: Is it true that people still see extraordinary things, as in the times of the Conquest, or before?"

"The devil take you! Have you got a smoke?"

I gave him a cigarette.

"Well, I'll tell you. For many years I have known these Indians as well as I know myself, and I have lived among them as though I were one of them. . . . I came here when I was but a lad, in the times of Maximilian. I was already a priest then, and I still am, and I'll die a priest, too, I expect."

"Yes?"

"Don't go poking your nose in there."

"You're right, padre. But if you'll allow me to take an interest in your strange life. . . . How have you managed for so many years to be a priest, a soldier, a man with a legend, living so long among the Indians, and even fighting in the Revolution with Madero? Didn't you say that Porfirio had won you over?"

Old Padre Reguera gave a great bellylaugh.

"So long as Porfirio had a grot's worth of respect for God, everything went along just fine—thanks, too, to Doña Carmen . . ."

"How's that, padre?"

"Well, just that. What happened is that the other gods . . ."

"Which gods, padre?"

"The gods of the earth . . ."

"But—do you believe in them?"

"Hush, boy, and have another swig of this tequila."

"Let's offer a drink," I said, "to Mr. Perhaps, who's gotten pretty far ahead of us up there."

"Mr. Perhaps! Perhaps!"

The Yankee didn't answer our calls.

"I'll go," I said to Reguera, "and see if I can catch up to him."

"Don't do that," he replied, looking into the depths of the forest. "Have your tequila."

The Aztec alcohol had infused a remarkable activity into my blood. After going on awhile in silence, the priest said to me:

"If Madero hadn't deluded himself . . ."

"About the politicians!"

"No, my son, about the devils . . ."

"Tell me of that. You know about the rumors of *espiritismo*."

"No, no, nothing of the kind. It's that he managed to establish communication with the old gods. . . . Yes, boy, yes indeed, and I tell you this because I may say mass, but that doesn't mean I'd deny what I've learned in this territory over so many years. I'll tell you one thing: we've done very little with the cross here. Inside and out, the soul and the forms of the primitive idols defeat us. . . . There were never enough Christian chains here to enslave the deities of the old days, and every time we've tried, now above all, those devils show themselves."

My mule gave a start backward, all agitated and shaking. I tried to make it go on, but the animal stood proverbially firm.

"Ssh, ssh," Reguera said to me.

He took out a knife and cut a withe off a tree nearby, and then he hit the ground with it several times.

"Don't be afraid," he said. "It's just a rattlesnake."

I then saw an enormous serpent lying dead across the road. And when we continued our journey I heard a muted laugh, the muted laughter of the priest. . . .

"We haven't caught up to the Yankee," I said.

"Don't you worry, we'll find him sooner or later."


We journeyed on. We had to pass through a large, dense stand of trees, on the other side of which we could hear the sound of water in a brook. And then a little ways in—"Halt!"

"Again!" I said to Reguera.

"Yep," he replied. "We're in the most delicate place that the Revolutionary forces hold. Have patience!"

An officer and several soldiers stepped forward. Reguera spoke with them and I heard the officer say:

"Not possible to go any farther. You'll have to stay here till morning."

For our resting place we chose a clearing under a great ahue-huete tree. It goes without saying that I couldn't sleep.

I had come to the end of my tobacco, and I asked Reguera for some.

"I have some," he said, "but it's got marijuana in it."

I took it, albeit fearfully, because I know the effects of that inebriating weed, and I lay back to smoke.

Immediately, the priest was snoring, but I couldn't sleep.

All was silent in the forest, but it was a fearsome silence, in the pale light of the moon. Suddenly I heard in the distance a sound like a long, ululating moan, which soon became a chorus of howls. I knew that sinister music of these savage forests: it was the howling of the coyote.

When I realized that the sounds were getting closer, I got up. My head was light, and I felt queasy. I remembered the priest's marijuana. Might that be it?

The howls grew louder. Without waking old Reguera I picked up my revolver and crept over to the edge of the clearing where the danger seemed to lie. I walked a bit farther, and even went a way into the woods, until I saw a kind of glow that was not from the moon, for the moonlight in the clearing had been silvery, while this, inside the woods, was gold. I continued on, deeper and deeper into the woods, until I heard the vague murmur of human voices alternating from time to time with the howls of the coyotes. I advanced as far as I could. And this is what I saw: A huge stone idol, which was idol and altar at the same time, rose in the midst of that glow that I have only barely described.

It was impossible to see anything clearly. Two serpent heads, which were like the arms and tentacles of the block of stone, joined at the top, above a kind of enormous fleshless skull, around which there was a braid, or wreath, of chopped-off hands on a necklace of pearls, and under that I saw, as though alive, a monstrous movement.

But above all, I observed a number of Indians, of the same group as those who had been carrying our equipment, silently and hieratically circling that living altar.

Living, because as I looked closely, and now recalling my

special readings, I became convinced that that was an altar to Teoyoamiqui, the Mexican goddess of death. And that upon that rock there writhed living serpents, which gave the spectacle a macabre and horrific air.

I stepped forward. Not howling, but instead in mortal silence, a pack of coyotes appeared, and the canine beasts surrounded the mysterious altar. I noticed that the serpents were now writhing in a ball, and that at the foot of the ophidian block, a body was wriggling, the body of a man. It was Mr. Perhaps!

I huddled behind a tree trunk with my terrified silence. I believed I was having an hallucination, but what actually was there was that circle formed by those New World wolves, those howling coyotes more sinister than the wolves of Europe.

The next day, when we reached the camp, the doctor had to be called for me.

I asked about Padre Reguera.

"Colonel Reguera," I was told by the person beside me, "is busy just now. There are still three left to go to the firing squad."

There came to my brain, as though written in letters of blood: *Huitzilopoxtli*.

# THE CASE OF
# MADEMOISELLE AMÉLIE

*A story for New Year's*


That Doctor Z—— is illustrious, eloquent, dashing, that his voice is deep and vibrant, his gestures hypnotic and mysterious, especially after the publication of his work *The Sculpture of Daydreams*—these things, you might be able to deny or accede to with certain reservations. But that his bald head is unique, remarkable, lovely, solemn, lyrical if you like—oh, *that,* you could never deny, I am certain! For how could one deny the light of the sun, the fragrance of roses, and the narcotic properties of certain verses?

Very well then: Last night, shortly after we saluted the midnight bells with a salvo of twelve champagne corks of the finest Röderer, in that lovely rococo dining room belonging to the sybaritic Jew Lowensteiger, the bald pate of Doctor Z——, haloed with pride, raised its burnished ivory orb, whose mirrorlike surface seemed to contain, by some caprice of the light, two sparks that formed, I know not how, a shape very like the glowing horns of Moses. The doctor directed his grand gestures and wise words in my direction. For there had issued from my lips, almost always closed, some banal phrase. This one, for example:

"Oh, if only time would stop!"

The look the doctor gave me and the sort of smile that adorned his mouth after hearing my exclamation, I confess would have unnerved anyone.

"Dear sir," he said, savoring his champagne, "were I not totally disillusioned with youth, did I not know that all of you who are beginning to live are already dead—that is, dead in the soul, without faith, without enthusiasm, without ideals, gray-haired on the inside, no more than mere masks of life—yes, did I not know that, yet not see in you something more than a fin-de-siècle man, I would tell you that that phrase you have just spoken, 'Oh, if time would only stop!' has found in me its most satisfactory response."

"Doctor!"

"Yes, I repeat—your skepticism prevents me from speaking as on another occasion I might."

"I believe," I answered in a firm, serene voice, "in God and His Church. I believe in miracles. And I believe, too, in the supernatural."

"Ah, well. . . . That being the case, I will tell you all something that will make you smile. And I hope my narration will also make you think."

Not counting Minna, our host's daughter, four of us had remained behind in the dining room: Riquet the journalist, Pureau the abbot just sent in by Hirch, the good doctor, and I. In the distance we heard in the gaiety of the salons the usual words of the first hour of the new year: *Hap-py new year! Happy new year! Feliz año nuevo!*

The doctor went on:

"Who among men is so wise as to say *This is so*? Nothing is known for a certainty. *Ignoramus et ignorabimus.* Who among men understands the concept of time? Who knows precisely what space is? Science proceeds by fits and starts, groping in the darkness, poking along like a blind man, and it sometimes thinks it has conquered when it manages to glimpse some vague glimmer of the true light. No one has ever been able to pull the snake's mouth from its tail in that endless symbolic circle. From the thrice-great Hermes to our own day, the human hand has been able to lift barely one corner of the mantle that covers the eternal Isis. Nothing has been learned for an absolute certainty about the three great expressions of Nature: facts, laws, and principles. I, who have attempted to delve into the immense field of mystery, have lost almost all my illusions.

"I, who have been called wise in illustrious universities and voluminous books; I, who have consecrated my life to the study of humankind, its origins, its ends; I, who have penetrated the Kabbala, the mysteries of the occult and of theosophy, who have passed from the material plane of the sage to the astral plane of the wizard and the spiritual plane of the magus, who know how Apollonius of Tyana and Paracelsus worked their wonders, and who, in our own day, have aided the Englishman Crookes in his laboratory; I, who have delved into the Buddhist's Karma and the Christian's mysticism, and know both the unknown science of the fakirs and the theology of the Roman priests—I tell you that *we sages have seen not a single ray of the supreme light*, and that the immensity and eternity of the Mystery form a single, frightful truth."

Then, addressing himself to me:

"Do you know what the principles of man are? Grupa, jiba, linga, sharira, kama, rupa, manas, buddhi, atma; that is, the body, the *force vital*, the astral body, the animal soul, the human soul, the spiritual force, and the spiritual essence . . ."

Seeing Minna put on an expression almost of desolation, I dared interrupt the doctor:

"I think you were going to explain to us that time . . ."

"Well," he said, "since you seem not to like dissertations for prologues, let's get right to the story I was going to tell you, which is the following: . . ."

Twenty-three years ago, in Buenos Aires, I met the Revall family, whose founder, a delightful French gentleman, had held a consular post during the times of the dictator Rosas. Our houses adjoined one another, I was young and enthusiastic, and in terms of beauty the three *mademoiselles* Revall would have given the three Graces a good run for their money. There is no need to mention, I suppose, that very few sparks were needed to light the bonfire of love. . . .

(*Lo-o-o-ove*, pronounced the obese sage, the thumb of his right hand hanging in the pocket of his waistcoat as his swift fat fingers drummed on his potent abdomen.)

I frankly confess that no one of them caught my fancy more than the others, and that Claire, Joséphine, and Amélie all held the same place in my heart. Or perhaps not the same place, because the both sweet and ardent eyes of Amélie, her gay red laughter, her childish piquancy. . . . I suppose I must say that she was my favorite. She was the youngest; she was barely twelve, and I was past thirty. For that reason, and because the young creature had a mischievous, jolly way about her, I treated her like the child she was, and between the other two shared out my incendiary looks, my sighs, my squeezings of the hand, and even my serious promises of matrimony—in a word, I confess to you all a most reprehensible and horrid bigamy of passion. But oh, little Amélie! . . .

When I went to the house, it was she who ran to greet me, with her smiles and her flattery: "Have you forgotten my *bon-bons*?" Oh, that sacramental question! I would feel overcome with joy, after my somewhat stiffly polite greetings, and I would shower the girl with rich rose-flavored caramels and delicious chocolate drops which she, open-mouthed, would savor with a loud palatal, lingual, and dental music. The reason behind my feelings for this little girl with the knee-length skirts and pretty eyes, I cannot explain to you, but the fact is that when my studies took me away from Buenos Aires, I feigned emotion when I bade farewell to Claire, who would look at me with large pained and sentimental eyes; I gave a false squeeze to the hands of Joséphine, who held between her teeth, so as not to cry, a batiste handkerchief; and upon the forehead of Amélie I bestowed a kiss, the purest yet most ardent, the most chaste yet wanton of all I have given in my life.

And so I embarked for Calcutta, precisely like your beloved and admired General Mansilla when he departed for the Orient, himself full of youth and his pockets full of resounding new gold coins. I sailed away, thirsting for a taste of the occult sciences, and it was my intention to study among the mahatmas of India those things that impoverished Western science still cannot teach us. The epistolary friendship that I had kept up with Madame Blavatsky had opened many doors for me in the land of the fakirs, and more than one guru, knowing my hunger for knowledge, put himself at my disposal, offering to guide me along the path to the sacred fountain of truth, and although my lips believed they would sate their thirst in its cool diamantine waters, there was in fact no quenching my bottomless thirst. I sought, I sought with great determination, what my eyes yearned to contemplate, the Zoroastrian Ke-herpas,[2] the Persian Kalep, the Kovei-Khan of Indian philoso-phy, the Paracelsan arch-oenus, Swedenborg's limbus.[3] I listened to the word of the Buddhist monks in the deep forests of Tibet; I studied the ten Sephiroth of the Kaballa, from that which symbolizes limitless space to that which, called Malkuth, contains the principle of life. I studied the spirit, air, water, fire, the heights, the depths, the Orient, the Occident, the North, and the South, and I almost came to understand and even know, intimately, Satan, Lucifer, Astaroth, Beelze-bub, Asmodeus, Belphegor, Mabema, Lilith, Adramelch, and Ba'al. In my desperate eagerness for comprehension, in my in-satiable desire for wisdom, just when I believed I had achieved my ambitions, I would find signs of my weakness and mani-festations of my poverty, and those grand ideas—God, space, time—would form a most impenetrable haze before my eyes. . . .

I traveled through Asia, Africa, Europe, and the Americas. I helped Colonel Olcot found the theosophical circle in New York. And of all of this—the doctor suddenly asked, staring balefully at blond Minna—do you know what true science and immortality is? A pair of blue eyes . . . or black ones!

"And the end of the story?" the young lady sweetly groaned.

The doctor, yet more seriously than before, said:

I vow to you, gentlemen and lady, that what I am telling is absolutely true. The end of the story? Just over a week ago, I

---

2. The "aerial form" or "astral image."
3. The envelope or "containant" of the human soul.

returned to Argentina, after twenty-three years of absence. I've
grown fat, quite fat indeed, and as bald as your kneecap, but in
my heart the flame of love, that vestal of the aging bachelor, still
lives. And of course the first thing I did was find out the where-
abouts of the Revall family. "The Revall girls!" I was told, "the
girls in the Amélie Revall case!" and these words were accom-
panied with a special smile. I came to suspect that poor Amélie,
the poor child. . . . And I searched and I searched until I found
the house.

When I entered, I was greeted by an old negro butler, who
took my card and asked me to step into a parlor in which
everything bore a hue of sadness. On the walls, the mirrors
were covered with crêpe veils of mourning, and two large
portraits, in which I recognized the two older sisters, looked
out, melancholy and dark, over the piano. Soon, Claire and
Joséphine:

"Oh, my friend, oh my friend!"

That was all. Then, a conversation filled with reticences and
timidities, broken phrases and sad, very sad smiles of intelli-
gence. From all I could manage to piece together, I gathered
that neither of these young women had married. As for Amélie,
I dared not ask. . . . My question might strike those poor
creatures as some sort of bitter irony, remind them perhaps of
some terrible and irremediable disgrace and dishonor. . . .
And just then I saw a little girl come skipping in, with a body
and face exactly—but exactly, my friends—like those of my
poor Amélie. She skipped over to me, and in that other girl's
very voice exclaimed:

"Have you forgotten my *bonbons*?"

I was speechless.

The two sisters looked at each other, stricken with a sudden
pallor, and shook their heads disconsolately. . . .

Muttering some words of farewell and making a *gauche* bow,
I rushed out of the house, as though pursued by some strange
gust of wind. Since then, I have learned everything. The girl that
I believed at that moment to be the fruit of a guilty love affair is
Amélie, the same young creature that I left twenty-three years

ago. She has remained a child; the course of her life has been halted. The clock of Time has been stopped, at a certain hour—who can say out of what unknown god's inscrutable plan!

Doctor Z—— was at that moment entirely bald . . .

# Myth and Legend

# PALIMPSEST I

When Longinus rushed away, spear in hand, after wounding the side of Our Lord Jesus, it was the sad hour of Calvary, the hour when the sacred agony began.

Across the arid hill, the three crosses threw their shadows. The multitude that had gathered to witness the sacrifice was on its way back to the city. Christ, sublime and solitary, the martyrized lily of divine love, hung pale and bleeding on the wood.

Near his crossed feet, Mary Magdalene, lover, her hair in disarray, was pressing her head with her hands. Mary was moaning maternally. *Stabat mater dolorosa!*

Later, a fleeting dusk heralded the arrival of the black coach of night. Jerusalem shimmered in the light to the soft evening breeze.

Longinus' feet were swift, and on the tip of the spear he carried in his right hand there glimmered something like the luminous blood of a star.

The blind man had recovered delight in the sun.

The holy water of the holy wound had washed from his soul all the shadows that prevented the triumph of the light.

At the door of the house wherein he had been blind, a grand archangel stood, its wings spread and its arms upraised.

Oh, Longinus, Longinus! From that day forth, your spear was to be an immense human good. The soul that it wounded was to suffer the celestial contagion of the faith.

Because of it, Saul came to hear the thunder and Parsifal was chaste.

At the very hour when, in Haceldama, Judas hanged himself, Longinus' spear flowered ideally.

These two figures have remained eternal in the eyes of men.

Who would prefer the traitor's noose to the weapon of grace?

# PALIMPSEST II

One hundred twenty-nine years had passed since Valeriano and Decius, cruel emperors, displayed the barbarous fury of their persecutions by sacrificing the children of Christ, and it happened that one bright azure day, near a brook in Thebais, a satyr and a centaur came face to face.

(The existence of these two beings is confirmed by the testimony of saints and sages.)

The two creatures were thirsty under the bright azure of the sky, and they quenched their thirst: the centaur by cupping the water in his hand, the satyr by bending down over the brook and lapping at it.

Then they spoke, in this way:

"Not long ago," said the centaur, "coming down from the North, I saw a divine being, perhaps Jupiter himself, in the disguise of a beautiful old man.

"His eyes were piercing and powerful, his thick white beard fell to his waist; he was walking slowly, leaning on a rough staff. When he saw me, he came toward me, made a strange sign with his right hand, and I felt that he was so great that he could have sent down a lightning-bolt from Olympus. I can explain it no other way than by saying that I felt I was in the presence of the father of the gods. He spoke to me in a strange tongue, yet I understood. He was seeking a path through my ignorance, and without knowing how, I managed to speak to him, obeying that strange or unknown power.

"I felt such fear, that before Jupiter continued on his way, I ran madly across the vast plains, my belly near the earth and my mane in the air."

"Ah!" exclaimed the satyr. "Have you perchance not heard that a new dawn is now opening the doors of the East, and that all the gods, all of them, have fallen before another God who is stronger and greater than they? The old man that you saw was not Jupiter, or any other Olympian being. He was the messenger sent by the new God.

"This morning when the sun rose, we were on the mountain near those where there is still an immense army of centaurs.

"We called to the four winds for Pan, yet naught but echoes responded to our calls. Our reed flutes do not sing as in days gone by, and through the leaves and branches we have seen not a single nymph of living rose and marble like those that once were our delight. Death pursues us. We have all raised our hairy arms and bowed our poor horned heads, praying for succor to this one who announces himself as the only immortal God.

"I, too, have seen that old man with the white beard, before whom you have felt the inrushing of an unknown power. Just a few hours ago, in the neighboring valley, I came upon him leaning on a staff and muttering prayers, dressed in rough cloth, his loins girded by a cincture. I vow to you that he was more handsome than Homer, who would speak with the gods and also had a long snowy beard.

"I happened to be carrying dates and honey. I offered him some, and he savored them like a mortal. He spoke to me, and I understood him without knowing his language. He wanted to know who I was, and I told him that I had been sent by my companions to find the great God, and to plead with him to intercede for us.

"The old man wept with joy, and above all his words and moaning, in my ear rang the harmonious sound of this word: Christ! Then he rained imprecations upon Alexandria, and I, like you, frightened, fled from there as quickly as my goat's feet would take me."

At that, the centaur felt a flood of tears falling from his eyes. He wept for the old paganism, now dead, but also, filled with a newborn faith, he wept at the appearance of a new light.

And as his tears fell on the black and fecund earth, in the cave of Paul the hermit, two white heads, two gray beards, two souls chosen by the Lord greeted one another in Christ. And when Antony had told the hermit about his encounter with the two monsters, and how he had come to the retreat in this barren place, the first of the hermits said to the other:

"In truth, my brother, they will both have their reward: half of them belongs to the beasts, which are cared for by God alone, and the other half belongs to man, which eternal justice rewards or punishes.

"I tell you that the reed pipe, the pagan flute, will grow and appear later in the pipes of organs in great basilicas, to reward the satyr that went out to find God, and because the centaur wept half for the antique gods of Greece and half for the new faith, he shall be condemned for the rest of his life to run over the face of the earth, until he takes a wondrous leap, and in virtue of his tears, ascends to the azure sky, where he will shine forever in the wonder of the constellations."

# THE RUBY

"Ah! So it's true! So that Parisian sage has managed to extract from his retorts and flasks the crystalline scarlet that encrusts the walls of my palace!"

And as the tiny gnome said this, he paced back and forth, back and forth, sometimes with tiny skips, through the deep cave in which he dwelled, and as he paced, his long beard quivered and the bell on the tip of his azure hat tinkled.

And indeed, the news was true: The chemist Frémy—a friend of centenarian Chevreul (quasi-Althotas)—had just discovered a way to make sapphires and rubies.

Distressed, perturbed, and filled with wrath, the gnome (who was expert in the arts of magic, and possessor of a lively genius) went on muttering to himself:

"Oh! wise men of the Middle Ages! Oh Albertus Magnus, Averroës, Raymond Lull! Your skills were not enough to make the great sun of the Philosopher's Stone to shine in your day, yet now—without studying the Aristotelian formulas, without one jot of the Cabbala or necromancy—comes a man of the nineteenth century to make in the light of day what we create here, in our subterranean chambers. And what is the spell he has cast? A twenty-days' fusion of a mixture of silica and lead aluminate, coloration with potassium bichromate or cobalt oxide—words that truly seem to be in a diabolic tongue."

Bitter laughter.

Then he stopped.

The evidence of the crime was there, at the center of the grotto, on a massive rock of gold: a tiny round ruby, softly gleaming, like a pomegranate seed in the sun.

The gnome blew a horn (which he wore always at his waist) and the echo resounded throughout the vast halls of the cavern. Soon there was a bustle, a trampling sound, a noise of jubila-. tion. All the gnomes had arrived.

The cave was broad, and filled with a strange white light. It was the light of the carbuncles that sparkled in the ceiling over-head—encrusted, one upon another, into many-celled spot-lights. A sweet light, that illuminated the entire cave.

The carbuncles' gleam revealed the wondrous mansion in all its splendor. On the walls, veins of gold and silver, strata of lapis lazuli, and precious stones formed strange designs, like the arabesques of a mosque. The crystal irises of diamonds as white and clean as drops of water peeked out from the gloom, and there were agates hanging in stalactites, emeralds of green radiance, and sapphires in weird masses, in sprays and festoons like great blue shivering flowers.

Golden topazes and amethysts girdled the cave, and on the floor, with curds of opals, upon the polished chrysoprase and chalcedony, a tiny stream of water leapt up from time to time, falling then with a musical sweetness, in harmonious drops like those of a silver flute played ever so softly.

Puck, mischievous Puck, had played his part in this! He had brought the evidence of the crime, the false ruby—there, upon the rock of gold, like a profanation among the sparkle of all that enchantment—to the cavern of the gnomes.

When they were all gathered at last—some still carrying their mallets and short picks, others dressed as for a celebration, wearing scarlet and gold capes pavéed with gems, and all curious—Puck spoke:

"You have asked me to bring proof of the new human falsification, and I have done as you wished."

The gnomes, sitting crosslegged like Turks, tugged at their beards, or thanked Puck with a slow inclination of their heads, or (those closest to him) gazed in rapt amazement at his pretty wings, like those of a dragonfly.

He went on:

"Oh, Earth! Oh, Woman! Since that day I saw Titania I have been but a slave to one, an almost mystical adorer of the other."

And then, as though speaking from the pleasures of a dream:

"Those rubies! In the great city of Paris, flying invisible, I saw them everywhere. They gleamed in the necklaces of courtesans, on the exotic medals of parvenus, in the rings of Italian princes, and in the bracelets of prima donnas."

And then with his usual mischievous smile:

"I slipped into a certain pink *boudoir* very much in vogue . . . there was a beautiful woman lying there, asleep. I snatched a medallion from about her neck, and from the medallion, I snatched the ruby that lies before you. . . ."

What hilarity at that! And what a tinkling of tiny bells!

"Well done, friend Puck!"

And then came the opinions of that false gem, that work of man—or worse yet, scholar.

"Glass!"

"A spell!"

"Poison! Cabbala!"

"Chemical!"

"To think, imitating a fragment of the rainbow!"

"The rubicund treasure of the depths of the earth!"

"Made of solidified rays of the setting sun!"

The eldest gnome, approaching on his twisted legs, with his snowy beard and wrinkled face and patriarchal figure, spoke as follows:

"Gentlemen! You do not know what you are talking about!"

Silence. All the gnomes were listening.

"I, who am the eldest of you, since I hardly have the strength to hammer out the facets of the diamonds, I, who have watched these deep caverns form, and have carved out the bones of the earth, and have molded up the gold, and have smashed my fist into a wall of rock and fallen into a lake where I violated a nymph—I, the oldest gnome of all of you, shall tell you how the ruby was first made. Listen . . ."

Curious, Puck smiled. All the gnomes drew around the Old One, whose white hairs grew even paler in the gleams of the gems and whose hands cast wavering shadows on the gem-encrusted walls like canvases of honey onto which grains of rice had been tossed. And these were the words the old gnome spoke to them:

"One day, my brigade and the others who were charged with toiling in the diamond mines went on a strike that inspired the entire earth, and we walked out through the craters of the world's volcanoes.

"The earth was gay, and all was youthfulness and vigor. The roses, and the cool green leaves, and the birds whose mouths peck at seeds and send forth songs, and the entire countryside saluted the sun and the fragrant spring.

"The woods were flowering, and all was harmony—birdsong and bee-buzz everywhere. It was a nuptial ceremony of light, and in the trees the sap ran hot, and among the animals, all was quivering and bleating and song, and among the gnomes, all was laughter and pleasure.

"I had come up out of a dormant crater. Before my eyes lay a broad meadow. I leapt up into a great tree, an ancient oak. And then I climbed down the trunk and found myself near a brook, a small clear stream in which the water tittered and told glassy jokes. I was hungry. I wanted to drink that water. . . . Now, listen closely.

"Naked arms, backs, breasts, roses, lilies, ivory hillocks crowned with cherries; echoes of golden, festive laughter—for there, among the bubbling spray, among the shattered water, under the green boughs . . ."

"Nymphs?"

"No, women."

"I knew where my grotto was. I rapped on the ground, the black earth opened, and I dropped into my domain. You poor young gnomes have much to learn!

"Under the tender shoots of new green ferns I scuttled, across rocks washed by the burbling, bubbling spray, carrying the woman, the lovely creature, under this once-muscular arm, about the waist. She screamed, I rapped the ground, and we descended. Amazement, astonishment, remained above; down below, the proud, victorious gnome.

"One day I was hammering an immense hunk of diamond. It shone like a star and shattered into pieces under my mallet.

The floor of my workshop looked like the shards of a shattered sun. My beloved woman was resting nearby, a rose of flesh among the flower-beds of sapphires, empress of gold upon a rock-crystal bed, all naked and splendid as a goddess.

But in the depths of my domain, my queen, my beloved, my beautiful one, was unfaithful to me. When humans truly love, their passion penetrates all things, and is capable of piercing all the earth.

My human woman loved a human man, and from her prison she was sending him her sighs. The sighs passed through the pores of the earth's skin and found him, and he, still loving her, would kiss the roses in a certain garden, and she, his beloved, would have sudden convulsions—I noticed them, of course— in which she would pucker her pink, cool lips like the petals of a damask rose. How did these two sense one another's love? Being the creature that I am, I do not know.

I had finished my work. A large pile of diamonds finished in one day. The earth opened its granite fissures like thirsty lips, awaiting the brilliant shattering of the rich crystal. At the end of the day's work, tired, I gave one last hammer-blow, which split a rock, and I fell asleep.

I awoke some time later when I heard a sound like a moan.

From her bed, from her mansion more rich and luminous than all the queens' of the Orient, my beloved, the stolen woman, desperate for a human's love, had fled. Oh! And trying to escape— beautiful, and naked—through the crack opened by my granite mallet, she had torn her body—so white, so soft, so like orange blossom and marble and rose—on the sharp edges of the broken diamonds. Blood flowed from the wounds along her sides and flanks; her moaning moved me to tears. Oh, what pain!

I awoke, took her in my arms, gave her my most burning kisses, but her blood flooded the cave, and the mass of diamonds was stained as though by cochineal crimson.

I thought, when I gave her a kiss, that I caught the smell of a sweet perfume, exhaled by that fiery mouth. Indeed, it was her soul. Her body lay lifeless.

When our great patriarch, the demigod centaur of the bowels of the earth, came by, he found that mass of blood-red diamonds. . . .

Pause.

"Have you understood my story?"

The gnomes, very grave, stood.

They examined the false stone, the product of the Parisian sage, more closely.

"Look, it has no facets!"

"What a pale gleam it throws!"

"Imposture!"

"As round as a beetle's shell."

And then—one here, another there—they went to the walls and tore from them the pieces of the arabesques: rubies as big as oranges, as red and blazing as diamonds turned to blood. And they said:

"These are ours, oh Mother Earth!"

It was an orgy of light and color.

And they tossed the gigantic, luminous stones into the air, and laughed.

Suddenly, with all the dignity of a gnome:

"And now, the contempt!"

They understood. They took the false ruby, shattered it into pieces, and threw the fragments—with terrible disdain—into a hole that dropped into an ancient jungle, now turned to coal.

Then, upon their rubies, upon their opals, in the cavern of gleaming, shining walls, they joined hands and danced a wild, echoing farandole.

And they howled with laughter to see themselves made gigantic in the shadows on the walls.

Now Puck was outside, in the bee-buzzing gold of the newborn morning, flying toward a flowery meadow. And he whispered to himself, smiling cheerily:

"Earth . . . Mother . . ."

Because you, oh Mother Earth, are grand and fecund, and your breast is inextinguishable, and from your brown womb issue forth the sap of the robust trees, and gold, and the diamantine water, and the chaste fleur-de-lis. All that is pure, and strong, and unfalsifiable! And you, Woman, are spirit and flesh, and wholly love.

# THE BIRTH OF CABBAGE

In the earthly paradise, on that glowing day when the flowers were created, and before Eve was tempted by the serpent, the Evil One approached the most beautiful new rose just at the moment when, at the caress of the celestial sun, she spread the red virginity of her lips.

"You are beautiful."

"I am," said the rose.

"Beautiful and happy," the devil went on. "You have color, grace, and fragrance. But . . ."

"But?"

"You are not useful. Do you not see those tall trees covered with acorns? Those, besides being leafy and giving shade, give food to multitudes of animate creatures that pause beneath their branches. Oh Rose, being beautiful is so little . . ."

The rose then—tempted as, later, Woman would be—wished for usefulness, and she wished so desperately that a paleness crept over her crimson.

And God passed by the next morning, just after dawn.

"Father," said that princess of the flowers, trembling in all her perfumed beauty, "would you make me useful."

"So be it, my child," replied the Lord, smiling.

And it was then that the world saw its first cabbage.

# QUEEN MAB'S VEIL

Queen Mab, riding on a ray of sunlight in her coach made of a single pearl and drawn by four beetles with golden carapaces and wings of pavéed gemstones, flitted in through the window of a garret in which there were four thin, bearded, impertinent men, complaining like wretches.

It was back in those years when the fairies had shared out their gifts to mortals. To some they had given the mysterious little wands that fill the heavy casks of trade with gold; to others, wondrous stalks of wheat which, when the tiny seeds were stripped from their tips, piled the granaries full of riches; to yet others, crystals that allowed the possessor to discover gold and precious gems within the bowels of mother earth; to some, full heads of hair and muscles like Goliath's, and enormous sledge-hammers with which they struck the red-hot iron; to others, strong feet and agile legs with which to ride on swift steeds that drink the wind, their manes streaming out behind them.

The four men were complaining. One had been given a quarry, another the rainbow, another rhythm, and the fourth the azure sky.

Queen Mab overheard their complaints. The first one was saying: "Ay! Here I am, struggling with my dreams of marble! I have wrestled forth the block and I have the chisel. You others have gold, or harmony, or light, while I dream of divine white Venus, displaying her nakedness under a roof the color of the sky. I want to give the mass line and plastic loveliness, and I want a colorless blood, like that of the gods, to flow through the statue's veins. I have the spirit of Greece in my brain, and I love nudes in which the nymph flees and the faun stretches out his arms. Oh, Phidias! You are for me as peerless, as august as a god in the realm of eternal beauty, a king who stands before an army of beauties that throw off their magnificent chitons to display to your eyes the splendor of their bodies of rose and snow.

"You strike, wound, and tame the marble, and the harmonic blows of your chisel resound like a poem, and you are adored by the cicada, lover of the sun, who hides among the tendrils of the virgin grapevine. For you, the blond, glowing Apollos, the severe and sovereign Minervas. You, like a wizard, transform rock into likeness, elephant's tusk into celebratory goblet. And when I look upon your grandeur I feel the martyrdom of my own insignificance. Because the age of glories is past. Because I tremble before the eyes of today. Because I contemplate the immense ideal, and the forces spent. Because, as I chisel away at the block, I am gnawed by disheartenment."

And the next man said: "Today, I shall break my brushes. Why should I want the rainbow and this great palette of flowering fields, if when I am done, my painting will not be admitted into the Salon? What shall I paint? I have passed through all the schools, all possible artistic inspirations. I have painted the visage of Diana and the visage of the Madonna. I have borrowed the countryside's colors, and its hues; I have worshipped the light like a lover, and have embraced it like a mistress. I have been an adorer of the nude, with its magnificences, its flesh tones, and its fleeting half-tints. On my canvases I have drawn the saints' nimbuses and the cherubs' wings. Oh, but always the terrible disappointment! The future! Selling a Cleopatra for two pesetas in order to eat!

"If only I could, in the shudder of my inspiration, paint the great painting that I have down here inside me! . . ."

And the next man said: "In my great hope for my symphonies my soul is lost, and I fear all disappointments. I listen to all harmonies, from Terpander's lyre to Wagner's orchestral fantasies. My ideals shine forth in the midst of my inspired audacities. I have the perception of that philosopher who heard the music of the spheres. All sounds can be caught and imprisoned, all echoes are capable of being combined. Everything fits within the line of my chromatic scales.

"The shimmering light is an anthem, and the melody of the forest finds echo in my heart. From the deafening noise of the storm to the song of the bird, everything mixes and joins and intertwines in infinite cadence. And meanwhile, I see nothing but the multitude that snorts and bellows, and the prison cell of matrimony."

And the last man: "We all drink the water of the Ionian spring. But the ideal floats in the azure, and in order for spirits to take delight in its light supreme, they must ascend. I possess the verse that is of honey and of gold, and the verse that is of red-glowing iron. I am the amphora of celestial perfume; I possess love. Dove, star, nest, lily—you all know where I dwell. For my incommensurable flights I possess the wings of the eagle, which with magical strokes can part the hurricane. And to find conso-nants, I search in two mouths whose lips come together—the kiss explodes, and I write the line of poetry, and then, if you see my soul, you will meet my muse. I love epics, for from epics springs the heroic breath that sets banners rippling above the lances and crested helmets; lyric songs, because they sing of goddesses and love; and eclogues, because they are fragrant of verbena and of thyme, and of the holy breath of the ox crowned with roses. I would write something immortal, but I am crushed by a future of poverty and hunger."

And then Queen Mab, from the back of her coach made of a single pearl, took out an azure veil, as impalpable as though it were made of sighs, or the glances of pensive blond angels. And that veil was the veil of dreams, the sweet dreams that make one see life all rose-colored. And she cast it over the four lean, bearded, impertinent men. And they immediately ceased being sad, because hope penetrated their breast, and the happy sun penetrated their head, with the imp of vanity, which consoles poor artists in their profound disappointments.

And since then, in the garret rooms of brilliant wretches,

where the azure dream floats on dust motes in the sun, men think of the future as they think of the coming dawn, and laugh a laughter that banishes sadness, and dance strange capers around a white Apollo, a pretty landscape, an old violin, a yellowing manuscript.

# Fables

# THE PALACE OF THE SUN

To you mothers of anemic daughters goes this tale, the story of Berta, the girl with the olive-colored eyes, as fresh as a branch of peach-blossoms, as glowing as the dawn, as gentle as the princess of a fairy tale.

You will see, wise and respectable ladies, that there is something better than arsenic and iron for rekindling the crimson of lovely virginal cheeks, and that the doors of your enchanting little birds' cages must be opened, especially when the springtime comes and there is ardor in the veins and sap, and a thousand atoms of sunlight are buzzing in the garden like a swarm of gold among the half-open roses.

When she turned fifteen, Berta began to grow sad, and her blazing eyes were ringed with a dark and melancholy cast.

"Berta, I've bought you two dolls . . ."

"I don't want them, mamá . . ."

"I've sent for the *Nocturnes* . . ."

"My fingers ache, mamá . . ."

"Well, then . . ."

"I'm sad, mamá . . ."

"Then we'll send for the doctor."

And in came the tortoise-shell spectacles, the black gloves, the illustrious bald spot, and the double-breasted frock coat.

Let's have a look, then. . . . No, everything quite normal. The girl's age, you know; the pangs of adolescence. . . . Clear symptoms: a lack of appetite, a sort of oppression in the chest, sadness, an occasional throbbing in the temples, palpitations. . . .

Perfectly normal. Give her a few drops of arsenious acid, then showers. That's the treatment.

And so when spring began, the cure began to be administered for her melancholy: drops of arsenious acid and showers—Berta, the girl with the olive-colored eyes, as fresh as a branch of peach-blossoms, as glowing as the dawn, as gentle as the princess of a fairy tale.

But despite everything, the dark circles around her eyes persisted, her sadness did not abate, and Berta, pale as a precious piece of ivory, came one day to the doors of death. Everyone in the palace wept for her, and the wise and sentimental mamá had to think about the white palms of a maiden's coffin. Until one morning the languid anemic went down to the garden, all alone and still with that air of vague melancholy lethargy, just as the dawn was laughing. Sighing, she wandered aimlessly here and there, and seeing her, the flowers were sad. She leaned on the pedestal of a magnificent, noble faun whose marble locks were wet with dew and whose splendid nude torso was bathed in golden light. She spied a lily raising its white chalice to the azure sky, and she stretched out her hand to pick it. Hardly had she . . . —yes, this is a fairy tale, my dear ladies, but soon you shall see its applications to sweet reality—hardly had she touched the flower's cup, when a fairy sprang from it, in a tiny golden coach, and the fairy was dressed in dazzling impalpable threads, with a sprinkling of dew, a diadem of pearls, and a little silver wand.

Do you think that for one second Berta was frightened? Hardly! She clapped her hands gaily, was revived as though by magic, and to the fairy spoke the following words:

"You're the one that loves me so much in dreams?"

"Climb in," replied the fairy.

And as though Berta had suddenly grown very, very tiny, she found herself seated very comfortably inside the golden coach, which was of course nestled into the curved wing of a swan floating on the water. And the flowers, the proud faun, the soft sunlight watched as the fairy's chariot flew away on the wind—bearing Berta, the girl with the olive-colored eyes, as fresh as

the dawn, as gentle as the princess in a fairy tale, smiling peace-
fully in the sun.

When Berta—the divine coachman had brought the coach back
down to earth—ascended the smaragdite-green terraces of the
garden toward the sitting rooms of the palace, everyone—
mamá, Berta's cousin, the servants—were waiting for her, their
mouths making a perfect O. She was skipping like a bird, and
her face was full of life and crimson; her lovely swelling bosom,
receiving the caresses of a long stray lock of chestnut hair, was
half-exposed, and free; her arms were naked to the elbow, half
showing the web of her almost-imperceptible azure veins; and
her lips, half-open in a smile, looked ready to break out into
song.

Everyone exclaimed: "Hallelujah! Gloria! Hosanna to the
king of the Aesculapiuses! Eternal fame to the drops of arse-
nious acid and the triumphant showers!" And while Berta ran
to her own room, where she dressed herself in rich brocades,
gifts were sent to the old gentleman in the tortoise-shell specta-
cles, the black gloves, the double-breasted frock coat, and the il-
lustrious bald pate.

And now, listen closely, my dear mothers of anemic
daughters—for there is something better than arsenic and iron
for rekindling the crimson of lovely virginal cheeks. And you
shall know that it was not the drops, and it was not the show-
ers; nor was it the pharmacist who brought health and life back
to Berta, the girl with the olive-colored eyes, as gay and fresh as
a dawn, as gentle as the princess in a fairy tale.

As soon as Berta found herself in the fairy's coach, she asked:

"Where are you taking me?"

"To the palace of the sun."

And of course the girl felt her hands grow warm, and her lit-
tle heart leap, as though swollen with impetuous blood.

"Pay attention now," the fairy went on. "I am the good fairy
of adolescent girls' dreams; I am the fairy that cures chlorotics
by nothing more than taking them in my golden coach to the
palace of the sun, where I am now taking you. Be careful not to

imbibe too much nectar of the dance, and not to swoon away at the first bursts of gaiety. We're arriving now. Soon you will return to your own room. A minute in the palace of the sun leaves years of fire in the body and the soul, my child."

And indeed they were now in a pretty enchanted palace, where the sun seemed to feel right at home. Oh, what light, what fires! Berta felt that her lungs were being filled with country air, and sea air, and that her veins were being filled with fire. In her brain, she felt a spreading harmony, and she felt as though her soul were growing, and expanding, and swelling, and as though her delicate womanly skin were becoming so much smoother and more elastic. Then she saw real dreams, and heard intoxicating music. In vast dazzling ballrooms, filled with light and fragrance, silks and marbles, she saw a whirlwind of couples swept up by the invisible yet overpowering waves of a waltz. She saw many other anemic girls like herself, who would enter pale and sad looking and breathe that air and suddenly be caught up in the arms of vigorous, slender young men, whose ringleted hair and downy upper lips glowed golden in the light, and those girls would dance, and dance, and dance with them, in an ardent embrace, hearing mysterious sweet whispered compliments that went directly to their souls, and from time to time smelling their breath, which bore the scent of vanilla, of new-mown hay, of violets, of cinnamon, until— feverish, panting, exhausted, like doves wearied from long flight—they would fall upon silk cushions, their bosoms heaving, their throats rosy, and lie there, dreaming, dreaming of intoxicating things. . . . And she, too, was drawn into that whirlwind, that beckoning maelstrom, and she danced, exclaimed, strolled, as she experienced the spasms of a fluttering pleasure, and she remembered then that she was not to become too tipsy on the wine of the dance—although she never stopped looking at her handsome companion with her big springtime eyes. And he would pull her through the vast ballrooms, put his arm about her waist and whisper in her ear in an amorous, rhythmic language of peaceful words, of iridescent, fragrant phrases, of crystalline, Oriental periods. And at that, she felt that her body and her soul were being filled with sunlight, with powerful exhalations, and with life. . . . No, I can say no more!

The fairy returned Berta to the garden of her own palace, the garden in which she would cut flowers wreathed in perfumes that rose mystically up to the tremulous branches, where they floated like the wandering soul of the dead lilies.

Oh, mothers of anemic girls. I congratulate you on the victory of the good doctor's arsenates and hypophosphates. But I tell you the truth: One must, for the sake of pretty virginal cheeks, open the doors of your enchanting little birds' cages, especially in the springtime, when there is ardor in the veins and saps, and a thousand atoms of sunlight buzz in the gardens like a swarm of gold in the half-open roses. For your chlorotic daughters, sun on their bodies and on their souls. Yes, to the palace of the sun, from whence come girls like Berta, the girl with the olive-colored eyes, as fresh as a branch of peach-blossoms, as glowing as the dawn, as gentle as a princess in a fairy tale.

# THE DEATH OF THE EMPRESS OF CHINA

As fine and delicate as a human jewel was that little girl of pink flesh who lived in the little house with a little parlor with wall coverings of faintest and most delicate azure. It was the jewel-case into which she had been clasped.

Who was the owner of that gay, delicious songbird of black eyes and red mouth? For whom, when Mlle. Spring showed her smiling face as golden as the triumphant sun, and the flowers of the countryside opened wide, and the nestlings began to twitter in the trees—for whom, I say, did this songbird trill her sweet song? Suzette, this tiny little creature was called, and she had been put into the cage all silk and lace and velvet by a dreamy artist-hunter who'd caught her one May morning when there was much light in the air, and many opening roses.

Recaredo—paternal whim! it was not the artist's fault that his name was Recaredo!—had married her a year and a half ago. "Do you love me?"—I love you. And do you love *me*?—"With all my heart. . . ."

Glorious golden day, when the priest had joined them at last! They went out into the spring-new countryside, to taste in free-dom the pleasures of love. There, the campanulas and wild violets (whose fragrance sweetened the air of the creek-side) whispered to one another from their green-leafed windows as the lovers passed—his arm about her waist, her arm about his, their red lips in fullest bloom bestowing kisses upon one an-other. Later came the return to the great city, to the nest filled with the perfume of youth and the warmth of good fortune.

Did I mention that Recaredo was a sculptor? Well, if it slipped my mind, let me say so now. Recaredo was a sculptor.

He had his studio in the little house, and it was a profusion of marble busts and plaster casts and bronzes and terra-cottas. Sometimes passers-by would hear, through the jalousies and wrought-iron railings, a voice's song and a hammer's clear high metallic ringing. Suzette, Recaredo—the throat from which the song sprang, the blow of the hammer and the chisel.

It was an endless nuptial idyll. On tiptoe, she would come to the place he was working and pour a flood of dark hair over his neck and give him a quick peck. Quietly, quietly, he would steal to the *chaise longue* where she drowsed, her feet in slippers, her limbs clad in black silk stockings, the book open on her lap, and he would kiss her lips—a kiss that would steal her breath away and make her eyes, her ineffably glittering eyes, fly open. And in the midst of it all, the wild laughter of the blackbird, a blackbird in a cage—and when Suzette plays Chopin on her piano, the blackbird turns sad and stops singing. The wild laughter of the blackbird! It was not insignificant.

"Do you love me?"—Do you not know it? And do *you* love *me?* "I adore you!"

Now the silly animal was pouring more and more cackling on the air. They would take it out of the cage and it would flutter about the azure drawing-room, perch for a moment on the head of a plaster Apollo or the javelin of an old bronze Germanic warrior. *Tiii-iii-iiirit!* . . . *rrr-rrr-rrr-rtch fi-i-i-i-i!* . . . Oh, sometimes it could be so naughty, so very very insolent! But it was pretty when it perched on Suzette's hand and she cooed to it and petted it and kissed it and held its beak between her teeth until it flapped its wings in desperation and then scolded it (with a voice quivering with tenderness), *Monsieur Blackbird, you are a crafty fellow!*

When the two lovers were together, they would touch each other's hair, arrange a curl or a straying lock.

"Sing for me," he would say to her.

And she would sing, slowly, and although they were no more than two poor children in love, they looked so lovely, so glorious, so real—he would gaze at her as though she were his Elsa, and she would gaze at him, her Lohengrin. Because Love—oh! young bodies filled with blood and dreams—sets an azure pane of glass before one's eyes, and gives infinite joy and happiness!

How they did love one another! In his eyes, she was higher than the divine celestial stars. His love ran the entire scale of passion—it was now contained, now tempestuous in its desire, and sometimes almost mystical. Sometimes one might even call that artist a theosophist who saw in his beloved wife a thing supreme and more than human, like Rider Haggard's Ayesha. He would breathe her fragrance as though she were a flower, he would smile at her as though she were a star, and his heart would swell with pride when he held her adorable head against his breast, to think that he had conquered this bright creature who, when she sat still and pensive, was comparable only to the hieratic profile of a Byzantine empress on a gold medallion.

Recaredo loved his art. He had a passion for form. He could bring forth from the marble elegant nude goddesses with calm, white, pupilless eyes; his workshop was a city of silent statues, metal animals, terrifying gargoyles, griffons with long vinelike tails, gothic creations inspired, perhaps, by his studies in the occult and, above all—his great love!—*chinoiseries* and *japonaiseries*. In this, Recaredo was an original. I do not know what he'd have given to have been able to speak Chinese or Japanese. He was familiar with the finest albums; he had read all the good *exotistes,* he adored Loti and Judith Gautier, and he made sacrifices in order to purchase good things from Yokohama, Nagasaki, Kyoto, Nankin, and Peking: knives, pipes, masks as hideous and mysterious as the faces in his hypnoid dreams, tiny Mandarins with cucurbitacean bellies and circumflex eyes, monsters with the open, toothless mouths of batrachians, and tiny soldiers from Tartaria, with wild countenances.

"Oh!" Suzette would say to him, "I detest this house of sorcery, that terrible workshop, that strange ark that steals you away from my caresses!"

He would smile, leave his workbench, his temple of rare gimcracks, and run to the little azure drawing room, to watch his graceful living *netsuke* and hear the mad gay blackbird laugh and sing.

That morning, when he entered, he saw his sweet Suzette lying half-asleep near a large vase of roses upon a tripod stand. Was this the Beauty in the Enchanted Forest? The white throw molding a delicate body, the chestnut hair across her shoulder, the vision respiring a soft feminine fragrance: she was like a delicious figure in one of those tales that begin "Once upon a time there was a king . . ."

He awakened her:

"Suzette, my love!"

His face was all happiness; his black eyes gleamed beneath his red work fez; a letter was in his hand.

"A letter from Robert, Suzette. The scoundrel is in China! *Hong Kong, January 18 . . .*"

Suzette, still a bit drowsy, had sat up; she now took the letter from him. So that globetrotter was all the way on the other side of the world! "Hong Kong, January 18." He was so amusing. An excellent chap, Robert, with such an itch to travel! He would go to the ends of the earth. Robert, such a dear friend! Like a member of the family! He had left two years ago for San Francisco, California. Could you imagine such an idea!

She began to read.

*Hong Kong, January 18, 1888*

My dear Recaredo,

I came and saw, but I still haven't conquered.

I learned of your marriage while I was in San Francisco, and I'm so very happy for you. I leapt the pond and landed in China. I'm here as the agent for a California firm, an importer of silks, lacquers, ivories, and other such Chinese wonders. With this letter I am sending you a small gift—which, given your love of things of the Yellow Kingdom, should make you jump with glee. My very best to Suzette (I throw myself at her feet, you may tell her). Cherish the wedding gift in memory of your own. . . .

Robert

And that was that. They both laughed out loud. And the blackbird made its cage ring with an explosion of musical shrieks.

A crate had indeed arrived with the letter—a middling-size crate covered with labels and black numbers and letters that insisted to all and sundry that the contents were most terribly fragile. When the container was opened, the mystery was revealed. It was a fine porcelain bust, an admirable bust of a smiling woman, very pale and most enchanting. On the base were three inscriptions, one in Chinese characters, one in English, and the third in French: *L'Impératrice de Chine.* The empress of China! What Asian hands had molded those lovely mysterious forms? The empress's hair was pulled back tight, her face was enigmatic, her eyes low and strange, like some celestial princess with the smile of a sphinx, a long neck on dovelike shoulders covered by a silken wave embroidered with dragons, all lending magic to the white porcelain with its tones of immaculate silk. The empress of China! Suzette ran her pink fingers over the eyes of that graceful sovereign—slanting eyes, with epicanthic curves under the pure, noble arcs of the eyebrows. She was pleased. And Recaredo was proud—proud to possess his porcelain. He would make a special cabinet for it, so that it might live and reign alone, as the Venus de Milo lived and reigned in the Louvre—triumphant, sheltered most imperially by the ceiling of that sacred place.

And so he did. At one end of his workshop he made a small space with screens adorned with rice paddies and cranes. Yellow was the predominant hue—the color's entire gamut: gold, fire, Oriental ochre, autumn leaf, even the pale yellow that dies into white. At the center, on a gold and black pedestal, laughing, stood the exotic empress. Recaredo surrounded her with all his Eastern curiosities and he sheltered her beneath a large Nipponese parasol painted with camellias and widespread blood-red roses. It was so droll that one might almost laugh, to see the dreamy artist leave his pipe and his chisel and come to stand before the empress, his hands crossed over his chest, to bow as the Chinese do. Once, twice, ten, twenty times he would visit her. It was a passion. Upon a lacquer plate from Yokohama he would lay fresh flowers every day. Sometimes he would be seized with bliss before the Oriental statuette whose delightful, immobile majesty so moved him. He would study the monarch's tiniest details, the whorl of her ear, the arch of her lip, her polished nose, the epicanthus of her eyelid. An idol, was this empress! Suzette would call him from afar:

"Recaredo!"

"Coming, my love!"

Yet he would continue in rapturous contemplation of the work of art. Until Suzette came to take him away, in a flurry of kisses.

One day, the flowers in the lacquer tray disappeared as though by magic.

"Who took the flowers away?" shouted the artist from his workshop.

"I did," came the vibrant trill.

And Suzette, all pink and smiling, her black eyes flashing, pulled back a curtain to peek.

In the depths of his brain, Recaredo the sculptor said to himself:

"What the devil's got into my little wife?" She hardly ate. Those lovely books, their pages deflowered by her ivory letter-opener, lay unopened on the little black side table, pining for her soft pink hands and warm fragrant lap. She seemed to Recaredo sad. "I wonder what the devil's got into my wife?" At table, she refused to eat. She was serious—so serious! He would look at her out of the corner of his eye, and he would see those dark pupils wet, as though she were about to cry. And when she answered him, it was like a child that one has refused a bon-bon. "Here, here, what's got into my little wife, eh?"—Nothing. And that "Nothing" would be spoken in a tone of grief, and between the two syllables there would be tears.

Oh, Recaredo! What's got into your little wife is that you are an abominable, hateful man. Have you not noticed that since the empress of China arrived at your house, the little azure drawing room has turned sad, and the blackbird no longer sings, no longer laughs its pearly laughter? Suzette wakens Chopin, and slowly draws from the echoing black piano the pale, wan, sickly, melancholy song. She is jealous, Recaredo! She is sick with jealousy, which suffocates and burns her like a fiery serpent squeezing the life out of her soul. Jealous! And perhaps he understood that, because one afternoon he spoke these words to the darling of his heart, face to face, through the steam from a cup of coffee:

"You are too unfair, my love. Do I not love you with all my heart? Do you not read in my eyes what is in my soul?"

Suzette broke into tears. He *loved* her? No, no, he did not love her. The sweet, radiant hours had all flown, and the kisses, too, like birds in flight. He did not love her anymore. And what was more, he had left her—her in whom he saw his very religion, his delight, his dream, his queen, his Suzette (for those were the names he had for her)—for that other woman!

Another woman?! Recaredo leapt back, startled. She was most terribly mistaken. Was she saying this about golden-haired Eulogia, for whom he had once, long ago, written madrigals?

She shook her head: No. . . . Then did she think it was that filthy rich Gabriela, with long black hair, and skin as white as alabaster—whose bust he had done? Or Luisa, who loved to dance, Luisa with her wasplike waist, the bosom of a wet nurse, and incendiary eyes? Or the young widow Andrea, who when she laughed stuck her red feline tongue out between her gleaming ivory teeth?

No, no, it was none of those. —Recaredo was utterly perplexed, then.

"Listen to me, child, tell me the truth—who is it? You know how I adore you. My Elsa, my Juliet, my soul, my love . . ."

So much true love trembled in those halting, almost sobbing words that Suzette, with red eyes (though now dry of tears), stood up straight and tall and raised her heraldic head.

"Do you love me?"

"You know I do!"

"Then let me avenge myself on my rival. Choose, Recaredo—her or me. If it is true that you adore me, will you allow me to put her forever out of your life, so that I alone may know your passion?"

"Yes, whatever you say, my love," Recaredo answered. And seeing his jealous, stubborn little bird go out of the room, he sat sipping at his coffee, which was as black as ink.

He had not taken three sips when he heard a great crash. The noise came from his workshop.

He hurried there. And what did his astonished eyes behold? The statue had disappeared from its black and gold pedestal, and among diminutive fallen Mandarins and dangling fans, pieces of porcelain lay scattered across the floor; they crunched and cracked under Suzette's little feet—for flushed, and laughing silvery laughter, awaiting his kisses, her hair loose about her neck and shoulders, she stood among the ruins.

"I am avenged! The empress of China is dead to you now forever!"

And when the ardent reconciliation of their lips began, in the little azure drawing room all filled now with joy and mirth and happiness, the blackbird, in its cage, almost laughed itself to death.

# JUAN BUENO'S LOSSES

This is the story of a fellow called Juan Bueno—"Johnny Good-fellow," you see. People called him that because from the time he was a boy, when someone would give him a smack on one side of the head, he would turn his cheek for another. His schoolmates would take away his candies and cakes, strip him almost naked in the street, and when he got home, his parents, one on one side, one on the other, would pinch him and slap him until his ears rang. And so he grew up, until he became a man. How this poor Juan suffered! He got smallpox, but he didn't die, though his face was left looking as though a dozen hens had been pecking at it. He was sent to jail in the place of another Juan—Juan Lanas. And he suffered all this with such patience that all the townspeople, when they said *"There goes Juan Bueno!"* would laugh out loud.

And then the day came when this fellow got married.

One morning St. Joseph, in excellent humor, with his halo of glory upon his head, a new cloak upon his back, bright new sandals upon his feet, and his long flowering staff to aid him, went out for a walk through the village in which Juan Bueno lived and suffered. Christmas night was near, and St. Joseph was thinking about his baby, Jesus, and the preparations for his birth; he strolled along blessing the good believers and from time to time softly humming some carol or another. As he was walking along one street he heard a great racket, and much moaning and lamenting, and he found—oh, grievous sight!— Juan Bueno's wife, *bam, bam, bam,* giving her wretched spouse what-for.

"Halt!" called out the putative father of the divine Savior. "I'll have no such rows in my presence!"

Just that short and sweet. The fierce Gorgon grew calmer, the couple made their peace, and when Juan told his tale of woe good St. Joseph consoled him, gave him a pat or two on the back, and as he bade him good night, he said to him:

"It will all be all right, my son. Soon your troubles will be over. In the meantime, I'll help you as much as I can. You know, with whatever comes along. You can find me in the parish church, the altar to the right. So long, now."

Happy as could be, was good Juan Bueno at these tidings. And it may well be imagined that he went off, day after day, almost hour after hour, to visit the shoulder he knew he could cry on. —Lord, this has happened! Lord, this other! Lord, can you imagine what's happened now! He asked for everything, and everything was granted. Well, not quite everything, because he was too embarrassed to tell the saint that his tyrant of a wife had not lost the habit of boxing his ears. So when St. Joseph would ask him, "What's that bump on your head there?" he would laugh and change the subject. But St. Joseph knew very well . . . and he admired Juan's forbearance.

One day Juan came in terribly sad and downcast.

"I've lost," he moaned, "a bag of silver I'd put away. Could you find it for me?"

"Well, that's really St. Anthony's job, but we'll see what we can do."

And indeed when Juan returned to his house, he found the little bag of silver.

Another day Juan came in with his face all swollen and one eye practically falling out of its socket.

"The cow you gave me has disappeared!"

And the kind saint replied:

"Go home, you'll find it."

And another time:

"The mule you were so kind as to give me has run off!"

And the saint replied:

"Now, now, off home with you, the mule will come back."

And so on, for many months.

Until one day the saint was not in the cheeriest of moods, and Juan Bueno came in with his face looking like an overripe tomato and his head all squashed out of shape. When the good saint saw him, he went, "Hm, hm."

"Lord, I come to ask another favor of you. My wife has left me, and since you are so good . . ."

St. Joseph's patience with Juan Bueno had reached its limit. He lifted his flowering staff and smacked Juan Bueno on the very top of his head, at a spot exactly between his ears.

"To hell with you—where you'll find her for yourself, you blockhead!"

# FEBEA

Febea is Nero's panther.

Softly domestic, like an enormous royal house cat, she sprawls beside the neurotic Caesar, who caresses her with the delicate, androgynous hand of a cruel and corrupt emperor.

She yawns, and as she does, her flexible, wet tongue appears between her two rows of teeth—sharp, white teeth. She feeds on human flesh, and in the mansion of the sinister demigod of decadent Rome she is accustomed to seeing three red things at all time: roses, the imperial crimson, and blood.

One day, Nero brings into his presence Leticia, a snowy-skinned young virgin, the daughter of a Christian family. Leticia, fifteen, has the loveliest face, the most adorable little pink hands, divine azure eyes, the body of an ephebe about to be transformed into woman—worthy of a triumphant chorus of hexameters in one of Ovid's metamorphoses.

Nero has been seized by a whim for this woman: he desires to possess her through his art, his music, and his poetry. The maiden—mute, unmoved, serene in her white chasteness—listens to the song sung by the formidable *imperator*, who accompanies himself on his lyre, and when he, the artist on the throne, concludes his erotic hymn (rhymed according to the rules of his great master Seneca), he sees that his captive, the virgin of his lustful whimsy, remains mute and innocent, like a lily, like a modest marble vestal.

At that, the great Caesar, filled with disdain, calls Febea and points an imperial finger at the victim of his vengeance. The powerful, proud panther stretches languidly, showing her sharp, gleaming claws, and she slowly yawns, her massive jaws gaping, and then, shaking off her stupor, her tail swings slowly, from side to side.

But then a remarkable thing occurs; the beast speaks the following words to the emperor:

"Oh, admirable and potent Emperor, thy will is that of an immortal; thy aspect is that of Jupiter; thy broad forehead is crowned with the glorious laurel—but I beg that today you allow me to inform you of two things: my fangs will never act against a woman such as this, who scatters splendors like a star; and thy verses, dactyls, and pyrrhics are truly abominable."

# FUGITIVE

Pale as a wax candle, or a sickly rose. Her hair is dark, her eyes ringed with azure circles, the signs of hectic labor and the disillusionment of so many dreams now vanished. . . . Poor girl!

Her name is Emma. She married the tenor of the company, when she was very young. When her puberty bloomed, sending forth the splendid aurora of a triumphant flower, he committed her to the boards. She started out among the "extras," and she received the false kisses of the feigning lovers in the comedy. Did she love her husband? She did not quite know, herself. Constant quarrels; inexplicable rivalries from those women that Daudet might have limned; a struggle for life in a harsh, mendacious field—the field in which the garlands of one-night flowers bloom, and the rose of fleeting glory: bitter hours, half-erased, perhaps, by moments of mad revelry. The first child, the first artistic disappointment. The prince of the golden storybooks who never came! And, in a word, the outlook for a rocky road ahead, with no glimpse of a smiling future.

Sometimes she was pensive, inward. On the night of the performance she is a queen, a princess, the dauphin, or a fairy. But under the vermilion lies paleness and melancholy. The spectator sees an admirable, firm form, lustrous dark curls, a bosom swelling in harmonious curves; what he does not see is constant worry, unwavering thought, the sadness of a woman in the disguise of an actress.

She is gay for one minute, completely happy for one second. But desperation, hopelessness lies in the depths of that delicate, sweet soul. Poor thing! What does she dream of? I couldn't say.

Her looks would deceive the best observer. Do her thoughts go out to the unknown country they travel to tomorrow, to the contract she has been promised, to her children's bread? Now the butterfly of love, the breath of Psyche will never visit that languid lily; now the prince of the golden storybooks will never come—she is sure, at least of that: he will never come!

Oh, you flame almost extinguished, bird lost in the wide human forest! You will go far, far away, you will pass like a quick vision, and you will never know that there has been a dreamer near you, who has thought of you and written a page in your memory—a dreamer in love, perhaps, with that waxen pallor, that melancholy, the enchantment of that sickly face, with *you*, in a word, dove of Bohemia, who knows not which of the four winds will blow beneath your wings tomorrow!

# GYRFALCONS OF ISRAEL

In the ship's parlor, there are four small desks. From early morning, they are all occupied by four passengers, in whose faces one can distinguish a mark of their race: one would think that they have been copied from one of Drumont's *menageries*.

Nearby, several other passengers and I are conversing.

"Speak," a Frenchman says, "the word *argent*, and you will see all four of them immediately turn their heads this way."

*"Parce-que l'argent . . ."* I said aloud.

All four of the writing men's heads rose, and they looked toward our group. The proof was there. They were four heads of robust health, of good rosy color—the heads of birds of prey, with hooked noses and pursuer's eyes. One could see that those businessmen, those exploiters of prey, were possessed by their ancestral demon, and that their religion, more than in the synagogue, was celebrated in the bank, in the golden houses of Frankfurt, Vienna, Berlin, Paris, London. They were four gyrfalcons sent by the great eagles and hawks of Europe to continue the hunt in the Americas.

And each of us in the group apart—in our conversation—expressed a thought, or told a tale, or narrated a humorous anecdote.

"There's a very well-known one," someone said. "Once a little Negro fellow and a Jew were passengers on a ship carrying a load of oranges, and a terrible storm swept over them. And after many hours struggling with the tempest, they realized that they had to lighten the load. The skipper threw the oranges overboard. And then a wooden bench. And then the little Negro fellow. And then the Israelite. And it so happened that when the storm had passed, a huge sea creature was caught in those waters, near the shore. And when the beast's belly was slit open, they found the Jew sitting on a bench selling oranges to the little Negro fellow."

"I'll tell you, those people were forced by necessity to see that the prophecies came true and that Israel became the master of the world, even if they were despised and persecuted. They were looked on as worse than lepers, they were abominated, they were stoned and spat upon everywhere, they were condemned to the ghetto, enslaved, even sent to the stake. They were forbidden to have land. So they found their country in money. They were avaricious and skillful, and Shylock sharpened his indestructible knife. And as civilization has gradually advanced, the power of that race so accursed, yet so active and fearsome, has gradually increased; as the search for gold has grown more and more rapacious, the omnipotence of capital has become a reality, and a cosmopolitan aristocracy of worldwide influence has been created—an aristocracy whose parchments are checks and whose supremacy has invaded all spheres, whetting all appetites. This is the work of the falcons of Mammon, the gyrfalcons of Israel."

The four Israelites had gotten up from their chairs, but they had left, in a sign of possession, their valises upon the desktops. They were out on the deck, smoking thick cigars, speaking loudly, making grandiose gestures, and walking with great strides upon their long, broad feet. And in them there was a malign and aggressive animality.

# THE STRANGE DEATH
# OF FRAY PEDRO

Not long ago, on a visit to the monastery in a Spanish city, we chanced to pass by the community's cemetery, and the amiable friar who was acting as our cicerone pointed out to me a gravestone that bore only the following inscription: *Hic iacet frater Petrus.*

"This brother," he said, "was one of those defeated by the devil."

"That old devil who's now pretty far along in his dotage," I muttered.

"No," the friar replied. "The modern demon that hides behind Science."

And he told me the following story.

Fray Pedro of the Passion was a soul tormented by the evil spirit that instills in men the lust for knowledge. Thin, angular, nervous, pale, he divided his monastery hours between prayer, the brotherhood's disciplines, and the laboratory he was allowed to keep because of the profits it brought the community. He had, from a very young age, studied the occult sciences. In his hours of conversation he would mention, with some emphasis, the names Paracelsus and Albertus Magnus, and he held a deep admiration for that other friar, Schwartz, who did us the diabolical favor of mixing saltpeter with sulfur.

Through science, he had even managed to penetrate certain astrological and chiromantic arcana; Science had turned him from contemplation and the spirit of Scripture. The sickness of curiosity—that canker that infected our first parents—had taken up residence in his soul. Even prayer was many times forgotten, when some experiment held him, cautious, feverish, in its spell. Since he was allowed any sort of reading, and he had access to the monastery's rich library, his authors were not always the least questionable, or least misleading. And so he even decided one day to try out his powers as a water-dowser, and to test the effects of white magic. There was no doubt that his soul was put in great peril by this thirst for knowledge, this ability to forget that science was, in principle, the weapon employed by the Serpent who is the Antichrist's essential potency, and this neglect to remember that, for the true man of faith, *initium sapientiae est timor Domini.*

Oh, happy Ignorance, holy Ignorance! Fray Pedro of the Passion did not understand thy celestial virtue, which has created the certain Celestines! Huysmans has expatiated upon thee, oh virtue—who, amidst the mystical splendors and miracles of hagiography, cast a special nimbus around some of those followers of St. Francis de Paul so beloved by God.

The doctors of the Church go to great lengths to explain that in the eyes of the Holy Spirit, the souls of love are more greatly glorified than the souls of understanding. In the sublime *vitraux* of his *Physionomies des saints,* Ernest Hello has depicted those made worthy by charity, those favored by humility, those dove-like beings, as simple and white as lilies, clean of heart, poor in spirit, blessed brothers of the Lord's tiny birds, looked upon with affectionate, sisterly eyes by the pure stars of the firmament. In that marvelous book in which Durtal is converted to Catholicism, Joris-Karl—so deservedly blessed, perhaps hereafter sainted, despite his literature—clothes in paradisal splendors the lay swineherd who brings down to the sty the hosannas of choirs of archangels and the applause of the potencies of heaven. Fray Pedro of the Passion did not understand that simplicity. . . .

He, of course, believed—believed with the faith of an unquestionable believer. But the lust for knowledge goaded his spirit, propelled him to ferret out secrets of life and nature—so avidly, in fact, that he failed to remember that that thirst for knowledge, that indomitable desire to penetrate into the forbidden things, the arcana of the universe, was a sin, and a snare laid by the Evil One to prevent Fray Pedro's absolute dedication to the adoration of the Eternal Father. And the last temptation would be fatal.

The case occurred not many years ago. Into Fray Pedro's hands there came a newspaper that spoke in detail of all the progress achieved in radiography thanks to the discovery, by the German scientist Roentgen, of a process by which photographs might be taken through opaque bodies. The friar learned what was involved in the Crookes tube, the cathode-ray tube, the X-ray. He saw the facsimile of a hand whose anatomy could be seen clearly through the now-transparent skin, and the patent shape of objects contained in tightly sealed boxes and packages.

From that moment on, he was unable to keep his mind still, because something—a lust in his believer's desire, although he did not see the sacrilege in it—pricked him on. . . . How might he, Fray Pedro, get his hands on a device like the machines created by those wise men, so that he might to put into practice a certain occult thought in which his theology and his physical sciences were intermingled? . . . How, in his monastery, could he perform the thousand experiments that thronged his fevered imagination?

In the hours set aside for the liturgy, and for prayers, and for chanting, all the other members of the community would see that Fray Pedro would sometimes be lost in thought, sometimes agitated, as though startled, or frightened, sometimes his face would be flushed by a sudden rush of blood, sometimes it would have a look almost of ecstasy, and his eyes would be fixed on some high spot on the wall, or on the ground. And that was the work of the sin that had made its dwelling in the depths of that combative breast—the biblical sin of curiosity, the omnitranscendent sin of Adam as he stood beside the Tree of the Knowledge of Good and Evil. And there was much more than a mere tempest in that cranium. . . . Many a strange idea filled the brain of the poor friar who could find no way to secure one of those precious devices. What would he not give—how many years of his very life—to see one of those savants' outlandish instruments in his poor laboratory, and be able to perform the hungered-after proofs, do the magical exercises that would open the door to a new era of human wisdom and conviction! . . . He would offer more of what St. Thomas offered. . . . If the interior of our bodies could now be photographed, soon man would be able to uncover to sight the nature and origin of the soul, and, applying science to divine matters, as the Holy Spirit surely should allow him, why not also be able to capture the visions of ecstasy, and the manifestations of the celestial spirits, in their true and exact forms?

If only there'd been a Kodak at Lourdes, during the times of Bernadette's vision! If only it were possible for the camera oscura to catch those moments when Jesus, or his Holy Mother, favored certain faithful servants with their bodily presence! . . . Oh, how the unbelieving, the infidels would be convinced, and how religion would triumph!

Thus the friar meditated, thus he furrowed his brow and exerted his brain—tempted as he was by one of the fiercest princes of darkness.

And then the day came when, during one of those moments of meditation, one of those instants at which his desire was at its most intense, one of those hours when he should have been in his cell, devoting himself to discipline and prayer, there appeared before him one of the brothers of the community, bringing him a package under his habit.

"Brother," he said, "I have heard you say that you wished for one of those machines, one of those that the world is marveling at even now. Well, I have found one for you. Here you have it."

And depositing the package in the hands of the astonished Fray Pedro, the other friar vanished, without Fray Pedro's having the time to see that under the habit the brother, just as he was vanishing, had shown two hairy goat's feet.

From the day of that mysterious gift, Fray Pedro dedicated himself to his experiments. With the excuse of a chill, a catarrh, a runny nose, he missed matins, failed to attend mass. The provincial would reprimand him, and all the others would see him pass by, odd and mysterious, and fear for the health of his body and his soul.

He pursued his *idée fixe*. He tested the machine on himself, on fruits, on keys tucked inside books, and the other usual things. Until one day . . .

Or one night, rather, the unfortunate friar dared, *at last,* to test *his idea*. Stealthily, with muffled footsteps, he made his way to the sanctuary. He slipped into the nave and went to the altar where, in its tabernacle, the Holy Sacrament was displayed. He took out the goblet. He picked up a thin, round communion host. And he rushed back to his cell.

The next day, before Fray Pedro's cell, stood the archbishop with the provincial.

"Most holy father," the provincial was saying, "we have found Fray Pedro dead. He had not been quite right in the head of late. It was those studies of his that I believe were not good for him."

"Has your reverence seen this?" said the archbishop, showing him a photographic plate he had picked up from the floor, on which there appeared, with his arms freed from the nails and a sweet look in the divine eyes, the image of Our Lord Jesus Christ.

# THE NYMPH

*A Parisian story*

In the castle recently purchased by Lesbia, that capricious and fiendish actress whose extravagances have given the world so much to talk about, six friends found ourselves one evening at the table. Our Aspasia was presiding, and just then she was entertaining herself by sucking, like a little girl, on a moist lump of sugar, white between her rosy fingertips. The hour for the *chartreuse* had come. In the glasses on the table it looked like nothing less than dissolved jewels, and the light of the candelabras played among the half-empty wineglasses, where some of the burgundy's purple, the champagne's boiling gold, the *mente*'s liquid emeralds still remained.

After a good meal, there was enthusiastic talk of some promising artists. We were all artists, some more, some less, and there was even an obese sage who flaunted on the whiteness of his immaculate shirtfront the large knot of a monstrous cravat.

"Ah, yes, Frémiet!" someone said.

And from Frémiet the conversation passed on to his animals, his masterful brush, two bronze dogs, both nearby, one of which, nose to the ground, was tracking its prey, the other, as though looking at the hunter, raising its head and the thinness of its stiff, erect tail. Who of us mentioned Myron? It was the sage, who recited an epigram from Anacreon in Greek: "Shepherd, pasture thy flock at a little distance, lest thinking thou seest the cow of Myron breathe, thou shouldst wish to lead it away with thine oxen."

Lesbia finished sucking on her sugar cube, and with an Argentine burst of laughter, said, "Bah! Give me satyrs. How I would like to give life to my bronzes! And if that were possible, my lover would be one of those hairy demigods. But I tell you, even more than satyrs, I adore centaurs, and I'd let myself be carried away by one of those robust monsters just to hear the groans of the satyr I'd been stolen from, for his flute-song would be filled with sadness."

The sage interrupted.

"Satyrs and fauns, hippocentaurs and sirens, have existed, as have salamanders and the Phoenix."

We all laughed, but through the peals of laughter there rose, irresistible, enchanting, the notes of Lesbia's, whose lovely flushed face seemed to beam with glee.

"Yes," the sage went on, "what right have we moderns to deny those facts asserted by the ancients? The gigantic dog seen by Alexander, as tall as a man, is as real as the Kraken that lives at the bottom of the seas. When St. Antony went at the age of ninety in search of the old hermit Paul, who lived in a cave— Lesbia, don't laugh—he found himself one day making his way through the barren waste, leaning on his walking stick, not knowing where to find the man he was searching for. And after walking for so many days, do you know who told him what road it was he should follow? A centaur, 'half man and half horse,' says St. Jerome, who has told us of this wonder. The creature spoke as though it was angry; it fled with such speed that soon it was out of sight—galloping away, the monster, 'its hair blowing in the wind and its belly low to the ground.' On that same journey, St. Antony saw a satyr, 'a little man of strange figure, beside a streambed; he had a hooked nose, a harsh, wrinkled forehead, and the extremities of his misshapen body ended in goat's feet.'"

"A perfect description," Lesbia whispered to me, "of that charming M. de Cocureau, future member of the Institute!"

The sage went on:

"This, as I say, is attested to by St. Jerome, who in the times of Constantine the Great led a live satyr into Alexandria, its body being preserved when it died. It was seen, too, by the emperor in Antioch."

Lesbia had refilled her glass with *crème de menthe*, and she was wetting her tongue in the green liqueur like a feline might.

"Albertus Magnus says that in his day two satyrs were captured in the mountains of Saxony. Enrico Zormano declares that in the lands of Tartary there were men with a single foot, and a single arm in their chest. Vincencio saw a monster brought to the king of France; it had the head of a dog (Lesbia laughed), but its thighs, arms, and hands were as smooth and hairless as our own (Lesbia squirmed like a little girl being tickled); it ate cooked meat and drank wine like water."

"*Colombine*!" cried Lesbia. And Colombine entered, a little lap dog that looked like a cotton ball. Its mistress picked it up, and amid the explosions of the guests' laughter, said "Did you hear that, my love? A monster with your head!"

And she kissed the dog on the mouth, while the animal wriggled and flared its nostrils as though filled with voluptuousness.

"And the first-century historian Philegon," the sage concluded elegantly, "affirms the existence of two species of hippocentaurs, one like elephants."

"Enough erudition," said Lesbia. And she finished her *crème de menthe*.

So far I had not opened my mouth, but I was gay.

"Oh!" I exclaimed. "Give me nymphs! I should like to gaze upon their nakedness in the woods and groves and around pools of water, even if, like Actaeon, I were torn to pieces by dogs. But there are no such things as nymphs!"

That happy concert ended in an exodus of sparkling laughter, and of guests.

"So you say," Lesbia said to me, her faun's eyes burning into me, her voice low, so that only I could hear. "Nymphs exist. You'll see them for yourself!"

It was a spring day. I was wandering through the castle's parklike grounds, looking no doubt like a confirmed dreamer. The sparrows were shrieking among the new lilacs, attacking the beetles that defended themselves from the birds' beaks with their shells of emerald, their armor of gold and iron. Among the roses, carmine, vermilion, the penetrating fragrance of their sweet perfumes; farther on, the violets, in large masses, with their peaceful color and their odor of virginity. Farther yet, the tall trees, the thick foliage filled with the buzzing of bees, the statues in the shadows, the bronze discus throwers, the muscular gladiators in their superb gymnastic postures, the perfumed gazebos covered with twining vines, the porticos, lovely *faux*-Ionic, caryatids all white and lascivious, and vigorous telamons of the Atlantic order, with broad backs and gigantic thighs. I was wandering through the labyrinth of these enchantments when I heard a sound, there in the obscurity of the woods, by the pool where there are white swans like alabaster carvings, and others half of whose long neck is ebony, like a white leg in a black stocking.

I drew closer. Was I dreaming? Oh, Numa! I felt what you felt, when you saw Egeria in her grotto the first time.

In the center of the pool, among the disturbed and restless stirring of the startled swans, there was a nymph, a real nymph, her rosy body bobbing in the crystalline water. Her thighs and maidenly girdle sometimes appeared gilded by the dull light that managed to penetrate the leafy canopy. Oh! I saw lilies, roses, snow, gold; I saw an ideal with form and body, and I heard, among the echoing burbling of the wounded water, a burlesque and musical laughter that stirred my blood.

Suddenly the vision fled—the nymph emerged from the pool, much like Cytherea on her wave, and, gathering her hair, which cascaded diamonds, she ran through the rose bushes, behind the lilacs and violets, past the leafy glades, and was concealed from my sight, ay!, by a turning in the path. And there stood I, lyric poet, eluded faun, watching the grand alabaster fowl sport as though mocking me, stretching out toward me their long necks, on the end of which gleamed the burnished agate of their beaks.

Later, we friends of that night at Lesbia's lunched. Among us, triumphant, with his shirtfront and his magnificent dark cravat, the obese sage, future member of the Institute.

And suddenly, while everyone chatted about Frémier's latest

bronze at the Salon, Lesbia exclaimed in her bright Parisian voice:

"Tea! As Tartarin says: the poet has seen nymphs! . . ."

Everyone looked at her in astonishment, and she was looking at me, looking at me like a cat, and laughing like a little girl being tickled.

# THE BLACK SOLOMON

Then—as Solomon is about to go to his last rest, and in a hall of crystal weary groups of satans sleep—one evening he is suddenly puzzled: before his eyes, like a statue wrought of iron, there arises an extraordinary figure, a djinn or prince of darkness. What djinn, what shade-born prince is unknown to him? In the presence of this apparition, the power of his ring is rendered useless. He asks:

"Thy name?"

"Solomon."

Yet greater surprise and bewilderment for the wise king. He then notes the rare beauty of his face, his mien, his eyes—all so like his own. He would venture that it is his own person, sculpted in rarest jet.

"Yes," said the wondrous black Solomon. "I am thy likeness, thy equal, save that I am in all things thy opposite. Thou art the master of one side of the earth's disc, but I possess the other. Thou lovest truth; I rule in falsehood, whose existence is the only reality. Thou art beautiful as the day, and handsome as the night. My shadow is white. Thou receivest thy understanding of things from the illuminated side of the sun; I, from the side that is hidden. Thou read'st in the visible moon, I in the unseen. Thy djinni are monstrous; mine shine in splendor among the prototypes of beauty. Thou hast in thy ring four stones, given thee by the angels; the demons set in mine a drop of water, a drop of blood, a drop of wine, and a drop of milk. Thou believest that thou hast understood the language of the animals; I know that thou hast understood only the sounds, not the arcana of their tongue."

Solomon, mute thus far, exclaimed:

"By God Who is great! Maleficent spirit, which against Him and His greatest creation doth so blaspheme, how darest thou assert such a thing? Men may be polluted by error, but the animals of the Lord live in purity. How could their innocent thoughts have deceived me?"

And the black Solomon replied:

"Call up," he said, "that angel in the form of a whale that gave thee the stone on which is written *Let all creatures praise the Lord.*"

Solomon placed the ring against his head and the misshapen angel appeared.

"What is thy real name?" asked the black Solomon.

And the angel replied:

"Perhaps."

And it came unmade. Solomon called all the animals, and he said to the peacock:

"What were thy words to me?"

And the peacock replied:

"Judge not, lest thou be judged."

And he asked the same of all the beasts. And these were their replies:

THE NIGHTINGALE: "Moderation is the greatest good."

THE TURTLE-DOVE: "It would have been better for many beings had they not seen the light of day."

THE FALCON: "He who hath no pity for others shall find none for himself."

THE BIRD NAMED SYRDAR: "Sinners: convert to the love of God."

THE SWALLOW: "Do good, and thou shalt be rewarded."

THE PELICAN: "Praised be God in heaven and on earth."

THE DOVE: "All things pass; God alone is eternal."

THE BIRD NAMED QATA: "He who remains silent is more certain of speaking true."

THE EAGLE: "However long our life is, it comes always to an end."

THE CROW: "One lives one's life best far from men."

THE COCK: "Think on God, frivolous men."

———

"There, you see!" exclaimed the black Solomon. "You, peacock, you lie. And among the animals, as among men, trust leads lambs into the embrace of wolves. You, nightingale, you lie. Nothing triumphs save the exercise of power. Moderation is called mediocrity, or cowardice. Lions, great cataracts of falling water, tempests, are not moderate. You, turtle dove, you lie, for you do not speak of the weak. Weakness is the only crime, joined with poverty, on the face of the earth. You, falcon, lie seven times over. Pity can be imprudence. Woe to the pitying! Hatred is powerful; hatred is what saves us. Smash the small; put the wounded out of their misery; give no bread to the hungry; cut the legs off any man who limps. It is thus that the world may be brought to perfection. You, syrdar, lie. You are a bird of hypocrisy. God is named X; he is named Zero. You, swallow, lie. You are the falcon's lover. You, pelican, lie. You are the syrdar's brother. And you, dove, lie. You are the pelican and syrdar's mistress. You, qata, lie. The creature who roars or thunders, should not keep quiet; that creature is always right. Eagle, crow, and cock: I shall lock you all into the cage of unreason. That is as certain as that Solomon in his glory cannot overpower me, and that the cock's eye cannot penetrate the surface of the earth to find springs of water.

The beasts disappeared. The satans, now awake, peered through the crystal walls of their hall. Solomon, with vague anxiety, contemplated his own dark likeness in that Other who had spoken and whom he was unable to dominate with his spells. And the Black One was about to depart, when he asked again:

"What didst thou say thy name was?"

"Solomon," the Other answered smiling. "But I have another name as well."

"Yes?"

"Friedrich Nietzsche."

The sage grew desolate, and prepared to ascend, with the angel of infinite wings, to contemplate the truth of the Lord.

The Simurg flew in on rapid wing.

"Solomon, Solomon: thou hast been tempted. But rejoice, and beest thou consoled. Thy hope lies in David!"

And Solomon's soul melted into God.

# THUS SPAKE AHASUERUS

In a land whose name I do not wish to remember, and which likely appears in none of the cartographic atlases in any library, the inhabitants wished to know what the best form of government might be. These inhabitants were so rational in their pursuit that despite the many gray-haired wise men and illustrious politicians in their land, they went off to consult a poet, who answered them in the following way:

"Although I am terribly occupied just now, composing an epithalamion to a jasmine, a salutation to a nymph, and an epigram for the statue of a faun, I shall think about this, and soon I shall suggest how you might best continue. I ask for but three days before I give you my reply."

And since this poet was more of a poet than King Solomon himself, he spoke and understood the language of the stars, the plants, the animals, and all the beings in nature. And so, on the first day, he went off to the country, meditating on what the best form of government might be. Under a leafy oak tree he found a lion, resting before lunch, like Charlemagne under his pine tree.

"King," the poet said to him, "I know that Your Majesty might almost be Pedro de Braganza with a mane, and so I ask you—What is the best form of government for a nation?"

"Ingrate!" the lion answered. "I never thought that since the day Plato cast you humans so cruelly from your republic, you poets might doubt the advantages of a monarchy! Without the pomp and majesty of royalty and all its grandeur, you would have neither purple nor crimson nor gold nor ermine to deck your verses. Unless, that is, you prefer the bloody red of revolutions, the silver leaf of constitutions, and the white of Monsieur Carnot's shirt front, for example. Long-haired Numen has forbidden men to speak the word 'democracy' within his empire. Republics are bourgeois, and someone has said that democracy smells bad. For their dryness, Monsieur Thiers would have all Hymetus' bees routed. The honorable George Washington, or the equally honorable Abraham Lincoln, can be hymned only by a splendid savage like Walt Whitman. Victor Hugo, who heaped such praise on that immense and terrible Hydra called 'the people,' has been, nonetheless, the most aristocratic spirit of this century. So far as I'm concerned, the happiest countries are those that are respectful to tradition—and since the world was born, there is nothing that gives greater majesty to jungles than the roar of lions. And there you have my opinion, Mister Poet—absolute monarchy."

Soon after, the pensive poet came across a tiger, its paws resting on the bones of an ox he had just had for dinner.

"I," said the tiger, "recommend military dictatorship. You crouch in the branches of a tree or behind a nice big boulder, and when a herd of free buffalo passes by, or sheep, you shout *Long live freedom!* and pounce on the juiciest animal in the bunch, using your teeth and claws the very best you can."

Not long afterward, a crow came by and began to pick through the bones the tiger had left.

"I like republics," the crow exclaimed. "And especially the republics of Latin America, because they're the ones that leave the most bodies on the field of battle. We have these feasts so often that there's nothing better under the sun, unless it might be the slaughters of barbarian tribes. And I vow on Maître Corbeau that that's the truth."

From the branches of a laurel tree came the voice of a dove, answering the poet:

"I personally am theocratic. Incarnated in my body, the Holy Spirit descends upon the Pontiff, who is the highest of all priests and three times king, in the light of God. The happiest nation would be that land whose shepherd and guide is, as in Biblical times, the Creator of all things."

But the fox had an answer to that:

"My dear sir, if the people elect a president they will have acted very wisely. And if they proclaim a man king, and crown him, they will have merited my applause. I beg you to take my warmest felicitations to either one—oh, and tell them that if they send me a fat hen on the day of the celebration I will most gratefully accept it, and eat it feathers and all."

A bee answered:

"Once we bees tried to depose our queen—a monarch very much like Queen Victoria, because you no doubt realize that a hive has a great resemblance to the England of today in its form of government. But that one attempt went so badly for us that all that harvest's honey was spoiled. And what's more, we had an increase in drones and went through the worst time of our lives. Since then, we've taken an oath to be sensible about all this—our cell is always hexagonal and our leader is a woman."

"Long live the republic!" shouted a swallow, picking at the fruit on the tree it sat on. "Citizens of the forest, attention! I ask for the floor! Is it possible that since the Day of Creation we have been subject to the most heinous tyranny? My fellow animals! Our hour has come—progress shows us the road that must be followed. I come from the cities in which thinking bipedals live, and I have seen the advantages of universal suffrage and parliaments. I have seen a vessel called a ballot box, and I can tell you great things about *habeas corpus*. Who of you can deny the advantages of self-government and home rule? Lions and eagles must be brought down. Down with eagles! Miserable birds, begone! Let us declare the republic of the United States of the Mountain and the Air, let us proclaim liberty, equality, and fraternity. Let us establish our own government, of the animal, by the animal, and for the animal. And I will be happy to be elected this nation's first magistrate—as could be the respectable mister bear, or the very distinguished mister fox. But now—to arms! War, war, war! And later, we shall make peace."

"Poet," said the eagle, "have you heard what this demagogue says? I believe in monarchy—and why should I not, being myself a monarch of the skies and having always accompanied such crowned conquerors as Caesar and Bonaparte? I have seen the grandeur of the empires of Rome and France. My image is on the coats of arms of Russia and the great empire of the Germans. *Ave Caesar* is my finest salutation."

To which the poet objected that as the bird of Jupiter, if he spoke Latin in the land of the Yankees, it would be to cry out *E pluribus unum*.

"The best form of government," said the ox, "is that which imposes no yoke and requires no mutilation."

And the gorilla:

"Form of government? None. Tell that country of yours to return to the heart of nature, to abandon that system it calls civilization and return to the primitive, savage life, in which I believe it will find true freedom. As for me, I protest against Darwin's dreadful slander against my species, for I find nothing good about what the human animal does and thinks."

On the second day, the poet heard other opinions:

THE ROSE: "All we know of politics is what the four-o'clock whispers at nightfall and the sunflower says during the day. I, the empress, have my court, my splendors, and my poets to praise me. I admire both Nero and Louis XIV. I love this splendid name: Pompadour. I have no other opinion than this: Beauty above all things."

THE FLEUR-DE-LIS: "I defer to Her Most Holy Christian Majesty!"

THE OLIVE TREE: "Frankly, I advise a republic. A good republic, that is the ideal. But I must also tell you that in most of your republican nations not a year goes by that I am not left without a single branch, for the people pull them off to adorn their temples to peace . . . after the yearly war."

THE COFFEE TREE: "Compare the millions of hundredweights that were exported from Brazil in the time of dom Pedro with those that are exported today—that will be my answer."

THE SUGAR CANE: "I advise a republic, and I beg you all to work to free Cuba."

THE CARNATION: "And what about General Boulanger?"

THE PANSY: "The dress I wear, the color I bear, that is my opinion."

THE CORN: "Republic."

THE STRAWBERRY: "Monarchy."

That night, the poet consulted the stars, among which there exists the most luminous of hierarchies. Venus had the same opinion as the rose. Mars acknowledged the autocracy of the Sun. The only thing that disturbed the majesty of the skies was the fleeting demagogy of the meteors.

On the third day, the poet made his way to the city, where he was to deliver his reply to the inhabitants there, and as he walked, he thought: Which of all the multitude of opinions he had heard was the best, and which would be the most suitable for bringing happiness to a nation?

Suddenly he saw an old man as hunchbacked as an archway coming toward him. He had a long, long beard, as white as a torrent of snow, and above his white beard there was a curved Semitic nose, like a red beak about to peck his lips.

"Ahasuerus!" exclaimed the poet.

The old man, who was hurrying along with the aid of a thick walking staff, stopped. And when the poet explained to him what had brought him to this road today, the Wandering Jew spoke to the poet the following words:

"You surely know the saying that the Devil is not as clever as he is because he's the Devil, but because he's old. I am not the Devil, and indeed I hope one day to enter the kingdom of Heaven, but I have lived so long that my experience is greater than the waters of the ocean. And as bitter! But I must tell you that with respect to the way to govern nations, I couldn't really say whether this way is better than that. Since I have been wandering the earth I have seen the same evils in republics, empires, and kingdoms, for when the men on the throne, or in power because they were elected by the people, are not guided by wise principles of justice and right action and truth, only evil can come of it. I have seen good kings who were like fathers to their subjects, and presidents like the plagues of Egypt upon their people. The commonplace that each country has the government it deserves should always make one stop and think. It is true that when Attila passes, the nations tremble like poor flocks of sheep. Sometimes a Haroun al-Raschid comes, and sometimes a Louis XI. There are many republics, from the Republic of Plato to the republic of Boulanger, and from Venice to Haiti. . . . Nations are very much like children, and like women. One day they will love monarchy because of its golden crown, and the next they will adore the republic because of its red beret.

"Men slice open bellies with bayonets and shatter skulls with bullets. Today they grab up someone to direct their affairs and set him in a chair high above his station, and then not long after they pull him down and raise another. Or they hold celebrations of trickery and sham and call it democracy, and carry the chosen one—whom they call 'elected'—in triumph through the streets, to the sound of peaceful fifes and drums. I tell you, humanity has no idea what it is doing. In nature, one sees the order and justice of the eternal divine intelligence. Not so in the work of humans, where the reason that enlightens them seems to make them descend ever deeper into the abyss of darkness. That is why I must tell you, it is not the form of government that brings happiness to a people, but rather those who direct their destinies, whether they be heads of republican states or monarchs of divine right."

The old Jew said many more things, with words that seemed as wise sometimes as Solomon's, sometimes as Pero Grullo's. And so eloquent was the ancient man about the politics of the world that the poet repeated his advice word for word to the citizens gathered to hear his reply.

And no sooner had he stopped talking when a storm of cries and protests rose around him. A red citizen who had read many books from ancient Greece set a crown of roses upon the poet's brow, and then those citizens so judicious that they

consulted a master of poetry for answers to their public ques-
tions threw him, with great jubilation, out of the city, to the
smiles of the flowers, the cackling of the birds, and the aston-
ishment of the shining theories that run through the azure of
the stars.

# THE STORY OF
# MARTIN GUERRE

"Is it a story?" asked Pérez Sedano's wife.

"A true story," replied old M. Poirier. "A true story that is hard to believe true. How is it possible for a woman, no matter how many years have passed, to confuse her husband with another man?"

Pérez Sedano, recently married, happy, healthy, and cheerful, looked at his wife.

"Impossible!" she exclaimed, giving him, in turn, a speaking look.

"Well, I shall tell it one more time," M. Poirier said, "Just as I read it when I was a law student, in that work by Jean de Coras titled *De l'arrêt mémorable du parlament de Toulouse, contenant une histoire prodigieuse.* I assure you that it is as interesting as a novel. . . ."

Back in the year 1539, in Artigat, in the diocese of Rieux, in Gascogne, a wedding was celebrated between two people, very young and very much in love—Martin Guerre and Bertrande de Rols. They lived together for ten happy years—ten years!—and then suddenly the husband, *le petit mari,* disappeared, and no one knew where he might have gone. Eight years later, a man appeared who resembled him completely—same size, same features, same "distinguishing marks," as they are called: a scar on the forehead, a dental defect, a blotch on the left ear, and so on.

What joy for the abandoned wife, who took him in her arms and into her bed, and everything went swimmingly. But when three years had passed, it was discovered that this false husband was named Arnoult du Thil, alias *Pansette,* and that he had managed to dupe everyone, especially the wife of Martin Guerre. Who, speaking of the devil, appeared one day to reclaim his rights.

And so the case went to trial.

Of twenty-five to thirty witnesses, nine, or perhaps ten, swore that the impostor was Martin Guerre, seven or eight that he was du Thil, and the rest wavered. Two witnesses testified that a soldier from Rochefort had passed through Artigat not long before and was astonished to see du Thil passing himself off as Martin Guerre; the soldier had said quite loudly that this man was an impostor, because Martin Guerre was in Flanders, with a wooden leg, having been wounded by a bullet at St. Quentin on the mission to take St. Laurens. But almost everyone testified that when the defendant arrived in Artigat, he greeted everyone he met by name, without having ever seen or known them. And to those who said they didn't know him he would remind them: "Do you not recall when we were at such-and-such a place, ten, fifteen, or twenty years ago, and that we did such-and-such, and So-and-so was there, and he said such-and-such?"

And on that first night, he even said to his alleged wife: "Go fetch me my white breeches if you will, the ones lined with white silk that I left in such-and-such a trunk when I left." And lo and behold, there were the breeches.

The court found itself in great perplexity, but the good and powerful God, showing that He is always ready to assist Justice and not allow such an extraordinary transgression to remain hidden and unpunished, ordained that as though by a miracle the true Martin Guerre should appear—and Martin Guerre, come from Spain with a wooden leg, just as the soldier had said a year earlier, presented a complaint against the impostor.

The judges took him aside and asked him to secretly reveal to them something more private, which neither one side's interrogations nor the other's had yet uncovered. And when he had done this, they brought in the prisoner and asked him to do the same. He replied in the same way as the first, which astounded all who heard him and made people think that du Thil knew his bit of magic.

"There was, in truth," writes Jean de Coras, a man of un-

THE STORY OF MARTIN GUERRE

questioned and profound probity, in his curious annotations to this trial, "great reason to think that this well-prepared fellow had conversation with some familiar spirit. There can be no doubt that among the extraordinary and abominable tyrannies which Satan, since the creation of the world, has cruelly exercised against men, to entrap them and draw them to his kingdom, is that of the great storehouse of magic, an ever-open shop that traffics in such merchandise, and gives of it to men so prodigally that many of them have been reverenced with great wonder, and persuading many men that all is possible through the virtue of magic."

The judges called Bertrande, who, suddenly, after setting eyes on the man who had just arrived, cried out in desolation and, trembling like a leaf in the wind, her face bathed in tears, ran to embrace him, begging his forgiveness for the error which, through imprudence, though led by du Thil's seductions, impostures, and perparations, she had committed; and she accused Martin's sisters above all, for they had been too quick to believe, and had vowed that the prisoner was their brother.

The newcomer, though having wept to find himself once more beside his sisters, was unmoved by Bertrande's exceedingly great tears and moans, and showed not one groat's-worth of softness of heart for her. Indeed, on the contrary, he drew himself up and stood austere and aloof. And without deigning to look at her, he said to her: "Put aside that crying and weeping, which I neither ask for nor allow to move me, and do not put the blame upon my sisters, for neither father, nor mother, nor brothers and sisters should know their child or brother so well as a wife should know her husband, and no one is more blameworthy than you." And for this, the judges did censure Bertrande, but at this first encounter they could never soften Martin's heart, or his austerity.

The imposter du Thil, once discovered, received the following sentence: "The court . . . has condemned du Thil to make honorable confession to the church at Artigat, and there, kneeling and in his shirt, with head and feet naked, with the noose about his neck and holding in his hands a torch of burning wax, ask forgiveness of God, the king, and justice, and of Martin

Guerre and Bertrande. And this having been done, du Thil shall
be delivered up to the executor of high justice, who shall lead
him through the streets and other places of said locality of Arti-
gat, and, noose about his neck, shall lead him to the house of
Martin Guerre, where, on the scaffold, he shall be hanged and
garrotted, and after that, his body burned. . . . Pronounced this
12th day of September in the year of our Lord 1560."

The condemned man, led from the court to Artigat, was
heard by the judge at Rieux, to whom he made a long confes-
sion of his guilt. He testified, however, that what had first
led him to his project had been that seven or eight years ear-
lier, upon his return to the countryside around Picardy, some
there, who had been Martin Guerre's close friends and even
family, had taken him for Guerre, and thinking that many oth-
ers might also be deceived, he conceived the idea of making in-
quiries and informing himself, as cautiously as possible, about
Martin's profession, his wife, his relatives, what he would say
and how say it, what he had done before he'd left home—but
the condemned man always denied being a necromancer, or
having used spells or enchantments or any other sort of magic.
In addition, he confessed to having been *un fort mauvais
garnement*—a right rascal, you might say—in every way. As he
was about to climb up to the scaffold, he asked forgiveness of
Martin and Bertrande, with a great show of repentance and de-
testation of his deed, and begged God in a loud voice for mercy
through his son, Jesus Christ. And he was executed, his body
hanged and then burned.

"How extremely interesting!" everyone exclaimed.

"And to think," the acid Mme. Poirier said, with just a hint of
sarcasm, "that she might have been happier with the other one."

"As for my little wife," Pérez Sedano concluded, "I think
that however hard the impostor tried, she would never confuse
him with me. . . ."

And the little wife of Pérez Sedano, laughing, agreed with
what her husband had just said—but she turned as red-faced as
a rose. . . .

# Prose Poems

# IN THE ENCHANTED LAND

Far away in that tropical land, on the bank of a lagoon a melancholy willow stands, its green hair trailing in the water that mirrors forth the branches and the sky as though in its depths there were a land enchanted.

Two by two, birds and lovers visit the old willow, and there my eyes once gazed upon an evening when the sun was but a violet whisper fading away over the great volcano and the soft ripples, a waning rose like the loving light's shy caress, and my ears heard a rustle of kisses near the tree.

There they were, a young man and a maid, lover and beloved, on a rustic bench under the canopy of the tree. Before them lay the tranquil pool, with its flock of boats, the trembling trees along its banks, and beyond, amidst the green leaves, a picturesque chalet.

The lady was all loveliness; he, a noble lad caressing with his fingers and his lips the nymph's graceful hands and jet-black hair.

And over the two ardent souls there chattered, in their rhythmic, wingèd tongue, the birds. And the immense sky drew close, with its riot of clouds, its feathers of gold, its wings of fire, its fleece of imperial purple; the azure sky, fleur-de-lis'd with opal, poured over them the magnificence of its pomp, the sovereignty of its august grandeur.

Under the waters, like a whirlpool of living blood, swift fishes flitted, fins of gold.

In the evening splendor, the landscape seemed draped in soft gauze by the sun, and the two lovers were the scene's soul:

he, dark-haired, dashing, vigorous, with the sort of silken beard that women love to touch; she, fair-skinned—a verse by Goethe!—dressed in a lustrous grey gown, and upon her breast a fresh rose quivering, like her rose-colored lips, for his longed-for kiss.

# THE HONEYMOON SONG

My lady: That moon's honey is fashioned by the bees of the azure garden, which flit among the twinkling petals of the stars to suck their nectar. They fly, in iridescent swarms, from the blooms of Aldebaran to the daisies of the Bear, to the trembling, flickering carnation of Sirius. But the lightest, the most delightful, the most beautiful and paradisal of the bees alight upon the beckoning, sacred, mysterious calyx of Venus' golden rose!

My lady: The painter Spiridon has limned the blessèd land of happiness: a calm lake, a boat, a lass, a lad, and love to row them. Good breeze, good day, my lady!

There is a delicate, a divine lily that possesses all the proud candor of nuptial jewels, the paleness of the votive lamp that illuminates the altar, the transparency of the bridal veil, the perfumes and supreme enchantment of the newlyweds' sweet dreams. This lily is hope and happiness foreseen. A thousand times fortunate, she who can come to the end of her life with that celestial flower intact and fresh. For the wind is sometimes so bitter, and some nights there is so much frost! And at those times, when they see the holy, ideal lily wither and fade, poor souls lift their eyes to the great God. Oh! may powerful, invincible love guide you! Good breeze, good day, my lady!

Sweet nuptial dreams of adoration that make the pensive, virginal bride swoon!

Chaste lilies molded of the fine powdery snow from the highest peak of the sacred mountain!

Doves that nest in the green leaves of the myrtle!

Serene star of love!

Of all of you I ask: Is it not true that a breath of divinity passes, giving delight to the world's soul, when on a quiet night, in a solemn wood, the nightingale sings the crystalline melody, the lovely verses, of the song of the honeymoon?

# BLOODY

This evening has been all rose. From the broad whorl of its grand palette, the sky has chosen all the rose-pinks possible, but there has also been the blood-red of the bloody king, a furious red bursting from the sun in its death-agony, tinging the sea a sanguine scarlet. And then, after the wheel of crimson fire, of fire condensed and vibrant, unique and occidental, sank into the waves, the fantasy of reds dimmed, too, and the glare of hot, offensive yellows faded.

Slowly, almost imperceptibly, the scarlets dissolved into carmine, which gradually, in chromatic languor, swooned into pomegranate, then flamingo's wing, then moon-rose, then sweet anemic tea-rose.

The sea reflected back the glory of the setting sun. On the horizon, the curve that marks the eyes' limit seemed not consumed by flame. A thick dark cloud had split into two rotundas, upheld by a visionary architecture like none seen before on land. And there was a gigantic balustrade, above a pavement stained as though by a recent, luminous decapitation.

Birds of the hecatomb—an eagle as orange as though it had passed through a rainbow—spread their wings, whose tips seemed still wet from a shower of ruby-colored water. In one corner of the sky, where the hue was faintest and most languorous, the soft color brought to my mind a distant recollection. It was the memory of a rose petal, bloodless and forgotten, between the pages of a book of hours. It was a book printed in Brussels, of ancient manufacture. The page on which that relic rested, perhaps a page from some antique romance, had a red capital of exquisite archaic beauty, like those that illuminate missals and antiphonaries.

Then suddenly, the swift white flash of an electric light woke me from my vague thoughts. Behind the nearby hills, crepuscular mists heralded the night.

The city was turning on its lights. The last vibration of the evening's death throes was a fainting, desolate rose.

# SIREN-CATCHERS

Catch me one, oh satyr fishermen!, with gleaming scales, a metallic, iridescent radiance like the nacreous gold of sumptuous herrings. Catch me one with a tail, two-forked, that will make me dream of sea-peacocks, and gleaming flanks with fins like Oriental fans studded with pearls. Catch me one with green hair, like the hair of Lorelei, and eyes of strange phosphorescence and magical sparks; one whose salty mouth will kiss and bite when it is not singing songs like those that o'ermatched Ulysses' cunning. Catch me one with marmoreal breasts crowned with pink rosebuds, and with arms, like two divine white pythons, that will clasp me and bear me off to the depths, where we will live in an abyss of ardent pleasures in the hidden country where the palaces are made of pearls, of coral, and of nacre.

But those two satyrs sporting on the coast of some unknown Lesbos, Tempe, or Amathusia are not good fishermen. One, old and muscular, leans on a thick knotty stick and looks with comic puzzlement at the frightened, bedraggled siren his companion has fished up. The other pulls in the net, and seems unhappy with his catch. Water streams from the siren's hair, making concentric circles on the sea. Upon the two-horned, hairy heads, kissed by the day, a fresh leaf-growth spreads, while in a gala of gold, above clouds, land, and waves, the torch of the sun is upraised.

# OCEAN IDYLL

Beyond the solitary isles where voyaging birds rest, in the land ruled by Leviathan, upon a rock the Conqueress sits enthroned, in the irresistible omnipotence of her nakedness.

On her white skin is salt, the marine perfume of Anadyomene, and the serpent of the waves reveals once more, loving yet humiliated, the sovereign triumph of feminine enchantment: Europa on the bull's back, the Beauty and the Beast, the modern painter's Mundana, who, naked, cuts the lion's claws.

A hairy, scaly triton makes his hoarse seashell sing, while the monster is caressed by the temptress, the Woman, who, under the immense sky, offers her fatal loveliness in the abandon of her supreme immodesty.

# THE SONG OF WINTER

It is raining—black clouds across the azure sky, hiding the sun, that light which, illuminating and warming bodies, warms and illuminates souls.

It is cold; the day is dark. There is cold in the heart, too, and snow in the soul.

Raw winter, with its snows and the north wind that lashes, withers flowers.

In winter, the days are dark as nights.

In the tomb, there is eternal night.

When there is sweet sadness, we sleep, and then we dream and the dreams are rosy.

In the tomb, where we shall also sleep, what, oh God!, will the dreams be like?

And when we awaken, we smile at the memory of the delights we saw in our sleep. Then, we frown and our eyes darken, for we meet reality—the dreams were only dreams.

In the tomb, shall we not awake? Do wounding realities not come, after forged illusions? Is there no flowery perfume, stars' gleam, dawn's light, angelic laughter, celestial warmth in the spirit? Oh! surely souls do not have winter fogs, withered flowers, clouds that hide the stars, mists that shatter little boats, thorns or roses for the heart, brambles that tear the feathers off innocent doves.

In this world, after the warmth of the sun in the day and the silvery gleams of the moon, the luminous light of the stars, and sweet whispers on spring and summer nights, comes winter—winter that brings cold and withers flowers and illusions, and with them, life!

Winter is sad, it is gloomy for those who have no warmth to comfort the body, no gay illusions to animate the soul.

But blessèd art thou, old winter, when we hear the rain fall slowly, and the dense fog surrounds us and the cold comes with that idle ache that steals over us even as, wrapped in soft furs, in the soul we feel the light that Nature lacks, and in the heart, the spring so far away.

We hear the birds sing, the bees buzz, see the lilies totter on their graceful stalks, breathe the perfume of heliotropes and jasmines, hear the murmur of the breeze in the tall trees, and see the pearly dew that wets the green grass. All that, within our hearts.

Is there snow?

Welcome! How white that rain of swan's feathers is!

Is it cold?

We do not feel it. Within our breast there is a fire that gives life, heat, light.

Are all things musty, the roses dry and withered, the trees bare of leaves?

The soul is smiling. In the soul there are flowers whose perfume intoxicates; in the soul, divine plants sprout, grow, and are beautiful; in the soul there is music, harmony, poems that give life, while with eyes half closed we dream and are able to see, behind the gray mantle of the sky, the rose and azure of the dawn, with its soft twilight smile.

It is cold and it is snowing and it is raining. To the theater, to the ball, where a thousand lights are shining! In fireplaces, fires burn; music echoes triumphantly; and in the midst of playful laughter, couples dance dizzying waltzes, while dreams whirl and flutter like mad butterflies. Eyes gleam black and deep, or azure and tender, and pink lips murmur sweet nothings. And we listen to the rain fall, and in the light of street lamps we see the snow fall like a silver coverlet, and we say to ourselves: "How beautiful! Yes, the winter is very beautiful!"

How dreadful, though, when we feel it in our heart, and it reigns within our soul, and it brings the cold that kills. And the winter passes, and spring returns, yet winter remains.

But when the roses do not wither, and butterflies still flutter in our dream-garden, it is lovely to watch the roofs turn white, see the trees bare of leaves and the sky leaden. Gay, the rhythmic sound of rain caresses our ear.

Blessèd art thou, old winter!

# THE IDEAL

And then, an ivory tower, a mystic flower, a star to fall in love with. . . . It passed; I saw it as one might see a dawn—fleeing swift and implacable.

It was an ancient statue with a soul that peered out from its eyes, angelical eyes, all tenderness, all azure as the sky, all enigma.

It felt me kiss it with my eyes, and it lashed me with the majesty of its beauty, and like a queen and a dove it looked at me, but it passed—breathtaking, dazzling, triumphant, like a blinding vision. And I, poor painter of Nature and of Psyche, maker of rhythms and airy castles, saw the glowing fairy gown, the star of its diadem, and thought of the yearned-for promise of beautiful love.

But all that remained of that supreme and fatal ray of light in the depths of my mind was the face of a woman, an azure dream.

# BÖKLIN:
## "THE ISLE OF THE DEAD"

To what land of dreams, what funereal kingdom of dreams does that gloomy isle belong? It lies in a far and distant place where silence reigns. There, no voice issues from the water's crystal waves, or from the wind's light gusts, or from the black and mortuary trees' dark leaves—those mortuary cypresses which, in silent copses, resemble ghostly monks.

One sees, carved in the volcanic rocks gnawed and scarred by time, the mouths of crypts, dark niches where, under the mysterious and taciturn sky, the dead sleep. The specular sea reflects the walls of that solitary palace of the unknown. The ship of mourning approaches a mute gravedigger, as in that poem by Tennyson. What pale dead princess is rowed to the Isle of the Dead? . . . What Helen, what beloved Yolanda? —A soft chant in minor key, a chant of vague melody and profound desolation. Perhaps the silence is broken by a wandering sob, or by a sigh; perhaps a vision wrapped in a veil as though of snow. . . .

That is where Psyche's possession begins; it is within that blackness, poor dreamer, that you will see, perhaps, the dazzling wings of Hypsipyla sprout from the dark cocoon. To your solemn isle, oh Böklin!, goes pale Queen Bathsheba. And in a shroud of mourning goes, too, the wife of Mausolus, who poured ashes in her wine. And Hecuba—in what horrid trance!—silently, clenching her teeth against her howling, sinking her fingers into her aching maternal breasts. Venus, upon her clam shell drawn by white doves, approaches, to see whether Adonis' shade still wanders, moaning. The imperial throng of proud porphyrogenitors, who loved both love and death. Upon a divine bark, with an archangel at its tiller, comes the Virgin Mary, wounded in the breast by the seven wounds.

# SIRENS AND TRITONS

With more sonority than the sound of the conch rings the laughter of the triton, whose sea-satyr's head, crowned with otherworldly vines that grow in undersea gardens and with roses of a strange and unknown flora, cut in beds of lichens and floating medusas, emerges from the waves. Behind him puffs a batrachian face, fleshy red mouth, bulging eyes. The waves are dancing. On the breast of one, a nymph of opulent thighs, with fins upon her heels, gives a watery leap and plunges into the sea. Farther out, another nymph, her head crowned with algae, exhibits her breasts. With jocose astonishment, an aquatic centaurian Sancho swims by; his hindquarters thrash the waves, and the spray forms a boiling white ring about his belly, on which one sees his deep stain, like the sign of a blow with a palette-knife, his navel.

In the foreground, in the transparency of the water, a siren displays her forkèd, curving fishtail, all jet and silver; in the white spray quivers that double rotundity whose curves, in a human maiden, issue in the nether limbs.

The fearful eyes look out to a point where something is espied, and the finny female fails to mind the fauny triton that beckons her, inviting her to some sexual dalliance—as on the land, to lovemaking in the great forest, Pan would beckon the woodland's River-Nymph.

# THE CLEPSYDRA: THE EXTRACTION OF THE IDEA

## I

The Sun and the air and the still tongue of all things say to the good miner: It's a good day.

The worker, agile and naked, feels his blood sing, feels an impulsive need to work as it courses through his marrow. It's as if an inevitable radiant oil had charged his limbs with strength and levity, and he considers himself ready for any struggle and able to reach the heart of the earth with his pick.

The mouth of the hole calls out to him: the deep, cerebral hole beckons him to descend. The good worker peers over the edge and, far below, sees the precious stones shine.

Nature, like some maternal wet nurse, lends him a hand at the entrance to the mine, helps him go down. And he descends into the dark hole. Soon, there's a harmonious sound of the metallic pick, wounding the rock.

When the miner comes up again from his labor, the light from the sky illuminates a new treasure on the face of the earth. There are diamonds, gold rubies, chalcedony quartz, emeralds, the rich and varied gems that the good worker has extracted.

Happy and tired, he rests, while the old and mysterious Wet Nurse smiles.

## II

Is the Sun sick, perhaps? It has a dark veil over its eyes. The air jumps brusquely and steams, as if it were stepping from an icy bath. All things say to the good worker: It's a bad day.

The miner feels a deathly chill in his body. His arms can't lift the pick of his labor. He might think that he would keel over after a single step. The air around him does him harm: his eyes grow tired in their desire to drill through fog.

The hole, black and silent, seems to view him with hostility. The good worker peers over the edge and sees only darkness. Far below, he thinks he may hear the voice of an ill-fated cricket.

But it's time to go down. And, weak, with no help and no high spirits, he descends into the shadowy hole.

Every so often, there's the sound of the pick's strident blows. In the silent intervals, the mine's cricket sings.

At nightfall, the miner comes up like an ant on the edge of a glass. His hands and feet are destroyed. He hasn't extracted anything. Tomorrow, he won't be able to deal with the merchants. Exhausted, almost fainting at the entrance to the mine, he takes refuge in sleep.

Then, as he drifts off, the old Wet Nurse comes, holding a shaded lantern in silence. She casts light on his face and contemplates him in her mystery.

S. W.

# WAR

For you, oh ardent youth, war is beautiful! Filled with illusions of glory, you think you were born under a lucky star and that the enemy bullets will respect your life even if your comrades fall like ripe fruit from dry branches. You'll come out of this victorious, you say, so that when you return with their bodies you'll be able to cry with a winner's pride. You'll be lifted in acclaim as if you were one of the first sons of the Motherland.

As for you, Mr. Merchant, you'll stir your thick gravy, exploiting the needy patriots in your depravity and negotiating with the republic. You'll bless the discord that will have filled your pockets with money and your belly with the deepest satisfaction.

And you, Mr. Foreign Banker: you'll lend your money at an inflated interest. For you, Lord of Gunpowder and Killing Machines, death is a delectable dish, and you'll sell murderous steel for fabulous prices, blood and gold, at the expense of poor peoples cast into the sea, their grave, at the mercy of the wind.

And you, Mr. Politician: after the carnage, you'll rejoice in the remains of misfortune or, from your safe haven of victory, strut around in self-righteousness. And then you'll plot some new infamy so that when the nation has recovered its lost health and its veins are coursing with fresh blood, you can seek new conflicts with your brother and your neighbor, conflicts that will bring new adventures in hatred and envy.

And you, artist and thinker: may you find a field worthy of your praise, where you can set your fantasies free in the air.

But what about those aging women who will do nothing

more than cry? What about those pale women and those poor, orphaned children? What about those war benefits requested, that one light so late at night, those sad sewing machines? What about those black clothes?

S. W.

# ESSAYS, OPINIONS, TRAVEL WRITING, AND MISCELLANEOUS PROSE

# On Literature

# MODERNISMO

*November 28*

In Madrid's press, one sees constant allusions to *Modernismo,* references to the *Modernistas,* the Decadents, the Aesthetes, the Pre-Raphaelites—with *s* and all. Yet I cannot but be struck by the fact that I can find no reason whatever for the invective or the praise, or for any allusions at all. There is not in Madrid, or in all the rest of Spain, with the exception of Catalonia, any group, any "brotherhood" in which pure art—or, ye promulgators of rules, impure art—is cultivated in obedience to this "movement" that has recently been treated with such harshness by some, such enthusiasm by others. Traditional formalism, on the one hand, and the conception of a particular sort of morality and aesthetic, on the other, have produced a deep-rooted "Hispanicism" which, as don Juan Valera tells us, "cannot be uprooted no matter how hard one tugs." This has prevented the inflowing of any cosmopolitan breeze, as it has prevented also any individual broadening, or liberty, or (let us say the consecrated word and be done with it) anarchism in art—which is the basis on which any modern or "modernist" evolution must be founded.

Now, in the youth that yearns for all things new, what is lacking in art is the virtue of desire, or, better said, enthusiasm, passion, and, above all, the gift of *will.* Furthermore, the limited public teaching and knowledge of foreign languages, the absolute lack of attention that the press gives, as a general rule, to the manifestations of the mental life of other nations (unless it be those that touch upon the "great unwashed"), and, especially, the rule of idleness and mockery, cause there to be only a tiny few who take art in all its integral value. In a visit I made recently to Jacinto Octavio Picón, the newest member of the Real Academia Española, this most excelsus writer said to me: "Believe me when I tell you, sir, that in Spain there are great talents; what we need is will, and character."

Not long ago, Sr. Llanas Aguilaniedo, one of the few spirits among the new generation in Spain who accord study and meditation their due seriousness, said the following: "There are, furthermore, in this country idiotized by neglect and idleness, very few *active* spirits, for the general run of men are accustomed to the comforts of an easy life which demands little in the way of intellectual or physical effort. Most men do not understand how there might be individuals who find work of any sort to be a comfort, or a rest, and at the same time a tonic that expands the spirit. For true *workers,* with ideas and a true calling for labor, are, one might daresay, confined to the region north of the Peninsula; the rest of the nation, although one must not generalize absolutely in these matters, works when forced to, but without illusions and without enthusiasm." Where I do not agree with Sr. Llanas is that here, everything produced in other countries is known, everything is analyzed, everything is studied, and then none of it is followed. "No doubt," he says, "we consider ourselves elevated to a superior height, from whence we are content to observe what happens in the world, without its ever occurring to us to follow that movement."

Let me expand on this. It is hard to find in any bookstore works of a certain genre unless one asks the bookseller to have them on hand. The Athenaeum receives a number of "independent" reviews and journals, yet only the smallest handful of writers and others with a taste for literature have any familiarity with the production of other nations. I have observed, for example, in the editorial offices of the *Revista Nueva,* where many good Italian, French, and English magazines are received, not to mention books of a certain type of intellectual aristocracy unknown in Spain, that even my colleagues of great talent look upon them with indifference, disdain, and an utter lack of curiosity. It goes without saying that in every circle of younger writers, everything descends finally to jokes, more or less risqué wit, or caricature and cliché—there is an absolute avoidance of deep thought. Those who reflect on art, or worship it—there is no doubt that in such promiscuity, they suffer.

Those labeled "Symbolists" have not a symbolist work to their name. Valle-Inclán is called a Decadent because he writes in a careful, polished prose of admirable formal merit. And Jacinto Benavente is called a *Modernista* and an Aesthete because if he philosophizes, he does so under the sun of Shakespeare, and if he smiles and satirizes, he does so in the manner of certain Parisians, who have nothing to do with the Aesthetes or *Modernismo*. Everything becomes a joke. For the first time, *Modernismo* was talked about in Madrid, and our aforementioned Sr. Llanas Aguilaniedo had the following to say: "The 'hardware store' of the Athenaeum functioned as a sort of oracle, where Oscar Wilde was remembered. . . . The court's newspapers and magazines came out playing with words and measuring all the idolaters of beauty by the yardstick of the founder of the school, abusing the term [*'Modernismo'*] so much that by now, even López Silva's barbers consider the name offensive, and take umbrage at the epithet. That road leads nowhere."

Nor does *Modernismo* have any representatives in painting, aside from a few Catalonians, unless it be the "draughtsmen," who believe they have done it all by simply leading their silhouettes as in *vitraux*, imitating the wood-shaving ringlets of Mucha's women, or copying the decorations in German, French, or Italian magazines. The Catalonians have, however, done everything possible—perhaps even too much—to add their bit to the progress of modern art, from their literature, which numbers such luminaries as Rusiñol, Maragall, Utrillo, to their painting and decorative arts, which have, once again, Rusiñol, Casas (whose wit and skill are worthy of all praise and attention), Pichot, and others who, like Nouell-Monturiol, have made reputations not only in Barcelona but also in Paris and other cities of art and ideas.

In Latin America, we had this movement before Castilian Spain, and for reasons of the utmost clarity: our immediate material and spiritual commerce with the many nations of the world, and also because there is, in the new Latin American

generation, an immense desire for progress and an intense en-
thusiasm, which is that generation's greatest potential and by
which, little by little, it is triumphing against the obstacles of
tradition, the walls of indifference, and the oceans of medioc-
rity that confront it at every turn. I have great pride here in
showing books by Lugones or Jaimes Freire, among the poets;
among the prose writers, such poems as that vast, strange, and
complicated trilogy by Sicardi. And I always say: This is not
*Modernismo,* but it is *true,* it is the reality of a new life, the cer-
tificate of the intense *force vital* of a continent. And other
demonstrations of our mental activity—not the activity that is
profuse and rhapsodic, the activity of *quantity,* but rather the
activity of *quality,* limited, very limited, but that makes a good
presentation of itself and, by the criteria of Europe, triumphs
indeed: studies in the political and social sciences. I am just as
proud of those. And I remember certain words by Juan Valera,
speaking of Olegario Andrade—words in which there is a
good, and probable, vision of the future. Speaking of Brazilian,
South American, Spanish, and North American literature, Valera
said that "the literatures of these nations will continue to be En-
glish, Portuguese, and Spanish, which does not mean that with
time—perhaps even tomorrow—Yankee authors will not emerge
who are better than any so far in England, or that in Rio de
Janeiro, Penambuco, or Bahía, writers [will not emerge] better
than any Portugal has produced, or that in Buenos Aires, Lima,
Mexico City, Bogotá, or Valparaíso, the sciences, letters, and arts
may not flourish with more health and freshness, and more love-
liness, than in Madrid, Sevilla, or Barcelona."

Our *Modernismo,* if it can be called that, is beginning to give
us a place apart, a place that is independent of Castilian litera-
ture, as Rémy de Gourmont says in a letter to the editor of the
*American Mercury.* What does it matter that there are so many
wits—*grotesques,* if you will, dilettantes, cynics? Those who
are truly consecrated know that it is not a matter of schools,
formulas, codes.

In France, England, Italy, Russia, and Belgium, those who
have triumphed have been writers and poets and artists of en-
ergy, of artistic character, and of tremendous culture. The

also-rans have sunk, have faded away. If in the *salons* and chapels of Paris there are and have been laughingstocks, it has been, in fact, the *precieux*. Many would be forgiven, *pour l'amour du grec,* if our dear Professor Calandrelli knew them. Today, artists and writers do not produce *Modernismo*—nor have they ever—with simple plays on words and rhythms. To-day, the new rhythms imply new melodies that sing the words of magical Leonardo in the depths of every poet: *Cosa bella mortal passa, e non d'arte.* No matter how often the playful, lightsome *wits* and aged, bitter children speak of this move-ment's "failure," the only writer who fails is the writer who does not bravely and with firm step enter the cage of that di-vine lion Art—which, like that art created by da Vinci for the great king Francisco, has a chest covered with lilies.

There is no such thing as *Modernismo* here, then, save that which is brought to our arts by a proximity to a fashion that is not understood. Neither character nor way of life nor sur-roundings aid in the consecration of an artistic ideal. People have talked about a theater, which when I first arrived I thought might be feasible, but today think absolutely impossible.

The only "brotherhood" I see is the brotherhood of car-icaturists, and if we are talking about poetic music, the only innovators, surely, are the smiling rhymers of the caricature-newspapers.

A very different case arises in the capital of Catalonia. From *L'Avenç* to *Pel y Plom,* which today are sustained by Utrillo and Casas, we have seen that there are elements for exclusively "modern" publication by an artistic and literary *élite. Pel y Plom* is a periodical similar to the more popular *Gil Blas Ilus-tré,* without losing its thorniness, its "edge," and on its first page there is always a drawing by Casas, which is applauded by the *crayons* of Munich, London, and Paris. Per Romeu, whom I have spoken about because of his famous café the *Quatre Gats,* has, with the aid of Casas, been publishing a similar periodical of remarkable artistic merit.

In this capital there are none but the graceful, elegant, if tentative, drawings of Marín—whom the great Puvis has been pleased to praise—and of one or two others. In literature, I repeat, nothing that justifies an attack, or even allusions. The rich and elegant procession of beleaguered "modern art" has had but a few vague parodies, if that . . . . Does my reader recall in Apuleius the dream-vision that preceded the entrance of Spring in the festivals of Isis?[4] (Met., XI) Well, pay heed.

4. Isis instructs Lucius, who has been turned into an ass, how to return to human form: In the procession to welcome the Spring, Lucius is to pretend to kiss the hand of the great priest, who will be holding a bunch of roses, but at the last minute he is to snatch away the roses. And having done this, Ceres/Isis/ Diana/Aphrodite tells Lucius: "Know thou this of certaine, that the residue of thy life untill the houre of death shall be bound and subject to me!" Darío believed that this was the most desirable state a man could live in: First, in a state of daring and bravery and then, subjection to the goddess that brings forth all poetry.

# THE STORY OF MY BOOKS

## AZURE . . .

This bright spring morning I have sat down to leaf through my beloved old book, that firstborn that initiated a mental movement that was to have so many triumphant consequences in the years that followed, and I browse through its pages like a man rereading old love letters—with an affection mixed with melancholy, and a twinge of *saudade* in remembering my distant youth.

It was in Santiago, Chile, where I had landed, from remote Nicaragua, in search of an environment suitable for intellectual study and other such labors. Despite Chile's having produced until then only statesmen and jurists, grammarians, historians, journalists, and (at the most) rhymers—traditionalists and academics descended directly from the Spanish motherland—I found there a new air for my eager flights, and found, too, a generation of youths filled with desires for beauty and noble enthusiasms.

When I published the first stories and poems (which bubbled up from the usual canonical founts), I was greeted with incomprehension, astonishment, and censure from the professors, but cordial applause from my companions. What was the origin of the novelty? The origin of the novelty was my recent encounter with the French authors of the Parnassus, for at the time the Symbolist struggle was just beginning in France and so was not known abroad, much less in our Americas. Catulle Mendès was my true initiator—and a Mendès translated, at that, for my French was still somewhat raw. Some of his lyrical-erotic stories, one or another poem among those contained in the *Parnasse contemporaine,* were a revelation to me. Later, I read other authors, prior to Mendès and superior—Gautier, the Flaubert of *The Temptation of St. Anthony,* Paul de Saint-Victor—and from them I got a theretofore unknown (to me) and instantly dazzling conception of style. Accustomed as I was to the eternal cliché of the Spanish *Siglo de Oro* and Spain's indecisive modern poetry, I found in those French writers a mine of literary gold that was there to be explored, and exploited: I applied their way of employing adjectives, certain syntactical habits, a verbal aristocracy, to my Spanish. The rest was given by the character of Spanish itself, and the talent of yours truly. And I, who know Baralt's *Dictionary of Gallicisms* by heart, realized that not just a well-chosen Gallicism but also certain particularities from other languages might be extremely useful, might even be of incomparable efficacy in a certain type of "transplant." Thus, my knowledge of English, of Italian, of Latin were to serve later in the pursuit of my literary ends.

But my penetration into the world of the verbal art of France had not actually begun in Chile. Years earlier, in Central America, in the city of San Salvador, and in the company of the fine poet Francisco Gavidia, my adolescent spirit had explored the immense jungle of Victor Hugo and had contemplated his divine ocean, which contained all things.

Why that title, *Azure . . .*? I had not yet heard or read that Hugo-esque phrase *"l'Art, c'est l'azur,"* although I had read that musical strophe from *"Les châtiments"*:

> *Adieu, patrie*!
> *L'onde est en furie*!
> *Adieu, patrie,*
> *azur!*

But blue, azure, was for me the color of daydreams, the color of art, a Hellenic, Homeric color, a color oceanic and firmamental, the *coeruleum* which in Pliny is the simple color that resembles the sky, and sapphires. And Ovid had also sung it:

Respice vindicibus pacatum viribus orbem qui latam Nereus
caeruleus ambit humum.[5]

Into that celestial color I concentrated the spiritual flowering
of my artistic spring. That first book—for one can hardly count
the incomplete volume of verses that appeared in Managua un-
der the title *First Notes*—was composed of a handful of stories
and poems that might be called "Parnassian." *Azul* . . . was
printed in 1888 in Valparaíso under the auspices of Eduardo
Poirier and the poet de la Barra, for the patron to whom the
book was dedicated (under the suggestion of the second of
these friends) did not even acknowledge receipt of the first copy
that I sent him.

The book was not particularly successful in Chile. A few
people gave it a look when the great poet Juan Valera took note
of its contents in one of his famous "American Letters" for *El
Imparcial*'s literary section, *Lunes*. Valera saw much, expressed
his surprise and smiling enthusiasm—why are there those who
insist on seeing pins in that ducal outstretched hand?—but he
did not realize the full breadth and importance of my attempt.
For if this little book had some relative personal merit, then
from that was to derive all of our future intellectual revolution.

Those who were taken aback by the originality of this new
manner thought it strange, indeed, that a person of such impec-
cable credentials as Juan Valera might note that the work was
written "in excellent Spanish." Other praise was bestowed by
"the treasure of the language," as the Conde de Navas was
known at the time, and from that moment onward the book
was sought after and talked about in both the Americas and
Spain. Valera observed, in particular, the completely French
spirit of the volume. "None of the men of letters of the Penin-
sula that I have known with more cosmopolitan spirit, and that
have resided for a longer time in France, and that have spoken

5. "Behold, a world pacified by your protective strength, / where sea-green
[*caeruleus*: dark blue] Nereus circles the wide earth" (Ovid, *Heroides*, IX:
15–16).

French and other foreign languages better, have ever seemed to
me so deeply filled with the spirit of France as you, sir: not
Galiano, not Eugenio de Ochoa, not Miguel de los Santos
Alvarez." And he added a little later: "It seems that here, a
Nicaraguan author who never set foot out of Nicaragua except
to go to Chile, and who is an author so *à la mode de Paris* and
with such 'chic' and distinction, has been able to anticipate
fashion and even modify and impose it."

It is true; a whiff of Paris animated my efforts at that time.
But there was also, as Valera himself noted, a great love for clas-
sic literatures and a knowledge of "all European modernity." It
was not, then, a limited and exclusive project. There was, above
all, youth, a yearning for life, a sensual *frisson*, a certain pagan
dewiness—and that, despite my religious education and profes-
sion of the Catholic, apostolic, and Roman faith. Certain het-
erodox notes are explained by certain readings.

As for the style, it was a time when there was a great love of
"artistic writing" and elegant dilettantism. In the story titled
"The Bourgeois King," I think I can recognize the influence of
Daudet. The symbol is clear, and is summarized in the artist's
eternal protest against the dry, practical man, the dreamer's chaf-
ing against the tyranny of uncultured and uneducated wealth. In
"The Fat Satyr," the procedure is more or less that of Mendès,
though there are also echoes of Hugo and Flaubert. The models
for "The Nymph" are the Parisian stories of Mendès, Armand
Silvestre, Mezeroi, with the superaddition that the setting, the
plot, the details, the tone belong to the life of Paris, the literature
of Paris. There is no need to note, is there, that I had never voy-
aged outside my native country, as Valera said, except to go to
Chile, and that both subject and composition were what one
might in all justice call "bookish"?

In "The Bale," the then-much-in-vogue Naturalist school
triumphed. I had just read certain works by Zola, and the
reflection was instant; but as this mode suited neither my tem-
perament nor my fancy, I have never again followed that road.
In "Queen Mab's Veil," on the other hand, my imagination did
find a suitable subject. Shakespearean dazzle possessed me, and
for the first time I produced a poem in prose. More than in any

of my other attempts, I sought in this story to achieve rhythm and verbal sonority, a transposition of music into words—a feat until then (as everyone acknowledges) unknown in Castilian prose, for the periodic cadences of some classics are another thing. "Gold's Song," *El canto del oro,* is also a prose poem, but of another genre. Valera calls it a litany. And here, allow me to insert an anecdote. I sent several Parisian men of letters copies of my book, the moment it came out. Some time later, in Péladan's *La Panthée,* there appeared a *"Cantique de l'or"* that bore more than a passing resemblance to mine. Coincidence? Perhaps. I hesitated to make anything of the matter, because between the great aesthete and me, there was no clarification possible, and in the long run I would have been, despite the chronology, the author of "Gold's Song" plagiarized from Péladan.

"The Ruby" is another story in the Parisian manner. A "myth," Valera calls it. A springtime fantasy, rather, as is "The Palace of the Sun," where the use of the *leit-motif* may be noted. And then another tale of Paris—lighter, despite its significance to life—"The Azure Bird." In "White Doves and Dark Herons," the subject is autobiographical, and the setting is the Central American land in which I was born. Everything in it is true, though gilded with youthful illusion. It is a faithful echo of my lovelorn adolescence, the awakening of my sense and my spirit under the influence of the enigma of universal palpitation. The section of the volume titled "In Chile," which contains "In Search of Paintings," "Watercolor," "Landscape," "Etching," "The Virgin of the Dove," "The Head," another "Watercolor," "A Portrait of Watteau," "Still Life," "In Charcoal," "Landscape" [*sic,* original title in English], and "The Ideal" are essays of color and drawing that had no antecedents in our prose. These transpositions of the pictorial into the verbal were to be followed by those of the grand Colombian J. Asunción Silva, and that, chronologically, resolves the doubt expressed by some that the work of the author of "Nocturne" may have been prior to my own. "The Death of the Empress of China"—published recently in French in the collection titled *Les Mille Nouvelles Nouvelles* —is an innocent sort of tale, with little intrigue, and with a slight echo of Daudet. In "To a Star," a song of passion, a romance, a prose poem, the idea is joined to the musicality of the word.

Then comes the part of the volume devoted to verse. In the poems, I followed the same method as in the prose: the application to Spanish of certain verbal superiorities from other languages, in this case mainly French. The pieces evidence an abandonment of the usual rules and regulations, the sanctified clichés; an attention to interior melody, which aids in the success of the rhythmic expression; a novel use of adjectives; a concentration on the etymological meaning of each word; an application of timely erudition, lexical aristocracy. In "Springsong" ("*Primaveral*")—in the section titled "The Lyrical Year"—I believe I added a new note to the orchestration of the romance, even acknowledging such illustrious predecessors as Góngora and the Cuban poet Zenea. In "Summersong" ("*Estival*"), I attempted to render a piece of force. . . . In "Autumnsong" ("*Autumnal*") the influence of music returns—an intimate music, chamber music, containing the pleasant yearnings of my salad days, the nostalgia for what had yet to be found—and is almost never found as one dreamed it, anyway. Then immediately— clashing with the poems that went before—there comes a version of "Autumn Thought" by Armand Silvestre. It is well known that despite his Rabelaisian particularities and his excessive *galoiserie,* Silvestre was a poet who could be delicate, refined, and sentimental.

"Ananké" is an isolated poem, which has little patience with my Christian foundations. Valera quite rightly censures it, and it has no possible *raison d'être* save a moment of disenchantment and the bitter taste of certain readings not likely to raise one's spirit into the light of the supreme truths. The most intense theologian could rip to shreds the poet's reflection in that pessimistic moment, and demonstrate that the hawk and the dove are equally necessary elements of the Oneness of the universe. . . . The little book concludes with a series of sonnets: "Caupolicán," which introduced the alexandrine sonnet *à la française* into Spanish, at least so far as I know. A similar experiment, a formal poem of fifteen-syllable lines, may be found in "Venus." Another very French sonnet, with a Parisian theme, is "On Winter." Then come some lyrical portraits, "medallions" of poets I admired at the time: Leconte de Lisle, Catulle Mendès, the Yankee Walt Whitman, the Cuban J. J. Palma, the Mexican Díaz Mirón, whom I imitated in certain poems added to later editions of *Azure* . . .

And that was my first book, the origin of several that came after, which has come to me on this bright spring morning to awaken the most pleasant, fragrant memories of my past life, there in the beautiful land of Chile. If my *Azure* . . . is a production of pure art, with nothing of a pedagogical or moralizing purpose, it is also not *elucubrated* in any way that might cause even the slightest morbose delectation. With all its defects, it is among my favorites. It is a work, I repeat, that contains the flower of my youth, that externalizes the most inward poetry of the first dreams and yearnings, and it is impregnated with both love of art and love of love.

## PROFANE PROSE PIECES

It would be futile to attempt an exegesis of my book *Prosas Profanas,* (Profane Prose Pieces), after the painstaking study by José Enrique Rodó in his masterful, celebrated essay, reproduced as an introduction to the Paris edition by Veuve C. Bouret, though an oversight by the publisher caused the omission of that illustrious author's name. But I hope, nonetheless, that I may be permitted to express my personal sentiments, to speak for a brief while about my methods and the genesis of the poems contained in this volume. They belong to a period of hard intellectual labor that I was to go on pursuing, along with my companions and followers, in Buenos Aires, in defense of new ideas, the freedom of art, the anarchy—or, looked at rightly, aristocracy—of literature. In a few words of introduction I have concentrated the scope of my intentions.

*Azure* . . . had already appeared in Chile; *Los Raros, (The Misfits)* had already appeared in the Argentine capital. The publication of manifestos was much in vogue back then, in the Symbolist struggle for recognition and existence in France, and many young friends of mine asked me to do in Buenos Aires what Moreas and so many others were doing in Paris. I replied that we were not in Paris, and that such a manifesto would be neither useful nor opportune. The atmosphere and culture of that ancient Lutetia[6] was hardly the same as that of our continental state. If in France there were so many Rémy-Gourmonts, "*celui-qui ne comprend-pas,*"[7] how could our situation be any different. The type abounded in our ruling class, in our general bourgeoisie, in letters, in our social life. There was, then, only an "élite" and above all the enthusiasm of young persons yearning for reform, for a change in their way of conceiving of and cultivating beauty.

Even among some who had put aside, a bit, the former ways, the value of study and constant application was not well understood, and it was believed that with nothing more than effort, talent might be persuaded to yield up the prize. An aesthetic of individualism was proclaimed, the expression of the concept, but what was also needed was a grounding in knowledge of the art to which one consecrated oneself, an indispensable erudition, and the necessary gift of good taste. I stepped forward to prevent prejudice against all imitation, and holding at arm's length especially the young catechumens who wished to follow in my footsteps. . . .

Disgusted and horrified by the social and political life that kept my original country in a deplorable state of embryonic civilization—nor were things better in the lands most closely neighboring mine—I found the Republic of Argentina to be a wonderful refuge, and its capital, though filled with commercial bustle, to have an intellectual tradition and a more favorable environment for the broadening and expansion of my aesthetic

6. A "town of Belgic Gaul, on the confluence of the rivers Sequana and Matrona, which received its name, as some suppose, from the quantity of clay, *lutum,* which is in its neighbourhood. J. Caesar fortified and embellished it, from which circumstance some authors call it *Julii Civitas.* Julian the Apostate resided there some time. It is now called *Paris,* the capital of France" (Lemprière's *Classical Dictionary*).
7. "The uncomprehending."

faculties. And though the lack of a basic fortune obliged me to labor in journalism, I was able to devote my free moments to the exercise of pure art and mental creation. But abominating that democracy which is poisonous to poets (*pace* such worshipers of it as Walt Whitman), I looked toward the past, toward ancient mythologies and splendid histories, and incurred the censure of the nearsighted. For in all the Spanish Americas no one held any end or object for poetry save the celebration of *native* glories, the events of Independence, the *American* nature: an eternal hymn to Junín, an endless ode to the agriculture of the torrid zone, and stirring patriotic songs. I did not deny that there was a great treasure trove of poetry in our prehistoric times, in the Conquest, and even in the colony, but with our subsequent social and political state had come intellectual dwarfism and historical periods more suitable for the blood-dripping penny dreadful than the noble canto. Yet I added: "Buenos Aires— cosmopolis! And tomorrow!" The proof of this prophecy can be found in my recent "Canto to Argentina."

As for the ideological and verbal question, in the face of the most sonorous Spanish glories—Francisco de Quevedo's, Santa Teresa's, Gracián's—I proclaimed an opinion that would later be seconded and upheld by egregious geniuses on the Peninsula. There is one phrase that must be commented upon: "Grandfather, I must tell you: my wife is from my homeland, my mistress is from Paris." In the depths of my spirit, despite my cosmopolitan outlook, there lies the inextirpable vein of the race; my thought and my feeling continue a historical, traditional process—but from the capital of art and grace, of elegance, of clarity and good taste, I had to take those things that might be used for beautifying and decorating my autochthonous productions. And I made that clear to one and all. Adding, by the way, that essences were drawn not just from the roses of Paris—but from all the gardens of the world.

Then I set forth the principle of *inner music*: "Since each word has a soul, there is, then, in each line, in addition to verbal harmony, an ideal melody. Music comes, many times, from simply the idea." Then I professed disdain for criticism by blind hens, for the honking of geese, and I stirred up the fires of stimulus for work, for creation: "Let the eunuch snort: when one Muse gives you a child, the other eight get pregnant"—a phrase quoted recently in a production by a young Spaniard and attributed to Théophile Gautier! . . .

In "Era un aire suave . . . ," which is itself a soft air, I follow Verlaine's precept of Poetic Art: *"de la musique avant tout de chose."* Landscape, characters, tone: they are presented in an eighteenth-century ambience. I wrote as though listing to the king's violins. My senses were possessed by Rameau and Lully. But the young abbot of madrigals and the blond viscount of defiant challenges, faced with laughing Eulalia, maintain an ages-old feminine felinity against the surrendering male: Eve, Judith, Ophelia, worse than all the suffragettes. In *"Divagación"* there is a course in erotic geography: an invitation to love under any sky, a passion for all colors and all times. There I made the hendecasyllable as flexible as I possibly could. "Sonatina" is more rhythmic and musical than the rest of these compositions, and has received the warmest response in Spain and the Americas, perhaps because it contains the cordial dream of every adolescent woman-child, of every woman who awaits the moment of love. It is the most private and inward desire, yearning melancholy, and it is, thus, Hope. In *"Blasón"* ("Coat of Arms") I praise the swan, for those lines were written in the album of a lovely French marquise with a fondness for poets. In *"Del Campo"* ("On the Country") I stood in the shadow of Banville, for a "nativist" subject and atmosphere. In the song of praise titled *"A los ojos negros de Julia"* (To Julia's Black Eyes), I madrigal'd most whimsically. *"Canción de Carnaval"* (Song of Carnival) is also *à la Banville,* an ode to tightrope-walking, of Buenos Aires flavor. Two gallantries follow, posies for a Cuban lady. They were written in the presence of my ill-starred friend Julián del Casal, in Havana, more than twenty years ago, and inspired by a lovely lady, María Cap, today the widow of General Lachambre.

"Bouquet" is another whimsical madrigal. *"El faisán"* (The Pheasant), in monorhymed tercets, is a product of Paris—conceived in Paris, written in Paris, filled with the air of Paris.

*"Garçonnière"* (Bachelor Flat) speaks of artistic, fraternal

hours in Buenos Aires. *"El país del sol"* (The Country of the Sun), formulated in the manner of Catulle Mendès' "Lieds de France" and as an echo of Gaspard de la Nuit, makes concrete the nostalgia of a little girl from the isles of the tropics, animated by art, in the frigid, hard city of Manhattan, in imperial New York. "Margarita"—which has met the not incomprehensible fate of remaining in so many memories—is a melancholy recollection of passion, life, although in the true story, the sensual beloved was taken away not by death, but rather by mere separation. *"Mía"* (Mine) and *"Dice mía"* (He Says Mine) are sports for music, suitable for singing, *lieder* calling out for a voice.

In "Heraldos" I demonstrate the theory of inner melody. One might say that in this little poem, when one imposes the ideal notation, the line does not exist. The game of syllables, the sound and color of the vowels, the name cried out heraldically, evoke an Oriental, biblical, legendary figure, and tribute, and correspondence.

The "Colloquy of Centaurs" is another "myth," exalting natural forces, the mystery of universal life, the perpetual ascension of Psyche, and then addresses the fatal, terrifying arcanum of our inevitable end. But in a renewal of a pagan concept, Thanatos is not presented as in a Catholic vision: a horrific figure, or a skeleton armed with her scythe, or the medieval queen of the plague and empress of war. Instead, she stands beautiful, almost seductive, smiling, pure, chaste, with no anguished visage, and with Love sleeping at her feet. And under a panic principle, I exalt the unity of the Universe on the illusory Island of Gold, before the vast ocean. For, as the divine visionary John has said: *"Et tres sunt qui testimonium dant in terra: spiritus, et aqua, et sanguis: et hi tres unum sunt."*[8]

*In "El poeta pregunta por Stella"* (The Poet Asks after Stella), the poet recalls an angelic being who is no longer with him, a sister to Poe's lilylike women who has ascended to the Christian heaven. Then you will read a lyrical prologue, which

8. "And there are three that bear witness in earth, the Spirit, and the water, and the blood: and these three agree in one" (I John 5:8).

I called "Portico," written long years ago in praise of the excellent poet, the vibrant, sonorous, and copious Salvador Rueda, the glory and decorum of Andalucía. And since at about that time I visited what is all too popularly known as the Land of Holy Virgin Mother Mary,[9] and, finding myself infected with the joy of castanets, tambourines, and guitars, I could not but pay tribute to that enchanted sunny region. And I wrote, among other things, *"Elogio de la seguidilla,"* or "In Praise of the Seguidilla."[10]

In Buenos Aires, initiated into the secrets of Wagner by a Belgian musician and writer, M. Charles del Gouffré, I rhymed the sonnet titled *"El cisne,"* The Swan—eternal bird!—which ends in the following way:

> Oh swan! Oh sacred bird! If once white Helen
> from Leda's azure egg emerged, with grace infused,
> the immortal princess being beautiful,
> under your white wings the new Poetry
> conceives in a glory of light and harmony
> the pure, eternal Helen who incarnates the Ideal.

*"La página blanca"* (The White Page) is like a dream whose visions symbolize the effort, the anguish, the pains of existence, brilliant fate, hopes and disappointments, and the unpardonable epilogue of eternal shadows, the unknown Beyond. Oh! Nothing has brought more bitterness to the hours of meditation in my life than the tenebrous certainty of the End. And how many times, seized by the horror of death, have I sought refuge in some artificial paradise.

*"Año nuevo"* (New Year) is a calendric decoration, animated, one might say, by a breath of theology.

*"Sinfonía en gris mayor"* (Symphony in Gray Major) entails the inevitable memory of magical Théo, exquisite Gautier, and his *"Symphonie en blanc majeur."* Mine is annotated *"d'après nature,"* under the sun of my tropical native land. I have seen

9. Andalucía.
10. The *seguidilla* is a dance characteristic of southern Spain.

those stagnant waters, the burning coasts, the old sea-wolves who loaded wood for dye into schooners and brigantines and set sail for Europe. Taciturn or jolly drinkers would be singing at dusk, on the aft deck, accompanying their Normandy or Breton airs on the accordion, while the nearby woods, the estuaries ringed with mangroves, exhaled warm, malarial breezes.

"*Epitalamio bárbaro*" (Barbarian Epithalamion) is a song, on the lyre, to the loving triumph of a great Apollonian. The "Response" to Verlaine proves my admiration and cordial fervor for "*pauvre* Lelian," whom I met in Paris in his sad and saddening Bohemian days, and I show the two faces of his panic soul: that which is turned to the body and that which is turned to the soul; that which turns to the laws of human nature and that which turns to God and the Catholic mysteries—in parallel. In "*Canto de la sangre*" (Song of the Blood), there is a series of symbolic correspondences and equivalences under the enigma of the sacred liquor that sustains the vitality of our mortal bodies.

The title of the following part of the volume, "Archaeological Recreations," indicates its content. These are echos and manners of past times, and a demonstration, for my disconcerted and misguided detractors, that in order to achieve reform, in order to achieve the modernity that I have undertaken to achieve, I have needed to study the classics and the primitives. Thus, in "*Friso*" (Frieze) I take up elegant *vers libre,* whose last plausible use in Spain occurs in Marcelino Menéndez y Pelayo's famed "Epistle to Horace." There is more architecture and sculpture than music in it, more brush than string or flute. The same can be said for "Palimpsest," in which the poem's rhythm approaches the reverberations of Latin meters. In "*El reino interior*" (The Inner Kingdom), one feels the influence of English poetry, Dante Gabriel Rossetti, some of the coryphaei of French Symbolism. (Good God! In one line I have even alluded to Powell's "Glossary"! . . . ) "*Cosas del Cid*" (On El Cid) contains a legend narrated in prose by Barbey d'Aurevilly and continued by me in verse.

The *"Decires, leyes y canciones"*[11] renew old poetic and
stanzaic forms; thus, I express new loves in verses composed and
arranged in the manner of Johan de Duenyas, Johan de Torres,
Valtierra, and Santa Fe, with unusual and suggestive verbal
compression and rhythmic combinations that yield a graceful,
euphonious result. . . .

And to conclude: In the series of sonnets titled *"Las ánforas
de Epicuro"* (Epicurus' Amphorae)—with one "Seascape"
slipped in—there is a sort of exposition of philosophical
ideas: in *"La espiga"* (The Stalk), the concentration of a reli-
gious ideal in Nature; in *"La fuente"* (The Fountain), self-
knowledge and the exaltation of personhood; in *"Palabras de
la Satiresa"* (Words of the Female Satyr), the conjunction of
praise to both Pan and Apollo (which Moreas, as a clever cen-
sor of mine has made clear, had prefigured—and so much
better!); in *"La anciana"* (The Old Lady), an allegorical affir-
mation of survival; in *"Ama tu ritmo . . ."* (Love Your
Rhythm . . . ), once again the exposition of the inner potency
of the individual; in *"A los poetas risueños"* (To Cheery Po-
ets), a pleasure, an impetus that leads to gay, comforting clar-
ity, with the exultance of hymns to joy; in *"La hoja de oro"*
(The Golden Leaf), the arcana of autumnal sadness; in *"Ma-
rina"* (Seascape) a bitter true page from my life; in "Syrinx"
(for the sonnet that appears in other editions erroneously un-
der the title "Daphne" should be called "Syrinx"), I paganize
as I sing the spiritual concretion of metamorphosis. *"La Gi-
tanilla"*[12] is a rhymed anecdote. I then laud an ancient, delicious
Spanish zither-player; I cast forth a song of encouragement
and spirit, I reveal my dreams.

And that is the nature of this book, which I love intensely yet
delicately—not so much as a work of my own as because when
it appeared a whole mountain range of poetry, inhabited by
magnificent young spirits, was awakened in our continent. And
our dawn was reflected in the sunny old man.

11. These are the names of types of poems in older Spanish literature.
12. A type of Spanish song.

# SONGS OF LIFE AND HOPE

If *Azure . . .* symbolizes the beginning of my spring and *Profane Prose Pieces* my spring full blown, then *Songs of Life and Hope* contains the saps and essences of my autumn.

I have read praise to autumn (I no longer remember by what hand), but who better than Hugo has sung that praise with the profound enchantment of his forest of lyrics? Autumn is the season of reflection. Nature communicates her philosophy wordlessly, with her pale leaves, her taciturn skies, her melancholy glooms. Our daydreaming is impregnated with reflection. With its peaceful inner light, recollection illuminates the sweetest secrets of our memory. We breathe, as though it were a magical air, the perfume of bygone roses. Hope exists, but its smile is a discreet one. Love acquires that same sweet gravity. This was not understood by many, for when *Songs of Life and Hope* appeared, many lamented the absence of the auroral tone of *Azure . . .* and the princess who was sad in *Profane Prose Pieces* and the eighteenth-century capriccios, my beloved, high-born Versailleings, the gallant, precious madrigals, and all the rest that in its time helped renew the taste and forms and vocabulary of our poetry, which had been straitened within the stiff pedagogical-classical poetics of the Renaissance, or, at best, had clung to the prosaico-philosophical (or baritone and bell-like) formulas of masters who, however illustrious, were nonetheless limited. . . .

By the time I wrote *Songs of Life and Hope* I had explored not just the field of foreign poetics but also the ancient poets, the work—whether complete or fragmentary—of the primitives of Spanish poetry, and I had found there a richness of expression and grace that will be sought in vain even among the immensely celebrated poets of centuries nearer to our own. To all this, add a spirit of modernity that I found fitted me perfectly in my polyglot and cosmopolitan incursions. In a few introductory words and the hendecasyllabic epigraph, I explained the nature of the new book. The history of a young-manhood filled with sadness and disappointment, despite the springlike cheer;

the struggle for existence from the beginning, with no family support, no aid from a friendly hand; the sacred and terrible fever for the lyre; the worship of enthusiasm and sincerity against the snares and betrayals of the world, the flesh, and the devil; the dominant, invincible power of the senses in an idiosyncratic character warmed by the tropical sun in mixed Spanish and Chorotegan or Nagrandano blood; the seed of Catholicism juxtaposed against a tempestuous pagan instinct and complicated by the psycho-physical need for thought-modifying stimulants, dangerous combustibles, suppressors of disturbing perspectives, but which put at risk the cerebral machine and the vibrating tunic of nerves. I had recovered from my optimism. A Spaniard of the Americas and an American of Spain, I sang, electing as my instrument the Greek and Latin hexameter and placing my faith and trust in the renaissance of old Hispania in my own homeland, the renaissance of the other side of the ocean in the chorus of nations that in the emotional scale act as counterweights to the strong, daring race to the North. I chose the hexameter because it was in the Greek and Latin tradition and because I believe, after studying the matter, that in our language, *malgré* the opinion of so many scholars, there are, indeed, long and short syllables, and that what is lacking is a deeper and more musical analysis of our prosody. . . .

Our alexandrine rendered more flexible, then, by the application of what Hugo, Banville, and later Verlaine and the Symbolistes brought to French, it was cultivated, perhaps a bit too enthusiastically, in Spain and the Americas. One must note here that the Portuguese had already benefited by these reforms.

There is, as I have said, a great deal of Hispanicism in this book of mine. Whether the optimist in me was making his salute, or I was addressing King Oscar of Sweden or President Roosevelt, or celebrating the Swan or evoking anonymous figures from centuries past, or making Diego Velázquez or Luis de Góngora speak, or praising Cervantes or Goya, or writing the "Litany of Our Lord Don Quixote"—Hispania forever! I had already lived for some time and my ancestral past had been reborn in me. . . .

The title—*Songs of Life and Hope*—though it corresponds in large part to the contents of the volume, is not fully sympathetic to certain notes of disillusion, disappointment, doubt, and a degree of fear of the unknown, the Beyond.

"*Los tres reyes mago*" ("The Three Wise Men") establishes my absolute deism. In "*Salutación a Leonardo*"—written in French *vers libre* . . . —there are games and enigmas of art that can only be understood, naturally, if one has undergone certain initiations. In "*Pegaso*" ("Pegasus"), the value of spiritual energy, the will to creation, is proclaimed. "*A Roosevelt*" ("To Roosevelt") preaches the solidarity of the Spanish-American soul in the face of the possible imperialist incursions of the men of the North; the following poem considers poetry as a special gift, a divine gift, and points to the lighthouse of hope in the face of mean democracy and terrifying equality. In "*Canto de esperanza*" ("Canto to Hope") I turn my eyes to the immense splendor of the figure of Christ, and call out for his return as a salvation from the disasters of an earth poisoned by men's passions, and farther on I once more give a glimpse of the meditative philosophers, the poets who undergo transfiguration and the final victory. "Helios" proclaims Idealism, and, always, infinite omnipotence. "Spes" ascends to Jesus, who, "against cruel hell," is asked to bestow "a grace to purify us of wrath and lechery." "*Marcha triunfal*" is a "triumph" of decoration and music. There is a part titled "Swans." Love for this beautiful symbolic bird since ancient times—

*ignem perosus,*
*quae colat, elegit contraria flumina flammis . . .*[13]—

has made both me and the Spaniard Marquina the butt of censure by one Spanish-American critic, who over the white bird Leda prefers the owl—a dark fowl, though Minervan. (Though I daresay Sthenelus' son [Cycnus] was happier in his metamorphosis[14] than Ascalaphus was in his.[15] And allow me to note, in

13. Now Cycnus is a swan, / and yet he fears to trust the skies and Jove, / for he remembers fires, unjustly sent, / and therefore shuns the heat that he abhors, / and haunts the spacious lakes and pools and streams / that quench the fires. (Ovid, *Metamorphoses*, II: 379–380, trans. Brookes More, 1922).
14. Into a swan.
15. Into an owl.

my defense, that in several places I affirm the owl's wisdom. . . .) In *"Retrato"* ("Portrait"), I present in evocative canvases figures of grandeur, and of Hispanic character, from the past, four gentlemen and an abbess. Then I rhyme the spring's influence in a romance which I suddenly truncate. In *"La dulzura del Angelus"* ("The Sweetness of the Angelus") there is a kind of mystical dream, and I present belief in the Deity and the purification of the soul, and even Nature itself, as a true refuge, through the intimate grace of prayer.

*"Tarde del trópico"* ("Tropical Evening") was written many, many years ago, when for the first time I felt under my feet the vast waters of the ocean during my voyage to Chile. At that time, the demigod Hugo was everything to me in poetry. The "Nocturnes," on the other hand, speak of a later culture; my spirit had now been anointed by the great "humanists," and thus I exteriorized in transparent, simple, musical verses (inner music, that is) the secrets of my embattled existence, the blows of destiny, the inevitabilities of fate. There may be too much despair in some places; the blame lies only with the marked instances in which a hand from out the darkness plucks the martyrizing strings of our nerves. And with the truths of my life: "a vast pain and small cares," the "voyage to a vague Orient on glimpsed ships," the "grains of prayers that flowered in blasphemies," the "confusions of the swan among the pools," the "false evening azure of unloved dissipation. . . ." Yes, more than once I thought I could be happy, had not "rude destiny" interposed. Prayer has always saved me, and faith, but I have also been attacked by the forces of malignity, which have created in my understanding hours of doubt and anger. But have not the greatest saints endured worse aggressions? I have slogged through mudholes. I can say, like the vigorous Mexican,[16] "There are plumages that cross the swamp and are not sullied; my plumage is one of those."

As for that "unloved dissipation," would I have wasted so many hours of my life in white nights, the artificial and exorbitant euphoria of alcohol, the wasting-away of a too-robust

---

16. Salvador Díaz Mirón (*q.v.*).

youth, if fortune had smiled upon me and if another person's caprice and sad error had not kept me, after a cruelty of death, from the formation of a home? . . .

And let us give thanks to the Supreme Reason that I am able to exclaim, with the line that opens this book, "If I did not fall, it was because God is good!" In the *"Canción de otoño en primavera"* ("Song of Autumn in Spring") I bid farewell to the years of youth in a melancholy sonata which, if one must offer comparisons, has a melody like a sentimental echo of Musset. It is, of all my poems, the one that has conquered the greatest number of soft and fraternal hearts.

*"Trébol"* ("Three-Leaf Clover") is an homage to Spanish glories; in "Charitas," a theological aspiration sends up incense to the most sublime of virtues. In the following lines, *"¡Oh, terremoto mental!"* ("Oh Mental Earthquake!"), the menace of maleficent powers passes, and farther on there is talk of the danger of the eternal enemy, the lovely Varona who offers us the apple. . . . "Filosofía" addresses the truth of the natural world and divine reason against ugly, harmful appearances; in "Leda" I sing once more the glories of the Swan; *"Divina Psiquis"* ("Divine Psyche") tends, in its lyrical whirlwind, toward the ultimate consolation, the consolation of Christianity. The *"Soneto de trece versos"* ("Sonnet of Thirteen Lines"), whose misunderstood meaning has rendered more than one critic of not particularly malicious intent a babbling fool, is a game, *à la* Mallarmé, of suggestion and fantasy. The lines that follow it elevate moral miseries to ideality, and lighten their burden. Then comes a paternal recollection, a hymn to the mysterious enchantment of the female, a song of praise to the Great One-Handed, a madrigal of occasion, a song to the always attractive (to me) Thalassa, a philosophical meditation, followed by others: a biblical silhouette, allegories and symbols.

There is a sonnet with a sad history: "Melancholía." It is dedicated to a poor Venezuelan painter whose last name was the same as the Liberator's.[17] He was a man of grief, possessed by his art, but mostly by his despair. I met him in Paris; we

17. i.e., Domingo Bolívar.

were the best of friends; he showed me the wounds to his soul. I attempted to encourage him. After a short time, he left for the United States. And I soon learned that in New York, at the end of his bitter rope, he killed himself.

*"Aleluya"* praises the gift of joy in the Universe and in human love. *"De otoño"* ("On Autumn") explains the difference between the Mays and Decembers of the spirit; in the poem *"A Goya"* ("To Goya") I bow before the power of that prince, that genius of lights and shadows; in *"Caracol"* ("Sea Shell"), alongside the mystery of nature I set my own unknown mystery; in *"Amo, amas"* I lay the secret of life upon the holy universal fire of love; in *"Soneto autumnal al marqués de Bradomín"* ("Autumn Sonnet to the Marquis de Bradomín"), in praising a great wit of Spain I praise the aristocracy of thought; in another *"Nocturno"* I speak of the sufferings of incorrigible insomnia when the spirit trembles and listens; in *"Urna votiva"* ("Votive Urn") I pay my debt to friendship; in *"Programa matinal"* ("Dawn Program") I set forth a poetic epicureanism; in "Ibis" I point out the danger of poisonous relationships; in "Thanatos" I shudder at the inevitable; *"Ofrenda"* ("Offering") is a light, rhythmic Banvillesque compliment; *"Propósito primaveral"* ("Spring Proposition [or 'Purpose']") once more presents a goblet filled with wine from the amphorae of Epicurus.

*"Letanía de Nuestro Señor Don Quijote"* ("Litany for Our Lord Don Quixote") once again affirms my deep-rooted idealism, my passion for all things elevated and heroic. The figure of the Symbolic Gentleman is crowned with light and sadness. In this poem I attempt the smile of "humor"—like a memory of Cervantes' portentous creation—but behind the smile lies the visage of human torture by realities that do not touch Sancho. In *"Allá lejos"* ("There, Far Off ") there is a recollection of tropical landscapes, a memory of my hot native land, and in *"Lo fatal"* ("Mortal"), against my deep-rooted religiosity there rises, like a fearsome shadow, the ghost of desolation and doubt.

There has most certainly existed within me, from the beginning of my life, a profound preoccupation with the end of life, a terror of the unknown, a horror of the tomb, or rather, of the moment the heart halts in its uninterrupted task and life disappears from our body. In my desolation I have clung to God as a refuge; I have clutched at prayer as though at a parachute. I am filled with grief and despair when I examine my beliefs deeply, for I have not found my faith to be sufficiently strong and well founded when the conflict of ideas has made me waver, and I have felt that I am bereft of a constant, secure support.

All philosophies have seemed to me impotent—and some, detestable, or the work of madmen and malefactors. From Marcus Aurelius to Bergson, on the other hand, I have gratefully saluted those who give wings, who impart tranquility, peaceful flight, and who teach us to understand as best we can the enigma of our existence on this earth.

And so the principal merit of my work, if it has any, is that of great sincerity, of having displayed "my heart naked," of having flung the doors and windows of my interior castle wide open, so as to show my brethren the dwelling place of my most private ideas and dearest dreams.

I have known the cruelties and madnesses of men. I have been betrayed, paid with ingratitude and calumny, misunderstood in my best intentions by ill-inspired men, attacked, vilified. And I have smiled sadly. After all, everything is nothing, *la gloire* included. If it is true that "the bust survives the city," it is no less true that the infinity of time and space—both bust and city and, ay!, the planet itself—shall disappear before the gaze of the only Eternity.

# AZURE

Great God! What hand has scriven that evangel of despair that appeared yesterday in the columns of *La Tribuna*?

Through the dark and bitter sentences one can see the will-o-the-wisp of talent. It makes one want to repeat to that soul who poured so much bile into his ink the words spoken by Sainte-Beuve to Baudelaire: "My son, you must have suffered greatly."

Fortunately, the world is not the way the pale lovers of Misfortune see it.

The sun shines, women laugh, the air vibrates, and the lips of the roses sing their fragrant songs.

And in order for a man to seek the praise of that woman "who, unique in the world, has no breasts," as Matías Behety wrote, one's soul must lack any spark of the divine light of hope.

Humanity is sick, it's true. But what a way to cure it! The preachers of death do not see that the cure is worse than the disease.

It is not disdain for life, it is not horrifying surgery or suicide that will cure the sickness. It is hygiene, moral hygiene that is needed—one must raise one's eyes to the firmament, cool the heart with the dew of the ideal, fumigate oneself against the most horrible contagions of the plague, look at the invading wave and foresee its force, the bitterness of its white spray, be worthy of human nobility and divine goodness, be strong, and bear the saving *sursum!*[18] always in one's soul. That is handsome action; that is the rule.

18. "Upwards!" or "Onwards!"

And it is the easiest thing in the world to do. One learns this lesson from a little book that was once read a great deal but that today is relatively forgotten: the catechism.

This little book has never once been found in the pockets of children who kill one another.

And above all, oh writers!, it is good not to be one of the preachers of the tomb.

Blessèd be those who announce the dawn.

Do you think because you suffer you have the right to poison the world with your complaints?

Writers, your first duty is to give humanity all the azure possible.

Death to black!

Azure! Azure! Azure!

# FRONTISPIECE FOR "THE MISFITS" [19]

Pan, divine ancient Pan, rises at the entrance. But since the voices that one day announced his death did not lie, that Pan that rises in the night, upon the black mountain enchanted by the moon, is the theophany, the god-appearing. Look at his mummy arms, how they hold up the seven reeds of his pipe; look at that eyeless head, that dry chin to which some relic of the savage beard still clings, like sepulchral vegetation. That mouth which knew so much of laughter, kisses, and sensual love-bites and which blew so brilliantly songs upon the flute, today breathes forth a cold wind over the dead instrument, from which emerge weird sounds of music—the music of dreams, melodies of profound mysteries.

This Mountain of Visions, impregnated with the breath of night, raises its towers of dark trees filled with wandering, sobbing spirits. Look, look into the blackest part of the mountain, and sometimes you will see eyes of fire gleam forth. The vast and arcane mountain keeps its deepest secrets, and only those who have been lost in their pilgrimage and have heard—oh!— the sound that issues from the lipless mouth of the spectral Pan will know the wordless voices of the visions.

The moon's pale light enchants this fearsome, mysterious, perilous place, where often one may see, dancing in the wan and sickly moonglow, Madness who plucks the petals off daisies, and Death, crowned with roses.

From time to time, in the midst of the silent bosks, the

19. Never published with that volume; published in 1895 in the *Revue Illustrée du Río de la Plata.*

moonlight reveals the roundness of a snowy thigh, and if one pricks up one's ear, one may think one hears the vibrant laughter of a nymph.

I see the young walker coming, with his knapsack and his lyre. The bloodthirsty star comes to hide himself; he comes with his lovely hair still wet, because he has secreted the dew of dawn in it; with his cheeks rosy with kisses, because it is the time of Love; with his arms strong, to squeeze fleshly torsos— and so he comes, making his way to the black mountain!

I run, run toward him, before he reaches the place where, in the empire of the night, the head of the god-appeared rises, with horns, and without eyes: "Oh, young walker, go back," I say to him, "you have taken the wrong road. This road, you may be sure, takes you not to the peninsula of naked graces, fresh loves, pure, sweet stars. You have taken the wrong way: This is the road to the Mountain of Visions, where your beautiful hair will turn white, and your cheeks wither, and your arms grow tired, because upon this mountain is the spectral Pan, to the sound of whose pipes you will tremble before enigmas you can only glimpse, before mysteries you can only vaguely see. . . ."

The young walker, with his knapsack and his lyre, as though he had not heard my voice, continues on his way, unhalting, and soon he is lost to sight upon the Mountain, which is impregnated with the breath of night and enchanted by the Moon.

# THE MISFITS
## (*LOS RAROS*; EXCERPTS)

### EDGAR ALLAN POE

*Fragment of a study*

It was a cold, damp morning when I arrived for the first time in the immense nation of the United States. The steamer moved slowly, and the foghorn sounded, for fear of hitting another vessel. Fire Island and its erect lighthouse lay astern; we were just off Sandy Hook, from which the Health Department lighter set forth to meet us. The barking Yankee slang could be heard everywhere, under the canopy of stars and stripes. The cold wind, the nasal whistles, the smoke from smokestacks, the movement of machines, the big-bellied waves of that leaden sea, the steamer making its way into the great harbor—everything said *All right!* Through the fog and haze loomed islets and ships. Long Island showed us the immense ribbon of its coast, and Staten Island, as though framed in a vignette, stood in all its loveliness, tempting the pencil if not, due to lack of sun, the photographer's camera. The passengers gathered on the deck: the paunchy merchant, stuffed as a turkey, with a curving Jewish nose; the bony clergyman in a long black frock coat, a broad-brimmed felt hat, and, in his hand, a small Bible; the girl who wears a jockey's cap and throughout the crossing has sung in a phonographic voice, to the strumming of a banjo; the robust young man as smooth-skinned as a baby; an amateur boxer whose fists look as though he could knock out a rhinoceros with a single blow. . . . In the Narrows, we begin to make out the picturesque and flowered land, the Forts. Then, raising her symbolic torch above her head, the Madonna of Liberty, whose plinth is an entire island. From my soul there rises a salutation: "To thee, prolific, immense, dominant. To thee, Our Lady of Liberty. To thee, whose bronze breasts suckle multitudes of souls and hearts. To thee, who standest solitary and magnificent upon thy island, raising the divine torch. I salute thee as my steamer passes, and I prostrate myself before thy majesty: Hail, and *good morning!* I know, divine icon, oh great and grand statue, that thy mere name, the name of the great beauty thou incarnat'st, has made stars bloom above the world, like the Lord's *fiat lux*. There they are, shining upon the stripes of thy flag, the stars that illuminate the flight of the eagle of America—this, thy formidable blue-eyed America. Hail, Liberty, full of strength, blessed art thou above all women. But wouldst thou know an unhappy truth? Thou hast been wounded a good deal by the world, and thy splendor hath somewhat dimmed. Abroad in the earth there is another, who has usurped thy name, and instead of a torch bears a flaming brand. She is not the holy Diana of incomparable arrows; she is Hecate."

My salute done, my eyes look upon the enormous mass before me, that land crowned with towers, that region from which you can almost feel the breath of a terrible, subjugating wind. Manhattan, the island of iron. New York, the bloody, the cyclopic, the monstrous, the stormy, the irresistible capital of Capital. Surrounded by lesser islands, she is flanked by Jersey on the one side and linked to Brooklyn on the other by the enormous bridge, the Brooklyn Bridge, upon whose palpitating breast of iron there lies a bouquet of bell towers.

One thinks one hears the voice of New York, the echo of a vast soliloquy of figures, numbers. How unlike the voice of Paris, when one thinks one hears it—as seductive as a love song, a song of poetry and youth! Out of the soil of Manhattan one thinks that at any moment there might rise up some colossal Uncle Sam, calling all the people of the earth to a grand auction, and the auctioneer's hammer will fall upon cupolas and roof-tops, making a deafening metal racket. . . .

The men of Manhattan live in their towers of stone, iron, and glass, as in the castle-fortresses of days gone by. In their fabulous

Babel, they shout, bellow, thunder, roar; they cheer on the Stock Market, the locomotive, the forge, the bank, the printing press, the dock, the ballot box. Within the iron and granite walls of the Produce Exchange gather as many souls as in a small town. . . . Here is Broadway. Seeing it, one feels a sensation almost like pain, an overpowering vertigo. Down a grand canal whose banks are formed by monumental houses with their hundred glass eyes and sign tattoos flows a powerful river, a confusion of merchants, runners, horses, trams, omnibuses, sandwich-men dressed in advertisements, and fabulously beautiful women. As one's eyes take in the immense artery with its constant agitation, one begins to feel an anguish like that of certain nightmares. This is the life of ants: an anthill whose inhabitants are gigantic Percherons yoked to the monstrous tongues of every kind of wagon. The newspaper boy, pink and smiling, flits like a swallow from tram to tram, shouting at the passengers *Eentramsooonwooood,* which means he is hawking the *Evening Telegram,* the *Sun,* and the *World.* The noise is dizzying, and in the air there is a constant vibration—the clatter of horses' hooves, the echoing rumble of wheels—and it seems to grow louder every second. Every second, one would fear a collision, an accident, did one not know that this immense river flowing with the force of an avalanche moves with the precision of a machine. In the thickest mass of the crowd, in the most convulsive wave of motion, an elderly lady in her black cape, or a blond "miss," or a nanny with her baby will want to cross the street. A corpulent policeman raises his hand, the torrent halts, and the lady crosses—*All right!*

"Those cyclops . . . ," says Groussac; "those fierce Calibans . . . ," writes Péladan. Was Péladan right when he called these men of North America by those names? Caliban does rein on the island of Manhattan, and in San Francisco, Boston, Washington, as well—indeed, throughout the land. He has managed to institute the empire of *Matter,* from its mysterious state with Edison to its apotheosis in the hog, in that awe-inspiring city of Chicago. Caliban saturates himself with whiskey, as in Shakespeare's play he does with wine; he grows and prospers, and, slave to no Prospero, martyred by no genius of the air, he grows fat and multiplies—his name is Legion. By the will of God there rises up amidst those powerful monsters some being of superior nature, who spreads his wings before the eternal Miranda of the ideal. At that, Caliban mobilizes Sycorax against him, and banishes him or kills him. The world has seen this with Edgar Allan Poe, that ill-starred swan who best knew the world of dreams, and death. . . .

Why did the image of Stella, Alma, my sweet queen, so soon gone forever, come to my mind on that day when, after wandering along thronged Broadway, I sat down to read the verses of Poe—whose Christian name Edgar, harmonious and legendary, itself contains such vague, sad poetry—and saw the procession of his chaste beloved women pass before me, in the silvery dust of a mystic daydream? It was because you, my adored one, are sister to the lilylike virgins sung in that misty English tongue by the unhappy dreamer, prince of *poètes maudits*. You, like they, are a flame of infinite love. Your sisters pass before the white-rose-bedecked balcony in Paradise from which you look out with generous, deep eyes, and they salute you, in the wonder of your virtue—oh my consoling angel! oh my wife!—with a smile. The first to pass by is Irene, with her strange pallor, the bright lady come o'er far-off seas; the second is Eulalie, sweet Eulalie with yellow hair and violet eyes lifted up to heaven; the third is Lenore, named by the young, radiant angels in distant Eden;[20] the next is Frances, the beloved whose memory soothes your cares; then comes Ulalume, whose shade wanders the misty region of Weir, near that gloomy tarn of Auber; then Helen, she who was seen for the first time in the pearl light of the moon;[21] next is Annie, Annie of kisses and caresses and prayers for the adored one; and then there is Annabel Lee, who loved with a love coveted by the winged seraphs of heaven; and after her comes the other Isabel, she of the loving colloquies in the moonlight; Ligeia, at last, meditative, wrapped in a veil of otherworldly splendor. . . . This is a choir of Oceanides, who console and cool the brow of our lyrical Prometheus chained to the Yankee promontory, where a

20. In "The Raven" (1845).
21. Darío is referring to the 1848 "To Helen," not the more famous poem of the same title written in 1831.

raven, crueler than the Aeschylan vulture, seated on a bust of
Pallas, tortures his poor heart, stabbing him with the monoto-
nous syllables of despair. And so you are for me: In the midst of
the martyrdoms of life, you refresh me and encourage me with
the air from your wings, for though you departed in human form
upon the voyage that has no return, when my strength fails me
or when pain flogs me with its black lash, I feel the coming of
your immortal being. Then, Alma, Stella, I hear the invisible gold
of your angelical shield near by me. Your luminous, symbolic
name rises in the sky of my nights like an incomparable guiding
star, and by your ineffable light I bear the gold and frankincense
and myrrh to the manger of eternal Hope.

## The Man

Poe's influence on the world's literature has been deep and tran-
scendent enough that his name and his work shall be remem-
bered forever more. From the time of his death to today, there
has been almost no year in which, whether in book or periodical,
critics, essayists, and poets have not sung this finest of American
poet's praises. Ingram's book illuminated the man's life; nothing
can increase the glory of the wondrous dreamer. Indeed, the pub-
lication of that book, whose translation into Spanish was carried
out by Sr. Mayer, was intended for the wider public. . . .

Poe, like some Ariel made man, passed his life, one might say,
under the floating influence of a strange mystery. Born in a land
of practical, material life, the influence of his surroundings
worked upon him in reverse. Out of a land of calculations arose
this stupendous imagination. The gift of mythology seems to
have been born in him out of some distant atavism, and one sees
in his poetry a bright ray of the land of sun and azure where his
forebears had been born. Reborn in him was the chivalric spirit
of the knights Le Poer, praised in the chronicles of Gambresio. In
Ireland in 1327, Arnold Le Poer hurls this terrible insult at the
knight Maurice, Earl of Desmond: "Thou art a rhymer." And for
that, the men take up their swords and a dispute begins that is
but the prologue to a bloody war. Five hundred years later, a de-
scendant of the provocative Arnold will glorify his line, erecting

upon the rich pedestal of the English language, and in a new world, the golden palace of his rhymes.

Poe's noble family is of no interest, of course, except to "those who have a taste for discovering the effects produced by their country and their lineage on the mental and constitutional peculiarities of men of genius," as the noble Mrs. Whitman has noted. Indeed, it is Poe, not the family, that gives honor and worth to all the Protestant ministers, storekeepers, investors, and street-hawkers that bear his name in the land of the honorable father of his country, George Washington.

We know that in the poet's lineage there was a brave Sir Roger who battled alongside Strongbow; a daring Sir Arnold who defended a lady accused of witchcraft; a heroic, virile woman, the famous "Countess" of the times of Cromwell; and passing over several genealogical confusions, a general of the United States, Edgar's grandfather. And yet after all that, this tragic creature, whose story is so strange and romantic, uttered his newborn's cries under withered laurels; he was born to an actress, who gave birth to him in the empire of her fiercest love. The poor playeress had been orphaned at an early age; she loved the theater; she was intelligent and beautiful; and out of that sweet grace was born the pale, melancholic visionary who gave art a new world.

Poe was born with the enviable gift of physical beauty. Of all the portraits I have seen of him, none gives any idea of that special beauty that many persons who knew him have insisted upon in their descriptions of the man. There can be no doubt that in all the Poean iconography, the portrait that best represents him is that which Mr. Clarke used, an engraving of the poet during the time he was working in that gentleman's establishment. Clarke himself protested against the false portraits of Poe that were published after his death. If not so much as those who calumniated his lovely poetic soul, those who disfigured the beauty of his face are worthy of the world's sternest censure. Of all the portraits that have come into my hands, those that I have been most struck by are Chiffart's, published in Quantin's illustrated edition of the *Extraordinary Tales,* and the engraving by R. Loncup for Mayer's translation of Ingram's biography. In both, Poe has reached a mature age. He is not,

then, that somewhat dashing, sensitive young man who, intro-
duced to Elena Stannard, was rendered speechless, like the
Dante of the *Vita Nuova*. . . . No, he is the man who has suf-
fered, who knows at first hand how life can wound the flesh and
spirit. In the first of these portraits, the artist seems to have
wanted to produce a symbolic head. In the almost ornithomor-
phic eyes, in the air, in the tragic expression of the face, Chif-
fart has attempted to paint the author of "The Raven," the
visionary, the unhappy artist more than the man. In the second,
there is more realism: that look of infectious sadness, that
pinched mouth, that vague gesture of pain, that broad, magnif-
icent brow on which the fatal pallor of suffering is enthroned,
show the poor man in his days of worst misfortune, perhaps
those just before his death. The other portraits, such as Halpin's
for Armstrong's edition, give us *types* of the period, dandies,
faces that have nothing to do with the beautiful, intelligent head
that Clarke describes. Nothing truer than Gautier's observa-
tion: "It is rare for a poet, say, or an artist, to be known under
his first, enchanting aspect. Reputation comes only much later,
when the fatigues of study, the struggle to earn a living, and the
tortures of passion have altered that primitive physiognomy,
leaving but a mask, a worn, withered mask on which every
pain, every suffering has left a stigma, a bruise, a wrinkle."

Even as a child, Poe "promised great beauty," according to
Ingram. His schoolmates speak of his agility and his robust-
ness. His imagination and his nervous temperament were coun-
terbalanced by the strength of his muscles. The friendly, delicate
angel of poesy could double his fist and use it. . . .

When he entered West Point, a fellow student, Mr. Gibson,
has noted his "weary, tedious, jaded eyes." When he became a
virile young man, the bibliophile Gowans remembers him in
this way: "Poe had a remarkably agreeable exterior, and what
the ladies would call 'beauty' most certainly predisposed one to
him." A person who heard him recite in Boston says, "He was
the finest realization of a poet, in physiognomy, air, and man-
ner." A fine portrait by a female hand: "A stature a little less
than the middle height, perhaps, but so perfectly proportioned
and crowned by a head so noble, and carried so regally, that in

my girlish opinion, he gave the impression of an overtowering
stature. Those bright, melancholy eyes seemed to look down
from a great height." Another lady recalls the strange impres-
sion made by his eyes: "Poe's eyes, in truth, were the feature
that most impressed one, and it was to them that his face owed
its peculiar attractiveness." I have never seen anyone else's eyes
that resembled them. They were large, jet black, with long eye-
lashes; the iris was steel gray, and of a crystalline brightness and
transparency. The jet black pupil would expand and contract
with every shade of thought or emotion. I observed that his eye-
lids would never contract, as is so common in most people,
mainly when they speak, but his gaze was always full, open,
and without shrinking-back or emotion. His habitual expres-
sion was that of the dreamer, the sad man; sometimes he had a
way of giving a slight glance, out of the corner of his eye, at
some person who was not watching him, and with a calm, fixed
gaze he would seem to be mentally measuring the caliber of
that person, who would be totally unaware. "What enormous
eyes Mr. Poe has!" a lady said to me. "It chills my blood to see
him turn them slowly toward me and fix them upon me when
I am speaking." This same lady adds, "He wore a black, care-
fully trimmed mustache, but it did not completely mask a tight-
ness of the mouth and an occasional tension in his upper lip, as
though in mockery. This mockery was easily kindled, and it
manifested itself in a barely perceptible yet intensely expressive
movement of the lip. There is nothing of malevolence in him,
but there is a great deal of sarcasm." We know, then, that that
potent, strange soul was enclosed in a lovely vessel. It appears
that distinction and physical gifts must be innate in all bearers
of the lyre. Is Apollo, the long-maned lyrical Numen, not the
prototype of masculine beauty? But not all his children are born
with such splendid gifts. The privileged ones are named
Goethe, Byron, Lamartine, Poe.

Because of his vigorous and cultivated constitution, our poet
was able to resist that terrible condition that an author who was
also a physician quite rightly calls "the illness of sleep." He was
sublime and passionate, a nervous man, one of those divine
half-madmen necessary for human progress; he was a pitiable

Christ of art, who out of love for the eternal ideal had to walk the street of bitterness, and wear his crown of thorns, and bear his cross. He was born with the adorable flame of poetry, and it nourished him at the same time it martyred him.

He was orphaned as a child, but he was taken in by a man who was never able to recognize the intellectual stature of his adoptive son. Mr. Allan, whose name would pass into the future in the bright light of the poet's name, could never imagine that the poor boy who cheered evenings at home by reciting poetry would later be one of the great princes of art.

In Poe, daydreaming reigned from childhood. . . . On the one hand, his strong mind possessed a faculty for music; on the other, a faculty for mathematics. His "daydreaming" is filled with chimeras and figures, like some astrological chart. . . . He went to school to Mr. Clarke, in Richmond, where at the same time he was nourishing himself upon the classics and reciting Latin odes he was boxing, even becoming something of a student champion. In foot races, he would have left Atalanta in his dust, and he aspired to Byron's swimming laurels. But if he shone intellectually and physically among his schoolmates, and indeed stood head and shoulders above them, the scions of the families of the flabby aristocracy of the city looked down on the actress's son. How much bile must that delicate creature have had to swallow, humiliated as he was by origins which in later years he would proudly boast of? Those were the first blows, and they began to engrave upon his countenance the bitter, sarcastic creases of his mouth. At a very early age he knew the lurking wolf of reason; that was why he sought to communicate with nature, so healthful, so fortifying.

"I hate above all things and detest this animal called Man," Swift wrote Pope. Poe, in turn, speaks of the "mean-spirited friendship and gossamer fidelity of mere men." In the book of Job, Eliphaz the Temanite exclaims, "How much more abominable and filthy is man, which drinketh iniquity like water?"[22] Our lyrical American did not seek the aid of prayer; he was not a believer, or at least his soul was never mystical. . . . Science

22. Job 15:16.

prevented the poet from spreading his wings and attaining the atmosphere of ideal truth. His need for analysis, the algebraic nature of his fantasy, made him produce infinitely sad effects when he dragged us to the verge of the unknown. Philosophical speculation blinded him to faith, which, like every true poet, he must have possessed. In all his works, if I am not mistaken, only twice does the name of Christ appear (though he has a hymn to Mary in *Poems and Essays*). He did, nonetheless, profess an adherence to Christian morals, and as for man's destiny and fate, he believed in a divine Law, an inexorable Judgment. In him, equations overpowered belief, and even with respect to God and His attributes, he, like Spinoza, believed that things invisible and things that are the right object of understanding can be perceived only through the eyes of demonstration. This, forgetting the profound philosophical declaration *Intellectus noster sic se habet ad prima entium quae sunt manifestissima in natura, sicut oculus vespertilionis ad solem.*[23] He did not believe in the supernatural, as he himself declared, but he said that God, as creator of Nature, could, if He chose, change it. In the story of the metempsychosis of Ligeia there is a definition of God, taken from Grandwill, that Poe seems to maintain: "God is but a great will pervading all things by nature of its intentness." . . . In "Mesmeric Revelation," on the heels of certain philosophical digressions, Mr. Vankirk, who, like almost all the characters in Poe, is Poe himself, affirms the existence of a material God, which he calls "ultimate, or unparticled, matter." But he adds, "The unparticled matter, or God, in quiescence, is (as nearly as we can conceive it) what men call mind."[24] In the dialogue between Oinos and Agathos[25] he pretends to sound the mystery of the divine intelligence, as in the dialogues of Monos and Una[26] and

23. "As the eyes of bats are to the light of the sun, so is the intelligence of our soul to the things most manifest by nature" (Aquinas, *Summa contra gentiles,* bk. 1, chap. 3, quoting Aristotle, *Metaphysics,* bk. 2, part 1).
24. Here, in the Spanish, Darío uses the word "spirit" instead of "mind," perhaps because of a faulty translation by "Sr. Mayer." Poe's words in "Mesmeric Revelation" are as quoted above.
25. In "The Power of Words," 1850.
26. In "The Colloquy of Monos and Una," 1850.

Eiros and Charmion[27] he penetrates the unknown shadow of Death, producing, as few have, strange glimpses into his conception of spirit in space and time.


## PAUL VERLAINE

At last you will be at rest; at last, oh poor divine old man!, you have stopped dragging about your lamentable stiff leg and your existence filled with pain and dreams. No longer will you suffer *mal de vie,* complicated in you by the malign influence of Saturn.

You died, no doubt, in one of the hospitals you taught your disciples to love—one of those "winter palaces" of yours, the spas and rest homes that were home to your vagabond bones when you writhed from implacable attacks of rheumatism and the harsh miseries of Paris life.

You have died, no doubt, surrounded by your loved ones, your spiritual children, the young officiants of your church, the students of your school, oh lyrical Socrates of an impossible time!

But you die at a glorious moment, when your name begins to triumph and the seeds of your ideas have started to become magnificent flowers of art, even in countries distant from your own. For today we can say that now, around the world, your figure—your nimbus—shines resplendent among the chosen few of diverse languages and climes, as it does before the throne of immense Wagner.

[One critic] has portrayed Verlaine as a leper seated before the door of a cathedral—pitiable, mendicant, awakening compassion, a groat's-worth of charity among the entering and departing faithful. [Another] compares him to Benoit Labre,[28] the living symbol of disease and misery; León Bloy had once called him the Leper, and had painted him in the triptych *Un brelan d'excommuniés,* alongside the Enfant Terrible Barbey d'Aurevilly and the Madman Ernesto Hello. Ay, such was, indeed, his

27. In "The Conversation of . . . ," 1850.
28. St. Benedict Labre (*q.v.*).

life! Seldom is a creature born of woman's womb so fated to bear upon his shoulders such a weight of pain and grief. Job would say to him: *Mon frère!*

I confess that after plunging into the agitated waters of the gulf of his books; after penetrating into the secret of that unique existence; after seeing that soul scarred and incurably wounded; after hearing all those echoes of celestial or profane music, always deeply enchanting; after contemplating that imposing figure in its pain, that superb head, those dark eyes, that face with its hint of Socrates, Pierrot, and a child; after gazing upon the fallen god, punished, perhaps, for Olympian crimes in some prior life; after knowing the sublime faith and furious love and immense poetry whose dwelling was that wretched, hobbling body—I felt a dolorous love being born in my heart, alongside my great admiration for this sad master.

As I passed through Paris in 1893, Enrique Gómez Carrillo offered to introduce me to him. My friend had published an impassioned "impression" . . . in which he spoke of a visit to a patient in the hospital in Broussais. "And there I found him, always ready with a fierce word of mockery, in a narrow hospital bed. His huge, friendly face, whose extreme paleness reminded me of the figures painted by Ribera, had a hieratic aspect. The nostrils of his small nose dilated often, to sniff at the delicious smoke of a cigar. His thick lips, which half-opened to lovingly recite several lines from Villón or curse the poems of Ronsard, always had upon them that bitter grimace in which vice and goodness mingle to form the expression of a smile. His blond Cossack beard had grown a bit, and had turned much grayer."

Through Carrillo's agency we penetrated into some of Verlaine's inner thoughts. This was not the time of the worn, spent, feeble old man that one might imagine; he was, rather a "robust old fellow." One might venture that he suffered from dreadful nightmares and visions in which the memories of the dark and mysterious legend of his life mingled with the sadness and terror of alcoholism. He passed his hours in illness, sometimes in pitiable isolation, abandoned and forgotten despite the kind initiatives of the likes of Mendès and León Deschamps.

My God! That man born to wear the crown of thorns, and to suffer the slings and arrows and afflictions of the world, looked to me like the living symbol of angelic grandeur and human misery. Angelic, Verlaine most surely was: No lute, no psaltery since Jacopone da Todi's, since the *Stabat Mater,* has praised the Virgin with the filial, ardent, yet humble melody of *Sagesse*; no tongue, save perhaps the tongues of prostrate seraphim, has better sung the flesh and blood of the Lamb; in no hands have the sacred coals of penitence burned hotter; and no penitent has flagellated his naked back with greater ardor of repentance than Verlaine when he has rent his very soul and its fresh, pure blood has spilled forth in rhythmic roses of martyrdom.

Those who have looked into his *Confessions,* into his *Hospitals,* into his other intimate books, will understand the man—inseparable from the poet—and find that in that sea, tempestuous at first, dead calm later, there are treasure-stores of pearls. Verlaine was a wretched son of Adam in whom the paternal bequest was stronger than in other men. Of the three Enemies, the World did him the least harm. The Devil hounded and attacked him; he defended himself from the onslaught, as he could, with the shield of prayer. The Flesh, however, was invincible and implacable. Seldom has the serpent Sex bitten the human brain more furiously, and more venomously. The poet's body was the lyre of sin; he was an eternal prisoner of desire. When he walked, one was tempted to look in his footprint for the cleft of the hoof. It was odd not to see upon his brow two little horns, for in his eyes one could see visions of white nymphs flit past, and upon his lips, once familiar with the flute, there oft appeared Pan's rictus. Like Hugo's satyr, he would have said to Venus, upon the splendor of the sacred mount: *Viens nous en! . . .* [29] And that carnal pagan's lust did not ebb, but waxed eternally, primitive and natural, as his Catholic conception of guilt grew stronger.

And yet—Have you not read those lovely stories, renewed recently by Anatole France, in which there are satyrs who

29. "Come along, then!"

worship God and believe in His heaven and His saints and even manage upon occasion to become satyr-saints? That to my mind is the case of Pauvre Lelian—half, horned flute player in the forest, violator of hamadryads; half, the Lord's ascete, the hermit who, ecstatic, sings His psalms. The hairy body suffered the tyranny of the blood, the imperious domination of the nerves, the flame of spring, the aphrodisiac of the free and fecund mountain; the spirit was consecrated to praise of the Father, the Son, and the Holy Spirit, but as well, and above all, the chaste, maternal Virgin, so that when Temptation sounded its clarion-call, the spirit, eyeless, did not look, but remained as though in a stupor, to the music of the fanfare of the flesh. There were times when the satyr would return from the forest and the soul would recover its empire and look up toward God; the remorse would be profound, and the psalm would issue forth. And so he would live, until, through the thick leaves of the woods, he would glimpse Calixto's thigh again. . . .

When Nordau published his famous work on Dr. Tribulat Bonhomet, the figure of Verlaine—almost unknown to the general public, and among that general public I include many of the *élite* in other spheres—appeared for the first time, in the most curiously abominable of portraits. The poet of *Sagesse* was presented as one of those supposedly patent illustrations of the pseudo-scientific claim that contemporary aesthetic fashions are forms of intellectual decay. I will give a brief excerpt of Nordau's presentation of the "case": "We have before us the neatly-delineated figure of the most famous of the *Symbolistes*. We see a horrid degenerate with an asymmetrical cranium and a mongoloid face; an impulsive vagabond; a dipsomaniac; . . . an erotomaniac; . . . an emotional dreamer, weak in spirit, who struggles painfully against his evil instincts and finds sometimes in his anguish, moving moans and whimpers; a mystic whose smoky consciousness is filled with representations of God and the saints; a doddering old fool . . ."

Many writers were attacked; some defended themselves. Even the cabbalistic Mallarmé, descending from his tripod to give a lecture on Music and Literature in London, felt himself obliged to demonstrate the lack of intellect of that Austro-German "professor." Pauvre Lelian did not defend himself, although several friends and disciples did, Charles Tennib perhaps with greatest vigor and aplomb, and his beautiful, justified diatribe was a fit reply to Nordau's attack. . . .

Of the works of Verlaine, what is there to say? He has been among the greatest poets of this century. His work is scattered over the face of the earth. It is now seen as shameful for the official, earthbound writers of today not to quote Paul Verlaine from time to time, if only to damn him with faint praise. In Norway and Sweden, the young friends of Jonas Lee extend the master's artistic influence. In England, where he was wont to give lectures, and thanks to new writers such as Symons and the contributors to the *Yellow Book,* his illustrious name is well known: the *New Review* has printed his verses in French. In the United States, even before the publication in *Harper's Magazine* of Symons' famous essay "The Decadent Movement in Literature," the poet's fame was firmly established. In Italy, D'Annunzio acknowledged him as one of the masters who aided his rise to glory; Vittorio Pica and the young artists of the Tavola Rotonda expound his doctrines. In Holland, the new literary generation salute him—Werwey's study is a notable example. In Spain, he is almost unknown, and shall continue to be so for a long time; it is only Clarín, I believe, and the perspicacity of Clarín, that has held him in high esteem. Nothing worthy of Verlaine has been written in Spanish, save perhaps a few things published by Gómez Carrillo, for the notes and impressions by Bonafoux and Eduardo Pardo are very slight, indeed.

Let these lines serve, then, as an offering to the moment. On another occasion I shall consecrate to the grand Verlaine the study he so fully merits. For today, this shall be all.

"This sick leg does make me suffer some; on the other hand, it is easier to bear than my verses, which truly bring me anguish. . . . And if not for the rheumatism, I couldn't live on my income—if one is well, the hospitals won't have one."

Those words paint the fraternal tragedy of Villon.

He was not evil; his *animula, blandula, vagula*[30] was ill. . . .
God has taken him into heaven as though into a hospital!


# COMTE AUGUSTE DE VILLIERS
# DE L'ISLE-ADAM

*Va oultre!*
— Motto of the house of Villiers
de l'Isle-Adam

"This was a king . . ." Thus, as in a fairy tale, should begin the
story of the *monarque raté mais poète formidable*[31] who in this
life was known as the Comte Auguste de Villiers de l'Isle-
Adam. A fragment of his ideal history might be constructed
thus:

"At that time—in the middle years of the indecorous nine-
teenth century—Greece saw a rebirth of its ancient splendor. A
prince like the princes of antiquity was crowned in Athens, and
he shone like a royal star. He was descended from the Knights
of Malta; in him there was a pinch of Prince Hamlet and much
more of King Apollo; silver trumpets announced his coming; he
would ride through the countryside in a heroic chariot drawn
by teams of white steeds; he evicted from his realms all the cit-
izens of the United States; he showered largesse upon painters,
sculptors, and rhymers, and soon the Attic bees began to buzz
again to the sound of lyres and brushes. He filled the woods
with statues; the eyes of shepherds were met once again with
visions of nymphs and goddesses. He received the state visit of

30. *Animula, vagula, blandula* is the correct sequence of this famous three-word
phrase; Darío seems to have had a *lapsus menti*. It is the first line of a poem at-
tributed to Hadrian (A.D. 76–138) on his deathbed: *Animula, vagula, blandula /
Hospes, comesque, corporis, / Quae nunc abibis in loca, / Pallidula, rigid,
nudula?*, translated as "Sorry-lived, blithe little, fluttering sprite, / Comrade and
guest in this body of clay, / Whither, ah! Whither, departing in flight, / Rigid,
half-naked, pale minion, away?" Thus, Darío understands these words to refer,
wryly, to the soul.
31. Failed monarch, formidable poet.

a sovereign named Louis of Bavaria, a gentleman as handsome as Lohengrin, beloved by Lorelei, who lived beside an azure lake dotted with snowdrifts of swans. He brought Wagner to the harmonious land of Olympus, so that the beautiful sun of Greece might set its golden halo upon the divine brow of Euphorion. He sent embassies to the lands of the Orient, and closed the gates of his kingdom to the Western barbarians. Thanks to him, the glory of the Muses returned, and when he died, no one knew whether it was an eagle or a unicorn that bore his body off to a mysterious place."

But fate, oh sire!, oh poet sublime!, would not allow that happy dream to come to pass, in these times which have taken the abominable figure of a Franklin to the highest apotheosis.

Villiers de l'Isle-Adam is a being rare among the rare ones. All those who knew him preserve the impression of an extraordinary personage.

In the eyes of sublime, hermetic Mallarmé he was a man of dreams, a solitary, like the most beautiful gems and saintliest souls; in addition, in all things and by all things, he was a king—an absurd king, if you will, poetic and fantastic, but a king all the same. And then, a genius. "The most magnificently endowed youngster of his generation," Henri Laujol has written. In 1884, Mendès wrote the following about Villiers:

"How wretched and unfortunate are the demigods! They are too far from us for us to love them like brothers and too close to be adored as teachers." The type of the *demi-genius*, described by the poet of the *Panteleia*, is apt. We might name more than one man who might have have been, like a spark of the celestial fire from which God forms geniuses, a complete genius, a total genius, but who, like an eagle with clipped wings, could neither reach the supreme heights, like a condor, nor flit about the woods like a nightingale.

Demi-geniuses have more than talent, but they lack the voice to say to the gates of the Infínite, as on that page by Hugo: "Open. I am Dante." And thus they float, alone, isolated, unable to rise to the titanic strength of Shakespeare, unable to seek refuge in the flowery stalls of Gautier. And they are wretched.

Today, when all the works of Villiers de l'Isle-Adam have been published, there is hardly any reticence to salute him as one of the august and superior spirits. His genius is that which creates and that which dives deepest into the divine and mysterious. Villiers was, indeed, a genius.

He was born to triumph, yet he died without seeing that victory. Descendant of a noble family, he lived in poverty, almost abject penury. An aristocrat by blood, art, and taste, he was obliged to frequent surroundings unsuitable to his delicacy and royalty. Verlaine was right to include him among his *poètes maudits*. That proud man, of a pride that sat comfortable upon his shoulders, that artist who wrote, "What does justice matter to us? Any man that is born without his own glory in his breast will never know the real meaning of that word," made his pilgrimage through the world accompanied by suffering, and he was one of the damned.

According to Verlaine, and especially according to Villiers' biographer and cousin R. du Pontavice de Heussey, he began by writing verses. He awakened to poetry in the Breton countryside, where, like Poe, he had an ill-starred love affair, a sweet, pure dream snatched away by Death. It is curious how all the great poets have suffered the same pain—and it perhaps explains that beautiful constellation of divine dead maidens who shine so brilliantly in the sky of art, and whose names are Beatrice, Lady Rowena de Tremain, and that sublime lady made to vibrate by the lute of Daniel Gabriel Rossetti. Villiers, at seventeen, was already singing:

> *Oh! Vous souvenez-vous, forêt délicieuse,*
> *de la jolie enfant qui passait gracieuse,*
> *souriant simplement au ciel, à l'avenir,*
> *se perdant avec moi dans ces vertes allées?*
> *Eh bien! Parmi les lis de vos sombres vallées*
> *vous ne la verrez plus venir.*[32]

32. Oh! Do you remember, delicious woods / that pretty girl who gracefully passed by / smiling innocently at the sky, at the future, / wandering with me through these green allées? / Well, among the flowers of your shady valleys, / you will never see her come again.

Villiers never again loved with as much fire as in his youth; his had been an almost childlike passion, and it was "the love of his life."

Gautier, speaking in his *Grotesques*[33] about Chapelain, notes that Chapelain's parents, contrary to a family's usual horror of a literary career, pushed their son into poetry. The result was that French letters were provided with an excellent bad poet. This was not, by any means, the case of Villiers. From his earliest years, his parents encouraged him in his struggle to become an artist; the family possessed, from time immemorial, a sense of greatness and a trust in every victory. The fond parents—especially that proud marquis, seeker after treasures—never lost hope; they always believed that their Mathias' head was destined to wear a crown, whether it was the gold of kings or the fresh green laurel of poets. Although this latter diadem was beginning to be seen in the last days of his life—Verlaine went so far as to call him *trés glorieux*—another crown, this one of thorns, had always graced the brow of the unhappy dreamer.

When Villiers arrived in Paris it was the dawn of the Parnassians. In all those brilliant warriors for art, his arrival inspired awe and amazement. Coppée, Dierx, Heredia, Verlaine—they all saluted him as though he were a triumphant captain. "A genius!" exclaimed Mallarmé. And so we understood him to be. The genius revealed itself from the first: a few poems published in a volume dedicated to Comte Alfred de Vigny. Then, in the *Révue Fantastique,* edited by Catulle Mendès, he gave life to the most surprising character ever to animate this century's literature: Dr. Tribulat Bonhomet. Only a breath of Shakespeare could have made the stupendous *type* that so perfectly symbolizes our incomparable age live and breathe and *work* in the way Villiers did.

33. A series of "literary exhumations" performed by Théophile Gautier; his subjects included François Villon, Cyrano de Bergerac, and Jean CHAPELAIN (*q.v.*). In a sense, this work is comparable to Darío's own *Los Raros,* though Darío's portraits of these "misfits," "rare birds," decadents, the misunderstood and despised, are of his contemporaries.

Dr. Tribulat Bonhomet is a sort of tragic and malignant Don Quixote, pursuing a Dulcinea of utilitarianism; his figure is painted in such a way as to make a strong man tremble. The deep, mysterious influence of Poe prevails in the creation of this figure, there can be no doubt of that. . . . Both Shakespeare and Poe have, of course, produced similar flashes of brilliance— flashes that half illuminate, if only just for an instant, the shadows of Death, the dark kingdom of the supernatural. In Villiers, this impulse toward the arcana of life persists, and we find it in later works such as *Cruel Tales, New Cruel Tales, Isis,* and one of the most powerful and original novels ever written: *The Eve of the Future.* . . .

His life is another novel, another tale, another poem. Let us look, for example, at the legend of the king of Greece, which appears in narrations by Laujol, Verlaine, and B. Pontavice de Heussey. Heussey's version is as follows: "In the year of grace 1863, at a time when imperial governments shone with their greatest brilliance, the Hellenes were in need of a king. The great powers that protected the tiny, heroic nation for whom Byron sacrificed his life—France, Russia, England—set about seeking a young constitutional tyrant for their protectorate. During this period, Napoleon III had a determining voice in the congresses of Europe, and there was great concern whether he might present a candidate, who of course would in the course of things be French. The newspapers were filled with rumors, commentaries on this burning matter: the 'Greek question' was the order of the day. Periodicals gave free rein to their imagination, for while other nations seemed to have chosen the son of the king of Denmark—the ruler so justly called 'the taciturn prince' by Charles Dickens, his friend of gloomy days—the Emperor, studious Napoleon, kept his own quiet counsel. And so things went on until one morning in early March when the grand marquis (the father of our Villiers) rushed like a hurricane into the sad sitting room on rue St.-Honoré, waving a newspaper about and exclaiming in a veritable apoplexy of excitation—a state soon shared by the entire family. This, in a nutshell, is the strange news published that morning by many

Parisian dailies: 'We have learned from a reliable source that a new candidate for the throne of Greece has just emerged. The candidate today is a great French gentleman, well known throughout Paris: none other than Comte Auguste de Villiers de l'Isle-Adam, the last of the noble line which produced the heroic defender of Rhodes, and the first Grand Master of the Knights of Malta. In the most recent reception hosted by Napoleon, the emperor, asked by one of his court about the success that this candidate might meet, simply smiled enigmatically. All our votes to the new aspirant!' Those who have followed my story thus far will surely imagine the effect that this news produced on the minds and imaginations of the family of Villiers. . . ."

Now of course there might be some sort of joke in this report, but however the case may be, the young pretender was granted an interview at the Tuilleries, where the matter was to be taken up. And the well-dressed—though not, let it be said, with the mantle, or uniform, or suit of armor of his grandparents—young count was received in the royal palace . . . by the Duke of Bassano. Villiers lived in a world of dreams, and any modern monarch would have been naught but a good bourgeois to him, with the possible exception of Louis of Bavaria, the madman. The eccentricities of Mathias I, the poet, left the royal chamberlain a bit disconcerted: the youth believed he had been the victim of occult enemies; he thought this whole thing was some sort of Shakespearean tragedy; he refused to speak with anyone but the Emperor himself. *Il vous faudra donc prendre la peine de venir une autre fois, monsieur le comte, dit le duc en se levant; sa majesté est occupée et m'a chargé de vous recevoir.*[34] And so ended Villiers' pretension to the throne of Greece, and the Greeks' chance to see the age of Pindar reborn under the rule of a lyrical king who would have had a real scepter, a real crown, a real mantle, and who, banishing Western abominations—umbrellas, beaver hats, newspapers, constitutions, etcetera—Civilization and Progress, with

34. You will have to take the trouble to come another time, then, monsieur le comte, the duke said, getting up; his majesty is occupied and has asked me to receive you (Heussey).

capital C and capital P—would have made the old groves fabulous once more, would have celebrated the triumph of Homer in temples made of marble, under the curvets of doves and the soaring flights of bees, and to the magical sound of illustrious cicadas.

There are other admirable pages in the life of this magnificent unfortunate. The beginnings of his literary life have been affectionately and admiringly described by Coppée, Mendès, Verlaine, Mallarmé, Laujol; the last moments of his life, no one has portrayed like the admirable Huysmans . . . .

A couple of anecdotes and a few words by Coppée:

The story was told of Villiers arriving at one of the Parnassians' soirées: Suddenly the group rose as one and cried "Villiers! It's Villiers!" as a young man with pale azure eyes and unsteady legs, biting on a cigarette, twisting his short blond moustache, and tossing his long, unruly hair entered the room a bit distractedly. He embraced the poets all round, shook hands and so on, and then went straight for the open piano, where he sat and poised his fingers above the keyboard. Then he began to sing in a voice that quivered yet had such a magical quality about it that none of the men present were ever to forget it. It was a melody that he had just conceived as he walked over that night—a vague and mysterious melody by which he accompanied Baudelaire's gorgeous sonnet:

> *Nous aurons des lits pleins d'odeurs légères,*
> *Des divans profonds comme des tombeaux* . . . [35]

Then, when everyone was thoroughly charmed, the singer abruptly interrupted himself, stood, turned from the piano, and went off to hide himself in a corner of the room, where he rolled another cigarette, gave his astonished audience a sidelong, unsure look, a gaze like Hamlet's at the feet of Ophelia. . . . This was

35. On couches filled with odors faint and failing, / Divans profound as tombs, we shall recline ("La Mort des Amantes" / "The Death of Lovers," trans. Clark Ashton Smith [www.eldritchdark.com/wri/poetry/death_of_lovers.html, as of June 12, 2004]).

Comte Auguste de Villiers de l'Isle-Adam eighteen years ago, in those friendly soirées on the rude de Douai, in Catulle Mendès house. . . .

When Drumont fired his first anti-Semitic salvo with the publication of *France Juive*, the powerful Israelites of Paris began looking for a writer who might victoriously respond to the broadside writer's formidable text. Someone mentioned Villiers, whose poverty was common knowledge; they thought to buy his clean conscience, and his pen. An envoy was sent to him for this purpose, a man of the world, a merchant who commanded, in addition to a fortune, fine words and elegant bearing. The envoy entered the humble apartment of the famous poet, flattered him with his best-constructed and most unctuous praise, raised him above the roof of the synagogue itself, explained to him the persistent and implacable injustices done the community by rabid Drumont, and, lastly, pleaded with the descendant of the defender of Rhodes to name his price for his writings, for he would be paid in shining gold louis on the instant. Villiers may not have eaten that day, but he gave the following incomparable reply: "My price, sir? It has not changed since the days of Our Lord Jesus Christ: thirty pieces of silver!"

To Anatole France, when France appeared one day to ask him questions about his family:

"What! You want me to tell you about my forebears the illustrious Grand Master and the famous field marshall, just like that, in broad daylight, at ten o'clock in the morning!"

At the table of Naundorff, the pretender dauphin of France, on the occasion of a fit of snobbery and contempt by Naundorff toward a good retainer, the comte F—, just when the old fellow was leaving the room in tears, abashed:

"Sire, I drink to your majesty. You have proven your titles unimpeachable—you have the ingratitude of a king!"

In his last days, to a friend:

"My flesh is ripe for the tomb!"

And like these, so many memorable phrases, ripostes, witticisms—enough to fill a volume.

His work forms a lovely zodiac, impenetrable to most people: shining and filled with the omens and portents of initiation for those who can find their place in its marvelous light. In the *Cruel Tales,* a book that Mendès rightly calls "extraordinary," Poe and Swift applaud.

Mysterious and profound pain is manifested sometimes with an indescribable, false, pained smile, sometimes with the wet shine of tears. Few have laughed so bitterly as Villiers. . . . *The Eve of the Future* has no precedent; it is a cosmic, unique work, the work of a wise man and a poet, a work that cannot be summed up in few words. Let it suffice to say that upon its title page one might well engrave, as its symbol, the Sphinx and the Chimera; that the gynoid (that is, the female android) created by Villiers can be compared to nothing, no female creature at all, unless it be to the Eternal Father's own Eve; and that when one finishes reading the last page, one has been moved, for one believes one has heard what the Mouth of Shadows whispers. When Edison was visiting Paris in 1889, someone introduced him to that novel in which the Wizard is the main protagonist. The inventor of the phonograph was astounded: "Here," he exclaimed, "is a man who outdoes me! I invent; he creates!" . . .

There is no room within the brief confines of this article for a complete review of the works of Villiers, but I would be remiss not to recall *Axel,* the play just performed in Paris thanks to the efforts of a brave and noble writer, Mme. Tola Dorian.

*Axel* is the victory of wish over reality, ideal love over possession. It goes so far as to renounce nature, in order to achieve ascension to absolute spirit. Axel, like Lohengrin, is chaste; the only possible consummation of that burning yet pure passion is death.

This dramatic poem, written in luminous, diamantine language and performed by such wonderful actors—and applauded by a mob of admirers, poets, select listeners— . . . would have been an unparalleled victory in life for Villiers. But he who was so ill-starred never saw the realization of one of his most fervent dreams back in those days when he would wear a pair of his cousin's pants and eat nothing but a cup of broth a day.

In 1889, in the hospital of the Frères de St.-Jean, in Paris, Comte Auguste de Villiers de l'Isle-Adam—descendant of the noble family of Villiers de l'Isle-Adam, of Chailly, originally of the Isle de France, and among whose ancestors were Pierre, grand master and *porte-oriflamme de France*; Philippe, grand master of the Order of Malta and defender of the isle of Rhodes during the siege laid by the forces of Suleyman the Magnificent; and François, marquis and *grand louvetier de France* in 1550—married, on his deathbed, a poor uneducated girl with whom he had had a child. The reverend father Silvestre, who had helped Barbey d'Aurevilly die, married the count and his bride, who had loved and served him with adoration in the bitter hours of his illness and poverty, and that same priest prepared him for his last, eternal journey. Then, after receiving the sacraments, surrounded by only a few friends, among them Huysmans, Mallarmé, and Dierx, he gave up his soul to God—that most excellent poet, that king, that dreamer. It was August 20, 1889. Sire, *va oultre!*


## RACHILDE

*Tous ceux qui aiment le rare,*
*l'examinaient avec inquiétude.*
— MAURICE BARRÈS


She is a strange, shocking, scabrous woman, a unique spirit, sphinxly solitary in these *fin-de-siècle* times. She is a curious and disturbing "case," a writer who has published all her works under that pseudonym "Rachilde."[36] She is the satanic flower of decadence, piquantly perfumed, mysterious, enchanting, and as evil as sin.

Some years ago, in Belgium, she published a novel that attracted a great deal of attention and was, rumors say, condemned by the courts there. It was not one of those neurotic books that made the publisher Kistemaekers famous in the times of Naturalism, nor one of those boxes of aphrodisiac bonbons *à la* Mendès. It was a demonic book, impregnated with an unknown or forgotten lust, a book whose abysses had never been

---

36. Her real name was Marguerite Eymery (1860–1953).

treated in those manuals used by confessors, a work that was complicated and refined—the triple-refined essence of perversity, in fact. It was an unprecedented book, for it burned with a different flame than the burning, bloody coals of the "divine Marquis," and it was nothing like the prurient collections held hostage in the private reading rooms of libraries. This book's title was *Monsieur Venus,* and it is the best-known of a series that contains the strangest and weirdest creations of a malignly female and outlandishly infamous brain.

Yes, a woman was the author of this book—a sweet, adorable nineteen-year-old virgin who seemed to Jean Lorrain (who went to visit her) to be a strange being with a pallor "like that of a studious schoolgirl, a true *jeune fille,* somewhat thin, somewhat frail, with small, restless hands and the grave profile of a Greek ephebe or a young Frenchman in love . . . and eyes—oh, what eyes!—big, big, big, water-clear eyes heavy with unreal-looking lashes, eyes that know nothing, so that one could almost believe that Rachilde sees not with those eyes, but with others, deep in her head, which seek out and discover the rabid peppers with which she spices her works."

That woman, that "virginal schoolgirl," that *child* was the planter of mandrake, the cultivator of venomous orchids, the decadent *jongleur,* the charmer of snakes and concocter of Spanish flies whose books, in times to come, will shock, as though with an incredible hallucination, the documentarians who write the moral history of our century. Powerful painters, says Barbey d'Aurevilly, can paint everything, and their painting is always moral, at least when it is tragic and shows us the horror of the things it portrays. The only immorality comes from the Impassive and the Mockers.

Rachilde is not impassive—how could that mass of nerves trembling in constant, contagious vibration be impassive! Nor is she a mocker: There is no room for laughter in those dark depths of Sin, or at the sight of the lamentable deformities, those cases of psychic teratology presented to us by the foremost immoralist of all times.

Imagine the sweet, pure dream of a virgin, filled with whiteness, delicacy, softness—a eucharistic celebration, an Easter of lilies and swans. Then a devil—Behemoth, perhaps, . . . the devil of black masses—appears. And into that chaste white dream he introduces the red flower of sexual aberration; essences and aromas that attract incubuses and succubuses; mad visions of unknown and devastating vices; poisonous, bewitched kisses; the mysterious twilight in which love, pain, and death mix and intermingle.

The virgin tempted or possessed by the Evil One writes down the visions she has seen in her dreams. And that is the origin of those books which should be read only by priests, physicians, and psychologists.

Maurice Barrès puts *Monsieur Venus* beside, for example, *Adolphe*,[37] *Mlle. de Maupin*,[38] *Crime d'Amour*[39]—in which certain rare phenomena of the sensibility of love have been studied. But Rachilde, examined closely, has no predecessors, unless it be *Justine*,[40] or perhaps certain old books whose names are never more than whispered by bibliophiles of love (or the Libido) such as that Englishman that animates D'Annunzio in his *Il Piacere*.[41] . . .

The greatest attraction exerted by the works of Rachilde depends upon the reader's pathological curiosity regarding the autobiographical part, the direct and noneuphemistic presentation by the observer of the soul of a woman, of a *fin-de-siècle* girl

---

37. A novel (1817) by French political theorist and writer Benjamin Constant (1767–1830); *Adolphe* is considered to be the first psychological novel.

38. A novel (1835) by Théophile GAUTIER (*q.v.*); the title character "dresses as a man and calls herself Théodore in order to move freely in male social spheres, combines delicate features with a masculine attire and seduces both the male narrator, Albert, and his mistress, Rosette. Albert confesses his love for the consummately androgynous, and therefore irresistible, Théodore: 'What I feel for this young man is truly incredible; never has a woman troubled me in this way.' At the same time, Rosette manages to lure Theodore into her bed, and the discovery she makes there does nothing to cool her passions" (*Blithe House Quarterly:* www.glbtq.com/literature/french_lit2_19c.html).

39. A novel (1886) by Paul Bourget (1852–1935), French literary critic (*Essais de psychologie contemporaine* [1883], in which the time's most important authors, including Baudelaire, Flaubert, and Stendhal are discussed) and "master of the psychological novel."

40. A scandalous novel by the Marquis DE SADE (*q.v.*).

41. A novel of cynicism and sexual passion; its English title is *Child of Pleasure*.

with all the complications that the *mal de siècle* has inflicted upon her. . . . How have such equivocal creations been born to that well-educated girl? That, indeed, is the curious, beguiling problem. One can only believe that distant influences have been at work in her; that atavistic forces afflicting this delicate being with generations-worth of perversity have inspired in her the awakening, discovery, or invention of ancient sins, utterly forgotten, erased from the face of the earth by the fires and waters of chastising skies.

A listing of the titles of her works may given some idea of the infernal jewels of this female Antichrist: *Monsieur de la Nouveauté, La Femme du 199ème, Monsieur Venus, Queue de Poisson, Histoires Bêtes, Nono, La Virginité de Diane, La Noise du Sang, A Mort, La Marquise de Sade, Le Tiroir de Mimi-Corail, Madame Adonis, L'Homme Roux, La Sanglante Ironie, Le Mordu, L'Animale*. They resemble nests of shining, brightly colored vipers, beautiful, red, poisonous fruits, jams that will drive a man mad, harsh peppers, fobidden gingers. I could not go into details here unless I did so in Latin, or better yet, in Greek, for Latin would be too transparent, and the Eleusian mysteries were not, most decidedly, brought into the light of the sun.

The *types* in her works are all exceptional. *La Sanglante Ironie,* for example, presents a young man deranged, *detraqué*. He has murdered his beloved in a moment of hallucination. Now in prison, he tells the story, explaining the succession of causes that led him to commit this act. The figure of Sylvain d'Hauterac, the madman, is one of Rachilde's finest creations, but the critics have called it improbable, like nothing in nature. That does not prevent the work from presenting a life of intensity and a study of admirable psychological insight.

She has written a play called *Madame la Mort*. The action revolves around the main character's desperate struggle between Life and Death. . . . Paul Gauguin has drawn this figure, a symbol for Madame la Mort: a spectral ghost against a dark background of shadows. One can just see the anatomy of a figure, a large head; the specter is holding one hand to its brow—the long, disproportionate, thin hand of a skeleton. One can clearly make out the bones of its jaw; its eyes are sunken into their orbits. The visionary artist has evoked the manifestations of certain nightmares in which we see corpses walking, approaching their victim, touching him, embracing him, and in that horrid dream we can feel the waxen flesh press against us and we breathe the familiar, horrendous smell of the tomb. . . .

*Monsieur Venus* is the product of an incubus. Jacques Silvert is Sporus to the cruelly passionate female Nero—a vulgar, smiling, passive Sporus with soft lamblike eyes. Raoule de Vénerande, a sort of female Des Esseints, falls in love with this exquisite porcine creature—falls in love as in Shakespeare's sonnet: *A woman's face, with nature's own hand painted.*

Raoule de Vénerande is cousin to Nero and that legendary, terrible Gilles de Laval, the sire of kings, who died at the stake. . . . As for the castrated and detestable Jacques, a ridiculous Ganymede to his vampire lover, he is a curious clinical case, and could be a patient of Krafft-Ebing's, or Molle's, or Gley's. The florist's androgyny is explained by Aristophanes in Plato's *Symposium,*[42] and Krafft-Ebing would classify him as a case of "eviration," or *transmutatio sexus paranoia.* . . .

A woman, a delicate, intellectual, cerebral young woman reveals terrible secrets to us: that is the highest praise, and the most tempting of attractions. Yet note that in her works we enter a most hard and unknown country—unnatural, forbidden, perilous.

There is a portrait of Rachilde at twenty-five. In profile: her throat is naked to the swelling of her breasts; her hair is rolled up at the back, at the nape of her neck, like a black serpent, and upon her brow, it is cut in the fashion of some years ago, straight across, though covering her entire forehead. Her gaze—such a gaze!—and eyes that say everything and know everything. A delicate, slightly Jewish nose, and a mouth—oh, mouth! companion of the eyes. And in it all, the divine and terrible enigma of Woman: *Mysterium.* On her white bosom lies a spray of white rosebuds.

---

42. i.e., that humans were once "one," or unitary, and that they were divided by Zeus as punishment; ever after, they have sought their missing half; we were once, then "androgynes," men-women.

I know of one man who, while he was in Paris, refused to be presented to Rachilde, for fear of losing another youthful illusion. Today, Rachilde is Mme. Alfred Vallette; she has put on weight, and is not the enigmatic dominatrix of the portrait of twenty-five years ago, that adorable and fearsome god-daughter of Lilith.

Married to Alfred Vallette, she is the "lady of a house" today, but she has not stopped producing intellectual offspring. She writes novels, stories, reviews.

Rachilde has a quick critical sense, and with her woman's swift and skillful perspicacity is able to discover in the works she analyzes the most hidden meanings. . . .

"In our days," says Rachilde, "there are instigators of ideas (as before there were *meneurs de loups*),[43] because in this 'modern' era of ours, a thousand times more sinister than the bloody Middle Ages, there is need of apparitions a thousand times more flagellant; and those *meneurs,* driving their murderous ideas to the murder of old theories, old principles, madly throwing open the eyes of the spirit, are also precursors of the Angel. Those who fail to understand that the time is coming when the herders of ideas shall come, one after another, with astonishing swiftness, over the shadowy horizon, are quite mad." And am I not right, then, in calling Rachilde Mme. Antichrist? She understands, she knows, and she is also an omen, a portent. . . .

## LE COMTE DE LAUTRÉAMONT

His real name is not known.[44] "Comte de Lautréamont" is a pseudonym. He says he is from Montevideo, but who knows the truth of that shadowy life, which was perhaps a nightmare dreamt by some sad angel martyred in the empyrean by the memory of celestial Lucifer? He lived a life of misfortune and

43. Drives or herders of wolves; i.e., those who drive wolf packs.
44. Actually, it was Isidore Lucien Ducasse. He was French, but born in Montevideo, Uruguay, in 1846.

hard luck, and he died a madman. He wrote a book which would be unique, except for the prose pieces of Rimbaud—a diabolic, mocking, howling, cruel, terrible, strange book, a book in which one hears, at once, the groans of Pain and the sinister hissing of Madness.

León Bloy was the true discoverer of the Comte de Lautréamont. Furious St. John of God said of the sores on the soul of blasphemous Job, that they were filled with light. But today, in France and Belgium, no one outside a tiny group of initiates knows the poem called *Chants de Maldoror,* into which is poured all the horrific anguish of the wretched yet sublime poet, whose work it was my fortune to make known to Latin America in Montevideo. I will not advise our youth to drink from those black waters, however much they might see the marvels of the constellations reflected in their depths. It would not be prudent for young spirits to have much conversation with that spectral man, whether on account of his literary "dash" or in search of new delights. There is a very sensible piece of advice in the Kabbala: "There is no need to judge the specter, for soon enough one will be one." And if there is a dangerous author in this regard, it is the Comte de Lautréamont. What hellish, rabid Cerberus bit that soul, down there in the regions of mystery and darkness, before it was incarnated in this world? The cries of the theophobe make all who hear them shiver. If I were to take my muse near the place where the madman is caged and shouting into the wind, I would put my hands over her ears.

Like Job, his sleep is tormented and he is tortured by visions. Like Job, he might exclaim: "My soul is weary of my life; I will leave my complaint upon myself; I will speak in the bitterness of my soul."[45] But "Job" means "he who weeps"; Job wept, yet poor Lautréamont does not. His book is a satanic breviary, impregnated with sadness and melancholy. "The evil spirit," says St. Francis de Sales in his *Introduction to the Devout Life,* "delights in sadness and melancholy because it is sad and melancholy, and will be so for all eternity." Even more: the man who

45. Job 10:1–3.

has written the *Chants de Maldoror* might very well have been possessed. We must recall that certain cases of madness, today classified by science with technical names and set down in the catalogue of nervous disorders, were and still are seen by the Holy Mother Church as cases of possession, and in need of exorcism. "Soul in ruins!" Bloy exclaims, with words moist with the tears of compassion.

Job: "Man that is born of a woman is of few days and full of trouble."

Lautréamont: "I am the son of man and woman, or so I am told. I find that strange. I thought I was more than that!"

The author with whom he has most points of contact is Edgar Allan Poe. Both had the vision of the supernatural; both were persecuted by terrible enemies of the spirit, infernal "hordes" that drive a man to alcohol, madness, or death; both felt an attraction toward mathematics, one of the three roads, with theology and poetry, that can lead a man to the Infinite. But Poe was celestial, while Lautréamont was infernal.

Listen to these bitter fragments:

"I dreamt that I had entered the body of a pig, that it was not easy to get out again, and that my feet were sunk into the most horrible of mudsties. Was this some recompense? Object of my desires: I no longer belonged to humanity! That was how I interpreted it, as I experienced the most profound joy. But I searched and searched, trying to remember what act of virtue I had committed to merit this wondrous gift of Providence. . . . But what man knows his innermost needs, or the cause of his pestilential delights? This metamorphosis never appeared to my eyes as anything but the high, magnificent repercussion of a perfect felicity that I had so long been waiting for. At last, the day had come when I was transformed into a pig! I tried out my teeth on the bark of a tree; I eyed my snout with delight. There was not the slightest particle of divinity in me; I was able to raise my soul to the immense height of this ineffable voluptuousness." . . .

Hear again the macabre voice of this rare visionary. In this little prose-poem he is speaking of dogs at night, which jangle the nerves. The dogs howl: "sometimes like a child crying out in hunger, or a cat wounded in the belly, under a roof; like a woman giving birth; like a dying man assailed by the plague, in the hospital; like a young woman singing a sublime melody— they howl at the stars of the North, at the stars of the East, at the stars of the South, at the stars of the West, at the moon, at the mountains, which look, from a distance, like gigantic boulders, lying in darkness; at the cold air they breathe in lungsful, that turns the inside of their noses red, burning; at the silence of the night; at owls, whose oblique flight brushes their lips and noses, and who are carrying a mouse or a frog in their talons, sweet living nourishment for their chicks; at the rabbits that disappear in the blink of an eye; at the thief who flees on a galloping horse after committing his crime; at the serpents that part the grass and make the dogs' flesh crawl and their teeth chatter; at their own barking, which frightens even them; at the frogs, which they burst with one gnash of their teeth (why did they leave their pond?); at the trees, whose leaves, softly soughing, are yet further mysteries they do not understand, although they peer at them with intelligent eyes; at spiders suspended between their long legs and that scurry up the trees to save themselves; at the crows that have not found anything to eat during the day and so return to their nests on weary wing; at the rocks on the ocean's bank; at the fires that look like the masts of invisible ships; at the muffled sound of the waves; at the big fish that swim by, showing their black fins, and then plunge into the abyss; and at the man who enslaves them. . . .

"One day, with glassy eyes, my mother said to me, 'When you are lying in bed and hear the howling of the dogs in the countryside, hide in your sheets. Don't laugh at what they are doing; they have an insatiable thirst for the infinite, like I do, like all humans, for the *figure pâle et longue*. . . .'"

"And I," he continues, "like those dogs, suffer a yearning for the infinite. I cannot, I cannot fill that need!" It is irrational, delirious, "but there is something down deep that makes reflective men shiver."

He is a madman, no doubt about it. But we must acknowledge, too, that the *deus* drives oracles mad, and that the divine fever of the prophets produced similar fits, and that the author "lived" that, and that this is not a "literary work," but rather the cry, the howl, of a sublime being martyred by Satan.

He almost mocks beauty itself—like Psyche, out of hatred of God—as we can see in these following comparisons, which I have taken from other little poems:

"The grand duke of Virginia was beautiful, as beautiful as the memory of the curve traced by a dog running after its master." . . .

The beetle, "as beautiful as the trembling of the hands in alcoholism. . . ."

The adolescent, "as beautiful as the retractable talons of a bird of prey," or even "as the muscular movements in the ulcers on the soft parts of the posterior cervical region," or perhaps . . . "as the chance meeting, on a dissecting table, of a sewing machine and an umbrella. . . ."

The fact is, oh serene and happy spirits!, this is a cutting and abominable "humour." . . .

He never thought about literary glory. He wrote only for himself. He was born with that supreme flame of genius, and it was that flame that consumed him.

The Prince of Darkness possessed him, entered his soul by way of sadness. He allowed himself to fall. He abhorred Man and detested God. In the six parts of his work he planted a sick, leprous, poisoned Flower. His animals are those that remind one of the workings of the Dark One: toads, owls, vipers, spiders. Despair is the wine that intoxicates him. Prostitution is for him the mysterious symbol of the Apocalypse, glimpsed by exceptional spirits in all its transcendence. "I have made a pact with Prostitution, in order to sow disorder in families . . . Ay! Ay!" exclaims the naked woman, "someday men will be just. I will say no more. Let me depart, let me go hide my infinite sadness in the depths of the ocean. There is nothing but oneself and the hateful monsters that seethe in those black abysses, monsters that do not scorn me."

And Bloy: "The indisputable sign of a great poet is the prophetic 'unconscious,' the disturbing faculty of speaking, to men and to time, words never heard before, and whose meaning the poet himself cannot fathom. That is the mysterious stamp of the Holy Spirit upon sacred or profane brows. However absurd it may be today to say that one has discovered a great poet, and discovered him in a madhouse, I must in conscience say that I am certain I have done just that."

Lautréamont's poem was published seventeen years ago in Belgium. Nothing is known of its author's life. Great "modern" artists of the French language speak of the volume to one another as a symbolic, rare, indiscoverable prayer book.


# IBSEN

It has not been long since intellectual explorations of the Pole began. Leconte de Lisle has gone off to contemplate Nature and learn the song of the *runoja*;[46] Mendès, to see the midnight sun and converse with Snorr and Snorra, in a poem of blood and ice. In those distant boreal regions strange and hitherto unheard-of beings have been discovered: tremendous poets, cosmic thinkers. One of these beings has been found in Norway, a strong, rare man with white hair, a shy smile, and a profound gaze who writes profound works. Is he, perhaps, possessed of Arctic genius? He is indeed perhaps possessed of Arctic genius. He seems to stand as tall as a pine tree; he is small of stature. He was born in his mysterious land; the soul of the earth there, in its most enigmatic manifestations, revealed itself in him when he was but a child. Today he is an old man; upon his head much snow has fallen; the halo of glory sits upon his brow like a magnificent aurora borealis. He lives far away, in his land of fjords and rain and fog, under a sky of capricious and elusive light. The world sees him as a legendary inhabitant of the polar realm. There are those who think that he is extravagantly generous, shouting to other men from his cold retreat the words of his dream; there are those who believe him to be an unapproachable and stand-offish sort of apostle; there are those who think he is mad. Great visionary of the snows! His eyes have looked upon the long nights and red

46. *Runoja* is the Finnish word for "poems" (sing, *runo*); Darío is simply noting that Leconte de Lisle has become interested in Finnish poetry.

sun that bloodies the dark winter; they have gazed upon life's night, the dark side of humanity. His soul shall be bitter unto death. . . .

"His nose is strong, his cheeks red and prominent, his chin vigorously marked; his large gold spectacles, his thick white beard into which the lower part of his face is sunken, give him *l'air brave homme,* the appearance of a provincial magistrate, grown old in the job. All the poetry of his soul, all the splendor of his intelligence has taken refuge in the long, thin, slightly sensual lips, at whose corners there is an expression of haughty irony; his gaze, which is veiled and as though turned inward, is now sweet and melancholic, now swift and aggressive, disquieting, tormented, and under it one trembles, for it seems to delve into one's very being. The brow is especially magnificent— square, solid, of powerful dimensions, a brow heroic and genial, as broad as the world of thoughts it contains. And dominating the whole, and accentuating yet further that impression of ideal animality that one feels in his entire physiognomy, there is a wavy shock of white, untamable hair. . . .

"A man, in a word, of special essence and strange appearance that disquiets one and is striking, overpowering; his equal, there is none—a man one could never forget, though one lived a hundred years."

All men have an inner world, and superior men have one that is superior, and thus the great Scandinavian found his treasure trove within his own inner world. "I have looked for everything within me; everything has arisen from my heart," he says.

It was within himself that he discovered the richest lode in which to study the human principle. He performed a vivisection upon himself. He put his ear to his own breast, his fingers to his own pulse. And everything arose from his heart. His heart! The heart of a sensitive and nervous man. It beats for the world; he is sick with humanity.

His vibrating organism, predisposed to collisions with the unknown, was further tempered in that realm of phantasmal nature, the alien atmosphere of his native land. From out the shadows, an invisible hand seized him. Mysterious echoes called to him from the fog.

His childhood was a flower of sadness. He was anxious,
filled with daydreams; he had been born with illness. I picture
him, a silent, pale child with long hair, on cloudy, misty days.
I picture him in the first shivers produced by the spirit that
must have possessed him, in a perpetual twilight or in the cold
silence of the Norwegian night. His tiny child-soul, squeezed
into a hard home; the first spiritual blows against that small,
fragile, crystalline soul; the first impressions that caused him
to see the evil of the land and the harshness of the road ahead.
Later, in the years of his young-manhood, more harshness.
The beginning of the struggle for life and the revelatory vision
of social concern. Ah! he recognized the hard machinery and
the danger of so much toothed noise, and the error in the di-
rection of the machine, and the perfidy of the bosses, and the
universal degradation of the species! And his soul became a
tower of snow. And within him there appeared the fighter, the
combatant. Armored, helmeted, armed, the poet emerged. He
heard the voice of the peoples of the earth. His spirit went
forth from its restricted sphere of nation; he sang foreign
struggles; he called for the nations of the North to unite; his
word, which was hardly heard within his own land, was ren-
dered dumb with disillusion; his compatriots did not know
him; for him there were only stones, satire, envy, egoism, stu-
pidity; his land, like all native lands, was a hard stepmother
that swatted at the prophet with her broom. . . . Yet after dis-
enchantment his young muse found songs of enthusiasm, life,
love once more.

In the years of the first struggles to earn a living, he had been
a pharmacist. Then a journalist. Then director of a traveling
theater company. He traveled, he lived. . . . He was poor; he
didn't care; he loved. He was mad with love; so mad that he
married. The sweet daughter of a Protestant pastor was his
wife. I figure the good Suzannah Thoresen must have had hair
of the most glorious gold, and eyes divinely azure.

After his *Catilina,* a simple essay of his youth, the playwright
emerged. . . . Let us hear something from *The Vikings at Helge-
land,* that rare and visionary work:

HIÖRDIS

The wolf there—close behind me; it does not move; it glares at
me with its two red eyes. It is my wraith, Sigurd! Three times
has it appeared to me; that bodes that I shall surely die to-night!

SIGURD

Hiördis! Hiördis!

HIÖRDIS

It has sunk into the earth! Aye, aye, now it has warned me.

SIGURD

Thou art sick; come, go in with me.

HIÖRDIS

Nay, here will I bide; I have but little time left.

SIGURD

What has befallen thee?

HIÖRDIS

What has befallen? That know I not; but 'twas true what thou
said'st today, that Gunnar and Dagny stand between us; we
must away from them and from life; then can we be together!

SIGURD

We? Ha, thou meanest——.

HIÖRDIS

[*With dignity.*] I have been homeless in this world from that day
thou didst take another to wife. That was ill done of thee! All
good gifts may a man give to his faithful friend—all, save the
woman he loves; for if he do that, he rends the Norn's secret
web, and two lives are wrecked. . . . [47]

47. *The Collected Works of Henrik Ibsen*, vol. 2, *The Vikings at Helgeland*,
trans. Wm. Archer, NY: Charles Scribner's Sons, 1906, Act. 4, pp. 108–109.

Later came *The Pretenders [to the Crown]*, in which there is an admirable dialogue between the Skald[48] and the King; this play must have had a direct influence on Maeterlinck's manner of writing dialogue in his symbolic plays. . . . Here is an excerpt:

KING SKULE

Let that wait. Tell me, Skald: you who have fared far abroad in strange lands, have you ever seen a woman love another's child? Not only have kindness for it—'tis not that I mean; but love it, love it with the warmest passion of her soul.

JATGEIR

That do only those women who have no child of their own to love.

KING SKULE

Only those women——?

JATGEIR

And chiefly women who are barren.

KING SKULE

Chiefly the barren——? They love the children of others with all their warmest passions?

JATGEIR

That will oftentimes befall.

KING SKULE

And does it not sometimes befall that such a barren woman will slay another's child, because she herself has none?

JATGEIR

Ay, ay; but in that she does unwisely.

KING SKULE

Unwisely?

48. Poet.

JATGEIR

Ay, for she gives the gift of sorrow to her whose child she slays.

KING SKULE

Think you the gift of sorrow is a great good?

JATGEIR

Yes, lord.

KING SKULE

[*Looks fixedly at him.*] Methinks there are two men in you, Icelander. When you sit amid the household at the merry feast, you draw cloak and hood over all your thoughts; when one is alone with you, sometimes you seem to be of those among whom one were fain to choose his friend. How comes it?

JATGEIR

When you go to swim in the river, my lord, you would scarce strip you where the people pass by to church; you seek a sheltered privacy.

KING SKULE

True, true.

JATGEIR

My soul has the like shamefastness; therefore I do not strip me when there are many in the hall.

KING SKULE

Ha. [*A short pause.*] Tell me, Jatgeir, how came you to be a skald?
Who taught you skaldcraft?

JATGEIR

Skaldcraft cannot be taught, my lord.

KING SKULE

Cannot be taught? How came it then?

JATGEIR

The gift of sorrow came to me, and I was a skald.


KING SKULE

Then 'tis the gift of sorrow the skald has need of?


JATGEIR

*I* needed sorrow; others there may be who need faith, or joy—
or doubt—


KING SKULE

Doubt as well?


JATGEIR

Ay; but then must the doubter be strong and sound.


KING SKULE

And whom call you the unsound doubter?


JATGEIR

He who doubts of his own doubt.


KING SKULE

[*Slowly.*] That, methinks, were death.


JATGEIR

'Tis worse; 'tis neither day nor night.[49]


*Love's Comedy* shows the fine humor that is also in Ibsen, its
lens always turned on the ills of society, and open to the holy
human instinct of love.

With the hostility of the players under his direction and the
clamor of hatred and outrage turned upon him by certain jour-
nalists, he had to have shoulders of iron, a hard head, firm fists.
His land turned its back on him, disdained him, hated him,
poured calumny upon him. So he shook the dust from his

49. Ibid. *The Pretenders*, Act 4, pp. 258–261.

boots—he left, muttering verses against the herd of fools; he left, banished by the fossilized family of retardates and puritans. But deep in his heart still lay the sentiment of social redemption.

The revolutionary went off to see the golden sun of the Latin nations.

After this time of bathing in the sun, those works were born that raised him into the empyrean of modern dramatists, set him beside the great Wagner, upon the pinnacle of contemporary art and philosophy. . . . He gave life to those strange symbolic characters of his, from whose lips came denunciations of the deeply rooted evil of the new doctrine. The poor found in him a great defender; he was driven by the desire for social redemption. He was a giant architect who wished to raise his monumental edifice to save souls by prayer into the very sky, face to face with God.

The man of visions . . . found that there are finer mysteries in the common things of life than in the kingdom of fantasy; the greatest enigma lies in man himself. And his dream has been to see the coming of a better life, the rejuvenation of man, the destruction of the social machinery of our age. The Socialist was born in him; he became, if you wish, a second redeemer.

And so arose *The Wild Duck, Nora, The Enemy of the People, Rosmersholm, Hedda Gabler*. He wrote for the masses, for the salvation of the masses. Machinery has been dealt rude blows by the enormous hammer of the Scandinavian god. The hammering has been heard around the planet. The intellectual aristocracy has been with him. He has been greeted as one of the world's great heroes. But his work has not produced the effect he desired. And his efforts have been veiled by a shadow of pessimism.

And in the Latin nations he found struggles and horrors, disasters and sadness; his soul has suffered for the bitterness of France. There came a moment when he believed the soul of the race was dead. And yet hope did not entirely abandon his heart. He believed in the future resurrection: "Who knows when the dove will bring the olive branch of promise in its beak? We will see it. So far as I am concerned, until that day I shall remain in my little padded room in Sweden, jealous of my solitude, arranging distinguished rhymes. The wandering crowd will undoubtedly be angry, and treat me as a renegade, but that crowd terrifies me. I don't want to be splashed with mud; I want to await the dawn that is sure to come, wearing my spotless clean wedding-suit."

Ah, poor lost humanity! That strange redeemer wants to save it, find a remedy for evil and a path that leads to true good. But every minute that passes deals a death blow to a dream. Men are marked by an original taint. Their very organism is infected, and infectious; their soul is subject to sin and error. Their road leads them through mudholes, or bramble-patches. Life is a field of lies and pain. Evil are those who come to know the face of happiness while the immense mass of wretches writhe under the leaden weight of fatal misery. And the redeemer suffers the pain and grief of the multitude. His cry is not heard; his tower does not wear the crown it merits. And so his agitated heart is in mourning; and so from the lips of his new characters pour forth terrible words, raging condemnations, harsh and flagellating truths. He comes to his pessimism "by the back door." He has glimpsed the Ideal, like a mirage. He has followed it; his feet have been bloodied and tattered on the rocks of the road, and he has reaped harvests of naught but disillusionment. His fata morgana has vanished.

Yet his symbolic progeny are animated by a wondrous and eloquent life-force. His characters are beings who live and move and act on this earth, in the midst of today's society. They have the reality of our own existence. They are our neighbors, our brothers and sisters. Sometimes we are surprised to hear our own innermost thoughts issue from their lips. For Ibsen is brother to Shakespeare. . . .

The *types* are observed, taken from life. Even national peculiarities, the setting of Norway, allows the playwright to accentuate the universal traits of man. He, the creator, has squeezed out his heart, has plumbed the depths of his mental ocean, has entered his dark inner jungle—he is the deep-diver of the common mind, into the depths of his own. And there must have been a day on which even in his mother's womb his soul was filled with the virtue of art. His suffering must be the sublime suffering of genius—of a peregrine genius, in which are joined all the occult psychic energies of all those distant lands in which he has believed there may be found, in certain manifestations, the reality of the Dream. And that "unapproachable," "stand-offish" man, that excellent man, that hero, that almost-superman, lived through a holocaust, was the apostle and martyr to the incontestable truth, was an immense thunderclap in the desert, an ominous flash of lightning in a world of blind men. And he sought examples of evil because evil saturates the world. From Job to our own days, the verbal flesh of dialogue has never given such jolting and such shock to the spirit as in the works of Ibsen. Everything speaks—bodies and souls. Sickness, dream, madness, death all speak; their speeches are impregnated with the Beyond. They are "Ibsenian" beings through which the essence of the centuries flows. We are transported thousands of leagues away from Literature, that high and pleasant branch of the Fine Arts, to a different, mysterious world, in which the thinker has the stature of an archangel. We feel, in the surrounding darkness, a breeze that blows from the Infinite, that realm whose muffled waves, beating against the seashore, we hear from time to time.

His language is constructed of logic, yet it is animated by mystery. Ibsen is one of those who has most deeply peered into the enigma of the human psyche. He rises to God. The river of his thought flows down from the mountain of primordial ideas. He is the moral hero. Solitary and powerful man! he comes down from his tower of ice to exercise his trade—tamer of the races, regenerator of nations, savior of humankind—a grand trade, ay!, for he does not believe he will live to see the longed-for day of transfiguration.

We must not be surprised if mysterious fogs hang over his titanic *oeuvre*. As in all sovereign spirits, as in all the hierarchs of thought, his Word is veiled in mists, like the fissures and vents of hot springs, or the craters of volcanoes.

As consecrated to his work as a priest, he is the most admirable example of the unity of action and thought that may be found in all the history of human ideas.

He is the formidable mystery of an ideal religion which with unparalleled courage preaches the truths of its evangel even to the civilized arrows of the white barbarians.

If Ibsen were not a rebelling Titan, he would be a saint, for sainthood is genius in character, moral genius. And he has felt on his face the breath of the unknown, the arcane, and in his explorations of the shadows of his own abyss he has obeyed that breath. And in the midst of the pains of mankind he wanders through the world, and he is the echo of all the groans and sighs. Here are his lines to the swan:

"Innocent swan, forever mute, forever calm! Neither pain nor happiness disturbs the serenity of your indifference. Majestic protector of the Elf that dozes, you have glided across the waters without a murmur, without a song.

"All that we gather upon our paths, vows of love, anguished glances, hypocrisies, lies—what do they matter to you! What do they matter to you?

"And yet on the morning of your death you sighed out your agony, you whispered your pain. . . .

"And you were a swan!"

The snow-white Olympian bird sung in such a melancholy way by the Arctic poet . . . is, for him, the nuncio of the otherworldly Enigma.

That is why the inviolate Unknown will always appear—strong, silent—wrapped in an impenetrable cloud; its strength, the end of all strengths; its silence, all harmonies alloyed together. . . . Authority, the constitution of society, the conventions of deceived or perverse men, religions turned to tainted uses, the injustices of the law and the laws of injustice, the entire old system of the civil organism, the entire apparatus of modern society's culture and progress—all of great and monstrous Jericho hears the luminous enemy's trumpets. But its walls do not fall, its factories remain standing. Through windows and battlements, the enemy sees the pink faces of the women who live in the city smile, and the men shrug their shoulders. And the enemy trumpet sounds against the deceptions of society; against the opponents of the ideal; against the Pharisees of the public good; against the bourgeoisie, whose chief representative will always be Pilate; against the judges who mete out false justice, the priests who preach false doctrines;

against Capital, whose coin, if it were broken, like the host in
the story, would drip human blood; against the exploitation
of poverty and misery; against the errors of the State; against
the leagues, rooted in centuries of ignominy, that conspire
against man and even against nature; against the idiotic rabble
that stones prophets and worships the golden calf; against all
that has deformed and reduced the brain of womankind and
made her, through immemorial centuries of opprobrium, a pas-
sive and inferior being; against the gags and chains of the sexes;
against vile trade, mud-bespattered politics, and prostituted
thought. The trumpet sounds in *Hedda Gabler,* in *An Enemy
of the People,* in *The Master Builder,* in *The Pillars of Society,*
in *The Pretenders,* in *The League of Youth,* in *Little Eyolf.*

Sincerity is the guardian archangel of huge Ibsen. Other an-
gels escort him—Truth, Nobility, Goodness, Virtue. He is also
generally accompanied by the cherub Eironia. . . .

Laurent Tailhade, praising the excellencies of *An Enemy
of the People,* said, "If there is anything that can ever mitigate
the damnation earned by the [Parisian] public for those first
performances—men and women of the world, stockbrokers,
pillars of men's clubs and scribblers for newspapers, idiots and
snobs of every stripe, the astonishing incompetence that distin-
guishes them, the monstrous appetite they generally show for
every sort of rubbish—it is the reception given, for these last
three years, to two geniuses whose bitterness has nothing to do
with what is so justly called 'the French taste.' I am referring to
Richard Wagner and Henrik Ibsen." If this is said of Paris, then
pay heed, you centers of thought in other nations! May the ex-
cellencies of national taste pour forth and ascend to the high
pinnacles of Idea and Art; may the doctrine of the chosen
guides be heard; may the "demon of stupidity" be exorcised
with the holy water of the ideal.

Ibsen does not believe in the triumph of his cause. That is
why irony has drawn sardonic lines upon his face. But is there
anyone who dares affirm that the white, untamable hair of that
proud, catastrophe-prophesying Precursor of the Future shall
not finally be gilded by the sun of the long-awaited dawn?

# JOSÉ MARTÍ

The cortège for the funeral of Wagner would require the solemn
thunder of *Tannhäuser*; to accompany the casket of a sweet bu-
colic poet there should be, as in antique bas-reliefs, flute players
making their melodious double flutes lament; for the ceremony
at which the body of Melesigenes[50] was burned, vibrant cho-
ruses of lyres; to accompany—oh! allow me to speak his name
before the great epic Shade; at any rate, you evil smiles that
might appear, he is now dead!—to accompany, I say, the fu-
neral of José Martí, his own language would be needed, his for-
midable organ with all its many registers, its powerful verbal
choirs, its golden trumpets, its wailing strings, its sobbing
oboes, its flutes, its drums, its lyres, its zithers. Yes, ye Ameri-
cans of the Spanish tongue, we must tell the world who this
great man was, this man who now has fallen.

He who writes these lines, which rush out from heart
and mind, is not one of those who believe in the riches of the
Americas. . . . We are very poor. . . . So poor that our spirits, if
not for foreign nourishment, would starve. And so we should
weep many tears for this man who has fallen! The man who
died there in Cuba was one of the best of the little we poor peo-
ple have; he was a generous millionaire; he constantly emptied
out his pockets, yet as though by magic he was always rich.
Among the enormous volumes of the collection of *La Nación*
there is so much of his fine metal and precious gems that the
finest statue could be made of it. . . . Never did our tongue find
better inks, ideas, splendors. . . . And what agile grace, and
what natural strength so long-sustained, so magnificent!

Another truth: . . . What we call genius, that fruit that is
borne only upon hundred-year-old trees, that majestic phenom-
enon of the intellect elevated to its highest power, that high cre-
ative marvel—Genius, that is, which has never yet been born in
our Republics—has tried to appear twice among us: once, in an
illustrious man of this land, Argentina, and again in José Martí.

50. A name sometimes given to Homer.

And Martí was not, as might perhaps be thought, one of those demi-geniuses that Mendès talks about, unable to communicate with men because his wings raise him over their heads, unable to rise to the sphere of the gods because his wings' strength is not sufficient and the earth will always pull him downward. No, this Cuban was *un hombre*—he was a man. More than that, he was what the true superman should be: grand and virile, possessed of the secret of his excellence, in communion with God and with Nature.

In communion with God lived this man of soft yet immense heart, this man who abhorred pain and evil, this amiable lion with the breast of a dove who, though able to cut, smash, wound, bite, rip, was always kind and gentle, even with his enemies. And in communion with God he was, having ascended to God by the firmest and surest stairway—the stairway of Pain. Mercy found in this creature its temple: through it, one might say that his soul followed the four rivers mentioned by Ruysbroeck the Admirable: the river that ascends, and leads to the divine heights; the river that leads to compassion for captive souls; the other two rivers that enfold all the miseries and sorrows of the lost and wounded human flock. He rose to God by the path of compassion and by the path of pain. Martí suffered much!—from the consuming robes of temperament and illness to the immense sadness of the chosen one who feels himself unknown among the general stolidity that surrounds him; and, lastly, brimming over with love and patriotic madness, he consecrated himself to following a sad star, the solitary star of his Island, the deceiving star that led this ill-fortuned wise and wizardly king to fall suddenly in the blackest death. . . .

Oh, Cuba! You are very beautiful, most certainly, and great and glorious service is done you by your sons who struggle because they wish to see you free. And bravo, too, to that Spaniard who will not yield peace because he fears to lose you, Cuba admirable and rich and a thousand times blessed by my tongue. But the blood of Martí did not belong to you—it belonged to an entire race, an entire continent; it belonged to a spirited generation of youth that lost in him perhaps the foremost of its teachers. He belonged to the future!

When Cuba shed its blood in the first war, the war of Cés-
pedes, when the efforts stemming from a desire for freedom
bore no fruit but death and fire and butchery, much of the
Cuban intelligentsia left the country. Many of the best went
into exile—disciples of José de la Luz, poets, philosophers, edu-
cators. That exile is still going on for some of those who have
not left their mortal remains in a foreign land, or have not now
returned to the jungle. José Joaquín Palma, who left when he
was the age of Lohengrin, with a blond beard like his, and more
elegant than the swan of his poetry, after traveling from repub-
lic to republic, cooing his *décimas* "to the solitary star," saw
snow invade that golden beard, though he always longed to re-
turn to that Bayamo from whence he had sallied out into the
field to fight after burning down his house. Tomás Estrada
Palma, cousin to the poet, an upright, discreet man, filled with
intelligence, and today elected president by the revolutionaries,
made a living as a school teacher in distant Honduras. Antonio
Zambrana, an orator of well-deserved fame in the United
States, was about to go off to the Spanish Cortes,[51] where he
would have done honor to his Americans, when he took refuge
in Costa Rica, and there opened his law office. Eizaguirre went
to Guatemala; the poet Sellén, the celebrated translator of
Heine, and his brother, also a poet, went to New York, where
they made calendars for the Lamman and Kemp pill company,
if rumors are to be believed. Martí, the great Martí, wandered
from country to country, here in sadness, there in abominable
penny-pinching due to a lack of income on foreign soil; now
triumphing, because after all, the fighting spirit will always
overcome misfortune, now suffering the consequences of his
antagonism to human stupidity—newspaperman, professor, or-
ator, his body wasting away and his soul bleeding to death,
squandering the riches of his soul in places that would never
know the value of his high intelligence (although he would also
be assailed by the praise of the ignorant). He did derive, on the
other hand, great pleasure from the understanding of his flight
by the rare souls who knew him profoundly, from the abhorrence

51. The parliament.

of the fools, from the reception given him by the *élite* of the Latin American press in Buenos Aires and Mexico for his correspondence and articles.

He wandered, then, from country to country, and at last, after remaining some time in Central America, he settled in New York.

There, in that cyclopean city, did that noble gentleman of thought finally land, and he worked and struggled there more than ever. Discouraged—he, so great and so strong, my God!—discouraged in his dreams of Art, he riveted into his brain, with three strong iron rivets, the image of his solitary star and, allowing things their due time, began to forge arms for war, using words for a hammer and ideas for a furnace. Patience, he had; he waited and watched, as though for some vague fata morgana, for his dreamt-of *Cuba libre*. He went from house to house, working in the many households of Cubans living in New York. He did not disdain the humble man; that serene and indomitable hero, that fighter who could have spoken, like Elciis, for four days straight to powerful Oton, surrounded by kings, spoke to the humble man like a good older brother.

His labor grew from moment to moment, as though the sap of his energy drew fire from the fervor of that great city. And he would pay a visit to the Fifth Avenue doctor, the stock broker, the newspaperman, the executive, the cigar-roller, the black stevedore, all the New York Cubans, trying to keep the fire alive, trying to maintain the urge to war, struggling against more or less clear rivalries, yet loved and admired by all. He had to live, he had to work, and so there poured forth those cascades of writing, columns that went off to dailies in Mexico and Venezuela. There can be no doubt that this was the best time of José Martí's life. It was now that he showed his intellectual personality most handsomely. In those miles-long epistles, if you except one or another rare branch without flower or fruit, you will find . . . diamonds like the Koh-i-noor.

It was there that one saw Martí the thinker, Martí the philosopher, Martí the painter, Martí the musician, Martí the poet (always). With incomparable magic, he portrayed the United States alive and palpitating, with its sun and its souls. That colossal "nation," the "plains" of years gone by, was presented in his columns, at every posting from New York, in thick floods of ink. Bourget's United States delight and amuse; Groussac's United States make one think; Martí's United States are a stupendous and enchanting diorama that one might almost say heighten the color of reality. My memory loses itself in that mountain of images, but I do recall a martial Grant and a heroic Sherman, handsomer and smarter than I have seen anywhere else; the arrival of heroes from the Pole; the Brooklyn Bridge, the *literary* bridge, but so like the bridge of iron; a herculean description of an agricultural fair, as vast as the Augean stables; flowering springs and summers—oh!—better than any natural season; Sioux Indians that spoke in Martí's tongue; the Manitou that inspired in him snowfalls that made one truly cold; and a patriarchal, prestigious, lyrically august Walt Whitman long before the French learned through Sarrazin of that biblical author of *Leaves of Grass*.

And when the famous Pan-American Congress came, his letters were quite simply a book. In those dispatches he spoke of the dangers of the Yankee, of the careful watch Latin America needed to keep on its older sister, and of the depth of the words with which an Argentine speaker countered the words of Monroe.

This was the Martí of nervous temperament, the thin Martí with lively, kindly eyes. But his soft and delicate word in familiar conversation changed when it stood at the podium, to take on violent, coppery, oratorical tones. He was an orator, and an orator of great influence. He inspired multitudes. His life was a combat. He was soft-spoken and extremely polite to the ladies; the Cuban *damas* of New York held him in just esteem and affection, and there was one society of females that took his name.

His culture was legendary, his honor intact and crystalline; any person who approached him, left him loving him.

And he was a poet, and he made verses.

Yes, that prose writer who, always faithful to classical Castalia, drank of its water every day, was unsatisfied with being "merely" classic, and so he communed with all things modern and savored his universal and polyglot knowledge, and in the course of things formed a manner most special and particular to himself, mixing in his style Saavedra Fajardo with Gautier, with Goncourt—with whomever you like, for it has a bit of everything—constantly employing English inversions, launching his fleet of metaphors, twisting his spirals of figures, painting now with Pre-Raphaelite minuteness the landscape's tiniest leaves, now with broad strokes, or sudden touches, smears of the spatula, giving life to his figures. That strong huntsman made verses, and almost always small verses, simple verses—was there not a book of his by that title?—verses containing patriotic sadness, grief over love, rich with rhyme and harmonized always with great tact. A first, rare collection is dedicated to a son whom he adored and whom he lost forever: "Ismaelillo."

The *Versos Sencillos—Simple Verses*—published in New York in a lovely little edition . . . contains true gems. There are other poems, and among the loveliest "*Los zapatitos de rosa,*" "The Little Pink Slippers." I think that as Banville has employed the word "lyre" and Leconte de Lisle the word "black," Martí has used "pink." . . .

The children of the Americas were especially dear to the heart of Martí. There is a newspaper, unique of its kind, whose few editions were written especially for children. In one of them there is a portrait of San Martín, a masterpiece. There is also the collection called *Patria* and several works translated into English, but all that is the least of the literary *oeuvre* that will be read in the future.

And now, teacher and author and friend, forgive those who loved and admired you for bearing you some small ill-will for having gone off to expose, and lose, the treasure of your talent. The world will know soon enough who and what you were, for God's justice is infinite, and to each man grants his due and legitimate glory. Still . . . Martínez Campos, who has ordered that your body be laid out for the public's viewing, continues to read his two favorite authors: Cervantes and Ohnet. It may take Cuba some time to give you your due. The youth of the Americas, however, salutes you, and grieves your passing. Oh, Maestro, what have you done!

And it seems to me that in that voice of yours, kindly, warm,

you are scolding me, you who adored La Patria until the death
of that luminous and terrible idol, and you are speaking to me
of the dream in which you saw the heroes—the hands of stone,
the eyes of stone, the lips of stone, the beards of stone, the
sword of stone. . . .

And then your voice repeats the poem's vow:

> Yo quiero, cuando me muera,
> sin patria, pero sin amo,
> tener en mi losa un ramo
> de flores y una bandera![52]

52. When I die, without homeland / but without master, I want there to be /
upon my grave a spray of flowers / and upon my gravestone, a flag!

# On Poetry and the Poet

# AN EXCERPT FROM "FROM A BOOK OF INTIMATE PAGES"

In my opinion, while on one side a poet leans toward nature, and in that he approaches the estate of the plastic artist, on the other side he is of the race of priests, and in that he rises toward the divine. Ergo, the symbol, which manifests an idea with the enchantment of form and is animated by a vague yet powerful mystery. To draw that rare spirit of the poet into the agitations that stir the common race of men is to cause him to trip on his own wings. That is the case of Baudelaire's "Albatross":

| | |
|---|---|
| *Le poète est semblable au prince des nuées* | The poet is like this monarch of the clouds, |
| *Qui hante la tempête et se rit de l'archer;* | Familiar of storms, of stars, and of all high things; |
| *Exilé sur le sol au milieu des huées,* | Exiled on earth amidst its hooting crowds, |
| *Ses ailes de géant l'empêchent de marcher.* | Her cannot walk, borne down by his giant wings.[53] |

53. Though this translation is unattributed, it can be found at www.shanegaron .com/Capra7/ArtStudio_htmls/poets_writers/baudelaire/34.html.

# AN EXCERPT FROM "THE LITERARY LIFE"

There are few, very few athletes of thought who in the midst of the rude battles of every day continue to worship the Muses and their arts. Most men, disillusioned by this age of positivism and scepticism, have closed themselves up into a despairing muteness that ill befits their artistic nature. . . .

A sad and disappointing fate is art's among us!

Ask booksellers how many editions they have published and how many copies they have sold of great poetry, of books of travel, of novels—ask them, and the reply will be terribly mortifying to your spirit! . . .

It is not enough to have an Atheneum and an Academy; there must be what one might call an *artistic audience,* an audience that loves science, poetry, art, the beautiful things of the spirit, an audience that reads the verses of our conscientious historians, the scientific texts of our men of thought.

It is truly painful that in a city of six hundred thousand inhabitants like Buenos Aires, there are not a hundred readers of the nation's books.

Here, aside from the gaucho poems of Estanislao del Campo, José Hernández, and Hilario Ascasubi and the detective stories of Eduardo Gutiérrez—which are widespread in our pampas—the only works that have had the honor of more than a single edition are the histories of San Martín and Belgrano written by General Mitre. . . .

It is time to concern ourselves with Argentine thought, because (as Luther said) "the prosperity of a country depends not on the abundance of its rents, nor the strength of its fortresses, nor the beauty of its public buildings; it consists in the number of its cultured citizens, in its men of education, enlightenment, and character. This is where one finds a nation's true interest, its principal strength, its true power."

What can one add to those heartfelt and vibrant words? . . .

# THE 1001 NIGHTS

A lovely and glorious work has just been completed by Dr. J. C. Mardrus: the complete translation of the *Book of the Thousand Nights and a Night*, brought into French literally from the Arabic. It is a priceless gift that we Westerners cannot sufficiently give thanks for. The last volume will leave in dreaming souls an inevitable nostalgia. A spirit as rare as it is subtle has made this complaint: "*The Thousand Nights and a Night* is a loving epic of the globe from the moment of its creation down to our own days. The globe is an egg incubated, in turn, by Love and Night. Is it possible that humanity is no more than the accident of a daydream? So long as Love and Night fan us with their wings, the earth will continue, I dare believe, to turn. But behold, the morning comes . . . ay!, ay!, the East turns white . . . the East grows old! Who will rock our dream of people of the North?"

Yes, Rachilde is right. In order to approach even the illusion of happiness, we need the deliciousness of Night and the enchantment of Love. And that is the *ambience* of these magical stories that the European scholar has coaxed from their secret Oriental shelters.

Dr. Mardrus is a noted Orientalist, whatever may be said to the contrary by an emir (a friend of Claretie) who has found "certain imprecisions" in this version, which one feels to be so filled with enchantments. A most conscientious laborer, Dr. Mardrus spoke from the outset of the magnitude of his undertaking. Before him, no one had made a complete, exact, literal translation into French, out of fear that the nakedness of Arabic expression might wound, more than our Western modesty, the universal puritanism of Christian literatures. In English, there are the faithful versions, today extremely rare, of Payne and Burton, but those were limited subscribers' editions and thus were, so to speak, secret. Mardrus knows, also, of a second edition of Burton, but it is expurgated. The erudite French translator gives the origins of his sources. The basis of *The Thousand Nights and a Night* (for thus its title should be rendered) is a Persian anthology, the *Hazar Afsanah*.

There have been several narrators who, taking the original pieces, fantasized at will. Persian stories were mixed with legends from other nations. "The entire Moslem world, from Damascus to Cairo and from Baghdad to Morocco, was reflected in the mirror of *The Thousand Nights and a Night*." A mixture of dialects, of various idiomatic phrases, which are found in manuscripts produced at different times, prevents us from fixing a date for the marvelous book in which it would seem that all the fantasy of the Orient intermingles. Recent studies, however, have shown that the stories that appear in all the texts date to the tenth century. Those stories are: the story of King Shahryar and his brother King Shahzaman; the story of the merchant and the Ifrit; the story of the fisherman and the Ifrit; the story of the porter and the three young ladies; the story of the woman cut into pieces, the three apples, and the black slave Rayhan; the story of the vizier Nur al-Din; the story of the tailor and of the hunchback; the story of Nur al-Din and Anis al-Jalis; the story of Ghanim ben-Ayyub; the story of Ali ibn Bakkar and Shams al-Nahar; the story of Kamar al-Zaman; the story of the ebony horse; and the story of Jullanar of the sea. The second story of Kamar al-Zaman and the story of the Mearuf date to the sixteenth century; most of the stories are from the tenth to sixteenth centuries, and the stories of Sindbad the Sailor and King Jali'ad are prior to all the others.

According to the note that stands at the beginning of Madrus' edition (which began to be published by the *Revue Blanche* and has been completed by Fasquelle), there are seven critical editions of the original texts of *Alf Laylah wa Laylah:* the (unfinished) edition of sheik El Yemeni, 2 vols., Calcutta, 1814–1818; the Habitch edition, 12 vols., Breslau, 1825–1843; the Macnaghten edition, 4 vols., Calcutta, 1830–1842; the Bulaq edition, 2 vols.,

Cairo, 1835; the Ezbekieh editions, Cairo; the cut, corrected, quirky edition by the Jesuits, 4 vols. Beirut; and the four-volume Bombay edition. Doctor Mardrus has preferred the Bulaq, but has had recourse, too, to Macnaghten's edition, in addition, principally, to the various Arabic manuscripts.

I have no knowledge of any literal German, or Italian, or Spanish translation. *The Thousand and One Nights* that we know in Spanish is translated from the French translation by Galland, "a curious example of the deformation that a text may suffer when it passes through the head of a scholar in the time of Louis XIV." Galland's adaptation, done for the Court, was systematically emasculated of all things *risqué* and filtered of all its wit. Even as an adaptation it is incomplete, for it contains barely a quarter of the stories. Before Mardrus, the stories that make up the other three-quarters were unknown in France, or, better, the world.

In order to translate a work of poetry one must be a poet. And in order to translate this peerless work of poetry, what was needed was a poet learned in things of the Orient—a man such as Dr. Mardrus, who has lived the Oriental life in the same places where, in prestigious and abolished imaginations, these extraordinary tales were born.

That the translator is a notable poet will be seen in the pearl of an introduction, a handful of harmonious words that I must set down here as a gift to my readers: "I offer," it says, "all naked, virginal, intact, innocent, for my own delight and the pleasure of my friends, these Arabian nights—lived, dreamed, and translated, in their native land and on the water. They were sweet to me during the vagaries of long journeys, under distant skies. That is why I offer them. They are innocent, ingenuous, and smiling, and they are filled with ingenuity, like that Moslem Shahrazad, their succulent mother, who bore them in mystery, fermenting uneasily in the bosom of a sublime prince—lascivious and fierce—under the tender eyes of clement, merciful Allah. From the moment of their coming they were caressed by the hands of auroral Dinarzad, their aunt, who engraved their names on golden leaves sparkling with moist jewels, and secreted them under the velvet of her eyes until pure adolescence, when she sprinkled them, voluptuous and free, over the Oriental world, made eternal with her smile. I judge them and I give them as they are, in the freshness of flesh and rose. For . . . there is but a single method, honorable and logical, for translation—'literalness,' impersonal, hardly attenuated by one's quick blink and long savoring. . . . This sort of translation, which is suggestive, produces the greatest literary power. It creates evocative pleasure. It recreates by suggestion. It is the surest guarantee of truth. It sinks, firmly, into the stone's nakedness. It sniffs the primitive aroma and crystallizes it. It winds and mixes . . . fixes. Of course, if literalness enchains and tames the digressing spirit, then it restrains the infernal facility of the pen. I will not complain of that.

"For where is one to find in a translator the simple, anonymous genius free of *la niaise manie de son nom*?[54] Yet the difficulties of the native land—difficulties so very unyielding for the professional—would not, under the fingers of the lover of the Eastern way of speaking, be concentrated in more whorls and knots than those needed for the enjoyment of unbinding them. As for the reception. . . . The mannered West, made pale in the stifling atmosphere of verbal conventions, feigned confusion at hearing the frank, simple, whispered yet sonorous language, and the laughter, of those dark-skinned healthy girls who inhabited those vanished tents.

"Those houris see no harm in that. And the primitive peoples call things by their name, and find in what is natural almost nothing blameworthy, or in the expression of what is natural nothing licentious. (By 'primitive peoples' I mean those who do not yet have any defect of flesh or spirit, and who are born into the world under the smile of beauty . . .) Of course pornography, that hateful product of spiritual old age, is utterly unknown to Arabic literature. The Arabs see everything under the aspect of hilarity. Their erotic sense leads only to joy, to gaiety. And they laugh out loud at what the Puritan would think scandalous. Any artist who has wandered through the Orient and lovingly cultivated the sometimes rickety benches

54. "The foolish mania of his name."

of the popular cafés in true Arab, Moslem cities—old Cairo
with its cool streets filled with shadows, the *souks* of Dam-
ascus, Yemen, Mascata, or Baghdad; who has slept on the
bedouin's immaculate mat in Palmyra, fraternally broken
bread and tasted salt in the glory of the desert with sumptuous
Ibn-Rachid, that perfect type of the authentic Arab, savored all
the exquisite pleasure of a conversation of ancient simplicity
with Sharif Hussein-ben Ali ben-Aun, the pure descendant of
the Prophet, emir of holy Mecca, will have been able to remark
upon the expression on the picturesque physiognomies gath-
ered there. A unique sentiment reigns over all existence: a mad
hilarity. It flames up in the vitals shaken by every frank remark
of the heroic, gesticulating public narrator, animating all listen-
ers, leaping from one delighted spectator to another. . . . And
so the drunkenness rises in one, for one finds oneself aroused
by the words, by the sounds, by the perfume or the aphrodisiac
of the air, by the soft under-odor of hasheesh, that last gift of
Allah! . . . And it floats through the air in the night. . . . Allah
is not applauded; that barbaric gesture, inharmonious and
fierce, that undeniable vestige of the ancestral Carib races
dancing around the post of colors, which Europe has taken as
the symbol of the horrid bourgeois delight of men and women
crowded together in the gaslight, is essentially unknown. To a
song, the notes of reeds and flutes, a complaint from the qanun
or oud, a rhythm from the deep darbukkah, a song from the
muezzin, or an almeh,[55] a piquant story, a poem of cascading
alliterations, a subtle fragrance of jasmine, a flower-dance or
deep-throated cadence of the bukkah, a song from the muezzin
or from a pearl upon the belly of a ripe undulating courtesan
with starry eyes—the Arab responds quietly or with his entire
voice, with an Aa-a-ah! a-a-ah! . . . long, wise, modulated, ec-
static, architectural. The Arab is intuitive, but refined and ex-
quisitely so. He loves the pure line and the unrealized riddle.
But . . . he stretches, wordlessly, infinitely.

"And now, I can promise, without fear of misstating, that the
curtain will rise only on the most astonishing, most complicated,

55. A woman who improvises verses and dances for a living.

and most splendid vision that a narrator's fragile instrument has ever, upon snowy paper, lighted."

That is the prologue that opens the mysterious and talismanic portals of those kingdoms of dreams so human yet so divine. Nor does Doctor Mardrus announce his work in vain. Among the strangest and most prestigious decorations, the most unlikely yet magnificent scenes begin to unfold. From the narration emerge the most varied of dews; one hears the most astounding sounds, sees the vastest visions. The joy of a humanity without complications flowers freely, healthily, and freshly, in all its pristine nature.

Bread is called bread, and wine, wine, and the functions of love, as in Moses' decalogue. There is nothing deformed; neither the sin of our theologies exists there, nor the shame of our guilty modesties, nor the malice of our civilized perversities. There is, however, a superior culture that casts justice and goodness upon souls. And the unknown seems natural, and the prodigious seems usual, and dream enters life and life mingles with dream, as it should. One perfectly understands that wish of Stendhal, who desired to "forget two things, *Don Quixote* and *The Thousand and One Nights,* so that every year I might, as I reread them, experience a new voluptuousness."

Of myself, I will say that no book has so liberated my spirit from the tediums of our common existence, our daily aches and pains, as this book of pearls and gems, magic spells and enchantments, realities so ungraspable and fantasies so real. Its fragrance is sedative, its effluvia calming, its delights refreshing and comforting. Like any modifier of thought, but without the inconveniences of venoms, alcohols, or alkaloids, it offers the gift of an artificial paradise. To read certain tales is to enter a pool of warm rosewater. And in all, there is delight for the five senses—and for others that we hardly suspect.

In no way shall I recommend that Mardrus' version be read by any persons save men of letters, men of education, *men.* Unless they be judicious, quiet ladies stuffed with literature, none of our females is prepared for this work, which would undoubtedly scandalize them. The Oriental nude is yet more natural than the nude of classical Greece. As for young unmarried ladies, they simply cannot read it. Suffice it to say that the morality of Mohammedan damsels is quite other than that taught in nuns' schools, finishing schools, and the like, where the doctrine of Christ is taught.

Happy the person who can with naturalness and simplicity, without irony or evil thoughts, wander through these flowery, perfumed gardens of delights! Fortunate the person who can anoint himself with the exhalations of the poets of the East as though with a fine unguent of poetry. That person will feel that for a moment centuries-old chains will have fallen from the wings of his soul. And as Doctor Mardrus, that new Sindbad who brings us miraculous stories from the lands of wonder, says, the reader will feel himself to be "an aerial sailor through the night."

# MARINETTI AND FUTURISM

Marinetti is an Italian poet writing in French. He is a good poet, a notable poet. The world's intellectual *élite* know him. I know that personally, he is a kind soul, and he is worldly. In Milan, he publishes a lyrical, polyglot review, *Poesia,* which is luxuriously presented. His poems have been praised by the best lyric poets in France. His major work—so far—*Le roi Bombance,* is Rabelaisian, pompously comic, tragically burlesque, exuberant, and it achieved well-merited success when it was published, though it probably will not when it is performed in Paris under the direction of the very famous actor Lugne-Poe. And Marinetti's book against D'Annuzio is so well done and filled with such ill will that the Imaginificus must be most pleased with the satirical homage. . . .

Marinetti's poems are violent, sonorous, and unbridled. They give the effect of the Italian fugue played upon a French organ. And it is curious to see that the author whom he most resembles is the Flemish poet Verhaeren. But the reason for making Marinetti the subject just now is a survey carried out today about a new literary school that he has founded, or whose principles he has proclaimed with all the music of his considerable instrument. This school is called Futurism.

The problem is, Futurism was founded by the great Mallorcan Gabriel Alomar. And I have spoken about this in *Dilucidations,* which prefaces my *Canto errante.*

Did Marinetti know the pamphlet in Catalan in which Alomar put forth his *pensées?* I believe he did not, and that this is just another of those coincidences. But however the case may be, one must recognize the priority of the expression, if not altogether the doctrine.

What is this doctrine? Let us see.

1. "We intend to sing the love of danger, the habit of energy and daring." In the first proposition it seems to me that Futurism becomes Past-ism. Is all this not in Homer?

2. "The essential elements of our poetry shall be courage, audacity, and rebelliousness." Is all that not already in the entire classic cycle?

3. "Literature having up to now magnified pensive immobility, ecstasy, and slumber, we intend to exalt aggressive motion, feverish insomnia, the gymnastic gait, the mortal leap, the punch, and the slap." I think that many of these things are already in Homer, and that Pindar is an excellent poet of sports.

4. "We declare that the splendor of the world has been enriched with a new beauty: the beauty of speed. A race car, its hood adorned with thick tubes like serpents with fiery breath . . . a roaring automobile that seems to run on machine-gun bullets, is more beautiful than the Victory of Samothrace." I fail to understand the comparison. Which is more beautiful, a naked woman or a storm? A lily or a cannon-blast? Should one, as Mendès suggests, reread the preface to *Cromwell*?

5. "We intend to sing hymns to the man at the wheel, whose beautiful ideal is launched forth from the Earth into the circuit of its orbit." If not in the modern way of understanding, one could always return to antiquity in search of Bellerophon or Mercury.

6. "The poet must spend himself in heat, light, and prodigality, in order to increase the enthusiastic light of the primordial elements." Plausible. Of course this is an impulse of youth and consciousness, of one's own vigor.

7. "There is no beauty except in struggle. There is no master-piece that is not aggressive in nature. Poetry must be conceived as a violent attack on unknown forces, in order to impose on them the sovereignty of man." Apollo and Anphion inferior to Herakles? The unknown forces are not tamed with violence. And at any rate, for the poet there *are* no unknown forces.

8. "We stand upon the last promontory of the centuries. . . . Why look behind us, since we must break through the doors of the Impossible? Time and Space died yesterday. We live now in the Absolute, for we have now created eternal, omnipotent speed." Oh, Marinetti! The automobile is a poor carapaced thing in a dream before the eternal Destruction that is revealed, for example, in the recent horror of Trinacria.

9. "We intend to glorify war—the world's only hygiene— militarism, patriotism, the destructive work of anarchists, beau-tiful Ideas that kill, contempt for women." The innovative poet has revealed himself to be Oriental, Nietzschean, and in thrall to an anarchistic and destructive violence. But why, then, all these articles and rules? As for War being the world's best and only hygiene, there is always the Plague.

10. "We intend to demolish museums and libraries, to combat moralism, feminism, and all opportunistic, utilitarian forms of cowardice."

11. "We shall sing hymns to the great multitudes stirred by work, pleasure, and uproar: the many-colored, polyphonic tides of revolutions in the capitals of the modern world, arsenals vi-brating at night, shipyards under violent electric moons [ . . . ],[56] gluttonous stations that swallow smoking serpents, bridges leap-ing gymnastically over the diabolical cutlery of sunny rivers, adventurous steamers sniffing at the horizon, broad-chested

56. Darío has omitted an item in the Futurist Manifesto: "factories hung on clouds by the ribbons of their smoke."

locomotives pawing at the rails like huge iron steeds bridled with long tubes, and the sleek flight of aeroplanes with propellers that crack and clatter like flags and cheering multitudes." All this is wondrously enthusiastic and, above all, wondrously juvenile. It is a platform of youth, and because it is, it has its inherent virtues and its inescapable, essential weaknesses.

The Futurists, speaking through their main leader, say that this manifesto has been proclaimed in Italy (though it is written in French, like all respectable manifestos must be) because they want to "free Italy from its gangrene of professors, archaeologists, *ciceroni*, and antiquarians." They say that Italy must no longer be the *grand marché des brocanteurs*.[57] We are not, of course, in the full bloom of Futurism when it is Italian professors who call upon a Theodore Roosevelt or an Emilio Mitre to educate their respective nations.

It is very difficult to transform widely held ideas, and infiltration into human collectives must be done through successive layers. The museums are cemeteries, you say? Let us not *peladanicemos*[58] too much. There are dead men in marble and bronze in parks and along boulevards, and although it is true that some aesthetic ideas resist the agglomeration that occurs in those official edifices, for the moment we have not been able to discover anything to replace those orderly catalogued exhibits. The *Salons*? That's another thing.

Marinetti's main idea is that everything lies in the future, and almost nothing in the past. In an old painting he sees nothing but "the laborious contortions of an artist throwing himself against the barriers that thwart his desire to express his dream completely." But has modernity achieved complete expression? If it is at most a bouquet of flowers every year that one is to be allowed to take, funereally, to the *Gioconda,* what shall we do with the contemporary painters of golf and the automobile? And "Onward!" he says. But where? If Time and Space no longer exist, is it not the same to go Backward as Forward?

57. One big second-hand store.
58. Write like PÉLADAN (*q.v.*); that is, hermetically, mystically, platonically.

The oldest of us, says Marinetti, is thirty years old. That says it all. They give themselves ten years to do their work, and then they immediately turn themselves over to those that come next. "They will rise against us—*when the Futurists are forty!*—panting with scorn and anguish, and all of them, exasperated by our proud and tireless courage, will rush to kill us, with a hatred the more implacable the more their hearts are drunken with love and admiration for us."

And in that tone the ode continues—with the same speed and impetus!

Oh, how wonderful is youth! I feel a certain nostalgia for impulsive spring when I consider that I shall be among the devoured, for I am over forty now. And, in its violence, I applaud Marinetti's intention, because I see it from the standpoint of a poet's work—a poet anxious, yearning, courageous, who wants to ride the sacred horse off into new horizons. You will find in all these things a great deal of excess; the wound of war is too impetuous, but who besides young men, who have that first strength and that constant hope, can manifest impetuous and excessive attempts?

The only thing that I find worthless is the manifesto. Although Marinetti has, with his vehement works, proven that he has an admirable talent and is able to fill his mission with Beauty, I do not believe that his manifesto does anything but inspire a goodly number of imitators to do "Futurism" to an extreme— many of them, surely, as always happens, without the talent or the poetry of an innovator. In the good old days of Symbolism, there were also manifestos from leaders of schools, from Moreas to Ghil. And where did all that get us? The Naturalists also "manifested," and several ephemeral schools, such as Positivism, found echo in Brazil. There have been other schools since, and other aesthetic proclamations. The oldest of all these literary revolutionaries has not been thirty.

Bald D'Annuzio, I don't know how old he is now, and look, Marinetti—the glorious Italian still enjoys marvelous health after that lovely bomb that tried to demolish him. Gods depart, and that is all to the good. If they didn't, there would be no room for us all in this poor world. D'Annuzio will be departing soon enough. And other gods will come, and they will go when their day comes, and so on, until the final cataclysm blows this ball we are all riding to eternity to bits, and with it all the dreams, all the hopes, all the impetus, and all the illusions of the ephemeral king of creation. The Future is the unending cycle of Life and Death. It is the past backward. We must take advantage of the energies in the moment, joined as we are in the process of universal existence. And afterward, we shall sleep quietly for ever and ever. Amen.

# On Art

# RICHARD LE GALLIENNE

*The Influence of the Sense of Beauty*

*. . . egli tenne lontano il volgo profano dal temple belisimo ed accesible al soli iniziati in cui sée compiaciutu de collocare la sua meravigliesa poesia.*—D. OLIVA

## I.

The English author Richard Le Gallienne, who is scandalized by the young men of the *Yellow Book,* has recently published a volume containing things quite miscellaneous: disheartening judgments on modern art, psychological digressions, something on Copernicus and on "humour," and other pieces—a stew, a salad of things, all with a vague hue of scholarly sentimentalism. And in this book, one may read the following declaration:

*It is quite curious that in our time, among those artists called* decadents, *the influence of the sense of Beauty is affirmed not as "spiritualizing" but rather, on the contrary, as "materializing" and degrading. Even when—as I dare say in its worst forms—decadent art is not the expression of a mental and spiritual disease, even when it retains a certain innocence and a certain health, it does all it can to wrap itself in pure sensuality.*

*It directs itself only to the sensual eye, the sensual ear, and it desperately attempts to limit beauty to form and color, ignoring and disdaining the sensibilities of the heart and the spirit.*

## II.

These ideas—which seem so terribly unfair to one who knows the tendencies, the fundamental ideas of those seekers of the ideal who throughout the world (and especially in France) proclaim the kingdom of unified and sovereign Art—should surprise all those who have entered the sanctuary of the school rubber-stamped by journalists and official critics with the seal of Decadence. Without going so far as to the greater stars—to Poe and Wagner, the great, chaste beings who have given life to Ligeias and Parsifals—the penetrating observer who takes an unprejudiced, honest look at the matter will see that the work of these new writers occupies mainly the region of Pure Ideas, Daydream (some may say Fantasy), and Mystery. To whom do we owe the recent yearning after spiritual flight, the greater impulse toward the unknown, the tendency to the knowledge of first causes, the renaissance of mysticism, the renewal of the antique symbols, the exploration of the immense ancient forests of History in which the occult temples of past religions may be found?

The "Decadents," it is true, have consecrated a great part of their concern to the excellencies of form, but they have not dwelled only in the marmoreal world of Greece, so beloved of the academic schools for its nature limited, linear, and comprehensive. No, they have sought everywhere for the profound manifestations of the universal soul; they have seen in the Orient a world of strange initiations; they have found in the North a vast region of dreams and mysteries; they have recognized and proclaimed the immanence and totality of Art; they have cast off all the ballast that weighed down the wings of the psyche; they have attempted to achieve a definitive form, and with it the immortal, triumphant life of the Work of Art. Never, since the times when the great works of mysticism flowered, has the soul had a greater number of priests and soldiers; never has there been such thirst for God, such desire to penetrate the unknowable and the arcane, as in these times, when there have appeared messengers of a high victory, worshipers of a supreme ideal, those great artists who have been called Decadents.

It is to them that the world owes the current triumph of Legend, by which forgotten visions of Poesy have been illuminated;

to them is owed the holy impulse toward Faith, and today's defenses and dikes against the perilous trials of science; to Wagner, the immaterial flowering of artistic ecstasy and the most profound understanding of the Mass; to Verlaine the Catholic, the most admirable liturgical hymns, the finest cantos since Jacopone da Todi to that purest and most august of symbols, the adorable Mystery of the Virgin; to Baudelaire, the unknown decorations of Sin, illuminated by the "new light" of his visionary lyrics; to Mallarmé, rare sensations of the immaterial life and graspable veils of the attire of dream. . . . Who but Poe and his followers have penetrated the night of Death? Who more than Léon Bloy has glimpsed the formidable and apocalyptic enigma of Prostitution?

## III.

What repulses Le Gallienne in Decadent art is, no doubt, the inevitable appearance of carnal love in all its manifestations. Carnal love can turn even the head of St. John the Divine, when he contemplates one of his most portentous and terrible visions: "And there came one of the seven angels [and] he carried me away in the spirit into the wilderness: and I saw a woman sit upon a scarlet coloured beast, full of names of blasphemy, having seven heads and ten horns. And the woman was arrayed in purple and scarlet colour, and decked with gold and precious stones and pearls, having a golden cup in her hand full of abominations and filthiness of her fornication: And upon her forehead was a name written, MYSTERY, BABYLON THE GREAT, THE MOTHER OF HARLOTS AND ABOMINATIONS OF THE EARTH. And I saw the woman drunken with the blood of the saints, and with the blood of the martyrs of Jesus: and when I saw her, I wondered with great admiration. And the angel said unto me, Wherefore didst thou marvel? I will tell thee the mystery of the woman, and of the beast that carrieth her, which hath the seven heads and ten horns."

Or Dante, to whom appears

| | |
|---|---|
| . . . una lonza leggera e presta molto | A panther light and swift exceedingly, |
| che di pel macolato era coverta. | Which with a spotted skin was covered o'er! |
| e non mi si partia dinanzi al volto, | And never moved she from before my face, |
| anzi 'mpediva tanto il mio cammino | Nay, rather did impede so much my way, |
| ch'i' fui per ritornar più volte volto. | That many times I to return had turned. |

(Trans. Henry Wadsworth Longfellow)

This eternal female mystery, the omnipotence of whose manifestations overmasters the human being, is that which constantly arises before the eyes of the artist, and it is that which makes such critics as the clergyman I am speaking of now affirm that Decadent art has eyes and ears only for the colors and sounds of sensuality. Where is one to turn one's gaze, though, so as not to come under the influence of Eves and Venuses? Where is a man of flesh and blood not to find the red eyes of the mysterious serpent? That is why great artists—at once strong and delicate—are seized by an invincible obsession, for every great artist is a solitary in his Thebais or on his Zenobii, and it is solitaries who are visited by the invisible, unknown forces, whether they be in the form of the tempting devil or the divine *daimon*.

Thus Huysmann, thus poor grand Verlaine, thus Gabriel d'Annunzio.

# RANVIER

*"The Infancy of Bacchus"*

## I.

His is not the triumphant Bacchus that marched off to India, embossed upon vases and medals; his, not the great obese Bacchus crowned with clusters of grapes, that god painted by a court painter to please an imperial prince. Following his inspiration, Ranvier has chosen his subject from the mythology of ancient Greece, and its central figure is a strong, jolly god at the very moment of his birth—hatched from the thigh of father Jupiter like a chick from the egg, the son of Semele, as he is portrayed on the old Etruscan mirror. This is the Bacchus beloved of the Greek culture, the vigorous Dionysus in his childhood. In terrifying Eleusian mysteries he sits beside the fecund and bountiful Demeter and Corë, daughter of great Ceres. The child Bacchus in the arms of the swift winged god, as though Mercury, Prometheus' interlocutor in the Aeschylean tragedy, were the conductor of a symbol of fertility and power.

Where does the scene in Ranvier's painting take place?

We should believe that it is in Nysa, on the coast of Euboea, on the banks of one of the lyrical rivers that lent inspiration for the songs of the ancient poets, and where the foot of nymphs left hardly a trace.

In this painting there is a pure sky. Bacchus is not yet the triumphant child on the back of the lion—as later Venus will be set.

The bearded Silenus has not yet appeared to teach his favorite disciple. There is not yet the sound of thyrsi, cymbals, and other musical instruments, no dancing by the bacchantes.

Here, this child-Bacchus is learning to swim; he is bathed as he is held in the arms of a naked white nymph—I assume she is Mystis, whose long, luxurious hair is hymned in Greek verses, though Ranvier does not paint it. On the bank, among the leaves, there are other nymphs, also naked, white, and lovely.

Beautiful Mystis is poetic and meritorious, because she is the inventor of the vibrant bell, the gay rattle, and the ringing tabour; it was she who first cried "Euoi!" with joyous unction, and she was crowned with the cool crown of grapes from the virgin vine.

## II.

From the legendary painters to sovereign Velázquez, the brush has given Bacchus perpetual triumph. On amphorae his grapevine is preferred over Pan's pea-vine; in bas-reliefs, the faun is his acolyte and the satyr his officer; in murals he makes the spreading grapevine bear fruit, and about him dance the bacchantes, called "Maenads," or *the furious,* because of their mad frenzies. In his youthful aspect, he is painted with the belly of an ephebe, because in that way painting may reflect the verses of the Anacreontic ode, and when artists have wanted to give an idea of his poetic sovereignty and pomp, they have portrayed him as a serene and regal Bacchus—the Indic Sardanapalus—a Bacchus majestic and pontifical.

Ranvier's subject is not new. Poussin's *Education of Bacchus* is the greatest of this painting's elder siblings. The name and deeds of the divine conqueror shall be an eternal subject for artists.

From the time of the first Greek poets until the greatest poet in the world, great Victor Hugo, Dionysus has always had an *Euoi!* and a crown of green grape leaves.

## III.

Before me I have Aristophanes' *Thesmophoriazusae,* or *Women at the Festival of Demeter,* and I read the following words, which are a hymn: "Do thou, oh divine Bacchus, who art crowned with ivy, direct our chorus; 'tis to thee that both my hymns and my dances are dedicated; oh, Evius, oh, Bromius, oh, thou son of Semele, oh, Bacchus, who delightest to mingle with the dear choruses of the nymphs upon the mountains, and who repeatest, while dancing with them, the sacred hymn, Euios, Euios, Euoi! Echo, the nymph of Cithaeron, returns thy words, which resound beneath the dark vaults of the thick foliage and in the midst of the rocks of the forest."

The vulgar Bacchus, the drunken god, the patron of the intoxicated and the lost, that god appealed to by the late-night revelers of all times and places, is fat, lardy, with a belly full not, like the cicada, of dew, but wine—a heavy, red-faced, rotund epicurean Bacchus.

Ranvier's painting portrays that lovable childhood among the soft pink flesh of guardian nymphs, beside a peaceful river that reflects a sweet, serene sky; and while there is precise truth in the way he treats the female bodies, with their firm fleshiness and their precise movement, under that sky that has all the light of reality, the atmosphere of the scene is no less ideal—a page from myth and eclogue, bathed in ineffable, delightful poetry.

# On Himself

# THE COLORS OF
# MY STANDARD

*La fin de dix-neuvième siècle verra son poète (cependant,
au début, il ne doit pas commencer par un chef d'oeuvre,
mais suivre la loi de la nature): il est né sur les rives améri-
caines, à l'embouchure de la Plata, là où deux peuples, jadis
rivaux, s'efforcent actuellement de se surpasser par le pro-
grès matériel et moral. BuenosAyres, la reine du Sud, et
Montevideo, la coquette, se tendent un main amie, à travers
les eaux argentines de grand estuaire.*
—Lautréamont, Les Chants de Maldoror

I must, at last, speak of my own work and of myself, *pro domo
mea,* for a writer worthy of my reply and my respect has ex-
pressed certain judgments that I believe myself obliged to con-
tradict. This writer is M. Groussac, and the judgments to which
I refer have appeared in the most serious and aristocratic peri-
odical in the Spanish language today: *La Biblioteca,* which is
our own *Revue des Deux Mondes.* M. Groussac has proclaimed
my modesty. It is true: before the authority of the masters, before
superior spirits, I am modest and respectful. In the face of inept
praise and censures, my modesty turns to absolute indifference.
In the face of ineffable hostility—for example, the inoffensive
sniff of a Galician snout that rummages in the fields of
Córboba—my modesty is higher than Ossa upon Pelion.

M. Groussac has written, upon the publication of my book
*Los Raros (The Misfits),* phrases that I must say delight me. He
is not known to be facile or grandiloquent. Behind his back,
timidly or angrily mutter herds of the wounded and the threat-
ened. I have been relatively fortunate. What is there that is
sweeter than honey or stronger than the lion? I have found
honey in the mouth of the lion, and I have survived!

He must have perceived something in the part of the soul that comes out in the eyes [when I met him several years ago], for he has been very kind in his words. Had he been able to see even deeper he might have read this most intimate confession: "Sir, when I published my *Azure* . . . in Chile[ . . . ]the decadents had hardly begun to sharpen their quills in France. Verlaine's *Sagesse* was yet unknown. The masters who have led me to the 'mental gallicism' that don Juan Valera accuses me of are a handful of Parnassians in verse, and you, in prose."

Yes, Groussac, with his theater criticism for *La Nación* in Sarah Bernhardt's first season was the man who taught me to write—for well or ill—the way I write today.

My success—it would be absurd not to confess it—has been due to novelty. And this novelty, what has it consisted of? A mental gallicism. When I read Groussac I did not know he was a Frenchman writing in Spanish. But he taught me to *think in French*; after that, my young, happy heart claimed Gallic citizenship.

In truth, I live on poetry. My dreams have a Solomonic magnificence. I love beauty, power, grace, money, luxury, kisses, and music. I am naught but a man of art. I am good for nothing else. I believe in God, and I am attracted to mystery. I am befuddled by daydreams and death; I have read many philosophers yet I know not a word of philosophy. I do espouse a certain epicureanism, of my own sort: let the soul and body enjoy as much as possible on earth, and do everything possible to continue that enjoyment in the next life. Which is to say that *je vois la vie en rose*.

My adoration for France was, from my first spiritual steps, deep and wide. My dream was to write in French. And I even perpetrated certain verses in that language; they merit forgiveness, for I have not repeated that error. . . . As I penetrated into certain secrets of harmony, of nuance, of suggestion that one finds in the language of France, I believed I might discover those same secrets in Spanish, or apply them.

The oratorical resonance, the brasses of Castilian, its ardor— why could they not take on the intermediate notes and dress the indecisive thoughts that the soul tends most frequently to manifest itself by? After all, both languages are, in a way, made of the same stuff. As for the form, there are identical artifices in

both. The evolution that might bring Castilian to that Renais-
sance would have to take place in the Americas, for Spain is
buttressed and girded by tradition, walled in and bristling with
Spanishness—"What no one will uproot from us," says Valera,
"no matter how hard they pull." And so, thinking in French
and writing in a Castilian that might have been praised by the
pure Academicians of Spain, I published the little book that was
to begin the current Latin American literary movement out of
which, according to José María de Heredia, the mental renais-
sance of Spain also derived. And I tell you that since there is
great sincerity and truth in all this, my modesty is intact.

Azure . . . is a Parnassian book, and therefore French. For the
first time in our language the Parisian "tale" appears, French
adjectivization, the Gallic turn injected into a paragraph of
classic Castilian: the trinkets and stage-dressings of Goncourt,
the erotic *câlinerie*[59] of Mendès, the verbal compression of
Heredia, and even a soupçon of Coppée. *Qui pourrais-je imiter
pour être original?*[60] I asked myself. Why, everyone. From each
I took what I liked, what suited my thirst for novelty and my
delirium for art: the elements that would go on to constitute a
medium of personal expression. And it turned out to be origi-
nal. "You have stirred everything up in the alembic of your
brain," says the oft-quoted Valera, "and have pulled out of it a
rare quintessence." *Azure . . .* sounded the first note, then, and
it found fortune in Spain and even in France, where Péladan
openly imitated my *Song of Gold* in his "Cantique de l'Or,"
which is the prologue to *Le Panthée.* . . .

In Europe I came to know some of the so-called Decadents in
their work and in person. I met the good ones and the extrava-
gant ones. I chose those whom I liked for the alembic. I saw
that the useless ones fell, that the poets, the true artists, rose,
and that satire made no headway against them. I learned the
song of the panpipe from Verlaine and the music of his Pom-
padour clavichords. "If I could only bring all this into Span-
ish!" I said to myself. And from the bunch of grapes in the

59. Cuddling.
60. Whom can I imitate in order to be original?

Latin Quarter I ate the freshest fruit, tasted that which was past its prime, and, as in the verses of cabbalistic Mallarmé, blew on the skin of the empty grape and looked at the sun through it.

I saw in the *salons,* among the useless acolytes and true failures, a few great poets and men of wisdom. It is from them that the *Revue des Deux Mondes* issues.

Grotesques there were, there still are. As there are in the Americas. . . . The Classics, the Romantics, and the Naturalists had them. The grotesque Classics produced a beautiful book by Gautier; the grotesque Romantics were Petrus Borel and company; there have been grotesque Naturalists even in Spain, grotesque Decadents, even in the Americas. Oh, you young men who call yourself Decadents because you imitate one or two gestures of some strange and exquisite poet—to be a decadent like the true decadents of France, you must know a very great deal, study hard, and fly high.

So who, then, are these Decadents?

In one of his latest epistles to *La Nación,* Doctor Schimper mentioned an entire conference, in Vienna, given over to the real name that should be given the modern artists who have come together under the light of the new art.

They have no special mark that would distinguish them as members of a particular school. Some seem Classicists, like Moréas, who leans toward Racine; others, pure Romantics; yet others, like Huysmans, seem offshoots of Naturalism and employ their own language and isolate themselves in an unmistakable way. Some, like Louÿs, are clearly Hellenists, or are Latinists, like Quillard; others, like Albert, do France the service of revealing the secrets of the literature of the North; others become "official" and go to the *Revue des Deux Mondes,* like Wyzewa or Régnier, whose entrance into the journal-foyer of the Académie does not surprise me, for if his father-in-law's daughter published pieces there at the age of eleven, the wife's husband might well do so at thirty.

And if Europe has stamped with the stamp of Decadence all those who have left the vulgar, common road—among us, in our language, M. Groussac,—the last *boulevardier* magazine writer to write with some care for his style would be a most egregious Symbolist. There are those among us, that is, who take Sarcey and Ohnet to be Decadents.

And while we are about it: M. Groussac is mistaken when he states that Verlaine and Régnier never accepted such epithets as "decadent," et cetera. These are trivialities of the *salon* that there is no reason for the maestro to know. . . .

That group of artists has given the world, in these last years, the knowledge of great genius: Ibsen, Nietzsche, Max Stirner, and above all, the sovereign Wagner and the prodigious Poe. Among them, anonymous or unknown, they have translated and commented upon, published and promoted. The Pre-Raphaelites are their brothers, and the work of those Pre-Raphaelites is their own: Swinburne has declared as much. It was their influence that led to the commencement of what de Vogüé called the "Latin Renaissance," with Gabriel D'Annunzio, whom M. Groussac looked upon not so long ago with disdain but who has today entered—despite the attacks and the well-known accusations of plagiarism—the *Revue des Deux Mondes*. All these men follow the star of Beauty. There are obscure writers among them; there are bright, indeed crystalline ones. In painting and music they are followed by other brothers-at-arms. What high spirit does not feel today at least a distant influence from the Titans of modern art!. . . .

Our poetics, furthermore, is based on melody: rhythmic caprice is personal. French *vers libre,* today adapted by the moderns in all languages and initiated by Whitman, mainly, is subject to "melody." And with that, we arrive at Wagner, but we will not enter that deep woods for now. Great poets often make mistakes. People have said that hexameter is impossible in Spanish; but it exists, and there are admirable examples. Poe denied it in English, which did not keep Longfellow's *Evangeline* from being in hexameters.

Whitman, maestro Whitman, broke all the rules and, guided by instinct, went back to the Hebrew line. And I must concur with the diagnosis of the Jew Nordau with respect to the immense poet of *Leaves of Grass,* that rare, strange—passing strange, *degenerate* Whitman—yet honored, too, Maeterlinck's master, that strong, cosmic Yankee. We, dear maestro, the young poets of the Spanish Americas, are preparing the way, because our own Whitman must be soon to come, our indigenous Walt Whitman, filled with the world, saturated with the universe, like that other Whitman of the north, chanted so beautifully by "our" Martí. And no one would be surprised if in this vast cosmopolis, this alembic of souls and races, where Andrade of the symbolic *Atlántida* lived his life and this young savage Lugones has just appeared, there might appear some precursor of that poet heralded by the enigmatic and terrible Montevideo madman, in his prophetic and terrifying book.

# PRO DOMO MEA

Things I should point out to don Leopoldo Alas after reading Clarín's piece published in yesterday's *La Prensa*:

- Clarín has "read grandiloquent praise of don Rubén Darío in many places," but Clarín has never read a single word *written* by yours truly.
- Rubén Darío . . . bears no responsibility for all those *modernista* (if we can call them that) atrocities that have appeared in Latin America since the publication of his *Azure* . . .
- Rubén Darío is more outraged than Clarín at all the purveyors of Frenchified preciosity, the gawky imitators, the makeup artists, etc.
- In Latin America there is no such *pléiade* of new writers—not even remotely. There are some ten, or twelve, writers and poets, unknown in Spain, whose works would surely win the praise of Clarín himself, if he only read them. The rest, the *herd*, is no worse, however, than the bad writers of the Peninsula. We have the same blood, both the blood of El Cid and the blood of Carulla. Neither the heroes nor the bad poets of Latin America have anything to envy Spain's.
- I am not constantly writing prefaces to other men's books. I admire and love Salvador Rueda; he asked me to write a prologue for his book of poetry. So I wrote it in verse! And in a rhythm that was a *novelty!* Except that when I very proudly read the lines to don Marcelino Menéndez

Pelayo, he informed me that though my verses were "very pretty," their rhythmic novelty had been discovered over a thousand years earlier, and that they were a form of hendecasyllable. . . .

In case Clarín doesn't know, they are called *Galician* gaita *hendecasyllables.*

- The young writers of *La Pluma,* in San Salvador, are almost children. Ambrogi, the *enfant terrible,* is sixteen years old!

- I do not make a dilettante's literature; I detest snobbery. I write for *La Nación* and *La Tribuna,* in Buenos Aires, for the *Revista Nacional,* and for two foreign periodicals. And it is all very well paid, because, as Clarín says, "I want no unpleasantnesses on account of literature, which serves me for a very different end."

- I am not the leader of a school, nor do I advise youngsters to imitate me, and the "army of Xerxes" may be overlooked, for I have no intention of preaching Decadence or of applauding literary extravagance or dislocation.

- Not long ago, in one of those harsh but amusing pieces of his, Clarín criticized some verses by Batres Montúfar, of Guatemala—specifically the poem "The Watch," a true jewel of Latin-American literature, and this is not just my opinion, but that of Menéndez Pelayo, Boris de Tanneberg, Val, et cetera. Clarín thought he was dealing with a mockingbird; he found a fragment of "The Watch," took the humorous poem seriously, and applied to a poet of the early nineteenth century the same yardstick as he would use on a contemporary today.

- Clarín should seek to become more familiar with those things meritorious in Latin American letters. One day he wrote, more or less, "Why should I know about Latin American poets, or those of great China?" Let him study us, and he will be able to fairly gauge the good among us. And let him not, for a gallicism or neologism, damn an entire work.

- Furthermore, he might ask some of his better-informed friends—Campoamor, Núñez de Arce, Valera, Menéndez Pelayo, for instance—for information about those of us who write in Latin America.

As for myself, I received, along with Clarín's piece, a letter containing this sentence: "My admiration, my friendship, my affection, my constant reading—you have all those." If Clarín should wish to know who wrote those lines, he should look for the highest summit of Spain, among the highest in the world.

# THE JOURNALIST AND HIS LITERARY MERITS

. . . Today, and always, "journalists" and "writers" must of necessity be confused with one another. Most essayists are journalists. Montaigne and de Maistre are journalists in the broad sense of the word. All observers of, and commentators on, life have been journalists. Now, if you are referring simply to the mechanical aspect of the modern profession, then we can agree that the only persons who merit the name *journalist* are commercial "reporters," those who report on daily events—and even these may be very good writers who with a grace of style and a pinch of philosophy are able to turn an arid affair into an interesting page. There are political editorials written by thoughtful, high-minded men that are true chapters of fundamental books. There are chronicles, descriptions of celebrations or ceremonies, written by reports who are artists, and these chronicles might not be out of place in literary anthologies. The journalist who writes what he writes with love and care is as much a "writer," an "author" as any other.

The only person who merits our indifference and time's oblivion is he who premeditatedly sits down to write, for the fleeting moment, words without the glow of burnishing, ideas without the salt taste and smell of blood.

Very beautiful, very useful, and very valuable volumes could be made up if one were to carefully pick through newspapers' collections of "reports" written by many persons considered to be simple "journalists."

# On "Modern Life"
# and Politics

# MUSINGS ON CRIME

Canon Rosenberg-Montrose and banker Boulain have, in the annals of notoriety, displaced the remarkable swindles of the fictional Mme. Humbert.

A canon who steals, in the coldest of cold blood, from stupid lambs and sheep, his most excellent flock—a man standing upon the Roman curia, an apostle of good and a philosopher of the ideal Jerusalem—is no small thing. So banker Boulain must take second place. He is but a vulgar *escroc*[61] with whom the Parisians amuse themselves until another, greater scandal comes along.

There can be no doubt that these resounding malefactions are more comic than tragic, though they leave many poor wretches in poverty. What is comic is that the victims are all so much like the perpetrators; that is, they are conned because they thought they were in on a con, or greedy souls who did not see the wolf's ears peeking out from the sheep's clothing.

There are, then, comic crimes; what is not easy to accept, despite the most vivid paradoxes, is that there are beautiful crimes. De Quincey, the opium-eater, wrote a famous essay titled "On Murder Considered as One of the Fine Arts," and Gómez Carrillo has made it known in Spanish. This marvelous work of humor is parallel to Swift's memoir on the anthropophagic leanings of children. There are no artists of crime; there are, that is, criminal talents, as there are such rare bloodhounds as Sherlock Holmes.

61. Swindler.

Many think that there are in fact artistic crimes, while others, such as Osmont think this way: If one adopts an exclusively moral point of view, there is no beautiful crime, and there could never be one. The contingent circumstances that might give some luster to a generally blameworthy action must seem all the more horrific the more they appear to be, as the old metaphor that M. Prudhomme still favors has it, flowers that decorate the abyss. That concession made, let us confess—Osmont adds—that there are very few people who place themselves in a purely moral point of view, and stand firm there.

And here enters the question of "taste." If an aesthete were allowed to legislate morals, clearly there would be "beautiful" crimes. It would be as puerile to deny that as to write—someone has said—that a poisonous flower is never beautiful. Look at the monk's-hood, the hellebore, the foxglove with its lovely purple blooms. When a crime is profoundly horrific, and no low motives are intermixed, and the situation in which it occurs does not disturb one's emotions, then in order for the reader not to see the direct horror of the spilled blood and the writhings of agony, some sort of savage grandeur must be part of the true tragedy, and there are those who would applaud as though it were a well-made play. The recent Italian drama in which the Conde de Bonmartini was the victim is what they call "a beautiful crime." Why? M. Osmont tells us: Because passion alone—but what monstrous passion!—guided the murderers' hand. The shocking risk run by the culprits, if they should be discovered, because a man, and especially a woman of high estate, loses not just liberty and inner honor but the respect of others, and that luxury, enjoyed since childhood, has been a kind of air in which one lives; the shocking dramas revealed by the final catastrophe—all that makes a strong impression on one; it is disconcerting, disturbing—yet in some way thrilling. In that crime in Bologna, a figure emerges who strangely dominates the case: Senator Murri. That Roman virtue, that stoic courage could not occur but in a similar circumstance—very grand for our shriveled times. And as is required in a drama in which eternal justice appears to intervene, the crime will have its punishment, virtue its just reward in the carrying-out of a terrible duty. For—and this is to answer a likely objection—no one, I should think, admires a "beautiful crime" in itself. It is an image of violent hues, a moving drama. Its telling can make an *aesthetic* impression. Is there a person alive who has not admired, with horror, the scenes of torture painted by Spanish painters, or the nightmares of Goya? I do not wish to speak about political assassination. Here, a new element appears: faith. That is enough to elevate the act to sacrifice. When all is said and done, even if we agree on the existence of the "beautiful crime," one must say that it is a most lamentable spectacle, and that it is not a school in which brains and hearts should be formed. And so, admiring in a book, or a newspaper, occasionally, the murder in Bologna, it seems to me that crimes, beautiful or not, occupy too much space in journalism and literature. They bloody every page and perpetuate in the people the Byronic idea of the sublimity of crime and the elegance of desperation. One should rather—or also—show virtue, let it be seen as it is—a superior beauty. Osmont's ideas seduce me more, I confess, than aesthetic originalities and deviations of sensibility. Erudite Thomas de Quincey, "who at fifteen composed odes in Greek, and by twenty had read all the ancient books," seems to me not to have been quite in his right mind, *pace* Baudelaire (another of the same sort) and my friend Carrillo.

I will not get mixed up with the Nietzscheans, but I will make reference to those, like M. Colah, who believe that the word "hero" can be given a dark reverse. Certainly, M. Colah says, from the philosophical and moral point of view crime is unworthy of admiration, but the fancy, faced with the success of certain evil deeds, falls into a state that is none other than admiration. One admires any sort of hero for his audacity, the ability he has employed in surmounting the insurmountable, the contempt for danger he has shown in carrying out an act of patriotic or social abnegation. Is it because the assassin acts antimorally that the obvious courage, the incredible wiles, the irrational audacity, the terrible temerity—the thousand difficulties that must, in the final analysis, come together to create the "beautiful crime" and that have, in fact, been met and conquered—that even in his astonishing success he should be denied the label "hero"? He is a hero in an evil cause, but nonetheless a hero! What we admire is not the outcome, the final scene, but rather the complications almost wiped away, the dangers almost shrugged off, that precede it. For a "beautiful crime" should most certainly be labored over, weighed, reflected on, sagely premeditated—while still it entails combinations which cause the triumph to be more or less fortuitous. A drama of poverty and squalor, the sad ending of a love affair, the tragic result of a scene of jealousy cannot produce a "beautiful crime," for those are committed under the pressure and blindness of desperation, of despair, of wrath, of passion.

Before M. Colah, J. J. Weiss, in the third volume of his *Annales de Théâtre,* wrote the following words on the melodrama *Fualdès*: "For a beautiful crime, the criminal must act out of temperament, not out of a fortuitous and unique impulse. It is also required that the base details that almost always accompany a murder be excused in some way, their ignominy erased, for chance has disposed them so that they seem an effort of art, a contrast created and arranged by a mysterious rhetoric of things. Guilt must be demonstrated by the evidence, and yet there must lie over the motives and the execution of the crime a hint of mystery that one will always wish to penetrate, yet never manage to. It is necessary that bystanders be mixed into the story of the crime, which affects them in no way whatever. . . . It is necessary, if possible, that an entire city, or an entire class of society, be moved and appalled. It is necessary, etc. . . . (there is an endless list)." This theater critic's good sense is immediately obvious.

No, there are no beautiful crimes, no matter how aesthetic they may be, save in the sphere of the philosophy of cruelty or the persuasions of egoism. There are no beautiful crimes, just as there are no beautiful diseases.

Only physicians find "lovely sores" and "pretty cases." There are criminal artists, like Benvenuto, and sick artists, like the author of *Les fleurs du mal,* which buttress the new theories put forward by the philosophers of crime.

As for *buffo* criminality and comic criminals, they are indisputable. Criminals of the stripe of Mme. Humbert and Canon

Rosenberg await a vaudeville libretto, a songsmith for the stage. They are *types* that allow us to more clearly see the grotesque and malignantly hilarious side of the human creature. Their work is set in motion by lust, concupiscence, avarice. Many innocents fall into their clutches, but in the skin of every innocent lamb there is often, in the world of business, the soul of a canny wolf. Paris, like New York, like London, like Buenos Aires, gives both shelter and a wide field to the Carlo Lanzas, the Artons, the Boulains, the Humbert-D'Aurignacs. The latest work by former police chief Macé is rich in lessons in that regard.

In the comic crime there is often blood, as a consequence, but what there is most of is gold—the gold of the deceived, swindled, double-crossed, which evaporates into the strongboxes of the deceivers, swindlers, and double-crossers. Then, the majority applauds, laughs. "Ah!" say some. "Mme. Humbert is the greatest woman France has ever produced, a veritable Joan of Arc! She should have a statue on the Champs Elysée." And there is more than pity—smiles for the swindled. For the world cultivates, in one way or another, the art of deception.

I have heard the following story: Not long ago, several pieces of Empire furniture, put up for deposit on a famous *hôtel* by a calculating upholsterer, were sold to a buyer in Latin America for a large sum of money. "The Empress Joséphine's *mobilier*!" an advertisement to recover the pieces exclaimed. "Historical, family heirlooms, etc. . . ." The Empress Joséphine's *mobilier* came from the rue de la Pépinière. A certain marquis collected a fat commission, and a journalist another. Those are common practices. And the world smiles indulgently. Unfortunately, the "Latin American buyer" is growing rarer and rarer. . . . He is beginning to mistrust.

# TO THE RIGHT REVEREND ABBOT SCHNEBELIN

*London, Friday, 22—The explosive substance known as Schnebelin, invented by the French abbot Schnebelin, possesses admirable qualities and completely satisfies English experts.*

Father, the prank your brother Bertoldo Schwartz played on the world has turned out to be a very expensive one for the race of Adam. A most refined Frenchman has caused a sound like that slow weeping of the strong knight Roland, his tears falling upon his sword, to come over the world, for that same sword, now transfigured, can in one blow cleave a mountain. The German friar who, tempted by the devil, invented that cold black pepper that is so tasty to the mouths of cannons and the pale lips of death, has done great harm to sacred, lovely poetry. He has stolen from us the brave struggle of hand-to-hand combat, the horses caparisoned in iron, the noble tourneys, the formidable strength of Tizona, the immense majesty of Durandal. I said Frair Schwartz had been tempted by the devil, and I will confirm that with a cloven-footed witness, Baudelaire, who addresses these two lines to Satan:

| | |
|---|---|
| *Toi qui, pour consoler* | Thou who, to console frail man |
|    *l'homme frêle qui souffre,* |    that suffers, |
| *Nous appris à meler le salpêtre* | Taught'st him to mix saltpeter |
|    *et le soufre. . . .* |    and sulfur. . . . |

I do not believe it is the job of shepherds of men's souls to practice diabolic chemistry. Our king Christ told them, "Go and teach all men"—but not to make explosives! The fire for your hands, Father? The fire of the censers, or the sacred, divine fire of charity.

Generally, I must say, I like inventor-priests. When L'Epée discovered a way to allow deaf-mutes to communicate, I was overjoyed. When Sechi discovers something new, I am second to no one, save the sun itself, in my applause. If any *dom* whatever discovers in his monastery the way to make a liqueur from the gold of honey, like that nectar we savor after our coffee, I take my hat off to him. While I do not kneel before the seraphim of fire, like Francis of Assisi, I love those good jolly friars who cultivate their bellies and dedicate their great, immortal books this way: *Bonnes gens, buveurs très illustres, et vous goutteux très précieux.* . . . [62]

That seems to me more evangelical than teaching men to blow each other's heads off in an entirely new way. One must harken to the words of that Jehovah who "maketh wars to cease unto the end of the earth; he breaketh the bow, and cutteth the spear in sunder; he burneth the chariot in the fire," according to the words of holy Job.[63] Your invention, sir, will be of great value; it may even come to outshine the brilliance of dynamite, melinite, and plancastite. But what is unpardonable and unacceptable is that it be your reverence who has his hand in that sort of witchcraft—the salts with which the devil seasons the triumphs of those whose kingdom is this world.

Father, judging by the success announced in the wire report, your holiness merits a couple of pistols. If that wise gray head had discovered something more elevated and more worthy of his ministry—a new sausage, for example, or a new cake, or some cowled liqueur for an after-dinner cordial—he would merit a proper, priestly gift, a box of snuff, say. Unless he preferred a load of chocolate.

62. "Good folk, most illustrious bibbers, most precious tasters . . ."
63. These words are actually from Psalm 46.

# GOLD'S CHOLER

Our dear, dashing poet Leopoldo Díaz has told us in lovely free verse (with all the splendors of Hugo) how bronze rages. It is time that metals make their humors known. Silver has complained through the words of *Salamandra*. Lead impatiently awaits the hour of its battles. Not long ago, I heard gold, on a high hill, speak. It was so high that I could barely hear it, but this is more or less what I made out:

"I do not know why people say that worship of me is more widespread today than ever. The truth is, one hardly sees me anywhere. In times gone by, I incarnated the idolized calf and was exhibited to the eyes of all, so that all men might take pleasure in my divine radiance. Today, I am hoarded up and locked away in cellars. Of course I am also cut into pieces in a mint and stamped with this or that Caesarean profile, but at least here, in this great Buenos Aires, I am shown as no more than a rarity in the display cases of some Shylock or Isaac Simon. The fractional and ungainly 'bill' has replaced me. As condor, I have flown; as eagle, I live in Uncle Sam's house; as pound, I have fled to London. My radiance can hardly be seen even in the showcases of jewelers. I am not all that glitters. Accompanying the *straß*,[64] which struts about like a *parvenu*,[65] is gold plate.

"But then again, I must frankly say: although the anarchists raise the red flag for me, I am no anarchist—I am an aristocrat. The face of the man in the street has never looked good on a

---

64. Paste gem, rhinestone.
65. Upstart, social climber.

bright new gleaming gold coin. I take the face of an Augustus, an Ivan, a Bonaparte magnificently. Once, I gleamed with my most triumphant radiance on imperial scepters, but since—as someone has said—kings laid down their scepters and took up brollies, I tend to shine most brightly in museums. In the times of the brave Indians, I was *everything*: God in the idol, jewel, palanquin, sandal, necklace, diadem; today I am a rare invalid whose pulse is taken on the Bourse every day.

"And I must make another confession: I am the friend not of tradesmen and financiers, but rather, to their amazement, of poets!, however proverbial my material distance from all the Orpheuses may be.

"Yes, of poets and women, who know better than any others how to value my marvels and my splendors. I have never reigned more proudly than when, as messenger of an Olympic love, I fell like an incomparable rain upon the breast of Danaë, or when, transformed into the most harmonious of lyres, I made the divine aether vibrate when the blond-haired poet-god sang."

At that, I addressed myself, in the most clearly amiable and courteous way, to the proud metal: "Friend gold, how welcome are those words. You have spoken with a most plausible oracular voice. Poets have always sung your praises, and today, when they are obliged to be rich, they seek you and pursue you with the same zeal as the owner of the rotisserie and the manufacturer of matches. One of my most beloved teachers put the matter this way: For us poets, and for our brothers the artists, is it better to be rich, or poor? My teacher showed that in the past, it had been better to be poor, when poverty could be carried off well and having genius without having money was a way of life and a social position. But he advised rhymers to be rich, simply because 'the world wants it that way' and because Néstor Roqueplan quite rightly noted that no one is truly beautiful unless he follows his nation's, and his time's, fashion; doing otherwise is wearing a disguise. Unfortunately, in this century rhymes have been worth very little, and it has been the rare poet who, like Catulle Mendès, has possessed you purely because of his lyric jewels. Because really, who can make better use of you than poets and artists?

"Who would have used you better than Pindar, Gautier, Barbey d'Aurevilly, Edgar Allan Poe, Villiers de L'Isle-Adam?

"I picture to myself the incredible architecture, the crystallized dreams, the Oriental magic, the august wealth, the creative fantasy of a multimillionaire poet. For him, the Wagners, the dreamers of art. For him, castles on solitary islands, or beside mysterious lakes blooming with swans. They say that Louis of Bavaria was mad. He adored himself as a king and a poet, and he lived his life in a fairy tale. He was the last of the princes whose life can be told by beginning with the words 'This man was a king. . . .'

"As for your wrath, divine Gold, at being imprisoned in the strongboxes of a simple banker, some vulgar millionaire, some member of the clan of idle rich—it is just, and moving. You serve for gentlemen's gambling, serve to pay the English tailor and the industrialist and the lawyer, and so that honorable and distinguished fingers may have many rings. I, for my part, celestial Gold, adorable Gold, do not call you vile, or dirty, like tatterdemalion poets and writers who never get paid—I would know how to make you into admirable tunics and radiant slippers for all nine Muses, necklaces of wondrous pearls for the Hours, and all sorts of diamond-bedecked trinkets for the Games and the Graces, and for Laughter. And I would forget no one in the crystal palace with cupolas of gold, for each time the roses bloomed, I would send a gown sewn by a fairy to Pierrot's gay little wife. I would spare myself the suffering of vulgar humankind; I would go as far as I might, to be admired by my companions, and my *Messages* would come from the heart of Persia, or the illustrious city of Samarkand."

"Ay!" said Gold. "Now I really think it's unlikely that you and I could live together! . . ."

# IRON

The apotheosis of iron may be said to have been proclaimed in this century, in which men have attempted to give it a high place as a material for art. Huysmans attributes the triumph of iron to the utilitarianism of the age. "The age of utilitarian lust that we are now living through has nothing to envy the Stone Age, which stratified, in a certain way, high impulses and prayers, but it may be embodied in monuments that symbolize its activity and its sadness, its cleverness and its lucre, in works that are strange and hard—or at least new. And the matter of which they are made is iron."

Indeed, for as in luminous ages and intellectual countries marble was the material in which the architect symbolized an artistic ideal, so iron, in this harsh and cyclopic century, is the Numen's favored matter.

It was the Saxon who first raised metallic, cold, and heavy monuments. Now from mere nails, rails, and the portentous planking of bridges, iron has passed on to become the principal element of modern constructions. The artist is replaced by the engineer.

Does the Yankee take pride in his Brooklyn Bridge? Well, Paris allows the black skeleton of the monstrous Eiffel Tower to humiliate that Gothic jewel, the great H of Notre Dame.

Wise was that author who declared the Eiffel Tower to be the spire of a temple consecrated to the worship of gold, whose mass is read by the American pope Jay Gould, who would raise in his hands, to the sound of electrical doorbells, the host of the check.

For you, Greek, celestial Apollo, marble; for your churches, Holy Mystical Christ, stone; for Pluto, houses of iron, cellars of iron, strongboxes of iron.

And this is true in all the world, from New York, which is Rome, to the Great Republic of La Plata, which is the Promised Land.

One cannot complain about Buenos Aires. A splendid chapel dedicated to its worship has been dedicated on Calle Piedad—a grandiose chapel, which honors Buenos Aires' trade, thanks to Messrs. Staud and company.

Which of our great-grandchildren will engender the architect who will decide that it is *marble* that the Athenaeum—or the place, call it what you will, consecrated to Art and Letters—will be built of?

The universal credo rings out, and all of us repeat it:

"I believe in Gold Almighty, god of earth, and in Iron his son. . . ."

# THE TRIUMPH OF CALIBAN

No, I cannot and will not be a part of those buffaloes with silver teeth. They are my enemies, they abhor the Latin blood, they are the Barbarians. And thus shivers every noble heart today; this is the protest of every worthy man in whose veins there still runs a drop of the she-wolf's blood.[66]

I have seen those Yankees, in their overwhelming cities of iron and stone, and the hours I have lived among them, I have spent in a state of vague dread and anguish. I seemed to feel the oppression of a mountain upon me, I seemed to be drawing breath in a land of Cyclops, eaters of raw meat, bestial blacksmiths and ironmongers, inhabitants of the houses of mastodons. Red-faced, corpulent, gross, they make their way down their streets pushing and shoving one another, brushing against one another like animals, on a hunt for the mighty dollar. The ideals of these Calibans are none but the stock market and the factory. They eat and eat and eat, and calculate, and drink whisky, and make millions. They sing "Home, Sweet Home" and their home is a checking account, a banjo, a black man, and a pipe. Enemies of all idealism, in their progress they are apoplectic, perpetual mirrors of expansion, but Sir Emerson, rightly classified, is like the moon to Carlyle's sun; their Whitman with his hatchet-hewn verses is a democratic prophet in the service of Uncle Sam; and their Poe, their great Poe, a poor swan drunk on alcohol and pain, was the martyr to his

66. Legend has it that the twins Romulus and Remus, the founders of Rome, were suckled by a she-wolf. Thus, Darío is referring to the "Latin" race, as opposed to the Anglo-Saxons, and by extension, citizens of the United States.

dream in a land where he will never be understood. As for Lanier, he is saved from being a poet for Protestant ministers and for bucaneers and cowboys by the drop of Latin blood that gleams in his name.

"Ours," they say, "is the biggest in the world"—no matter what they are talking about. And indeed, one feels oneself in the land of Brobdingnag: they have Niagara Falls, the Brooklyn Bridge, the Statue of Liberty, twenty-story boxes, dynamite and cannons, Vanderbilt, Gould, their newspapers—and "they've got a nerve," as they themselves put it. From their towering heights (they stand head and shoulders above us, physically), they look upon those of us who do not wolf down beefsteak and do not say "all right" as inferior beings. Paris is a *grand guignol* for those gigantic *enfants sauvages*.[67] They go there to "have fun" and leave their dollars, for among them, even amusements are hard, and their women, though very beautiful, are of elastic rubber.

They imitate the English like *parvenus* imitating gentlefolk with generations of noble breeding.

They have temples to all the gods, but believe in none; their great men are named Lynch, Monroe, and that Grant whose figure my readers may find in Hugo, in *l'enfant terrible*. In art, in science, they imitate everything, twist and deform everything, those enormous red gorillas. But all the winds of the centuries will not be able to polish the enormous Beast.

No, I cannot and will not be a part of them; I cannot be a part of the triumph of Caliban.

That is why my soul was filled with joy the other night when three representatives of our race went to a solemn though receptive gathering to protest the Yankee's aggression against noble and now-exhausted Spain.

One of these men was Roque Sáez Peña, an Argentine whose

---

67. *Grand guignol*: a dramatic entertainment (a *"guignol"* is a puppet-show; the Grand Guignol was a theater in Paris) in which short horrific or sensational pieces are presented for the entertainment of a sometimes jaded audience. *Enfants sauvages*: wild children, children raised in a state of nature, prior to or removed from civilization.

voice in the Pan-American Congress, unlike the boasting "slang" of Monroe, took an elevated tone of continental grandeur, and showed the redskin in his own house that there are those in our own Hispanic republics who stand as sentinels against the ravenous maws of the Barbarians.

Sáenz Peña spoke movingly of Spain on that night, and one could do no less than dream of his triumphs in Washington. It must truly have surprised that Blaine of the political confidence games, that Blaine and all his cotton-growers, bacon-makers, and railroad-builders.

In his speech at this gathering, the ever-cordial Sáenz Peña stood and spoke as a statesman. He repeated what he has always spoken of—his conception of the peril presented by those boa-constrictor jaws, ready to swallow still more, even after the enormous dinner it made of Texas; the greed of the Anglo-Saxon, the appetite the Yankee has shown, the political infamy of the government of the North; and how useful, how necessary it is for the Hispanic nationalities of the Americas to be prepared for the boa constrictor's next strike.

Only one soul has been as farsighted in this matter, as farsighted and persistent, as Sáenz Peña, and that soul was—time's strange irony!—the father of free Cuba, José Martí. Martí never ceased urging the nations of his blood that they be careful with those men of prey, that they not be lured into those pan-American schemes, but rather look to the Yankee businessmen's traps and snares. What would Martí say today when he saw that under the colors of aid to the troubled Pearl[68] the monster was swallowing it, oyster and all?

In the speech I have referred to, I have said that the man of cordiality and the statesman were arm-in-arm. That Sáenz Peña is both things is attested to by his entire life. Such a man should appear in defense of the noblest of nations, fallen into the booty-sack of those Yankees, in defense of the unarmed gentleman who accepts the duel with the dynamite-carrying, mechanic-overall-wearing Goliath.

68. Cuba is called the "Pearl of the Caribbean."

On behalf of France, Paul Groussac. A comforting spectacle, the sight of that eminent, solitary man emerging from his book-filled cavern, from the scholarly isolation in which he lives, to protest against injustice and against the material triumph of Power. The great writer is no orator, but his reading moved the audience and filled the intellectuals among it, especially, with enthusiasm. His address, couched in the periods of high literary decorum, like all his writings, was vigorous and noble Art coming to the aid of Justice. And it gave pleasure to hear him say "What? Is this the man that eats nations alive? Is this the butcher that cuts his prey into pieces? Is this the constable of cruelty?"

Those of you who have read his most recent work—concentrated, metallic, solid—in which he judges the Yankees, their adventitious culture, their civilization, their instincts, their proclivities and tendencies and danger, would not have been surprised to hear him at this gathering, after the playing of the "Marseillaise." Yes, France must be on Spain's side. The vibrant Gallic lark cannot but curse the hatchet that chops at one of the finest vineyards of the Latin vine. And Groussac's emotional cry—"¡Viva España, with honor!"—never inspired a finer response from Spanish throats than this one: "¡Viva Francia!"

For Italy, Signore Tarnassi. In thrilling, fervent, Italian, Manzonian music,[69] he expressed the vow of Latius;[70] the ancient mother Rome spoke in him and through him—warlike, the decasyllables of her clarions sounded, with bravura. And the large audience was stirred by this fiery *squillo di tromba*.[71]

All of us who listened to these three men, the representatives of three great nations of the Latin race, thought and felt how right this unbosoming was, how necessary that attitude, and we saw a palpable manifestation of the urgency to struggle to ensure that the Latin Union is no longer a fata morgana of the kingdom of Utopia—for when the moment comes, and the politics and policies and interests of another species rear their

69. Referring to the Italian novelist and playwright Alessandro Manzoni (*q.v.*).
70. The surname of Jupiter in Rome.
71. "Trumpet blast," or clarion call.

heads, our peoples feel the rush of common blood and the rush of common spirit. Do you not see how the English enjoy the triumph of the United States, locking away in the vault of the Bank of England their old rancors, the memory of past struggles? Do you not see how the democratic, plebeian Yankee throws up his three *hurrahs!* and sings "God Save the Queen" when a ship flying the Union Jack passes by? And together, they think: "The day will come when the United States and England own the world."

And that is why our race must unite, as body and soul unite, at moments of tribulation. We are the sentimental, feeling race, but we have also been masters of power; the sun has not abandoned us, and the renaissance is ours, by ancestral inheritance.

From Mexico to Tierra del Fuego, there is an immense continent in which the ancient seed has been sown, and the vital sap, the future greatness of our race, is about to begin once more to run. From Europe, from the universe, there comes a vast cosmopolitan wind, which will help to invigorate our jungle. And yet still the North extends its tentacles of rail lines and locomotives, its arms of iron, and opens its many greedy mouths. It will not be the buccaneer Walker that those poor republics of Central America will have to wrestle, but rather the canal-building Yankees of Nicaragua. Mexico's eye is peeled, for it still feels the sting of mutilation; Colombia has its isthmus larded with U.S. coal and iron; Venezuela allows itself to feel the fascination of the Monroe Doctrine and what happened in that recent emergency with England, not realizing that Monroe Doctrine and all, the Yankees allowed the soldiers of Queen Victoria to occupy the Nicaraguan port of Corinto. In Peru there are demonstrations of fellow-feeling upon the triumph of the United States, and Brazil—sad to say, sad to watch—has shown more than visible interest in the you-scratch-my-back-I'll-scratch-yours policies of Uncle Sam.

When the perilous future is laid out for all to see by leaders and thinkers, and when the greed of the North is there for all to see, one can do no less than prepare a defense.

But there are those who will say to me: "Do you not see that the Yankees are the strongest? Do you not know that there is a

Law that says that we are bound to be swallowed or crushed by the Colossus? Do you not recognize their superiority?" Yes, of course; how can I not see the mountain formed by the mammoth's hump? But no matter what Darwin and Spencer say, I am not going to docilely put my head on the block so that the Great Beast can crush it.

Behemoth is huge, but I am not going to throw myself under its enormous feet. And if it catches me, at least my tongue shall give one last curse, with my last breath of life. And I, who have always favored a free Cuba—if only so that I might share the dream of so many dreamers, share the heroism of so many martyrs—am nonetheless a friend of Spain's when I see it attacked by a brutal enemy whose ensign is Violence, Force, and Injustice.

"But have you not always attacked Spain?" Never. Spain is not all priestly fanaticism, and stiff pedantry, and the wretched *domine*, disdainful of a Latin America that it does not know. The Spain that I defend is a Spain of Nobility, Ideals, Chivalry; its name is Cervantes, Quevedo, Góngora, Gracián, Velázquez; its name is The Cid, Loyola, Isabella; its name is Daughter of Rome, Sister of France, Mother of the Americas.

Miranda preferred Ariel; Miranda is grace of spirit; and all the mountains of rock and iron and gold and bacon shall never make my Latin soul prostitute itself to Caliban!

# THE HIPPOGRIFF

Everyone has been mad these days—madder than usual—on account of the newest automobile craze, the Paris-Madrid race. Newspapers have given over long columns to it; *camelots*[72] have sold thousands of programs and maps; those who attended the trial have been much more numerous than ever before; the names of Michelin, Mors, Mercedes, Panhard, Renault, and other marques of swift machines are on everyone's lips. It is a time when a skilled and daring driver enjoys ovations that a Berthelot, a Pasteur, an Anatole France would never be accorded. The madness of speed, which I believe has already been studied by physicians, has invaded, rather alarmingly, the city of young and old walkers. And now the women are mixing in. Yesterday it was a former café *chanteuse* who occupied the reporters' pens; today it is Mme. Du Gast, the *dame au masque* of the echoing, worldly process, for whom the hand of a certain French nobleman struck the cheek of an old attorney—Mme. Du Gast, who is going to drive for kilometers, at more than a hundred thirty-some per hour, in her "auto" decorated with her colors, yellow and red: *"Vive l'Espagne, olé!"* And a huge crowd has gotten up at some ungodly hour of the morning to go see the racers depart, and has launched cries of enthusiasm never heard by swift-footed Greeks and lyrical charioteers sung by Pindar. Frightful collective delirium, a madhouse without walls . . .

Even before the first stage, there have been seven deaths, among them wealthy sportsmen, and many injuries. Aside from

72. Street vendors.

the madmen at the wheels, the victims have been poor souls standing along the roadways, eviscerated by the swift, heavy iron-and-rubber cockroach. Adulators of industry *à outrance* say that the accident is insignificant, that business is business, and that "to make an omelette, one has to break eggs." And when the Cabinet here [in France] decided to suspend the race on French soil, it appears that young Alfonso of Spain did everything in his considerable power to ensure that the fearsome race continue on the Spanish portion of the course. Why? Aside from his adolescent caprice and curiosity, because there had been *expenses* paid out . . . to greet the automobiles, and because there, like here, a certain part of the public was beside themselves with happiness. A certain part of the public, which is "the people," in some places received the hippogriff with stones:

> Violent hippogriff
> That kept pace with the wind,
> where, thunderless lightning-bolt,
> featherless bird, scaleless fish,
> and brute of no instinct
> natural—where, in the confused labyrinth
> of these naked cliffs and rocks,
> do you fall upon your face,
> head over hooves in the dirt,
> and fall from the high precipice?

Several violent hippogriffs fell on their faces, and others fell from high precipices and smashed into trees.

And the *aficionados* and impassioned expect even greater speed, which will be the unprecedented coronation of French industry, for it is in France that this branch of sport prevails and conquers with greater force and more elements than in any other country—a coronation that will bring progress to certain manufacturers and certain champions on a field of smashed skulls and fractured bones. Already, the populace sings: *J'en ai soupé de l'automobile!*[73] And the automobile has *soupé*[74] and

73. I've had it up to *here* with automobile!
74. A pun: has dined.

continues to dine on poor pedestrians who have the rotten luck to find themselves on the same street or highway with the great hulking homicidal beast.

With progress have come those ungainly (to our tongue) English words *trust, record, looping-the-loop, cakewalk* . . . ; with "progress," I say, which attempts to possess all the infinite universe by overcoming time and space. Everything created by human advances, everything invented by inventors, is created in the service of that god-like desire: to conquer time and space. In modern "sport," that desire is complicated by the collective neurosis. Everything leads to excess: an excess of pleasure, an excess of business, a fever for speed. And the Yankee spirit, invading the entire world, decides that records will be set. And the world finds that it must understand English: *trust, record, looping-the-loop, cakewalk. All right!*

Was an Englishman the author of that Nietzschean-culinary saying "if you want to make an omelette, you have to break eggs"? It could as well have been the Spaniard Pero Grullo or the Frenchman M. de la Palisse. But the fierce and pitiless application of the homily is, I believe, quite modern, and in fact resides among the wise sayings of Zarathustra. It is an excellent philosophy for those who eat, though unsettling for those that are eaten. In the case of the *super-chauffeur,* the wretch who has the miserable luck to be run over by the automobile counts for nothing. The *super-chauffeur* is the representative of human energy and the omnipotence of industry, of capital: Beware, those who stand in his way! It happens, however, that he, too, the *super-chauffeur,* may smash his person into a tree or fall off a cliff. All that is perfectly fine. The boss requires that his factory triumph, that industrial might increase, that Moloch breakfast on his omelette—and to breakfast on omelettes, there are eggs that must be broken.

The logic of this principle is applied likewise to larger matters. It was quite an omelette savored by Moloch when Great Britain smashed little Transvaal. Business is business, and the appliers of the Zarathustrean law are named Cecil Rhodes, are named Chamberlain. An age truly more shocking than any other in the history of mankind. The world's heart is sick; life causes harm;

the universal disquiet is manifested in a thousand ways, and much worse than in the year 1000. Because in the year 1000 there was still faith and hope, and the man of today has murdered both. Everything is reduced to the victory of the moment—by force, by violence, by skill. Glory is threatened with extermination, as is old Honor (already on its deathbed), and Modesty, and Charity. The degenerates from above are about to be supplanted by the lunatics from below. Kings flee, and the people know not where to turn. And the future arrives in an automobile, swiftly, madly, killing, exploding. The socialist mediocrity believes that some time ago it saw in today's progress, there in the distant Orient, a dawn. But it is a conflagration—unless it might be an eruption, a Vesuvius or a Montagne Pelée.

Everything that once might have been seized upon and put to use in the service of the dreamed-of fraternity of the races, in the service of Christian ideals, is applied now to war and destruction; war, which Victor Hugo dreamed might disappear in the early twentieth century, has ever greater scope, despite the diplomatic leg-pulling and pacifying idylls of retarded ideologues. From the moment when money began to replace the ancient ideals, the dispute over land and wealth became more and more fierce, more and more bitter, and the shattering of morality leads to the most absolute disaster. The human being has never been less an angel than today, never more the savage and bloodthirsty beast. And this is the case with automobiles, with wireless telegraphy, with cinematography, with the omnipotence of the machine in industry and gold in everything.

All this is irrational. But all of life, says Tolstoy, is irrational. It is irrational for men to have useless organs, and for horses to have the vestige of a fifth toe—it is a useless waste of energy. Useless wastes of energy, however, are authorized by progress. The usefulness of an automobile race? Absurd. That is what happens in the kingdom of the irrational. A man who is rich, healthy, perhaps even happy, goes off, leaves his comforts, his house, his home, his beautiful wife, his children, and speeds off to devour space. And he dies. He dies, and kills. Once upon a time he went on crusades; earlier still, Jason went off in search of the ideal.

Today, heroism tends toward speculation on the one hand and annihilation on the other. A race of unquiet men, of *Bovaristes*,[75] of neurasthenics, marches toward infinite confusion. And Moloch grows fat upon his omelettes: Moloch, the eternal, the indestructible, the god of appetite and of cruelty.

*Oh, que la vie est quotidienne*,[76] Jules Laforgue the Montevidean would say. Laforgue should have lived to see the twentieth century, because this age would have found in his Hamletlike and ultramodern irony its true poet. But he, too, died, run over by his time, mortally injured by the common ill.

Oh, the deliciousness of mediocrity! Not to think; to isolate oneself in unconsciousness! Oh, to wax enthusiastic over bicycle riders!

One can hear the sound of the skull's bones cracking. I hurry to bring this to a close, for this newspaper article runs the risk of winding up as a prose poem. And that would be serious, indeed.

---

75. *Bovarisme* is yearning after the impossible; the state of being impossibly romantic and unrealistic, of being constantly unsatisfied with one's lot (after *Madame Bovary* by Gustave Flaubert).
76. "Oh, how quotidian life is!"

# TO THE VENERABLE
# JOAN OF ORLEANS[77]

*In heaven*

It is a holy day, venerable Joan, the day of your triumphant feast.[78] Look how an illustrious Pontiff—the White Pope—raises the lily of your sanctity in the last days of a century of struggles. All the red of wars was born this century. Much has been thought, and many combats fought. You, formidable Maid, have been chosen by divine disposition to reign over this century's end, which shall witness your elevation to the sovereignty of altars. And the shepherd who consecrates you is he who—in a time of hatred of the holy hierarchy and of human hierarchy, as well—stands impeccable, admirable, serene, upon his snowy-white and immaculate dais. He is looked upon by all men as the Sublime One; his genius dazzles, his power impresses, and more than once the world has watched as eagles have paid homage to the symbolic dove. And while the blood of the races throbs in tempests and miseries, in the uprisings of secular rages, agitations, and protests, in hours when there are many prayers too few, you come, diadem'd celestially, Joan of France, new saint, chaste light of Orléans.

The fairies in the pagan oak of your village called to you, called you to the feasts of love and life, but the divine will was with you, and when the hour of your predestination came, the archangel of war, as in the case of Judith, put in your hand a conquering sword.

77. Joan of Arc was not sainted until 1920; thus, Darío is addressing her on the day of her official canonization.
78. May 30.

Young, white, intact, the ancient Penthesilea carries her virginity before the armies of Amazons. Clorinda is at your side, like a page or an aide-de-camp, but none bears, as you do, the consecrated bouquet of paradisal lilies.

Joan of France, who touched the keys of a marvelous organ to make the highest lauds, the most thrilling antiphons, the most excellent prose, under the arches of the most wondrous of cathedrals, resound in you?

If I were an image-maker, an artist in stained glass, I would decorate the windows of your church with all the poems in crystal that might be held within the vibrations of the rainbow: Biblical dreams and legendary deeds, the actions of the prophets, the struggles, the lives of the holy kings, the luminous works of the prophecies—all, to exalt, most high Maiden, the excellencies of your predestination, the beauties of your sanctity, and the splendors of your strength.

There, in the forest of Domremy, the same fairies who in the days of your childhood sang to you soft songs of love, gay songs of first life, saw that you had arrived at absolute happiness, and that your lips received no kisses of mortal love, for you were destined for the passion of heaven, after the struggles and that cruel sacrifice.

An incomparable feast-day is yours, and an incomparable feast-day is the high kingdom's, too, when you arrive, trailing your ermine roles of sanctity, treading with renewed life upon the crimson of your martyrdom.

What perfume, the perfume of celestial flowers! What white joy, the joy of ineffable lilies! What red triumph, the triumph of martyrs' roses! What sounds, the sounds that Cecilia draws from the sweet organ that the Father has set under her alabaster fingers!

When you, Joan, were a poor girl, the deities of your native forest saw in you a sweet enemy of the pagan gods.

Later, Voltaire's inkwell shattered at the feet of your marble figure! The arrows of the skinny old sagittarius could not touch the radiant candor of your wings.

In the Apocalypse, Venerable Joan, there is a grand incarnation of Evil, and she is called Whore. When the world is heated by social monsters, and threatened by immense calamities, you come, you bring the combatant's sword, the saint's nimbus, and the Maiden's fleur-de-lis.

# Travel Pieces and Vignettes

# VIEUX PARIS[79]

Vieux Paris, April 30, 1900

I am in Vieux Paris, that curious reconstruction by Robida. Although, like the entire Exposition, it is not entirely completed, the impression is pleasant. From the river, the view of the ancient buildings resembles a stage-setting. Houses, towers, roofs, an entire *quartier*—called up out of the past by the talent of an artist both learned and touched with genius—greet the spectator with their picturesque perspective.

As one enters, one is welcomed by costumed players—perhaps a harquebusier, perhaps a lancer—strolling before the portals, past the souvenir vendors who, behind their display cases and tables, wear atop their heads those high pointed caps whose name, in Old French, has just escaped me. The sun filters down through the wooden scaffolding, shatters on the jewels and gold filigrees of the merchandise for sale and the soldiers' gleaming armor, and a breeze of *life* blows through it all, the breeze that Spring brings to the immense, magnificent Exposition and to all of Paris. And since fantasy generously contributes to this moment, one inevitably finds it shocking when a morning coat, a pair of the very most modern and prosaic trousers, and a bowler hat interrupt this scene of wonder, casting a terrible blotch on the page of *vielle vie* that one is trying

79. "Vieux Paris" was, as historian Arthur Chandler puts it (charon.sfsu.edu / publications / PARISEXPOSITIONS / 1900EXPO.html), a sort of "medieval village theme park erected by the city of Paris" for the Exposition Universelle of 1900. Historical records and descriptions portray it substantially as Darío does here.

so hard, just now, to live in. If things of today were only slightly other, then one would enter this fair in ancient garb and speaking archaic French. Meanwhile, we resign ourselves to the semi-fantasy.

The portal of Saint-Michel stands there, and the great rose window above it, its broad ogives facing the Seine. The rue des Vielles-Écoles leads one into a picturesque quarter, its angular facades, its balconies and windows; in the broad passageways one hears the gay laughter of visitors. In one street, a follower of Nostradamus will, for a few *centimes*, read one's fortune if one asks, and there are *badauds*[80] who ask, and who deliver the few *centimes*.

But I think something is missing in this scene: the figure of the Sarrazin-olive man, strolling through the streets as he does in Montmartre, handing out his Rabelaisian advertisements and selling his tasty wares.

Robida, the recreator, is, as we all know, a skilled draftsman and witty writer. His artistic and archaeological erudition are manifested in this attempt, as his picaresque, future-gazing talent has been in imagining customs, architectures, and scientific advances—all of which he traces in the most charming drawings. In this work that I have visited, and which will surely be one of the main attractions of the Exposition, he has attempted something varied, though reduced. This is a structure composed of several individual constructions and which therefore revisits, in a single piece, several motifs that remind archaeologists of one or another bygone "type."

The amusements of Vieux Paris are still not open, with the exception of a theater in which some of us have experienced quite a come-down. Imagine: it is no small thing to find in Vieux Paris not the recitations of troubadours or the pranks of jugglers, but rather a children's theater with Caballero's operetta *The Little Old Lady*! Still lacking are places where one might taste ancient dishes served up on ancient tableware, and taverns with their lovely bar-girls serving beer—or mead. Still lacking is the Paris-past of *les Écoles*, where one might see a little of the life lived by

80. Passersby, strollers.

the *escholiers* of the classics, who, when their counterparts from Salamanca or Oviedo came, with their *bandurrias*[81] and their guitars, greeted them in Latin. . . . It is a pity that in the kiosks selling beverages, or jewelry of goldplate and paste, there should be this mixture of medieval dress and modern touches, for one often sees anachronisms that bring an involuntary smile to one's lips. There should also be a section on the occupations of Old Paris, and the street-hawkers' and craftsmen's cries should be revived, to cheer one's ears. Animation is lacking in the medieval quarter and the merchants' quarter, where the seventeenth century is recreated: a complete replica of rues de Foire-Saint-Laurent, Châtelet, and Pont-au-Change. When everything is once open and available, the aspect of the place cannot but be most very attractive. What to my mind is not appropriate is the concessions made to progress and comfort, to the sacrifice of authenticity. At night, instead of the soft lanterns of the time, one encounters in the reconstructed quarters the glare of electric lights!

Soon, the advertisements declare, there will be festivals, jousts, and tourneys, and perhaps courts of love. It is a pity that all those necessary things were not ready today, so that the visitor might not leave the place a bit unsatisfied after a walk through the unfinished city. Among those things that call one's attention now are the varied shops' signs and the kiosks, copied from old engravings. As one passes by, names from bygone ages call to one: Villon, Flamel, Renaudot, Etienne Marcel. Perhaps in a few days these things will have a soul, and as we stroll past Molière's house we will be persuaded that we actually see the old fellow, and in another place believe we spy the editor of the *Gazette,* and in front of the church of Saint-Julien-des-Ménétriers hear the sounds of a viol and the cries of *saltimbanques.*

My readers would not forgive me if I slipped in a dissertation here on architecture and began a technical explanation, with nomenclature, of the buildings, streets, and *quartiers.* But I beg their indulgence for a first, quick impression, on a peaceful golden afternoon, when the pleasant, archaic panorama passed before my eyes.

81. A Spanish type of mandolin.

From afar, the colors of the vast decoration softened, the vision of the Pont d'Alma and the Palais des Armées of land and sea is delightful. As one's *bateau-mouche* advances, one recognizes, in the gold of the setting sun, the Archbishop's tower and the two naves of the chapel, the picturesque construction of the Palais, with its Grand Salle; the Moulin, the Gran Chatelet, with its sharp tower, the Cour de Paris café and, near the hôtel of the Ursinos, the Coligny mansion; Louis XII's great Chambre des Comptes; the church of Saint Julien-des-Ménétriers and a good number of other buildings that my reader will have seen in engravings and on maps, even the door of Saint-Michel and the portal of the charterhouse of Luxembourg.

And as the spirit gives itself over to this pleasant return to the past, in one's memory appear the thousand events of history and legend associated with all those names and places: love affairs, acts of war, the beauty of times when life was not wearied with practical prose and progress as it is today. The lays and villanelles, the rondels and ballads that poets composed for beautiful, chaste ladies who held another ideal for love and poesy than that we hold today, were not drowned out by the noise of industry and modern traffic.

At night, it will be a pleasant refuge for lovers of dream-visions. I know not whether the passersby who love their Baedeckers, those angular Englishmen and others from all parts of the globe who come to amuse themselves in the most *swell* sense of the word, will delight in the imaginary recreation of so many scenes and canvases. . . . As for the poets, the artists, I am certain that they will find there a free field for more than one sweet reverie.

So much the worse for those who, amidst the agitations of turbulent, overwhelming life, cannot have, even once, the consolation of extracting from their gold mines one enthralling illusion.

# [ON WOMAN]

## THE WOMAN OF THE AMERICAS

In modern times, all civilized societies have become aware of the vast importance of the education of women, given their immense influence on a nation's citizens.

It becomes necessary not simply to impart instruction, but also to ensure that those who have inherited from God the privilege to live without work, learn to live honorably.

The benefit goes especially, and directly, to the poor. In the home of the "people," heroines from the Age of Romance are impossible; in the workingman's house, what is needed is a worker.

Work gives moral beauty to poor women, and endows them with a certain domestic, homely strength that somewhat alleviates their natural weakness.

Today, all the nations of the world believe in work as a way to the aggrandizement of woman. And nowhere so much as in the United States.

The woman of the United States wishes to compete with the man. There, she may set her sights on all professions and public offices. The number of female inventors there is incalculable. The American woman has made, and is continuing to make, great contributions to the progress and greatness of the land of Washington.

Germany, as the *thinking* country, now has some five million women in its factories.

England, where poverty is rampant, has fewer: four million five hundred thousand; France, three million seven hundred thousand; Austria and Italy, three million five hundred thousand working women each.

In Spanish America, Chile has the most female workers. Aside from their special labors, Chilean women work in telegraph and telephone offices and in railway companies. And that is good. Keeping occupied, having a profession keeps women out of brothels; it increases marriage among the working classes and allows a breath of well-being, which is tonic and refreshing, to blow through the soul of the people.

The working mother will make hardworking children, and good citizens.


## THE WOMAN OF SPAIN

March, 1900

A few days ago, during the recent Carnival, in the palace of a distinguished lady married to a millionaire Mexican diplomat, there took place a most elegant, if spur-of-the-moment, masked ball, the praises of which have been widely sung by the usual chroniclers of society, especially my tireless, pleasant friend the Marqués de Valdeiglesias. What most distinguished the party was the attendance by many of those beautiful, aristocratic women who affect the picturesque *mantilla* and other no less national adornments. And the enthusiasm was immense: there were even those who exclaimed *Olé!*, with the excuse, of course, of days of celebration. But the enthusiasm was only natural. It is so difficult among the Spanish aristocracy to find a purely Spanish beauty! For Spanish high society, like all the upper classes of the world, has been invaded by Britainism on the one hand and Parisianism on the other. It is lamentable. A Goya *maja*[82] dressed by Chaplin is enchanting and disconcerting, but my reader will, I am sure, confess that a Goya *maja* dressed by

82. A black-haired, black-eyed Spanish woman, often something of a coquette, of the type painted famously by Francisco de GOYA.

Goya is infinitely better. Not that I would have these modern-day *duquesas* return to the high comb, perpetual mantilla, and strolls along the tree-lined avenues of San Antonio de la Florida, but foreseeable to all lovers of living human statuary is the disappearance of one of the most beautiful *types* that have ever graced art: the *type espagnol,* whose line has been bastardized and confused (and ourselves, confounded) by French curves and English angularity. Fashion—*that* is the enemy! And in that appreciation I am buttressed by a talent who, more than perfectly aesthetic, is a woman: Emilia Pardo Barzán. Doña Emilia considers that heavy English attire with its masculine cut a traitor to the classic Spanish grace: those long "mackintoshes" and overcoats, certain shoes, and, above all, those *chapeux formidables* from Paris.

Nature proceeds and teaches logically; Nature has ordered the creatures and things of the earth according to their place on it, and Nature knows why the Scandinavians are blond and Abyssinians black, why the English have swan's necks and Flemish women opulent handholds. Spanish females were given several models, depending upon their region in the Peninsula, but the true type, the type best known through poetry and art, is the olive-skinned beauty, somewhat *potelée,*[83] neither tall nor short, with wondrous large dark eyes and wavy black hair that falls in cascades, all this animated by a marine, Venusian quality that has no name in any other language: *sal.*[84]

In his time Gautier said that to see real Spanish dancing one had to go to Paris; today, in painting, those who cause the world to wonder at the feminine grace of Spain are foreigners such as Sargent and Engelhart. Will we be content, in a few years, to find in old canvases and prints what was once the original graceful Hispanic beauty? Fashion has begun to do its damage in our education. For every young woman of good family who plans to go off and study abroad, the indispensable "governess," almost always English or German, sometimes French, is brought in. The

83. "Full-figured," as the phrase is today.
84. Salt; a spark of piquant wit, mixed with physical grace.

governess begins her molding, and the native Spanish grace is forced into the angular cage of discipline, usually one that is "veddy English." Clothing, of an equally angular cut, aids in the reformation of the original curvilinear charm. Once the girl is grown, her tastes and customs will tend toward the foreign.

There was once a "Spanish" elegance; now, it is remembered once in a rare while at a costume ball. Today, because fashion demands it, the opulent black locks are dyed blond or red; the proud, elegant carriage of yesteryear is transformed, gestures are "learned." First our Spanish females turned *chic,* then *vlan,* then *pschut,* then *smart,* and now *swell.* They do not read good Spanish books—yet what *señora* would not blush if she had not read Ohnet in the original? One travels, one summers, one adores Worth, Laferrière, Doucet. Our ladies dress in great luxury, yet are seldom confused with a Parisian; disdaining their own wealth, they still cannot seem to find the other country's treasure. . . .

The court is so sad because the shadow of the Queen falls over it. That huge, gloomy, lavishly bedecked old palace that so startled and frightened the fine French canary named Réjane, is in fact a vast basilica of sadness, which—if it is not to infect the entire country with its witchy spell—needs gay, cheery queens, like Isabella, and easy, gallant kings, like Alfonso. The Regent, who from the time of her religious duties as an unmarried woman still preserves the convent's gravity, and whose married life was not pleasant with respect to its private moments, and whose life has been so hemmed in by caretakers and managers, penalties and misfortunes, has little reason, in truth, to dress in pinks and pastels. The only thing that adds its note of gaiety to the royal mansion is the Infanta Isabel, the people's Infanta—a friend to artists, a bit of a virago, a lover of the hunt, of horseback riding, a valiant sportswoman, a generous, charitable very *Madrid* sort of woman who loves music and whose spontaneousness makes her attractive and *simpática* everywhere she goes, especially among the people. . . .

There are no literary *salons* in the French sense of the word. Doña Emilia Pardo Bazán often invites guests to soirées at which there is no hint of the intellectual, and don Juan Valera has had his *samedis* which, outside the ladies of his family and the daughters of the Duque de Rivas, only men have attended. From time to time the dukes of Denia invite certain artists and men of letters to share their table, as does the Baron del Castillo de Chirel. But the intellectual barometer indicates the level of conversation: the aristocracy's favorite poet is Grilo. There are cultured, intelligent ladies who, as I have said, travel and gain an education, but they are the black pearls or blue roses of their kind. The Duquesa de Alba takes an interest in works of scholarship and history, and she puts her house's inexhaustible archives at the disposal of scholars; the Duquesa de Mandas is quite knowledgeable in the sciences; the duquesas de Medinaceli and de Benavente are patronesses of letters; the Condesa de Pino Hermoso and the Marquesa de la Laguna bring their spirituality to gatherings. Gloria, the daughter of this lastnamed lady, is famous for having added new salt and pepper to the grace she has inherited from her mother.

The middle class, whether well-to-do or not, follows the lead of the upper class. All it takes is the slightest observation to see that since the time, in the not too distant past, when a young lady hardly knew how to read and write, great strides have been made in primary education. I refer, of course, to the common run, because both before and after Oliva Sabuco of Nantes and St. Teresa there have been notable Spanish females who could compete with the males in the mental disciplines. . . . In this century, there has been an army of female literati and poets, so many in fact that one author has published a volume with a catalog of them—which does not include them all! Among all the dense and useless foliage, one discerns a few great trees: Coronado, Pardo Bazán, Concepción Arenal. These two last-named authors, particularly, with their virile minds, honor their nation. As for the countless majority of affected, romantic, sentimental Corinnas and confectionery Sapphos, they are part of the abominable international sisterhood to which Great Britain has contributed so many "authoresses." In order to arrive at the palace of that much-talked-about Eve of the future, they will have to exchange their Pegasus for a bicycle. . . .


# THE WOMAN OF NICARAGUA
# (FROM "JOURNEY TO NICARAGUA")

The Nicaraguan woman is not markedly different from those of the rest of Central America, but there is something special about her that distinguishes her from the others. It is—and I have remarked on this elsewhere—a kind of Arabian languor, a native-born insouciance, joined to a natural elegance and looseness in her movements and her walk. As in the Antilles, as in almost all the South American republics, the skin color is olive, the hair black, and yet blonds are not rare—although the climate does not allow the gold of the early years to last very long. Thus, the golden or light blond turns chestnut, the wavy locks darken, leaving only the enchantment of blue eyes. The mane of ebony or jet is of copious richness. The Spanish legacy is clear: the ancestors from Extremadura, Castile, or Andalucía. One is pleasantly surprised by the great number of tall, svelte bodies, which walk with remarkable elegance. "In a way," says Havelock Ellis, "the gait of the Spanish woman can be attributed to her anatomical peculiarities. Her walk—which is seen also everywhere women have the custom of carrying bundles on their head, such as in the steelyards of the Albanian hills and some parts of Ireland—is erect and dignified, accompanied with sober movements, like a priestess bearing the sacred vessels. At the same time, the Spanish woman's walk, not lacking proud human dignity, has something of the grace of a feline animal, whose body is still quick and whose movements are measured, with no excess or superfluity whatever."

All this is applicable to the Nicaraguan woman, especially the woman of the people, for in the more well-to-do families it is not unusual to find a *señorita* educated in European cities who has acquired foreign airs and mannerisms; for example, among those who have been at religious schools, the *Sacre Coeur* calm, or among the young ladies educated in the United States, American gestures, manners a bit too Amazonian for a graceful race. For myself, let me say that after so many years of absence, visiting so many nations, I found in my female compatriots an enchantment that on the one hand seemed to me to possess an exotic charm, while on the other revived in me impressions almost lost in the mists of my early years. Accustomed to the bustle of great cities, to the widespread and well-known elegance of women in the populous metropolises, I felt myself sweetly enthralled and as though *captivated* by the figures of mystery that in that voluptuous setting I would see in drawing rooms, visible from the street—drawing rooms in which, at night, they rock lazily, tropically, in rush-bottomed rocking chairs, or on warm mornings at the doors of their houses, as is the custom, where one admires the gentility of so much pale and large-eared beauty, not far from the garden that wafts such flowery perfumes on intoxicating breezes that one is seized as though with anguish. The development of the human plant is prodigious in that clime. There are splendid girls, like roses or fruit. In the town of Léon, in the marketplace, for example, I have seen girls of twelve, thirteen, fourteen years already ripe for maternity in the most precocious of adolescence. And I remembered Maurice Donnay's amusing *boutade:*[85] "... *et tu n'ignores pas que dans les pays chauds, on est plus vite arrivé à l'age de puberté que sous nos froids climats d'Europe; les républiques sudaméricaines ayant pour devise: Puberté, Egalité, Fraternité!*"[86] And indeed one can find that type of adolescent *à l'orientale* that is described so whimsically in *The Arabian Nights,* translated by Dr. Mardrus.

It is not in the balls or receptions, which are more or less the same in every civilized country, that the ladies of that land exhibit their special poise and grace, but rather in certain country outings, and especially in the celebrations held on the shores of a lake or at the seaside. There, they most elegantly sing and

85. Quip, witticism.
86. "And you will surely know that in warm countries, young people arrive at the age of puberty earlier than in our cold European climates; the South American republics have for their motto 'Puberty, Equality, Fraternity!' "

dance the airs and songs of the country, or perhaps it is gay fandangos and songs of Spain, which have remained since the times of the colony. All that is quite patriarchal—quite primitive, if you like; but for me it is an irreplaceable delight. . . .

"Modernity" has not yet reached the home, and large families abound, for there is extraordinary fecundity and the people have not heard, nor do they wish to hear, of Malthus. Despite the victory of radical principles in politics, women, as in almost all countries, continue to maintain their religiosity and their practices of devotion. . . . For example, the Iglesia de San Juan de Dios, in Léon, owes a great deal to the munificence of the wife of one of the most meritorious of Nicaragua's public men; I am referring to doña Soledad de Sánchez. Likewise, in the Cathedral, in altars and paintings, the name of a beloved aunt of mine, now deceased—doña Rita Darío de Alvarado—is prominent. . . .

In Nicaragua, courage, sacrifice, and abnegation are qualities that are admired greatly in a woman, and there are many proofs of that assertion in the many wars that have shaken the country, from the war of independence down to our own time, and in the times of Spanish dominion examples of bravery and feminine decisiveness were much admired and exclaimed upon. "Among the Spanish women," says Ellis, "in past times, despite the Moorish customs of withdrawal and enclosure, valor and warlike qualities were common," and H. D. Lea, in his *History of the Inquisition in Spain,* says that women "fought and defended their side in the factional intrigues with more ferocity than the men." When Nicaragua was attacked by pirates—about which Oexmelin writes such curious things in his strange *History of Piracy*—there was one case of womanly valor that Gámez reports in the following way: "But at the same time the pirates were threatening the Realejo, four hundred French and English buccaneers were disembarking in Escalante, a southern port twenty leagues from Granada, which they immediately set upon. The Grenadines, upon hearing of the imminent arrival of the enemy, hurried to fortify themselves with fourteen large artillery pieces and six petraries.[87] On April 7, 1685, at two in

87. Stone-throwing mortars.

the afternoon, the enemy appeared, and after a brief exchange of fire took possession of the city. The next day they demanded a ransom for the town, and as it was not given them, they burned the convent of San Francisco and eighteen of the principal houses, sacked the populace, and retreated with a loss of thirteen men, passing through Masaya and other towns until they reached Masachapa. With the memory of this alarming event still fresh in people's memory, on August 21, 1685, the buccaneers, under the command of the pirate Dampier, disembarked on an estuary next to the Realejo and, making their way along a river that runs down to the beach at Jaguei, they entered Léon, intending to surprise the town. But they could not prevent the townspeople and the authorities from rushing to the defense, although hurriedly and without much order. When the enemy appeared, the governor's mother-in-law, doña Paula del Real, banged the drum, and for that reason her name was given to the estuary by which the English entered."

If doña Paula del Real bangs drums, señorita Rafaela Herrera fires cannons—not against a certain young English mariner named Nelson, who was later at Trafalgar, for Nelson was in Nicaragua on another occasion, but rather at other enemies, though still English. . . . Nineteen years later, the Spanish government issued a royal decree granting Rafaela Herrera a pension for life as reward for her heroic defense of the Castillo de la Concepción in 1762. In just that way the Nicaraguan women of today, the women of the people, go off to campaigns—as sutlers,[88] canteen-operators, or companions to the soldiers; and more than one has been seen manfully fighting with her rifle, like the bravest of the men. And in her house, that same woman is good, hard-working, quiet, and excellent for love—what the Nicaraguans call a *mengala,* which is their word for a working woman, those who wear not the *chapeau* of the affluent classes but rather the ancient shawl (which, like those of India, they decorate most beautifully) draped over their shoulders, which are as bare as a lady's in a ballgown. Among these *mengalas* there are delicious examples that one would swear were the

88. Merchants who prepare and sell food to the soldiers.

flowers of Andalucía complicated by the ancestral dream and voluptuousness of the native peoples.

And three girls in the Léon market, cloth-vendors, will remain in my memory as though I had seen them in an Arabian Nights *souk* in the times of the great caliph Haroun al-Raschid, before the imposition of the veil.

# THE POSTER IN SPAIN (EXCERPTS)

When I wrote up my first impressions of Spain, upon my arrival in Barcelona, I mentioned that one of the particularities of that city was the luminous joy of its streets, which were decked out, as though with flowers, in springlike *affiches*.[89] However much Buenos Aires may still be nursing from a bottle in this respect, at least Spain has graduated to short pants. Léon Deschamps declares that this is the case with art in general and more especially with the decorative arts. The French gentleman exaggerates. Had he laid his eyes on a study recently published in the *Revue Encyclopédique* by Mélida he would have been convinced of the contrary. If in this general *anomie* there is one thing that sustains the ancient spirit of the glorious nation, it is art. Expositions—although the most recent one left something to be desired—follow fast on one another; they are nourished by the Fine Arts Circle in Madrid and the municipal government in Barcelona. The little illustrated magazines do what they can to develop the public's taste. Architecture quests after amplitude and grace in new styles. The decorative arts attain a notable height in Catalonia. Theater design . . . is making great and visible strides. The old art of Spain has a nucleus of passionate devotees in the Sociedad de Excursionistas, and in the Atheneum, the chairs of Archaeology and History of Art are well filled. The problem, so to speak, as I have said before, is that support and protection by the wealthy classes is nil, nor does the government bother, as in times of illustrious memory, to grant its favors in the cultivation of Spanish talents. In the

89. Posters.

last exposition there was much talk when a lady of the aristoc-
racy bought a painting by Sorolla. . . .

But let's talk about the poster, the *affiche* . . .

For many years now, colorful posters have been used in Spain
to announce the famous *ferias* in Seville and Valencia, the feast
of the Virgen del Pilar in Zaragoza, and bullfights on feast days.

These posters are not, of course, the genre of the commercial
posters of today. They seek above all to attract the passerby's
attention with the *criarde*[90] reproduction of picturesque provin-
cial *types* or *majas* with big eyes and crimson lips, and bulls,
and bullfighters. In the background the city's cathedral often
appears.

Recently, posters have been seen announcing art exhibits,
Carnival, and a few plays. These in small numbers, although
the habit is becoming established.

The bullfighting posters, like those for provincial festivals
and, one might hazard, most of this new crop, employ the ear-
splitting cry of colors, the fierce call of color, with its deceiving
tyranny—this terrible potency of color which, as Barbey d'Au-
revilly says, makes one believe in the truth of lies.

Deschamps is rightly surprised by this accentuation of crude
coloration and pronounced golds. The lack of originality is no-
torious, but really, not just in Spain—in the rest of Europe as
well. There are four, or perhaps six—let us say *ten*—original *af-
fichistes*. The rest combine several techniques or frankly imitate
this or that manner. In "modern" art, in literature, as in every-
thing, an air of kinship, a family resemblance, one might say,
can been seen in the production of many nations in many
climes. Primitivism, English pre-Raphaelism, has infected the
entire world. The decorative art of William Morris and his cir-
cle has been reflected in the decorative art of the world for
several years now. And with respect to the poster, Aubrey
Beardsley lives on in a phalanx of artists in England, the United
States, and other countries. Even the Yankee Bradley, who has
his own personality, would not deny the influence of that ill-
starred, mysterious master. Dudley Hardy has also spread his

90. Strident.

suggestion to many of his contemporaries. And in France, the name Cheret can clearly be attached to works designed and signed by others, who have calqued his figures, been seduced by the mad flames of his colors. In our attempts in Buenos Aires, can one not see Mucha? Therefore, it should hardly be surprising that here, the art of the poster is an art of reflection.

Some time ago, a very well-known industrial concern—the manufacturer of the world renowned anisette "Mono"[91]—held a competition to advertise its liqueur. One noted for the first time that in Spain there were a number of quite remarkable poster artists, more than one had suspected. "Three hundred monkeys going through three hundred thousand monkeyshines" suddenly appeared. But the best of the monkeys, the first-prize monkey, was that by the Catalonian Casas, who presented two posters, with their respective monkeys accompanied by two zoologically perfect Spanish ladies. In one, the simian, perched upon a tripod, is pouring on the Spanish beauty, wrapped in a luxurious mantilla, a glass of anisette; in the other, the Spanish beauty—a dazzling model, upon my word!—is holding a glass in her right hand and with her left is clutching the monkey. Casas is one of the best artists in Spain today; with Rusiñol, he is the wise and sensible pillar of a well-understood *modernismo* in the capital of his Catalonia. There are those who point out manners "borrowed" from foreign models, and Deschamps notes that one of his most recent productions, *Pel y Plom,* owes something to Ibels and Lautrec. Admitted—the fact is, Casas and Rusiñol, and the "new" artists of the young Catalan school, and the authors of the region, are all aware of what is being done around the world in contemporary art, and they follow in foreign thought what ought to be followed: *the methods,* as Juan Agustín García has so wisely said. . . . After that, one may develop one's own conception in one's own surroundings and in the appropriate medium. I find nothing else than this in the works of art and literature of the admirable Sitges artist Casas.

Rusiñol has done posters worthy of note. . . . In all Rusiñol's

91. The symbol of Mono is a charming, sometimes mischevous monkey.

posters, his spirit shines through, as it does in all his paintings, in everything of his, in fact—(and if they are all different from one another, as M. Deschamps disapprovingly notes), each subject should have its own interpretation. . . .

Riquer is an enthusiast. . . . He knows modern art wonderfully well. His illustrations, his drawings have been done with admirable originality. In his posters there is the same inquisitive, happy talent. He is a skillful symphonist of color, though the colors may "detonate" too loudly in his gracious combinations. His *Chrysanthemums* are delicious in their clear Saxon origins; Bradley himself has few posters superior to this one. His little figure for Grau and Company's cookies and cakes is an undeniable delight upon the harmonious decoration of the wrapping. Utrillo has been compared with Steilen. There is no doubt that the image for *Ferros d'art* and the figure for the *Anuario Riera,* for example, appear to be by the hand of the Parisian, but what about the exquisite poster for the Cardo waters? Utrillo is strong, he is vigorous, but when he is brushed by a soft breeze, grace is with him.

Marcelino Unceta, like Pérez, specializes in bullfights. His picadors, his powerful horned beasts, his *espadas,* all the figures in the national circus that inspire his pictorial talent, are first-rate. But his posters, examined closely, do not correspond to what one understands by the term "poster art." They are figures that might be used in a genre painting, or a study for a *real* painting.

I do not consider the caricaturist Xaudaró as belonging to the same line as the Catalan poster-makers, even the new ones, like Gual, who shows indisputable brio and talent. Xaudaró takes his caricatures to the poster: the eternal macrocephalic dwarf, the exaggeration of gesture, the deformation—not, let it be understood, out of an excess of understanding of drawing. So much repetition of his *bonshommes* tires one, I fear. They lie outside one's expectation for the poster; one sees that they have come from their creator's albums, or have emerged from the humorous pages of weekly magazines.

Navarrete merits mention on account of the forthrightness of his drawing and coloration—always with the national exaggeration, of course. Both he and almost all of Spain's draftsmen have used and abused the thick line that outlines the figure, as in the leading of *vitraux*. Since the appearance of the posters that have brought Alphonse Mucha such renown, that tendency to heavy outlining has increased, as, in imitation of the *affichiste* of Sarah Bernhardt, has the unbinding of figures' hair into volutes and ribbons and ringlets.

I have not had the fortune to come across those posters described by M. Deschamps—who, I understand, has not actually *been* in Spain—in which Spanish painters have attempted to create a national art of the poster here. What I have seen, however, are many reflections, many imitations, many calques. There is a great deal of talent, and many good intentions. It would not be surprising if that creation were achieved. Of course one sees that in the Spanish poster the artists go beyond seeking to attract attention with the nude. I do not know what reason there might be, except for the eternal beauty of the nude, to advertise a sewing machine, or pills, or light fixtures, with naked women, as most French posters do. But here, in this land of lovely female faces, this true empire of flowers, there are many beauties to portray, to the delight of the public's eye; Sattler, in that fantasy of his in the land of the North, was clever enough to have his *affiche* for the magazine *Pan* blossom from a rare flower. What things, in the clear light of day, might the Spanish palette not say, with the aid of the truth of its sun?

# A DIPLOMATIC MISSION

The extraordinary German diplomatic mission, led by Prince Albrecht, has been much talked about in recent days. He is a good Teuton giant, a worthy representative of his military, iron nation. He has brought the Black Eagle to adolescent King Alfonso XIII, who in the palace ceremony gave a very pretty speech in French. There have been no military reviews, out of very sensible considerations. But the foreign princes have seen much of great, indestructible Spain; they have seen the Velázquez gallery in the Prado, have had several impressions that have given them to understand that however much the actions of bad governments may bring ruin and disaster to the Spanish nation, there is a wealth of fecundity and life from which a Spain that is the master of its own future may arise.

The other night they were also able to admire, in the Teatro Real, the superb fount of loveliness that belongs to this people filled with such nobility and enchantment. The aristocracy showed off such jewels of youth and beauty as few countries can boast of, whether it is the "type" with large black eyes and hair of incomparable richness falling over shoulders as harmoniously as the capillary burden that wearies a virginal *annunziana* of the rocks; or the semi-Arabic type, which reveals its Andalucian heritage; or the solid woman of the north who, in her opulence, bears all the pride of a generous race.

And while Darclee performed her brave Manon, I watched the German colossus examine the box seats through his opera glasses. Before him lay the fragrant human flora of the sunlit nation that has lived in an environment of knightly heroism under a sky of poesy; there, the descendants of the highest names of Spanish nobility, still preserving all the grace painted by so many illustrious brushes and sung by so many luminous poets.

And something by don Alonso Quijano "the Good" whispered to my soul: "Let the dum-dum bullet be tried on the Boer, and let the end of the nineteenth century be a time of blood and slaughter, reasoned or unreasoned. Someone has said that Krupp is Hegel and the Chamberlain is Darwin. There is no cause for despair. These heartless scientists may be succeeded by reasonable and necessary lyrical links. Don Quixote is never a bad thing. And William II writes verse and paints pictures and composes operas and hymns. Spain should not think of war now, or of things that it has been shown by the variety of its fortune or the fragility of greatness. And when the Germanic Caesar sends a black eagle, the gift in return should be a white dove."

# ¡TOROS!
# (EXCERPTS)

The gay peach trees are sporting fresh spring pink, the Retiro is all green, and with the springtime come the bulls. The city is beginning to see its usual profusion of Cordoban sombreros, tight pants in an absurd callipygian display, the smooth-skinned faces of the men of the bullring and their assistants. The day of the beginning of the bullfight season was a day of great celebration. On Alcalá, I was able to salute the spirit of Gautier several times. It was the same atmosphere as in the time of Juan Pastor and Antonio Rodríguez: the calashes lining the boulevard, the mules with pompoms and bright bunting, the carriages passing by filled with *aficionados,* the mantillas adorning the many enchanting heads. The very breeze seemed filled with enthusiasm; no one could think of anything but the next performance, no one could talk about anything else. Colored cravats exploded on men's shirtfronts; jackets seemed to have multiplied; bells jingled as vehicles rumbled by; the petulant figure of El Guerra appeared everywhere on the brightly colored posters.

—El Guerra! His name is like the blast of trumpets, or a flag. He stands a head taller than Castelar, Núñez de Arce, and Silvela; today, it is he who triumphs, he who is the lord and master of a fascinated city. El Guerra! Salvador Rueda, so very Andalucian, finds nothing more to say to me about his beloved *torero* than "He is Mallarmé!"

Let us go, then, to the bullfight.

"It has been repeated almost *ad nauseam* that the taste for bullfights, those famous *corridas de toros,* is waning in Spain, and that civilization will soon see that they disappear. If civilization does that, so much the worse for it, because a bullfight is one of the most beautiful spectacles that man can imagine." Who wrote that? Great Théo, magnificent Gautier, who came from "over the mountains" to see the fiestas of blood and sun; later, Barrès was to discover the *sang, volupté, et mort.* It is easy to understand the impression made upon that man who "knew how to think" by the cruel circus pomps. It is undeniable that the spectacle is magnificent, that so much color, so much gold and crimson, under the golds and purples of the sky, is singularly striking and seductive, and that the vast ring in which those jugglers of death, gleaming in silks and metals, exhibit their talents has a Roman air about it, a certain Byzantine grace. Artistically speaking, then, those of you who have read descriptions of a *corrida,* or who have witnessed one for yourselves, cannot deny that it is a thing whose beauty makes an impression. The gathering of a sun-people in these celebrations in which instinct and vision are rewarded, is justified, and from that justification derives the deification of the bullfighter, the *torero.*

*Nodier raconte qu'en Espagne. . . .* [92] It is easy to imagine Gautier's enthusiasm for this "Espagne" of his, which appeared in the Romantic period to be a peninsula from a fairy tale: the Spain of *châteaux,* the Spain of Hernani, and another, more fantastical Spain if you like, which, even if it did not exist, had to be invented. That Spain came forth in the fantasies of Gautier, and the bulls seen by him were seen through the magic of the imagination. On Calle Alcalá he was swept up, and swept along, by the picturesque crowds; the coaches, the mules adorned as for a fair day, the princely riders, the violent hues heated even further by the afternoon sun, the characteristic national "types." Art seized him at every moment, and if a brace of mules brought to his memory a painting by Van der Meulen, a pass with the *torero*'s cape reminded him of an engraving by

92. This is the first line of a poem by Théophile Gautier, "Inès de las Sierras," about a flamenco-dancing ghost in a haunted castle, the "apparition of the Spain of times past." This poem is, in turn, based on a fantastical novel by Charles Nodier.

Goya. Here he found the famous *"manola,"* that young woman of Madrid's lower classes, who would bring him to write a no less famous song whose *"¡alza! ¡hola!"* would be repeated in the future in all the café-concerts of Paris. He was fascinated by details; we smile now at the sincerity with which he corrected his compatriots in search of "local color": one should say *torero,* not *toreador;* one should say *espada,* not *matador.* Later, he amended Delavigne's essay, telling him that the Cid's sword was called *tizona,* not *tizonade,* and correcting an error in his use of Spanish in the description of a bullfight. Oh! the Spanish of the French would yield up many curious quotations, from Rabelais to Maurice Barrès, and including Victor Hugo and Verlaine. The bulls captured the eyes of the poet of *Enamels and Cameos:*[93] "When I was about to sit in my place, in the seats," he says, "I experienced a dizzying, dazzling sensation. Torrents of light flooded the ring, for the sun is a high, high chandelier (which has the advantage of not spraying kerosene about). . . . A throaty, roaring murmur floating like a haze of sound above the sand. On the sunny side of the *plaza* thousands of fans and parasols fluttered and sparkled. . . . I assure you that twelve thousand spectators in a theater so vast that its ceiling can only be painted by God himself, with the splendid azure that He extracts from the urn of eternity—that sight is an *admirable* spectacle."

Later were to come the vicissitudes of the games, the magnificence of the suits and capes, the bloody incidents—disemboweled horses, wounded bulls—and the tempestuous audience, an audience whose equal could not be found unless one traveled back to the circuses of Rome. And all this with sun and music and trumpeted fanfares and fiery *banderillas.*[94]

"The bullfight had been a good one," he concludes: "eight bulls and fourteen horses dead, one of the bulls' keepers slightly wounded—one could not ask for anything better." We can accept that for reasons of imagination and artistic sensibility men

93. Gautier.
94. The lances, with ribbons tied to their ends, that are stuck into the bull's neck.

such as Gautier were infected with a taste for the bullfights of
Spain; but the case is, that infection spreads to foreigners who
are wholly "intellectual," so that it is not unusual to see, up in
the seats, a blond *commis-voyageur*[95] giving clear signs of the
most overflowing sort of contentment.

As strongly rooted as bullfights are in Spain, it is inconceiv-
able that there should come a time when this violent hobby
should no longer be. Before and after Jovellanos, there have
been those who have protested against the practice, and they
have broken their best arrows against the centuries-old bronze
of this most immovable of customs. In the provinces, the same
thing happens as in Madrid. Sevilla seems to water its red
carnations with the blood of those fierce *soavetaurilias*; there,
bullfights—which they call *fiestas de toros,* bull-feasts—are
inseparable from the fire of the sun, the warmly amorous
women, the manzanilla sherry, the furious happiness of the
earth. The *corrida* is another aspect of the land's voluptuous-
ness, and Bloy's opinion as to the sensuality of the spectacle
would find its best support in the truly sadistic enjoyment taken
by certain women who attend the bloody performance. The
Sevilla of Mañara's sword-thrusts, Moorish languor, females
for whom Gutierre de Cetina dissolved, the bloody scenes of
Zurbarán, the feminine flesh of Murillo, little Gypsy girls, gen-
erous bandits, must be the Sevilla of the classic bullfight. Under
Ferdinand III, the young men of the nobility had their own spe-
cial ring in which to practice their favorite sport. Royal births
and the taking of Zamorra were celebrated with bullfights. The
cardinal Archbishop Rodrigo de Castro forbade bullfights dur-
ing one particular jubilee year; the city protested to His Excel-
lence and won, with the support of Philip II. The bullfight went
on. . . .

In the times of Philip IV "don Juan de Cárdenas, one of the
duke's jesters, a man of excellent humor, fought bulls, and with
such skill and princely nobility that he gave the most furious
bull a good sword-thrust: His Majesty killed three bulls with a
harquebus," said one chronicler of the time. Philip V attempted

95. Traveling salesman.

to replace bullfights with "intellectual games," but the French part of him was defeated by the Spanish part. Yesterday, as today—*toros* forever! . . .

Nevertheless, there are certain passionate followers of the sport who lament the decadence of bullfights; they say that today there is no "love of the art," that the *espadas* (Frenchmen and others, read: "matadors") have become simple businessmen, and that the breeders, even the descendants of Columbus, offer—according to Pascual Millán, notable taurographer—"rickets-ridden animals, without blood or bravery or power." Some days ago I met, in Aranjuez, a hospitable, friendly man who, through his knowledge of the pigtail, showed a certain refinement and a liking for Latin America. He spoke to me about the Río de la Plata, and Chile, and his friend Agustín Edwards. This was the famous Angel Pastor. He is suffering greatly. At the top of his career, when he was still strong and young, he had the misfortune to break an arm. He will no longer be able to "work," as he calls it; the bad luck has hit him worse than an angry bull, and has crippled him. And Pastor also spoke about how bad bullfighting is today, how the art has fallen into decay; and he spoke about the "classical" and the "modern" forms, like some professor of literature or painting. But he lacks not the fat diamond on the finger and the admiration of everyone. The best hotel in Aranjuez is his. And the traditional gentility and chivalry are his, too.

Decadent or not, the bullfights will go on in Spain. There is no king, no government that dares end them. Charles III had that bad idea, and soon enough his other defects appeared, too. Jovellanos, in his letter to Vargas Ponce, was not ashamed to maintain that the diversion is not, strictly speaking, *national,* since Galicia, Léon, and Asturias care little about bullfighting. "What glory do we derive from it?" he exclaimed. "What is Europe's opinion in the matter? Rightly or wrongly, do they not call us barbarians because we preserve and defend these *fiestas de toros*?" He claimed that *toreros* were not, in fact, brave men, and derided their general stupidity outside the bullring. He pointed out the damage that the sport causes agriculture, for raising a good bull for the bullring costs as much as raising fifty oxen for the plow; and to industry, for nations who attend bullfights are not, generally speaking, the most hard-working. As for customs, the paragraph that Jovellanos dedicates to the influence of bulls upon customs and traditions would be perfect if inserted into a chapter of Léon Bloy's *Cristophe Colomb devant les taureaux*. . . . [There is a theory that] the basis for a taste for those cruel diversions may be found in the sediment of animality that remains even after society has evolved. This theory is not new, and before it was sustained by scientific arguments it was already cemented in the wisdom of most nations.

But if there is no doubt that the Spaniard, collectively, is the clearest example of regression to primitive ferocity, there is also no doubt that in every man there is something of the Spaniard in this regard—not to mention a bit of the perversity that Poe reminds us of. And the proof of this is the contagion, individual or collective—the contagion of a traveler who goes to the bullfight out of curiosity, or the contagion of an entire population, or a large part of it (such as that of Buenos Aires or Paris), into which this entertainment has been imported, with the risk that if curiosity is drawn, first, by exoticism, then later will come the sport and all its consequences.

In Buenos Aires, despite the numerousness of the Spanish colony and the Spanish blood that still prevails among the inhabitants, the spectacle could not be sustained for long, but once one passes over the cordillera, and in countries less Saxonized than Chile, the case is different. From Lima to Guatemala and Mexico, there is still enough Peninsular "essence" to give life to the taste for the bullring.

"In any people," says Varona, "this public spectacle would be noxious to the culture; among the Spaniards and their descendants, it is infinitely more so. All the propensities of their character, which are the product of their race and their history, incline them toward violent, even homicidal passions. So far as I personally am concerned, I am simultaneously drawn and repulsed by the spectacle; I have still not been able to slit the throat of my beloved little suckling pig."

Given that the multitudes must have their diversions, must have some way to manifest their *joie de vivre,* I, too, would prefer that nations congregate on their holidays to enjoy a double, noble, mental and physical pleasure by listening, *à la greque,* to a declamation under the canopy of the heavens while seated upon the rising tiers of an open amphitheater, or that a procession of men, women, and children wind their way up into the mountains or along the seashore in harmonious liberty, singing songs to nature. But since no nation on earth has such traditions today, and since our customs tend increasingly to diverge from the eternal poetry of bodies and souls, then let there be bullfights, I say, let there be enormous bullrings like ancient circuses, filled with beautiful women, and sparkling eyes, and glints and gleams of steel and jewels, and shouting, and gesticulating. . . .

I assure you that my sympathies are always on the side of the animals, and between the *torero* and his horse, I would choose the horse, and between the bullfighter and the bull, my applause is for the bull. Courage, bravery, has very little to do with this sport, wherein what is most required is good eyesight and agility. I would not be the one to cheer the establishment of a bullring among us, but I would also not cheer the day that Spain abandoned those lovely exercises that are a manifestation of her national character.

The river of people turned down Calle Alcalá; past the Cibeles Fountain flowed a constant stream of carriages; the evening was turning to night, and the golden globe of the Banco de España reflected the glory of the West, where the sun, like an incandescent peacock tail, or the spokes of a gigantic Spanish fan, red and yellow, cast from a diamantine center its symmetrical and outspreading rays. The radiant eyes of the women sparkled tempestuously under their graceful *mantillas*; springlike vendor-girls offered their white tuberoses and red roses; golden dust motes floated in the air; and from every body, blood and desire sang forth a hymn to the new season. The *toreros* passed in their carriages, making the fleeting evening light all the brighter; there was the sound of distant music, and the Prado thrilled with children's laughter.

And I understood the soul of that Spain that does not perish, that Spain that is the queen of life, empress of love, joy, and cruelty—that Spain that will always have conquistadors and poets, painters and bullfighters.

Castles in Spain! the French say. Yes, of course: castles in the air and on the ground, filled with legend, history, music, perfume, nobility, color, gold, blood, and iron, so that Hugo may come and find in them everything he needs to sculpt a mountain of poetry. Castles in which Carmen lived, and Esmeralda, and where the Gautiers, the Mussets, and all the other artists of the world may drink the most intoxicating wines of art. And as for you, don Alonso Quijano the Good, dear beloved Don Quijote, you know that I will always be on your side.

# "BLACK SPAIN"

A few days ago I paid a brief visit to Aranjuez. If Versailles holds the memory of an enchanting lady who limped, Aranjuez still breathes the perfume of a bewitching one-eyed lady. A trip to that lovely *buen retiro*[96] of Castilian royalty is most worthwhile, a journey to pay homage to that Princesa de Eboli. Among the evocative, fragrant woodlands, the distant scenes rise up again, and in the air of the groves and gardens there are sleeping echoes that await only the lover or poet to bid them wake. In the Royal Palace and the "Workman's House," a spirit of sadness comes over you from the moment you step inside the sumptuous, solitary rooms. As you wander the countless rooms and apartments, adorned with centuries of gold, silver, marble, onyx, agate, silk, ivory; as you gaze upon those ceilings that have sheltered so many tragic, gay, or mysterious hours in the lives of so many Spanish monarchs, you are overcome by the somberness and gloom: This place and its furnishings have been so long without life; the mirror that held so many images in the past, the Manuel Rivas clock that has stopped; the pillow on which Philip II laid his head; the fresco, the painting, the locket, the old stove with its odd, sad beauty. . . . And the guide who pronounces his rote story yet removes his cap before a painting that portrays a chapel in El Escorial where mass is being said. . . . What comes to mind is Black Spain.

I had just finished reading that recent book by Emile Verhaeren and Darío de Regoyos, *La España negra,* and Barrès' Spanish novel *Un amateur d'ames,* and that positive volume on

96. Retreat.

Spain's political and social evolution by Yves Guyot—and in all of them I found that observation, suggestion, and detail produced the dark note that contrasts, in this land, with the luxury of sunlight, the perpetual feast of light. On account of some spectral effect, so much color, so much polychrome gleam, produces, with the turning of the wheel of life, the color black.

This is the land of happiness and gaiety—the reddest of happiness, in fact: the bulls, the Gypsy festivities, the sensual women, Don Juan, Moorish voluptuousness. But for that very reason, the cruelty is all the more cruel, and lust, the mother of melancholy, all the more unbridled. Torquemada, immortal, still lives in this land. Granada lies open to the sun like the pomegranate that gives it its name, perfumed, sweet, acidly pleasing, but there is a Toledo, a concretion of time, that is as dry and immutable as a stone, and inside its walls a burst of laughter would be rare indeed, and out of place. There, in the heat that bakes Castile to aridity, there can be no love affairs but those that end in sadness or fatal tragedy, and the passion that makes this place bear such bitter flowers has the sinister, ardent savor of an act of incest. Verhaeren notes his dolorous impressions, copies onto his engravings hot, desiccated landscapes, displays the country's violent, barbarous souls as though they were the products of a lush, rare, tropical flora. His Belgian blood is overmatched, atavistically, by the fierce savagery of a Spain that enchained his ancestors in the irons of the Duque de Alba. Through the optics of theory he sees the bloody crystallization in the subsoil of this race, whose natural energies are roiled and complicated by the crude need for tortures, and the concept of death and grace are decked with mourning by a feverish, exacerbating Catholicism, by a fierce tradition that has lighted the most horribly beautiful bonfires and imposed the most crimson, exquisite martyrdoms. Art reveals that incomparable history. The symbolism of religion turns the naves of churches and cathedrals into morgues, and I can understand how they moved Verhaeren, as they move all thinking visitors whose footsteps take them through these bloody sanctuaries in which Rivera or Montañés, to mention just two, exhibit to human horror their lamentable crucifixions.

A talented Spaniard says this to me: "In every one of us there is the soul of an inquisitor." It is true. Tell me that José Nakens is not the living parallel—into infinity itself, like geometric lines—of Torquemada. One sees in him the same fierce and terrible faith, the intransigence that becomes blindness, the desire to impose the rack on all and sundry, the certainty of salvation through suffering, so magnificently illuminated in the plays of Hugo. In the Americas, the conquistadors and friars simply worked instinctively, under the impulse of their native proclivities: The Indians torn to pieces by dogs; the acts of subtlety, deceit, and violence; the deaths of Guatimozín and Atahualpa; the enslavement; the fires and swords and harquebuses—all these things were *logical,* and only an exceptional heart, a foreign soul among them, like Las Casas, could be grieved and astonished by that manifestation of Black Spain. . . .

The political glooms of yesteryear are repeated today, though of course without that lost magnificence. . . . The shadow of Rome still falls over the palace in Madrid, the confessors still play their role, and the intrigues are the same, the only difference being the players and the mental aptitudes. *Oh, Spain will change!* That is the cry the moment the Yankees' injustice and strength are felt. And what changes is the Ministry.

The national verbosity overflows from a hundred mouths and pens belonging to self-appointed regenerators. It is a new national pastime. Yet the Gypsy celebrations are not interrupted. "Spain," says a French author, "is attempting, no doubt, to imitate those great ancient Eastern nations that crumbled into public drunkenness." But that is not correct; it is not trying to imitate anything. It works from its own impulses. Its gaiety is a native product, among so much tragedy; it is the red carnation, the red flower of Black Spain. Thus, when the conservatives returned to power, it was believed abroad that the reaction would bring on a revolution. . . . But nothing happened. Silence. Stagnation. . . .

# SEVILLE

Though it is winter, I have found roses in Seville. The sky has been pure and openly hospitable, after the first few hours of the morning. La Giralda stands tall against the splendid field of azure. Then the women of Seville, glimpsed through the wrought-iron gratings that stand at the entrance to the marmo-real, flowering patios, show reason for the city's fame. I have seen wonders.

Not without reason is this the city of Don Juan and Don Pe-dro. Poetry, legend, tradition forever come out to greet you. Estrella, the Burlador, the cruel Monarch, the Barber. . . . [97] Tourism arrives, fashionably, during Holy Week. Not so much out of holiness as to pay outrageous hotel bills, sleep on a bil-liard table if nothing else presents itself, and watch the pro-cessions pass by—the crowds of irreligious Catholics, macabre saints, livid, bloody Christs with human hair. At the same time, the traveler will hear the cries of the *saetas,* those extraordinary Flamenco songs sung at only this time of year, and the wails of the *carceleras,* those songs bemoaning the harshness of impris-onment. During the day, he will go to see the cigar-makers in the factory, with their suggestive *deshabillés;* if he has read Pierre Louÿs' *La femme et le pantin,* so much the better, and he will return to his country saying that he felt the enchantment of Seville.

But the enchantment of Seville lies, most certainly and unar-guably, elsewhere. Holy Week and its celebrations are singular notes, and the cigar-rollers help the local color that one has

97. Characters in operas set in Seville.

gleaned from one's readings, but the soul of Seville has little to
do with all that compulsory picturesqueness. Or with the indus-
trialism and commercial life that bustles about the boats on the
banks of the Guadalquivir, either. Or even with the battalion of
callipygian *toreros* that wines and dines itself along the narrow,
winding Calle de las Sierpes. No, the intimate enchantment of
Seville lies in what it communicates to us of its past. Its soul
speaks in silent solitudes—as does the sad soul of all Old Spain.
The ancient byways whisper their secrets in the hours of night.
And nothing compares with the grave melancholy of the city's
gardens, those gardens that have been interpreted so masterfully
in paint, in melodies of color, by the exceptional, profound talent
of Santiago Rusiñol—that "nightingale"[98] of strong Catalonia.

Seville! The injustices of reputation have little foundation:
Shun, then, the famous Street of the Serpents, where there was
once a celebrated flamenco café called El Burrero. . . . Shun
even the *manzanilla,* that sherry so famous yet so oily and
unlovable; shun, even if you are drawn to the bullfights, the
*toreros* outside the ring. But worship, in ecstatic wonder, to the
delight of your inner kingdom, the gardens of the Alcázar, as in
Aranjuez, as in magical Granada. Of all the things my eyes
have looked upon, one of those that has left the greatest mark
upon my spirit is those cool, delightful retreats. Neither the
moldy, ages-old walls of the city, which still attest the ancient
power of the Roman conquerors, nor the remains of the Visi-
goths, nor the svelte Mauritanian Giralda, whose name delights
like a flag snapping in the wind, nor the Tower of Gold on the
banks of the river, nor the magnificences of the Alcázar, which
stir in my memory the sensations I experienced in the Alhambra
in Granada—nothing, nothing has made me meditate and
dream like these gardens that have seen so many sights of his-
torical grandeur, so many mysteries, and so many voluptuous
encounters. And the culprit for all this wonder is, in large part,
that Don Pedro who had so much of the Don Juan about him.

When one enters, to one side of the galleries that bear the name
of that strange monarch who understood the beauties of the

98. A "Rusiñol" is the Spanish word for "nightingale."

Moors, who was so very Eastern, so very much like the Haroun al-Raschid of the Arabian Nights, the first thing that will move one is the softest of silences, disturbed—if disturbed can be said of such a calming sound—by the burbling of a fine stream of water falling from a vessel into the broad pool of greenish water. The soft breeze stirs the leaves of two large magnolias. And among the rose gardens and the myrtles, two terraced lawns descend, and one glimpses what is called "the baths of María de Padilla." There is a long pool, under a canopy of low Gothic arches. That is all. But what does it matter? Painters have tried to revive the sensual chapter of that beautiful novel of life. Let yourself be seduced by your imagination. Do you not hear the singing of the birds of spring? Do you not see the monarch as he approaches through the garden's luxuriant new flowers? Do you not hear the sound of the transparent water in which the pink body of the royal mistress makes diamond circles all around her? She laughs, and the hard king smiles. Nearby, there are white doves with plumage that the light makes iridescent, and a peacock, dressed in gala finery, displays his gems, like a vizier from the East. That, *that,* is the enchantment of Seville.

Farther on you will enter the garden of the Grotto, and there the myrtles form a famous, childlike maze, and in a rustic pavilion, under a strange vault, you will find a white statue of two women joined at the back—the four breasts pour forth four streams of water. A decorative Neptune greets you in the Grand Garden, as it is called, and in the Garden of the Lions there are, indeed, leonine beasts: HIC SUNT LEONES. It is here that the circular garden of the caesarian Carlos V is still preserved. Here, among the marbles and polychrome tiles and intricately carven wood screens, the imperial eagles preserve the pride and nobility of their attitudes, and they recall the much-faded presence of the proud—even arrogant—sovereign.

When you leave, you will take with you an ineffaceable impression. . . .

There in the church of the charity hospital, I have bowed before illustrious names—names of mosaic-makers, painters, and sculptors: Murillo, for one, multiplied in excellent works, such as a Child Jesus, leaning on the world, all grace, and a Moses in

which Bartolomé Esteban has demonstrated that celestial soft-
ness and sweet brush strokes do not prevent one, when one is
determined, from striking a note of forcefulness. And then the
realistic, macabre Valdés Leal, singing in the sculpted rhymes
of Gautier, renewing in more than one painting the triumph of
death and the cadaverous visions of the frescos of the Pisan bur-
ial ground.

A certain chronicler tells us that Murillo, seeing decomposi-
tion painted in so deathlike a manner upon a coffin, turned to
the artist and said, "My friend, people will have to hold their
nose when they look at this." But pass on to the sacristy. Do not
stop at the vision of San Cayetano, or Céspedes, or Roela's St.
Michael.

Look at that portrait of Old Time, look at that knight signed
by Valdés Leal, and look at that ancient sword, which in these
days of contemptible prose there is no hand worthy of describ-
ing. That proud knight, whose statue has been inaugurated
only recently, is a *revenant*, is an inhabitant of dreamland, is a
citizen of the city of eternal illusion, is a hero of poetry, a ghost
of sword and cape. That man is the murderer of love and the
champion of voluptuousness. He is Don Miguel de Mañara,
celebrated in the immortality of art under the name Don Juan.
And that is his sword. He is in a sacristy because, as you know,
when the devil got old he became a friar.

There is much to admire in the cathedral, and the guides go
into great detail about it, but there, too, as everywhere else, it is
the past, with its page from history or legend, that makes us
pause. Thus, from that pulpit which you will find in a court-
yard, where illustrious men such as the vigorous Vicente Ferrer
once preached, you will pass on to the marvels of the naves,
where glorious palettes left tapestries of great value and fame.
And the traditional anecdote awaits you in every chapel and
corner, from the colossal St. Christopher, at the Gamba altar, to
the small Child Jesus, which the people call "the mute one," the
work of Montañés. And here we come upon a curious note.

You will find people of years-long devotion, to whom you
will address some word or question, and you will find that how-
ever much you speak to them, they will never answer you.

These are fanatics who have made the blond child upon the altar a promise of silence for a certain length of time. In one of the chapels—and here the anecdote is modern—is the famous St. Antony, by Murillo, a painting that was mutilated by a visitor from the United States who thought it best to isolate the saint from the rest of the composition, for the saint's own good. The Spanish consul in Boston received a report of the fragment's whereabouts and managed to rescue it. Today, thanks to the art and ability of an eminent painter, the painting has been restored, and no sign of the Yankee robber's amputation is to be seen.

I will not stop you before the many famous art works kept here, for there are so many, and of such quality, that there are entire books, written by scholars such as Cean Bermúdez, dedicated to them. But I must tell you that you will see a certain funereal monument near Pérez de Alesio's *Christoforo,* a modern and very cerebral monument, composed of four figures holding up an urn—surely it will be familiar to you from the illustrations. In that urn—hats off, if you please!—repose the ashes, the controversial ashes, of Christopher Columbus, which were formerly deposited in the cathedral in Havana. I believe that even the most impassive and indifferent of Latin Americans must feel at least some vague emotion before that handful of dust. Although later, eternal Eironeia may appear and remind us that the favor he did us is not, perhaps, such a great one.

The evening was gay and golden when I crossed the Triana bridge to make my way into the quarter of that name, so oft-song in certain folksongs. Shall I say that I had more than one illusion shattered? Aside from one and another window filled with the usual flowerpots of Andalucía, and one and another face out of a lithograph or the label on a box of matches, I was unable to satisfy my curiosity as to the particular beauty of Seville. I saw many a young man in coat and tight pants, conversing loudly on the corners not far from the docks on which the Sevillan stevedore sweats as he takes part in the modern world's bustle. I saw unswept and unmopped entryways and salt-fish markets, and one old-fashioned stagecoach, traveling alongside the tram tracks with its load of people and luggage. I saw the Tower of Gold bathed in the gold of the afternoon, and the river a sort of dirty yellow color, and in the distance the heights that were beginning to fade, to turn smoky in the twilight. And if I did not return happy with Triana—given that I went with the idea of a fantastic and imaginary Triana, either impossible or too much *á la française*—at least I gathered some consolation from the vision of a beautiful girl and an old duenna as they came out of an old church. Doña Inés of my soul, and her inseparable chaperone.

# CÓRDOBA

A modest train station; an omnibus bumping along the street, through mud and potholes.

Bad weather. That is my first impression in centuries-old, illustrious Córdoba. But soon, despite the inclement day, the green orange trees and flowers in the nearby gardens have made up for that initial disappointment. The hotel at which I am staying is on the city's principal thoroughfare, the tree-lined avenue called the Great Captain, in memory of that magnificent warrior Don Gonzalo, whose birthplace was here. When the rain relents and I am able to go out, I see groups of people along the avenue, the eternal gatherings of a Spanish city, conversing and "killing time."

Off this tree-lined boulevard, which the inhabitants of this city are rightly proud of, the other streets are markedly typical; they descend from the higher part of the city to the lower, the Ajerquia. With each step I have taken in ancient Andalucian Córdoba, I have thought, as though inevitably, of that other Córdoba, in Argentina. Not that they bear any resemblance to one another, mind you, aside from the spirit of the race that fills the men of the colony as well as those of the motherland; it is the name that brings the memory, and the fact that this grandmother city has been a center of study and of knowledge since time immemorial, like that newer city in more recent days. . . .

But as I was saying, the streets of the city strike me as remarkably *typical,* and there is good reason for that, for according to Ramírez' historico-topographical monograph on the city, "in terms of neither direction nor breadth have the streets undergone any substantial alteration since the most remote ages, and they are, in general, as in all ancient cities, narrow and tortuous, or ill-aligned, so that it is worthy of note that in the center of the city one finds a few streets of some breadth." In neither Granada nor Sevilla nor Málaga have I found this atmosphere of antiquity that I have found here in this capital illuminated by—or in fact the focus of—universal wisdom. And in the narrowness and solitude of the streets, I am entranced by the constant wrought-iron grilles, the barred windows so well-fitted for discreet midnight courtships, the mysterious courtyards that one glimpses as one passes. In one place, a sort of circular plaza, one finds the name of Seneca, and one recalls that admirable philosopher and journalist *avant la lettre,* while a familiarity not quite so ancient presents itself to one in those houses on the narrow byways, from which there often bursts, all unexpectedly, the sound of a piano. . . . In one or another of these houses, the illustrious Juan Valera may have been born, for as we know, he, like Góngora, is from Córdoba.

From ancient times, Córdoba retains traces of the Caesars, but there are also vestiges of its masters before Rome, the Carthaginians. Its place as a Roman colony is attested to by medallions, and histories tell us that it was notable. One of the city's historians even declares that when Marcus Claudius Marcellus was praetor of the Spanish lands, "the city was expanded and ennobled with luxurious buildings, and apparently it became fashionable in Rome, at that time, to possess a 'country house' in the pleasant countryside of Córdoba." Today, of those grandeurs there remain only gravestones, inscriptions on monuments, milliary columns,[99] Augustan coins that present blurry problems for numismatists, and a venerable bridge, which is still upheld over the turbid Guadalquivir by its heavy arches. The city belonged to the Goths and then to the Arabs, and the Islamites raised it to its highest potency and preeminence. To read this history is to penetrate into the almost fabulous life of an imperial capital, an empire from an Arabian Nights tale.

99. That is, small columns on the side of the road, marking a distance of one thousand paces by the Roman army, the Roman "mile" (one can see the etymology of the word in *mille,* one thousand); the equivalent of mile-markers on modern highways.

Today there is almost nothing in comparison to the ancient splendors of the caliphs, but what does remain—the mosque converted into a cathedral, a transformation that must anger every artist-traveler—gives one an idea of what sort of brain was covered by those venerable turbans. What must that magnificent Rusafa, or royal garden, have been like, in which the puissant Abd al-Rahman I—who, like so many men of the East, was a prophet—stole a poetic march on the Cuban José Martí and sang to his compatriot, a solitary palm tree, like the caliph a stranger in a strange land, of his nostalgia for the desert? And what setting can compare for the story of Prince Camaralzahman and Princess Badura, or the other young princes and princesses in whom Dinarzad took such interest, with that Garden of Azhara built by Abd al-Rahman III—a garden that took its name from the king's favorite in the harem? The truth is, King Solomon himself might have resided in this place, in the company of the Queen of Sheba. I will not repeat here the somewhat prosaic information given by Christian chroniclers such as Díaz de Rivas, although I cannot pass over a description given by Arab authors who lived in the times of that splendid caliph:

"The houses, built to a uniform design, with great taste and magnificence, and crowned with rooftop terraces, had gardens planted with orange trees, and they suited the grandeur and luxuriousness of the alcázar (fortress) to which they had been added. For the construction of this royal compound, Abd al-Rahman put immense sums at the disposition of his dream. The workmen employed in the construction numbered one thousand; one thousand five hundred were the mules; and four hundred, the camels that brought materials. The labors were overseen by the most famous architects of Baghdad, Tosthat and Qairoan, and from Constantinople, sent by the caliph's ally Constantine VI, who also gave him forty granite columns, the most beautiful he could find. Abd al-Rahman had more than one thousand two hundred varieties of marble brought to him, at great cost, from the provinces of Spain, France, Italy, Greece, Africa, and Asia. The exterior of the Alcázar, as well as the interior, contrary to the custom of the Arabs, was adorned with

the same devotion and wealth of detail as the rest of the build-
ing, and the interior contained all the beauty and enchantment
that art, seconded by wealth, could create. The walls were en-
crusted with arabesques of great taste, the windows and doors
were of cedar adorned with precious carvings, and the ceilings
were painted a celestial azure and enameled with gold.

"But as is only natural, for exquisite beauty, richness, and de-
tail, nothing compared with the room that was the caliph's bed-
chamber. The decorations upon the walls were formed of gold,
pearls, and other precious stones, and in several places, as was the
custom, Koranic hallelujahs were inscribed. Into a magnificent
alabaster fountain, set in the center of the chamber, several gold
animals poured forth water from their mouths, and in the foun-
tain's center swam a swan of that same metal. Above the bowl
hung a pearl of extraordinary price, which had been presented to
the caliph by the emperor Leon, of Constantinople. The alcove
that contained the bed of the caliph's favorite was closed off by a
carved screen covered with hammered gold and iron, and stud-
ded with precious stones, and in the midst of the splendor cast by
the oil lamps of a hundred pendant chandeliers, there flowed a
stream of mercury, whose liquid silver fell into a lovely basin of
alabaster.

"Above the main door of the alcázar stood a statue of the
lovely slave-girl, to the indignation of the most austere Mus-
lims, who censured the caliph's impiety, for in contempt of the
express teaching of the Qur'an he had dared portray the human
figure. The gardens surrounding the palace were in keeping
with the rest in splendor and beauty, for the most fertile fantasy
had lavished upon them all things that might please the senses.
Woods of myrtles and laurels were mixed with olive trees,
whose verdure was reflected in the crystalline waters of the
pools; rare animals wandered through gardens designed for that
purpose, and birds of lovely plumage and pleasing song ani-
mated the enchanting mansion." As we suspend this descrip-
tion, can my reader not hear the voice of Dinarzad: "Sister, will
you tell one of those lovely stories that you know?" Of those
glorious mansions, there remains no more today than the most
superb of crowned heads, and they can only be contemplated,

with the aid of the imagination, in the famous narrations that I have quoted, and which have been brought into the light, and art, of modern times by the wise and admirable talent of Dr. Mardrus.[100]

Wandering from one point to another, and becoming lost sometimes in the labyrinth of these Oriental streets, I have come upon fountains, ruins, a curious monument to the angel Gabriel (who, according to legend, has freed the city time and again from plagues, storms, and calamities), and at last I found the only thing that truly attracts foreigners: the mosque. In this case, as in others, there is no reason at all to describe it, as there are hundreds of guide books and dozens of travel narratives that save me that effort. Suffice it to say that this building of faith overwhelmed me, as have so many buildings of war and love left by the Arabs in their beloved Al-Andalus, and that I joined my voice to the thousand others that have deplored the religious vandalism of the Catholics who believed it was right to demolish works of art and uglify the place of Allah in order to better worship Jesus Christ.

The forest of columns, the profusion of arches make one think of what this place might be without the dark doors, with natural light pouring in. A vast petrified palm grove, no doubt. And thank goodness there are still some of the architectural and mosaic splendors, like that prodigious *mihrab*, or Muslim chapel, which is the admiration of those who know about such things. Although in the Spanish intruders' construction there is remarkable work, such as the choir, the visitor's only thoughts must be for the people of Islam, who were able to build such glorious tabernacles to prayer. When one enters, one is seized with the desire to remove one's shoes and put on a pair of slippers and murmur, "Only Allah is great."

100. See the essay "The 1001 Nights," in this volume, for a full appreciation by Darío of J. C. MARDRUS.

# [TRAVELS IN ITALY]

## TURIN

September 11, 1900

From the bustle of the Paris Exposition, under that sad gray sky that serves as a canopy for so much joy, I move on to this land of glory that smiles under an azure dome of purest and most pleasant sky. I am in Italy, and my lips murmur a prayer similar in fervor to that formulated by the serene, free mind of harmonious Renan before the Acropolis. A prayer most very like in fervor, indeed—for to my spirit Italy has been an innate adoration. In its very name there is so much light and melody that it seems to me that if the lyre were not called lyre it might be called, for reasons both euphonic and platonic, *Italy*. Here one instantly recognizes the ancient vestiges of Apollo. Here, for good reason, pilgrims from the four corners of the earth have come in search of beauty. Here they have found so much: the sweet spiritual peace that issues from contact with things consecrated by the divinity of understanding; the vision of soft landscapes, incomparable firmaments, magical dawns and enchanting sunsets, through which a rich and loving Nature is revealed; the hospitality of a lively race, a people who love the singing and dancing that they have inherited from primitive, poetic beings who communicated with the Numens; and marbles divine in loveliness, bronzes proud in their eternity, paintings in which perfection has touched human effort, works of art which preserve legendary figures, signs of greatness, those simulacra that give to the artist exiled today among ancient

fragrances, memories of yesterday, those alphas that begin the
mysterious alphabet in which the omegas of the future are hid-
den. Blessed for the poet is this fecund and fecundating land in
which Tityrus[101] played so his goats might dance. Here, oh Pe-
trarch, the doves of your sonnets still fly. Here, beloved old Ho-
race, the vine you planted still grows; here, egregious celebrants
of Latin love, your roses still bloom, as in days of old, and your
games and kisses are played and kissed again. Here, Lamartine,
the Graziellas still laugh and cry; here, Byron, Shelley, Keats,
the laurels speak of you still; here, old Ruskin, the seven lamps
are still lighted; and here, huge Dante, your somber, colossal,
imperious figure, your occult demiurgic force still towers over
the echoing woods, the beings and things of this land, with the
majesty of an immense pine among whose branches one hears
the oracular voice of a god.
[. . . . ]

# ROME

October 3, 1900

The arid landscape of the Roman Agro behind me, I arrive in
Rome at dusk. The first impression is of a sad, neglected, ugly
city, but all that is erased by the influence of the sacred soil, the
evidence of a glorious land. In the trip from the station to the
hotel, through the windows of the omnibus appear, before my
yearning eyes, one after another monumental vision that I rec-
ognize: the baths in ruins, the column of Marcus Aurelius. My
spirit teeming with thoughts and memories, I sleep in a room in
a hotel on the Piazza Colonna which, perhaps out of an excess
of archaeological zeal, makes its customers light their chambers
with simple candles. In my opinion, any antique candelabra
someone had dug up, or even a wondrous chandelier, would
have served better.
    In the morning, a look at the city. . . . A long narrow street,

101. A shepherd in Virgil's Eclogues.

filled with trade, in the evening filled with people strolling along, and from time to time the imposing façade of a palazzo whose name is a page from history. I warn you: the sin of wanting to turn Rome into a modern metropolis could not be committed without spoiling the grandeur of this Catholic capital, but since Rome is—whatever you might want to say about it—the Pope's city, not the King's, no governmental decrees will ever fully prevail against it.

And this *is* the Pope's city. What has been left to it, down through the centuries, by religious events, the long domination by the pontiffs, and an ecumenical worship that converges on that place where Christ set his Rock, cannot be destroyed by political events or interests of a more partial nature. Through the Porta Pia little entered and nothing left.

While I make my way toward the Piazza Venecia, where I will take the tram that will take me to St. Paul's,[102] I am engulfed by a cosmopolitan army, its insignias on its breast and its guidebooks in its hand. People speak here in German, over there in Hungarian, farther on in English, Spanish, French, the dialects of Italy—every imaginable language. They are the members of various pilgrim groups who have come this Jubilee Year. They trample one another, jostle one another, push and shove one another to get a place on the streetcars. I see sad and ridiculous scenes. Clusters of humanity scatter as one of the vehicles pulls away. An old woman with a singularly odd cap clutches at the skirts of an obese priest, and both tumble to the paving stones. Since the coachmen are all on strike, this struggle is continual, though one constantly sees covered wagons passing with cargoes of pilgrims. Old folk, men of various ages, children, nannies with babies, friars of every feather, priests of every vintage

---

102. St. Paul's "outside the walls," a basilica built over the supposed burial place of the apostle Paul, was constructed over the centuries by popes and cardinals, but its greatest flowering occurred in the twelfth and thirteenth centuries. The church was added to down through the years, and its decorations increased. Then, on the night of July 15, 1823, the basilica was struck by a fire which burned it almost to the ground. Thus, Darío is going to visit the "new" basilica, as he will note later, which was not fully completed until 1931, but parts of which were completed by 1900, when he visited it.

have poured in from every corner of the globe. They come here
to visit sanctuaries, kiss stones, admire temples, and, more than
anything, see a little ivory-colored old gentleman (barely able
to raise his almost hundred-year-old right hand) sketch in the
air, in the immense basilica, the sign of a papal blessing.

And all of them bring gold, whether much or little, which
will remain in the Holy City, in the treasuries of the Vicar of
Christ and King of Rome—contributions from the greater part
of humanity. Oh, the de Savoies[103] know very well that that
mysterious white dove must be kept locked up tight in his
colossal marble and gold cage!

At the door of St. Paul's, the new basilica, I see the same mob
scenes repeated. Everyone shoves to get in first, as though free
samples of something were being passed out inside and they had
to get in before closing time. I, too, make a lever of my elbows
and shoulders, and all attentive—*Beware of pickpockets!*—I am
in! Enormous basilica, filled with luxury and happy spirit. Gold,
mosaics, columns of majestic elegance: wide, bright naves. These
magnificent things keep prayer a bit at arm's length, of course,
and one cannot help but think of an orchestra about to launch
into a waltz, or the foyer of a stupendous café-concert hall.
Teeming throngs on the polished floor tiles, admiring, calculat-
ing, fixing their eyes on the rich ceiling-work or the pope's
medallions and then unfixing them to stand in awe before the al-
tars, the craftsmanship, the marmoreal portraits. And the univer-
sal question: I wonder how much all this cost? But the answer is
in their pocket. The priests, shepherds to their various groups of
pilgrims, lead their flocks here and there, from one point of inter-
est to another, having some of them pray, some read from guide-
books; some of the cicerones lecture, some do not.

I leave St. Paul's with another spirit than that with which I
entered. . . . St. Paul's is the fin de siècle cathedral, where all
that is lacking is the note of *liberty* in art. When, I wonder,
shall we have the "modern style" basilica? St. Paul's is the club-
church, the tea-room church, the five-o'clock cocktail church.

103. Ruling family of Italy; the king at this time was Umberto II de Savoie,
Umberto I having died in July of 1900.

It is the cathedral of worldly religiosity, where one goes to flirt. An imposing place, indeed. Oh, the serene, severe religious spirit of old cathedrals, made for people of faith in times of piety and fear of God—and how far from these pompous Alhambras, imperial Empires, Casinos to Our Lord! And note that all this corresponds fully to the policies of the Vatican Chancellory—tourism to Lourdes, that sort of thing. Zola was largely right, and one must come here to see it.

To the sound of water falling in the fountains, I enter the vast hemicycle of columns and approach the basilica of basilicas [St. Peter's], which rises gigantically, heavily. It looked very large; as I approach it, it looks even larger. And as I penetrate it and lift my eyes toward the apse, its enormousness presents itself in all its reality. It is a building made for nations. The waves of visitors, which increase at every moment, appear to be no more than small groups moving here and there. Under the cupola, light falls in broad golden streams. The grand baldacchino with its serpentine columns stands magnificently; the railing around the tomb of St. Peter, with its lamps lighted, attracts a crowd of the curious. To one side, the bronze Jupiter, the black St. Peter, with its famous toe, worn away by kisses, receives the endless homage of the groups, who follow one another in infinite procession. The tombs of the popes, with their various chapels and their statues, the fabrics, the magnificent decorations give the sensation of a museum. This sensation increases when one sees visitors everywhere with little opera-glasses, notebooks, manuals, and English, French, and Italian guidebooks. And one word vibrates within you: *Renaissance*. From the black St. Peter to the nightshirt-clad statues, equivocal angels, symbolic virtues, figures made by pagan artists for paganizing popes, everything speaks of that admirable time in which the gods made a pact with Jesus Christ. It was there, then, that faith began to wither and die, the soul to soar ever lower in its ascetic flights.

I love this magnificence, but it does not make me feel, sense the presence of the doctor of humility. . . . Under the dome that rains down light, I feel the Bramantes, the Michelangelos. This pomp is Oriental, it is Solomonic. (Solomon, after all, was more a vizier than a priest.) The white figures of the virtues incite one to caresses more than to prayers, and the cherubs are more Olympian than paradisal. The colored marbles, the white marbles, the onyxes, the agates, the gold, the silver, the gold, the bronze, the gold, and even the crimson hangings—everything speaks of the pride of the earth, the glory of the senses, Caesarean pleasures, a delight in the things of this world. High up there, a phrase: *Tu es Petrus et super hanc petram aedificabo ecclesiam meam.*[104] . . .

October 7, 1900

The Pincio, a path that curls up, around, to the summit of a hill. From a platform there, one has a view of almost all of Rome. Cupolas everywhere, though I cannot be inspired to count the three hundred that one particular traveler, the admirable and exuberant Castelar, recorded. The pathway is not overly crowded at this season; much of Roman society is summering. There are a few carriages, a very few strollers, and, on the benches, the clients that discover the shady spots and parks and tree-lined walks everywhere one goes: the solitary gentleman reading or lost in meditation, the lady dressed in black, perhaps with a melancholy little girl beside her, and, in certain shady corners, under the affectionate trees, children laughing and playing. But here in Rome there is also the young seminarian, the couple of religious students, the venerable figure of an old priest, and, inside his carriage, the silhouette of some Eminence. And then there is the amiable lady who, with more or less luck, is in search of admirers—a lady as distant from the triumphant Parisian "mistress" as she is from her predecessor, the Roman courtesan.

And always in Italy, you find the luxury of marble. Here you will see the illustrious stone carved into bas reliefs at the entrance, statuary all along the monumental steps, and the long series of busts of Terminus throughout the woods and copses. These spots are impregnated as though with the perfumes of

104. "Thou art Peter [*Petrus*], and upon this rock [*petram*] I shall build my church."

love, of readings from breviaries; they are filled with the whispers of worldly conversations. And over there, to one side, by one of the great walls, there is a spot to which death beckons. It is the wall from which suicides leap, the point chosen by the desperate, from which they can erase the nightmare of their lives; it is the refuge of the poor in faith, the prisoners of destiny. Paris has her Seine; London, its Thames; Madrid, its viaduct; Rome—the Pincio wall.

In one corner of the Pincio is the Villa Borghese. Both are entered through the Piazza del Popolo: the Pincio, via the monumental steps; the villa, via a broad door at which a municipal employee stands and collects the entry fee. Even at the gates one can see how vast and harmonious this park is. It is filled with enchanted spots and delicious shady retreats and secluded corners perfect for lovers. Cypresses, ilexes, pines rise tall, evocative, in the vast convent of trees. Crumbling columns, invaded by vines and ivies, illustrated with archaic inscriptions, and temples and fountains of venerable antiquity delight one with their classic grace. One strolls past a structure in the Egyptian style and comes, among pagan figures, flowers, and leaves that stir in the soft sweet breeze, to a lovely lake, composed with lyrical taste, upon which a loggia, reached by a little bridge, stands in the midst of the transparent emerald water that is inhabited, above, by silent swans, below, by schools of rosy trout. On the shore of the lake I see an old painter, copying a place where stalks of water lilies rise. . . . Before me lies a marvelous view, out to the Roman suburbs. From this magnificent lookout one sees valleys and hills and picturesque profiles in a landscape like those favored by magical Leonardo for the background of his paintings. The sun is setting in a soft drowsy haze; the light slowly dies, in an endless twilight sigh. The statues, the peristyles, take on a mysterious splendor of gold and violet. And when I bid my sad farewell to this paradise, and make my way along a new path, I see a luminous fluttering of pheasants. In my poet's spirit, I feel the loving health of the earth, the generosity of nature. The pines, with their aristocratic elegance, raise toward the firmament their thick, dark parasols in a gesture of praise and offering; the cypresses' bow is long and languid;

the centuries-old ilexes display the same nobility as the poems
and paintings of this city. In a second, a past world comes to
life again—a heraldic world of cardinals and royalty and em-
perors and popes, a world of valor, of culture, of strong virtues
and noble vices, a world of crimson, of marble, of iron and
gold, a world that there, in the villa's museum, is eternalized in
the glories of an age of beauty and struggle and life. And it fills
me with real sadness and grief and *bother* that I have to go say
hello to people, to communicate with so many persons that are
strangers to me, to enter once more into the abomination of my
contemporaries. . . . In the Piazza del Popolo I buy a newspa-
per. . .

October 12, 1900

As I leave the Immortal City, to the hoarse noise of the train, I
make an inventory of memories. One, of course, is of an after-
noon spent in the Forum and the Coliseum, the revelation of a
stone, Ruskin's "bread," ruin, a broken column, a gravestone,
a statue, an inscription. . . .

In the Coliseum I recalled that remark by the Goncourts:
"Like a circle-dance suddenly violently interrupted, and with
some of the dancers fallen over on their backs: one entire side
of the Coliseum tumbled to earth." Colossal, cyclopean,
enormous, a place of lions and emperors. And I imagine the an-
cient circusian spectacle to which nothing is comparable today
save perhaps bullfights. The fact is, however, that as I stood be-
fore these ruins—as I had stood earlier before the Aqueduct,
the Cloaca Maxima, the Baths—the usual phrase came to mind:
The work of the Romans. In our days, the Yankees, on account
of their tendency to make, or have, "the biggest one in the
world," claim for themselves that saying. I read, for example, in
an article on the upcoming Exposition in Buffalo, where an
enormous stadium is to be built: "The stadium will offer sports
fanatics the most spacious and splendid arena ever constructed
in the United States. The Athletic Carnival to be held during the
Grand Exposition will be the most remarkable in the history of
sports in the United States, for the finest promoters of athletic

games, contests, and matches in the country have pledged their support. . . ." Rome's Coliseum, built in the first century of the Christian era, is said to have held eighty thousand spectators. The Pan American stadium will be 129 feet longer, though only 10 feet wider, than the historic amphitheater in Rome, but the gladiatorial arena will be larger, so that there will be seats for only twenty-five thousand persons. Such a reaching toward the colossal, the *Coliseum*. But for me there is no hesitation between those fairground "matches" sponsored by egalitarian democracy and the formidable performances in which Caesarean magnificence watered with blood the ground on which the symbolic tree of Christ would be raised.

They say there are tourists who pay to see the Coliseum illuminated with torches, and romantics who go on nights when there is a full moon to remember Eudora and Cymodoce.[105] The first are afflicted with an excess of Baedeker; the second, an excess of anachronism. The Coliseum surprises and overwhelms even in broad daylight, bathed in sunshine—the immense stone armature, the crumbling arches, the walls rent and cracked by centuries, carved by the ceaseless passage of hours, the vast, superb body mutilated by barbarians both ancient and modern.

As I stepped outside the vast amphitheater, there passed before my eyes, like some great insect, a man on a bicycle.

Later, dawn came to the outskirts of Rome, near the enchanted places that gave Poussin his magnificent landscapes. The Tiber ran slowly through hills and the cool countryside. The light had barely begun to creep into the eastern sky; the horizon was tinged with a sweet violet; and a wash of pearl softened a pale eruption of gold. And little by little, hills and countryside were illuminated with progressive splendor. From the earth there rose a haze of life. This was not the poisoned breath of the Pontine Marshes, but a healthful, life-giving respiration. To the soft flight of a breeze impregnated with the perfume of the countryside, the amber grasses and the leaves of the

105. Nereids.

wild anemones trembled, and the fiery star of a fine golden
flower opened on the river's edge. And in a skiff caressed by the
current, we floated on, a dreamy friend and I, upon the waters
that mirrored back the colors of the sky. A solitary fisherman
was mending a net. From the houses nearby came the shrill cry
of a cock. And suddenly, there was a feast, a celebration of sun-
light in the Roman firmament. . . .

And it was a luminous day in the Piazza del Capitolio,
whether before the long stairway to Ara Coeli or before the
Palazzo Cafarelli, among the statues of Castor and Pollux or
alongside the cage of the living she-wolf that embodies the orig-
inal symbol of the city of Romulus. I remembered, as I contem-
plated the statue of Marcus Aurelius, the traditional superstition:
I looked to see whether the statue was becoming more golden,
and whether it might once again be gold from head to toe, at
which point the end of the world would come, accompanied by
the end of the villa no longer eternal, but perishing, like all the
works of man. . . .


# NAPLES

Naples! The Vesuvius is still a pyre worthy of the funeral cere-
monies of Patroclus. Are we truly in the Christian era? One has
to put a strong bridle on one's imagination to think so. The
morning burns, docilely, with an impeccable azure. I have
climbed to the heights crowned by Castel Sant'Elmo, the classic
point from which to look out over the city, so that I may *see
and conquer* before I plunge into that noisy world that whirls
and laughs at my feet. And I tell you, my friends, that we are
under the empire of the Augusti—nothing here reminds one of
the Nazarene's cross, nothing his religion of suffering and an-
guish. This sun, which even in the fullness of autumn roasts the
roses, which flower twice a year, is the same jovial sun that
gilded Seneca's venerable forehead.

The Bay of Naples, softly curving, palpitating, like a swath of
azure silk upon an immense lap, still sings the *cum placidum*

*ventis staret mare,*[106] in its perpetual idyll with the islets of Sirenusa, choirs of fair Oceanides. The brilliant azure of the sky, the historic azure of that immortal sky, mocks the twenty centuries that have passed since in the pious sweetness of Mt. Pausilypus the sweet Mantuan who cooed eclogues[107] lay down for his eternal rest. To its right, the Isle of Capri casts upon the waves glints of aventurine[108] veined with living gold. . . .

106. "When winds had stilled the sea"; from Virgil's Second Eclogue, "Alexis." The lines in this part of the poem speak of the glassy, mirrorlike surface of the sea giving back the image of a lover.
107. Virgil, whose tomb is believed to be here.
108. A translucent quartz spangled throughout with scales of mica or other mineral.

# HAMBURG, OR THE
# LAND OF SWANS

Huysmans has been unfair with Hamburg, and his harsh humor
has been expressed in bitter paragraphs. Clearly, Durtal did not
visit the paradise of swans, and M. Folantin ate badly at two
marks fifty. Hamburg is gay, with almost Latin gaiety, at least so
far as is admissible in a Saxon center. Hamburg is a working,
trading, independent city, with its strict Senate, its factories, its
canals, its grand hotels, its large warehouses, and is also a city
that amuses itself, prettifies itself, flirts with the foreign visitor: it
has a St. Pauli that resembles Montmartre as beer resembles
champagne, open-air cafés on the bank of the Alster, which in
turn is vibrant with yachts and plied by little steamboats—and
on Sunday, comely lasses flirting to the sound of music. It has a
large wealthy neighborhood which some call "Judea," because
powerful Semites enjoy, in their villas and "cottages," the happi-
ness lent by money. Huysmans vents his spleen against men and
women from Caracas whom he found in this commercial empo-
rium. I have found no compatriots of Bolívar, although it is not
unusual to hear Spanish spoken, because the city has many Latin
American residents, and Hamburgians who have returned to set-
tle here with their criollo families after making fortunes in warm
distant lands. Various architectures arise among the green of gar-
dens or beside the orderly tree-lined avenues.

Helkendorf, fresh and flowery, has delicious corners in which
one may rest, court, and daydream, for it is not impossible to en-
gage in that delicate enterprise of dreaming in a city whose in-
habitants, however practical they may be, have a poetic place in a
turn in the river where a large number of swans is maintained
by the public treasury. These poets have no occupation but to

consecrate themselves to beauty, to be white—there are some black ones—and to glide nobly along, with the dignity bequeathed them by Jupiter. They meet those obligations most exactingly, and besides the daily ration put out for them by their keepers, the public gratifies them with bits of bread. The pool is crystalline, the river bank carpeted with flowers; the golden afternoons rain a magical grace over that divine spectacle that would put even Doctor Tribulat Bonhomet into a meditative mood. And the lyrical inhabitants of that glassy pond that multiplies their Olympian figures enjoy the sweetest beatitude in the capital of counterfeiters and Teutonic merchants. Although if truth be told, I have felt a bit uneasy when, eating in the company of my friend the Semitic exporter, he has told me, with an air of gluttonous satisfaction, that the swan, like the goose, well-prepared, is—oh!!—so very tasty.

And while we are speaking of lyrical swans, let me tell you that Hamburg has a Montmartre called St. Pauli. . . . Or so I had been told, at least. A Montmartre? . . . For sailors. With one or two cafés of note, where one can eat to the soft music of an orchestra. But otherwise, the theaters are squalid, with *chanteuses* much past their prime, heavy moo-ers of romantic ballads, or skinny Parcae who shriek songs in English or in German. There is not a single cabaret, a single long-haired poet (or a short-haired one, for that matter) who might evoke a memory of Privas, Rictus, or Montoya. In a great working-class auditorium, a military band gives concerts. On the town square, a guignol attracts a large crowd; the electric sign promises marvels, but inside, the entertainment is third-rate and tiresome. But then there are the restaurants, with their sweet soups, their sausages, their braten, and their excellent beers. M. de Folantin in one way was right. But—oh, *Des Esseintes*!—what about the swans?

# THE SECESSION

In 1900, when I visited the Grand Palais to see the section devoted to the Viennese Secession, what I found were quite a number of sincere worshipers of freedom in art, seekers after the new, the strange, if that suited their temperament, or personal interpreters of ancient artistic traditions, all without worldly *blague*,[109] without Montmartrean aestheticisms, without the absurd monstrosities which, among a very few works of talent, were being exhibited at the time by so many wretched painters in the Parisians' Salon des Indépendants. Was the air different in Vienna? Was the struggle for *la vie et la gloire* different there? The fact is that in all the efforts of the artists of the Secession, I sensed a sincerity and a noble independence and a consecration to the ideal and realization of beauty very unlike the extravagant and *arriviste épateurs* that abound in Paris.

In their own building, built and decorated according to the aesthetic tastes and ideas of the organizers of the museum, the work of the Secession is exhibited in the Austrian capital as an undeniable testimony to the tenacity, the energy, and the talent of its pure artists. The museum is an "exceptional" museum, as Vittorio Pica would say. Nothing in it is vulgar or common, and in everything one sees a gift of high grace and a desire for loveliness and a strength of thought that marvelously honor and elevate the Austrian mentality of struggle. Here one sees that there is no attempt to *épater les bourgeois*,[110] but rather offer them a

109. Joking, or irony/sarcasm.
110. *"Épater les bourgeois"* ("shock the bourgeoisie") was a motto of the "art for art's sake" or Decadent movement. These artists, however, are "newcomers," in the sense of those who have not "paid their dues" and are riding the wave of the success of those who have truly innovated.

new revelation of beauty. Here, noble priests show dreams, a life of mystery, and the brush and chisel speak the profundity of the unknown, the arcane depths of our human existences, and the enigma that throbs in all things. Whether synthetic or complicated, they express their meditations and the inner visions, or in a strange symbolic apparatus draw forth an aspect of a possible truth, or make the light of the soul bloom, or crystallize the indecisive and the recondite. And there is frank, open expression, and a disdain for all routine. This is the only museum in the world where not only has the academic fig leaf been destroyed, but men have had the courage to reveal the most private things, the courage not to hide the most hidden—to the point that one recalls certain memorable quartets by Théophile Gautier. The legend has its cultivators. I see a hundred canvases that do not attract me; I will not mention the names of their creators, for they are not on the paintings and I have no time to produce an entire catalog. I will, however, recall potent Franz Metzner, the Austrian Rodin, the creator of that superb marble poem called *The Earth,* and of admirable decorative studies and busts and statues of an imposing and comprehensive originality. Metzner's *The Earth* is exhibited in a special little gallery, decorated only with expressive telamons[111] and its unique, impressive, elegant simplicity. And the figure in which earthly life and rhythm and natural strength is expressed, reposes on its base like the majesty and mystery of a sacred simulacrum. What the Secession has sent to the St. Louis Exposition testifies to the value of its painters, decorators, sculptors, ceramicists, and furniture makers. Ferdinand Andri sends his valiant figures, which in some ways renew archaic Assyrian art; Metzner, his superb creations, his synthetic expressions of the human person; Klimt, his symbolic paintings of such extraordinary workmanship and profound meaning, such as *The Golden Apple, Life Is Combat, Jurisprudence,* and *Philosophy,* which caused such controversy when it was exhibited in Paris at the last Universal Exposition.

I leave the Secession delighted to have found a true temple of

---

111. Human or legendary figures holding up a part of an architectural or artistic element (e.g., an Atlas or a turtle or dragon); "bearers."

art in times when temples of art are in the hands of the merchants, the insincere, the second-rate, the histrionic. And I salute that generous effort, with the hope that in our lands of nascent art the individual energies of the pure, the uncontaminated may come together to make something similar, far from the shoddiness of the schools of limitation and atrophy and the vain fashions that have nothing to do with the eternity of beauty.

# BUDAPEST

Budapest . . . the king . . . Maria Teresa . . . the blue Danube . . . paprika . . . Tokay wine . . . and an old operetta that delighted the years of my childhood, *The Magyars,* in which a chorus sang:

> *Come, gentlemen,*
> *to the fair in Buda,*
> *for today is the day*
> *to buy and sell . . .*

And the colorful apparel with its bright loop-and-button fastenings, its galloons and braid, and the little lay-brother in the convent:

> *Ego sum, ego sum*
> *the little lay-brother of the convent,*
> *Ego sum, furthermore,*
> *the bell-puller and the sacristan.*

And I was enthralled with the dashing city (or rather the twins, the two cities joined by magnificent bridges), its climate, its flowers, its walks, its elegant, modern neighborhood in which almost all the new buildings are *art nouveau,* or Secession, whimsical mansions belonging to the grand aristocracy and the proprietors of huge tracts of the lucrative *puszta.*[112] It is delightful to stroll through the *kiralyi var,*[113] and to admire the

112. The Hungarian steppes, where herds of horses are raised.
113. The royal palace, located on a hill above the old city of Buda.

city's palaces and greenery beside the blue waters of the bur-
bling river. There are splendid edifices, such as the magnificent
Parliament building, which is reflected in the Danube. The
city's broad squares, streets, and avenues, and, above all, the
most beautiful women in the world make this place seem an
earthly paradise. Oh! every country has lovely places and beau-
tiful women, but the city of love and loveliness, believe me, is
Budapest. There is one spot, in a suburb of the city of Pest,
which is called Ó Buda Vára[114]—garden, walks, an evening fair
filled with attractions, little theaters, kiosks selling all manner
of things, glowing castles, flowers, perfumes, national songs,
picturesque apparel—and there, I have seen a collection of
beauties that would have set King Solomon himself (a man
known for his exquisite taste) to meditating.

There has been one particular moment of national mourning—
or more than mourning, glorification, apotheosis: the death of
Jokai. Filled with the enchantments of this fascinating city, I at-
tended the funeral ceremonies for its poet, its novelist, its na-
tional philosopher. The funeral cars laden with wreaths of
flowers passed down Andrassy, on which the poet had, in life,
resided; the cortége was solemn and magnificent. Representatives
of the government attended the ceremony at which the memory
of the old revolutionary was honored; colorful, picturesque
uniforms of all types—military, university, heraldic—filed by in
strict and rigorous procession. And on the balconies above,
adorned with black crepe, there stood a multitude, with divine
faces out of which gleamed marvelous Hungarian eyes. And at
that splendor, that wonder of feminine beauty, when the coach
with the freshest wreaths passed by—sent by the city's students—
I bought a bunch of roses from a flower seller and, unknown
poet from a distant land, with beating heart, in a shiver of emo-
tion, I, too, tossed my offering to old Jokai.

114. The old Buda "citadel," the oldest part of the city.

# APPENDIX
# SELECTED LETTERS

To Dr. Gerónimo Ramírez

My dear friend:
I dedicate this little poem to you, a person who takes such plea-
sure in things of the mysterious Orient, a friend of all things
luxurious and imaginative, someone who is so fond of that style
in Zorrilla's legends that is half pearls and half honey and flow-
ers, to you, my dear Dr., since you are so benevolent with all
that comes from my poor pen. You may remember when you
suggested that I write something along the lines of the piece I
have enclosed. Here it is. I am sorry that it did not turn out as
I had hoped, but, unfortunately, I have been unable to find any
of Theophile Gautier's hashish anywhere. What are we to do!

    Yours always,
    RUBÉN DARÍO


(Managua), May 12, 1886

Rosario:
This is the last letter I will write you. Soon I'll be taking the
steamer to a very distant country and I don't know if I'll return.
Before we're separated, perhaps forever, I take my leave of you
with this letter.

    I met you, perhaps, to my great misfortune. I loved you and I
still love you a great deal. Our personalities are opposites and
despite how much I have loved you, it is necessary that our love

come to an end. And since it would not be possible for me to stop loving you if I saw you all the time and knew how you suffer and how you have suffered, I have made the resolution to leave. It will be very difficult for me to forget you. If you were me, you would understand how I suffer, too. But my trip is arranged and soon I will say farewell to Nicaragua. I always wanted to fulfill our dreams. My conscience is clear, because, as an honest man, I never imagined that I could stain the purity of the woman whom I dreamed of making my wife. God grant that if you come to love another man you will have the same feelings.

I don't know whether I'll be back. I may never return. Who knows? I might die in that foreign land! I go, loving you the same as always. I forgive you for your childishness, that little girl in you, your groundless jealousy. I forgive you for the fact that you have come to doubt how much I have always loved you. If you were to remain as you are now, by moderating your character and your frivolousness, if you could continue in the same way as we did while we were first in love, I would return. I would return to fulfill our desires. You loved me a great deal, but I don't know whether you still love me. Girls and butterflies are so fickle! . . .

If you love another, you will remember me. You'll see. I have no desire but that you be happy.

If, while I am so far away, I were to receive news that you are living peacefully, happily, married to an honest man who loved you, I would be filled with joy and I would remember you sweetly. But if, in Santiago, Chile, I were to hear something to the contrary, some news that, even if I were to imagine it, would make my blood boil, if some friend were to write and say that you couldn't bear to look into my eyes as we once did. . . . I would be ashamed of having placed my love in a woman unworthy of it. But this will not happen, I'm sure.

As God is my witness, I swear to you that the first person I kissed in love was you. . . .

I hope that we can see each other again with the same tenderness as always, remembering how much I loved you and still love you. Good-bye, then, Rosario.

RUBÉN DARÍO

Buenos Aires, February, 1896

Román Mayorga Rivas
San Salvador

. . . And, to be honest, do I have anything to return to? No. Family? Have I by chance ever had a family among all those people with my surname that is mine alone today?

. . . I have a son and a sacred memory: that is my family. "Friends?" you might ask. Well, yes, my childhood friends are the only ones, but they're gone, too. Some have died, others have distanced themselves. Some, when I see them, look at me as if I were a foreigner: they have treated me without the intimacy of our early years. I have discovered a new generation that was still in its infancy when I left.

So, each time I have returned to the land where I was born, I have suffered. Oh, Román, you know about the emotional sadness of my childhood, the sorrows of my youth: you also know, my dear friend, about the painful things that affect me as a man today . . . !

What else can I tell you about myself? That my life is my work. That I have given the press, especially *La Nación,* enough material over the last three years for three or four books. That I continue and will continue in the struggle . . .

RUBÉN DARÍO

Buenos Aires, (early 1896)

To Luis Berisso
Conchera de las Flores,
Gualeguay, Entre Ríos [Argentina]

My dear friend:
It was only a question of time before misfortune struck. The rosy part of life had repeated itself too much. Then came the gray or black part, the continuous parties that caused countless physical ailments and emotional sorrow. From the last time we saw each

other until today, my brain has been on the verge of exploding, my blood nearly paralyzed; pain, fainting spells, a disaster. Then the immense disgust that considers death itself a refuge.

And then, bad news, and betrayal, and again my life grew dark at a time when it was beginning to brighten a little. Today, I was unable to eat with Doctor Iraizos because I was too sick. I have been alone, completely alone, at a time when this was least advisable. And letters that arrive, bringing terrible news, and things that I regret, and rumors and bad things!

Tomorrow, Sunday, some conversation with you would do me good. I have thought about priests, I have thought about dying—it would be for the best!—and I have gone through some horrible hours.

I need to go to some spot in nature, and not breathe this atmosphere. Come early if you can. The letters are the least of my worries; but they are a symptom. I have deceived myself, and when I least expect it, my enemies descend upon me, worse than what happened to Lugones, and I don't even have Lugones' enthusiasm or years of experience.

And then, some lines by Bartrina:

> If I wanted to kill
> my worst enemy,
> I would have to commit suicide.

I will not go to the Ateneo. I will wait for you in my room. Good night! I will get over this somehow. It will be the third night of insomnia and black ideas. God willing, I will see you tomorrow.

RUBÉN DARÍO

To Miguel de Unamuno
Madrid, April 21, 1899

My distinguished friend:
Your letter and then your article found me in bed and so sick that the worst was expected; but, fortunately, this was absurd, and I am back on my feet and happy again.

I believe that our ways of thinking are joined in spite of differences in terms of means and methods. Insofar as Hispanic-American literature is concerned, I am of the opinion, of course, that *there is nothing there,* or at least very little, but what little there is deserves respect. What *there is* is unknown here. Here, what is known is a ridiculous and stupid bulk of work; but there does exist a small, worthwhile core.

With regard to myself, I appreciate your kind judgments, but I think I am still unknown to you just the same. I will confess to you that I do not consider myself a *Latin-American* writer. I wrote about this in an article I was obliged to write when Groussac honored me by writing a critical piece about my work. Prof. Rodó, from the University of Montevideo, has developed this idea more fully than I have. I am including this piece. But I am even less Castillian. I am embarrassed to admit it, but I do not think in Castillian Spanish. Rather, I think in French! Or, better still, I think *ideographically,* which is why my work is not "pure." I am referring to my most recent books. My first works, up to *Azul* . . . , come from an undeniably Spanish stock, at least in their form.

We will speak at greater length in the near future if I follow through on my resolve to visit you in that centuries-old city that attracts me like an ancient grandmother with many stories to tell me.

Sincerely, your friend,
Rubén Darío

P. S. Your beautiful gift is even now on its way to Buenos Aires.

To Juan Ramón Jiménez
Paris, November 20, 1903

My very dear poet:
Each letter from you is a pleasure. And as one who has lost many sympathics and gained enemies for not writing letters, I write to you most willingly. Because, disgusted as I am with

men of letters and with all the nastiness of the so-called literary life, I see in you a true poet with a healthy heart. You see far and fly high, you live in your dream of beauty. For a long time, I have seen up close, to my misfortune, only opportunists, elegant men of malice, fraudulent art, falseness disguised as friendship.

That is why your letters filled with fragrant ideas and pure sentiments are such a comfort to me.

I hope to God that disillusion comes to you as late in life as possible—for it can prove fatal.

I always like your poetry and your prose, your prose and your poetry. *Helios* is full of mental distinction; may your seriousness last and may harmful elements or mediocre things that are simply useful not find their way into your life. One must maintain the greatest orthodoxy in the most ample spirit of freedom. No pink pigs and whoring!

I'm leaving for Barcelona, finally, on the 30th, and from there I will travel to Málaga. I won't pass through Madrid on my way back, but if you want, we can meet in Granada. That would be beautiful and most welcome.

Many thanks to Martínez Sierra, whose progress I have followed with pleasure. Give him my affectionate regards.

And to you, my dear poet, my complete *cariño*.

    RUBÉN DARÍO

To Miguel de Unamuno
Paris, September 5, 1907

My dear friend:
First of all, my response to an allusion you made. I am writing you with a quill [*pluma*] that I pluck out from under my hat.[115] And the first thing I do is complain about not having received your latest book. There might be mental differences between

---

115. In 1916, the year Darío died, Unamuno admitted with regret that he once told Valle-Inclán that one could see the feathers of an Indian protruding from under Darío's hat.

you and me, but it will never be said that I don't recognize in you—especially after reading your most recent work—one of the most powerful minds, not just in Spain, but in the world.

However, I would also appreciate some benevolent words from you regarding my cultural efforts. I would not say that you have been taken seriously at any point in your human career, because those who are born to be national leaders are always, to their great misfortune, victims of something even more serious: the influence of the life that surrounds them. And then, I am one of the few who have seen the poet in you. It doesn't surprise me when people speak of your wisdom or your work as a professor. Your role in the university makes one a believer of these ideas, and one should never scorn the truly convincing power of science. But who, besides the poets, would see the gift of poetry in this kind of man? And in terms of how this relates to me, a consecration of a life such as mine deserves some regard.

The independence and severity of your way of being announce you as a man of justice. Sober and isolated in your family happiness, you should try to understand those who do not have such advantages.

You are a spiritual director. Your concerns about eternal and final matters oblige you to seek justice and kindness. Please, then, be just and good.

*Ex toto corde.*
RUBÉN DARÍO


To Santiago Argüello
Madrid, January 12, 1909


My Dear Santiago:
Thanks for your letter of December 31. I'm glad that *La Torre de Marfil* is being published again, protected now by the Government. I will see about getting friends to contribute, and I will send you what I can. For now, I'm sending you some poems that I published in the *Heraldo* about the catastrophe in Italy.

I really appreciate your good conversations with the General. Others might have had bad ones. In any case, you will understand that, with my character and nerves, it's not very comfortable to live trying to keep my balance perpetually on a tightrope.

I know the person who, with good reason, you call a "boiling pot of intrigues in the circle of our Government." But you're wrong when you speak of my "trusting illusion of a poet's soul and a good man." To believe that I am lost in the clouds is a general mistake, but it wouldn't be a good idea to contradict this too much. *Homo sum*. And, besides, if you take a close look, I'm a little bourgeois. So, don't think that anything that could happen would surprise me. After all, you've seen how I live and what life is like in Madrid. For everything, they give me 1,000 pesetas, and the new Minister of Relations tells me that from that sum official cablegrams must be paid. . . . You might ask, "But why don't you resign?" The answer: So I don't give satisfaction to those you graphically call reptiles. You're no doubt aware that Medina is the person who pays my salary. Well, for the last four months, I haven't received a cent! All this time I've had to use my scarce resources, that barely cover me as Rubén Darío, to maintain the decorum of the Ministry of Nicaragua before his Royal Catholic Majesty. And what if I were to tell you that I had to sell (at a terribly low price) a copy of *Páginas escogidas* and my piano in order to make do in this situation? Despite the dignity of the position and the official treatment, this is all hardly enviable, as you can see. I've stopped asking and I don't complain, but I am keeping records of my expenses in case something happens later.

On to an urgent matter. My book entitled *El viaje a Nicaragua,* which, for a long time, has been appearing in *La Nación* in Buenos Aires, will soon appear [in Spanish and] simultaneously in London. I'm talking about everything. Naturally, in the sections on intellectuals, I write a great deal about you. For the English edition, which will be illustrated, I need you to send to me, as soon as possible, photographs of landscapes, monuments, and national personalities. I have a good portrait of you. But I don't have any of the President, or

Luis, or other people. I also need some portraits of beautiful women. So, please send me one of doña Blanca and others, of course, beginning the list with your house. This is a rush job since I have already signed a contract with the editor.

I also urge you, as my friend, to send me *La isla de oro,* which remained with you and from which you published a chapter.

I haven't heard anything from Luis. I sent him an urgent cable, which he answered, promising a letter. I hope to God that his silence doesn't have anything to do with some family sickness.

Wishing you happiness, and with cordial greetings to your family, I remain fraternally yours,

    RUBÉN DARÍO

Madrid, June 11, 1908

Dr. D. Rodolfo Espinosa
Minister of Foreign Relations, Managua

I have the honor of communicating to Your Excellency that, after a short stay in Paris, I moved to Madrid and took up provisional residence in the Gran Hotel de Paris.

On the day following my arrival, I made the indispensable calls to the Secretary of State and to the Introducer of Embassadors, both of whom returned them immediately. On June 2, the day indicated by his Royal Majesty the King, according to communications I received through the office of the Secretary of State, on the 1st of the current month, at 7:45 P.M., I was received in a solemn Audience for the presentation of my Credentials as Resident Minister of the Republic of Nicaragua in this Court. From the Royal Palace, two coaches were sent, in keeping with standard protocol—one of half-gala, which corresponds to my position as Resident Minister, and another out of respect. Immediately, the committee was organized in the Hotel de Paris, and I went in the first coach, accompanied by the Introducer of Embassadors and the Head Stableman.

I returned to my residence, where I showed them the honors that put an end to the ceremony.

Afterwards, I made the usual call to the Secretary of State, who greeted me with deference.

I requested Audiences from the Secretary of State to greet the princes for an appropriate time in the future. I will not be able to do this until the autumn since they are currently away from Madrid. Upon their return, they will be here only a short time, whereupon they will leave to spend the summer months on the beaches in the north.

I would also like to inform you that the Legation has been installed at Calle Serrano, 27.

Hoping, Mr. Minister, that the first act of my mission meets with the approval of our Supreme Government, I have the honor of submitting this to Your Excellency.

    Sincerely,

    R. D.

 

                                        (September, 1910)

My Dear Manuel Ugarte:

You have an up-to-date knowledge of the events that were provoked in Mexico due to my arrival as a diplomatic representative of Nicaragua at the celebration of the Mexican Centennial as well as the commentaries about this that appeared in *The Times* of London and the press in the U.S.A.

The new government of Nicaragua, in its violent organization, has not had time yet to send me my letter of resignation as Minister before the Spanish Court. I doubt that Nicaragua will be a dependent of the United States. And I say this despite what the newspapers maintain and what the origins of the Nicaraguan revolution that the new government has put in place would lead one to believe. Since I have no desire to be a Yankee, and since the Republic of Argentina has been, for me, my intellectual motherland, and since when I published my *Canto a la Argentina* the press of that beloved country clamored that I be given Argentine *citizenship,* I want to do this, should do it and can indeed become an Argentine citizen.

Since you, my dear friend, have done so much for our Latin America, I am communicating to you my determination to do this.

You know how much I have loved the Río de la Plata and I know that, there, everyone will approve of my preference for the Sun of the South over the Stars of the North.

    RUBÉN DARÍO


                   To Rodolfo Espinosa

                   Legation of Nicaragua
                         Confidential
                        29-12-1911

Your Excellency:

Despite the confidential communications of June 22 and the 11th of the current month, in which I requested that the President of the Republic officially declare my current diplomatic status as representative of our Republic before His Majesty the King of Spain, neither I nor the Spanish Government has received any announcement regarding my resignation. For this reason, I feel obliged to directly inform Your Excellency that this irregular situation has produced consequences that our Government cannot ignore. I cannot remain indifferent either, since this is really about the good name and the credit of the Republic.

However painful it may be, I find myself obliged to break the silence that I had been determined to keep in terms of how this affects me personally, limiting myself to point out, respectfully and as an individual, the disdainful role played by our country[. . .]concerning the aforementioned lack of official documentation regarding my resignation.

But there is still something more, Mr. Minister.

When I carried out the mission that the previous Government of Nicaragua requested of me in Mexico, I was forced, due to the anomalous circumstances, to compromise my personal credit to the sum of 20,000 pesetas, money that was used to pay my salary as Minister. I mention this especially since the Government of General Zelaya already owed me three months of wages. From that time to this very day, I have received as an allotment for my trip to Mexico only 5,000 francs that the ex-Minister in Paris, Don Crisanto Medina gave me.

If I had the money to cover this debt to individuals, some of whom are foreigners, I would gladly sacrifice it for the good name of the Republic. But, unfortunately, this is not the case, and my creditors threaten to take the matter to court.

If this were to happen, I would have no choice but to transfer to them my credit with this republic, which, officially speaking, currently owes me twenty-nine months of salary that I have not received. I reiterate that neither I nor the Spanish Government has yet received any communication regarding my resignation.

In this sense, allow me to direct Your Excellency's attention to this matter, assuring you once again that only the extreme urgency of the situation forces me to take this step, which I sincerely would have preferred to avoid for the convenience of the republic and the tranquility of our Government.

This is also why I have given this note a confidential classification.

I hope that Your Excellency understands this letter and accepts the major concerns I have in keeping with the honor I have of serving you.

Sincerely,

R. D.


To Francisca Sánchez (in Barcelona)
Guatemala, August 12, 1915

My dear Francisca:
I have not written to you sooner because, once again, I have been at death's door. I look like a skeleton and I can barely walk. There have been complications with my illness here. It requires a great deal of care and I'm not supposed to work. I went to

confession. I live on what the President gives me. For months, I haven't earned a thing, and if I can send you money, it's thanks to the nobleness of that woman whom you call my wife,[116] who came when I was about to die upon the advice of the Archbishop of Nicaragua. She is the first one to tell me that my top priority should be taking care of you and our son, and she has lent me money to send you. I have taken the necessary steps to request that the President give me sufficient funds so that you receive a pension each month. If I live, I will always watch over you and Güichín, and if I die, his education will be assured.

You've never had confidence in me. I forgive you. The actions will speak for themselves, whether or not I return to Europe.

Rubén Darío Trigueros[117] was here. He left. He's a scoundrel. I didn't receive the First Communion portrait of Güichín. Tell him that I am going to write and send him more postcards. Be strong. Eat well. Buy some hens. I always remember you and I pray to God for both of you. I will also write to my excellent friend Mr. Terán. But this will be all for today. I embrace you and I will never forget you,

TATAY


P.S. Go to confession and take communion. Now you will be able to do it. Soon I will get more money to send you.


Managua, first week of January, 1916

Mr. Emilio Mitre y Vedia
Director of *La Nación*
Buenos Aires


I find myself in my motherland, sick.
The doctors are all wrong: some think I have tuberculosis, others think it is dropsy, and some even think I'm half-crazy. . . . I really want to get a little better so that I can go to

[116] Rosario Murillo
[117] The poet's firstborn and only child with Rafaela Contreras

the countryside, enjoy the solitude and some good food and ride a burro like Sileno to the sun and feel the breeze in the hills. Or, if I can't recover, I'll opt for the Epicurean life—until I explode! I get exhausted thinking about the situation of my son in Europe, in misery, abandoned. And Francisca! Ah, this is terrible!

I want to thank you for the opportune check you sent, which reached me in New York at a dramatic moment. I will never forget *La Nación* or, you, my noble friend. It makes me cry when I think about never seeing Argentina again! I ask you to watch over my son, alone now. He will be my only heir. I say good-bye to you with the appreciation that I owe you for all your care and attention. I have served *La Nación* with all my thought and also you with my most devoted respect.

RUBÉN DARÍO

# GLOSSARY

Rubén Darío's esthetic constellation extends in every direction: into philosophy, European and Latin American history and politics, the Bible, ancient mythology, geography, academia, literature and the arts. The effort has been made to note significant references that were current in the late nineteenth and early twentieth centuries:

**Achilles:** The petulance of Achilles, ancient Greece's greatest warrior, came close to costing the Greek invaders a victory in their war against Troy. But when his friend and lover Patroclus was killed by Hector, the resultant blood lust of Achilles was sufficient to ensure the downfall of Troy. Of more interest to readers of Darío, perhaps, is the fact that Achilles' sea-goddess mother, Thetis, was a shape-shifter. Her mortal husband Peleus conquered her, according to legend, by holding on to her while she was taking on different forms—everything from animals to fire.

**Actaeon:** In Greek mythology, a hunter who came one day upon Diana, the virgin goddess, as she was bathing in a pool. To punish Actaeon for seeing her naked, Diana changed him into a stag, and he was torn to pieces by his own dogs.

**Aeschylus:** "First and greatest of the three Athenian writers of tragedy, was born at Eleusis 525 B.C. . . . Of the ninety tragedies which he is said to have produced, only seven have come down to us . . . ; in probable order of composition they are *Suppliant Women, Seven against Thebes, Persians, Prometheus Bound, Agamemnon, Libation Bearers, Furies*" (*Lemprière's Classical Dictionary*). Legend has it that Aeschylus was killed when an eagle, mistaking his bald head for a stone, dropped a turtle on it to break the turtle's shell.

**Aesculapius:** God of medicine and healing (from the Greek *Asklepios*), Aesculapius entered Rome as a snake during a pestilence;

hence, the snake twining around a staff became his (and Medicine's) symbol. He was physician to the Argonauts, we are told by Lemprière's Classical Dictionary.

**Alas [y Ureña], Leopoldo [Enrique García] "Clarín":** (Zamora, Spain; 1852–1901) Novelist and literary critic, probably the best-known and most influential critic in Spanish letters of the late nineteenth century. He adopted the *nom de plume* Clarín for his reviews and other, often barbed, commentaries in newspapers and literary magazines. Clarín was relentlessly logical, incisive, and antimystical, and was a kind of astringent to the sometimes syrupy writing and literary appreciations of his time.

**Albertus Magnus:** Albert the Great (c. 1206–1280) of Cologne, a famous Dominican scholastic philosopher, called *doctor universalis*; popular tradition paints Albertus as a great alchemist. He was said to have control over the weather: He threw a garden party for a visiting prince in the middle of the winter. Albertus is also reputed to have constructed a curious automaton, which he invested with the powers of speech and thought. The Android, as it was called, was composed of metals and unknown substances chosen according to the stars and endowed with spiritual qualities by magical formulae and invocations; the labor on it consumed over thirty years. Thomas Aquinas was one of Albertus' Paris students, and he reportedly received all of Albertus' alchemical secrets (including the secret of the Philosopher's Stone, which supposedly changed base metals into gold), but he killed Albertus' Android after the master's death, saying that it was a creature of the devil.

**Alexander:** (356–323 B.C.) Warrior-king of Macedonia who conquered much of the ancient world and founded the Ptolemaic dynasty in Egypt that eventually produced the last Pharaoh, Cleopatra.

**Alomar [y Vilalonga], Gabriel:** (Palma de Mallorca; 1873–1940) Alomar was a Futurist poet who wrote in Catalán; he was also a politician, political theorist, and diplomat. He wrote several books of poetry, including *El futurisme* (1904).

**Alphonse:** (1221–1284) Alphonse X, "the Wise," a medieval Spanish king who wrote poetry and music, fostered Christian, Muslim, and Jewish coexistence, and founded the School of Translators in Toledo.

**Althotas:** This mysterious figure was the mentor and guide to a notorious eighteenth-century "alchemist"/sorcerer and con-man named Count Alessandro di Cagliostro (probably born in Palermo, Italy, as Giuseppe Balsamo). Cagliostro, who claimed not to know who his parents were or how they had died (etc.), told that he had spent his childhood in Arabia, where he was raised under the name Acherat or Acharat; he was attended by four persons, one of whom was the mysterious Althotas. This Althotas led the young "count" on long journeys, initiating him in the occult sciences, and bringing him at last to Europe, where he could practice his arts. In associating Chevreul the chemist with Althotas, Darío is probably alluding to Chevreul's advanced age and the "fact" that in 1774 Althotas claimed to be a hundred years old.

**Amathusia:** *Lemprière's Classical Dictionary* gives the following information on this fabled place: "Amathus, now *Limisso,* a city on the southern side of the island of Cyprus, particularly dedicated to Venus. The island is sometimes called AMATHUSIA, a name not infrequently applied to the goddess of the place." Thus, it is a place from which beautiful women, even goddesses, come.

**Anacreon:** A Greek lyrical poet (born c. 570 B.C.), whose name is used for certain types of odes, either because of their meter or their subject matter, which was generally love and wine. Lemprière gives the following customarily charming information: "He was of a lascivious and intemperate disposition, much given to drinking, and deeply enamoured of a youth called BATHYLLUS. His odes are still extant, and the uncommon sweetness and elegance of his poetry have been the admiration of every age and country. He lived to his 85th year, and, after every excess of pleasure and debauchery, choked himself with a grape stone and expired."

**Andrade, Olegario:** (Brazil; 1839–1882) Poet, journalist, and diplomat, Andrade was born in Brazil but lived almost all his life in Argentina, early in Entre Ríos province and later in Buenos Aires. He began writing as a boy, and he had a distinguished career as a journalist. He had several fallings-out with the governments of Argentina, but was "rehabilitated" under the Autonomist Party and served as a diplomat in Paraguay and Brazil. His *Atlántida: A Hymn to the Future of the Latin Race in the Americas* earned him great recognition at the end of his life, although his poetry had been acclaimed since the mid-1870s.

**Andri, Ferdinand:** (Austria; 1871–1956) Painter, graphic artist, and sculptor who studied at the Vienna Academy and was a member (president from 1905 to 1906) of the "VIENNA SECESSION." He revived fresco painting.

**Antony:** (83–30 B.C.) In 37 B.C. Marcus Antonius, Roman Imperator and soldier, settled in Alexandria as Cleopatra's lover. He gave himself up to pleasure, and after his fleet met defeat at the hands of an invading Roman navy off Actium, committed suicide, under the false impression that Cleopatra was already dead.

**Apollo:** Apollo was the son of Zeus and Leto, and the twin brother of Artemis. He was the god of music, prophecy, religious healing, poetry, and light. A legend exists that he was Hector's father, and that he guided the arrow that killed Achilles. He was the destroyer of rats and locusts, and held sacred the wolf, dolphin, and swan.

**Apuleius:** A Numidian (Africa) Latin poet (125–?), he is most famed for his picaresque novel *The Golden Ass,* in which the hero, turned into an ass, is returned to human shape by Isis. The novel contains an interpolated story of Cupid and Psyche, which is also quite famous and often quoted.

**Aranjuez:** Castilian town, at the confluence of the Tagus and Jarama Rivers. In its Garden of the Island, built for Spanish royalty, are fountains dedicated to Bacchus, Apollo, Neptune, and Cybele.

**Arenal, Concepción:** (Spain; 1820–1893) One of the most outstanding public women of the nineteenth century in Spain, a pioneer of feminism, organizer of the Red Cross in Spain, and a prolific writer for newspapers and other periodicals, as well as a minor novelist, poet, and playwright.

**Aristophanes:** (ca. 450–ca. 385 B.C.) A great Greek comic playwright, famed for his satires of public officials and leaders. Eleven of his plays, the only remnants of the so-called Old Comedy, have come down to modern times; they are marked by ribald ("though never prurient," says one authority) language and situations. Lemprière says the following: "Aristophanes is the greatest comic dramatist in world literature; by his side Molière seems dull and Shakespeare clownish"; not all critics would agree with this assessment.

**Ascasubi, Hilario:** (Argentina; 1807–1875) A journalist and *Gauchesco* poet, known for semi-documentary narrations of gaucho life and long narrative poems such as *Santos Vega,* which tells the story of two twins, one good and one criminal, in the Argentine pampas.

**Atahualpa:** (1502–1533) Last king of the Incas.

**Atlántida:** (*See* ANDRADE, OLEGARIO.)

**Bacchus:** Son of Zeus and Semele. After being struck with madness by the jealous goddess Hera, he wandered the earth until Rhea cured him, and was thereafter dedicated to the cultivation of grape vines. He is the subject of a famous painting by VELÁSQUEZ.

**Banville, Théodore:** (France; 1823–1891) A French poet associated with the PARNASSIANS, Banville was a staunch opponent of the "new realism" in poetry and the novel, and also of the tearful side of Romanticism, although he himself was a late-Romantic. His taste for Greece preceded LÉCONTE DE LISLE, and his work had considerable influence on such poets as MALLARMÉ, VERLAINE, Catulle MENDÈS, François COPPÉE, and Alphonse DAUDET. He espoused the aesthetic of *l'art pour l'art*, art for art's sake.

**Barbey d'Aurevilly, Jules Amédée:** (France; 1808–1889) Writer and critic. Barbey was an aristocrat and monarchist who supported himself by journalism. He admired Balzac and Baudelaire and was a harsh critic of naturalism. His best-remembered book is *Les Diaboliques* (1874), consisting of hallucinatory tales with a satanic motif, and thus Barbey could be considered one of the "decadent" writers of the time.

**Barrabas:** According to the New Testament, the Roman procurator Pontius Pilate was sure that if the Jews of Galilee were given the choice between the release of the infamous thief and murderer Barrabas or of the religious heretic Jesus, they would choose Jesus.

**Barrès, Maurice:** (France; 1862–1923) Nationalist politician and exponent of a theory of radical individualism or "egoïsme," Barrès was perhaps most famous for the trilogy *Le culte de moi* (*The Cult of Myself*), in which he divided the world into the *moi* and the Barbarians. He harbored a deep hatred for Germany, which led him to adopt a xenophobic French nationalism and to become a follower of the notorious General BOULANGER, although his volume of travels in Spain, *Du sang, de la volupté, de la mort,* is remarkable for its perceptiveness and affection for Spain. His style is convoluted and often obscure.

**Bartolomé Esteban:** (*See* MURILLO.)

**Bathyllus:** Lemprière tells us that Bathyllus was "a beautiful youth of Samos, greatly beloved by Polycrates the tyrant, and by ANACREON."

**Batres Montúfar, José:** (San Salvador; 1809–1844) A Guatemalan poet in the classical vein.

**Behety, Matías:** Argentine literary historian and scholar, author of *Historia de la literatura hispanoamericana*.

**Bellerophon:** A prince and accomplished archer who managed to tame the winged horse Pegasus. After he had accidentally killed a man, he had to redeem himself by performing heroic tasks, such as killing the lion-goat-snake monster Chimaera. When he decided to ride Pegasus to Mount Olympus, he was thrown from the horse and crippled, and spent the rest of his life wandering the earth.

**Bello, Andrés:** (Venezuela; 1781–1865) Venezuelan philosopher, grammarian, and poet. Bello spent two different periods in Europe, where he became imbued with the liberating waves of humanism in the early nineteenth century. From 1829 to 1865 he was in charge of reforming the educational system of Chile, and he founded the University of Santiago there. He introduced the ideas of Locke, John Stuart Mill, and Berkeley to Latin America, but perhaps his greatest contribution was philological: the *Grammar of the Castilian Language* (1847), which, with some additions, is still used today. In a debate with Sarmiento, Bello defended neoclassicism against Romanticism, although he himself translated Byron and Hugo. The long poem *Silvas a la agricultura de la zona tórrida* (1826) celebrated nature in a Virgilian manner.

**Benedict Labre, St.:** (1748–1783) A mendicant priest. The *Penguin Dictionary of Saints* indicates that "between 1766 and 1770 [Benedict] made several attempts to join one or other religious order, but was rejected as too young, too delicate, or of insufficiently stable disposition. He then went on pilgrimage to Rome, on foot and begging his way." He wandered about Europe for several years, but beginning in 1774 he remained in Rome, sleeping outdoors and wearing rags until he was forced by ill health to seek a shelter for the poor. He is more like the Eastern wandering holy man than the usual Western saint, but the people of Rome had no doubt of his saintliness, and he was finally canonized in 1881.

**Berthelot, Pierre Eugène Marcelin:** (France; 1827–1907) Berthelot was a distinguished French chemist, one of the founders of modern organic chemistry. He was one of the first to produce organic compounds synthetically (including the carbon compounds methyl alcohol, ethyl alcohol, benzene, and acetylene), thereby playing a major role in dispelling the old theory of a vital force inherent in organic compounds. He also did valuable work in thermochemistry and in explosives. He wrote a text on the history of alchemy.

**Blavatsky, Madame (Helena Petrovna):** (1831–1891) A Russian-born spiritualist medium, magician, and occultist who founded the Theosophical Society; famed for her book *Isis Unveiled*, which was influential around the world, with such writers as W. B. Yeats devoted followers.

**Bloy, Léon:** (France; 1846–1917) Novelist and essayist/critic. Early in his life, under the influence of BARBEY D'AUREVILLY, he turned from his materialistic ways and became a mystic: *Plus on approche de Dieu, plus on est seul. C'est l'infini de la solitude.* Bloy was known above all as a polemicist, a judgment that may to a degree have obscured the fine "poetic" prose of his work, which was influenced by both Romanticism and Symbolism. He was widely quoted (his *bon mots* and well-turned phrases made him often memorable: *"Un* *homme couvert de crimes est toujours intéressant. C'est une cible pour la Miséricorde"*) and his opinions were widely respected, if sometimes feared as well. The *Brelan d'excommuniés* is an essay on the three authors mentioned in "Los Raros: Verlaine": VERLAINE, Barbey d'Aurevilly, and Ernest HELLO.

**Böcklin: "THE ISLE OF THE DEAD":** Arnold Böcklin (1827–1901) was a Swiss-German artist in the German Romantic tradition (heavily atmospheric landscapes, lowering thunderstorms, lonely mountains); late in life he took up the tenets of Symbolism, though in among the landscapes and still lifes he still painted mythological subjects. The painting of the title (at least four versions of which are extant today) depicts a craggy island, with a boatman ferrying a shrouded figure to the afterlife; Dario's prose poem recreates the scene.

**Bonafoux (y Quintero), Luis:** (Spain, b. in France; 1855–1918) Known popularly as "Aramis," Bonafoux was a journalist and polemicist-critic whose ironic and sometimes bitter humor won him the favor of readers.

**Bonhomet, Tribulat:** "Erudite and materialistic" hero of at least one novel (eponymous) and more than one short story by VILLIERS DE L'ISLE DE ADAM.

**Borel, Petrus:** (France; 1809–1859) Pseudonym of Joseph-Pierre Borel D'Hauterive, French novelist, poet, and translator who was trained as an architect but became a writer. He was the most extreme of the *bousingos,* a group of extravagant young Romantic artists and writers; he loathed the bourgeoisie and believed in the hatred of men for one another. Due to his radical ideas and behavior, he was unable (or unwilling) to earn a living as a writer (or anything else), and so Théophile GAUTIER found him a job in the civil service. Borel's works were intended to shock and horrify; today they seem merely melodramatic.

**Boulanger (General), Georges:** (France; 1837–1891) An opponent of the Third Republic, Boulanger's personal ambition led him, after his election to Parliament, to conspire (with royalists and his own followers) to overthrow the Republic. An order for his arrest on charges of treason was issued, however, and he fled the country, dying a suicide some years afterward.

**Braganza, Pedro de:** (Dom Pedro II of Brazil; Portuguese; 1825–1891). (Last) Emperor of Brazil, 1831–89. The son of Pedro I, Pedro II succeeded to the throne at the age of five, on his father's abdication, although he was subject to a regency until he reached his majority in 1840. Pedro had a lifelong interest in science and was a patron of the arts. He opposed slavery, which he gradually phased out of

Brazilian life—outlawing the slave trade in 1850, initiating a process of emancipation in 1871, and finally abolishing slavery altogether in 1888. Under his rule Brazil fought a costly but successful war with Paraguay (1864–70), gaining some territory as a result. Although impartial toward Brazil's rival political groups, Pedro's use of the wide powers given to him by the imperial constitution caused resentment, which, along with dissatisfaction among slave owners, led to his overthrow and the establishment of a republic in 1889. It is interesting that six months before becoming Emperor of Brazil, Pedro sat for one of the first daguerreotypes taken in the New World; his fascination with the process no doubt led to his lifelong interest in science and the applied sciences.

**Buffon, Georges Louis Leclerc de (Comte):** (1707–1788) French naturalist best known for his *Histoire naturelle* in thirty-six volumes (1749–88) and his *Théorie de la terre* (1749). His works deal with the earth, minerals, animals, and humans, and he laid the foundations for nineteenth-century "natural science"; he was perhaps the first to write about a series of geologic stages in the evolution of the earth. He is also known as a remarkable stylist, and in his address to the French Academy in 1753, he proclaimed, "Style is the man."

**Burton, Sir Richard Francis:** (1821–1890) An English explorer and travel writer with an extraordinary facility for languages, Burton threw himself into the life and culture of the Middle East and Africa, and he is famous for passing himself off as a wandering dervish in a pilgrimage to Mecca and Medina (if found out, he faced certain death for the imposture). During his explorations of Africa, Burton discovered Lake Tanganyika; in Arabia, he was so captivated by the storytellers of the *souks* that he undertook to translate the *1001 Nights,* and his translation has become an English-language classic.

**Cafre:** Part of a racist system of categorization used to identify slaves from the eastern part of South Africa. It also described slaves considered by the ruling class to be especially primitive or violent.

**Calamus:** Latin word for reed, from Greek *kalamos*. The hollow stemlike main shaft of a feather, often used for writing with ink.

**Calderón [de la Barca], Pedro:** (1600–1681) Spanish soldier and dramatist who specialized in revenge dramas. The best known of the two hundred plays that he wrote is *Life Is a Dream*.

**Campo, Estanislau del:** (Buenos Aires; 1834–1880) A journalist, soldier, and *gauchesco* poet (disciple of ASCASUBI) whose most famous work is *Fausto,* which is based on a performance of Gounot's opera

*Faust* given in Buenos Aires: a gaucho who goes to the opera believes he has seen an actual act of magic in the theater. This tradition of comic portrayal of the gaucho culminates in José Hernández' *Martín Fierro,* one of the acknowledged masterpieces of Argentine literature.

**Campoamor, Ramón de:** (Asturias, Spain; 1817–1901) A Spanish post-Romantic who had some influence on Darío's poetics. While having a vocation for religious studies, Campoamor finally devoted his life to politics and literature. Even while acting as governor of three Spanish provinces, he produced a considerable body of poetry and literary theory; his *Poetics* argued for a poetry of clarity and ideas, with vivid images and an avoidance of empty "poetizing," in reaction to the effusions of Romanticism.

**Carmañola:** "La Carmañola Americana" is an antimonarchy, revolutionary song that was widely sung in the early nineteenth century when Hispanic America was seeking its independence from Spain.

**Casal, Julián del:** (Cuba; 1863–1893) Modernist poet influenced by GAUTIER, Baudelaire, Zorrilla, and Bécquer. When del Casal's family lost their sugar plantation, the young man became a clerk. He began writing newspaper articles attacking the Spanish government in Cuba. As a poet, he preferred "beauty" to "nature," as he noted in his "Song to Morphine": ". . . artificial joy / which is true life." He can be considered both a Symbolist and a Parnassian, and is sometimes compared to Darío himself with respect to his formal and metrical innovations. He died of tuberculosis at thirty.

**Casas, Ramón:** (Barcelona; 1886–1932) Catalonian painter who early went to Paris to study art, where he apprenticed with the famed Carolus Duran. On his return to Spain, he became fascinated with bullfighting. He, UTRILLO, and RUSIÑOL, with the property's owner Per Romeu, opened the famous bar Els Quatre Gats (four cats, an expression indicating "just a few people"), which became the center for the Barcelona avant-garde. A tireless poster-maker and collaborator in periodicals such as *Pel y Plom* and *Quatre Gats,* he also did many portraits. Picasso was a frequent visitor to Els Quatre Gats, as were other younger artists and important musicians such as Albéniz and Granados.

**Castalia:** Also "Castaly"; a fountain of Parnassus sacred to the Muses; its waters inspired those who drank them with the fire of poetry.

**Cetina, Gutierre de:** (Seville; before 1520–1557?) A poet greatly influenced by the Italians, he translated Petrarch and Ariosto.

**Chamberlain, Joseph:** (British; 1836–1914) British statesman who held many important positions within the British government. In

1895, Chamberlain became colonial secretary; by 1899, Britain was at war in the Transvaal, and Chamberlain's aggressive imperialism proved lethal. The British pursued a scorched-earth policy in South Africa, interning thousands of people in camps. When the war ended, Chamberlain sought a "conciliatory" peace, and indeed the Union of South Africa was formed, although even today, despite often the best intentions of many of its inhabitants, the region continues to be plagued by problems of race and politics. Thus, for South Africa, Chamberlain's legacy is not altogether a happy one.

**Chapelain, Jean:** (France; 1595–1647) French poet and man of letters. Chapelain's father intended him for the law, but his mother determined that he would be a poet (she had known Ronsard), so at an early age he studied Greek and Latin under a tutor while teaching himself Italian and Spanish. He became the tutor to the children of the grand provost of France, and he worked in this position for seventeen years, even coming to manage the provost's vast fortune. His first published work came late, a translation of Mateo Alemán's novel *Guzmán de Alfarache,* and four mediocre original odes, one dedicated to Richelieu. In 1656 he published the first twelve cantos of his remarkably unfortunate epic *La Pucelle ou la France Delivrée* (*The Maiden* [i.e., Joan of Arc], *or France Delivered*), which was roundly satirized by Boileau and others. His reputation as a critic was undamaged, however, and his erudite and general kindliness endeared him to many readers and younger poets. Chapelain is credited with introducing the unities of time, place, and action into French drama.

**Chevreul, Michel-Eugène:** (France; 1786–1889) Very important French chemist who, though renowned for the breadth of his work, is especially known for two lines of research: in chemistry, the constitution of fats, and in physics, the harmony of colors. The former led to practical corollaries such as the establishment of the great industry of stearin candle manufacture, the introduction of glycerine into commerce on a large scale, and, later, the creation of margarine. His position as director of the Gobelins, to which he had been appointed by Louis XVIII, led to important discoveries in both the chemistry of dyeing, previously little understood, and the physics of color and color effect. His great work, "The Law of Simultaneous Contrast of Colours," was published in 1839, setting forth the laws governing changes in intensity of tone and shade or modification of color, and particularly the influence of one color on another in juxtaposition. A practical application of this knowledge, together with practical results from the study of dye-stuffs and the blending of colors in dyeing, served to bring this art to a perfection which, increased again by the variety of dyes obtainable from benzol, has been of the utmost use industrially. Chevreul also participated in many of the philosophical debates of his century. He strongly combated scepticism and materialism, and constantly asserted that the harmony of the universe and nature, and of man's life and place in them, demonstrated a wisdom which he believed must be called Divine.

Chibcha: Wealthy, highly developed indigenous people of the Andes who lived in what is now Colombia. Their religious ceremonies included human sacrifice, and the source of the legend of El Dorado is attributed to them.

Chiron: Born a centaur because Kronos begot him in the shape of a horse. Known for wisdom, justice, and his interest in medicinal herbs. Mentor of Achilles and Jason.

Chorotegan or Nagrandano: Chorotegan: Aboriginal people and language group of Honduras, Nicaragua, and Costa Rica. Little is known of the Chorotega, who were contemporaneous with the Maya to the northwest and inhabited principally the Ulúa River valley and the Mosquito Coast. With other tribes to the south and the Chibcha of Colombia, they formed a cultural link between the peoples of the Andean area and those of Mexico. The Chorotega culture became extinct in the Spanish colonial period. The Nagrandando were a related people.

Clarín: *See* ALAS Y UREÑA, LEOPOLDO ENRIQUE GARCÍA.

Cleopatra: (69–30 B.C.) The last Pharaoh of Egypt, mistress of Caesar, with whom she had a son, and later the ill-fated Marc Antony (Marcus Antonius). Committed suicide with an asp after Antony's death.

Clepsydra: An ancient device that measured time by marking the regulated flow of water through a small opening.

Clorinda: Heroine of a poem by Torquato Tasso (1544–1595), *Jerusalem Liberated,* a romanticized account of the First Crusade (1095–1099), during which parts of the "Holy Land" were seized from their Arab Muslim rulers by western Roman Catholic armies. In the scenes used by Monteverde for his opera, the *Combattimento di Tancredi e Clorinda,* the Western knight Tancredi is in pursuit of Clorinda, a woman disguised as a Muslim warrior (with whom he has already fallen in love). The battle that ensues made Clorinda a proto-feminist hero; the motif was used not just in operas but in paintings, sculptures, and other art works throughout the eighteenth and especially nineteenth centuries.

**Coppée, François:** (France; 1842–1908) French novelist and playwright, archivist of the Comédie-Française for a time. Known for his devout Catholicism. His one-act play *Le passant* won great success, and was the first play in which the great Sarah Berhhardt appeared. In poetry, he is associated with the PARNASSIANS.

**Corbeau (Maître):** Maître Corbeau is "Mister Crow," a character in Jean de la Fontaine's famous French animal fables, who is often outwitted by the fox (Le Renard). Thus, when Darío's character, the crow, swears on Maître Corbeau that "that's the truth," there is some irony: the self-important crow can be deluded by those more subtle than he.

**Coronado, Carolina:** (Spain; 1823–1911) A poet and, to a less successful degree, novelist whose first volume of poetry, published in 1843, won her considerable acclaim. Best known for her love poems, which took love to almost mystical heights.

**Cromwell, Oliver:** (England; 1599–1658) Puritan leader and Lord Protector of the Realm from 1653 to 1658, after his defeat of the Royalists and the beheading of Charles I. He refused to be crowned king but ruled with near-absolute power. He allowed some religious toleration in England and Ireland.

**Cuátemoc:** (1500?–1525) "Descending eagle," more often spelled Cuauhtemoc. Chosen from the monastery school of Calmecac, where he studied military tactics and religion, to become emperor of the Aztecs after Moctezuma and Cuitlahuac were killed in the war against the Spanish invaders, Cuauhtemoc fought valiantly in defense of the Aztec capital, Tenochtitlan, until he was captured by Cortés and hanged on February 28, 1525.

**Cuzco:** The ancient Incan capital. Known to the Incas as Qosqo or Cusco, "navel of the earth," it was founded around 1100 A.D., making it the oldest continuously inhabited city in the western hemisphere. According to Peter Frost, it was a "Holy City, a place of pilgrimage with as much importance to the Quechuas as Mecca has to the Muslims."

**Cybele:** "Great Mother of the Gods," wife of Saturn, also known as Rhea to the Greeks and Ops to the Romans. She is often represented in a chariot drawn by lions, and as such, depicted in a great fountain at an important intersection, is a familiar landmark to visitors and inhabitants of downtown Madrid.

**Cythera:** Southernmost of the Ionian Islands, near which Venus, the goddess of love, arose full-grown from the sea, Cythera served as inspiration for the theme of love in many French poems, ballets, operas, and paintings. "What is that black, sad island?" Baudelaire wrote. "We are told / it's Cythera, famed in songs of old, / trite El Dorado of worn-out roues." ("A Voyage to Cythera," trans. Frederick Morgan.)

**D'Annunzio, Gabriele:** (1836–1938) Italian poet, novelist, and playwright whose works are characterized by fin de siècle decadence, sensuality, pleasure, and what D'Annunzio called "perfect passion," with sybaritic characters who reject the bourgeois ethic. He is famed for his love affair with the actress Eleonora Duse and, late in life, for his support of the Fascist Party.

**Dante Alighieri:** (1265–1321) Florentine soldier, poet, and diplomat, author of *The Divine Comedy*. In 1302 he was sentenced (in absentia) to death by burning at the stake, and spent the last twenty years of his life in exile.

**Darclee, Hariclea:** (Braila, Romania; 1860–1939; d. Bucharest). Darclee was a very famous opera singer (soprano) of the late nineteenth and early twentieth century. She studied in paris with J.-B. Faure and made her debut in 1888 at the Opéra in *Faust*. In 1890 she sang at La Scala in *Le Cid* and was immediately engaged by all the leading Italian theatres. Between 1893 and 1910 she appeared in Moscow, St. Petersburg, Lisbon, Barcelona, Madrid, and Buenos Aires, returning also several times to La Scala. She was especially revered for having created the role of Tosca in Puccini's opera of the same name. The *Grove Dictionary of Music and Musicians* tells us that among "her exceptional qualities were power, beauty of tone, evenness, agility and excellent technique. She was extremely handsome, with a stage presence as elegant as her vocal line. A certain coldness of temperament, however, diminished her conviction in the *verismo* repertory."

**Daudet, Alphonse:** (France; 1840–1897) Novelist of the Naturalist school, noted for keen observation, sympathetic portrayal of character, and vivid presentation of incident. His novels deal with life in Provence and the various social classes of Paris.

**de Laval, Gilles:** (*See* GILLES DE LAVAL.)

**De Lisle, Léconte:** (*See* LECONTE DE LISLE.)

**de Sade, Marquis:** (*See* SADE, DONATIEN ALPHONSE FRANÇOIS, COMTE DE.)

**De Vogüé, Émile-Melchior (Viscount):** (France; 1848–1910) French critic, novelist, and historian who wrote many volumes on a wide variety of subjects, and among other accomplishments is credited with introducing the Russian novel to France in the late nineteenth century. De Vogüé served in the army during the Franco-Prussian War, and when the war ended he entered the diplomatic service, although his heart seems always to have been more in literature than affairs of war or state.

**Decadents, Decadence:** The *Penguin Dictionary of Literary Terms and Literary Theory* tells us that the term "Decadence," in the context to which Darío belongs, is used for "the late 19th century symbolist movement in France, especially French poetry. The movement emphasized the autonomy of art, the need for sensationalism and melodrama, egocentricity, the bizarre, the artificial, art for art's sake, and the superior 'outsider' position of the artist *vis-à-vis* society, particularly middle-class or bourgeois society. Much 'decadent' poetry was preoccupied with personal experience, self-analysis, perversity, elaborate and exotic sensations." Figures allied with this movement were VILLIERS DE L'ISLE-ADAM, RIMBAUD, VERLAINE, and Laforgue. "Disenchantment, world-weariness, and ennui pervaded their work." A DECADENT, then, is a follower of this literary movement.

**Des Esseintes** (*see also* HUYSMANS): The *Penguin Dictionary of Literary Terms* notes that "Huysmans' novel *A rebours* (1884) was what Arthur Symons described as the 'breviary' of the Decadent movement. Des Esseintes, the hero, exemplifies the decadent figure who is consumed by *maladie fin de siècle*. He devotes his energy and intelligence to the replacement of the natural with the unnatural and artificial. His quest was for new and more bizarre sensations."

**Deschamps, Léon:** French critic of art and literature at the turn of the nineteenth and twentieth centuries. In 1889, Deschamps founded the literary review *La Plume*.

**Desmond, Maurice, Earl of:** (Ireland; ?–1355) Second son of Thomas, Maurice rose to earlhood on the early death of his older brother; his birthdate is unclear, though he married in 1312, so undoubtedly it was sometime in the last decade of the thirteenth century. Called "Maurice the Great," Desmond was active in the war against Bruce in Scotland. The mention by Darío has to do with the following event: "In consequence of his having been insultingly termed 'rhymer' by Baron Arnold le Poer, at a public assembly, this Maurice embarked in a fierce intestine strife, the nobles of Ireland banding themselves on the opposite sides. Such ravages were committed that the towns were obliged to provide garrisons for their own protection, and royal writs were issued from England ordering the Le Poers and Geraldines [the family of Maurice] to desist from levying forces for the purpose of attacking each other, but to little purpose" (Alfred Webb, *A Compendium of Irish Biography*, Dublin: M. H. Gill & Sons, 1878, p. 137).

**Díaz Mirón, Salvador:** (Mexico; 1853–1928) Son of the governor of
Veracruz, Díaz Mirón at first seemed to follow in the footsteps of
his father, but then turned to letters. A journalist for many years, at
one point he was deported to New York by the government, but he
returned to follow his profession. He began to write poetry young,
and continued to do so throughout his life. His early poetry, espe-
cially, followed the tenets of Romanticism, with such poems as an
"Ode to Victor Hugo."

**Díaz, Leopoldo:** (Argentina; 1862–1947) Though originally a writer
of fine sonnets, Díaz changed his style completely with the arrival of
Darío in Buenos Aires; *Bajorrelieves* ("Bas-Reliefs," 1895) shows
this influence. His translations, collected in *Traducciones,* intro-
duced Edgar Allan POE, LECONTE DE LISLE, and D'ANNUNZIO to
Latin America. Though he continued to write sonnets, they now
bore the imprint of HEREDIA and other PARNASSIANS.

**Díaz, Porfirio:** (*See* PORFIRIO DÍAZ.)

**Dierx, Léon:** (France; 1838–1912) Born, like LÉCONTE DE LISLE, on
the island of Réunion, Dierx spent a happy childhood in the large
family (ten children) of a merchant trader. He produced his first
verses at age fifteen, and by twenty had published a volume of po-
etry, *Aspirations.* After traveling through North Africa and parts of
Europe to assuage his heart broken by a failed love, Dierx returned
to France and began his life as a poet and young boulevardier. He
frequented the gatherings at the house of Léconte de Lisle, and his
poetry shows some influence by him. Later he became, in fact, one
of the most distinguished of the PARNASSIANS. These early verses
were delicate and profoundly melancholy, and they were very popu-
lar, but when his mercantile family was ruined in 1867 he was
forced to go to work for the French railroad, where he was a writer
for their commercial office. He continued to publish poetry, gaining
more and more renown, and at the death of MALLARMÉ he was
crowned "Prince of Poets." The image he has left is of a hermetic,
misogynist poet.

**Doucet:** The House of Doucet was the oldest of the French *couture*
houses. By the 1870s, the creations of Mme. Doucet had achieved
royal patronage, and the same ladies who were shopping down the
street, at the House of WORTH, were shopping at Doucet's shop at
21, rue de la Paix. The famed designer Jacques Doucet is Mme.
Doucet's son.

**Drumont, Edouard-Adolphe:** (France; 1844–1917) French anti-Semite,
called in a recent publication "the pope of antisemitism," who in
1886 published *La France Juive* (Jews in France). He established a

radical anti-Semitic newspaper, *La Libre Parole,* which spread his vicious ideas. He gained lasting fame as one of the most strident accusers of Dreyfuss in the "Dreyfuss Affair."

**Durtal:** A character in novels by HUYSMANS generally taken to be Huysmans' alter-ego.

**Eheu!:** A Latin word that Horace used to begin one of his odes: *Eheu! fugaces labuntur anni.* (Alas!, our fleeting years pass away.)

**Elciis:** In Victor Hugo's poetic epic *La Légende des siècles* (Legend of the Centuries; 1859), Book XX contains the scene in which the old bald seneschal Elciis speaks for four days to King Oton and his twelve feudal under-kings, some from France, some from Italy and Germany. Oton was "emperor of Germany and king of Arles," and thus extraordinarily powerful and feared, but Elciis was summoned (the reason is not entirely clear) and he "spoke truth to power," comparing the current times to the better times of the past, and discoursing on war and the Church, the King and the people, natural and human disasters, and God.

**Electra:** In Greek mythology, Agamemnon's revengeful daughter.

**Empusa:** Vile, vampirelike creatures in Greek mythology, usually members of the wicked hordes in attendance on Hecate, the mysterious goddess of magic. They were described as demons who could assume from time to time the guise of flesh and blood. The most famous account of their activities was recorded by Philostratus in his *Life of Apollonius of Tyana,* which told of the handsome youth Menippus, who was enticed by an empusa disguised as a Phoenician woman. Confronted by Apollonius, the empusa revealed itself and admitted to fattening up Menippus so that she might devour him. The empusas were also mentioned by ARISTOPHANES.

**Engelhart, Josef:** (Austria; 1864–1941) Painter and sculptor, Engelhart studied at the Academies in Vienna and Munich, spent many years in Paris, traveled extensively in Spain and Italy (from whose paintings there, Darío no doubt takes Engelhart as one who "understands" Spain). He was a founding member of the SECESSION in Vienna; he painted scenes and characters from everyday life in Vienna, and from 1903 also worked as a sculptor there.

**Esteban, Bartolomé:** (*See* MURILLO.)

**Euphorion:** (275–220 B.C.) Lemprière tells us that Euphorion was "a Greek poet of Chalcis in Euboea, in the age of Antiochus the Great. His poems were full of difficult allusions, but Tiberius took him for his model for correct writing, and was so fond of him that he hung his pictures in all the public libraries. Cicero calls him *Obscurum.*"

**Europa:** A Phoenician princess, loved by Zeus. Disguised as a tame white bull, Zeus carried her off across the Mediterranean Sea to Crete, where she bore him several children and married the king. Another version of the myth suggests that Europa was willingly abducted by the King of Crete, who blamed his audacity on Zeus.

**Flamel, Nicholas:** (France; 1330–1418) Nicholas (or Nicolas) Flamel was a French alchemist. His house in Paris, built in 1407, still stands, at 51 rue de Montmorency, where it has been made into a restaurant. Flamel is supposed to have been the most accomplished of the European alchemists. It is claimed that he succeeded at the two magical goals of alchemy: He made the Philosopher's Stone that turns lead into gold, and he and his wife Perenelle achieved immortality. Flamel is supposed to have received a mysterious book from a stranger, full of cabalistic words in Greek and Hebrew. He made the understanding of this text his life's work, traveling to universities in Andalucia to consult with Jewish and Muslim authorities. In Spain, he met a mysterious master who taught him the art of understanding his manuscript. After his return from Spain, Flamel was able to become rich: one source says that "the knowledge that he gained during his travels made him a master of the alchemical art." He became a philanthropist, endowing hospitals and churches. He caused arcane alchemical signs to be written on a tombstone, which is preserved at the Musée de Cluny in Paris. His tomb is empty; some say it was sacked by people in search of his alchemical secrets. On the other hand, if he in fact achieved the secret of immortality, his empty tomb may have another explanation. Nicholas Flamel's story is alluded to in the first Harry Potter book, *Harry Potter and the Philosopher's Stone* (or *Sorcerer's Stone*).

**Folantin, Jean:** Protagonist of HUYSMAN's *A Rebours*. A minor office clerk, Folantin is a middle-aged, unmarried Parisian. He employs a slovenly, thieving servant—Mme. Chabanel, "an old hag, six feet tall, with moustachioed lips and obscene eyes." In Folantin's youth, he frequented prostitutes with disastrous consequences to his fragile health, and now the only thing left in Folantin's life is the question of where he should eat his next evening meal. Folantin earns just enough to allow him to eat at restaurants every evening, but unfortunately, he is doomed to a series of disgusting, unpalatable meals. In an attempt to improve his life (and his meals), Folantin begins haunting various establishments throughout Paris—trying to discover a decent meal for a cheap price. . . .

**France, Anatole:** (*nom de plume* of Jacques Anatole François Thibault; France; 1844–1924) Novelist, poet, and critic, France was known for his worldly sophistication, his refined sensibility in art and literature, his attitude of somewhat ironic detachment, not to say cynicism, and his graceful, witty, allusive writing.

**Frémiet, Emmanuel:** (France; 1824–1910) Sculptor noted for his vigorous portraits of animals, as the text implies. His equestrian statue of Joan of Arc is a landmark in Paris.

**Frémy, Edmond:** (France, 1814–1894) French chemist best known for his discovery of hydrogen fluoride and investigations of fluorine compounds. Among other compounds, Frémy investigated those of iron, tin, and lead. He also studied osmic acid, ozone, the coloring substances of leaves and flowers, and the composition of animal substances. He applied chemistry to the commercial saponification of fats, and to the technology of iron, steel, sulfuric acid, glass, and paper. He tried, but failed, to isolate the element fluorine. He also failed in attempts to make crystals of aluminium oxide, but instead found he could create rubies.

**Galland, Antoine:** (France; 1646–1715) First translator of the *1001 Nights, Arabian Nights, Thousand Nights and a Night,* or *Arabian Nights' Entertainment,* depending on the translation. It was from his translation (serially, 1704–1717) that the first translations appeared in English. All the commentators note that his edition is "expurgated," omitting all references to eroticism or sexual activity.

**Garcilaso [de la Vega]:** (1500–1536) Spanish soldier, lyrical poet, diplomat, confessed adulterer, political exile. He fought in Rhodes and North Africa, and died during an invasion of France.

**"Gaspard de la Nuit":** Prose-poems by French poet [Louis] Aloysius Bertrand (1807–1841); these writings evoke the Middle Ages with innovative images and fantastic subject matter.

**Gautier, Judith:** (France; 1845–1917) Daughter of THÉOPHILE GAUTIER, she was constantly in the presence of Flaubert, GONCOURT, Baudelaire, Gustave Doré, etc., who were her father's visitors. Her first published piece, which earned her the nickname "the Hurricane," was a critique of Baudelaire's translation of Poe's "Eureka." She became interested in Chinese literature and Eastern cultures and incorporated this Orientalism into her own works. In 1866, she married CATULLE MENDÈS, but soon divorced him, saying he was neither a faithful husband nor a good writer. She was greatly admired by many, among them VICTOR HUGO and Richard Wagner (whom she in a way "discovered" for France). The correspondence between Wagner and Gautier seems to indicate that Wagner was passionately in love, though the relationship does not appear to have been consummated; she does, however, seem to be the "muse" for *Parsifal*. A famous portrait of her exists by John Singer Sargent.

**Gautier, Théophile:** (France; 1811–1872) Poet and novelist; in his early career Gautier wrote works dealing with the fantastic and the macabre, while later he stressed the perfection of form, even adopting a poetics of "art for art's sake"; he is a forerunner of the French PARNASSIAN school (*q.v.*). In the context of Darío, he is important for his Orientalist, exotic leanings and his ideology of art and the artist.

**Ghil, René:** (*nom de plume* of Henry Guibert; b. Belgium; lived in France; 1862–1925) Philosophical poet and theorist-manifesto writer of Symbolism, with important and controversial ideas about synaesthesia (he wrote the book on this topic: *Traité du verbe*) and on such ideas as "symbolism and cosmic poetry" and "mystical positivism."

**Gilead:** A mountainous region east of what is now Jordan. The word means "hill of testimony."

**Gilles de Laval, Maréchal de France and Baron de Rais (Rays, Rayx, Retz):** (France; 1404–1440) Also known as Gilles de Rais. A noted soldier, Gilles was at Orléans with Joan of Arc. He was immensely wealthy, and was a patron of music, literature, and the arts. After his military retirement, however, rumors began spreading of satanic and vicious acts perpetrated by the maréchal; when brought to ecclesiastical trial, Gilles confessed to kidnapping more than one hundred children, most boys, and to murdering them after abusing them. For these crimes, he was executed. His attacks of sadism seem to have been irresistible, making him a kind of maniac. He would even sexually abuse the dead bodies of his child victims. He has been associated popularly with "Bluebeard," but this attribution is probably unfounded. Thomas Mann said that Gilles de Rais embodied "the religious greatness of the damned; genius as disease, disease as genius, the type of the afflicted and possessed, where saint and criminal become one." This seems to be the Decadent (and fin-de-siècle) view of such figures as DE SADE, Gilles, RACHILDE, etc., what one might call aesthetic monsters. (For this, see also TAILHADE.) HUYSMAN's novel *Là-Bas* deals with a writer, Durtal, obsessed with the legend of Gilles.

**Gley, Marcel Eugène Emile:** (France; 1857–1930) Professor of physiology in the Faculty of Medicine and Biology, Collège de France, Gley is deemed responsible for *"cette science née d'hier, que les progrès de la morphologie cérébrale et ceux de la physiologie expérimentale ont seuls rendue possible, la psychologie physiologique"* (that science, born just yesterday, which progress in cerebral morphology and experimental physiology have made possible: physiological psychology). Thus Gley is responsible for great strides in "clinical psychology," as it is called today. A street in Paris is named after him.

Gómez Carrillo, Enrique: (*nom de plume* of Enrique Gómez Tible; Guatemala; 1873–1927) Journalist, critic, and novelist. As a reporter for the newspaper *El Imparcial,* Gómez met Darío when Darío arrived in Guatemala, and he hired Darío to write for *El Correo de la Tarde.* Later, in Madrid and Paris, Gómez met and became friends with VERLAINE, LECONTE DE LISLE, and other writers, some of whom influenced his own writings. Aside from his journalistic work, he is perhaps best known for his travel writing, which deals especially with Greece and the East. His novels were not particularly successful, and are derivative of those of PIERRE LOUŸS and Gustave Flaubert.

Goncourt, Edmond (1822–1896) and Jules (1830–1870) de: French novelists, brothers, who often collaborated; they were early leaders of the Naturalist school, and are considered forerunners of Emile Zola and others. They researched their novels' subjects almost obsessively, striving for perfection in the details. They were interesting to Darío not only because of their writings, but also because of their connoisseurship of art and decoration; they were amateur Orientalists, and the first to introduce Japanese art to France.

Góngora [y Argote], Luis de: (1561–1627) Son of a Cordoban bibliophile, Luis de Góngora was raised in an educated, refined family. Leaving his formal studies due to gambling debts and problems with women, he entered religious orders, but was "too much" for his superiors, who sent him traveling throughout Spain. At court, he became chaplain to Philip III and became famous when he published ten romances and a few sonnets in two famous anthologies of the day. While in Madrid, he attacked Lope de Vega (a favorite at court) and QUEVEDO, who counterattacked. Over the long run, however, both Lope and Quevedo came to admire Góngora for the stunning perfection of his verses. Góngora was an exponent of what in his day passed for an "art for art's sake" aesthetic, and he crafted extraordinarily elegant, refined poems.

Gould, Jay: (American; 1836–1932) Speculator and "robber baron." A country-store clerk and surveyor's assistant, Gould rose to control New York City's elevated railroads, the Western Union Telegraph Company, and half the railroad mileage in the Southwest

United States. At the age of twenty-one, with savings of five thousand dollars, he became a speculator, particularly in small railroads. After some years he became a director of the Erie Railroad. Aided by James Fisk and Daniel Drew, he defeated Cornelius Vanderbilt for control of the Erie and manipulated its stocks in his own interest and that of his group, including New York political boss "Boss" Tweed. The Gould-Fisk scheme to corner gold in 1869 caused the Black Friday panic. Public protest forced the Gould group out of the Erie, ending with Gould's expulsion in 1872. He then bought into the Union Pacific and other western railroads. He gained control of four lines that made up the Gould system. For years his name was a symbol of autocratic business practice, and he was widely hated.

**Gourmont, Rémy de:** (France; 1858–1915) Essayist, novelist, playwright, philosopher, and prominent member of the Symbolist movement, influential also on English literature through T. S. Eliot, Ezra Pound, etc. Gourmont cofounded the important Symbolist review *Mercure de France* and published extensively, most importantly on style and aesthetics, often as applied to specific authors. Eliot called him "the perfect critic."

**Goya, Francisco de:** (Spain; 1746–1828) Painter, engraver famous for his *Caprichos* (1796–98), savagely satirical attacks on manners and customs and on abuses in the Catholic Church, and, after the Napoleonic conquest of Spain in 1808, his *Disasters of War.* As a painter, Goya was a portraitist and court painter, employing an early sort of Impressionism (so that he had a great impact on nineteenth-century French painting); as a lithographer, he made bullfighting prints and etchings. Some of his best-known work, such as *Saturn Devouring His Children,* has a ghastly, horrific quality.

**Gracián [y Morales], Baltasar:** (Spain; 1601–1658) Spanish baroque moralist, philosopher, and Jesuit scholar, whose works influenced La Rochefoucauld and, later, Voltaire, NIETZSCHE, and Schopenhauer. Gracián's first book, *The Hero,* criticized Machiavelli and defined the virtues that a great man, or leader, should possess. He was constantly criticizing the institutions of society, including the court, and thus was harshly disciplined by his order; his superiors called him choleric, ill-humored, melancholic. He published many of his works under pseudonyms, due to problems foreseen with censorship. Along with QUEVEDO he became known as an exponent of *conceptismo* (wit), an aesthetics that sought to express witty and original ideas through puns, antitheses, epigrams, twisted metaphors, conceits, and other verbal devices. In *Agudeza y arte de ingenio* (1648; freely translated, *Sharp Wit*) he defined the varieties of literary *agudeza* (ingenuity). Gracián achieved fame with the novel *El criticón,* which examined society and contemporary moral decline.

**Grilo, Antonio:** (Spain; 1845–1906) Applauded at only sixteen as a promising young poet, Grilo, as he was universally known, soon made a name for himself among the nobility. One critic notes that he was "charming, worldly, a great reciter of verses, and the salons of the [Spanish] Restoration opened their doors to him in Madrid, where he poured forth the vacuity of his rhymes. A poet 'of occasions,' his verse is so superficial that the monarchs who favored him with their friendship—Isabel II, Alfonso XII, María Cristina, and Alfonso XIII—knew some of his poems by heart."

**Groussac, Paul:** (b. Toulouse, France; Argentine; 1848–1929) Argentine by adoption, Groussac spent most of his life in Buenos Aires. Novelist and essayist, he was director of the National Library (before Jorge Luis Borges). While there, he founded *La Biblioteca* (The Library), a monthly journal of history, science, art, and literature, and through it and its successor *Anales de la Biblioteca* ("Annals," no doubt following the famed French journal of almost the same name), substantially raised the level of journalism in Argentina.

**Grullo, Pero:** By the fifteenth century, Pero Grullo was a popular folk character, a simpleton whose name is believed to derive from the crane (*grulla*), known for its slow movements, which were thus transferred to slowness of comprehension. The name Pero Grullo is now used for a fact or truth so obvious that even the simplest of understandings can grasp it; declaring that fact or truth is virtually fatuous.

**Guyot, Yves:** (France; 1843–1928) French journalist, politician, and economist who was generally "radical"; that is, he constantly attacked power, whether it be that of the Empire or that of the Republic, and he was several times imprisoned for his writings. In addition to his writings in politics and economy, he composed two satirical novels.

**Haceldama:** In Aramaic, "field of blood"; the name given by the people to the potter's field purchased by the thirty pieces of silver earned by Judas for his betrayal of the Christ, and the place where Judas may have hanged himself.

**Haggard, Rider:** (English; 1856–1926) A writer of suspenseful adventure novels set in exotic locales, usually Africa; known especially for *King Solomon's Mines, Allan Quartermain, She* (1887), and *She's* sequel *Ayesha* (1905). These latter two novels have a beautiful Amazonian heroine, who understandably captivated the imagination of many readers and writers.

**Heinsius, Daniel:** (1580–1655) One of the greatest of the scholars of the Dutch Renaissance, Heinsius was a professor of Greek and Latin, composed poetry and essays in Latin, and translated many classical authors.

**Hello, Ernest:** (France; 1828–1885) French journalist, staunchly Catholic, who founded a journal of Catholic defense but later free-lanced. Published several large religious volumes, among them the *Physiognomies of the Saints* referred to by Darío.

**Hercules:** The son of Zeus and the mortal queen Alcmene, who named him "glorious gift of Hera," after the wife of Zeus. He was renowned for his prodigious feats of strength, one of which was to strangle two snakes sent to his crib by an angry Hera. Hercules also killed the lion of Nemea, and in Book IX of Ovid's *Metamorphoses*, won a memorable battle against a shape-changing sea-god named Achelous which set in motion the revenge-driven death of Achilles.

**Heredia, José María de:** (Cuba; 1842–1905) Son of a Spanish father and French mother, Heredia was educated in France and lived in Paris. He studied law, but soon abandoned it for literature. He was one of the first PARNASSIANS. In 1894 he was named to the French Academy.

**Hermes Trismegistus ("thrice-great Hermes"):** Name originally given by the Neoplatonists to the Egyptian god Thoth, but later applied to the putative author of a body of alchemical and occult writings; thus, a great, if only legendary, alchemist. The French Symbolists reawakened interest in the Hermetic writings (and W. B. Yeats gave them some importance in English-language literature); the writings are an amalgam of Egyptian magical writings, Jewish mysticism, and Platonism.

**Hernández, José:** (Argentina; 1834–1886) The last of the *gauchesco* poets, and author of the famous *Martín Fierro*. Not influential on later literature, but immensely quoted and talked about by both admirers and detractors.

**Herod:** (d. 40 A.D.) Known as Herod Antipas. Tetrarch of Galilee, son of Herod the Great. He divorced his wife in order to marry his niece, HERODIAS, who was also the ex-wife of his own half-brother. According to the Gospel of Mark, John the Baptist criticized the king for this marriage, and was consequently killed. Herod ended his life in exile in Gaul.

**Herodias:** Matthew 14, 1–10: "For Herod had laid hold on John, and bound him and put him in prison for Herodias' sake, his brother Philip's wife. For John said unto him, It is not lawful for thee to have her. And when he would have put him to death, he feared the multitude, because they counted him as a prophet."

**Hugo, Victor Marie:** (1802–1885) French poet, novelist, dramatist, and leader of the Romantic movement in France. Unquestionably one of the greatest writers of the nineteenth century in European literature, and one of the greatest ever in France, Hugo as a poet experimented with rhythms and language, yet, spurning any idea of "art for art's sake," he believed in the poet's responsibility as a leader of the people (a Romantic notion *par excellence*). His novels today strike most readers as quite melodramatic, but they are concerned with the great drama to be found in the lives of common people (in novels such as *Les Miserables, The Hunchback of Notre Dame,* etc.). As a playwright, he broke from classicism and asserted the poet's right to experiment with mixtures of the comic and tragic (seen much in Darío), the use of colloquial dialogue, etc. Plays include *Hernani, Ruy Blas, Le Roi s'amuse* (which became Verdi's *Rigoletto*), and *Cromwell* (mentioned by Darío), whose preface became a manifesto for Romantic drama.

**Huysmans, Joris Karl:** (1847–1907) A Frenchman of Dutch ancestry, Huysmans was the leader of the French DECADENTS (*q.v.*). He himself was neurasthenic and perverse in his tastes, and his works are marked by an exquisite sensitivity, with fantastic descriptions, a great deal of the exaggerated and grotesque, and, when "naturalistic," sordid settings and situations. Today he is perhaps best known for his semi-autobiographical work *Là-Bas* and his novel *A Rebours* (*Against the Grain*), whose hero DES ESSEINTES, sick with ennui, goes in search of the rare and perverse and finds it in perfumes, music, painting, circus acrobats, and medieval Latin literature.

**Hypsipyla:** Although Hipsipyle was a queen of Lemnos who is associated with Jason and the Argonauts, the reference in "Böklin" is to a brown-winged moth, Hypsipyla, which actually is a pest, harmful especially to the South and Central American mahogany tree.

**Jaimes Freire, Ricardo:** (Bolivia, nationalized Argentina, 1916; 1868–1933) One of the "second" generation of *modernista* followers of Darío, Jaimes Freire was an ardent experimenter with rhythms in verse and with *vers libre*; he wrote a manual of versification in Spanish in which he concluded that free verse should be the basis of all poetry written in Spanish. In 1894, with Darío, whom he

GLOSSARY 627

considered his teacher and mentor, he founded the influential *Revista de América*. He was also a great friend of the master poet LEOPOLDO LUGONES.

**James [St.]:** (d. 44 A.D.) Santiago Matamoros, St. James the Moor-Killer, was an early Christian martyr called in a vision from his tomb to help the Christian population of Spain resist the Moorish invasion of 711.

**Janus:** Two-faced Roman god (or Numen) of gates and doors, beginnings and endings. He is represented with a double-faced head, each side looking in opposite directions.

**Jason:** In Greek mythology, a warrior-prince who led the Argonauts on their quest for the Golden Fleece. The victim of a hereditary struggle over the throne of Thessaly, Jason was raised in exile by the wife of the centaur Chiron, who taught him the art of medicine.

**Jiménez, Juan Ramón:** (1881–1957) Exiled Spanish poet who won the Nobel Prize in 1956 while living in Puerto Rico. Darío and Jiménez were lifelong friends and correspondents.

**Jokai, Maurus:** (1825–1904) Hungarian nationalist, novelist and poet. The 1911 *Encyclopaedia Britannica* describes him in this way: "Jokai was an arch-romantic, with a perfervid Oriental imagination, and humour of the purest, rarest description. If one can imagine a combination, in almost equal parts, of Walter Scott, William Beckford, Dumas père, and Charles Dickens, together with the native originality of an ardent Magyar, one may perhaps form a fair idea of the great Hungarian romancer's indisputable genius."

**Joris-Karl:** (*See* HUYSMANS.)

**Junín:** Site of a famous battle in the South American wars of independence; the Battle of Junín took place in the then-department of Peru, where, on August 6, 1824, a cavalry engagement was fought between Simón Bolívar's nationalist forces and the royalist forces under José de Canterac. The tide was turning against the independence forces until the royalist rear was attacked by a force of Hussars under the command of Isidoro Suárez—coincidentally, one of the forebears of Jorge Luis Borges.

**Klimt, Gustav:** (Austria; 1862–1918) The principal exponent of the *Jugendstil* ("young style," which in France was called Art Nouveau) and one of the founders of the Vienna SECESSION and the Wiener Werkstätte. Though essentially a decorator, his paintings after 1898, influenced by Japanese art and some modern painters, have become touchstones of the Art Nouveau and Secessionist schools.

**Krafft-Ebing, Richard Freiherr von:** (Germany; 1840–1902) German psychiatrist who wrote the (in)famous *Psychopathia Sexualis*

(1886), a study of sexual perversity dealing with fetishism, sadism, masochism, etc. Born in Mannheim and educated in Prague, Krafft-Ebing studied medicine at Heidelberg. After specializing in psychiatry, he worked in several asylums, but was discouraged by the treatment received by the inmates there and so went into private practice. Many passages in *Psychopathia Sexualis* are written in Latin, "to discourage lay readers." After interviews with many male and female homosexuals, Krafft-Ebing came to the conclusion that homosexuality was not a mental illness or perversion, but he did see it as a psycho-physiological "anomaly" that occurred during gestation of the fetus. In 1901 he rephrased the idea, saying that homosexuality stemmed from a "differentiation" during gestation. This nonpathological position was overshadowed by Freud's, but has now, of course, won the day.

**Laforgue, Jules:** (France; 1860–1887) A Symbolist poet and the "inventor" of *vers libre,* or free verse, Laforgue had considerable influence on Anglo-American Modernist poetry and fiction: Eliot, Pound, Joyce, Stephen Crane, Wallace Stevens.

**Lanier, Sidney:** (U.S.; 1842–1881) A Southerner, like POE, and like Poe concerned especially with musical effects in poetry (though not the "sensationalism" that Poe generally employs in his subject matter); thus, for Darío, Lanier is interesting for his formal poetics and for his poetry itself, which is similar to that of the Pre-Raphaelites, who often employed situations and characters from the English Middle Ages (Arthurian legend, etc.) in a rich and luxuriant style, or rather heavily moralizing Christian messages.

**Larva:** In Latin, "evil spirit, demon, devil"; this is a word that corresponds to the modern "ghost," but with more sinister implications. Because in Middle Latin the word came to signify a (terrifying) mask, it came to be used for the "larval" stage of insects, the mask before the true form was revealed. Here, however, Darío is casting back to Old Latin to mean a specter or horrible night creature.

**Laujol, Henri** (*pseudonym of* Henry Roujon): (France; 1853–1914) Though Roujon began studies in the law, he quickly abandoned them for a life as an educator in the Ministry of Public Education; in 1876, he was named to the Bureau of Primary (Elementary) Education. Over the next quarter century, he rose in the ranks of the bureau, and soon was made director of Fine Arts, a position he held until the year of his death. Outside his salaried professional life, Roujon became known as Laujol: He was first a contributor and then editor of the *République des Lettres,* a review founded by Catulle MENDÈS, and was famed for his caustic and humorous book and theater reviews. He also contributed to *Le Figaro* and *Le Temps*. He was made a Commander of the Legion of Honor and elected to the Académie Française.

**Le Gallienne, Richard:** Darío gives this author's name as "Richar" Le Gallienne, but that spelling is erroneous. Le Gallienne (1866–1947) collaborated in *The Yellow Book* series but was, indeed, given to the more "spiritual" aspects of the late Romantic movement.

**Le Poer, Arnold (Sir):** (?–1329) Seneschal of Kilkenny, Ireland, who defended one Dame Alice Kyteler ("the sorceress of Kilkenny") against charges of witchcraft. In the events leading up to the trial, Sir Arnold, an extremely powerful man and probably related to Dame Alice's fourth husband, attempted to persuade the civil and ecclesiastical authorities to stop their investigation of Dame Alice, accused of murdering her three previous husbands, offering sacrifices of animals to demons, consorting with spirits of the air, having an incubus who had carnal knowledge of her, etc. When persuasion didn't work, Sir Arnold resorted to threats, and he did indeed slow the investigation, since the bishop who was leading it was put under arrest by the civil authorities. Meantime, Dame Alice had the bishop cited for attempting to excommunicate her without her having been found guilty of heresy or other crimes or sins. The upshot was that when the bishop appeared in Dublin for his hearing, he and Sir Arnold somehow made peace. Learning of this, Dame Alice fled to England, where she was never heard of again.

**Le Poer, Roger (Sir):** First, one must say that the name Le Poer (Poher, Pore, Poore, Power, Powere) is a very common one, perhaps derived from the various families' status of poverty, or a vow of religious poverty. It is a name of Norman origins, and comes to the English Isles in 1066. Second, there were many Rogers prominent enough to figure in history books within the several (sometimes unrelated) families. One Roger was Lord Chancellor of England from 1135 to 1139. Another is reported to have accompanied Henry II when he invaded Ireland in 1171. One was mayor of Waterford (the city of Waterford was early a part of the Le Poer reward from Henry II) in 1179. Are these all the same person? It is difficult to tell, but any or all of them could be the Roger associated with Strongbow that Darío mentions. Another Roger was born ca. 1275, so he is disqualified from that distinction. The list of Rogers continues. However, there are two Le Poers mentioned in histories as accompanying STRONGBOW, one Roger and one Robert, and a Robert Le Poer is said to be mayor of Waterford in 1179. These waters are too muddy to be fished for these notes. One indisputable datum is that Strongbow went into Ireland in 1172, and all agree that a Le Poer accompanied him, later to be rewarded with huge tracts of land in County Waterford.

**Leconte de Lisle, Charles Marie René:** (France; 1818–1894) PARNASS-IAN poet, author of *Poèmes Barbares, Poèmes Antiques, Poèmes Tragiques*; translator of Theocritus, Homer, AESCHYLUS, Sophocles, Euripides, Horace; playwright. He was twice defeated for inclusion among the giants of the French Academy, but the second time Victor Hugo voted for him so ostentatiously that Leconte is quoted as saying, "Victor Hugo's vote is equivalent to my election; I shall not present my name again." Indeed, he succeeded to Hugo's chair on Hugo's death. His verses are "clear, sonorous, dignified, deliberate in movement, classically correct in rhythm, full of exotic local color, of savage names, of realistic rhetoric" (*Encyclopaedia Britannica*, 1911). "Coldness," however, "cultivated as a kind of artistic distinction, seems to turn all his poetry to marble . . . ; most of [his] poems are little chill epics, in which legend is fossilized."

**Leda:** In Greek mythology, a Spartan queen who was visited by Zeus in the form of a swan; the mother of Clytemnestra, Helen of Troy, Castor, and Pollux. Clytemnestra, in turn, gave birth to Electra, who plotted with her brother Orestes to kill their mother in revenge for the murder of their father, Agamemnon.

**León:** A major Nicaraguan city that Darío considered home. His tomb in the Cathedral of León is a great sculpted lion.

**Lesbos:** Lemprière: "A large island in the Aegean Sea, now known by the name of *Metelin*. . . . The Lesbians were celebrated among the ancients for their skill in music, and their women for their beauty, although the general character of the people was so debauched and dissipated that the epithet of *Lesbian* was often used to signify debauchery and extravagance."

**Loti, Pierre:** (*nom de plume* of Louis Marie Julien Viaud; French; 1850–1923) Loti's career in the French navy took him to many exotic places, which he later used for his novels, written in a sensuous and impressionistic style. It was no doubt his travel romances, rather than the later, more naturalistic works, that attracted Darío's attention; these romances are set in Constantinople, Tahiti, and Japan.

**Louÿs, Pierre:** (*nom de plume* of Pierre Louis; French; 1870–1925) Poet and novelist; Louÿs was a disciple of the PARNASSIAN school. His fiction was intended to shock the bourgeois morality; he was a devotee of form in literature, and wrote one collection of Hellenistic poetry as well as his other, more "decadent" works.

**Lugones, Leopoldo:** (Argentina; 1874–1938) Arguably the *other* most important *modernista* poet, along with Darío. Self-educated, Lugones absorbed many of the literary currents of his time. *The Mountains of Gold* was a Whitmanesque volume that Darío praised very highly. The range of Lugones' poetry is very wide, from baroque sonnets to scientific terminology to Realism to *gauchesco* verse; he was constantly seeking new modes and manners of expression, and his followers, the younger poets of South America, had some difficulty in adapting to the many styles he adopted over his career. His journalism and criticism concentrate on the history and traditions of Argentina, especially the gauchos and their literature. Late in life, he became a Fascist, defining his position in *La hora de España* (*Spain's Hour*).

**Lull, Raymond (Raimundo Llull/Lully/Lullio):** (Mallorca; dates uncertain, given as between 1225 and 1235–ca. 1315–16) Mystic, poet, philosopher, missionary, and recently beatified (by Pius IX in 1847). Late-medieval legends have muddied the biography of Lull (or Llull or Lully), but it is known for a fair certainty that he was born on the island of Mallorca, off Spain, to a wealthy family who had moved to the island from Barcelona (Lull is always thought of as Catalonian, as his patronymic also attests) with James I after James's conquest of the island from the Moors in 1229. Educated as a knight, Lull became seneschal to James II of Mallorca upon James's receiving the island from James I in 1253. At court, Lull was a profligate and a poet, but in 1257 his marriage to Blanca Piany is recorded, and the couple had two children. At about the age of thirty, Lull underwent a true religious conversion, after seeing the Christ crucified several times in a vision, and he conceived the three goals that would dominate the rest of his life: the founding of schools to teach missionaries the Eastern languages; the writing of a book to prove Christian doctrine; and the teaching of the Christian faith among the infidels. While educating himself in the doctrines of the Church (Augustine, Anselm, etc.), Lull learned Arabic from a Muslim slave in Mallorca and also studied at least some popular versions of Islamic theology and philosophy. Lull persuaded the pope, Honorius IV, to establish schools of Eastern languages for missionaries, and then taught at some of them, including Montpellier. He also traveled as a missionary to North Africa and Asia. Over the years, Lull debated and often refuted the Averroists, and wrote treatises on religious topics, such as the attributes of the godhead in his famous *Ars Magna* (whose name has been confused with, or given to, alchemical treatises never written by Lull). In the late thirteenth and early fourteenth centuries, Lull was traveling extensively on missionary and proselytizing expeditions all over the Middle and Near East, and then in about 1302 he set up in Genoa and Montpellier, where

he wrote a number of additional works. In his last years, he unsuc-
cessfully lobbied a series of popes and high Church officials for sup-
port for a crusade, or at least large missionary expeditions. His last
journey was to Tunis, where according to one probably apocryphal
tradition he earned martyrdom by being stoned to death, but from
whence he probably returned, to die at home in Mallorca early in
1316, where he is said to be buried in the convent of the Franciscans.
In the Renaissance, Lull was thought to be the author of many al-
chemical treatises, the first of which appeared, incongruously, six-
teen years after his death. There is a widely circulated and believed
legend which says that Lull went to England to make gold for Ed-
ward III (1312–1377), who would use it to fund a crusade. Suppos-
edly Lull kept his end of the bargain, while Edward reneged on his.
Lull never revealed the process. Thus, Lull's name is inevitably linked
to medieval alchemy, and he is believed to be one of the great mas-
ters, like Albertus Magnus and Hermes Trismegistus, although his
alchemical writings are almost certainly forgeries or misattributions.

**Lully, Jean-Baptiste:** (1632–1687) Italian composer, practicing in
France.

**Mab, Queen Mab:** The "fairies' midwife," notes Brewer's *Dictionary
of Phrase and Fable,* "i.e., employed by the fairies as midwife to de-
liver man's brain of dreams." (This authority also reminds the
reader that "When Mab is called 'queen' it does not mean sovereign,
for Titania as wife of King Oberon was Queen of Faery, but simply
'female' [O.E. *quén* or *cwén,* modern *quean*].") In English literature
Mab is mentioned perhaps most notably by Shakespeare, but she is
also described by Ben Jonson, Herrick, and Drayton.

**Machado, Antonio:** (1875–1939) Spanish lyrical poet. "Am I classic
or romantic?" Machado wrote. "I don't know. / I would leave my
verse as a warrior his blade: / known for the manly hand that made
it glow . . ." (trans. by Willis Barnstone). Machado had a doctorate
in philosophy; his favorite philosopher was Pythagoras.

**Madero, Francisco I.:** (Mexico; 1873–1913) Revolutionary who
served as President of Mexico from 1911 to 1913. Madero, from
one of the richest families in Mexico, of Portuguese descent, was ed-
ucated in Baltimore, Versailles, and at the University of California,
Berkeley. He opposed the dictator PORFIRIO DÍAZ, running for pres-
ident against him in 1910 as candidate for the Anti-Reelectionist
movement. He was arrested in June and then released conditionally
in July. Díaz was declared president, with an improbably massive
majority, in October 1910. Madero refused to recognize the result
of this clearly fraudulent election, and he assumed the provisional

presidency, designating November 20 to be the day on which what was later called the Mexican Revolution would begin. The coup was discovered and Madero fled to San Antonio, Texas, but the Revolution had spread in the north, where Francisco "Pancho" Villa occupied Chihuahua and Ciudad Juárez. The overthrow of Díaz came on May 25, 1911, when Díaz resigned and Madero assumed the presidency. He died in a coup d'etat two years later.

**Maeterlinck, Maurice:** (Belgium; 1862–1949) Winner of the Nobel Prize for Literature in 1911. Maeterlinck's writing (poetry, drama, and essays) is distinguished by a preoccupation with the mystery of existence, expressed through symbolic and somewhat dreamy images and language.

**Maistre, de:** Either Joseph (1754–1821) or his younger brother Xavier (1763–1852), though probably Xavier, who, though not as well known, wrote works that one might, stretching, call journalism: *Voyage autour de ma chambre* (*Voyage around my Room*; sufficiently famous to be alluded to by Borges in "The Aleph"); *Le Prisonniers du Caucase*; *Le Jeune Sibrienne*. Both brothers were anti-Revolutionaries and staunch, even fierce, Catholics; Joseph wrote political theory and was adamantly papist and counter-Enlightenment.

**Malachi:** An Israelite prophet of the fifth century B.C.; one of the "minor" prophets, the last prophet before the coming of John the Baptist four hundred years later; author of the book of Malachi in the Old Testament. Nothing is known of his life.

**Mallarmé, Stéphane:** (France; 1842–1898) Leader of the Symbolists and formulator of the Symbolist theories, though he, in turn, was influenced by Baudelaire, Poe, VERLAINE, and the Pre-Raphaelites. Mallarmé's poetry is characterized by a density and compactness of expression, with unorthodox syntax; it is unfailingly evocative and stirring.

**mandinga:** A descendant of an African slave originally from the Western part of Sudan.

**Manzoni, Alessandro:** (1785–1873) Italian novelist, poet, and playwright, a central figure in Italian Romanticism. Known especially for his historical novel *I promessi sposi*. A religious man, a Catholic, Manzoni was concerned to show the workings of providence in the everyday lives of people. His language was subtle and refined, and it became the model for modern Italian prose. Verdi honored him with the *Manzoni Requiem* (1874).

**Maragall, Joan:** (Catalonia, Spain; 1860–1911) Catalonian *modernista* poet, essayist, and translator, some of whose poems have been set to music to become songs and anthems very well known in

Catalonia and Spain. He was very active in the founding and development of the *modernista* movement in Catalonia, where he and RUSIÑOL were often allies, especially against the attacks of the *Noucentistes*.

**Marat, Jean-Paul:** (1743–1793) French revolutionary who was banished to England for his incendiary writing and later stabbed to death in his bath in Paris by a promonarchist assassin.

**Marcel, Etienne:** (France; 1315–1358) A wealthy, influential French merchant, Marcel was an antiroyalist, and in 1358 he led an uprising against the crown.

**Mardrus, J. C.:** (1868–1949) French Arabist, translator of many works, including (in addition to the *Thousand and One Nights*) "The Queen of Sheba," "The Muslim Paradise," "*Toute-puissance de l'adepte; transcription des hautes texts initiatiques de l'Égypte; le livre de la verité de parole,*" etc. His translation was used by Powys Mathers for Mathers' English translation of the Nights.

**Marinetti, Filippo:** (1876–1944) Marinetti was an Italian poet and publicist associated, as Darío indicates, with the Futurist movement. Unfortunately, "his career reached its apogee in friendship with Mussolini," as the *Penguin Dictionary of Art and Artists* tells us.

**Marquis de Sade:** (*See* SADE.)

**Mars:** Roman god of spring, growth, and fertility, but also of death and war. Reputed to be the father of Romulus and Remus, the founders of Rome.

**Martí, José:** (Cuba; 1853–1895) Martí is known as the "apostle of Cuban independence"; he vehemently opposed Spanish rule over the island, and indeed was killed in an insurrection he helped mount. As a poet, Martí is ardent, romantic, sometimes almost mystical, and is concerned with love, freedom, and death; he is seen as a precursor of *Modernismo* in Latin America. His prose essays are inspiring tributes to his faith in the greatness of Spanish America; he was also a keen critic of U.S. culture and politics.

**Martínez Campos, Arsenio:** (Spanish; 1831–1900) Spanish colonial ruler of Cuba before the Spanish-American War, but resigned before that war took place. He fought not against the Americans, but instead against the Cuban rebels seeking independence from Spain. He resigned in 1896, in acknowledgment of his inability to win against the rebels, and was succeeded by the more heavy-handed Valeriano Weyler. Thus, Martínez Campos was military ruler of Cuba when José Marti's remains were displayed for viewing.

**Maximilian:** (1832–1867) Ferdinand Maximilian Joseph, Archduke of Austria, became Emperor of Mexico when Napoleon III sought to extend French imperial power. Assured a French army, and believing that his appointment had a popular base, the idealistic young aristocrat and his wife, Carlota, were crowned in Mexico City on June 10, 1864. Almost immediately, Maximilian's policies antagonized his backers, as he upheld Benito Juárez's land reforms, educated the Indians and the poor, and encouraged U.S. Confederates to immigrate to Mexico. Too late, he acknowledged that his government was bankrupt. By the spring of 1865, the venture had failed. But when the French finally left Mexico in March of 1867, Maximilian remained behind, refusing to desert "his people" when Juárez and his army returned. Two months later, Maximilian was court-martialed, condemned to death, and executed.

**Mendès, Catulle:** (France; 1841–1909) French poet, critic, and novelist of the PARNASSIAN school. Though born in Bordeaux, he moved early to Paris, where he became notorious after the publication of his *Roman d'une nuit* (1861), which earned him a month's imprisonment and a fine of five hundred francs. His critics claim that his elegant verse is marked more by skillful imitation of other poets than by originality, but he was also well known for his critical writings and his fiction. Some of his work was made into operas, as for example *Ariane*, by Massenet. He married JUDITH GAUTIER, but the marriage did not last. In February of 1909 he was found dead in a railway tunnel in Saint-Germain.

**Menéndez Pelayo, Marcelino:** (Spain; 1856–1912) Recognized by many as the finest critic and historian of literature in nineteenth-century Spain. He produced anthologies in which he introduced and commented on lyrical and classical poetry, as well as countless volumes of erudite literary studies on an immense variety of subjects. One of the most respected academics and men of letters in all of the Spanish-speaking world.

**Mercury:** Messenger of the gods, also known as Hermes, and the god of commerce. Mercury guided mortals such as Orpheus and Dante in their descents into Hades.

**Minerva:** Roman goddess of wisdom, medicine, and the arts, but also of war.

**Mitre, Bartolomé:** (Argentina; 1821–1906) Statesman, general, historian, intellectual. As a young man, Mitre earned the hatred of perennial dictator Juan Manuel Rosas and went into exile in Chile, Bolivia, and Peru, but he returned in 1852 and took part in the overthrow of Rosas led by Urquiza. Mitre opposed joining Buenos

Aires to the new Republic of Argentina, but in 1859 Mitre's troops were defeated by Urquiza's and Buenos Aires was, indeed, made part of the nation. Mitre became governor of the Buenos Aires province in 1860 and the next year became president of the republic. In 1870, he founded the important newspaper *La Nación.* In 1874 and again in 1891 he was defeated in runs for the presidency. He left many historical writings, among them the *Historia de Belgrano y de la independencia argentina* (1857; 1876–77) and the *Historia de San Martín y de la emancipación sudamericana* (1887–1890).

**Moctezuma:** (1466–1520) Aztec emperor during the invasion by Spain.

**Montagne Pelée:** A volcano in Martinique, also known as Mont Pelée, which erupted disastrously in 1902, killing some thirty thousand people. Only two persons are known to have survived. The town of Saint Pierre, once called "Little Paris," was now called the West Indian Pompeii.

**Moréas, Jean:** (b. Athens, naturalized French; 1856–1910) Original name: Iannis Papadiamantopoulos. Moréas went to Paris in 1872, at the age of sixteen. He wrote two volumes of Symbolist verse, *Les Syrtes* (1884) and *Le Pèlerin passionné* (1891). With the publication of *Enone au clair visage* (1894) and *Eriphyle* (1894) Moréas returned to classical style, and in *Les Stances* (1899–1901) and his play *Iphigénie* (1903) he clearly reacted against the new movements in poetry.

**Mucha, Alphonse:** (1860–1939) Born in Moravia (part of later Czechoslovakia), Mucha went to Paris at age seventeen, where he studied for a while, then lived the life (literally) of a starving artist in a garret. In 1895, having created a poster for a play starring the legendary Sarah Bernhardt, he presented his "Art Nouveau" to the Paris public. The poster, *Gismonda,* is one of the most famous posters in history, making both him and Bernhardt icons. He was immensely successful, but always considered his success as for Czechoslovakia, not so much for Paris. Later in life, his *nouveau* art was not so new, and so he fell out of favor, although he was still important enough to be arrested by the Gestapo when they invaded Prague in 1939. Having been subjected to an interrogation and then released, Mucha died at his home some hours later.

**Murillo, Bartolomé Esteban:** (Spain; 1617/18–1682) The leading painter in Seville after Velázquez went to Madrid in 1623. A painter of religious subjects, especially Madonnas and Immaculate Conceptions, in a "warm style," which was followed by a "vaporous style";

his later works, most famously of street urchins, are characterized by a high degree of sentimentalism.

**Myron:** *Lemprière's Classical Dictionary* has the following charming entry on Myron: "A celebrated sculptor of Greece, peculiarly happy in imitating nature. His statue of the Discobolus, a youth throwing the discus, is famous; and he also made a cow so much resembling life, that even bulls were deceived and approached her as if alive, as is frequently mentioned by many epigrams in the [Greek] Anthology. He flourished about 442 years before Christ."

**Nakens, José:** (1841–1926) Spanish journalist, fanatically republican and anticlerical. To combat the Restoration and the influence of the Church in Spanish politics and life generally, in 1881 Nakens established a newspaper, *El Motin* (*The Riot*), which he used to attack all those whom he saw as standing in the way of Spain's return to Republicanism. Indeed, Nakens stated that he sought "a Republic brought forth by force—bloody, hard, avenging," though he never found the man to lead that entity. When the Conservatives came to power, Nakens became their fiercest enemy: over a period of two years, 84 actions were brought against his newspaper for various crimes relating to publishing; its editors were jailed several times; and Nakens himself and others were hit by a total of 17 excommunications issued by various bishops. Due to Nakens' fanaticism, the newspaper fell on hard times; it hardly sold on the street, and there were but a handful of subscribers; Nakens, however, blamed the Republicans, whom he saw as never sufficiently hardline. (That is, he attacked his allies as ferociously as he did his enemies.) Nakens was involved in (some say framed for) the attempted assassination of Alfonso XIII in 1906 (in the least incriminating of the versions of the story he sheltered the young man who planted the bomb) and was sent to prison for two years. This "martyrdom" helped newspaper sales enormously, which skyrocketed to some twenty thousand copies per issue. Subsequently, the newspaper had a number of vicissitudes, but Nakens died at last without much recognition as a creator of the modern state of Spain; his views were simply too harsh, invective-laden, and alienating to be useful in any political way.

**Nebuchadnezzar:** (?–562 B.C.) King of Babylonia who conquered Jerusalem after Zedekiah had entered into an alliance with Egypt, against the advice of his prophet. Zedekiah was captured, blinded, and imprisoned for life.

**Nemea:** An upland valley in central Greece, near the Gulf of Corinth.

**Nephelibata:** Cloud-walker (Greek).

**Nero (Claudius Caesar Augustus Germanicus):** (Rome; 37–68 A.D.) Nero's mother, Agrippina (the younger), was the daughter of Caesar Germanicus and the sister of madman-emperor Caligula, who banished the family. Upon Caligula's death, Agrippina was recalled from exile and later she married her uncle, the emperor Claudius, and persuaded him to adopt Nero, whose name, originally *Lucius Domitius Ahenobarbus,* was changed to reflect his new status. Nero was educated by Lucius Annaeus Seneca, and at the age of twenty-one, in 58 A.D., he married Claudius' daughter, his adoptive sister, Octavia. After Agripinna poisoned Claudius in 54, Nero became emperor. For the first five years of his rule, he was an exemplary ruler, abolishing capital punishment, outlawing bloodshed in the gladiatorial games, reducing taxes, and allowing slaves to take abusive masters to court. He was a patron of the arts and sponsored poetry competitions. In 59, however, he had his mother murdered (after several attempts to poison and strangle her, he finally managed to have her stabbed to death), and in 62 he divorced his wife to marry Poppaea Sabina, his mistress. These were the omens of the remainder of his rule, which was marked by cruelty, outrageous excess, and a hatred of Christians and Christianity. When Rome burned, in 64, he blamed the Christians, and ordered many killed in horrendous ways. In 65, he kicked his pregnant wife Poppaea to death because she had scolded him for coming home late, and a year later he married another woman, whose husband had just been murdered. In 66, he took the boy SPORUS as his lover, supposedly because of his resemblance to Poppaea. By this time, Nero's excesses were about to catch up with him; his enemies both in the Senate and among the general population were growing in number and strength. Finally, even his Praetorian guard turned on him, and the Senate sentenced him to death. In 68, he fled Rome, but eventually committed suicide. His last words are reputed to have been "What an artist the world loses in me."

**Netzahualcóyotl:** (1402–1472) According to Miguel León-Portilla, Netzahuacóyotl of Texcoco was born in the year One-Rabbit and died in the year Six-Flint. As a ruler in pre-Hispanic Mesoamerica, he is known as a poet, architect, legislator, and *tlamatini* (one who knows). In keeping with Nahuatl thought, his poem/songs are like flowers, meditations on human transience and permanence.

**Nicarao:** The indigenous leader who had a famous, sophisticated philosophical dialogue with the Spanish conquistador Gil González Dávila on the shores of Nicaragua's Gran Lago in April, 1523.

**Nietzsche, Friedrich:** (Germany; 1844–1900) Philosopher now perhaps most famous for his theory of the *"Übermensch,"* or superman, which he developed in *Thus Spake Zarathustra.* His work *Beyond Good and Evil* attempts, as does all his work, to go beyond the rational to the irrational. He rejected Christianity ("God is dead"), and was concerned with teaching people how to live in this world rather than prepare for the next. His values, then, were based on "survival," one might say, and he exalted the will to power, along with strength and "virility." These ideas (the race of supermen that would inherit the earth, the notion that "might makes right," etc.) strongly influenced German thought in World War I and the theories of Hitler and the Nazis in World War II. He was insane for the last twelve years of his life.

**Nimrod:** One of the greatest warriors and city-builders of the ancient world. From the cities he founded, Babylon and Nineveh, the Babylonians and Assyrians went on to conquer Israel.

**Nodier, Charles:** (1788–1840) A French Romantic novelist to whom such luminaries as VICTOR HUGO, Alfred de Musset, and Saint-Beuve recognized a debt, Nodier wrote fantastical novels and stories, including some about vampires, ghosts, and fairies (not necessarily all in the same work).

**Nordau, Max:** (1849–1923) Nordau (born Simon Maximilian Suedfeld) was an early Zionist. Attracted by Theodor Herzl's idea for a Jewish state, Nordau labored to found the World Zionist Organization. He achieved fame as a thinker and social critic with the publication of several volumes highly critical of society, religion, government, art, and literature. His works aroused much controversy and continued to be studied and discussed many years after their first appearance. Among his most famous publications are *The Conventional Lies of Our Civilization* (1883), *Paradoxes* (1896), and *Degeneration* (1895). He was a favorite of the authors of *Modernismo.*

**Numa:** Lemprière comes once more to our assistance: "Numa Pompilius, a celebrated philosopher, born at Cures, a village of the Sabines, on the day that Romulus laid the foundation of Rome. He married Tatia, the daughter of Tatius the king of the Sabines, and at her death he retired into the country to devote himself more freely to literary pursuits. At the death of Romulus, the Romans fixed upon him to be their new king, and two senators were sent to acquaint him with the decisions of the senate and of the people. Numa refused their offers, and it was only at the repeated solicitations and prayers of his friends that he was prevailed upon to accept the royalty. The beginning of his reign was popular, and he dismissed the 300 bodyguards that his predecessor had kept around his person, observing that he did not distrust a people who had compelled him to reign over them. He was not, like Romulus, fond of war and military expeditions, but instead applied himself to tame the ferocity of his subjects, to inculcate in their minds a reverence for the Deity, and to quell their dissensions by dividing all the citizens into different classes. He established different orders of priests and taught the Romans not to worship the Deity in images, and from his example no graven or painted statues appeared in the temples or sanctuaries of Rome for upwards of 160 years. *He encouraged the report which was spread of his paying regular visits to the nymph Egeria, and made use of her name to give sanction to the laws and institutions which he had introduced.* He established the college of the vestals, and told the Romans that the safety of the empire depended upon the preservation of the sacred *ancile* or *shield* which, as was generally believed, had dropped down from heaven. He dedicated a temple to Janus, which, during his whole reign, remained shut, as a mark of peace and tranquillity at Rome. Numa died after a reign of 43 years, in which he had given every possible encouragement to the useful arts, and in which he had cultivated peace, 672 B.C." (Emphasis added.)

**Numen:** In Roman mythology, one of a specific list of gods and spirits. Cupid, Janus, Priapus, and Terminus were Numens.

**Núñez de Arce, Gaspar:** (Spain; 1832–1903) Poet, playwright, and journalist, Núñez was sent to cover Spain's African campaign in 1859–60 and became a politician when he returned. In the 1870s he turned to poetry, becoming one of Spain's leading poets. He wrote of social problems and religious doubts.

**Nuño, Alfonso:** (d. 1143) Nuño distinguished himself in successful battles against the Moors in twelfth-century Spain, near Toledo. He built a castle there which he called San Servantes (Cervantes).

**Oceanides:** Sea nymphs. Lemprière has the following entry: "Daughters of Oceanus, from whom they received their name, and the goddess Tethys. They were 3000 according to Apollodorus, who mentions the name of 7 of them. . . . Hesiod speaks of them, and reckons 41. . . . The Oceanides, like the rest of the inferior deities, were honoured with libations and sacrifices. Prayers were offered to them, and they were entreated to protect sailors from storms and dangerous tempests. The Argonauts, before they proceeded on their expedition, made an offering of flour, honey, and oil, on the seashore, to all the deities of the sea, and sacrificed bulls to them, and entreated their protection."

**Oexmelin, Alexandre Olivier:** (France; ca. 1645–ca. 1707) (Last name also given as Exquemeling, Esquemeling.) Author, as Darío notes, of a history of piracy: *Les aventuriers et les bucaniers d'Amérique.*

**Ohnet, Georges:** (France; 1848–1916) French novelist, admirer of Georges Sand and opposed to realism in the modern novel.

**Olympus:** In Greek mythology, home of the gods.

**Ossa upon Pelion:** In the *Odyssey* (XI, 315), when the Giants tried to scale heaven, they set Ossa upon Pelion (or Pelion upon Ossa, depending on how this expression is transmitted) to make a scaling ladder. These are two peaks in Thessaly.

**Oton:** (*See* ELCIIS.)

**Ovid:** (43 B.C.–17 A.D.) "Art for pleasure's sake." At the age of fifty, Publius Ovidius Naso, Roman lawyer and poet, was banished from an easy life in the court of Caesar Augustus to spend his last ten years at Tomi (or Tomis, now Constanta), a seaport in Romania. Ovid found life away from Rome uninspiring, and his final poems and letters are tinged with remorse and sadness. Fortunately he had already completed his masterpiece, a harmonious rendering of Greek and Roman mythology, written in perfect hexameters, that he called the *Metamorphoses.* Darío's swans, beloved by Apollo, are perfect exemplars of the potential for unpredictable and often violent change that Ovid (and Darío) found in all creatures—human, animal, mythological or poetical.

**Palenque:** Mexican village, site of ancient Mayan ruins.

**Palisse, M. de la:** M. de la Palisse is the protagonist of a French song first sung during the sixteenth century. The real de la Palisse was a soldier killed at the battle of Pavie in 1525, under the reign of François I. The jingle sung by the other soldiers went like this: *M. de la Palisse est mort, // Mort devant Pavie. // Un quart d'heure avant sa mort // Il était encore en vie!* (M. de la Palisse is dead / Dead at the battle of Pavie // A quarter of an hour before his death / He was alive as you or me!) As the years passed, more and more verses were added to the song, and it was published in the eighteenth century; now some scholars have documented more than fifty verses.

**Palma, J[osé] J[oaquín]:** (Cuba; 1844–1911) Poet and educator who, after fighting in the War of 1868, fled Cuba and went finally to Guatemala, where he lived out his days. Palma composed the Guatemalan national anthem.

**Pan:** Elemental Greek goatherd, minor deity of mirth, and prankster who allegedly spent his days and nights in drunken revelries with the Maeneds and any other nymphs he could catch, playing his flute.

He dressed himself in virgin white fleece and seduced Semele, goddess of the moon, and reluctantly taught Apollo the art of prophecy.

**Pandora:** "All-gifted," Pandora was the first mortal woman. Each of the gods contributed a favorite trait to her, including an overdose of curiosity from Hera which led her to open the jar or box she had been entrusted with, containing all the evils of the world. When the evils flew out, the legend has it, only Hope remained.

**Paracelsus:** (*nom de plume* of Theophrastus Bombastus von Hohenheim; German; 1490–1541) "Paracelsus" means "above/superior to Celsus," the famous first-century writer and physician. Paracelsus studied alchemy and chemistry and wrote a number of treatises on medical and alchemical processes and theory. He was an innovator, and apparently by nature mistrustful of authority and tradition, which led him into disputes with many of the leading "scientists" of his time.

**Pardo Bazán, Emilia:** (Spain; 1851–1921) Novelist and short story writer; named countess in recognition of her literary achievements. Pardo Bazán was a feminist (which led to the breakup of her marriage) and militated for improvement in the situation of women, especially working women. Her novels and stories are naturalistic, dealing generally with the urban underclasses (for the first time in the history of Spanish literature); her style is polished. Late in life her novels took on religious overtones, perhaps under the influence of the Russians, whom she read approvingly.

**Pardo, Miguel Eduardo:** (Venezuela; 1868–1905) Author of poetry, novels, plays, short stories, and criticism best known for *Todo un pueblo* (1899), a Naturalist social satire of life in Caracas.

**Parnassians:** A group of late-nineteenth-century French poets in reaction to the Romantics. Led by THÉOPHILE GAUTIER, LECONTE DE LISLE, CATULLE MENDÈS, etc., the tenets of the group's aesthetics were that art was an end in itself (art for art's sake, with poetry being almost a religion, an idea that struck many at the time as shockingly "decadent"), that the poet was like a sculptor (hence analogies with the plastic arts), and that poetry should be objective, with the poet's personality or ego eliminated. Some of the forms used were renovations of older forms: the *ballade, rondeau,* and *villanelle,* for example.

**Passerat, Jean:** (1534–1602) Though also known for political satire, French poet Passerat was best known for his charming, lightsome poetry.

**Pasteur, Louis:** (France; 1822–1895) World-renowned French chemist and biologist, who founded the science of microbiology, proved the germ theory of disease, invented the process of pasteurization, and developed vaccines for several diseases, including rabies.

**Patmos:** Volcanic island in the Aegean Sea, where the exiled Christian disciple St. John wrote his Apocalypse (Revelations).

**Payne, John:** (British; 1842–1916) Poet and distinguished translator not just of the *1001 Nights* (1882–84), for which he is famous, but also Boccaccio, French poetry (especially François Villon), and Arabic and Persian texts, including some by Omar Khayyam. Some say his translation of the Nights is a bit ponderous, but it has the virtue of being translated "from the original Arabic," a claim that many English (and other) translators cannot make, as many translations were rendered from GALLAND.

**Pegasus:** Winged horse, born of the sea-foam and the blood of the slaughtered Medusa. When Bellerophon attempted to ride him to heaven, and was thrown off by an angry Zeus, the horse kept on flying and became a constellation.

**Péladan, Joséphin:** (1858–1919) French poet. Born into a Lyonnaise family fascinated by alchemy, magnetism (at the time an "occult" power), homeopathy, science, literature, and Christian mysticism, Péladan became a Rosicrucian and published a novel on occult themes, making him famous. In Paris, he fell in with a group of Occultists and attempted to organize a Rosicrucian chapter there. Interestingly, Péladan organized art shows that became very popular, as they drew heavily on the Pre-Raphaelite and Symbolist schools. Péladan is also known for his writing of mystico-Catholic and occultist poetry.

**Pelion:** (*See* OSSA.)

**Penthesilea:** Queen of the Amazons, slain by Achilles.

**Petronius:** (27–66 A.D.) The Imperator Nero's *arbiter elegantiae,* and alleged author of the *Satyricon,* which described, among other things, the sexual carnival that was Rome. "This is what Romans read for entertainment," writes one commentator. Petronius was once the consul of Bithynia, and then fell into a life of indolence and luxury, often reversing night and day. Betrayed by a rival and arrested, he cut his own wrists. "He made dying a leisurely procedure, attended by festivity. . . ."

**Philegon:** A first-century historian. His *Chronicles* have been lost, but he is mentioned and quoted by Africanus and Origen.

**Phocás:** Darío's nickname for his infant son, Rubén Darío Sánchez, taken from a poem by the French poet Vielé-Griffín. The child died in 1904 from pneumonia.

**Pichot Gironés, Ramón:** (Barcelona; 1872–1925) He began studies in Barcelona and continued them in Paris, and in 1894 he gave his first show in Barcelona, at the Fine Arts Exposition, where he was awarded an Honorable Mention. A painter mainly of local color who was well received by both critics and collectors, he was influenced by Parisian Modernism, which had been introduced to Barcelona by RUSIÑOL and CASAS.

**Pindar:** (522–438 B.C.) "Words have a longer life than deeds." Theban poet-for-hire who wrote paeans, religious hymns, and hundreds of victory odes in honor of winners at various games.

**Pléiade:** A group of young sixteenth-century French poets, with Ronsard and Du Bellay those best remembered today, who sought to renew French poetry through imitation of Greek and Latin writers; they became the models for French Renaissance poetry. Because there were seven poets in the group, Ronsard gave them the name *Pléiade* after the group of stars in the constellation Taurus. By asserting that there is no "pléiade" of *modernista* poets, Darío both rejects the general notion of a school and, by ironically harking back to the renovators of French poetry, admits that there is such a "conspiracy" afoot.

**Poil de Carotte:** Title character in a popular novel (1894) by Jules Renard (1864–1910), Poil de Carotte (carrot-top) was a miserably unhappy child of miserably unhappy-together parents. Renard and others made the novel into a play and several films.

**Porfirio Díaz:** Full name: José de la Cruz PORFIRIO DÍAZ (Mexico; 1830–1915) Dictator who ruled Mexico from 1876 until 1911 (with the exception of one four-year period), Díaz was of Mixtec Indian and Spanish ancestry. An army officer with humble rural roots, he became something of a hero due to his participation in the war against the French, where he won several important victories. In 1876 he overthrew the government of President Sebastián Lerdo de Tejada. Initially, he advanced a platform of reform, using the slogan "No Reelection" (for the President). After appointing himself President on November 29, 1876, he served one term and then dutifully stepped down in favor of Manuel González, one of his underlings. The four-year period that followed was marked by corruption and official incompetence, so that when Díaz declared his candidacy for the next election he was a welcome replacement, and there was no remembrance of his "No Reelection" slogan. In the event, Díaz had the constitution amended, first to allow two terms in office, and then to remove all restrictions on reelections. Díaz embarked on a program of modernization, attempting to bring Mexico up to the level of a modern state. His principal advisers were of a type called *científicos*, akin to modern economists, because they espoused a program of "scientific" modernization.

This included the building of railroad and telegraph lines across the country and the construction of factories in Mexico City. In 1910, elections were held. FRANCISCO I. MADERO ran against Díaz for president. Madero quickly gathered much popular support, but when the official results were announced by the government, Díaz was proclaimed to have been reelected almost unanimously, with Madero garnering only a minuscule number of votes. This massive electoral fraud aroused widespread anger. Madero called for revolt against Díaz, and the Mexican Revolution began. Díaz was forced from office and fled the country in 1911. He died in exile in Paris in 1915; he is buried there in the Cimetière du Montparnasse.

**Poussin, Nicolas:** (France; 1594–1665) The great master of the classic school of painting in Europe (Poussin worked mainly in Rome), Poussin is famed for his paintings of mythological, historical, and religious subjects. His style is incomparably clean and effortless appearing, with his ambition being to approach the calm, measured grace of classical sculpture. Though unquestionably masterful, even virtuoso, and immensely influential, his principles later became the basis of a sterile academicism.

**Pythagoras/Pythagoreanism:** (sixth century B.C.) Greek philosopher and mathematician. Born in Samos, he is sometimes represented as a man of science, sometimes as a preacher of mystical doctrines. Mistrust and jealousy forced him to flee from the religious/scientific community he had founded at Kroton, and he died in exile. The main tenets of his philosophy are that music is related to health; bodies, like musical instruments, are strung to a certain pitch; all things are numbers; and men can be classified as being lovers of wisdom, honor, or gain.

**Quevedo [y Villegas], Francisco de:** (Spain; 1580–1645) Poet, satirist, moralist, novelist, Quevedo is unquestionably one of the greatest and most prolific of Spanish writers. Jorge Luis Borges said that Quevedo was "more than a writer, a vast literature unto himself." He was never, perhaps, as popular as Cervantes or Lope de Vega, no doubt because of his complicated (tortured) style (*conceptismo*; see also GRACIÁN); he was also a master of the grotesque, as shown in his *Sueños* (*Visions*) and *La vida del buscón* (the Swindler).

**Quijano, Alonso:** The "real" name of Don Quixote de la Mancha (the hero of Miguel de Cervantes' famous novel) before he goes mad and begins his adventures; Quijano was a man of the lower, more or less impoverished nobility who lived a quiet life until his reading of chivalric romances convinced him that the world was filled with magi, knights-errant, etc.

**Quillard, Pierre:** (France; 1864–1912) One of the Symbolist/Decadent writers (poet, playwright, and translator) of fin-de-siècle France, he contributed writings to the *Mercure de France* from 1891 to his death. He believed in the relationship between anarchy and art, and was also a graphic artist of some note.

**Rachilde:** (*Nom de plume* of Marguerite Eymery; France; 1860–1953) Rachilde wrote over sixty works of fiction, drama, poetry, memoir, and criticism, including *Monsieur Vénus,* one of the most famous examples of decadent fiction (the novel is filled with sex reversals and steamy eroticism, though it is tame by today's standards). She was closely associated with the literary journal *Mercure de France,* inspired parts of Oscar Wilde's *The Picture of Dorian Gray,* and mingled with all the literary lights of the day.

**Rameau, Jean Philippe:** (France; 1683–1764) Composer and organist.

**Ranvier (Infancy of Bacchus):** Joseph Victor Ranvier, French painter, 1832–1896; the somewhat saccharine painting discussed in this essay was reproduced in lithographs and etchings countless times in the late nineteenth and early twentieth centuries.

**Régnier, Henri de:** (France; 1864–1936) Régnier was a Romantic poet much influenced by the Symbolists; his subjects tended to be classical, though he worked in *vers libre.* He was married to the daughter of famed Cuban poet (Spanish father, French mother) José María Heredia (1842–1905), a PARNASSIAN.

**Renaudot, Eusèbe:** (France; 1648–1720) A distinguished French Orientalist, recognized as possessing more knowledge of Eastern languages than perhaps any other person in France. Friend and sometime collaborator with ANTOINE GALLAND.

**Rhodes, [John] Cecil:** (1853–1902) A British imperialist entrepreneur, now remembered as an exploiter of southern Africa's natural resources and the effective founder of the state of Rhodesia, named after himself. (Southern Rhodesia became an independent African state in 1980 under its current modern name, Zimbabwe, "the big house of stone," after the ancient city, the Great Zimbabwe. Northern Rhodesia is now Zambia.) Rhodes was born the son of a vicar, and he traveled to South Africa as a young man for the benefit of his health. He soon began making a profit off mining the Kimberley diamond mines, and he formed his own company, De Beers Consolidated Mines, in 1888. Although he remained a leading figure in the politics of southern Africa, especially during the Boer War, he was dogged by ill health throughout his relatively short life. As a result of his will, the Rhodes Scholarships, which enable foreign nationals to study at Oxford, came into being.

**Ribera, Jusepe (Giuseppe):** (Spain; 1588–1656) Painter. Though born in Valencia and always signing his works "Jusepe de Ribera, Español," early on Ribera made his way to Italy—first to Rome, where he was taken in by a cardinal who saw him copying the frescos on a palace wall. Later, he went to Caravaggio, an eminently naturalist painter and part of the "Tenebrosi" or Shadow-Painters. When Caravaggio died in 1606, Ribera went to Parma and painted under the influence of Correggio until he finally ended up in Naples, where he spent the rest of his life. Throughout this time he was called *Lo Spagnoletto,* or "Little Spaniard." His work was extremely popular and sought-after, and he became court painter to the Spanish viceroy; in 1644, he was knighted by the pope.

**Robida, Albert:** (France, 1848–1926) Robida was a novelist and illustrator, for more than a decade editor of the popular magazine *La Caricature*. His amusing, satirical drawings reflected *la belle époque,* but he was best known for three futuristic novels in which he, like Jules Verne, predicted what life would be like in the twentieth century. In the case of *Vieux Paris,* however, it is Robida's view of the past that counts: In 1900, for the Universal Exposition in Paris, he designed and oversaw the construction of "Old Paris" on the banks of the Seine, as Darío describes it here.

**Rodó, José Enrique:** (Uruguay; 1871–1917) One of Uruguay's most important essayists and journalists at the turn of the century, Rodó produced several influential works. Two of these are *Ariel,* which was written just after the Spanish-American War of 1898 and celebrated the spirit-life of Ariel (the Hispanic world) over the materialism of Caliban (the United States), and an essay/biography on Darío in 1899.

**Rodrigo:** (1040–1099) Rodrigo Díaz de Vivar, Castilian military leader and national hero, also known as El Cid. His exploits against the Moors have been immortalized in a famous poem, *El Cantar de Mio Cid*.

**Roosevelt, Theodore:** (1858–1919) Twenty-sixth president of the United States. His military exploits in Mexico and Cuba led to his success in politics.

**Rueda [Santos], Salvador:** (Spain; 1857–1933) A young poet befriended by Darío. Though almost illiterate until the age of eighteen,

Rueda later worked with Núñez de Arce at a Madrid newspaper. His first book prefigures some of Darío's *modernista* innovations, and his style is free and exuberant. Darío wrote the preface to an 1893 volume of his poetry.

**Rusiñol [i Prats], Santiago:** (Catalonia, Spain; 1861–1931) Catalonian watercolorist and painter, very influential in the Art Nouveau and *modernista* movement in Spain, both in its beginnings and flowering and in its defense against *Noucentisme,* which opposed *modernista* aesthetics. Like Monet with Giverny, Rusiñol is associated with the town of Sitges, which he loved for its light and landscapes. Rusiñol was also a very well-received poet, dramatist, and essayist-critic.

**Ruysbroeck, Jan van** (*also* **Jean, John;** *called* **the admirable**): (Belgium; 1293–1381) Mystic, author of *Ornement des Noces Spirituelles* (*The Adornment of the Spiritual Marriage*; English translation *Spiritual Espousals*), and of "The Seven Steps of the Ladder of Spiritual Love." The *Espousals* were "discovered" and translated by famed German writer Maurice Maeterlinck in 1891, which is why so many authors of the period quote this rather obscure Flemish mystic. Beatified 1908.

**Saavedra Fajardo, Diego de:** (Spain; 1584–1648) Political writer and diplomat. Many of his writings have disappeared, but of those remaining, most famous is perhaps *Idea of a Christian Political Prince in One Hundred Emblems,* a Christian reply to Machiavelli. His style is of a "Senecan simplicity."

**Sabuco, Oliva:** (Spain; 1562–?) Health worker who dedicated her life to exploring the relationship between emotional and physical health. In 1587, Sabuco published "New Philosophy of Human Nature Not Known and Not Attained by the Ancient Philosophers, Which Improves Human Life and Health." She always urged physicians to treat the whole person: body, mind, and soul. Her work was allegedly plagiarized by later writers who claimed credit for it.

**Sade, Donatien Alphone François, comte de (Marquis de Sade):** (France; 1740–1814) Educated by the Jesuits, Sade went into the French army and fought in the Seven Years' War. After his marriage at twenty-three, the rest of his life was filled with violent scandals over his sexual conduct and with feuds, which caused him to spend some thirty years, off and on, in prison. Many of his works, which are of pornographic and blasphemous subject matter, were written in prison; titles remembered today include *Justine* and *120 Days of Sodom.* Many of his manuscripts were burned by the government.

Sade is widely viewed today as a precursor of Nietzsche and Existentialism, and he is considered to warrant a high place in French literature.

**Sáenz Peña, Roque:** (Argentina; 1851–1914) Sáenz Peña was a statesman and served one term (1910–14) as president of the Republic of Argentina. He was committed to electoral reform, and thanks to his work the Radicals, led by Hipólito Irigoyen, were elected to office to replace the landowning oligarchs who had theretofore run the country. In 1888 he was one of Argentina's delegates to the Congress on Private International Law in Montevideo, and in 1889–90 he spoke before the delegates of the First Pan-American Congress in Washington, declaring Argentina's opposition to U.S. domination of the hemisphere (through the paternalism of the Monroe Doctrine) and staking out Argentina's place as an important bridge between the Old World and the New. In 1898, he spoke out strongly against U.S. aggression in the Spanish-American War and reiterated his accusations of U.S. hypocrisy as manifested in the "altruism" of the Monroe Doctrine.

**Saint-Victor, Paul Bins, comte de:** (1827–1881) French writer dedicated mostly to journalism; his style was ornate, "beyond even that of Théophile Gautier," according to one encyclopedia. (He refused to use his title, as not in keeping with his democratic principles.)

**Salomé:** Israelite princess who was persuaded by her mother, HERODIAS, to dance before King HEROD in seven transparent veils for the head of John the Baptist. Painted by many great masters, she has also inspired drama, opera, and cinema.

**Samson:** Israelite judge and warrior, noted for his great strength. Betrayed by the infamous Philistine Delilah, who cut his hair.

**Sarcey, Francisque:** (France; 1827–1899) Journalist and drama critic, very important tastemaker for the stage in late-nineteenth-century Paris.

**Sargent, John Singer:** (American; 1836–1925) Sargent, the *Penguin Dictionary of Art and Artists* tells us, was "a virtuoso portrait painter who settled in London and painted High Society in Edwardian and Georgian times. He was born in Italy of American expatriate parents and was trained in Florence and Paris. . . . [He] is best known for his portraits and for his brilliant watercolours. . . . In 1880 he visited Spain, and the technical skill and simple colour schemes of most of his portraits reflect VELÁZQUEZ, seen through the eyes of Manet and Courbet."

**Saturn:** Roman god of agriculture, and a Numen. The festival of the Saturnalia, on December 17, was celebrated in his honor. No punishment of criminals took place during the days of this festival, gifts were exchanged, and slaves were served by their masters.

**Secession, Vienna Secession:** There were several groups of German and Austrian Secessionists in the late nineteenth century, groups of artists who resigned from established academic bodies in order to forward the aims of a modernist (often Impressionist) aesthetic. The artists of the Vienna Secession sought to revitalize (especially Austrian) art through exchanges with foreign colleagues and by promoting a more organic integration of the fine and applied arts. This latter goal found ultimate flowering in the Wiener Werkstätte, a design collective.

**Sheba:** The Queen of Sheba, from the ancient Arabian kingdom of Saba (near what is now Yemen), which flourished from 950–115 B.C. She visited the Israelite King Solomon to partake of his legendary wisdom. Nine months and five days after her last night in Jerusalem, the queen gave birth to a son—Menelik, who founded Ethiopia's Solomonic dynasty, and reputedly stole the Ark of the Covenant from Solomon's court.

**Sicardi, Francisco A:** (Argentina; 1865–1927) Distinguished physician and writer, author of *Libro extraño* (*Strange Book*), to which Darío is undoubtedly referring. Author of other works as well, but most remembered in Argentina for his work in cholera.

**Silenus:** "A demi-god who became the nurse, the preceptor, and the attendant of the god Bacchus. . . . Silenus is generally represented as a fat, jolly old man, riding on an ass, crowned with flowers, and always intoxicated" (Lemprière).

**Silvestre, [Paul] Armand:** (France; 1837–1901) A poet considered to be one of the PARNASSIANS, Silvestre also produced a considerable body of journalism as well as stories and a couple of novels, as well as three volumes of art criticism on the nude.

**spes:** Latin word for hope.

**Sporus** (*see also* **Nero**): A young man, or perhaps really a boy, who took Nero's fancy. Roman historian SUETONIUS tells us that Nero "castrated the boy Sporus and actually tried to make a woman of him; and he married him with all the usual ceremonies, including a dowry and a bridal veil, took him to his house attended by a great throng, and treated him as his wife. And the witty jest that someone made is still current, that it would have been well for the world if Nero's father Domitius had had that kind of wife. This Sporus, decked out with the finery of the empresses and riding in a litter, he took with him to the assizes and marts of Greece, and later at Rome through the Street of the Images, fondly kissing him from time to time."

**Stirner, Max:** (*nom de plume* of Johann Kaspar Schmidt; Germany; 1806–1856) Philosopher and social philosopher, the first to translate Adam Smith's *The Wealth of Nations* into German. Stirner was often branded a "radical," and his philosophy did in fact espouse anarchism (although he denied this). As a proponent of what he termed the Egoist philosophy, he is considered, also, one of the precursors of Existentialism, and he believed that all religions and ideologies are based on superstition (with nationalism, statism, liberalism, socialism, communism, and humanism explicitly included in this set of superstitions).

**Strongbow:** The name by which Richard fitz Gilbert de Clare, Earl of Pembroke (1130–1176), was known. The men of the de Clare family of Ireland were known for their prowess with an unusually long, strong bow; hence the name. Basically a noble warrior during the mid-twelfth century, during what is known as the "chaos" in Ireland stemming from disputes over ascendants to the throne.

**Suetonius:** (Rome; ?75–?150 A.D.) Full name Gaius Suetonius Tranquillus; Roman biographer and historian, best known for his *Lives of the Caesars,* or *The Twelve Caesars,* although *Famous Men* and *The Lives of the Poets* have also come down to modern days; unfortunately lost are such volumes as *Lives of Famous Whores, Greek Games, Roman Dress, The Physical Defects of Man,* etc. It is Suetonius' life of NERO (*q.v.*) that gives the story of Sporus.

**Tailhade, Laurent:** (France; 1854–1919) Born into the French bourgeoisie, Tailhade soon broke with that ethos and moved to Paris, where he joined the literary and artistic bohemia. Though he published a book of poems in 1880, he is most famous for his polemical anarchism; after an assassination attempt that left several bystanders dead, he is quoted, for example, as saying "What do the victims matter, if the gesture was grand!" After losing an eye in the bombing of a restaurant in which he happened to be eating, he became even more radical and libertarian. At one point he was tried and sent to prison for a year for writing an "incitement to murder," an article against the Czar of Russia. Strangely, in 1905 he abandoned anarchism and became a rabid nationalist. In literary terms, he is remembered as the translator of PETRONIUS' *Satyricon* and a novel, "The Black Idol," on opium. He himself was an opium addict.

**Tannenberg, Boris de:** (1864–1913) Of Russian and German descent, Tannenberg was a French-speaking literary critic and student of Spanish literature, the author of such works as *L 'Espagne litteraire* and *Poésie castillane contemporaire.*

**Tartarin:** A famous comic character created by ALPHONSE DAUDET (1840–1897); the hero of three novels, Tartarin, infected by his reading of Fenimore Cooper's exciting novels, is an amusing braggart who loves telling fantastic tales of his own escapades, such as hunting lions in Africa.

**Tempe:** *Lemprière's* dictionary tells us that this is "a valley in Thessaly, between Mount Olympus at the north and Ossa at the south, through which the river Peneus flows into the Aegean. The poets have described it as the most delightful spot on the earth, with continually cool shades and verdant walks, which the warbling of birds rendered more pleasant and romantic, and which the gods often honoured with their presence. . . . All valleys that are pleasant, either for their situation or the mildness of their climate, are called *Tempe* by the poets."

**Teoyoamiqui:** The goddess Teoyoamiqui's office was to gather in the souls of those killed in battle, which went to the mansion of the sun in heaven, where they were transformed after a time into hummingbirds.

**Teresa, St.:** (Avila, Spain; 1515–1582) Catholic mystic and founder of the "discalced" (barefoot) Carmelite order, to return the Carmelites to their original purity. Author of numerous treatises, among the most famous the *Life, The Interior Castle,* and *The Way of Perfection.*

**Termini:** Lemprière comes to our aid with this explanation: Terminus was "a divinity of Rome who presided over bounds and limits, and to punish all unlawful usurpation of land. His worship was first introduced at Rome by NUMA. . . . His temple was on the Tarpeian rock, and he was represented with a human head but without feet or arms, to intimate that he never moved, wherever he was placed." Thus, several of these armless busts of the deity Terminus were placed about the garden, and owls perched on them.

**Thanatos:** The personification of nonviolent death and the twin brother of Hypnos (Sleep). He was depicted as a winged god.

**Todi, Jacopone da:** (Todi, Umbria, Italy; 1230?–1306) Born Jacopo Benedetti to a noble family, Jacopone was at the end of his life a "fool for Christ" and one of the most important of the medieval Italian religious poets and composers. After studying law, probably at Bologna, Jacopo married Vanna di Guidone. After just a year of marriage, Vanna was killed when a balcony she was standing on collapsed at a celebration. When Jacopo discovered that his wife, in a constant act of penitence characteristic of the Middle Ages, was wearing a hair shirt, probably in penance for his, Jacopo's, sins (among which was no doubt avarice in the pursuit of the law), he was beside himself with grief. He left the law, entered the Franciscan order as a tertiary brother (St. Francis was orginally from Umbria), and for the next ten years lived a life of self-imposed poverty and penitence. The children of the town called him "Jacopone"—stupid Jacopo—and the name stuck. After the decade of penitence, Jacopone entered the Franciscan order as a monk and began to write the Umbrian-dialect *laudi* and the Latin hymns such as the *Stabat Mater* for which he became increasingly famous. By the end of his life, some called him the "second David."

**Tolstoy, Count Lev Nikolayevich:** (1828–1910) Russian novelist, experimental farmer, and social theorist.

**Triptolemus:** Mythological prince of Eleusis, who taught men to plant grain and is said to have invented the plow. He was one of a trinity with Demeter, goddess of the earth, and her daughter Persephone, who was abducted and raped by Hades, the god of the Underworld. Triptolemus was always represented in the winged chariot Demeter gave him, holding sheaves of wheat.

**Tutecotzimí:** A legendary indigenous leader in the Nahuatl-speaking world.

**Utrillo, Miguel:** (Barcelona; 1862–1934) Art critic, *modernista* painter, and writer, adoptive father of famed painter Maurice Utrillo (b. Maurice Valladon). Member of the Quatre Gats group of writers, artists, and assorted bohemians in Barcelona.

**Valdés Leal, Juan de:** (1622–1690) Spanish baroque painter who, though like MURILLO a religious painter, had a penchant for the grotesque and macabre. His paintings are marked by a sort of feverishness, with dramatic lighting, excited movement, and brilliant color.

**Valera [y Alcalá Galiano], Juan:** (Spain; 1824–1905) A much-read novelist and important critic in late-nineteenth-century Spain, Valera was enormously cultivated, and his criticism and reviews carried great weight. His novel *Pepita Jiménez* (1874) is perhaps the most-read book in Spain in the nineteenth century. He was one of the earliest critics to praise Darío's groundbreaking *Azure . . .*, and in a way "made" Darío's career, or at least caused Darío to be taken seriously from early on.

**Van der Meulen, Adam Frans:** (Brussels/Paris; 1632–1690) A Flemish painter of the Baroque whose work was often used to design tapestries. Court artist for Louis XV, who hired him to produce Göbelins, he specialized in military subjects, although he also painted hunts, still lifes, landscapes, etc.

**Velázquez, Diego:** (Spain; 1599–1660) A naturalist painter, Velázquez began by painting the common people but became court painter to Philip IV, for whom he painted his most celebrated masterwork, *Las meninas*. Velázquez is unquestionably one of the greatest Spanish painters of all time.

**Verhaeren, Émile:** (Belgium; 1855–1916) A poet of energy and vitality, Verhaeren is dreamy MAETERLINCK's opposite. He was influenced by the French Symbolists and became an important exponent of free verse. Before World War I he had faith in the possibility of universal brotherhood and human progress, which may have attracted Darío to his work.

**Verlaine, Paul:** (1844–1894) French Symbolist poet and professional decadent who suffered from rheumatism, cirrhosis, gastritis, jaundice, diabetes, and cardiac hypertrophy. His life was dominated by the duality of absinthe, or the "green fairy" as he called it, and the Catholic Church. He abandoned his wife for Arthur Rimbaud, but Rimbaud left him after Verlaine fired a shot at him but missed. (Verlaine's strength was metrics, not accuracy.) Darío met Verlaine in a Parisian café shortly before the older poet's death in 1894, when Verlaine was almost penniless and living in relative obscurity, as his life had spiraled into debauchery and sordidness after his imprisonment for the attempt on Rimbaud's life.

**Villiers de l'Isle-Adam, Comte Auguste de:** (France; 1838–1889) An aristocrat by birth, Villiers went to Paris to live the life of a bohemian. He produced plays in an unabashedly Romantic style; his stories are fantastic and macabre, and he is generally considered a precursor and then part of the French Symbolist, or DECADENT, movement.

**Villon, François:** (France; 1431–?) The finest poet of the Late Middle Ages, Villon was a "vagabond king"-poet. He was in and out of prison for most of his life (without much cause in most cases, it is believed, except for his killing of a priest in a brawl when he was a student), but he produced poetry that was admired for its virtuosity, especially the *ballades* and *rondeaux,* which have been translated by Dante Gabriel Rossetti, A. C. Swinburne, Bertold Brecht, and others. When a death sentence was commuted to ten years' banishment from France, Villon disappeared and nothing further was ever known of him. He has become quite the romantic (anti-) hero, with plays, operettas, and movies made of his rowdy, bohemian life.

**Vincencio Belovacense:** Author of the *Espejo Historial* (*Mirror of History*), which recounts the tale of the Bishop of Jaén meeting a devil on the road.

**Watteau, Jean Antoine:** (1684–1721) French rococo artist whose paintings depict his interest in theater and ballet. His masterpiece, now at the Louvre, is titled *The Embarkation for Cythera,* and shows lovers in party dress leaving France to seek love on the island of Cythera, under the statue of its goddess, Venus. Another oil painting, exactly the same size as *Embarkation,* now in Berlin, is either called *Return from Cythera* or *Pilgrimage to Cythera,* and shows the same group of lovers in considerable disarray, accompanied by a cavorting column of cupids.

**Worth, Charles Frederick:** (1825–1895) French/British fashion designer, founder of the House of Worth in Paris and London, which was the arbiter of women's fashions for over a century. Worth himself first designed silks and then became court dressmaker to Empress Eugénie of France and Empress Elizabeth of Austria. He is credited with the invention of the tailored woman's suit, for which Darío cannot forgive him.

**Wyzewa, Theodor de:** (b. Russia to Polish parents, d. Paris; 1862–1917) An important figure in journalism and musicology in late-nineteenth-century Paris, founder of the *Wagner Review,* frequent contributor to the *Revue des Deux Mondes, Le Temps, Gazette des Beaux-Arts,* and the *Mercure de France,* Wyzewa was also famed for his translation of the medieval book of saints' lives, *La légende dorée.*

**Zeboim:** (zi-bO'im) One of the cities destroyed along with Sodom and Gomorrah. Deuteronomy 29:23.

**Zurbarán, Francisco de:** (Spain; 1598–1664) One of the great Spanish painters of religious and devotional art. The *Penguin Dictionary of Art and Artists* notes that "the bleak austere piety of his early pictures of saints, painted for the more severe religious orders, made him the ideal painter of simple doctrinal altar-pieces, expressed in clear, sober colour, with figures of massive solidity and solemnity. . . . His ability to portray rather arid scenes from saintly lives, with a perfect union of the mystical and the realistic [gave way, after he moved to Madrid, to] a stronger feeling for Baroque magnificence. He still retained his hold on pure realism, but the splendour of his colour and the clarity and solidity of the masses . . . show how well he absorbed lessons learnt from Italian art."

# Index of Titles and First Lines

# CLICK ON A CLASSIC
## www.penguinclassics.com

*The world's greatest literature at your fingertips*

Constantly updated information on more than a thousand titles,
from Icelandic sagas to ancient Indian epics, Russian drama to
Italian romance, American greats to African masterpieces

•

The latest news on recent additions to the list, updated
editions, and specially commissioned translations

•

Original essays by leading writers

•

A wealth of background material, including biographies
of every classic author from Aristotle to Zamyatin, plot
synopses, readers' and teachers' guides, useful web links

•

Online desk and examination copy assistance for academics

•

Trivia quizzes, competitions, giveaways, news on
forthcoming screen adaptations

# FOR THE BEST IN PAPERBACKS, LOOK FOR THE

In every corner of the world, on every subject under the sun, Penguin represents quality and variety—the very best in publishing today.

For complete information about books available from Penguin—including Penguin Classics, Penguin Compass, and Puffins—and how to order them, write to us at the appropriate address below. Please note that for copyright reasons the selection of books varies from country to country.

**In the United States:** Please write to *Penguin Group (USA), P.O. Box 12289 Dept. B, Newark, New Jersey 07101-5289* or call 1-800-788-6262.

**In the United Kingdom:** Please write to *Dept. EP, Penguin Books Ltd, Bath Road, Harmondsworth, West Drayton, Middlesex UB7 0DA.*

**In Canada:** Please write to *Penguin Books Canada Ltd, 90 Eglinton Avenue East, Suite 700, Toronto, Ontario M4P 2Y3.*

**In Australia:** Please write to *Penguin Books Australia Ltd, P.O. Box 257, Ringwood, Victoria 3134.*

**In New Zealand:** Please write to *Penguin Books (NZ) Ltd, Private Bag 102902, North Shore Mail Centre, Auckland 10.*

**In India:** Please write to *Penguin Books India Pvt Ltd, 11 Panchsheel Shopping Centre, Panchsheel Park, New Delhi 110 017.*

**In the Netherlands:** Please write to *Penguin Books Netherlands bv, Postbus 3507, NL-1001 AH Amsterdam.*

**In Germany:** Please write to *Penguin Books Deutschland GmbH, Metzlerstrasse 26, 60594 Frankfurt am Main.*

**In Spain:** Please write to *Penguin Books S. A., Bravo Murillo 19, 1° B, 28015 Madrid.*

**In Italy:** Please write to *Penguin Italia s.r.l., Via Benedetto Croce 2, 20094 Corsico, Milano.*

**In France:** Please write to *Penguin France, Le Carré Wilson, 62 rue Benjamin Baillaud, 31500 Toulouse.*

**In Japan:** Please write to *Penguin Books Japan Ltd, Kaneko Building, 2-3-25 Koraku, Bunkyo-Ku, Tokyo 112.*

**In South Africa:** Please write to *Penguin Books South Africa (Pty) Ltd, Private Bag X14, Parkview, 2122 Johannesburg.*